R. M. Meluch's
Tour of the Merrimack:

THE MYRIAD
WOLF STAR
THE SAGITTARIUS COMMAND
STRENGTH AND HONOR
THE NINTH CIRCLE

TOUR OF THE MERRIMACK

Volume Two

THE SAGITTARIUS COMMAND

STRENGTH AND HONOR

R. M. MELUCH

DAW BOOKS, INC.

DONALD A. WOLLHEIM, FOUNDER

375 Hudson Street, New York, NY 10014

ELIZABETH R. WOLLHEIM
SHEILA E. GILBERT
PUBLISHERS

www.dawbooks.com

First Printing, November 2013
1 2 3 4 5 6 7 8 9

DAW TRADEMARK REGISTERED
U.S. PAT. AND TM. OFF. AND FOREIGN COUNTRIES
—MARCA REGISTRADA
HECHO EN U.S.A.

PRINTED IN THE U.S.A.

THE SAGITTARIUS COMMAND

TO JIM.

PART ONE

Emergence

1

THE HARSH WHITE SUN and the softer yellow day star shone directly overhead. Herius Asinius squinted against their combined light, searching for something wrong. Commander of Legion LXXI Draconis, Herius Asinius had a finely honed sense of wrongness.

Saw it. A smudge on the sky way up high among the icy streaks of cirrus clouds. More than one smudge. And they were moving.

Like veils of smoke or torn shreds of netting, they undulated in the lofty winds.

Sheets of the stuff rippled, furled, and spread back out, slowly falling. An edge of a broad sheet slipped, spilled the wind, dipped down quickly, caught the air, and spread itself out yet again.

Lower, closer, the cloudy sheets took on dimension, bigger, peppered, more like a swarm of gnats blowing in from a lake.

The lower they descended, the clearer it became that each gnat was a meter wide and haloed in tentacles.

Herius Asinius, on the stone rampart of the Roman fortress, lifted his wrist com, swearing and shouting into it for someone to identify the descending clouds. But he already knew what they were.

Mostly they were called gorgons or, altogether, the Hive,

as the gorgons in their countless millions seemed to compose one organized whole. A single vast alien entity characterized by an inexhaustible, indiscriminate capacity to eat organic matter.

And Herius Asinius threatened all ships in orbit with crucifixion for not alerting him to this latest wave's coming.

Someone should have detected the gorgons' distinctive spheres approaching the planet Thaleia before the damn things hit atmosphere.

No one answered from above.

The ships' coms could be out.

Or everyone up there could be dead.

The very first appearance of Hive swarms on Thaleia days ago might be excused as wholly unexpected. The Americans had led Rome to believe that the Hive could not possibly arrive in Near space for another hundred years.

But gorgons were here, on the Roman planet Thaleia, right now, less than fifty parsecs from Palatine. Been here for days.

Was it only days? How many? Felt closer to an eternity. How time crawls when you are in hell.

And how in bloody hell had *more* gorgons come to the planet without warning from the lookouts in orbit?

Herius did not care if Rome was desperately short of soldiers; someone was going to die for this. Someone besides Herius Asinius, who was pretty sure he was not getting out of this alive anyway. Whoever let gorgons approach Thaleia needed to hang on a cross for a while and have his children killed before his eyes, *then* get eaten by gorgons.

Herius roared orders to his legionaries as he hefted a beam cannon onto his shoulder, and trained it on those clouds. Fired.

The netted clouds were elusive. The gorgons splayed themselves flat, tentacles fanned wide to make themselves into a net of parachutes. Under fire, they split apart into individual parachutes, drifting on the wind. They fell in spidered rain, tipping and dodging, darting in the air currents like minnows. The fortress gunners scribbled the sky with fire. Oh, you hit some, but it was like trying to prevent every drop of rain from touching the ground.

Early in the siege, Legion Draconis had scorched a wide ring of land around the Roman fortress and brought all the residents from the surrounding region inside these stone walls. The burned fields around this place made it unattractive to the ravenous aliens.

Despite all the beam fire from the high ramparts, the rain of gorgons made landfall by the hundreds of thousands in the forested hills beyond the burn area.

The fortress was an ancient style structure, made of local red stone. The buildings within its thick walls were roofed in terra-cotta. It was a historical re-creation, never meant to serve as a real shelter in *Anno Domini* 2445. But when the invading aliens caused computerized systems to fail and made automated defenses turn on their makers, these primitive walls of stone became the place of last refuge.

The monsters continued to fall in the surrounding hills. The legionaries fired beam cannons until the sky was empty and all was dead quiet on the blackened perimeter.

Green birds came over the hills in a wheeling flock. Alighted on the ramparts, chattering, their double wings flicking.

Herius Asinius lowered his beam cannon from his shoulder. Dropped into a crouch on his heels, let his head hang. His back ached. His soul ached.

He had thought his legionaries were getting ahead of the monsters. Until this. A rain of gorgons.

How in the hell?

Heard footsteps on the catwalk. The sound halted a few paces away from him. "Are you hurt, *Domni*?"

Herius Asinius shook his bowed head and waved off whoever it was. The footsteps continued along the wall, paused once. The legionary fired a single shot over the wall. Walked on. It was a sometime dream of Herius Asinius to be the one to stand between Rome and its most deadly peril. In his dream, however, he had all the resources he needed to win the desperate battle.

Troops in the Deep End—two thousand parsecs away from here, on the far side of the abyss between galactic arms—those troops had weapons with which to combat these aliens. Legion Draconis did not. Legion Draconis was equipped to battle conventional enemies in Near space with modern weapons. Herius Asinius had never been trained in—or armed for—combat against gorgons. He felt set up, cheated. A naked slave thrown to the lions.

And he could not run—take his Legion, withdraw to his ship *Horatius*, and abandon the planet Thaleia to the predators.

It was unRoman.

It was unthinkable.

Herius Asinius was going to die here.

Sometimes certain death gave soldiers a weird sense of elation. Herius had seen that buoyant fire in the recordings of the last stand of the Roman 10th cohort of the Praetorian Guard at Corindahlor. The famed 300. Their faces damn near glowed. Some of them laughed. And died to a man.

The battle for the bridge at Corindahlor had been a defeat that opened the way to planetary victory. A defeat like Thermopylae, Masada, the Alamo. A defeat that made the 10th immortal.

Herius Asinius was not going down to immortality. His Dracs were just going to be eaten like sixty-four other Legions before his.

He stood up, stared at his own grave, this planet Thaleia.

The enemy was here. Now. And if here on Thaleia, they could be at the Roman capital Palatine within the year.

It fell to him to stop them.

It was too late for Herius Asinius to be careful what he wished for.

A voice sounding from his wrist startled him: "*Ave, Domni. Vivas tu?*" It was his ship's commander, his cousin Marcus.

Lifting his wrist com to his mouth—too hurriedly—Herius hit himself in the brow with his beam cannon. Stinging, furious, he rasped into the com in Latin, "Yes, I'm still alive, hang you! Where have you been!"

"The gorgons shut down the ship's systems," Marcus returned. "It's true what they say. With mobs of gorgons clustered on the shields, they shut down almost everything. We had to dive into the atmosphere to burn them off. We didn't have enough sharp objects to kill the ones that got on board."

The Americans had told them the only weapons that worked against gorgons were fire and a sharp edge, and even a sharp edge wouldn't cut the white ones.

"We set fires on two decks," said Marcus. "Oh, Heri, I messed up your ship."

Herius Asinius touched the rising welt on his forehead. It was bleeding. He had not slept. Anger sapped out of him. Remembered to worry about his younger cousin. "Are you okay?" Herius used the American word *okay*. Everyone did. Every nation on Earth. Every alien colony of Rome. Everyone knew that okay meant okay.

"I am—" Marcus could not say he was okay. Finished instead, "—unhurt."

A sudden boom split the quiet with a roar of heated wind. A rumbling vibration rolled through the ground. The noise thundered through everything, pounding.

No Roman ever took to space without sonic filters implanted in his ears, so the sound did not deafen Herius Asinius. But it dropped him into a crouch and knocked a chunk of the stone rampart over the edge.

"What is that!?!" Marcus' voice shouted from Herius' wrist com. "*Domni*, are you there!"

Herius stood up, turned toward the north where a blazing cloud mounted higher and higher above the horizon. He tried to remember the map of this side of the world. "The Ephesian munitions factory, I think."

Nothing edible in the factory, but masses of gorgons corrupted automated controls. Everything on this world was automated.

That's why we're hiding in this relic.

"Which way are the winds blowing?" Marcus demanded quickly.

"Northerly," said Herius. Away from the fortress. "There's a break."

"That's a first," said Marcus, sour.

Herius nodded. Marcus would know he was nodding. "Before you roasted my ship, Marcus, did you see gorgon spheres on approach?"

"No. There's nothing more coming."

"A million or more just fell."

Marcus was unintelligible for several moments. Finally choked: "Are you in danger?"

"Not immediately. They fell outside the burn area." And on the Ephesian munitions factory apparently. "Are you still blind up there, Marcus?"

"No, *Domni*. The systems came back on after we burned our gorgons off."

"What do you see coming toward the planet now?"

"Nothing! I didn't see anything before, and I don't see anything now! The Americans never told us gorgons could sneak up like that." Marcus sounded defensive. "They said gorgons travel through space in *spheres!*"

"There's a lot the Yanks didn't tell us," said Herius, watching the tower of fire in the distance. The gorgons had taken out a munitions factory. Convenient for the Americans.

"Heri? When is the last time you slept?"

Herius Asinius stammered in a fog. Admitted at last, "I'm due. I'm due. I'm overdue."

He would be of no use to anyone if he ran himself into the ground.

"I have your sky," said Marcus.

Herius glanced up. A silver glint passed overhead, horizon to horizon. His ship, the mighty *Horatius*.

"Marcus, check on my tribunes." Herius had split his Legion into its ten cohorts to defend the major population centers of Thaleia. Draconis, like most of the modern Legions, only numbered 3000—ten cohorts of 300 each—in addition to the crew of the *Horatius*.

Fortunately, Thaleia hadn't much of a population. The Dracs had gathered the citizenry into six refugee centers. Herius had no idea what was happening to them. "The other refugee centers—"

"I've *got* you, Heri," said Marcus.

Let go, Herius told himself. Herius Asinius never delegated well.

And it was not till dusk that Herius actually dragged himself down the ladder into the fortress. He set out on foot up the via Praetoria toward the center of the forty-acre complex.

Dazed refugees, wrenched from their automated homes, looked quite lost in the open air amid the stone buildings. The whole complex murmured fear, soft crying, a worried tone to all the muted voices.

God or gods, how had it come to this? How did we get treed like scared animals?

It began with the disappearance of a ship. The *Sulla*. At first few people even knew she was gone. *Sulla* was about secret business.

And those who knew kept the secret. Tried to. Rome never advertised its difficulties. The matter was to be handled quietly, done without anyone ever knowing there had been an incident in the Deep.

Rumors of *Sulla* got out. A shadow tale. A ghost story. The ship that never returned. You could not hear the name *Sulla* without a spectral cold lifting the hairs on your neck.

What had found *Sulla* then found more Roman ships. It destroyed warships, exterminated Legions, consumed worlds. Crushed the might of the star-spanning Roman Empire so that this proud people had to crawl under the heel of their hated enemy, the United States of America, to survive.

Hiding behind stone walls.

On one of the cross streets inside the legionary fortress, a hunched-over young woman, her mouse-colored hair hanging in front of her mouse-colored eyes, clutched a landing disk to her chest. Herius did not know where she thought she was going with that. Nobody was displacing off this world. No one ever displaced at all without a collar—and she did not have one.

"Drop it!" Herius barked.

The woman shied behind her mousy hair, quickly set the landing disk down, and scurried away.

"Pick up a sword!" Herius shouted after her.

Unlikely she would need one. The fortress was a secure place, unattractive to gorgons.

But just in case, his legionaries had hauled reproduction catapults and ballistae onto the ramparts of the reproduction legionary fortress.

Everyone had heard the stories. If the Hive moves on

you, you will be thrown back into the most primitive warfare you can imagine.

The reproduction siege engines were constructed of massive beams of wood—real wood from imported Earth trees. There was nothing remotely like wood growing native on Thaleia. Those giant-stalked spongy, corky, sinewy, rubbery things that sprouted leaves and passed for trees on this world did not make for suitable building material.

However, the native vines' twisted sinews served very well for the ballistae's torsion springs in place of horsehair, and sharpened native ironreeds could serve as projectiles for the ballistae.

Heavy round stones stood stacked next to the catapults in their historical role. But hurled stones were useless against gorgons. You can't crush a gorgon.

But you could set them on fire. So the Dracs and the refugees had wound strips of native saptrees tight into highly flammable balls, which could be catapulted at gorgons. Pressure-operated fire suppressants would keep the operators from torching their own catapults. If it came to that.

It could not come to that, Herius told himself. There was too much vegetation out there for gorgons to bother crossing the fields of ash to get at these stone walls.

This has got to be the safest place in the world.

In the fading double light, the battlements drew a surreal horizon against the alien sky.

Stars appeared quickly, winking behind wispy clouds. Two very bright ones were part of this solar system. MuCygni. The portside wing tip of the Swan as seen from Earth.

Herius Asinius came to the Principia at the center of the fortress. His standards were grounded here, the silver eagle staked beside his Legion colors, the gray dragon on a scarlet ground.

His men had prepared the commander's house for him.

Knew he had to sleep. Real sleep. The jack drugs would only carry him for so long before the nerve damage started.

The room was fittingly Spartan. A simple fresco of an ancient hunting scene on the walls. A simple mosaic on the floor. A single window.

A pernicious native vine had wedged itself between the window jamb and the sill with the slow force of plants everywhere. All native species of Thaleia were pernicious. Made terraforming difficult. In fact, terraforming had not really happened on Thaleia. Native life trumped the fragile imports.

Life emerged to survive conditions present.

Conditions on Thaleia were pernicious.

Herius did not undress. He stretched out on the plain chaff-stuffed linen pallet, his boots still on. Closed stinging eyes. Lay rigid and twitching.

It was hot. There were no climate controls. Alien smells carried on a thin breeze through the open window. He heard the quiet whir of the transports. Voices. Footsteps. Loading and unloading. Strange spiraling song of the green birds.

Insectoids, the kind called rotifers, flew in and out of the open window, keeping themselves aloft by means of a single flagellum like tiny copters. Rotifers normally made a humming sound, which became a whine when the creatures felt randy.

The room was filled with whining.

Herius bunched a chaff-stuffed pillow around his ears.

2

Woke flailing from a sleep he did not remember falling into. The rotifers were in a milling chaos. They bounced off his face. Sounded like tiny buzz saws. Their little copter whip-wings stung.

Crashed into his own aides in the doorway as they came to wake him. Blare of a general alarm filled the fortress.

It was dawn. Maybe. The sky had clouded over during the night.

Beam fire knifed down through the cloud bank and drew a circle around the legionary fortress.

Herius shouted into his com: "Marcus, what are you shooting at? What is happening!"

"Gorgons. They're massing. Looks like a coordinated attack on all refugee centers planetwide. Gorgons have surrounded every one. The numbers are crippling. When they close in, you won't be able to shoot."

"You have got to be—" Herius cut himself off. Kidding? No. "Which way are they coming at us here?"

"*All* sides. They're massing over the hills. You should be able to see them in the next several minutes. Our last beam salvo had no effect."

Herius knew the gorgons could generate a weak deflection field when formed in a sphere, but never singly on the ground. "How can that be?"

"Heri, you won't believe how much they look like a Roman tortoise right now. And—" Marcus' voice cut off. Herius could hear someone else speaking in the background. Marcus came back on the com, "The ship is under attack."

Herius caught himself about to demand how. If Marcus had seen the attack coming, it would not have happened.

Asked instead: "*Any* word of reinforcements?"

"No, *Domni*," Marcus said. His tone said, *Of course not*.

The United States of America, the League of Earth Nations, and most individual member nations of Earth had all promised aid to Thaleia. But they mobilized as fast as any other slug. All the really useful weapons were in the Deep End—where the gorgons were supposed to be. As for the Roman home guard, Legion Draconis was it. The Dracs were on their own.

"Marcus, get the ship cleaned off, then assist where you can at your discretion. *Valere*."

Herius waved down a transport on the via Praetoria. The party of soldiers on board squeezed together to make room for him, caught his arms as he leaped aboard, running. The transport sped to the front gate.

Herius scrambled up the ladder to the rampart in time to see a black mass shroud the dawn hills. He got out the order to open fire just before the coms died.

Beam fire from the ramparts affected nothing, glancing harmlessly off the top of the approaching mass. But beam fire from the ground, aimed at tentacle-level, killed the approaching gorgons.

For a moment it looked as if this would be easy.

Dracs stationed before the gates mowed down row on advancing row. Monsters stumbled over monsters, no end to them. The black sea flooded closer and closer, splashing in the remains of their own dead.

When the burn area was filled with nothing but black bodies and thrashing tentacles, the beam cannon would not fire anymore, and it became difficult to breathe.

Herius Asinius had been told about soldiers suffocating— or feeling like they were suffocating—when surrounded by crushing numbers of gorgons.

Herius issued orders for his gunners to fall back inside the fortress.

The massive wooden gates boomed shut. Legionaries took to the ancient weapons on the ramparts.

Stationed on the towers were men with crossbows, charged with repelling the enemy from the fortress' most vulnerable part, its edible gates.

Herius prowled the top of the walls, exhorted his men to keep fighting, and keep inhaling and exhaling. He reminded them the airless sensation was not real.

It felt real as hell.

Flaming balls tore from the catapulta with a screeching hiss and rain of sparks. Plunged into the sea of gorgons.

The monsters fanned in rings, scrambling on top of each other to get away from the flames. And kept coming.

Storms of crossbow bolts, flaming arrows, javelins, spears, and fragmentation grenades rained from the stone walls.

Odor of burning lead drifted in foul clouds. The legionaries had cauldrons of the stuff bubbling ready on the ramparts should the gorgons make it to the walls.

And they would.

We cannot win like this.

A ballista near Herius Asinius on the rampart let loose, its wooden arms slamming forward on twisted sinew, reverberated. The ironreed bolt hissed through the air. Tore through several gorgons before stabbing the ground.

The ballista's two-man team did not watch it go. Already they turned the winch, dragging the massive wooden arms back again, creaking, pulling the slide back in its channel. One man leaned heavily on the winch; the other secured the hook, set another bolt into the slide. The man at the winch, a hulking blond, scarcely got clear as the other, the broad dusky one, pulled the lever. The great wooden arms slammed forward again. Another bolt ripped the air. There was no aiming. There was no shortage of targets.

Too many. Too many.

An acrid smell of friction-burned sinew rolled off the ballista.

The two men had become part of the machine. Launch, wind, hook, load, launch.

The air was thin. Of moisture, there was none.

One of the men, the hulking blond, fell off the winch, his face bright red, his body shaking in huge spasms, overheated and dehydrated nearly to death.

Herius shouted for a hydrator and a medicus. The blonde crawled toward the shadows as the darker man labored at the winch. Herius took up the other side of the wheel himself.

Till the other soldier fell, too, his dehydrated body rebelling in tremors.

Herius muscled round the heavy winch alone.

Behind him, he heard someone else engage the iron hook for him and drop a bolt into the slide. Herius stepped away. Barked, "Fire!"

Heard the clack of the lever, the burning screech of the loosed bolt, the thunk of enormous wooden arms slamming forward. He seized the winch and started hauling the crank around again.

It became a mindless sequence, turn the wheel, listen for the lock, jump clear, wait for the bolt to fly, fall back on the wheel again.

His lungs burned. His muscles shook. He could not stop to rest with that hideous blackness closing in. Fired, cranked, locked, waited for another bolt to fall in the slide.

Waited. No bolt materialized in the slide.

Herius turned, snarling, "For your life, you idiot!"

It was the first time he had actually looked at his assistant. Saw why he got no help from him turning the winch.

A child. A civilian. Not even old enough to be a child soldier.

The crate behind the machine, which had been filled with ironweed bolts, lay empty. The boy was struggling to drag another crate of bolts along the catwalk.

Herius strode back, heaved the crate onto his shoulder. "What's your name, soldier?"

"Titus, *Domni*. Titus Vitruvius."

"Bring us some water, soldier," Herius ordered. "And hydrators if there are any left."

The curly-haired head nodded. Dashed away.

Herius turned toward the enemy. Face crinkled, twitching as if about to cry. Filled with a fierce pride. He loved Rome.

By now, it was apparent the hour of his death was at hand. It would be a Roman death. He only wished he could get Titus out of here.

Farther along the ramparts he glimpsed the cauldrons tilting. An angry sizzle and acrid metallic stench drifted his way.

The enemy were at the wall.

A splintering, shredding noise let him know they were also at the gates, chewing.

Shouts spiked from within the fortress. Herius caught a few words out of the uproar.

The gorgons were coming up the sewers.

They were in.

Herius was a twenty-fifth-century Roman. He barely knew what a sewer was. Never thought to secure them. Cursed any god that might be listening. This, *this* was so far beyond fair. Someone just *had* to re-create the fornicating *sewers*!

An ominous scritching sounded on the stones, very near, just below the ramparts. The gorgons were climbing.

There was no shooting straight down with a ballista.

The boy, Titus, returned with hydrators. Jammed one each into the necks of the fallen men, and presented another one to Herius Asinius, along with a slingshot.

The slingshot was technology right down there with sewers, but Herius could figure out how to work it. He shot himself with the hydrator, and accepted the slingshot. "Good man." Took up a bolt and climbed atop the ballista to look over the rampart.

Mouths looked back up, right *there* reaching on hell-black stalks.

Then the world began to shake.

Herius teetered, pitched toward the writhing blackness. He clutched at the ballista's wooden arm. Gorgon mouths snapped at his kicking feet. Reached.

Lost grip. The gorgon fell, flailing, knocking other gorgons off the wall.

But there were more rising.

Herius swung from the ballista's arm. Let go. Landed on the catwalk.

He pulled back the slingshot, bolt ready for whatever came over the wall.

Deep sounds rose from somewhere—below, above, around, echoing off the hills, rolling inside the low clouds like uneasy thunder. Without direction. A rhythm to it, arriving in a dopplered mash, sound over sound. A thumping baseline Herius felt up through the fortress stones.

Music.

Tremendously loud and coming closer.

A turbulence swirled the moody clouds.

Then a shape like the fin of an inverted shark tore at the cloud layer, music blaring.

"It's the cavalry!" someone shouted.

"That's not the cavalry—" someone else yelled. "It's bloody Judgment Day!"

More of the fin appeared, a goliath metal wedge. It was a spaceship's lower sail.

Slowly, the whole space battleship descended below the cloud layer. A spearhead shape—two wings, and an upper and lower sail round a single fuselage. *Monitor* class. The flag emblazoned on its hull was red, white, and blue.

The ship made a low pass over the fortress, then opened gunports and jetted hydrogen fire at the alien hordes on the ground. Mowed them back in a rolling burning wave.

The boy Titus jumped up, pointing at the ship. *"Merrimack! Merrimack!"*

The Americans had come to the rescue.

Down below, from within the fortress, cheers erupted.

Cheers for the most damned of ships. That was John Farragut's U.S.S. *Merrimack*.

Merrimack circled and made another pass like a fire-breathing dragon, scouring the gorgons, music booming.

Americans loved to make noise. So did Romans, but this was distinctly American noise in this Roman sky.

And Romans were cheering.

Gorgons died in the tens of thousands in the tsunami of fire. A wall of heat rolled up to the ramparts. Hit like a hammer, crouched you back behind the stone ramparts, shut your eyes against the blast.

And still gorgons climbed the walls. Herius could hear them scritching as the furnace blast subsided.

Merrimack could not dare fire on the walls.

Herius' young assistant Titus was not paying attention. The child's face was upturned and rapt as if beholding an angel.

Gorgon tentacles surmounted the wall, looped around the ballista. Titus shrieked. Herius thought he'd lost the boy to panic, but there was still a bolt in the ballista's slide, and as the gorgon paused to take bites from the ballista's massive wooden supports, Titus yanked the lever.

The bolt ripped through the black sack of a body. Wooden arms catapulted the remains into the air. Three torn tentacles remained clutching the ballista for a moment, then dissolved into heated brown slime.

Herius was staring at the steaming ooze dripping down the wooden supports, when another gorgon sprang up from the wall, spiderlike, onto the top of the ballista. The monster was a greasy-looking, black, shapeless sack the size of a pig, tentacles sprouting from all parts of it, each tentacle as thick as Herius' thumb, but more than a meter long and flexible, like a hose, each tentacle terminating in an open maw ringed with row within row of sharp teeth. The mouths tore at the twisted sinew of the ballista's firing mechanism.

Herius still had the slingshot in his hands. Loosed a bolt into the monster.

The bolt pierced the sack, in one side, out the other. The neat puncture wounds self-healed. The shot had done nothing but move the gorgon's interest from the ballista to Herius. The gorgon grappled over the arms of the ballista to get at the man with the slingshot.

Herius shot more bolts at the gorgon, two and three at a time. The gorgon tumbled down from the machine, dragged itself toward him by its tentacles, spilling its liquid insides.

Herius shot it again. The gorgon melted onto the catwalk.

Seven more gorgons clambered over the rampart.

Herius roared at Titus, "Fall back! Get down the ladder!" Backing away from the nests of tentacles, no bolts within reach.

Felt a hissing rip the air, ruffle his dark hair. The gorgon nearest him swayed. Another hiss sang over his shoulder. Another rupture appeared on either side of the gorgon and the one behind it.

The archers on the wall had spotted him. They ripped gorgons open with barbed arrows. The monsters splashed down dead round Herius Asinius.

And in the sky, *Merrimack* made another sweeping pass round the fortress.

Abruptly, he could breathe again. Then heard the wondrous sound of beam fire reports. The beam cannons were operational again. Legionaries were slapping powerpacks back into their hand cannons faster than a gorgon could jump.

This was a modern battle again.

Overhead, the enormous spearhead shape of the space battleship rose slowly, nearly vertically into the clouds in a grandstanding exit.

It was left to the legionaries now to shoot the remaining monsters that were scrambling to get out. They leaped from the high walls. Squashed flat on the ground and rebounded, unhurt, unless they hit the upturned stakes in the trench.

Herius climbed atop the rampart. Heat radiated up from the hard-baked ground, glassy now, like a kiln. The horizon was moving, black with the retreating multitude. An evil shadow withdrawing.

So many of them. So many of them still out there.

In time Herius' wrist com came back to life with reports from his centurions defending the other refugees centers around Thaleia:

Merrimack! Merrimack is here!

It was dusk when all the refugee centers reported in, secure for the moment.

In the moody twilight, the time of day called *inter canem et lupem* — between the dog and the wolf — Herius Asinius sat atop the rampart and watched the suns set, sharing a bottle of mead with his cousin Marcus. The mead was fairly nasty, but after four or five you didn't mind so much.

Herius felt protective of his younger kinsman. Never mind that Marcus was commander of his legion carrier *Horatius*. He was still little Marcus.

Marcus was taller, lighter skinned, his hair nearly blond. Gray-eyed, his cheekbones carved high. Handsome. There were no ugly Romans.

Herius had been a wild seed, spawned from a good lay. Marcus had been engineered. "That's why I'm better looking," Marcus always said.

Herius had a raw masculinity which genetic engineers could not encode. In a world where good looks were commonplace, it was Herius who captured attention.

The sounds rising within the ancient fortress were cheerful, citizens slopping through the disgusting remains. Voices of comaraderie and survival. Laughter. There was too much celebration down there, when we are where we were yesterday—only bloody now and robbed of several good lives. This was not a victory. Gorgons were still eating at Thaleia, still thriving on Rome's doorstep, poised to eat the heart out of the Empire. Herius did not want to go down there and have to smile for his people. He could not go down there and ruin their high morale.

His cousin knew his heart. Marcus was not smiling either. "If anybody had bothered to equip *Horatius* with hydrogen jets, we could have done that," Marcus said, nodding up where *Merrimack* had made its grand entrance.

"All hail John Farragut." Herius raised a flat toast and took a deep gulp of mead. Grimaced at the taste. "What took him so long?"

"So *long*?" Marcus pulled back in surprise. "How did he get here so *fast*? *Merrimack* is supposed to be in the Deep End!"

Herius nodded. "In the nick of time, was it not? A real *deus ex machina*, was it not?"

A god from the machine.

In stage plays in ancient times, near the end of a tragedy when all hope was lost, a god would be lowered onto the stage on a pulley to set the hopeless mess right.

Salvation came to Thaleia in a machine, but that was no god.

"*Merrimack* waited just long enough for us to get into shit deeper than our nostrils. The Americans staged that exactly right to make us look stupid."

"Heri!" Marcus' voice suddenly hushed, "You honestly think this was *planned?*"

"It could not be anything else." Herius hawked, spat over the wall into a brown puddle of deceased gorgon far, far below. "We were set up."

3

THE PERSONNEL LANDER MADE its teeth-rattling, spine-knocking descent into atmosphere; the Marines on board questioning the pilot's skill, parentage, and relationship with domestic livestock all the way down.

Weren't happy to begin with. Seven hundred and twenty U.S. Marines descending to a Roman world to give the Romans aid. Just wasn't natural.

And the Lander allowed more inertia than anyone was accustomed to, between the high winds and the pilot's warped sense of humor.

Made you pull the restraints tighter and hold on.

Knocked the language module out of one Marine's head—a she-dog from Baker Team. She unfastened her restraints and fished around on the bucking deck where her module rolled among Marines' boots. Caught it between Cole Darby's feet. Used Darby's knee to haul herself back up. "What you writing there, Darb?"

"Nothin'."

February 3, 2445

So here's Alpha Team, jammed into this space bus with two full companies of the 89th.

There's Flight Leader Ranza Espinoza. She started with

Alpha a year ago, same time I did, but Ranza's on her fourth tour so she had an easy entry. They never called her a CWAG (Civilian with a Gun).

The guy Ranza replaced got eaten by gorgons. Southern gentleman, third-generation military type named Hazard Sewell. Hazard didn't like trench mouths, so to honor his memory Ranza curses us out if we talk like soldiers. Her own mouth belongs in the head, so I think she's using that as an excuse to clean up. Arms and shoulders like a stevedore. Looks like she could bench-press Dak Shepard. I don't think she actually can, but I know for a fact she can bench-press me, and I'm 180 pounds.

Ranza has these extraordinary gray eyes. They're narrow and you can barely see them under those thick exotic lashes. You'd swear she had them enhanced, but the rest of Ranza is so raw you just know this man-jane would never sit still to have herself prettied up.

She talks like a baboon, but don't try and feed her a load of moon cheese. She'll smell it right away and ram it back up your moon.

The Personnel Lander gave a violent lurch that yanked everyone against his straps and sent up a howl and made Cole Darby clutch at his stylus.

Ranza has actually been married a couple times. I got a real hard time picturing that. (Those guys musta been looking at her eyes.) She even has some kids, back Earthside with their grandmom.

Dak Shepard laughed, swaying with the Lander's bucks and yaws. "Wish I coulda seen those lupes' faces when they saw the *Mack* come down from heaven. I'da paid money to see that. *Mack* comes plowing through all those gorgons. Like Noah parting the Red Sea. Yeah, I got their Roman superiority right here."

F/S Dak Shepard. Alpha Two. Reminds me of my old Neuf. I miss that dog. Dak don't drool like a Neuf, but he sweats, so either way you're real moist around a big happy guy. Horn toad. But who isn't? Strong guy. Great to have him on the team. Dak is an ox. Smart as one, too.

Reg Monroe had gone quiet. Her eyes shut. Her black face greenish at the moment. Her midriff gave a little heave, followed by a very hard swallow.

"Ho! No, no, no." Carly Delgado pointed warningly across the tight aisle. "Reggie? Listen to me, Reggie. No upthrowing in the box!"

F/S Regina Monroe. Alpha Three. Reg is not a lifer. She's just in the Fleet Marines so she can get into college. Short gal. Bow heavy. (Nothing wrong with that.) Cute face. Cute voice. Wants to be an engineer. She's the Smart One of us. Not saying the rest are stupid. They are so not. Except maybe Dak. They're just a different breed of real smart.

Carly was pulling her feet as far under the bench as she could, watching Reg go into the quick swallows.

F/S Carly Delgado. Alpha Five. Carly is the pointiest man jack or jane I have ever met. Woman is all elbows. Tough, vicious. Quick, quick, quick. You want Carly on your side. Carly plays with knives. Plays well. Maybe I've been out here too long, but Carly is starting to look fine.

Twitch Fuentes rummaged under the bench. Dug a weather hood out of a duffel bag and handed it across the aisle to Reggie just in time.

Of course it wasn't Twitch's duffel bag and it wasn't Twitch's hood. It was Dak's.

Carly is pretty tight with F/S Twitch Fuentes. I'm not sure I ever heard Twitch say much of anything besides, "Yes, sir," and "Alpha Four, aye."

Has a real sneaky sense of humor for a guy who don't talk. But in a furball, you can trust him at your back, and I guess that's all you need to know about a guy.

*   *   *

"Hey, Darb." That was Ranza. Motioned sideways with her head, "Go forward and relieve that foat-gucker at the controls."

"Aye, sir. I'll get right on that," said Darb. "Right after I walk the plank."

Me, I replaced the most popular man in the Company. A real cowboy named Cowboy. And you just try and tell me that didn't make for a fine welcome aboard the Merrimack, *Cole Darby. Most everyone has forgiven me for being here instead of him by now.*

The Lander gave a violent roll and yaw. The pilot's laughter carried all the way to the back. Sounds of mutiny carried all the way to the front.

Kerry Blue was not afraid or sick or angry. Kerry Blue was asleep, her face mashed against Dak Shepard's bulging bicep.

And what can I say about Kerry Blue? (I mean after she got over me replacing Cowboy.) Once the woman decides you're okay, she makes a man feel right at home, amen.

Easy Kerry Blue was a port in anyone's storm. The ship's cherry picker. Not that she was collecting. Young men just threw themselves at her. Because, unless a man was a complete pervenoid, Kerry Blue was kind. She did not post ratings, and a man never heard a performance review in the locker room when he fell down on the job. She wasn't any voluptuous wonder like the virtual babes a man could experience in a dreambox. But if you liked it real, Kerry Blue was as real as they came.

She had a light stride for a Marine in combat boots. She didn't stand in a stack. Rather, she walked as if her body were suspended from her shoulders. It gave her a free-swinging gait, which drew the Y-chromosomed eye and made a man want to fall in step.

Made Colonel TR Steele wish dead every man who looked at Kerry Blue.

Kerry Blue lived in the right here right now. Made her a superior soldier. Kerry Blue reacted in the moment. Never

looked beyond her own horizon. Kept her from freezing up
in anticipation in combat. Allowed her to fall asleep during
the Lander's turbulent descent.

Kept her from figuring out the obvious.

Like why, whenever possible, Colonel Steele kept her
out of his sight.

*Our CO is Lieutenant Colonel TR Steele. Don't ask me what
the TR stands for. TR Steele is a real hard brand of macho.
You could bruise yourself just looking at him. White. Real
white. Ice-blue eyes. His white-blond hair is cut short and flat
enough to set your drink down on. My team dared me to do
that once. Even I ain't that dumb. Steele is commander of our
half Bat of the mighty 89th, the Bull Mastiffs. Hoo ra.*

*I did something to make Steele want me dead. I got no
idea what.*

The Lander made a sudden surge up with its dropping of
one railroad-sized cargo car filled with equipment.

The Lander made a quick roller coaster arc, and immediately chunked down on the ground. All the Marines
bowed as far as their restraints would let them. Blessed the
pilot.

Kerry Blue woke up. The folds in Dak's sleeve were im-
printed on her cheek. "Are we there?"

Cole Darby snapped shut his notepad and stylus. Stuffed
them into a deep pocket of his cargo pants.

The hatch opened. Harsh sunlight and hot air spilled in.
The ramp extended.

Colonel Steele bellowed, "Red Squad! Forward Battery!
Fall out!"

Blue and Green Squads and the Rear Battery begged to
be let out, too. In the alternative, requested permission to
let the pilot out.

Ranza Espinoza led the way, descending the ramp at a
draft horse clomp.

Reg disembarked unsteadily, Darb right behind her,
keeping Reg's field pack balanced on her back so she
wouldn't weave off the ramp.

Dak Shepard paused in the hatchway to spread his arms

wide to the world. "Thaleia, behold your saviors! The 89th is here!"

Kerry Blue waited behind Dak. Her sleepy face was looking way too feminine for her to be allowed to stay in this Lander another instant.

Steele snarled at Dak. "Move your divine ass, soldier." Gave him a push.

Kerry Blue stopped in the hatchway, blinking at the sunlight.

Kerry Blue had kissed Steele once. But that was back when everyone thought Steele was going to die, so it didn't really count as a kiss.

That had been a year—a lifetime—ago, in a cold dark Roman hangar. Steele was going to a hero's death. And Kerry, like the Lady of the Lake, gave him a sword for his final battle. Okay, it was a red crowbar, but it got the job done.

It was a moment out of time. Her cold hands, either side of his head, drew him down to her and kissed him on the mouth.

He should have died there. But TR Steele found a ferocious will to live.

The woman owned him from the first moment he saw her.

"Marine, we are on a schedule!" he bellowed at her.

Kept scowling until the hatch shut her safely away from him.

Told the pilot to move it.

"Would you look at that!"

Kerry Blue had dropped her field pack and stood gawking at the hulking legionary fortress. The red stone walls, the crenellated battlements, the fanged trench, the massive wooden doors kind of chewed up around their iron bracing.

The Personnel Lander was lifting off, swirling ash high into the air under Thaleia's brutal suns, making the fortress look like it was on fire.

"Who lives there?" Darb shaded his eyes. "Ben Hur?"

Ranza Espinoza gave him a shove from behind, knocked him off-balance. "You looking for a tour guide, Marine? Get to work."

Auto loaders were moving skids out of the cargo car. Marines off-loaded crates from the skids. The Marines had brought swords, pikes, flamethrowers, and fragmentation grenades to Thaleia, along with frictionless face shields and acid-resistant clothing. "For our protectorate," said Carly Delgado sourly.

"Ha!" said Twitch Fuentes.

"We are arming our enemy, *why?*" Any one of the Marines could have said that. They were all thinking it.

"Rome is our ally," someone else said.

"Why don't we just turn a neutron hose on the whole planet and have done with it?"

"Can't. The Roman civilians won't evacuate."

"So?"

There really wasn't a good answer to that question.

Kerry Blue lost her grip on the handle of a crate, dropped her side of it. Darb, holding up the other side, said, "Gravity too strong for you, Blue?"

Kerry was still getting her land legs. Shipboard artificial gravity was not entirely consistent. And it was entirely unpredictable. Kerry was not accustomed to standing on ground that didn't move. Or gravity that didn't lose strength unexpectedly. She kept catching herself against burbles that never happened.

Cracks led out in a spray where one corner of her crate had hit ground. "What's with the dirt here?" It was hard, shiny, ceramic, an uneven color of red brown, coated with ash. Kerry kicked at it with her heel. "What *is* this stuff?"

"It's fired clay," said Darb. "We did that. *Merrimack* did. With the hydrogen jets."

A low sound started. From within the towering stone walls. Rhythmic as alternately firing pistons. A *tramp tramp tramp tramp* like hundreds of marching soldiers.

The Marines stopped unloading their skiffs to stare at the fortress.

Deep metallic thunk of crossbars pulling back. The massive wooden doors of the fortress parted, groaning from their own weight.

Out filed hundreds of marching soldiers.

They came in perfect martial precision. Could suspect

they were androids, but there was emotion in the stomps. Reined ferocity and smoldering hatred.

You immediately counted them. Six hundred of them to one hundred twenty of us. In crisp formation. Disciplined. They moved in unison in their knife-edge columns and dead straight ranks.

They were not wearing any armor, but each carried a beam cannon. Heads snapped left as one. Turned.

They wore field uniforms—loose cargo trousers with lots of pockets like any sensible modern soldier. Except theirs were black and covered with dust, where the Marines' trousers came from the factory already dust-colored. The Roman shirts were actually short, belted, black tunics. The legionaries wore their gun sights fixed either side of their eye sockets like Marines, but theirs had shapes—like fangs or wings—instead of plain black GI boxes.

The six hundred came to a halt with a stomp and a shout. Stood before the Marines, a sea of hostility. Dust and ash drifting up from the ceramic ground.

Into the pit of silence a Marine muttered, sardonic, "Yeah, that was pretty."

And there's Ranza, coming out slinging orders like she owned the fort, which she just about did as the ranking Marine here at the moment.

"Who's the guy in charge? Okay, *you.*" Ranza singled one out. Man on the right front. Muscular, not yet thirty years old, or maybe just. Romans bred for strength and looks. This one had both. He was perfectly proportioned. Big, but not outsized. Had loosely curled dark locks and smoky sultry brown eyes. And he had a presence. Bare-armed as he was, you could see his mark: *SPQR.* Not a tattoo on this one. This was a brand burned into his flesh. Tough guy. No one in the Roman company was wearing any rank insignia. But you didn't need a red-crested helmet to single out this one. Leader of the pack and sure of it. You could always spot them.

Ranza started in on him. She spoke fast and she spoke in English and didn't give a good squat who didn't habla.

"We are going to contain and destroy the alien threat. This here is the only gorgon outbreak in Near space! There are none on Earth and it's gonna *stay that way!* The enemy *will not leave* this planet!"

Ranza stalked along the expressionless first rank, bellowing.

"You *will* ID, locate, and disable all automated equipment! That means for the whole world, understand? You will get a census, then locate and secure the population of this planet."

Here the Roman commander interrupted her to demand, "Why do you need the census of a Roman territory?"

"I don't," said Ranza stalking back to him. "And I don't give a skat, 'kay? The census is for you. Account for all your guys. Or don't. The gorgons can eat all of yous for all I care, 'kay?"

A rotifer bounced off the Roman's face. He did not blink.

Ranza turned round to her Marines, who were standing about, slouching, in disorderly fashion around their crates of equipment, just watching the show.

Ranza shouted, "Hey, nobody told yous to stop working! Yous already know what you're doing!"

They knew. Just didn't like it. Resentfully continued offloading equipment for their dubious allies.

Ranza turned back to the Roman legionaries.

"You will be getting tools for the job at hand. All your fancy Roman weapons with your range finders and target locks and nanosecond adjustments are worthless in a concentration of gorgons! Gorgons can adjust your weapons to target your own guys. Yeah, they've learned how to do that, and first thing you tell these almighty Roman legionaries is to disable your fancy Tau sixties and do they listen? No! That's why most of them are dead and good riddance, too! DOES ANYONE HAVE AN INTACT TAU SIXTY HERE?"

The Roman ranks were motionless as a solid wall but for the breeze on their tunics.

"We are not morons," said the Legion commander.

"Well ain't chu just a Roman first," said Ranza. "What chu called?"

"I am the legate, Herius Asinius."

" 'Kay, Hairy Ass. My men are unloading weapons and training materials for those weapons. You'll be getting V masks to train yous how to use a sword."

Herius walked over to a crate, picked up a sword from it. Presented the sword dangling, its tip held between his thumb and forefinger. "This is the pointy end."

"Yeah?" said Ranza. "What the V mask is going to teach you—and I don't give a rat's ass if you learn it or not—is how *not* to kill each other in close combat. You are also getting fragmentation grenades." She paused, made eye contact with the legate. "You throw them."

Herius nodded. He got that part.

"At the enemy," Ranza added. "Watch the timing, 'cause the gorgons'll try to kick 'em back. Good thing gorgons can't throw. And you can just forget about setting minefields. Gorgons can smell 'em—or whatever it is gorgons do to sense 'em. Gorgons step around mines."

He may have heard someone say, "U.S. mines stink." But Ranza just kept on talking.

"Don't get predictable. Whatever you develop, the gorgons will come up with a countermeasure to it. The only thing that always works is slicing them open. Connecting the cutter to the cuttee is always the problem. Gorgons are smart in a swarm. By themselves, they ain't yet smarted a way to dodge a sword any better than you can. So in hand-to-tentacle combat, unless you're exhausted, you have a slight edge. But gorgons always have superior numbers, so you get exhausted and then you are uffed."

Another ship passed over the fortress.

Ranza glanced up at the sound. Commented, "Green guys are here." League of Earth Nations. The LEN flag was green. The LEN had remained neutral during the U.S./Roman hostilities. "They're here to evacuate your civilians."

"Our people are not leaving our world," said Herius Asinius.

Ranza already knew that. Might as well try to get a moray eel out of its hole.

"Good," said Ranza with a shrug of her broad shoulders. "We got nowhere to put yous."

Herius Asinius declared, "We leave Thaleia, we leave it like Telecore."

Rome had taken a neutron hose to its own colonial planet, Telecore. Left the world dead, utterly sterile.

"Don't get your nuts in a cracker, Hairy Ass." Ranza waved her hand aside dismissively. "So how did the gorgons get here?"

Herius stared, dumbstruck, at the she-ape with the striking silver eyes. If Herius Asinius had seen the gorgons coming, the gorgons would not have been allowed to approach the planet. He found his voice. "*Yous* told us to watch for *spheres*!"

Ranza shrugged. "'Kay. So how many spheres we got here?"

Herius opened his mouth. Could not speak for another second. *She is as stupid as she thinks I am.* "None."

"Then how'd they get here?"

Herius shook his head. *I am talking to a brick.* "You tell me."

"Any gluies?" Ranza asked. Got ash on her lips. Spat on the ground.

Herius had been expecting a different question. Got lost on the turn.

Gluies. The most horrible of the three kinds of gorgons. White. Hideous.

Herius collected his wits. Answered, "We have seen nothing that matches the description of a gluie."

"That's good. They're the worst. When I said slicing them open always works? I lied. You can't slice a gluie. Your sword just gets stuck. You can burn them."

Ranza turned to another crate. "You're getting handheld flamethrowers with backpacks. These are new. Never used 'em on shipboard. You can field test these. Let me know if they work. You're going to have to teach yourselves. We can't stay and babysit."

She walked away from the legate, fists on her hips, beautiful eyes narrowed appraisingly at the fortress walls. "You got a pretty good site here. I'm surprised the gorgons even attacked a place like this before they ran out of other stuff to eat. Did you resonate or something to bring 'em here?"

"No," said Herius, insulted. "We have all heard that gorgons can home in on a resonant pulse."

"Yeah. They do that. Don't know how they get a loc on

something that ain't got a loc, but they do that. 'Kay, Hairy Ass, that's all I got for you. My Marines are going to secure this here refugee center. We'll kill everything you missed. Then we got the rest of the planet to clean. Captain Farragut will be down here to give you your orders." And she yelled past him to his legionaries: "Fall out!"

Herius Asinius stood very still. Felt the stares of his legionaries on him like a physical thing. Stunned, offended at how that U.S. grunt talked to their commander. Angry. Embarrassed.

The Americans were quick to invade the fortress. They moved their junk in beneath the Legion's silver eagle and the Legion colors—the gray dragon on a scarlet ground.

If they try to run up Stars and Stripes, I will have to shoot someone.

Herius' cousin Marcus had taken a shuttle down from *Horatius* to the planet surface. He came to Herius now, holding one of the U.S. flamethrowers, disgusted. "We could have fabricated all this."

Herius did not seem to hear him. Lost somewhere inside himself.

Captain Farragut will be down here to give you your orders.

So John Farragut meant to put Legion Draconis under his own command. The American could do that under the terms of the surrender.

It was nearly a year ago now that Captain John Alexander Farragut had taken Rome's surrender from Caesar Magnus.

After the Hive had reduced Rome to scant shreds of its former might, Caesar had been forced to crawl to Rome's worst enemy for help.

Help had come at an awful price.

John Farragut had insisted on the Subjugation.

Legion Draconis had not numbered among the honored dead in Rome's desperate battle against the Hive. Herius Asinius and his Dracs were alive to walk under the arch of spears in humiliation. The surrender had put Rome's military forces under U.S. control.

The Americans had never enacted the provision of direct control in Near Space before now.

How convenient for the Americans to have gorgons here in Near Space. How convenient the excuse to invade Thaleia.

Thaleia was home to PanGalactic Automated Industries.

Suspicion, rooted deep, grew, pernicious as a Thaleian vine. Herius spoke his thoughts: "The U.S. imported the gorgons here to give them an excuse to come marching in and steal our technology."

"You think so?" said Marcus, naive as only an honorable man could be. "They would bring gorgons within seventy-one light-years of Earth? It's a stupid and dangerous thing to do."

"Americans are stupid and dangerous. *Ergo* . . ."

"Very well, Heri. Suppose, *arguendo*, the Yanks brought the gorgons here. How did they *pack* them without getting eaten by their own cargo!"

"Marcus, I don't know."

"Anyway, only a perfect madman would use gorgons as a weapon," said Marcus.

"And, of course, there is no such thing as a perfect madman," said Herius. "There was never a Nero. Never a Tiberius. And Caligula never made his horse a Senator. And we cannot forget the local king, Constantine the Great of Thaleia. I think that colossal statue of his goddess mother is still here somewhere."

"Heri, I concede the existence of perfect madmen," said Marcus. "But you are suggesting that someone was clever enough, powerful enough, stupid enough, and mad enough to bring the gorgons into Near Space and endanger all human life."

Herius was looking toward a cluster of Yanks who were comparing their surveillance maps to the local maps. Herius knew what the Americans were looking for. And it was not civilians to rescue.

"No, Marcus, I am not suggesting. I am telling you that is exactly what happened here."

4

ONCE UPON A VERY recent time, rings and rings of sentinel satellites had defended Thaleia against outsiders. Thaleia was a Roman world. Because it lay closer to Earth than to Palatine, Thaleia had been heavily defended. Its sentinel satellites automatically destroyed any Earth ship foolish enough to enter the MuCyg solar system, no matter the Earth ship's nationality or internationality. No Earth ship could get permission to approach Thaleia even in an emergency. The sentinels recognized no exceptions.

That was until the arrival of the Hive. The Hive had caused all of Thaleia's rings and rings of sentinels to self-destruct.

The world was now open to everyone and his dog. All the nations of Earth were here now. They all came ostensibly to help. And all, except the dogs, asked the same stupid question: "How did the gorgons get here?"

As if they didn't know.

A shuttle descended—red, white, and blue—outside the walls of the legionary fortress. Marines nodded up, told Herius Asinius, "Farragut is here."

"Oh, happy day. John Farragut is here," Herius said.

Shuttles were a slow and cumbersome way to get about, and vulnerable to gorgon attack. Still, the shuttles were safer than displacement. Displacement was a precise operation. Gorgons could easily foul displacement sensors and next thing you knew you were mashed potatoes on Alpha Centauri.

Herius Asinius considered waiting here and making Captain Farragut come to him. But he was not in the mood for games. Wanted to get this over with. Marched out of the fortress to where the red, white, and blue thing set down on the hard glassy ground.

The hatch opened. First thing Herius Asinius saw was the smile. And it didn't stay still. The big guy who belonged to the smile came bounding down the ramp. An instantly attractive presence—the light colors, blue eyes, blond hair, white teeth, and sparkling energy.

Farragut must have been briefed, because he knew the Roman legate on sight, seized Herius' hand and the better part of his arm. And he was full of praises for the Dracs holding the fort and acknowledged how hard it had been for them.

In the onrush of seductive warmth and comaraderie, Herius Asinius just wanted to tell Captain John Farragut to go suck a squid.

Should not have let him start talking.

Farragut was talking heroics and grand purpose. "For the first time in the history of humanity, all the sons and daughters of Earth are on *one side*. United in a single purpose. It's awesome and humbling. It's a moment in history I'm glad I didn't miss."

Of course, Herius thought. *You're in charge.* Said aloud: "United but not unified. You realize we are together for one purpose only."

"Yeah." Farragut came back down to ground level, but still smiling.

This man wielded authority as a birthright. It was only in the natural progression of things for him—a rite of passage—like body hair, lower voice, stiff dick, wisdom teeth, command rank. For John Farragut, it was simply inevitable. The lack of it would cause more notice than the attaining of it. The universe was unfolding as it should.

And here comes the question. Herius steeled himself for it.

Just say it. I have a knife. Say it.

But out of John Farragut's mouth came not the hated, insulting, *How did the gorgons get here?*

"What can you tell me?" Farragut asked. And then waited, attentive. Brightness in his gaze. Alert and absolutely here.

Struck Herius dumb. Such an amazing question. The question assumed nothing. Demanded no more than Herius had to give. And Farragut was *listening*.

Herius had a natural loathing to give any information, including the time of day, to the enemy. But this was military necessity. Caesar had put all of Rome into this man's hands. Herius told the American his observations of the Hive.

Farragut's was an expressive face. Herius saw surprise in it at his description of self-parachuting gorgons. Farragut was amazed by the gorgons' tortoise formation and the beam fire deflecting off the top of it.

John Farragut listening to you transformed you to the center of the universe. He was intent on everything Herius had to say. The Roman ballistae and the catapults intrigued him. Farragut looked up toward the ramparts. "I gotta see those later," he said, like a boy promised new toys.

He was a big man, his frame carrying more weight than he ought. But it suited him. John Farragut, larger than life.

Herius could see why people gushed over him. Not so much the blue eyes and the white teeth. It was the life behind them.

A hail sounded from Farragut's wrist com. The captain looked honestly vexed at the interruption, told the caller, "Something better be on fire."

"Captain, you have a call from Earth."

Earth was in a 13-billion-person uproar. Of course there would be calls from Earth. Farragut said, "Unless it's President Johnson, don't bother us."

Herius supposed that was meant to make him feel important.

"It's the Chief Justice of the Supreme Court of the State of Kentucky, sir."

Farragut looked to Herius, chagrined. "I'm sorry." And he moved a few paces apart to take the call.

*　　*　　*

Chief Justice John K. Farragut would rather die than initiate contact with his son, Captain John A. Farragut. People came to the Chief Justice. The Chief Justice did not seek people out. And not his own boy.

Captain Farragut's chest felt tight. Wondered who had died. Spoke into the com: "Yes, sir."

There was no hello. The Justice came right to the point: "Should I be sending your mother and the young folk to the outer colonies?"

Captain Farragut closed his eyes and silently thanked God. The family was okay. He answered, "No, sir."

"You sure about that? The gorgons are on the doorstep!"

"We are talkin' about my mother, sir."

"Hmph." It was a mollified *hmph*. "That's what your sister Catherine said. But she's a politician. I want it straight from the front. If it all goes to hell, all the boats will be taken. You know those gorgons will be coming to Earth next."

"If it ever comes to that, I'll come and move y'all myself," said Captain Farragut.

"I have your word on that?"

"By God, yes."

"Well, then." The Justice grumped for something to say. "Carry on."

Farragut returned to the Roman commander, apologizing. "Sorry. My dad. Do y'all have bighorn sheep on Palatine?"

Wasn't a question Herius Asinius was ready for. "No," he said hesitantly. "I know what they are."

Farragut brought his fists together knuckle to knuckle. "They bash heads."

"I'm told you can hear them for miles," said Herius.

Farragut shook his head, no. "For light-years, son," he corrected him. "For light-years."

John Farragut and his father as bighorn sheep. The American was trying to make a human connection with Herius Asinius.

Don't call me "son." There was not a full decade between them. *I walked in Subjugation. I will never forgive you.*

Because Farragut used his hands to talk, Herius could not help but notice the surgical gauntlets encasing both of Farragut's forearms. His eyes followed them involuntarily. Herius guessed at them. "Gorgon wounds?"

Farragut gave a very sheepish smile. Shook his head. "Sword. Friendly hacking. Both hands. Zing." Re-enacted the astonishment of watching his hands fly away from him. "You can't believe what that looks like. Just before *all* the blood leaves your head. Oh, we got chewed *all* to pieces. Turned out to be a blessing in deep cover. That's why we were on Earth for a refit—me and the *Mack*. It put us close when y'all came under attack here. The boffins slapped us back together and here we are. I'm sorry I couldn't get here sooner. Not as late as it would have been if we hadn't got mauled first. This could have been a *lot* worse."

Farragut walked a circle around a stain on the ground. Obviously, he would recognize the mark of a deceased gorgon. "I should have known that something that could gut the Roman Empire would not be easy to kill. Still, I really thought I should have been able to save the universe by now and it's torquing me off to holy Jesus that I haven't done it." He clasped Herius on the shoulder like a brother-in-arms. "We'll get them."

Herius remained rigid. *I walked in Subjugation.*

"Sir?" said Herius thickly, in English. He would not call this American *Domnus*. "I have a request."

John Farragut listened.

"Do not raise the Stars and Stripes on Thaleia."

Farragut gave a long thoughtful pause. Herius silently invoked damnations on him. Knew it. Knew it. The American hero was going to claim the planet and plant his colors on Thaleia.

Farragut countered, "We may fly our flags from our transports on the ground."

The vessels themselves were not Roman ground, though they were *on* Roman ground. Made them rather like consulates. Herius allowed the compromise, "Fair."

"Done," said Farragut, and was immediately talking into his com to someone named "TR" regarding flag protocol. And back to Herius, "Is that it?"

Herius could not resist: "How did the gorgons get here?"

The impossible question did not offend Captain Farragut. "Now ain't that the question I can't afford to be holding the I-don't-know to? Just when I think I know the enemy, I don't. And I need to find that out *yesterday*."

Herius Asinius almost believed him.

The most sensitive of the insect telltales inside the legionary fortress did not settle until the sewers were cleared of crusted black lumps, which the Romans had not recognized as dormant gorgons.

"I came to a Roman planet to clean a Roman sewer?" F/S Reggie Monroe's high voice wailed up from the depths. Reg was small enough to fit into the sewers. "There is something not right about this! Who surrendered to whom? Yo! Is anyone listening to me? I'm filing a complaint with somebody! This ain't right!"

Once the legionary fortress was pronounced secure, the U.S. Marines prepared to move on to the civilian centers to make them safe for the civilians to go home.

"You want to move out of here, too," a Marine told Herius Asinius. This Marine was the she-ape Ranza Espinoza's superior, a big white bull named Lieutenant Colonel TR Steele. None of the captain's bonhomie in this one. This one radiated hatred.

"Why do I want that?" said Herius. And just how many of John Farragut's minions did he have to listen to?

"Not just you," said Steele. "All your legionaries. Get them out of here. You fired beams at the falling gorgons from your refugee centers. You got the gorgons' attention. When you make enough of them die, gorgons will leave off chewing on the closest thing and gang up on whatever is killing them. You brought them here. If you had just left the civilians alone in the fortress with the scorched earth around it and done your shooting from somewhere else, they would have been safe till we got here."

TR Steele left Herius stunned.

Marcus came to Herius' side. He was never far away. Marcus had heard all of it.

"He's saying we screwed up," Herius murmured.

"Well not exactly, no—" Marcus started.

"He's saying we screwed up."

Marcus struggled for explanations. Finally had to allow: "I think that's what he's saying."

Herius' mouth had gone sour and dry, colors gone flat before his eyes. *I screwed up.*

As the Marines were leaving the fortress, Flight Leader Ranza Espinoza paid a visit to Herius Asinius where he was going over his centurions' reports. She smiled a jarring, gap-toothed smile. "Gotcha a couple a going away presents, Hairy Ass."

Herius looked up from his field table. Said flatly, "I didn't get you anything."

"Shucks," said Ranza.

She set an ant farm on his table.

"You're on your own, Hairy Ass. Keep your eyes on your bugs, 'kay? All bugs react to gorgons. Some of 'em start shaking and shouting if they're in the same atmo. Some of 'em have to be in your time zone. Ants will get antsy if they're within a couple klicks." She tapped the ant farm with a surprisingly dainty finger.

"And these?" Ranza slapped down a clear canister of inert bugs onto the legate's field table. Picked it back up, gave the canister a shake to make sure the contents were still alive. Banged it down again.

Pale yellow-white Zakan moths fluttered briefly inside the canister, then went back to sleep.

"These are your best friends," said Ranza. "When these guys make a sound? Get out of the house."

5

THE CIVILIAN CENTER WAS called Antipolis. Looking at it from a distance, the Marines hesitated to call it a city. Antipolis looked like a titanic termite hill.

"That's not it!" cried Dak Shepard. "We're in the wrong place!"

The pictures Red Squad had seen in their briefing showed a wondrous place of fantastical spires, rainbow colors, enormous arched windows, flying buttresses, and roof gardens. There had been big graceful trees swaying, and tame exotic animals peacefully wandering by a dazzling waterfall that splashed down hundreds of feet from a tower into a glittering moat.

"This is the place," said Ranza.

This was Antipolis with the power turned off. A compact cloistered ziggurat perhaps a mile in diameter, spiraling five hundred feet high, with very few windows.

"The rest was just light dressing."

"Ugh," said Kerry Blue. "Put its clothes back on."

"This isn't a sightseeing tour," said Ranza. "We're here to kill things. We need to see exactly what we're doing."

The Dracs had sent a drone reconnaissance squad in ahead of the Marines. Romans used a lot of remote-controlled, unmanned craft.

"We call that skeet," Ranza had told the Roman Vee jock who had done the recon on Antipolis.

"Never lost a pilot," said the Roman pilot, just before his audio and video went black in a flurry of tentacles.

The pilot shrugged, signed out another recon drone.

Recon indicated a "residual" gorgon presence inside Antipolis. No more than fifty hostile units.

Red Squad was dispatched to eradicate the gorgon presence.

"Fourteen United States Fleet Marines against fifty gorgons," Carly Delgado sniffed. "Hardly worth our time."

The briefing had stressed that Antipolis was a civilian establishment. It was vital that the Marines get all the gorgons. "Do not miss one. Not one."

The objective was to secure Antipolis so the civilian refugees in the legionary fortress could go home.

"Well, there's a priority," said Reg Monroe. "How many million gorgons on this planet and we're gunning for fifty? I'll tell you one thing. I am *not* doing the sewers."

"It's a modern city," said Darb. "There aren't any sewers."

"I'm just telling you," said Reg, slapping at the insects that orbited her head.

The shuttle had put down one klick to the east of the city. Scrub vegetation persisted here. The gorgons, when they had attacked Antipolis, appeared to have descended on the ziggurat from above, then moved off to the west. The western ground was eaten to the dust.

Sounds carried on the scorching breezes. The Marines could hear the gorgons in the distance, countless bladed teeth in millions of mouths, crunching their way westward.

The Marines started walking toward the ziggurat.

"You gotta wonder why gorgons would choose to land on a structure this—this—" Darb waved his hand in the air as if a word would fall into it. "*Appetizing.* I mean, it's a sand castle. All the hologramic froufrou wouldn't have confused the gorgons. Someone in there must have resonated."

"A lot of someones," said Ranza. "This colony is a hundred fifty light-years from Palatine. You gots to know the

Thaleians aren't sending messages home by passenger pigeon."

Resonance originating from the ziggurat would have attracted the Hive in its swarms.

"So why didn't the gorgons go to Palatine first?"

Ranza stopped. Darb stopped. Both of them stared at Kerry Blue.

"What?" said Kerry. "What'd I say? Palatine's closer to the Deep End, isn't it? Palatine is swapping res pulses with Thaleia. Shouldn't the gorgons have stopped to eat Palatine first?"

Resonance exists everywhere at once, on infinite harmonics. Touch one harmonic, and no one will know unless he is tuned to listen on that precise harmonic—in which case the listener will pick up the pulse instantly. But the listener will not be able to trace the pulse back to its source, because resonance exists everywhere at once.

Unless the listener was a gorgon. Gorgons were drawn to resonant senders and receivers on any harmonic.

Gorgons had come to Thaleia and not to Palatine.

Why didn't the gorgons go to Palatine first?

"That's a hell of a question, Blue," said Darb.

The Hive seemed to have hopped straight over the Roman capital world. And gorgons never pass up a meal.

The Marines approached the city warily, taking care to step around the Thaleian mines. None of the Marines wore a personal force field, because the PFs did not work against gorgons. The force fields worked well against beam weapons, but were designed to allow low-velocity objects to penetrate—things like air. The PF allowed your feet to contact the ground, allowed your hand to draw your sword. Did not allow lethal projectiles or beam fire through.

Gorgons had learned at exactly what speed a personal force field would permit a tentacle through. They learned that a long time ago. Probably on board the *Sulla*.

And PFs would probably not protect the Marines against the Thaleian mines anyway. The mines were actually native plants. Chameleon-colored vegetation, the mine splayed its leaves flat to the ground, and it looked like the ground. But you step on it, and up come the nettled leaves, wrapped around your calf. If you're bare-legged, you are now screaming and bleeding. If you are in field fatigues, you're cursing and cutting the flat hairy leaves loose from your pant leg with your sword or knife, and—with gloved hands—peeling pieces of leaves off your fatigues with a sound like Velcro separating, then trying to get the leaves off your gloves. Then shooting the roots with your beam pistol-you're-not-supposed-to-be-carrying, just 'cause you feel like it.

"No wonder we let the lupes have this planet," said Carly, sheathing her knife.

"The whole world isn't like this," said Darb.

"Yeah, this is the garden spot," said Reg.

A place of scathing sun, searing air, vicious plants, and worse insects.

Insects darted and caromed round them.

Hive sign was ever present.

In the small, self-contained world that was a spaceship, any Hive sign meant you were in immediate mortal danger. The Marines were not accustomed to having panicked insects around them constantly. So here on the planet, they existed in nerve-scraping anxiety.

They carried canisters of Zakan moths wherever they went. The moths were natural Hive proximity detectors.

A canister hung from each Marine's belt. You checked your canister every ten paces to keep your sanity. If your moths were quiet, you probably weren't in imminent danger of being eaten.

But if your moths were quiet, you caught yourself worrying that they might be dead, so you were still on high alert.

Ranza sent Baker Team around to a southern entrance of the yellow-brown ziggurat. Took Alpha to the north side herself.

Alpha Team entered the enclosed city through an air lock, like a ship.

The inner door opened to cool soft air and total darkness. The Marines illuminated their lanterns.

The first chamber was as featureless as the outside of the ziggurat. But there were no insects banging around in here.

Kerry Blue sighed, ran her hand back through her sweaty hair. "That's better."

The place was silent.

Except for the Zakan moths fluttering and squeaking in the Marines' canisters.

"Heads up. Swords out," Ranza ordered, her lantern directed every which way. "Somebody's home. Keep your wits about you."

Darb muttered, "Let's see, I got my nitwit, my half-wit, my dimwit and my twit. All here. Ooof." Took an elbow in the kidney. Felt like Carly's.

Ranza said into her com, "Baker Leader, this is Alpha Leader. We have Hive sign."

"Roger that, Alpha Leader."

"I'll take first point," said Ranza. "Darb, you're ass end Charlie. The rest of yous, don't bunch up! We know they're here."

Alpha Team set out under low ceilings and featureless walls.

Ranks of doors all along the spiral corridor led into tight pigeonholes of living compartments. This sector of the ziggurat appeared to be a dormitory of sorts, with shared kitchen, dining, and bath facilities.

Romans were different. This was all unAmerican.

The Marines moved up the corridor, dorm room by little dorm room. All with low ceilings and no windows. Made the compartments easy to search.

They came to a compartment furnished with little more than a hammock of some synthetic weave that felt just like cotton sailcloth, and a small table that looked like woven cane but couldn't be, because there was not a single bite mark on it. There was one closet, which had quite a bit of storage space in it now that the gorgons had eaten all the natural-fibered clothes from it. They had also cleaned out the bar.

"How can anyone live this way?" said Kerry Blue, boots crunching on broken wine bottles, just as Carly turned on what looked like a light switch.

Gentle daylight filled the claustrophobic space, and the stuffy compartment was transformed. It breathed ocean air.

Soft breezes and subtle sounds gave the sensation of great space. The Marines were now on a balcony under an open sky.

They looked out to an empty beach. Snowy white seagulls squalled. Sunshine glittered on the great expanse of emerald-blue water. Rush of gentle breakers sounded as if coming from below.

"Okay, well, that's how," said Kerry.

Twitch Fuentes tried to lean on the white railing that wasn't really there, pitched forward and banged his head against the sky.

Ranza barked, "Hurry it up. I don't want to be here all day."

"I do!" said Dak, trying out the hammock. Knew that was real.

Carly turned off the holoimages, tipped Dak out of the hammock. "Compartment secure."

Ranza tagged the door. "Move on."

They checked for monsters under all the beds and in all the closets of all the rooms. All the tiny living quarters could transform into illusions of space, luxury, romance, or serenity. Or the tree fort, obviously a young boy's space. "Damn, I wish I'd had one of these!" Darb said.

The room illusions were a source of endless fascination. Until Ranza ended it, promising to bring up on charges the next Marine who powered one up.

Baker Team, on the far side of the ziggurat, had brought a rat terrier with them. A small, rat-looking thing named Godzilla. Godzilla had been set loose in the ziggurat's vent system. Alpha Team could hear Godzilla's little claws tippy tapping through the extensive ductwork.

"I *hope* that's God," said Dak on second thought.

They all listened. It was a definite four-footed tapping, not a gorgon blunder.

They had started taking the compartments two at a time. Three Marines in each, one keeping watch in the corridor.

"Who *built* all this?" said Kerry Blue, slapping a tag on yet another door.

"Automatons," said Cole Darby. "This planet is headquarters of PanGalactic Automated Industries. Haven't you ever heard of Constantine Siculus?"

"Sure," said Kerry. One of those historical names everyone had heard of but did not necessarily know anything about.

In the last century, Constantine Siculus had founded Pan-Galactic Automated Industries, a core of machines that could design and build other machines or entire factories that would manufacture whatever you needed made. Pan-Galactic did not invent, but it could engineer or reverse engineer, and organize your entire supply chain from raw materials to working product. "All you do is decide what you want done, you pay up, and you get your—your—" Darb searched for an example. He stooped to pick up a silver disk the size of a dinner plate lying in the corridor. Presented it like a finished product: "You get your landing disk."

"You can keep that one." Kerry curled her lip and pushed the offered LD away from her.

Alpha Team had found quite a few of the Roman landing disks in the ziggurat. Roman LD's were smaller than U.S. make. They lacked the reassuring heft of government issue.

Marines displaced all the time, so they stopped thinking about how dangerous and precise an operation displacement was until faced with someone else's equipment. Then your first thought was: You will never catch me on one of those.

Safe displacement required three signal termini. One signal from the sending station. One at the destination—which was normally a landing disk (LD) like this one. And a third signal on the thing in transit—for human beings that was the displacement collar. U.S. Marines wore dog collars. Romans wore torques. For cargo you used a strap.

Neglect the displacement strap on your cargo, you had better own the insurance company.

Nothing in God's own galaxy could make a U.S. Marine trust a Roman landing disk.

Alpha Team took to bowling the flimsy silvery disks down the ramps until Ranza stopped that, too.

Beam fire resounded somewhere within the hollow ziggurat.

Ranza spoke into her com. "Baker Leader. This is Alpha Leader. What is your status?"

"Little busy here, Alpha Bitch!"

From the com you could hear swords meeting stone walls. Grunts and snarls as Marines swung at the enemy.

"Do you need assistance, Baker?"

"Negative. Get your own."

Ranza clicked off. "Baker got first ooze."

"Oh, shhhhhh—" Kerry started in disappointment, met Ranza's warning scowl. Finished, "—inbone."

A frantically paced tap-tap-tapping and a loud yap-yap-yapping blurred together in the ductwork.

Sounds of a rat terrier moving near light speed.

"God!" cried Dak Shepard. "Where is God?"

There was also a blundering, thumping and thrashing in the vents. The sound seemed to be everywhere.

Gorgon.

Godzilla had shared sewer duty with Reg Monroe in the legionary fortress. Reg shouted, terrified, "Godzilla?"

Dak yanked off the nearest vent cover, called, "Here, God! Here, God!"

Carly turned her head sideways, trying to separate out the sounds. "Where is he?"

"Here, boy!" Dak called.

The fast-clattering toenails sounded closer and closer.

"Here he comes."

A white football of dog rocketed out of the open vent, sailed into Dak's arms. The rest of the team had swords drawn. Hacked down the tentacles that bloomed from the opening.

The dog quivered, licking Dak's face.

Ranza spoke into her com: "Hey, Baker. We got your dog."

The dog was wagging itself.

A pat on the head, pop him into the vent, and Godzilla was clicky-clacking back into the hunt.

Darb walked point now.

Rounding a bend in the spiraling ziggurat, Cole Darby suddenly stopped with a gasp. Sounded no warning, just stopped there.

Kerry moved up behind him. Looked round the bend.

A young woman with an impish smile and blue-gray gaze, which met Darb's with seemingly genuine interest, spoke in a light, pretty voice, "*Ave*. May I help you find something?"

The woman spoke Latin. Kerry Blue knew what she'd said because Kerry was wearing a language module.

Darb gawked at the woman, could not talk.

Kerry could. "Yeah, gorgons," she answered in English, at the same time that Ranza came stalking round the bend, "Darb, you afthole, what kind of point man are y— *Lady, what are you doing here!*"

The woman, clad in pastel mufti, tilted her head and asked, in English this time, "Oh, have you mistaken me for a human being?"

Alpha Team had never seen Ranza speechless before.

Kerry answered for her, "Uh, well, *yeah*."

"Uh," said Darb.

When Ranza found her voice, she had no time for the questions of fake people. Demanded, "Do you know what a gorgon is, chicky?"

"Yes," the gynoid said pleasantly. "One of the monsters."

Ranza hauled the gynoid about-face and gave her a push up the corridor. "You can help us find the *monsters*."

"Well, most of them left the city," the gynoid said as she might apologize for being out of Ranza's brand of beer. "But I think we might be able to find some for you. This way, if you like."

The gynoid led the way, her hips rolling, skirt swishing. She had a soft, civilian shape to her.

"Hey. Hey, you. Girl thing." Dak moved up the column. "What are you called?"

The gynoid glanced back with a pretty smile. "I am Kayle."

Carly scrunched her face. "Like the vegetable?"

"K-A-Y-L-E," said Kayle.

"She's really well made." Dak poked at the soft supple skin of Kayle's arm. "Who makes them this good?"

"PanGalactic Automated Industries," Kayle said brightly.

Reg called from the rear, "How do we know she won't lead us into a trap?"

"Trap," said Kayle. "That would mean you don't know

the monsters are there." She turned round to ask, smiling, "Do you want to be surprised?"

Ranza seized the gynoid's arm, hauled her round, gave her a shove. "Find the gorgons, chicky. Sing out when you see 'em."

Sniggering, muttering among the Marines. Speculating on what the perky gynoid's song choice might be. Maybe *Mary Had A Little Lamb*?

"Oh, here we have a nice surprise," said Kayle.

A nightmare shape hurtled down a fire ladder from above.

Kayle moved out of the way. The gorgon rushed past Kayle, and leaped at the Marines.

Skewered itself on Ranza's barbed pike, knocking the pike out of Ranza's hands. Fell to the floor and thrashed itself to death on the barbs.

A round bite wound the size of a quarter bled on Ranza's cheek. She batted away Darb's attempt at first aid.

"Ranza, it's gonna scar. You have a nice face."

"Oh, get blown up," said Ranza.

Ranza's was a strong, square face. The top line of her nose described a graceful aquiline curve, but without the aquiline hook on the end. Her thick eyebrows were not quite a unibrow, but the two were very friendly.

Ranza rubbed the blood off her cheek against her shoulder, picked up her pike, and cleaned the melted gorgon's remains off it with Kayle's pastel skirt.

Kayle watched with an expression of well-isn't-that-nice on her face.

Alpha Team's U.S. insignia did not seem to disturb Kayle either.

Never having Americans on her world, Kayle did not recognize Rome's enemies when she was guiding them on a tour of her masters' citadel.

"She's not wondering why we're wearing U.S. uniforms," Kerry Blue muttered aside to Reg.

"It's a machine," said Reg. "It don't *wonder*."

Ranza batted them both up backside the head. "Spread out! You bunched up for a group photo shoot? Move. Move. Bring the arugula."

It was nightfall by the time the Marines secured the zig-gurat from the last gorgon presence. They had also cleared all the outbuildings.

A large stable outside the complex had been eaten clean of leathers. But there were no horse teeth in any of the stalls. Someone had thought to let the horses out before all the people fled to the legionary fortress.

Another cluster of buildings, furnished with very small furniture, had to be a boarding school. "Oh, they're so cute." Reg held up a child's chair.

"Baby Romans," said Carly. Spat on the schoolroom floor.

Another enclosure, dotted with beautiful statuary, turned out to be a necropolis. Modern Romans practiced cremation, so none of the graves had been dug up by hungry monsters, though something had eaten all the flowers.

Alpha Team met up with Baker Team inside the ziggurat. Lay on the ground of a faux outdoor mall, gazing up at a faux sky full of faux stars. The air was mild and smelled of grass, though the gorgons had eaten all the real grass. The Zakan moths lay quiet in their canisters.

Dak liked cute things. Could not get Reggie to sit on his chest, so God was sitting on Dak's chest, licking his face.

Reggie had curled up next to Dak, asleep, her cute face smooth, her big breasts stacked one on the other.

The stars overhead looked much the same as they did from Earth. Thaleia was only seventy-one light-years off-center from Sol.

Notably different in the star patterns was a bright yellow star, prominent in the false heaven, probably brighter than it ought to have been at a distance of seventy-one light-years. "Is that us?" Ranza pointed at the yellow star.

Darb nodded. "Yeah. That would be Sol."

"Why Sol? Why would Romans want to look at our sun in their fake sky?"

"Earth is Rome's home world," said Darb. "They want it back."

"Over my rotting carcass," said Ranza.

Kerry Blue and Big Richard from Baker Team had gone off to try out one of the fantasy bedrooms.

"Why do they call him Big Richard?" Darb asked, rankled at Kerry's choice of partners in her little expedition. "His name is Lawrence."

"Well, he don't have a big *Larry*," said Carly, her head resting on Twitch Fuentes' belly. "Figure it out."

Ranza Espinoza clicked on her com, signaled Legion Draconis. Told Herius Asinius he was clear to start sending the refugees back to Antipolis. "And nobody resonate, Hairy Ass, or I'll eat you myself!"

John Farragut stood in deep shadow within a vast crater. The shade was desert cold and dry. Native insectoids, the kind called cannibals, were thick down here. The cannibals' diet consisted solely of each other, just not their own brood. They would eat other broods, then seek out and inseminate their eggs.

The earth down here was a thin layer of windblown debris on top of bedrock, so little vegetation of any size grew on it. Some mobile blue-gray plants had wandered down, stuck their roots to the bedrock, and trolled for insects with their sticky, ciliate stalks. They feasted on cannibals.

Farragut's Marine guard watched him from the rim. Farragut had no real military purpose for being in the crater. But there was something about a crater that made you want to climb down into it.

And this crater was not supposed to be here.

Farragut checked and rechecked his map before hailing *Merrimack*. "Gypsy, I need a xeno. Can you put one on the com?"

He got two of them on the com. Doctors Weng and Sidowski.

"Gentlemen," Farragut announced. "I am standing in the middle of a big ol' crater a few miles across, and I am holding a surveillance map that shows a factory town at these coordinates. Now I think I'm reading this map right, and I think I'm reading my coordinates right, and I think I should be standing in the middle of a PanGalactic factory and I'm not. Any idea why I don't see a factory?"

"It's-ay one-gay." said Doctor Weng.

"Ot-nay ere-thay, aptain-cay," said Doctor Sidowski.

"Gentlemen, why are you speaking pig Latin?"

"It's a Roman world," said Weng.

"And all Romans are pigs," said Ski.

"When in Rome," said Weng.

"Y'all can belay that kind of talk as long as the truce holds," said Captain Farragut. "Clear?"

"Yes, sir."

"Yes, sir."

"Why does my map show a factory town here?"

"Old surveillance, sir," said Ski.

"Your survey was taken before the sentinel satellites and jammers went into orbit sixty years ago," said Weng.

"Sixty-one years ago," said Ski.

"But there was a town here sixty years ago?" Farragut asked.

"Sixty-one years ago," said Ski.

"Yes," said Weng.

"And now there is a crater," said Farragut. "Was there an asteroid impact here?"

"Negative," said Weng. "There is no mineral evidence of shock metamorphism. No concentric ridges round the point of supposed impact. No trees knocked over outside the crater."

"There aren't any native trees on Thaleia," Ski muttered.

"No debris fallout. No melt rocks. No fragments of ejecta in the surrounding area. No ash."

"Not an asteroid," Ski cut to the conclusion.

"Bomb?" Farragut guessed again.

"Negative," said Weng. "No burn layer. No residual radiation. No ash."

"Cleanly done," said Ski.

"Cleanly done by what?" said Farragut.

Murmurs of consultation on the other end of the com.

"Continental Knife," said Weng.

"Continental Knife," said Ski.

Farragut was astonished. "Was this some covert operation of *ours?*" Hijacking an entire factory town would certain qualify as industrial espionage taken to weird levels. Yet Farragut would not put it past the CIA to launch such an expedition.

"If it were covert, how would we know about it?" said Ski.

"However," Weng interjected. Could always count on these guys for a however. "It has the look of Roman work. Your crater is round. A U.S. Knife makes a more ovate footprint."

"Sixty-one years ago was the floruit of Constantine Siculus," Ski offered for consideration.

"End of floruit," said Weng.

"Rome gated him," said Ski.

Whether pearly ones or those of hell, Rome had shown Constantine Siculus a gate.

"With a Continental Knife?" said Farragut.

"The guy *was* PanGalactic Automated Industries. Brilliant man," said Weng.

"Yeah, real brilliant turning your empire into a stack of dominoes," said Ski, sarcastic. "It was a design flaw in Pan-Galactic's killer bots that allowed the Hive to detonate all the bots and kill *Legions*."

"Constantine Siculus had the power to knock over those dominoes himself," said Weng. "Maybe the domino flaw was intentional. And maybe that's why Constantine had to go. The Empire would have to feel well and truly threatened to rob itself of a brain like that."

"I don't think Rome killed Constantine with a Continental Knife," said Ski. "I think Rome used the knife to take Constantine's factory away from him."

Farragut cut in: "Gentlemen, it is not that I don't find Roman history and intrigue interesting. I do. But that's not what I'm doing in this crater. Just tell me: Can I cross this site off my list of human habitats to secure?"

"Pretty sure," said Weng.

"It's a hole, sir," said Ski.

Titus Vitruvius curled up in his own bed. Home at last. In Antipolis.

The air smelled of pine needles. Holoimages transformed the tiny compartment into a wooden tree fort. The night sky was always starry outside the window in his room. The moon above the trees was always full. It cast a gentle blue light in the pitch-darkness.

It had been a noisy night with a lot of thunder. A storm without clouds. He couldn't sleep.

He kept an ant farm by his bed, just like Legate Herius Asinius told him to.

He watched the ants pouring out of their tunnels.

And those boring, dead-looking Zakan moths, in the clear canister the legate had given him, stirred, fluttered.

Whining.

6

KERRY BLUE KICKED from a dream of gorgons to twilight awareness. Not sure where she was. Recognized the confines of her sleep pod, ship sounds and smells. She was on board *Merrimack*. Ranza was shaking her and bellowing: "We're going back to Antipolis *yesterday!*"

Kerry moaned into her pillow, already falling back to sleep. This had to be part of her gorgon dream. "We already secured Antipolis."

"It's under siege by gorgons. From the inside!"

Woke her up.

Stepped on Reggie as she fell out of her pod.

The ziggurat spouted smoke from many fires. The residents had tried to defend themselves. Legion Draconis was here by now. Legionaries with swords stood outside the ruin, thoroughly oozed.

The legate, Herius Asinius, was here. A boy, latched on to him tighter'n a tick, must be his son. The baby face at the legate's waist was fixed, grim. Dark eyes were wide and dry.

Colonel Steele was here, too. Looked like a UXB. Fair face red as fire, his scalp blazing red through white-blond buzz cut hair.

Steele roared down Ranza's throat as Red Squad arrived, "How could any troops of mine uf a site this bad!"

Ranza could not answer.

Kerry spoke up. Someone had to. May as well be Kerry Blue, 'cause Steele already hated her anyway. "Sir, we did it by the book. There weren't any gorgons here when we left. The dogs missed 'em. The *moths* missed 'em. *They weren't here.*"

Steele did not even look at her. Ordered: "Blue, back to the ship. Guard duty. Lower engine room."

Oh, yeah. Of course. Kerry snapped to attention. "Aye, sir!" *You just had to talk at him, didn'tcha, Blue? Why don't I just move my locker down to the bottom sail?*

Ranza Espinoza held her chin forward, her lips tight. Vibration in her throat betrayed that she was scared or pissed or both. Steele drilled her: "Where'd you mess up?"

Ranza's eyes were so narrow all you saw was a gleaming silver sliver between thick black lashes. "We were good, sir."

Steele shifted his glower to Baker Leader, who confirmed, "We were, sir. We were good."

And Steele nodded. Still mad, but not at his Marines anymore.

Because Steele was one of them. He picked up his Marines' dead albatross and wore it with them. "They got us," Steele growled. "Espinoza, find out how this happened. Report back to me. And I'll tell you this—it's not happening again. You got that!"

"Sir! Yes, sir!"

And—oh, no—here comes that man you really really don't want to face right now with an up screw this big.

Captain John Farragut moved in like a storm front. He looked big as a bull, his nostrils flaring. He was all but snorting.

The ziggurat belched black smoke, survivors huddled outside the settlement, crying. They had been safe inside the legionary fortress. They had been safe until the U.S. Fleet Marines had told them to go home.

Farragut's voice started very quiet. Worse than his roars.

"This is unforgivable." Farragut paced in front of Red Squad, turned round again. "Not just a lapse of security. This is titanic."

Colonel Steele stood like a stone. "Yes, sir."

The legate, Herius Asinius, unwound the boy's arms from his waist. Smoothed down the boy's curls, and sent him away.

Farragut was still pacing, outraged. "This site was pronounced clear. I come back to find gorgons *inside* the complex, eating their way *out*. That suggests there were gorgons *in* there when we left it, doesn't it?"

"Yes, sir," said Steele.

"And?"

"Sir. My Marines report that the Zakan moths, the resident automatons, the dogs, and my Marines all failed to detect any sign of Hive. The gorgons must be doing something new."

Farragut looked skyward. Nodded. "Gorgons threw a curve ball." Everyone already knew that gorgons were adaptable. "What exactly did they do to fox us? They can hide from the insects now? If they can do that, TR, we are hosed."

"Don't know, sir."

"Know." That was an order.

A crack like a thunderclap split the air. Came from somewhere inside the ziggurat. Not an explosion. Farragut had a long-practiced ear. Knew that sound at once.

Farragut hailed his exec on board *Merrimack*. "Mr. Dent. Identify whichever ship is making displacements to the surface, and escort it out of the solar system, please."

Commander Gypsy Dent's alto voice sounded from the com. "Aye, Captain."

Then Farragut called to anyone within earshot: "Did anyone get a direction on that? I'm going to clap someone in irons for that." And to Steele, "Do we have irons?"

The captain was probably not kidding. Steele said, "We could fabricate some."

The boy, who had not gone far from the legate's side, returned to Herius Asinius at a trot. Tugged on his tunic for attention.

The boy was holding a jar of Zakan moths.

The whole jar fluttered and whined.

"Holy God," someone said.

One of the Marines broke ranks to run apart from the others and throw up.

Captain Farragut met Herius Asinius' gaze. Farragut had his answer. The last answer he ever wanted.

It was an unspeakable horror.

The gates of hell were open. Gorgons had learned to displace.

The gorgons could displace from the Deep. They could go anywhere.

They could be home in a heartbeat.

Farragut's thoughts turned to his family. His mother, his father, his twenty brothers and sisters.

John Farragut had promised his father he would evacuate the family if he had to.

But there was nowhere in the universe to run.

7

BE CAREFUL WHAT YOU wish for, Herius Asinius.

He had wanted to see the American brought low, as low as the Legions of Rome.

So, John Farragut, welcome to a hopeless battle. A planetary siege with endless hordes that killed Legions. Welcome to despair, you who expected to save the universe.

A U.S. Marine, dismissed from the others, walked past Herius Asinius, making her way toward a shuttle set to leave the planet. Herius spoke at her in English, "Go on, American girl. You can always get in your ship and run. That tactic has always worked for the *Merrimack*."

Kerry Blue shrugged. Never gave much mind to what a Roman thought of her. The worse the better. And actually what the Roman said was true. *Mack* could always outrun a gorgon swarm. And Kerry Blue never had a problem with that tactic.

Mack wasn't running this time.

Problem here was, as Dak was saying: "Gorgons are on the five-yard line. Can't let 'em in the end zone."

"Yeah, that's profound, Marine," said Ranza, whacking Dak upside the head. "Ugly up, ladies, we got things to kill."

Kerry turned and called back to Steele. "Colonel! Can I stay and fight?"

Strange expressions moved across his red face. She thought he was going to shoot her. Steele roared: "NO!"

A Roman legionary approached the Americans upwind of the smoke. A very young legionary, no more than sixteen years old. He came at a run. Stopped well short of Captain Farragut and his guards. Announced: "The legate's compliments, Captain Farragut. There is something you need to see."

Captain Farragut let himself and his Marines be led to a cluster of buildings up on the hillside apart from the ziggurat on what used to be a grassy knoll, eaten bald.

Merrimack's civilian adviser, Jose Maria de Cordillera, came with them, looking out of place. A Terra Rican nobleman, Jose Maria dressed like Terra Rican aristocracy, in muted colors, simple lines, and the finest fabrics. Under Thaleia's harsh white sun he wore a flat-crowned broadbrim black hat, its silken cord drawn under his chin. Jose Maria was a wasp-waisted, trim, and striking man for all his sixty years. He wore his long glossy black hair held back in a silver clasp.

Merrimack's crew had long since stopped thinking of Jose Maria as a civilian. He was their *Don* Cordillera. Nobel laureate, microbiologist, expert swordsman, wealthy Renaissance man. Jose Maria was *Merrimack*'s sword master, the captain's confidant.

Jose Maria de Cordillera had joined the *Merrimack* on a personal mission to see the Hive exterminated.

Farragut was glad to have Jose Maria with him right now. He slowed the pace as he saw where he was headed, where the legate waited.

From the adjacent playground, the complex of low buildings on the hill looked ominously like a boarding school.

John Farragut knew he did not want to see this. But it happened under his protection, so he was obligated to look. Heard Jose Maria's murmur. Sounded like a benediction. This was going to be horrible.

And the Roman legate, burned, covered in soot and gorgon ooze, looked as if he were chewing venom.

Herius Asinius waited next to a bunker that had been

built against tornado, fire, or bomb. The bunker's metal hatch had been pried up, its stout metal hinges pulled off as if a giant starfish had torn open a steel-and-concrete clam.

Hive work.

Outside the twisted hatch lay a Roman helmet, a kevlar vest, some shredded synthetic cloth, black as a legionary's uniform. A pair of legionary boots ripped to pieces. A scatter of brass buttons. A kevlar glove. A Roman projectile side arm, its magazine spent. A sword.

The bare ground around the bunker was wet and muddy with puddles of brown ooze. What dead gorgons looked like.

The monsters had not got into the bunker without a fight.

Three Marines went down the concrete steps ahead of the captain. They came back out of the ground, their faces colorless, and pronounced the bunker clear in unsteady voices. They advised against the captain going down.

I don't want to see this. I have to see this.

Farragut descended into the bunker.

There were no torn boots or cloth down here. The victims must have been wearing natural fibers. There was little to see.

Only the scatter of shiny little pearls on the floor.

Tiny teeth.

Farragut knelt and gathered them. Saw the tremor in his own hand.

One of the Marine guards, who had followed the captain down, slung his weapon across his back and knelt down to help. The other stood watch, squinting up the steps, his mouth twitching.

Farragut rose, mounted the steps stiffly.

"Jose Maria, do you have a handkerchief?"

Don Cordillera produced a fine linen cloth. Farragut emptied his hands into it.

"Madre de Dios," Jose Maria murmured, folding the pitiful collection up gently.

Farragut excused himself and marched up the hill toward the school buildings, as if there were something he needed to check up there and only he could do it.

He marched round the back of one of the sand-colored buildings.

Alone, he fell back against a windowless wall, turned his face up at the pitiless blue sky. Tears fell like rain.

He slid down the wall into a crouch. His face wrinkled up. Had not felt this low since he had given *Merrimack*'s surrender to the Roman General Numa Pompeii.

Baby teeth. They should be under pillows, one at a time. Where was the love of God?

He swallowed sobs, fighting to stay silent. Breathed and breathed until he could breathe without sobbing, and he could hold his hand steady again.

A shadow crossed his hand. He had not heard anyone follow him up here.

He looked up. A long way up to a lean, tall figure. The man looked very lean because he was clad in black. Looked tall because he was very tall. He was six foot eight at least, his stony features, strong and regular, but too hollow, too taut and forbidding to be attractive. He stood over Captain Farragut, imperially proud, bitter, closemouthed.

Dignitos. The Romans owned that word, and this man had it. The power and the glory. His dignitos would have made him imposing. Even if he were not really, really tall.

"I didn't know anyone was here," said Farragut, voice gone gravelly.

"How do you live with yourself after this?"

The thought startled Farragut. Ought he to be feeling suicidal? "I have a job to do."

"No guilt?"

"It's just not helpful, Augustus." Farragut got to his feet.

Caesar Magnus had given Augustus to Farragut a year ago. Farragut had promptly given Augustus over to Naval Intelligence.

Farragut had not seen Augustus since.

The patterner's cables were hanging loose just now, disconnected, his wrist sockets empty. Nothing plugged in behind his neck.

Farragut did not know too much about the workings of patterners. Knew they could line up a shot that could pass through a space battleship's forward force field, or could ram a cannon barrel up a ship's gunport at speed without wrinkling the vessel that carried it.

Patterners were wicked creations, and you had to wonder why the Empire didn't make thousands of them. It could only be that the Empire *couldn't* make a lot of them. Probably couldn't make many of them, because these things were at least half human. And God knew *those* were always dicey to control.

Farragut was pretty sure patterners were *not* PanGalactic products.

He smeared his sleeve across his wet face, blurring the tear tracks. His eyes felt puffy, probably red, his lashes wet. He dragged the heel of his palm under his eyes, preparing to face his men.

The patterner stood like a critical tree.

"How do I look?" said Farragut.

"Like shit," said Augustus.

There was nothing for it. There were worse things than being caught crying for dead children. Farragut moved out of hiding with a squint like someone who has drunk too much, slept too little, or just run out of tears. He returned to the bunker.

Crouched next to the helmet and torn boots, searching in the caustic mud for an ID. Found it.

Decurion Melissa Asinius Atticus.

He collected her teeth. Picked up a kevlar glove, mostly empty. Felt like there might be a couple of bones left in the fingers. He held the remains in his two hands as if a person were attached, and he was holding Melissa's hand.

"Hero-making, John Farragut?" Augustus' voice sounded over his head. The patterner had followed him here.

Farragut murmured, "Seems to me she did that all by herself."

"She," said Augustus, *"died."*

"Something against heroes, Augustus?" He fished about in the mud for more of Melissa's teeth.

"I understand dying for your duty. The deification is useless to the dead and a danger to the living."

Farragut murmured to the teeth, as if Melissa still had ears. "You gave all you had. Sleep easy now. I'll see you home."

"She can't hear you," said Augustus.

"You speak for the dead, Augustus?"

"I have an insight you don't."

Irritated, Farragut retorted, rising to stand. "You having died when?"

"In my past life."

Farragut did not know what to make of the remark. Said, "This is my life."

"Good for you."

"I should like the respect of the dead."

"The dead are dead," said Augustus.

Farragut did not accept it. He repeated quietly, more to himself than to Augustus, "I should like the dead to think well of me."

He carefully gave over the glove, the teeth, and the ID into Herius Asinius' hands. "Make sure Caesar Magnus knows of this."

Herius nodded, conflicting expressions on his face, attempting, badly, to maintain no expression.

"Melissa Asinius Atticus," said Farragut. "Was she kin?"

Herius Asinius glanced at him as if Farragut had made a foul joke. The legate summoned his legionaries and left Captain Farragut with Jose Maria de Cordillera, the Marines, and Augustus.

"What did I say? Why did Herius look at me like that?"

"His kin," said Augustus, "are legion."

"Legion Draconis—"

"Is almost entirely from *gens* Asinius. There are millions of Romans named Asinius. Almost as many as there are Flavians."

An acrid cloud of black smoke scudded from the ruined ziggurat, up the bald hillock. Made Farragut cough.

Augustus said, "It is your fault this happened."

That rocked Farragut. "Fine. Yes. And where the hell have Naval Intelligence been!"

"I wouldn't know," said Augustus.

How could Augustus not know? Farragut had given Augustus to Naval Intelligence a year ago.

Farragut gazed back toward the smoldering ziggurat. Under his watch. This had happened under his watch.

The gorgons were displacing. Displacing *here*. Why here? Know your enemy. Couldn't.

"The Hive makes no sense," he said aloud.

"Yes, that would be of paramount concern when the universe was creating itself that it make sense to John Farragut," said Augustus.

"It makes sense to *you*?" Farragut challenged.

"It's all entropy," said Augustus. "The Hive. The universe. Entropy is a fundamental condition of the universe. It makes perfect sense," said Augustus. "It is the rest of this idiot's tale that signifies nothing."

Farragut demanded, tired of this, "Augustus, why are you here?"

As if in answer, Augustus flicked something at him. Farragut caught it on reflex. A lightweight, flimsy metal disk. The kind of thing that passed for a landing disk in Rome. John Farragut regarded the disk in his hand. Looked up at Augustus. "Can I have a more comprehensive answer?"

"Destroy them. All of them," said Augustus. He followed that command up with a message capsule, purportedly from the U.S. Joint Chiefs, instructing John Farragut to organize the destruction of all landing disks (LDs) manufactured by PanGalactic Automated Industries.

"I don't understand. Destroy all LDs? All LDs where? On the whole planet?"

"All that there are," said Augustus.

That raised all the eyebrows in the Marine guard.

The realization hit hard. "The gorgons are using our equipment," said Farragut.

"No. They are using *our* equipment," said Augustus. PanGalactic was a Roman firm. Roman displacement equipment was incompatible with U.S. equipment. "Do not miss any. Those in space. Those in orbit. All of them. And not just deactivate. Not just turn off. Destroy."

Farragut did a double-take. *Those in orbit?* "Who put LDs in orbit?"

"How very little you know."

"Augustus, we have been collecting data on the Hive for a solid year, and you are supposed to be a miracle machine at synthesizing data, so why *don't* we know?"

"No, John Farragut. I mean how little *tu* know."

Te was "you" singular in Latin, not *vos*, "you" plural.

Augustus was not saying that any collection of Americans was lacking in intelligence. He had said how little you—John Farragut—know.

Farragut kept his temper in check. He had a long fuse to begin with. And he had just let a civilian Roman settlement under his protection get eaten. He was willing to give the Roman a few miles of leeway. "Glory be, Augustus, just tell me what I don't know."

"Caesar Magnus thought he was serving Rome by giving me into your hands. Rome surrendered to you. *Te*. It was your responsibility to use—or not use—what you were given."

The com on the back of Augustus' hand began blinking. "My keepers summon." Augustus dismissed himself.

A Marine offered, "Brig the son of a bitch, sir?"

Farragut shook his head. Handed the Marine the orders from the JC. "Verify these orders, then start collecting Pan-Galactic landing disks."

He watched the tall bitter Roman go.

There was something he did not know.

8

WHAT WAS MAKING THE war in the Deep End near impossible was the inexhaustible numbers of gorgons out there. And, with displacement capability, gorgon numbers could become inexhaustible in Near Space as well.

But now the gorgons' invasion route to Near Space was known. The defense plan became simple: destroy the landing disks. That would end the invasion and limit the battle to those gorgons already in Near Space.

Thaleia was PanGalactic Automated Industries' headquarters. PanGalactic's central database contained a catalog of every PanGalactic landing disk ever manufactured. So locating every last one of the LDs was not impossible. Landing disks were made to be found. It was just a matter of doing it. Over and over and over.

There were over one billion units in circulation throughout the Roman Empire.

Caesar Magnus assisted in the collection and destruction by issuing a decree making it a capital offense for any Roman to maintain a PanGalactic LD.

At the same time, Caesar also declared that any bid coming from outside the Empire for the design and manufacture of replacement displacement equipment would not be considered. No outsider was going to benefit from "the sacrifice Rome makes in the name of human defense."

"Rome's sacrifice? Oh, my Aunt Fanny!" Kerry Blue cried, returned from her stint on guard duty in the ship's armpit. "The Romans bring 'em here, we clean up their mess!"

"You didn't have to do sewers," said Reg.

The landing disks were everywhere on Thaleia, which could be expected on their matrix world, but the LDs were in odd places. Under the sea. In the arctic. And yes, landing disks had somehow ended up in orbit around Thaleia.

The Marines did not even need to participate in the roundup of LDs on Thaleia. By now everyone and his squid had come to Thaleia to defend Near Space from the gorgons' invasion. Ships from all the nations of Earth, individually, and collectively from the League of Earth Nations came. The U.S. National Guard from all eighty-three United States was here. Citizen volunteers from Palatine came. From every Near Space colony and independent neutral world, people came.

The alien Vwakikikikik sent three ships. No one had ever known squid to make war, so their ships were not battleships. And the Vwakikikikik had no soldiers. What the squid sent to Thaleia were welders, equipped to burn the gorgons under the sea, and to collect the Roman LDs from the ocean floor.

"I never knew squid were friends of Rome," said Kerry Blue.

"They're not," said Cole Darby. "The war is coming home. They're practicing enlightened self-interest."

"Squids are enlightened?" said Dak.

No one found any sign that the gorgons were using either displacement collars or cargo straps in transit, which meant that the gorgons were not displacing safely.

There was no telling how many attempted displacements they had botched.

"Not enough," everyone agreed.

But if all landing disks were removed, the gorgons could never arrive at all. Displacement without a destination was unsuccessful one hundred percent of the time.

In hindsight, it made sense that it would be Roman equipment the Hive chose to use. PanGalactic displacement equipment had a resonant component, which would have. attracted Hive interest, where U.S. displacement equipment would not.

U.S. displacement did not involve resonance, which limited U.S. displacement range to well below one light-second. There was the one huge exception to that. The Fort Roosevelt/Fort Eisenhower Shotgun. The Shotgun did employ resonance to move ships across the two kiloparsecs from Near Space to the Deep End.

Any resonance attracted the Hive.

And Hive swarms were steadily closing in on Fort Eisenhower in the Deep End.

Unless the Hive was destroyed, Fort Eisenhower had five years to evacuate everyone from the Deep, and destroy the Shotgun after them. Even with that, humankind would not be safe from the Hive for more than two generations.

Jose Maria de Cordillera conferred with Captain Farragut. "Though I am heartily encouraged that we may be able to control this present Near Space invasion, it is a fleeting victory. I am gravely disturbed by this development of Hive displacement."

"As are we all, Jose Maria," said John Farragut.

"No, young Captain. Not just the act itself disturbs. It is the implication of a creative leap not seen before in the monster. It is one thing to cause Roman killer bots to detonate. That is the mere flipping of a switch. Quite another for the gorgon to link a displacement unit to a distant landing disk and *somehow* decide to send itself and then, *somehow*, do it. This is an evolution I would never believe, if it were not happening. In fact—no. I do not believe it. This is not happening."

"That's real scientific, Jose Maria." Farragut hazarded a smile.

"It is, actually. The conclusions we make now are based upon insufficient or flawed data. I aver: this is not happening."

"Bet?" said Farragut. "A case of Kentucky bourbon against—?"

"A case of Spanish brandy." Jose Maria clasped Farragut's hand.

"And I really wish you could win, Jose Maria, 'cause I really *really* hate the idea of creative gorgons," said Farragut. "But I'm fixin' to drink bourbon over our fleeting victory in Near Space."

"YeeeeeeeHA! Gotcha, gorgo!" Kerry Blue's Swift bore down on her target in a strafing run.

The destruction of the PanGalactic landing disks had worked. No more gorgons were arriving on Thaleia. Their numbers diminished under concentrated human attack.

And at some point the gorgons of Thaleia realized, if gorgons can be said to realize, they were in trouble. They were too spread out to use their combined energy to fox computerized systems. With no more reinforcements arriving, the gorgons were sitting ducks.

All the ships in orbit saw it first. "The gorgons on the planet surface are swarming!"

The Fleet Marine were issued immediate orders to keep the enemy from forming up in numbers. "Break 'em up. Cut 'em down."

Swifts were not designed to operate in atmosphere. Bombs were more aerodynamic than Swifts. A Swift's cooling system was only designed to get the Swift into space or onto the ground, not to fox-trot around in the middle. You only had minutes to fox-trot, then either park it on the ground or hightail to space, else roast yourself to tastes-like-chicken.

The Marine Wing tried picking off the gorgons on the ground from orbit, but the gorgons avoided the shots. Not that gorgons moved faster than light down there in the dirt. But they appeared to be sensing the Marine's sensors. Gorgons were allergic to targeting solutions. Shots missed by inches.

"Inches count," said Carly.

The only choice was to get in close.

The Swift pilots adjusted their displacement fields forward, to keep the thickest part of the field over bow and keel. The stern was open behind the engines.

Then they dove down there on the deck to fox-trot. Shoved shots up the gorgons' tentacle noses.

The Marines were not even bothering with targeting solutions. They took the enemy down the old-fashioned way, with messy, waste-a-crapload-of-shots strafing runs.

Dak shouted over the com: "Good night, Gretaaaaa!"

Carly: "Hoo ra!"

Reg: "They got their flapping butts here. They ain't ever leaving. Got one! I got one."

"Good. Do that twenty-five hundred more times." That was Ranza.

The gorgons galloped like obscene giraffes before the Swifts.

This close to the ground, you felt the speed, because you could see it.

"Cowboy would've loved this," Kerry sent over the com.

Cowboy's replacement, Cole Darby, sent, "*I* love this. Don't I count?"

Cole Darby was no Cowboy. Kerry hesitated, sent back: "You're a nice guy, Darb."

Twitch Fuentes cackled, and Dak gave a sympathetic moan on Darb's behalf. "Hombre, you can't love the sound of *that*."

Nice. The gals called him nice. Darb protested, "Why don't you just cut off my thing, why don't you?"

Carly: "Got bigger targets. Hoo ra!" Laughed at her own joke.

Dak: "They're cruel. They're cruel."

Darb, bleating: "I don't know if I can perform like this." But Cole Darby did bag his share of gorgons. Just couldn't bring himself to shout *Hoo ra*.

If Cowboy were alive, he would have augered in by now.

Reggie chasing a gorgon: "Come on. Come on. Come on. Come onnnnnn."

"You spend any more time with that thing, you're gonna have to marry it, Reggie girl."

"Shut up, Dak." Reggie jinked with her target. This gorgon had a wobble stop no-rhythm step going for it. Reggie brought her Swift down low on it.

The gorgon leaped.

"Shiiii—" Reg banked upward. "—ingles!"

Dak sang out: "Jumpin' gretas! Did you *see* that!"

"Yeah I *saw* that big bag of legs!" Reg cried, overheating. "I gotta go to the roof."

Reggie's Swift, Alpha Three, rocketed out of the atmosphere.

Kerry dove after Reggie's gorgon. "You don't get away with that, bagalegs!"

Carly snapped on the com: "Too steep, *chica linda*. Get your nose up."

Kerry yelling through the dive: "Yeeeeeee—"

The gorgon jumped. Caught her bow.

Alpha Six plunged deep into the ground and went silent.

9

"**K**ERRY!" TOOK A MOMENT to recognize that voice on the com. Alpha Four. Twitch Fuentes.

The Swifts of Alpha Team circled the site where Alpha Six had augered in.

Smoke issued from the hole in the ground.

"Chica!"

Ranza, in the dead calm voice of dire emergency, kept repeating, "Alpha Leader to Alpha Six. Alpha Leader to Alpha Six. Respond."

Utter nothing came back on the com.

"Merrimack. Merrimack. Merrimack. This is Alpha Leader. Do we have a reading on Alpha Six?"

"Alpha Leader. This is *Merrimack.* We are reading a distortion field at minimal. Tactical advises she should have survived that."

Alpha Three, Reg Monroe, scorching a path back into the atmosphere, sent: "Then why ain't she talking?"

Dak sent: "Kerry, why ain't you talking?"

Ranza checked her chron. Some of her birds had been down here too long. She ordered Dak Shepard to go upstairs and grab some vacuum.

Dak Shepard streaked heavenward. Cole Darby had to make a run for the roof as well. Could not talk. He was crying.

Ranza, continued mechanically: "Alpha Six. This is Alpha Leader. Respond."

Then she stopped sending. Listened to nothing.

TR Steele listened from *Merrimack*'s command deck, turned gray-white and still as a marble headstone. Dying in the silence.

Kerry Blue. The woman had become the center of his universe. He wanted to go down there and dig her out with his bare hands.

She was a Marine. She was born to fight.

She was his life.

Reg Monroe's voice, pitched high enough to deafen a bat, scared to anger: *"Kerry, say something!"*

Steele marched to the hatch to quit the command deck. He was going down there to dig her out with his bare hands.

The com had gone gravely silent again.

A tiny voice. Carly Delgado's. *"Chica?"*

The quiet lingered.

A cough.

A small voice on the com sounded disgusted: "Oh. *Shick*elgruber."

"Kerry!" All the rest of the voices.

And Colonel Steele barking into the com: "Wing Leader to Alpha Six. Marine, what is your situation."

"I'm stuck."

Ranza: "Wing Leader. This is Alpha Leader. I've got her, Colonel."

Kerry Blue fumbled in the dark. She had been flying in daylight. Then everything had gone dark as outer space. She found the switch for her cockpit light.

In the light she saw dirt and rocks and roots pressing against her distortion field, close and weird and claustrophobic. "This is too much like being buried alive."

"Uh. You *are* buried alive." That was Marcander Vincent at tactical on board *Merrimack*. He supplied her depth at twenty feet.

"Get me outta here!" Kerry yelled.

"Well, Kerry," said Ranza. "Come out."

"I can't move."

"Have you tried backing out the way you came in, mole-woman?" That was Reg Monroe.

Kerry unstrapped, turned round in her seat in the cramped cockpit to check her instrument reading with her own eyes. "No. It caved in."

"It's still the path of least resistance. Move your cow-catcher to the stern and back out."

The cowcatcher was the stoutest part of a ship's distortion field. *Merrimack*'s distortion field could hold off just about anything in the universe. The Swifts' fields were not as formidable. Loading most of the energy in the direction of travel—like a cowcatcher—offered the little spacecraft the most protection.

"Can't I just turn it off?" said Kerry. "I'm not moving, and I'm getting hot in here."

The cooling system on most spacecraft was heavily dependent on the ambient temperature outside being around three degrees Kelvin.

"Do NOT turn your field off!" Reg shrieked at her. "You'll be crushed. Vent out the sides."

A silence.

"Kerry! Did you hear me?"

"Uh-oh."

"Kerry? Translate that."

"I, uh." Too long a silence. You just wanted to reach through the com and throttle her.

"I'm not alone down here."

Carly figured it out first. "The gorgon that grabbed her crate! Where's the gorgon!"

"It's, um, smashed against my nose cone." Kerry knelt up in her seat, her head brushing the canopy. Stared at her bow.

Wadded up round her Swift's nose was a squashed amorphous blob of gorgon. Tentacles led off every which way like flattened hoses.

"You can't crush a gorgon!" someone had to shout.

"Uh, yeah," said Kerry, sour as hell.

It was moving. Slowly.

It was strange-looking, distorted through her distortion

field. She tried to focus on it through the distortion field. And that was it.

It was *through the distortion field*.

Or getting there.

Gorgons could do a lot of impossible things. Like travel faster than light in swarms. And move around in a vacuum.

And penetrate an impenetrable distortion field.

The gorgon was *in* the field itself. Kerry had seen this several times before on board *Merrimack*. *Insinuation* was the word the xenos used to describe how a gorgon wormed its way through an energy field.

"Kerry! Get out of there!"

It was too late.

The gorgon was part of her force field. If she moved her Swift, the gorgon was coming with her.

And it was coming inside.

"O God. O God. O God. O God."

"What?"

Fear quickly turned to anger. Kerry threw her Swift's clear canopy back hard in its slide. She eeled out of her cockpit, squeezing herself into the tight space between the hull and the distortion field.

The space battleship *Merrimack* had an enormous distortion field, with a spacious area between its field and hull. You could get out and *walk* on the *Mack*'s hull under her distortion field.

The Swift's distortion field was much thinner. Kerry had a *maximum* sixteen inches between her metal hull and a really hard energy shell in which to move.

She slithered on the hull, keeping her head low. Elbowed her way forward to where the first circular mouths were emerging from the inner surface of her force field.

Kerry pulled her knife from its sheath. Sliced the mouths off their stalks as they poked through the energy field and into her reach.

She muttered in a breathy snarl as she carved at the loathsome rings of teeth. "You couldn't cut yourself open on a sharp rock, could you? No, you foose-mucker. You just had to stick your faces where they don't belong." She sawed through another toothy maw. The angle was awkward, upward, close to her head, with nowhere to put her elbow.

She tried to shimmy backward. "Can't you just die like a good gorgon? Oh. Oh. Oh."

The severed mouths gave off an acidic gas as they disintegrated into brown residue and dripped down. Burned her hands. Watered her eyes. Stung her nose and closed her throat. "Oh."

"Alpha Six, what is your situation." Sounded like Steele.

"Fox-trotted!" Kerry cried.

Sweat threaded along her scalp. It was hot and hard to breathe. She jabbed her blade into a mouth right over her head. Little teeth popping out like corn kernels. Peppered her hair and dissolved into acidic gore. "Oh!"

Sudden pain and screaming. Hers. Kerry kicked wildly. Banged her head on the energy plane.

A tentacle had outflanked her within the force field, reached through and sunk all its teeth into her back. Tore out a dollar's worth of flesh from over one kidney.

Kerry writhed backward at panic speed, squid-fashion. Hit her chin on the hull. Another bite. Out of her scalp. A banshee shrieking, from every direction. Kerry Blue's voice rebounding on her.

But even in the throes of wild terror she found a strange stillness inside. Some part of her had detached. Watched herself writhe and scuttle and shriek. The animal carcass howling release, while the rest of her knew what to do. Contorted her arm around and continued to carve the hell out of the mouths. Sent them to hell.

Till the gorgon had no mouths, and all she could do was scream as it died on her.

Did not realize how frightful she looked when she reported to Ops for debriefing after the sortie. Figured it out when the Naval Intelligence Officer immediately summoned a medic for her. Spooks never looked out for you. And when Cole Darby said from behind her, "Uh, Blue. You look like you've been foully murdered."

"What?" Reached behind her for a tickling itch. Brought

her hand forward covered in blood. She had thought all that wetness was sweat.

Most of the blood was from the head wound. The gorgon had taken a shard out of her skull with that head bite, and had come within a millimeter of her kidney on the first chomp.

The ship's medical officer, Mohsen Shah answered the summons to Ops. He temporarily patched Kerry Blue's wounds with pink gel to hold her till he could cultivate new tissue and bone for her. Advised the interrogator, "Please be making this inquiry as short as is being possible."

The intelligence officer gave a curt nod. Put the question to all of Alpha Team: "Number of gorgons secured?"

"Pathetic," said Flight Leader Ranza Espinoza.

The IO recorded her answer.

"Observations?" the IO asked.

The Alphas glanced at each other.

"Gorgons jump," said Reg Monroe.

"Gorgons jump high," said Kerry Blue.

"Any other observations?"

"Kerry Blue discovered a wormhole," Cole Darby offered.

The IO glanced up. Asked wryly, "Confirming that using a wormhole collapses the wormhole?"

Never knew IOs to have a sense of humor.

"Yes, sir," said Kerry Blue. The blood in her hair was starting to dry and get stiff.

Just then Lieutenant Colonel TR Steele barreled into Ops with a head full of pissed off.

But he found everyone in Ops smiling.

Locked up everything he meant to say.

If he let out shouting, he may as well drop trousers and show everyone how he felt about Flight Sergeant Blue. So he forced evenness, his face immobile. Asked the Navy interrogators: "Did anyone report the unscheduled mining operation by Alpha Six?"

Kerry Blue shrank a little. Wondered how that foul-up had already got back to Colonel Steele. Wasn't a huge deal. So she buried a Swift. She and her Swift were back on board *Merrimack* and functional. What was the big thing?

The IO answered the Marine CO: "Yes, sir. We thought a Swift ought to manage a depth greater than twenty feet." More spook humor.

Steele was amused as a block of ice.

The IO finished his debriefing. Snapped his file closed. Motioned at Kerry Blue as he spoke to Dr. Mo Shah, "Your man, Mo."

Steele intervened. Demanded a moment with his Marine before giving her over to the medics. Said ominously, "This won't take long."

All of Team Alpha turned toward Kerry Blue. She could only meet the stunned gaze of one of them. Carly. Eyes round with doom.

Heard Ranza speaking, trying to, "Colonel. This is my—"

"Dismissed, Flight Leader," Steele cut her off.

Kerry's mates filed through the hatch in a funereal procession, each giving one last glance back.

Till Kerry Blue was alone with Colonel Steele.

He stalked a circle round her standing at stiff attention. She was cooling down, the pain settling in.

Colonel Steele was going to take her wings. Or transfer her. Or sack her.

This is it.

"What the hell did you think you were doing?"

"Up screwing, sir."

He nodded. An accurate assessment.

Had heard the com. Had died over and over. Heard her screaming. Feeling like being torn open and his guts spilling out on the deck.

Hurt him to see her here. Her pretty shape smeared with gore. Blood clotted her brown hair, soaked the back of her uniform. The medical gel oozed pinkly from her hideous wounds. Her girl-soft cheek was too smooth for a soldier. Her nostrils quivered in fear, pain, or anger. He couldn't tell.

He had listened to her go silent on that cannonball dive into the ground. *Yeeeeeee—*

Cowboy Carver's last words had been *Eeeeeeeha.*

Had she been following Cowboy?

Steele never figured Kerry Blue as suicidal. But she had loved that bastard Cowboy.

Apparently, she loved him still.

Damn Cowboy. Cowboy was dead.

Would he *ever* leave?

"Does it ever cross your mind—" Steele stopped, began again, "Do you ever think *you could die out here?*"

Kerry seemed startled. Answered simply, "I *will* die out here." And to his blank stare, she said, "I live out here. Where else can I die?"

Struck him dumb. He had to gesture at her, because he could not even get out the word: Dismissed.

10

THE YELLOW DAY STAR was just setting. Jose Maria de Cordillera joined a group of Marines resting under the spreading branches of an imported elm, out of the direct light of the hard white primary sun overhead.

Red Squad had been dispatched to this island in the southern hemisphere to take out an enclave of gorgons, which had fled the attacks of the Vwakikikikik in Thaleia's oceans.

Jose Maria took off his hangar, set it aside, and sat on the ground, his arms loosely circling his knees.

Flight Sergeant Dak Shepard lay on the ground, sleeping like a baby. A baby with a handsaw. You could hear Dak Shepard snore in a vacuum.

Twitch Fuentes swatted a winged something out of his face. Native insectoids were plentiful, loud, and bad tempered even without gorgons present. It was tough to tell what was Hive sign and what was normal vicious Thaleian insectoid behavior.

Cole Darby came tromping in from the sunlight, sweating like Dak. He threw himself down in the shade of the elm. Jerked his thumb back the way he had come. "Never *never* use the word *idiosyncratic* to a bunch of grunts. Now Baker Team is trying to synchronize their idiots."

"Do we have to synchronize ours?" came a mumble from the ground.

"Shut up, Dak."

Heat sizzled. In the tree branches overhead, insect noise wound up in rattling whir. It was a calm sound for all its volume. No panic about it. The gorgon population was thinning out, and some insects—those with only close-range sensitivity to the Hive—had settled into normality.

Normality in these insects was loud.

"Are we almost done here, *Don* Cordillera?" Cole Darby asked, pulling off his boots and shaking them out. He angled his feet downwind. "I'm tired of dirt, and I wanna go home."

Home was the *Merrimack*.

Jose Maria nodded. "We are close."

Thaleia was nearly free of gorgons. The battle for Near Space was just about won.

There remained countless hordes in the Deep, closing in on the far colonies and on Fort Eisenhower.

"So what we gotta do to get this done?" Ranza asked, rolling up on her elbows. "Kill the queen?"

Jose Maria demurred with a tilt of his head. Even in the shade his glossy black hair reflected a rich sheen. "That suggestion is based on a misunderstanding of the role of the queen in any hive. The queen does not rule. The queen does not make decisions. The queen is not the brain. The queen is the egg layer. She is also replaceable. Unlike a brain."

"Maybe *your* brain, *Don* Cordillera," said Carly Delgado. "We're not sure about Dak's."

"Hey," said Dak.

"So let's take out the brain," said Cole Darby.

"No!" Dak cried, hands protectively round his head.

"There is no brain," said Jose Maria.

"Yeah, there is!" Dak yelped.

"I apologize, Flight Sergeant Shepard," said Jose Maria, smiling. "I meant in the Hive. The Hive has no brain. Despite the obvious adaptability, there is no evidence of higher intelligence in the Hive."

"They seem pretty smart to *me*," said Kerry, picking at a bite scab on her arm till Carly slapped her to leave it alone.

Jose Maria explained, "Certain organisms change their behavior in groups, according to circumstance. But survival mechanisms should not be mistaken for intelligence."

"Then what *is* it?" said Ranza Espinoza.

"Emergent behavior," said Jose Maria.

"Yeah," said Ranza. "And I still don't know what it is."

Jose Maria bowed his head, abashed. He often spoke above his audience, but never intended insult. "Emergence refers to the spontaneous formation of complex systems from simple organisms obeying simple rules."

"Nope." Ranza wagged her head side to side. "The Hive don't have a brain. I got that far. How's it do what it does?"

"The Hive . . . cooperates. Consider the Portuguese man-of-war. To see its top bladders and its cluster of long stinging tentacles, you would think you were looking at a single animal—a jellyfish. But the Portuguese man-of-war is a cooperative colony of specialized entities. Were you to push a Portuguese man-of-war through a sieve, it would re-form."

"Woolly Bully!" said Dak. "Can we try that!"

"Fortunately—I mean, alas, I do not believe *Merrimack* carries a Portuguese man-of-war on board," said Jose Maria.

Darb said, "Okay, so forget the brain. I've heard a theory that if we find the gorgons' res harmonic, we can uf *their* functions just like they uf ours."

Jose Maria gave a hesitant sideways nod. "It is not quite a theory. It is still a hypothesis. A very attractive hypothesis. If the Hive indeed owes its coherence to resonance, that would make it vulnerable in a way that no other life-form is. Human life—in fact all life excluding the Hive—is protected by its diversity and its degrees of separation."

"In English, doc?" Carly suggested. "Or Spanish?"

Jose Maria started over: "Consider a virus. Let us assume one of us carries a virus."

"Do not!" Kerry Blue cried. "It's a lie."

"A cold virus," Jose Maria specified. "One of us has a cold. The virus requires a vector—a means of transportation—to spread itself from its current host to someone else. The vector could be as simple as a sneeze. Now we—by 'we' I mean this convivial gathering underneath the kindly boughs of this elm tree—at one degree of separation from each other, we could all be exposed to the virus with a single sneeze from the infected person."

Cole Darby nudged Dak with his bare foot. "Cover your mouth next time."

"Though we may be infected, not all of us will express symptoms," Jose Maria continued. "Because of our varied genetics, some of us will clear the disease without ever knowing we were infected. That is the strength of a sexual species—our diversity. Now, instead of a cold virus, consider one of the extinct deadly viruses—"

"But it's extinct," said Kerry. "How can it do anything?"

"We are going back in time for this illustration, Kerry Blue. Back when there were such things as deadly viruses. Consider one for which the most common vector was a mosquito. Let us assume I am infected with the virus. A mosquito bites me, then lands on one of you. Or all of you."

The Marines were seized by an unconscious need to brush imagined pinpricks off their arms and backs.

"None of you will become infected," said Jose Maria.

"Why not?" Darb argued. "Mosquitoes pass blood from person to person."

"Mosquitoes do carry blood from person to person, and might spread a virus with it, but only if the mosquito ingested a virus along with my blood. The mosquito that bit me did not pick up a virus with her bite."

"And we're really really sure of this—why?" said Ranza.

"Because the concentration of this virus in the human bloodstream—or in the bloodstream of any mammal—is very very low. The mosquito only withdraws a small drop of blood from me. The chance of the mosquito ingesting even a single virus with that particular drop of blood is remote. So the mosquito cannot pass the virus from me to you. This virus does not pass from person to person."

"Then how did *you* get it in the first place?"

"Not from another person. The mosquito that infected me may have bitten an infected jay first. The viremia of our subject virus in the bloodstream of a jay or in any of the *corvidae* was great. When the mosquito bites the infected jay, the mosquito has a one-hundred-percent chance of ingesting the virus. But that mosquito may carry the virus to a dead end instead of to a fertile reservoir. When I mentioned degrees of separation, I refer to the number of links required to connect one individual to another. Only one degree separates you and me. We are linked because we know each other."

"So I'm like one degree separated from Dak, but I'm ninety-five-hundred degrees separated from the President of the United States," Reg Monroe said.

"Two degrees actually," said Jose Maria. "I had dinner with President Johnson last month. Two degrees separate you from the President."

"*Well*, then!" said Reg, straightening her back importantly.

"Returning to our deadly, mosquito-borne virus, our one degree of separation is an impassable canyon. The virus cannot negotiate our link. It cannot spread from person to person. So even before we exterminated the deadly viruses, life on Earth already had certain natural walls against the rampant spread of most viruses."

"Why didn't we kill off *all* the viruses—and mosquitoes!—while we were at it?" said Ranza.

"Extinction must be undertaken with only the most profound consideration," Jose Maria said gravely.

"The Hive," said Darb. "We *are* going to exterminate the Hive, aren't we?"

"After profound consideration, yes. The Hive is bound for extinction by my own hand, if no one else accomplishes it first—and anyone may beat me to it with all my love and blessings."

"You're gonna do it with a virus," Reg guessed.

Jose Maria nodded. "Of a sort. The Hive has no degrees of separation and no diversity. Because the Hive is cohered by resonance, and resonance is everywhere at once, the Hive is more like a computer network without firewalls than it is like any organic system. One well-coded computer-type virus could infect the entire Hive instantly, and, as Flight Sergeant Darby suggests, we could uf their functions quite thoroughly. That is a hypothesis I pray to God I may test."

Reg blurted, "*Don* Cordillera, you are so beautiful. Can I bear your child?"

Jose Maria chuckled.

Kerry Blue suddenly jumped up onto her heels in a crouch. "Holes!" she said, casting about her on the ground on all sides. There were a lot of the holes pocking the ground under the scrub grass, holes the size of a finger. Smaller than a gorgon's mouth, but lots of them. "What's in all these foxtrotting holes!"

Jose Maria put out a calming hand. "Nothing, Kerry Blue. Everything is already out."

"What!" Kerry screeched. "What came out!"

Jose Maria pointed up into the shady elm boughs over their heads. "The sounds you have been hearing." He paused as an insect sound wound up, became loud. "Seventeen-year locusts."

Jose Maria turned to Ranza. "Now *this*, Ranza Espinoza, this is emergent behavior. The spontaneous organization of simple organisms with no leader. For seventeen years these insects burrow in the ground, dark, silent, solitary, wormlike. Then comes the night when the entire brood, in its millions, crawls to the surface and changes form." He plucked an empty locust husk off the elm tree trunk. "And our isolated, mute, ground dweller transforms into a noisemaking, gregarious creature, swarming together with others of its kind in an insectoid Mardi Gras for a few brief weeks out in the light."

"They change into something slinky and throw an orgy every seventeen years," said Kerry Blue.

"Once, Kerry Blue. Only once. The offspring of these locusts will organize the next orgy in another seventeen years—all without a leader or a communal brain. There is your emergence. There is your Hive."

Ranza said only: "What Roman squid-for-brains imported uffing locusts to one of their own colonies?"

"It has the look of a mistake," said Jose Maria with a sigh, sitting back against the elm. "The locusts likely arrived inside the roots of imported trees like this one," he patted the elm's stout trunk. "This world was terraformed by a coarse and clumsy hand. Not the way my Mercedes would have done."

Jose Maria de Cordillera had first come aboard *Merrimack* on a quest to find his wife. Dr. Mercedes de Cordillera, an expert xenobotanist, had worked on a secret Roman terraforming project deep in the Deep End. A planet called Telecore by those who knew of its existence.

On her homeward voyage, Mercedes disappeared in the Deep with the Roman ship *Sulla*.

Rome kept the disappearance secret for a long time. Jose Maria's attempt to get information ran aground. Because even Rome's feared Imperial Intelligence did not know what had become of *Sulla*.

And then they discovered other secrets too terrible to tell.

Now it was clear that the crew and passengers of *Sulla* must have been the first human casualties of the Hive.

Sulla was never found.

"This planet was trench-terraformed," said Jose Maria, setting aside his locust shell. "A clumsy, reckless method. But the developer of Thaleia was a self-serving man."

"Constantine Siculus," Cole Darby named the self-serving man. "Founder of PanGalactic Automated Industries. Set himself up as Caesar of Thaleia. Then he decided he was God, so Rome dared him to resurrect himself."

Reg frowned, confused, missing a step. Her pert nose wrinkled up. "Resurrect? Wouldn't that mean he had to die first?"

"Oh, yeah," said Darb. "Rome killed him good."

"Didn't happen, then?" Reg guessed. "The resurrection part?"

"No. It did not."

Kerry Blue cranked her head round to stare at Darby as if her comrade-in-arms had grown a second nose. "Darb, how do you know all this stuff?"

"Our Darb knows lots of stuff," said Carly. "None of it very useful. You know, like Reggie's stuff. But he knows stuff."

Ranza's silver eyes lifted to some point beyond the shade of the elm tree. "You got company, *Don* Cordillera."

Jose Maria did not even look to see who was coming. Gave a secret smile. "I do not believe this visit is for me."

A big figure hove into view. Captain John Farragut, hiking up the hill. Motioned the Marines of Alpha Team down as they made to stand up. That big sunny smile on the captain's face was all for Reg Monroe.

Reg's breath caught with a little gasp. She started up on hands and knees. Farragut's grin got brighter. "Mail call, Mister Monroe."

Farragut noticed every sparrow that fell on his boat, and he knew his Marines by name. And knew that Flight Sergeant Regina Monroe was a short timer with applications out at several schools.

The vid stat in his hand showed the seal of the University of Southern California.

Reg's eyes tried to escape her head. Her face was as pale as a black woman's could be. She was utterly terrified.

Farragut arrived at the elm tree, held out the stat to Reg. "Congratulations, Flight Sergeant Monroe."

Reg sprang straight up with an ear-piercing squeal. She did a little dance that included jumping into Captain Farragut's arms. And him catching her and just chuckling like Saint Nick.

Dak frowned, confused. "What just happened?"

"I'm guessing our little Reggie girl got into college," said Darb.

Reg's face was awash with tears. She squeaked over and over, "USC! USC!"

"Hey, I heard of them," said Dak. "That's a real school. They got a football team."

Reg had only ever enlisted in the Fleet Marine so she could get an education on Uncle Sam's card. There were church mice with more spending money than Reg Monroe had.

Reg had spent four years with John Farragut in front of the front line and waded through gallons of gorgon guts to get here. But she had arrived. College bound. A scant one month and seventy-one light-years from home.

Flight Sergeant Reg Monroe was the happiest she-dog in the known galaxy.

"I own you for another month," Farragut told Reg. "You watch your stern. That's an order."

League of Earth Nations inspectors declared Thaleia free of gorgons, from pole to pole, ionosphere to bottom of the seas.

Celebrations and memorials and thanksgivings were held all across Near Space. It was the first time a planet had ever been cleared of Hive presence without killing the planet.

For Herius Asinius, victory had a bitter edge.

Once again, John Farragut had got off easy. The battle for Thaleia had not been the same as the desperate Roman battles in the Deep. There were no endless hordes of gorgons on Thaleia. No gluies.

There were endless hordes of *humans* here.

The gorgons' line of transportation had been cut. Their reinforcements completely blocked—thanks to *Roman* intelligence, did you mark that, John Farragut?

Legion Draconis had been sent in without tools to do the job. Left it to John Farragut to save the day. Herius still swore that the fireman had set this fire.

Captain Farragut thanked Herius Asinius and released Legion Draconis to continue its former duty on the Roman home guard.

Herius took it as an insult. As if Draconis were still not worthy of Deep End responsibility.

Herius toured every settlement on this Roman world before leaving. He bade farewell to the boy Titus Vitruvius at Antipolis. Titus Vitruvius was his one bright memory of this hole.

Herius felt a startlingly ferocious paternal bond with the child. Valiant little Titus Vitruvius, who desperately wanted to come with him and serve in Legion Draconis.

But the boy had a mother.

Most Romans began life in a petri dish.

Herius Asinius himself took pride in having been conceived in passion. His life began in a womb, even if he hadn't stayed there for the duration. An incubator had finished the job. Titus did him one better. This child had been born of woman. You don't break up a set like that this early.

Pretty sure Titus' mother would murder him if he accepted his enlistment.

Herius dropped on one knee to look up at Titus' teary eyes. "Not that I couldn't use a man like you, you understand, but you already have a duty." And ordered the boy to stand his post and protect his mother. Legion Draconis would wait.

Herius, with his cousin Marcus, returned to the ancient-style fortress where he had made his first stand against the gorgons just months ago. He had aged five lifetimes since then.

Marcus halted the skimmer, short of the fortress, where the road was blocked. Herius and Marcus both climbed out of the skimmer to stare at the construction.

Automatons of PanGalactic Automated Industries were at work building a monumental structure that spanned the approach road to the fortress.

"What the hell is that?"

"Heri!" Marcus seized his cousin's arm. "It's a triumphal arch!"

Herius blinked. The dead last thing he expected. "I'll be damned."

He walked toward it. Marcus ran ahead, round to the other side of the huge stone structure.

Marcus' face changed. Strange unreadable expressions.

Marcus picked up a clod of mud and hurled it at the towering arch.

That certainly boded ill. Herius continued at a measured walk, made the turn to face the thing.

Looked up.

Oh. By. Jove.

Read the inscription on the architrave. *I shan't be damned,* he thought. *I am already in hell.*

S P Q R
IMP. CAES MAGNVS
IOHN FARRAGVT AMERICANO
QVOD CVM EXERCITV EST ARMIS IVSTIS
VIC HOSTES ALIENIGENOS
ARCVM TRIVMPHIS FAC CVR H L

PART TWO

The Ides Of August

11

THE FACE ON THE RES COM screen registered astonishment.

"John!"

A perfect face. Without its frame of long lush chestnut hair—here pulled severely back—the face was naked, perfect. Almond eyes. Sultry. Elegant.

Hard to take seriously.

Captain Callista Carmel, former executive officer of the space battleship *Merrimack* had a beauty to open doors. It also shut them. Beauty was Calli Carmel's last choice for a weapon, but she never threw away a weapon.

Captain Carmel had to drop her ship *Wolfhound* down from FTL to collect a coherent res message from a stationary caller. Resonance exists everywhere at once, but when a caller's time is relative to the receiver of the message, only the mess gets through.

Calli's ship operated in Deep Space, on the far side of the Abyss, so Calli was surprised when John Farragut's image resolved on her res caller. She knew he was fighting the Near Space gorgons. She thought he had that battle won. Now this call. Scared her. She was accustomed to bad news over the resonator. Something had gone wrong. "John, what is it?"

"Cal. I need my Roman expert."

Calli almost laughed. "You're on a Roman planet. Aren't there one or two genuine Romans there you can consult?"

"Lots of 'em. Lookin' at me like I burned their ranch, stole their horses, and shot their dog."

"What'd you do?"

"Has something to do with this big ol' arch, like something you'd see in Paris, but this one is outside the legionary fortress here on Thaleia, and it has my name on it. I'm turning you round here. Stay with me. Here it is. Can you see this? Stop saying Omigod Omigod and tell me what this is."

"John, this is huge."

"Almost seventy foot high."

"No. I mean it's, it's, it's the Congressional Medal of Honor. Only greater."

"Honor doesn't get any greater."

"Oh, yes it does. You have to have done something like—well, like save Palatine. Which I guess you just did. There's a crown that goes with that."

"Oh—" Wanted to say all kinds of words. Said instead, "Shouldn't Caesar might maybe oughta've *told* me about this?"

"I don't know."

"Why not! You're my Roman expert!"

"Triumphs are rare. I was on Palatine during the peace." Calli had grown up in the U.S. Embassy on Palatine and had attended the Imperial Military Institute. "I don't know how these are done. And there's something else. Stop pacing. You're making me nauseous. Bring that image back. There. You see?"

Farragut looked back up at the arch. "No."

"Look for what's not there."

"Cal, I can't really read it. Romans use more abbreviations and acronyms and alphabet mash than even the U.S. Navy."

"*'Caesar Magnus and the Senate and People of Rome dedicate this triumphal arch in this place to John Farragut Americano, because he conquered the alien enemy with his army.'* Isn't Legion Draconis there with you?"

"Yes. Herius Asinius' boys. They've been here since the beginning."

"They're not mentioned on the arch."

"Oh, for Jesus." That explained much. "Is Magnus trying to get me murdered?"

"Any other Roman, I'd say maybe. But that's not Magnus' way. But he did slip something in there. 'John Farragut Americano.'"

"That doesn't just mean I'm from America?"

"No. That would have read 'John Farragut of the U.S.A.' This is styled as part of your name. Tacitly, it claims you as a citizen of Rome from the Roman province of America. Ever since the end of the Long Silence, Rome has insisted that the U.S. is a Roman colony, not the other way around, so it's not a new idea. But here it is set in stone, so to say."

"All right. That's it. I'm getting myself posted to the Deep End right now." The image of the arch disappeared from Calli's res caller.

"John, *don't* refuse the triumph," Calli said seriously. Would have been an order had she been his senior. "We can't do a two-front war. With Near Space secured, it's *our* colonies out here in the Deep who will be eaten first."

"It's Rome who can't afford to open the war back up," said Farragut, dead certain.

"What Rome can afford to do and what Rome *will* do for the sake of pride aren't necessarily one and the same."

Farragut reconsidered. Death before dishonor was a distinctly Roman notion.

And a large—nay, *huge*—segment of the Roman population was almighty pissed at John Farragut for insisting on the Subjugation.

Very well, it was the entire Empire.

"Hell, Cal, if Magnus wanted to thank me, why didn't he get me World Series tickets?"

"Accept the Triumph, John."

"I'll think about it."

Did not sound sincere. The only thing he was thinking about was how to word a polite refusal.

Until he received orders to accept. From his Commander in Chief, Marissa Johnson, President of the United States of America.

*   *   *

Julius Caesar Magnus on the vid. Looked old. Haggard. The weight of his ravaged Empire on him. He carried it like a cross.

The white on his temples had taken over his entire head of thinning hair. His cheeks had sunk. The jowls belonged on a bloodhound.

Saving his Empire meant stabbing himself in the heart, and Caesar Magnus had done it. Caesar Magnus had surrendered Rome to the hated United States of America. It was a living death.

Magnus was not holding this Triumph for John Farragut out of gratitude. It was a public claiming of the American as a Roman. Made America less of a conqueror and more of an estranged relative you really hated to ask for help.

Behold the Roman Empire, prodigal sons and all, standing together against the deadly alien menace from the Deep.

John Farragut had not faced Magnus since the surrender. Saw what he expected. Resentment. Crushing duty.

And there was no love going back the other way from Farragut. But the two men understood each other.

Magnus' voice had lost all its color. Sounded papery. "Because you are a plainspoken man, I will be plain. I do not expect you to walk up the Via Triumphalis. Someone would take a shot at you, and it is not my intention that you be shot."

Plain enough. "I appreciate that, Caesar."

"At the end of the triumphal procession, you in your *Merrimack* will pass over Roma Nova with the Imperial home guard. You will be required to disembark from your *Merrimack* to accept the *obsidionalis* from my hand."

Note to self: ask Cal what an *obsidionalis* is.

"That ceremony will take place in Fortress Aeyrie where we can control the attendees and eliminate any chance of sabotage. Yes, I realize you are not universally loved. Neither am I. A protocol officer will instruct you and your Vice President on all you need to know."

The Roman protocol officer informed Captain John Farragut that weapons could not be brought into Fortress Aeyrie, and that the captain would not be permitted a Marine guard. Farragut was allowed one officer to accompany him.

"What's Reed allowed?" Farragut demanded.

"The Vice President of the United States of America is permitted six attendants," the liaison said loftily. Status conscious. Put Farragut in his place. "Unarmed."

No wonder President Johnson passed on this circus.

"*You* may have one attendant," the liaison repeated.

Yeah, I'm just the guy getting the crown, Farragut thought, the warmth of his enthusiasm slipping into degrees below absolute zero.

Farragut's choice of a companion was immediate and obvious. He signaled *Wolfhound* again in Deep space.

Surprised to find Captain Carmel not on board.

Calli Carmel had come through the Shotgun on a Long Range Shuttle. She was now in Near Space, at Fort Theodore Roosevelt.

And she had already been invited to the ceremony. Not as a military officer. She was attending as consort to Caesar's son, Romulus.

"You're Romulus' *date?*" Farragut yelled into the com.

"Well, yes. That is the sordid truth," Calli sent back.

"What were you thinking!"

"I was thinking I should report the invite to Admiral Mishindi. Which I did. And next thing I know, the Joint Chiefs are on my resonator. All of them. And *they* were thinking it would be good to get another Naval officer in Fortress Aeyrie any way they could."

"They ordered you to accept!"

"They strongly advised it. This is good, John. It means they trust me upstairs."

"Cal, you never had a good thing to say about Romulus."

"I still don't."

Caesar's son Romulus had attended the Imperial Military Institute with Calli Carmel. Calli was the extraordinary beauty who always said no. Made her a must have.

Farragut said, "Some terms I remember, let's see, self-serving, cunning, opportunist. Shallow as pond scum. . . ."

"That was half a lifetime ago, and people change," said Calli. "But not that much. You're right. I don't think Romulus ever learned that the word 'no' can apply to him, too. I may have to stab him at the end of the evening."

"With what? We're not allowed weapons inside Fortress Aeyrie."

"With hair sticks," Calli retorted. "I'll find something. I could hit him with Sampson Reed's chin."

Vice President Sampson Reed had an absurdly deep, manly block of a chin with a deep dimple in it, and enormous white teeth above.

Farragut had to smile. "I'm glad you'll be there, Cal. Watch out for me."

"There can't be any trouble. Security can't get any tighter."

"It's *their* security."

"Their security is better than ours," said Calli. Comments like that got her in trouble with U.S. authorities, who were often allergic to the truth. So yes, it was good to see the Joint Chiefs trusting her with the enemy. But John Farragut did not trust the enemy with her.

"Cal, have I ever cried wolf?"

"Not without there being a wolf," Calli admitted.

"Well, listen to me: Wolf. Wolf. If I could get out of this, I would. When we get into Fortress Aeyrie, *their* security is going to grab you, me, and Sampson, truss us up onto one of those big ol' Roman altars and open up our throats for Caesar."

"That is not Magnus' way," said Calli reasonably.

"It'll be a surprise present from Romulus to his daddy," said Farragut.

"*Their* security doesn't allow surprises to Magnus. Anyway, if my throat were getting cut, Numa Pompeii would want to be there, and he's not coming."

Meant as a jest, but it was a comforting argument. Both Farragut and Calli Carmel had history with the Triumphalis, General Numa Pompeii. Numa Pompeii would not miss Farragut's and Carmel's executions for anything in the universe.

Numa wasn't coming. So maybe this ceremony truly was the presentation of a crown to John Farragut after all.

"What's an *obsidionalis?*" Farragut remembered to ask.

"It's a grass crown given to Roman victors who have rescued a place from a siege," said Calli.

Farragut considered this. Said at last: "What kind of grass?"

12

THE WOLF STAR WAS A white main sequence star with a wide orbiting white companion two hundred light-years distant from Sol in the constellation of the Southern Crown. Were the crown to be worn, the Wolf Star would present over the wearer's left ear.

The planet Palatine orbited the main star at 1.12 astronomical units.

Roma Nova had been founded on a river in the northern temperate zone. An exquisite city, orderly, textured, artistic. Rich with color—the deep browns and golds of its stone and stucco, terra-cotta red of its tiled roofs, varying greens of its trees and gardens. There were typically Roman arches and domes, villas, fountains, viaducts, classical colonnades and temples. There was also the best of every alien style the Empire could borrow, for nothing was more Roman than adopting someone else's good idea and someone else's gods. The soaring bright Kwindaqqin spires were of questionable artistry—Kwindaqqin pricks, their critics called them—but Rome was nothing without its vulgar side.

Palatine, and every planet in the Roman Empire, kept its own local calendar, calculated to the planetary motions of its solar system. On Palatine the local year was 2856 *ab urbi condita*—2856 local years from the original foundation of old Rome back on Earth.

In addition to local reckoning, Rome also maintained a common calendar across all planets of the empire, much as all of Earth kept Greenwich Meridian Time even though little of Earth's population actually lived in the Greenwich Time zone. No matter where you were, there was one uniform date everyone could reference.

Because Rome claimed Earth as part of its Empire, the official time and date of the Roman Empire was the time and date at Greenwich, England, Earth.

So when *Merrimack* swung into orbit around Palatine, the date here and everywhere was the 15th of August 2445 C.E.

New among Roma Nova's monumental public artworks was the Monument to the Conciliation.

Conciliation was the official name of the Subjugation, that pride-crushing moment when Caesar and his surviving Legions walked beneath an arch of crossed spears in surrender.

The term Conciliation only ever came out of official mouths. Everyone else still called it the Subjugation. When John Farragut took Rome's surrender over a year ago.

The Monument ignored that, and celebrated the joining of bitter enemies for the common human good. The soaring graceful sculpture formed two eagles, one bald, one golden, flying wing tip to wing tip.

Romans hated it.

The monument had even angered most of Earth. All the nations of Earth other than the USA were left completely out of it, even though many Earth nations were friends of Rome.

It was always the worst prodigal who got the fatted calf.

In emergency, Rome turned not to its friends but to its most powerful enemy for help.

What *Merrimack* saw from above that could not be seen from the ground, or even from the palace on its hill, because of the tilt of the eagles' wings, was that someone had egged the back of the bald eagle. Farragut wondered how many times a day PanGalactic automatons had to clean that off.

"Let me down there," said the specialist at the tactical station, oldest man in the control room. "I bet I could lob some dog exhaust onto the golden eagle."

"That will do, Mr. Vincent."

Marcander Vincent was forty-three years old. He had been at the same grade for ten years now. Would probably retire there.

Planetside, crowds gathered round the Capitoline. Whether because Caesar commanded or because this promised to be a hell of a spectacle, the Roman citizenry was there.

In space, waiting their turn, the crew of the *Merrimack* watched on its many monitors a Legion of really pissed-off Dracs leading the procession. There should have been a crown on their standard. There wasn't. Following Legion Draconis came formations of flag bearers, prancing horses, elephants, camels, giraffes, griffins, centaurs, and sphinxes. Physical things, not holoimages.

Qord Johnson, the cryptotech, looked from the sphinxes to Captain Farragut on the command deck. "PanGalactic products?"

"Without a doubt," said Farragut.

Then clouds rolled in with astonishing swiftness, covering the sky over Roma Nova.

"Is that real?" Farragut asked Tactical.

"No, sir," said Marcander Vincent. "Holo."

"Get me a bounce of the ground. I want to see what this looks like from down there."

Menacing clouds billowed miles high. Darkened the Eternal City. Jagged lightning darted horizon to horizon. Snaking trees of blue and red scorched angry tracks across the heavens.

Then a bright shining golden crack split the darkness. The glowering black clouds parted, and the gleaming golden chariot of the Sun appeared, pulled by fiery horses.

As up from the ground a fountain of opalescent water spouted, towering a thousand feet high. Leaping dolphins danced at the crests of the shining waters. The spume spread miles wide, shimmering all colors, and casting triple rainbows in the sunlight.

The billowing clouds had turned a snowy, scintillating white. In the midst of them a ghostly shimmering triumphal arch appeared like a gateway to eternity.

While on the ground, in the procession, sixty-four fallen Legions marched. These were holoimages of the dead. Legionaries who had fallen to the gorgons before the surrender.

The legionaries looked perfectly real and whole, carrying their colors. Crowns on their standards.

And rank by rank the ghost legionaries stepped into the air on an unseen wide spiral stairway. The legionaries grew in size as they climbed, become ethereal, the size of titans, their faces turned downward as if searching the ground for someone left behind.

Apparently, the images were masterworks of accuracy, expression, gesture, and nuance, because everywhere in the crowd people burst into tears, shrieked, pointed, and waved at beloved images.

The spectral legions marched a wide spiral skyward. At the shining archway, a ghostly she-wolf waited, her teats heavy, her mouth spread in lupine smile. She greeted each of her sons at the arch. And each specter turned for a last look back at a special someone before passing through to the shining hills beyond.

After all the Legions had ascended to the home of heroes—and the crowd was completely blinded by tears—it came *Merrimack*'s turn.

Merrimack descended into atmosphere, joined up with the Legion carrier *Horatius* to pass slowly, wing tip to wing tip, up the Via Triumphalis in the tracks of the dead.

As nothing was permitted to fly directly over the Capitoline, when the two ships arrived at the Monument of the Conciliation, the American and the Roman split left and right.

Exactly what's going to happen the moment the Hive is dead, thought John Farragut.

The display ended with ground-shaking, sky-burning fireworks—real ones that boomed and sizzled and left a gunpowder haze over the dispersing crowds.

The spectacle struck Farragut as more a public funeral than a triumph. A reminder to the Romans of what they had lost. A justification of what Caesar had done to preserve the survivors.

That had been the easy part. What Farragut dreaded was still to come.

Spaceship Two was already at Fortress Aeyrie in orbit around Palatine when *Merrimack* made rendezvous.

Merrimack's companies of Marines of the 89th Battalion were barking furious not to be allowed to go with their captain into the wolf's lair.

"No weapons! What kind of Roman guano is that?" Kerry Blue squawked. "Does Reed get guards?"

Sampson Reed, Vice President of the United States.

"Reed gets an honor guard," Cole Darby answered. "But they're not armed either."

"Oh!" Kerry Blue gestured outrage in the air. *"Colonel!"* Begging with just his name.

White-blond head nodded. Square jaw set hard. TR Steele was in complete sympathy with his mutinous Marines but could say nothing.

Steele had insisted that he be the one to accompany the captain into Fortress Aeyrie. He had been denied.

"So who's going with?" Kerry demanded.

Steele could not answer her. Was afraid he would babble. She derailed every thought in his skull.

Ranza answered, "Mr. Dent."

Commander Egypt ("Gypsy") Dent was imposing. Had a bold bone structure with bold musculature over that, head to heel. Gypsy was black. Blacker than Reg. Way blacker than Dak. Gypsy Dent looked like she could break you down quicker than you could break down your field piece, though she was usually pretty mellow. The enemy never saw Commander Dent mellow.

Kerry nodded approval to that at least. "Yeah, she'd be my pick to take with."

Commander Dent had come over from Captain Carmel's *Wolfhound* after *Merrimack* lost her short-lived Executive Officer Sebastian Gray. Mr. Gray had gone missing, presumed eaten, in a battle with gorgons over a year ago.

Mr. Dent had a real bad start on *Merrimack*. First thing, straight off, one of the ship's dogs ate the new XO's cat.

Someone shoulda warned the new Exec about the sheer volume of doggage on board *Merrimack*. And not a whole lot in the way of cattage. In fact, there were no pets on *Merrimack*, except for the lizard plant Kerry Blue had picked up in the Myriad, but that passed as a plant because it had leaves.

For the demise of Mr. Dent's cat, it had been a Doberman named Inga what done the deed. Not the brightest of the breed, Inga had just wanted to play. Bluebeard had not.

It was probably the ragdoll shake rather than the launch into the bulkhead that snapped the cat's neck.

Captain Farragut had apologized to Commander Dent, but you could tell the captain wasn't all that upset. Inga was crew. Bluebeard was a cat. And you could tell Egypt Dent was all kinds of smoked about it.

That was for starters. Next thing, Farragut ordered Mr. Dent to lose the hair.

Gypsy Dent had come aboard the *Mack* with this Medusan thing on her head. The hair was a work of art. The hair was scary. Coils of woven dreadlocks, each ending in a gold snake head.

Gypsy already had a device for removing and reattaching the headdress hair by hair, so the order was not hard to obey.

It was insulting.

"*That* is not serving on my command deck," had been the captain's words.

So when Farragut requested Commander Dent accompany him to his crowning on Fortress Aeyrie, Gypsy asked, "May I wear my hair?"

"Mr. Dent, I would be pleased all to Jesus if you would wear your hair."

And Kerry Blue decided, yeah, Farragut and Dent will be okay.

That left Lieutenant Commander Glenn (Hamster) Hamilton in charge of the *Mack* while the captain and the exec were on Fortress Aeryie.

The Hamster was thrilled. This never happened. Never had both the captain and the XO been off the boat at the same time. Everyone could just hear Hamster's husband Patrick saying to his wife, "Maybe something will happen to the captain and the exec, and you'll get to keep command."

Captain Farragut couldn't quite blame Patrick Hamilton

for wanting him dead. It wasn't quite the secret Farragut hoped it was that Farragut was too fond of Dr. Patrick Hamilton's wife.

Glenn Hamilton was petite, polished, smart. Had a big attitude. Stood no taller than Farragut's chin. Could handle this boat. Only needed more mileage on her. Glenn Hamilton was not yet thirty years old.

"Do you trust me?" Hamster asked as the captain prepared to depart.

"With everything I have," said Farragut. "Keep the guns ready and stay on high alert."

"John, are you expecting trouble?"

When Captain Farragut was uneasy, it made everyone uneasy.

He said, "It's just fixin' to be pomp and circumstance. There won't be any shooting."

Those were his words, but Hamster heard his thoughts: Something—*something*—is fixin' to go south.

Hamster said, "Anything goes wrong, you can smite them all with the jawbone of the Vice President."

Got half a snicker out of him. Little more than a breath out the nose.

Glenn reached up to fix his collar. It seemed a natural thing for a woman to do for a man. Natural to do for a man she was intimate with, not for her captain. Her hands were behind his neck before she realized what she was doing. Burned with a sudden blush.

So did he.

There would not be any shooting unless Patrick Hamilton walked in on this.

Hamster bowed her head, gave her captain's broad chest a pat with a guilty smile. She moved back away from him to check her work. "You clean up pretty, John Farragut."

And she left him figuring out how to lose this wood before he boarded Fortress Aeyrie.

Took a look at Gypsy's hair. All's well again. Loved that hair.

The boffins had planted a rover in Gypsy's snaky headdress so the command deck on *Merrimack* would see everything

Gypsy saw. Both the captain and the XO wore earpieces and collar phones, so they could hear the command deck and whisper back.

Both officers were tricked out in full dress blues, plenty of fruit salad on their chests. Hats tucked under arms.

A skiff ferried them into the spaceborne mountain that was Caesar's mobile palace, Fortress Aeyrie. The skiff was forbidden armament, but the Marines inside it bristled like pirates, carrying everything but knives between their teeth.

Kerry Blue tried to clench a blade between her teeth. Did not care for the sensation of metal against enamel *at all*. Made her teeth curl.

The Roman guards who met them at the dock were also armed. They allowed only Farragut and Dent to disembark. Checked them for weapons.

Most American men carried a pocketknife, if only because their daddies gave it to them. The guards at the dock confiscated Farragut's. Checked the snake heads in Gypsy's headdress for venom before admitting them to the inner fortress.

A ceremonial guard in ancient-style armor provided escort in from the dock, their faces more expressionless than automatons. They did not carry weapons.

Met up with a protocol officer who led Captain Farragut and Commander Dent through the fortress with chilly professionalism.

Caesar's audience hall had changed appearance since last time Farragut had been here. Where there had been a bridge and bottomless crevasse was now a spacious solid floor to accommodate many many dignitaries.

Everyone was standing. The only chairs in the entire hall were in front, behind a long table with a snowy cloth, and up in the balcony for the musicians.

The protocol officer stationed Captain Farragut and Commander Dent in the back. Farragut could see he was going to make a long walk up the center aisle to the raised dais in front to collect his crown.

Gypsy turned her head slowly to show the monitors on *Merrimack* the lay of the land.

From the front of the wide hall, two ramps led up both sides to a balcony in back. Unarmed guards in ceremonial regalia were posted throughout. There were no weapons to be had here. Nothing that could be used against its bearer. Not even ceremonial swords. God knew John Farragut could use a sword.

Most of the attendees here were Senators, garbed in ancient-style togas, and provincial governors wearing anything from suits to lion skins.

Gypsy paused her sweep of the room when Legate Herius Asinius came into her line of sight. Let the command crew get a long look at him.

"Now there's a man who looks like he took one hard up the stern," Farragut heard Hamster's voice in his earpiece.

Muttered back: "He did."

Herius did not look back at Farragut's entrance.

Farragut glanced over his own shoulder, encouraged to see no one parked behind him. What he'd felt looming back there was a statue of a beautiful Roman youth holding out a golden orb in its alabaster palm. Farragut had a boyish urge to pick up the orb, it being between the size of a baseball and a softball, and it really looked like it wasn't fastened down. He resisted. Faced forward.

"There's no LEN there," Hamster's voice sounded again.

"Don't see any," Farragut murmured back. Gypsy made a slow scan of the upper level, which revealed no League of Earth Nations guests there either.

The League participated in the defense of Thaleia. They were not being recognized for it here.

"No squid either," Farragut observed.

The Vwakikikikik had done a splendid job eliminating the gorgons in the sea. It hadn't been easy for them. Thaleian seawater was harsh on squid skin.

But the Vwakikikikik did not even know they'd been slighted. It was tough to offend a squid. Which was why there were no squid armed forces.

Farragut muttered into his com, "I shoulda made Augustus come here."

Augustus, more than anyone, had stopped the Hive incursion into Near Space.

"I'm sure Augustus would enjoy this every bit as much as I am."

"There!" said Hamster suddenly. "Commander Dent, hold it."

Farragut looked in the direction of Gypsy's line of sight.

"The man standing to the right of the head table," said Hamster. "Colonel Steele doesn't like him."

The target was a dignified older gentleman. His seamed face had gone to seed. He looked extremely uncomfortable. But there were a lot of people like that. Most of them in Senatorial robes.

There were several U.S. Senators here. But not Catherine. Catherine had taken her husband's name, so maybe the Romans didn't know she was a Farragut. Or, perhaps they realized they would need a bigger room if they started inviting John Farragut's brothers and sisters.

Invited but not in attendance was the Chief Justice of the Supreme Court of Kentucky. The press of business prevented His Honor from attending.

"Must be something very important to keep him away," the protocol officer had observed.

"Yes, the Judge is a very important man," Captain Farragut had told him.

Vice President Sampson Reed had a prominent place in front, seated behind the table. There were speeches to be made and decrees to be signed.

Beside Vice President Reed was seated the Roman Senator Gaius Bruccius Eleutherius Americanus. A stately man. Gaius had aged well. Calli Carmel confessed to having a crush on Gaius Americanus in her Imperial Military Institute days. Gaius was American born. Had risen to power the hard way. From American ex-con to Roman slave to freeman to general to Senator. Now Gaius Americanus was regarded as the second man in the empire. Of a different *gens* but the same mind as Julius Caesar Magnus.

Farragut was relieved not to see the Triumphalis General Numa Pompeii in attendance. The fourth man in the Empire. Ostensibly Numa's duties defending Rome in the Deep kept him away. Truth was Numa would rather eat gorgon tentacles than watch John Farragut be crowned in triumph.

Standing in front, off to the right, was Caesar's son Romulus, a younger man of dark indulgent good looks. Gorgeous, really. And decorating Romulus' arm was one of the true beauties of this or any universe, Callista Carmel, looking spectacular in mufti—a simple floor-length gown, strapless, empire-waisted, cut from rich fabric of the color called black emerald. A side slit flashed a great length of smooth leg. Emeralds shone at her throat. Farragut could hear voices in his earpiece from *Merrimack*'s command deck, "Holy mother-of-pearl! Look at Mr. Carmel!"

Romulus looked altogether smug and possessive, proud as a Caesar. A vain man, Romulus would need to be seen with a woman of Calli's voltage. The emeralds were probably his, because last time Farragut looked, Calli didn't own any.

Almost laughed out loud when he noticed she was wearing hair sticks.

There was the weedy crown waiting on a stand beside the altar. There was no way out of it. Farragut settled into resignation.

Trumpets blared from the balcony. Those dignitaries seated at the front table rose to their feet for the entrance of Julius Caesar Magnus.

Caesar wore a plain toga and a simple laurel wreath. Real laurel, not gold. He moved like a very old man.

There was a religious offering involving incense and a very small flame on the altar, a chorus of resonant male basso voices and an ethereal feminine counterpoint. Figures of ancestors appeared in the flames as the incense was tossed onto the altar with requests for benediction.

Then there were decrees to be signed, validating the Conciliation, recognizing America's assistance in the deliverance of Thaleia from the gorgons.

The Vice President of the United States, a handful of U.S. Senators, and a handful of Roman Senators took their seats with Caesar at the table. Parchments were read aloud and laid out for signature.

The man TR Steele didn't like was presenting the signatories with their pens. Pens were important at such occasions. These were destined to become museum pieces or part of someone's private collection or auctioned for stupid amounts of money.

Farragut's gaze wandered upward to the brilliant illusion of wide-open sky overhead.

So he didn't see the pen plunge into Caesar's eye socket.

13

HEARD THE SCREAMS. Saw the blood, the slumping body. Heard Lieutenant Commander Glenn Hamilton's voice in his ear calling *Merrimack* to general quarters. Commander Dent instructing the skiff to prepare for departure.

Farragut's eyes followed the running man pushing his way up the right-hand ramp to the upper level.

The man Steele didn't like.

Farragut made a reflexive reach for a sidearm that was not there. There were no weapons here.

Nothing built as a weapon.

But there was a golden orb in the alabaster hand of the statue behind him. And it turned out to be detachable.

John Farragut had briefly pitched minor league for the Akron Aeros. Never made the majors because he had only one pitch.

Still had it. Fast ball.

Low and way inside. Heard the crunch a split second before the animal screech. Dropped the assassin in an anguished heap on the ramp, curled round his shattered knee.

Wasn't a lethal hit, but the man was well and truly dead by the time the guards hauled him up, blue poison spilling from his slack mouth.

The man had to have known he had only the smallest chance of getting out of here. He had been ready for capture.

An authoritative booming voice demanded calm and order. Quickly brought the clamor down to a murmur.

Romulus.

Romulus summoning medics to resurrect his father.

Romulus calling on guards to seek out the assassin's family and associates immediately.

Gaius Americanus had run up the ramp and was calling for medics to make haste to revive the assailant. It went without saying that Gaius wanted the man alive and talking, but without the saying, Romulus seized the opportunity to take a verbal stab at the man Magnus had elevated above his own son. "Oh, yes, tend to the health of my father's attacker if you must, Gaius Americanus."

Romulus met Captain Farragut's eyes across the great hall. Told him the ceremony would not continue. "You should leave now." Sounded concerned for his safety.

"Not arguing," said Farragut.

The Roman mood in Caesar's hall, already foul, became menacing.

There were a lot of pens left.

Romulus also advised Vice President Sampson Reed and the U.S. Senators to go. They were already clotted around the forward exit, behind a half ring of Secret Service agents.

For everyone to hear, Romulus announced, "Hysteria and blind vengeance would be easy, but I do not imagine the United States were involved in a plot against my father. Our guests will leave. Until my father is revived, this is what I expect—"

As Romulus told his people his expectations, the Secret Service agents hustled the Vice President out of the chamber.

Calli Carmel took off her high heels and sprinted through the crowd to John Farragut, who had his jacket off and over her bare shoulders as soon as she joined up with him and Gypsy.

"I'm not cold, John," said Calli as his jacket surrounded her.

"I want that prick to see Navy colors and captain's stars when he watches you go out the door."

Calli did not pretend not to know who the prick was. "Romulus has no time to look at me."

Gypsy glanced back, corrected Calli as she followed the captains out the door. "Oh, yes, he does."

Farragut, Carmel, and Dent made it to the skiff and cleared Fortress Aeyrie without incident. Farragut did not count the gun pointed in his face at the dock as an incident worth noting. It was bluff and posture to see if the American hero would blink. He didn't. Neither did he tell the man to go ahead and shoot, because gunmen tend to obey you when you say that.

Farragut asked for his pocketknife back.

Once the skiff cleared Fortress Aeyrie's force field, *Merrimack* looped out an energy hook to enfold the little craft into its own protection.

In transit, Farragut ordered over the com, "Hamster, hail Spacecraft Two. Stay in contact. Advise them *Merrimack* will provide escort back to Earth. Then get me Admiral Mishindi at the Pentagon."

Glanced aside to a Marine staring at him. A rough sort of pretty gal. Everyone knew Kerry Blue. "Flight Sergeant Blue?" Farragut prompted.

"You didn't get your crown," said Kerry Blue.

"Sure didn't," said Farragut.

"Maybe that was the idea," Calli Carmel suggested. She pulled out her hair sticks and let fall her shining chestnut tresses. All the other Marines were staring at Captain Carmel. "Someone couldn't bear the thought of you with a crown."

Farragut shook his head. "Then why wasn't it *me?*"

As soon as the skiff was in dock and the hatch opened, Farragut exited like a cannonball. Nearly took out his Marine commander barreling up the ramp tunnel. "TR! You were dead on with the guy you didn't like. I shoulda listened harder."

TR Steele was true as the family dog. Just like Lily should have listened to the Farragut family dog when she went off and married that bum Eddie Ray. Doesn't do to ignore the dog. Didn't take a lot of intelligence to have a truckload of good sense. Bull mastiffs and TR Steele could sense bad faith.

"With respect, sir," said Colonel Steele, keeping up with

the captain's charge up to his command deck, "I changed my mind. I like him a lot."

"TR, what is happening here—this is *not* good."

Farragut arrived on his command deck in his shirtsleeves just as the Roman legion carrier *Horatius* cut across *Merrimack*'s bow.

"What the hell was that?" Hamster cried, giving over the command to Farragut.

"Saber rattling," said Farragut, watching *Horatius*' pass on the monitors.

"Roman Legion carrier is coming round again," Tactical advised.

"Oh, for—!" Farragut started, more exasperated than anything. "Punch us to the gate. Threshold velocity. Execute now."

The great battleship shot forward. Cut off *Horatius*' attempted maneuver. Came close to skinning the Legion carrier's nose.

Farragut opened a com channel. Used to be the Roman channel. The Romans had probably changed it by now, but Farragut sent anyway: "Marcus, you try that again, I'll drop you." Clicked off.

"What was he *thinking?*" Glenn Hamilton said, watching *Horatius* on the tac screen. The ship was turning back toward Fortress Aeyrie.

"I don't know," said Farragut, unprovoked. "What would you do if someone dropped President Johnson?"

"Drop Sampson Reed?" Tactical suggested.

"I did not hear that, Mr. Vincent."

Marcander Vincent had a habit of inappropriateness.

Merrimack had to keep her six engines at threshold to stay with Spacecraft Two, which had departed Fortress Aeyrie like solar ejecta. Even at that, the *Mack* was not going to catch up until Spacecraft Two came within range of the Earth home guard.

Merrimack took up a position on the Vice Presidential ship's stern, several light-years behind, and settled there for a two-day journey.

A maelstrom of messages whirled round the settled region of the galaxy.

At threshold speed, the only messages *Merrimack* sent or received were res pulses, and only messages in which the whole message could be conveyed in a single instant. Mostly that meant written text. *Mack* could converse well enough with Spacecraft Two, which was moving at the same pace, but voice messages from *Mack* arrived on Earth in a compressed mash, while Earth's messages to *Mack* were strung out in bits.

So the Joint Chiefs at the Pentagon got text answers to their questions mere instants after they asked them, while on board *Merrimack*, waiting for the next question from the JC was like watching a rock erode.

John Farragut and Gypsy Dent had missed dinner, so they went to the captain's Mess while they waited for the next grain of sand to fall off the rock.

It was the middle watch, ship's night. *Merrimack* stepped down from high alert, back into her normal routines. The lighting was subdued most decks, dark in the forecastle. Quiet as she ever got. The ship was never silent. Sounds had a comforting familiarity, hisses and clanks, the deep hum of the six mammoth engines, footsteps, voices carrying through metal decks and thin partitions. Thumping of joggers' feet on the elevated track. Air moving in conduits. Water in pipes.

Chef Zack got out of bed to feed the captain and the XO. Was disappointed that the officers could not tell him about the banquet. The food on Fortress Aeyrie was legendary and Zack had been expecting a full report.

Calli showed up at the Mess, clad in a badly fitting borrowed dress-down uniform. Gave Farragut his dress jacket back.

She offered to tell Chef Zack about the food in Fortress Aeyrie if he would feed her, too. "Rom took me to the galley when they were preparing for the banquet," she said, sliding into a chair at the captain's table. "It was overwhelming."

Farragut's brows lifted like a dog's ears. "Rom?" said Farragut. *"Rom?"*

Gypsy's dark, heavy-lidded eyes narrowed at her former CO, Captain Carmel. Gypsy had two young sons back on

Earth, so she had the mom look down cold. "And what did you think you were doing in the kitchen with Rom?"

"He was showing off," said Calli.

"Like 'You play your cards right, all of this could be yours' kind of showing off?" Gypsy suggested.

Calli let her head fall to one side, thinking. "I don't know. He has either grown up into a responsible man or he has turned into a perfect psychopath."

"That was some surprising statesmanship back there," said Farragut.

"Yes, it was," said Calli. "Surprising."

"So why was it Romulus instead of Gaius calling the shots?" said Farragut. "Isn't Gaius Americanus the Second Man in Rome?"

Calli shook her head. "Romulus just grabbed the wheel first. He was quick. He made Gaius look like an ass."

"He did that very well," said Farragut. "Cheap shot about the attacker's health. But it worked. And your Gaius didn't try to argue with him."

"Gaius doesn't answer cheap shots. And he doesn't make snap decisions when he knows he's missing strategic facts. Gaius will wait to see how things fall. If Magnus can be resuscitated, then Rom's sniping back there won't matter much."

"Did he know?" said Gypsy.

Calli's smooth face pinched at the edges of her almond eyes, her full lips. "Rom? Oh, yes. While we were getting it human in the kitchen he told me he bribed one of his father's friends to stab him in the eye."

"Sarcasm does not look attractive on you, Captain Carmel," said Gypsy.

"Romulus did talk like he's expecting Magnus to survive," said Farragut. "Did y'all notice that?"

"'Until my father is revived, this is what I expect,'" Gypsy recited. "That was a nice touch. Not what you'd expect a parricide to say."

It was either the natural refusal of a son to assume the worst or the calculated facade of a perfect psychopath.

On a sudden thought Calli fished in the pocket of her baggy uniform. Produced an emerald necklace. It sparkled in the low light, dangling from her long fingers. "Can I get a courier to send these back to Rom?"

Big brother to many, Farragut had long practice ordering, "Cal, I don't want you seeing that boy anymore."

Gypsy positioned herself shoulder to shoulder with him, her arms crossed, like the other disapproving parent. "Calli, honey, you know we only want what's best for you."

"Know your enemy," said Calli.

Gypsy frowned. "Honey, you don't need to know him that well."

The resonator finally coughed up a message dot, automatically slotting it into the player. All three officers leaned forward. Farragut's blue eyes moved quickly back and forth across the text of the Joint Chiefs' latest message.

"Caesar is dead."

Caesar died and stayed dead. Roman medicine could repair a lot of damage to the human body. But in this case it was the ink—injected directly into the brain—that prevented resuscitation.

Neither had the Roman medics been able to revive the assassin. The Americans had to wonder at that. In the assassin's case the poison had not been injected directly into his brain. Either he had been a very clever assassin or the medics had not been trying hard enough.

By the middle of the second day of the voyage home, the crew of the *Merrimack* had learned that the assassin had already lost his children to the Hive, and that his wife left him a long time ago in a truly bitter divorce, so there was no Roman vengeance to be had.

The lack of a suicide note or of a shouted declaration as he struck Caesar down left the motive muddy. Unless the death of his children drove the man to it. He had already suffered in the worst way, so might he just as well commit a crime equal to it? And if his ex-wife were executed on his account, so much the better?

The investigation unearthed a dirty little secret in the assassin's excessive admiration of young girls. But killing Caesar was no way to keep that a secret, so blackmail seemed an unlikely motive.

A Sargasson autopsy found no brain alteration that might have affected his behavior—no alteration other than the poison that killed him, and a mild sedative he had taken that morning.

The why of it appeared unknowable. But lack of evidence did not hinder the proliferation of theories and accusations in the least.

There was speculation that Magnus had arranged his own assassination to soothe his empire's wounded pride. Magnus, so the theory went, had made a pact with his trusted adviser to do the deed, using someone who had no family to suffer for his apparent disloyalty.

But in a society that valued honorable death, that idea was perfectly alien and was more popular on Earth than anywhere in the Roman Empire.

Romulus wasted no time on speculation and witch hunts. The assassin was dead and that would do for now.

For now, Romulus kept a firm hand on his disrupted empire. He showed a poise and gravitas not seen before in Magnus' callow late-born son. Romulus had risen to the occasion.

And kept rising.

Succession in the empire was not hereditary. Magnus had never publicly announced a successor. Romulus had just assumed the interim rule. And for his boldness, his decisiveness, his restraint, the Roman Senate let him.

Romulus left Magnus' last testament sealed. Magnus may have named a successor in the sealed testament, but that successor could not be vested in the office without the vote of the Senate. That could wait.

Now, said Romulus, was not the time for political dissension and debate. The future of Rome should not be decided in haste during a crisis. Rome must deal with the Hive first, then, in safety, unseal Caesar's last wishes and decide the path of the empire.

It was a bald power grab. Everyone knew that Romulus' name was probably not in that sealed testament. Especially Romulus. Romulus would also know that the one at the helm at the end of the storm had a high likelihood of keeping the job.

Many Romans considered Magnus' death an assassination waiting to happen.

The wrath of the conquered empire, if not abated, was mollified with the death of its betraying ruler who sold them into Subjugation. Romulus, in an address to the Empire—appearing very handsome, grave, and imperial—stated that he disagreed with the Subjugation, but that he loved and honored his father, and that second-guessing the past was not the way to move forward.

Neat trick, thought Farragut. To be in alliance with the U.S. without taking the blame for the act that got Rome there. Romulus had not made the agonizing decision. Magnus had. But Romulus reaped the benefit.

Magnus had died to save Rome.

Or had he?

Had fury at the Subjugation been the motive behind the killing? Seemed obvious.

But there was someone more responsible for the Subjugation than Magnus. Magnus had only submitted to it. Someone else had demanded it. Someone who left Fortress Aeyrie alive.

The question came back again and again:

Why wasn't it me?

Merrimack arrived at Earth hot on the stern of Spacecraft Two. The emeralds were on their way back to Fortress Aeyrie. And Calli Carmel was back in her own uniform.

John Farragut saw her to the Kansas spaceport, where a military transport would take her to Fort Roosevelt. From there it would be through the Shotgun and back to her own ship *Wolfhound* in the Deep.

Calli could not get out of Near Space fast enough.

A sidebar to the media circus *sans* bread that surrounded Caesar's assassination was an unfortunate plethora of video of Calli Carmel on Romulus' arm.

Calli was not a celebrity in her own right, but she had stellar looks and she was with the new emperor—so the media were calling Romulus—and that made her video fodder.

"Be careful going through Fort Ted," Farragut told her.

Calli, surprised and perplexed, said, "It's *our* fort."

"Gypsy wanted to make sure you saw this."

Handed her a vid sheet. She opened it.

The image of Calli and Romulus jumped out at her. The caption read: EMPRESS CALLI.

Calli left her mouth open for quite a few moments. Finally she said to John Farragut, "Oh, for Jesus."

14

ADMIRAL MISHINDI HAD LET himself age outwardly. The brindled hair, the seamed face, gave him an air of wisdom and authority. But the old man could run John Farragut round a squash court and smash that little green ball like a man half John Farragut's age.

Mishindi appeared sedate and venerable behind his desk in his office at the Pentagon.

Like Mishindi, the Pentagon had been much rejuvenated on the inside. The admiral's chamber might have been a compartment on a spaceship, except that the ceilings were higher, the furniture was not bolted down, and the hatch appeared like a door, though it sealed as securely as any hatch.

"Captain Farragut, the Joint Chiefs have determined because the Hive has adapted to our current tactics that a change of tactics is in order. Single ships have become more and more vulnerable. We are organizing our forces into Attack Groups. To that end, the *Merrimack* will be flagship of Attack Group One, comprising *Gladiator, Wolfhound, Rio Grande . . .*"

Farragut had shut his eyes at the word flagship and kept them shut. The honor from the Black Lagoon. It meant some damned admiral was fixing to plant his flag on John Farragut's command deck, while John Farragut, captain of the *Merrimack*, became a passenger on his own ship. He tried not to look crushed but that was difficult to do with his eyes shut.

Until Admiral Mishindi spoke into John Farragut's darkness, "Congratulations, Commodore Farragut."

Farragut's eyes flew open. Mishindi was slyly grinning.

"Me! I'm the damned admiral!"

"How damned you are, I cannot say. It is a field promotion, mind you."

Farragut spoke thickly past the lump in his throat. "Thank you, sir."

Mishindi looked impish. "Did I scare you?"

Farragut wanted to bluster *No*. But the admiral had him cold. "A little," Farragut admitted.

Mishindi sniggered, devilish.

"Okay. A *lot*," Farragut cried. "I'll get you for that, Mishindi."

The admiral cackled out loud.

Farragut said, "Well, seeing as how I just shipped Cal back to the Deep to rejoin *Wolfhound* instead of *Wolfhound* coming here, can I assume my theater of operations is the Deep?"

"You can, Commodore. The mission objective is to detect, locate, isolate, and prosecute the Hive nexus."

"Hive nexus? There is such a thing?"

"Newly uncovered evidence suggests there is."

"'Newly uncovered' means we've had the intelligence and someone's been sitting on it."

Mishindi sighed, folded his hands across his middle and sat back in his chair. "Information sharing has never been our country's long suit. The CIA just decided to share that."

"I gave Naval Intelligence a Roman patterner a year ago. Why don't we have our own answers?"

"Augustus is no longer with Naval Intelligence."

"What!" Farragut came out of his chair. Then, sitting back down, "Sir."

Mishindi allowed the outburst. Pained him to admit, "Augustus reports to the CIA."

Farragut about swallowed his tongue. Kept his voice level addressing his admiral, "How did the CIA get him?"

Mishindi's face pinched in pain. "Admiral Klein."

"What about Admiral Klein?"

"He hit him," said Mishindi.

"Augustus *hit* Admiral Klein!" Farragut could not believe it.

"No." Mishindi's face knotted up entirely. "Former Admiral Klein hit Augustus."

Farragut's blue eyes popped wide.

Mishindi continued, "Your patterner has a talent for igniting people and causing careers to spontaneously combust."

Farragut instantly knew what the CIA had done with Augustus from there. The spooks would be more concerned with limiting Augustus' access to U.S. data than using him to consolidate the data. The power of a patterner was his ability to synthesize great masses of disparate information. Augustus' great power had been squandered in the clutches of the CIA.

John Farragut was on the edge of his chair, nearly on top of Mishindi's desk. "Get him back, sir. *I'll* take him. Patterners are amazing. We can't just piss him away because he's pissy. We need to use him. *I* need to use him."

For Jesus, no wonder Augustus hated him. Augustus' venom made sense now. *How little you know.*

"Do remember, John, this is the man—if you can call him a man—who shut down Fleet communications several years ago."

The patterner had discovered that sending the complement of a resonant harmonic whites out both harmonics. Augustus had got hold of the Fleet common harmonic and generated its complement at random intervals. Because some messages got through, the Fleet were slow to realize that other messages were not, and still slower to actually believe it could be happening.

"This is that guy," said Mishindi. "*Not* friendly."

"I know what he is."

"The CIA does not trust you, John. Something about 'idiot ideas of fair play.'"

"Idiot ideas of fair play are why the *Mack* is still alive. That patterner had a clean shot at my stern."

"And sorely regrets not taking the shot," Mishindi finished for him.

"He says that. But it's a Roman creed—if you win the battle and lose your honor, what have you won?"

Mishindi's dark face purpled, exasperated. Fingers curled as if to cage the air and throttle it. "John, *I* would have taken the shot!"

"You're not Roman."

"It's also a fact that Romans are the sneakiest, most self-serving, back-stabbing bastards in the known galaxy."

"I got the right Roman," said Farragut.

Mishindi shook his head, reluctant, relenting. "I can get you Augustus. But I don't know about getting you the files he wants. The CIA says that Augustus is trying to know his enemy."

"God bless America!" Farragut roared like a curse. "That's what he's for!"

"Us," said Mishindi. "They're afraid he will know *us*. Knowledge is power, and no one knows that better than the children of the wolf. There's a reason the CIA is mighty tightfisted about their information."

"Then cut off their fists. I mean it. We can't fight the Hive blindfolded."

"Here's the thing, John. What they're afraid of— What *I'm* afraid of— Are you listening to this part, John? We're afraid that your patterner will figure out how the Hive is getting a loc on a res pulse."

Before humankind's first encounter with the Hive, getting a location on a resonant pulse's point of transmission or reception was widely accepted as impossible. It was simple fact. But the Hive did it and most insects did it. And the United States needed to do it before the Romans.

"Yes, this is the guy who can figure that out," Farragut agreed. "And best he figures it out while we're still allied, 'cause otherwise he'll just figure it out after the Hive is gone and he's working only for Rome again."

Mishindi rolled the suggestion around. Said finally, "That argument has *some* merit. You do know that Augustus is a five-star monster when he is enabled?"

"Glory, I sure hope so, 'cause that's what I need to step in the ring with the Hive."

The admiral spread his hands, giving in. "I have never regretted taking a risk on you. I will requisition your patterner immediately. Mind you, this is not Androcles' lion you're getting here. You stuck the thorn *in* his paw."

Captain Farragut took delivery of the patterner in Mishindi's office.

Augustus. A stone basilisk who had refused the invitation to sit. Standing, Augustus could use his imposing height to intimidate.

Someone had provided him with U.S. drab to wear instead of the Roman black Farragut had always seen Augustus in, but still the patterner looked dark and forbidding. He had been given the rank of colonel, but was not a line officer.

Admiral Mishindi told Captain Farragut that information was being provided to *Merrimack*'s data banks. Copies of certain Pentagon databases were being sanitized, and irrelevant files omitted.

"You are no judge of relevance," said the patterner.

Mishindi countered, crossly, "What *is* relevant—and we haven't been able to *get*—are the Thaleia files. Thaleia is a Roman world. Your people are protective of their proprietary information. And Romulus won't release the information."

"Romulus?" Augustus echoed. Little expression, but Farragut sensed confusion and unease from him. Augustus asked carefully, "And what does Caesar say?"

A pall held the chamber. Even Mishindi was mortified.

Someone with a gift for making sense of data had been given less than none.

He doesn't even know Caesar is dead!

Farragut, mouth dry, asked, "Augustus, what information did the CIA give you access to?"

The head turned robotically, dark, dark eyes directed at him like weapons. The wrath.

Augustus finally spoke, soft as a whisper, gentle as a sadist before he cuts you. "Apparently even less than I thought. Where is Caesar?"

Silence fell thick and stayed.

Augustus waited.

Farragut answered at last, *"Ad patres."*

Gone to his forefathers.

Gone light speed. Gone from this life.

Augustus gave no reaction. In truth, it was the only answer Augustus could have expected after that long a silence.

Without expression, Augustus said/asked, "Assassination."

"Yes," said Farragut.

"How did you know?" Mishindi challenged.

"After Caesar acceded to the Subjugation, and without me there, it became only a question of when. Who?"

Mishindi supplied the name. Augustus dismissed it at once. "Who else?"

"No one that we know of."

Augustus appeared skeptical of that. Of the unknowing. Of the absence of others. "If I had been with Caesar, no one could have got to him. He should never have given me away."

"It was his decision," said Farragut. "He gave you to me."

"And that killed him," said Augustus.

"Maybe there were things more important to Caesar than staying alive."

Augustus looked genuinely shocked. As at a pig quoting Shakespeare. John Farragut had said something inadvertently profound. Or was it advertent? Augustus had not expected an American to know of things more important than his own life.

"There were," said Augustus. "But Caesar would have been sorry to give his life for— Just what did Caesar give his life for?"

Farragut took responsibility for that one. He should have checked up on Augustus. Made sure that Caesar's patterner was being used for important things.

Yet even in data starvation, Augustus had managed to puzzle together the fact that the Hive was using PanGalactic technology to displace to Near Space.

"Augustus, what do you need to do what you do?"

"Data."

"Exactly what data?"

"All that there is."

"Any particular format?"

"Any format."

Mishindi daunted, hesitated. "Exactly how much do you retain once you're unplugged?" He nodded toward the cables hanging from Augustus' forearms and the back of his neck.

"Things of interest," said Augustus, a dare. The look on his face said he expected to be locked away again.

"You'll have it," said Farragut. Thought he might have seen Mishindi flinch.

Spoken promises meant little to Augustus, but he said, "Then may I also request you get from the Empire anything surrounding the assassination. I could not prevent Caesar's murder. I can, at least, avenge him."

Farragut would have put a reassuring hand on the shoulder of anyone else at this point. But Augustus was remote, glacial. Farragut gave him his distance. "I'll request that information from Imperial Intelligence for you."

Augustus' wicked little Striker spacecraft had been locked down inside one of *Merrimack*'s docks. The Striker looked fast and evil, and it was. With its patterner installed, a Striker was an extraordinary war machine. The hull of this one was black and red, Flavian colors.

En route to Fort Theodore Roosevelt, the patterner was permitted to plug into *Merrimack*'s main database. Augustus' left-side forearm cable could adapt to any physical or electromagnetic dataport.

He made the connection and vanished from conscious presence. Sat. Hollow-eyed. Facial muscles slack.

Whether from pride or determination, his mouth did not hang open.

He did not eat or drink for two watches. Ignored you when you asked if he was okay. And when you persisted, he said from far away: "Don't talk to me."

The Naval Intelligence officers advised Farragut that a

patterner's time sense was altered when enabled. And human speech became as whale songs with their thirty-minute-long phrases. Like listening to mud flow.

Very well if you are a whale and in no great hurry. This being was compiling unimaginable amounts of data.

Farragut looked in on him every hour. The xenos and medics came and went, observing, speculating what the cables were for. One suggested they were analogous to express lanes added to a congested highway. There were synthetic neural pathways within those armored cable sheaths.

After seven hours—Palatine hours—Augustus lifted a somnambulant arm. Reached slowly behind his head. Pulled the cables out of the sockets at the base of his skull.

Looked cadaverous.

He detached his arm cable from the dataport. Unplugged a data module from behind his ear, where most folks wore their language modules.

Tossed the module carelessly onto the console.

Stood up. Threw up. Or spit up. There was very little to throw. Lay down on the deck and passed out.

John Farragut thought they'd killed him.

The intelligence officer seized the module. Several xenos and Jose Maria de Cordillera immediately withdrew from the compartment to review the contents.

Farragut summoned the medical officer.

Doctor Mo Shah was the only man Farragut knew who could react swiftly and remain utterly serene. Mo Shah did not seem surprised to see the patterner crumpled on the deck in the data vault. Regarded the motionless figure with deep hound dog eyes. "Yes, I have been reading about this happening. Your patterner will be continuing in this state for many hours."

"This is *supposed* to happen?"

Mo tilted his head to one side then the other. "Not so much supposing to as simply happening."

"Can you do anything for him?"

"Your Roman has forbidden me to be touching him," said Mo. "'*Primum non nocere.*'"

Farragut knew that one. "First, do no harm."

"I am not knowing if moving him would be harming him."

Farragut planted his fists just behind his hipbones, and strolled a half circle round the body on the black deck grates. Blue eyes lifted. "Well, I didn't take that oath, Mo. And neither did y'all," he said to the MPs at the hatch. "Get something comfortable underneath this officer."

Farragut could not see how getting Augustus off the deck grates could hurt.

And if he died, at least he would not look as if he had been killed with a waffle iron.

Everyone who reviewed the patterner's report looked like they had found religion. They were awed. Even Jose Maria de Cordillera.

"It is an astonishing piece of work, young Captain. How someone can identify and distill all these bits of scattered evidence and disparate minutiae into a coherent pattern is beyond my comprehension."

More than the method, Augustus' conclusion hit with the force of a bomb. "The gorgons did not displace themselves. They were delivered."

"Delivered?"

"There was an intelligence behind the act. There had to be. The Hive are not intelligent."

"No," Farragut rejected the idea. He launched into agitated pacing, with big stalking steps and big arm motions and big voice. "Augustus can't tell me some alien intelligence is using our own technology to sling gorgons at us from the Deep!"

"No. He cannot. And he is not," Jose Maria said, composed as a cat on a windowsill. "It is a human intelligence. And the patterner has put a name on it. The difficulty is that we are ninety-nine percent certain that the man who belongs to the name is dead."

The pacing stopped. Farragut guessed, "So we're looking at the other one percent here?"

"We are ninety-nine percent sure that we are. Rome killed him sixty-one years ago on the planet Thaleia. But because death is not always prohibitive anymore, your Roman is confident in saying that the intelligence behind the Hive is the aforesaid dead man. His name is Constantine Siculus."

15

Augustus woke up hours later. Lumbered like a drunken zombie—a drunken zombie with a homing beacon—through *Merrimack*'s corridors, its laddered shafts, the ramp tunnel, to the dock where his Striker was locked down.

A wicked little hornet of a spacecraft, colored red and black, the Striker crouched in the spacious dock between the bigger, placid, boxy, gray shuttles. Gave an impression of speed in the stillness, implacable anger in the dark.

The Striker's side hatch opened at Augustus' approach. Augustus climbed inside and slept some more.

Augustus' sleeping compartment was not large, but it was grand—opulent, draped deck to overhead in richly textured fabrics of deep red and brilliant gold against forest greens and browns. Very Roman. Augustus sprawled corpselike, with a brocade tapestry pulled half across him. The bed was longer than U.S. standard, built to accommodate Augustus' six-foot-eight frame. Still, he'd managed to miss the target, and one foot still hung off the end of the bed, the other off the side.

A voice intruded into his head-thumping dark: "You asleep?"

Without opening his eyes, Augustus croaked, "No."

"What's that about?"

Augustus had to crack one eye in a pained squint to see what "that" was.

Captain Farragut stood at the foot of his bed, looking straight down.

Augustus was sporting a toe tag on one bare foot.

"I woke up with it," said Augustus, voice raspy. "Not your work, then, I take it."

"No. I apologize—"

"Don't," said Augustus. The corner of his mouth made a hard curl. "I see the humor in it."

The toe tag was most likely the work of the FNG (New Guy), Flight Sergeant Cain Salvador. Replaced Reg Monroe in the Alpha Three spot. Reg Monroe had just left for home on an LRS headed from Fort Theodore Roosevelt to Earth.

Cain Salvador's new squad mates would have put him up to the tagging.

"Why are you here?" said Augustus.

"Stopped in to see if you were dead."

Augustus lifted his tagged foot. Considered. "Could be."

"Dead like Constantine?"

Augustus nodded, not lifting his head from the mattress. "About that dead."

"Anything I can do for you?"

Farragut had been advised that Augustus was dominant homosexual with sadistic inclinations, so he might have expected the reply he got.

The captain did not react to the obscenity. Just shook his head. "That won't be happening. But there's probably a dreambox programmed for that sort of thing."

"Then what do you want here?"

"Constantine Siculus."

"You have my report."

"Your report is extremely detailed."

Augustus had noted all his references and explicitly linked every miniscule point of evidence back to its conclusion.

"I came for the executive summary."

"The moron's version?" Augustus translated.

Farragut leaned back against a faux marble pilaster,

crossed one ankle over the other, ready to listen to a story. "Please."

You just could not insult the man. Well, you could, but it had no effect. Your opinion of John Farragut did not change him, and he knew it.

Augustus half rolled, elbow-crawled to get all of himself onto the bed, flopped back down, his back to Farragut. "Constantine Siculus is alive and coexisting with the Hive in the Deep."

"Not possible. Gorgons have never spared anything."

"Nothing," said Augustus. "Except each other."

Heard the amazed realization at his back: "He's got the Hive harmonic. He's resonating on the Hive harmonic."

"He is," said Augustus. "Coexisting with the Hive like a clown fish inside an anemone in very deep Sagittarian space."

"Can't be," said Farragut. He knew something of Constantine Siculus. "If someone is out there, it can't be Constantine."

Constantine Siculus. Born Conrad Nelson one hundred and thirty years ago in the United States of America. His mother was a Roman mole, working in the Pentagon. She fled to Palatine with her son as she was about to be brought in for questioning. There she ditched her husband's name, and assumed her true *nomen* of Siculus, and renamed her son Constantine.

Constantine became a systems engineer. Undertook the terraforming of Thaleia, where he founded PanGalactic Automated Industries.

The name of his business said a lot about the man. PanGalactic—when humankind had only explored a fraction of the galaxy.

Megalomania. The word was older than Rome.

The death of Constantine's mother unhinged him. He demanded that Caesar deify her. Caesar—Caesar Daisius at that time—refused, so Constantine declared himself Caesar and ordered the citizens of Thaleia to worship his mother.

Rome dethroned him.

"Rome blew him up," said Farragut. "They found pieces

of him. There was a Sargasson analysis. Those weren't cloned pieces. That was Constantine's body."

"Pieces of it," said Augustus. "You know, if you're going to stay here, I'm going to do illegal drugs."

He punched his headboard. Tubes eeled out, found their way to a vein in the crook of his elbow. Made a connection, hissed briefly, and withdrew back into the headboard.

Augustus sat up, looking marginally more human. Said, "They found an original heart, an original lung, an original kidney, and original bone of Constantine's at the blast site."

"That would make him pretty dead," said Farragut.

"There is a sublegal clinic on Palatine, which identifies its patients only by file number. It's a clone farm. Patient one thousand fifty-eight had a heart, kidney, lung, and bone replaced with cloned parts. Patient one thousand fifty-eight's stay at the clinic coincided with a time period in which no communications with Constantine were recorded on Thaleia."

"Not conclusive," said Farragut. "Lack of evidence is slim evidence."

"Patient one thousand fifty-eight was unique at the clinic for his demand to take his old parts with him."

Looked to Farragut for a return argument. There was none coming. Only astonishment.

"He was premeditating his own fake death," said Farragut.

Constantine had known Rome was gunning for him, and he'd been ready.

Augustus watched Farragut closely. "Do you remember when Numa Pompeii planted a resonator on your ship as gorgon bait?"

All resonance attracts the Hive. Numa Pompeii had found one harmonic that provoked gorgons into a ravenous frenzy to the exclusion of all else. Numa had planted a reso- nator on board *Merrimack* transmitting on that harmonic in order to draw gorgons off of his own ship *Gladiator*.

Farragut cracked a bright white smile and snorted. "Won't forget that unless you blow my brains out."

"Don't tempt me," said Augustus. "Ever wonder where Numa got that harmonic?"

"Are you nuts?" Of course he wondered.

"Sixty-one years ago, Imperial Intelligence found a note in Constantine's files on Thaleia with the notation: *This is the harmonic.*"

Augustus watched the captain's fair face go blank, then smolder with deepening wrath. Finally, in the soft voice of complete outrage, Farragut murmured, "That bastard."

"Numa or Constantine?"

"Both, but I was talking about Constantine. How—how could any human being—"

Anger. Augustus had got white-hot anger out of John Farragut.

But it wasn't the selfish little anger of most men. It wasn't for pride or for challenged authority or threat to himself, or even blasphemy against his idea of God. It was a pure sort of anger from a man faced with an amoral monster who let tens of thousands die. May have even caused their deaths.

Farragut was just now realizing that Constantine Siculus knew about the Hive decades before *Sulla* disappeared.

Farragut was in motion, pacing, too angry to put together a sentence. "Sixty-one years ago—! And he didn't—!"

Constantine had never warned anyone about the existence of the Hive.

"Damn him," Farragut said finally, softly. "Damn him to hell."

"Trying," said Augustus.

Farragut calmed down. Shook his head, brows drawn together. "Constantine was never *in* the Deep End. How did he discover the Hive?"

"Constantine had himself a private little Deep End terraforming project on the side. He'd been siphoning resources off Thaleia ever since he got there. He used automatons for everything. No loose lips on a machine, so he kept absolute secrecy. There was no Shotgun in those days, not that he would have been allowed to use it. So it was very slow work. But machines on board unmanned spacecraft don't mind slow work. At some point—probably when his automatons tried to transplant vegetation onto his target world, or when the automatons sent a resonant message back to their boss—Constantine Siculus discovered the Hive.

"By this time Rome was highly suspicious of Constantine. His PanGalactic products were in use across the Empire—his killer bots, his displacement equipment. He was dangerous, and he was unstable.

"Caesar Daisius sent his patterner—the patterner Secundus in that era—to Thaleia to tap into Constantine's computer network.

"Constantine was ready for that move. Probably hoping for it. He had a Trojan Horse program ready and waiting to corrupt Secundus' programming."

Farragut looked startled. "Y'all really are programmed?"

"To a degree, yes."

"If Secundus was a patterner, why didn't he see the trap?"

"No doubt Secundus was given insufficient information on Constantine before he was sent in. The technology for creating patterners was still new back then—Secundus was only the second of our kind ever made. Powerful creations that can think for themselves cause distrust. People are still very reluctant to give patterners enough information to get the job done. Did you know that?"

"I've gotten that drift, yes."

"Using information gathered by Constantine's drones in the Deep, Secundus would have divined both the provocative harmonic and the Hive's own harmonic."

"Of course," said Farragut, ironic. "A human being couldn't have figured it out. A discovery that extraordinary must be made by one of you cyborgs."

"Yes. Except that I am not a cyborg, yes," said Augustus. "When Secundus failed to return from Thaleia—with or without Constantine's head—that prompted drastic measures. If the size of the bomb was any indication, Rome was plenty afraid of Constantine. When they found his charred organs, Imperial Intelligence assumed they got him. They had a Sargasson check the parts for authenticity. Someone should have known that Constantine got away when they found no remains of Secundus or his Striker.

"Constantine is alive, in an area of space scummy with

Hive. Your Admiral Mishindi thought it was the breeding ground or nerve center of the Beast. It's Constantine's refuge. It's Attack Group One's target in deep Sagittarian space."

"You're a patterner," said Farragut. "Why can't you come up with the Hive harmonic?"

"I don't have any of the information Secundus had from the automatons on Constantine's Deep End world. The only shred of data that Constantine left behind regarding his secret project was the harmonic that gets you the Hive's undivided attention."

Farragut nodded. "Good work, Augustus." He headed toward the hatch.

"I don't need an atta boy from John Farragut."

"Then don't take it."

"The files you gave me are incomplete," said Augustus as Farragut opened the hatch.

It had the sound of an accusation.

Farragut turned sharply. "What are those CIA weasels withholding?"

"Wrong weasel," said Augustus. "There is nothing at all in your data banks concerning Caesar's assassination."

Merrimack dropped from FTL to take a res call from Admiral Mishindi. Farragut heard disbelief in the admiral's voice, "Captain Farragut, did you put in a request to Imperial Intelligence for their files concerning Caesar Magnus' assassination? *Twice?*"

"Yes, sir. I did."

"What the hell for? Did you used to play with hornets' nests back in Kentucky? And did you take too many stings to the head while you were at it! Internal Roman politics are not within the purview of the U.S. Naval Fleet! Romulus is stinging mad!"

Farragut had not considered how his information request might look to the Romans. Did it look like he was trying to interfere in the Roman government? "I asked for it at Augustus' request. He has some conspiracy theory and thinks he could smoke out other plotters in Caesar's assassination if he had access to the data. I didn't see the point in denying him that."

"Ever consider that your patterner's search for another conspirator could be a search for *self*?" said Mishindi.

Farragut blinked. Augustus as assassin? Yes, he could see Augustus as an assassin. But as a traitor? "Not for a heartbeat, sir."

"Well, John, I am holding here—in my hand—an extradition order served on the Joint Chiefs, issued by Caesar Romulus, to arrest Augustus on suspicion of complicity in Magnus' assassination. It orders us to return Augustus to Palatine—immediately. Dead or incapacitated."

"What did the JC answer?"

"Didn't. Passed it to me. And I'm passing it to you. You have an answer to this?"

"Yes, I do, sir. The answer is no."

Farragut expected an argument, a rebuke. Instead he got an extended silence that ended in, "I accept your refusal of Caesar's order. Romulus' stated reason for wanting Augustus lacks credence. I think he just wants the patterner back for his own use. But *you* are going to have to accept Caesar's refusal to hand over the files. I'm not going to war over this."

"It was a request, sir," said Farragut. "I didn't expect a war."

Reg Monroe called the bet and raised a lot. Her shirt gapped loose as she leaned forward to push the pile of money into the pot. A tactic as old as the invention of breasts and lace. Jarred the poker faces loose.

"Who let them play!" Enzo yelped.

"No fair, Reg." Tad, the dealer, gave the player to his right a shove. "So what are you doin'? You in or you out?"

The man stared, stupidly blissful, struck senseless by the vision. Mumbled, "I have no idea."

Long Range Shuttles moved at a tedious pace. But Reg Monroe was on her way home to Earth. For good. She was flying. Whiled away the time with a couple of bull mastiffs on leave—Tad from Delta flight and Enzo from Echo, and a station rat from Fort Ted.

"I—uh—fold," the station rat said finally. "I can't compete with that."

"Dealer calls." Tad pushed his money in.

Enzo studied the huge pot. Looked hard at Reg. At her eyes. "You got nothin'." Pushed all his money in. "I wanna see 'em."

"Me, too," said the station rat, dreamily.

"That was cheap, Reg," Tad scolded.

"Cheap?" Reg straightened her back, indignant. "How dare you say that to this elegant hag. Or this elegant hag." Reg lay down the queen of diamonds. "Or this elegant hag." Queen of spades. "Or this elegant hag." Hearts.

Tad and Enzo howling misery with every hag.

A cluster of bangs, like muffled explosions, rocked the LRS. Sent the money sliding off the table. Alarms sounded. Another series of hits. Dipped the lights.

The station rat was on the deck. The Marines kept their seats.

"What did we fly into?" said Enzo.

A voice on over the loud com announced, laconic: "We are under attack by the Roman Legion carrier *Horatius*. We are about to be boarded."

The clank of a *corvus* sounded on the hull.

Reg threw down her last two cards. "Oooo, they've been itchin' for a fight since we saved their sorry little planet for them. Let's have it! Come *on!*"

"We got this, Reggie girl," said Tad, rising.

"Stay in the back, short timer," said Enzo.

"Short timer?" said Reg. "I'm *done*! I crawled in a fox-trotting Roman sewer for those folf-wuckers! The elegant hag does NOT do the *back!*"

16

SIX BELLS, AND ONE OF the guys in the forecastle was screaming as if he'd found something dead in the sleep pod with him. Some laughter sounded, too, so no one was really dying.

Flight Sergeant Cain Salvador screamed bloody murder.

Apparently the toe tag had found its way back. Cain had woken up with it. And not on his toe.

Cain pounded on the partition that separated the jacks from the janes. "Kerry Blue! This better've been you!"

Kerry giggled in her sleep pod. "'Fraid not."

Cain wailed, "Aw, no. *Lie* to me, babe!"

The other men in the forecastle were altogether creeped. Kerry Blue could hear a case of the squirms and dancing yewies like never. Sounded like the guys just wanted to crawl out of their own skins and have 'em fumigated. Didn't want to think how that tag got there. There but for the grace of God.

Flight Leader Ranza Espinoza was up and trying to muster some kind of command to order, but she was *this far* from belly laughs. Could see the guffaws moving around in her midriff like snakes. Her eyes were upturned crescents, gleaming merry tears.

Dak Shepard pleaded through the partition, "Kerry Blue, can I sleep with you tonight? I'm scared!"

The sound to general quarters ended all that, with the Marine Wing throwing on clothes and running to their Swifts.

Commodore Farragut burst onto the command deck, still dripping, carrying his clothes under his arm except for his pants which were on him. The commodore had one of the three water showers on board *Merrimack* and had been in it when the alarms sounded.

Lieutenant Colonel Steele was already on the command deck. The XO, Gypsy Dent, was there, too, demanding the nature of the threat from the Officer of the Watch, Lieutenant Glenn Hamilton.

"Not sure, sir," Glenn Hamilton confessed. "The Emergency Action Message from the Joint Chiefs called *everyone* to red alert."

"Everyone?" Commander Gypsy Dent and Commodore Farragut said at the same time.

"The United States of America. Everyone," said Hamster. "There was a Roman attack. No declaration of war. No one knows what it means."

"Oh, for—" Farragut started. Then: "Tactical, who is out there?"

"Just us chickens, Commodore. We are still fifty light-years from Fort Theodore Roosevelt and there is no one within thirty light-years of the *Mack*."

All the monitors showed nothing but stars, and Marine Swifts out there in the big dark looking for a target and nobody laughing.

"Okay, turn off that alarm and back us down to yellow," said Farragut, slightly nettled at someone giving orders to his ship from a couple dozen light-years away. "Give me that EAM."

Farragut popped the EAM into his player. Glanced up from the reader. "Has this been authenticated?"

Glenn Hamilton stiffened as if she'd been called stupid. But it was only protocol. She answered evenly, "Yes, sir."

The cryptotech, Qord Johnson, echoed, "Yes, sir."

Farragut read the Emergency Action Message while he pulled his shirt on. "This is crazy."

A U.S. Long Range Shuttle had been attacked by a Roman Legion carrier. The *Horatius*. Two light-years outside the solar system. Three Marines had been killed trying to repel boarders.

No one could say if the U.S. and Rome were at war or not. Whether this was Pearl Harbor or piracy or something else, no one seemed to know.

The Emergency Action Message ordered all armed forces everywhere to expect other attacks. Or at least be ready for them.

"Request confirmation," Farragut ordered. A single silver star glinted from either collar tab as he buttoned his shirt.

The com tech and the cryptotech acknowledged. Sent the request.

The tall, ominous figure of the Roman patterner Augustus appeared in the hatchway to the command deck. Marines flanking the hatch instantly drew arms.

Augustus halted.

Difficult to read his expression. No fear. Disdain for the Marines and their splinter guns. Some curiosity. Looked to Farragut as if for explanation.

Farragut asked, "Augustus, are we at war?"

"I can hope," said Augustus.

"Are we at war?" Farragut repeated.

"If we are, I have not been informed," said Augustus.

"Neither have I, but there's been some shooting," Farragut told him. "Confine yourself to quarters until one of us knows."

Augustus had been moved out of his Striker in the ship's dock and given quarters on board *Merrimack*.

The patterner turned smartly about-face in the hatchway.

Farragut added at his back: "Whoever knows first *will* have the courtesy to inform the other."

Augustus lifted a hand, acknowledging that. Withdrew from the hatchway.

Steele ordered the guards, "Make sure he gets to his quarters and keep him there."

Surprised to hear the commodore speak over him, "Belay that. Stay at your posts." And to Steele, "Put a guard in the dock."

Lieutenant Colonel Steele, who never challenged orders, was trying hard to contain himself. He flushed. Looked like a tower of pink granite. Eyes of artic blue glared with accusation.

Farragut answered the unspoken objection. "TR, he's one of us right up until he's not."

Civility was vital in space warfare.

Which was why it was incomprehensible that *Horatius* would commit piracy.

Another EAM came in, summoning *Merrimack* back to the solar system.

Horatius had not responded to any hail. A pack of Rattlers in pursuit been fired upon and turned back. A request from the White House for clarification of the nations' status still awaited answer from Fortress Aeyrie.

"TR, bring your birds in," Farragut ordered. "Mr. Dent, as soon as everyone is aboard, turn this boat around."

Farragut returned to his quarters to finish his shower.

Merrimack hurtled toward Earth at threshold velocity. Covered vast distances without word from Earth. In the com silence, you had to wonder if Earth was still there.

The hard part was the not knowing.

Wondered about the Romans and Americans in the Deep End, serving side by side. Suddenly they had to watch their sides.

Updates dripped in with scant information.

Twelve hours later, the message everyone waited for came in: Rome had not declared war and had not ordered the attack.

"So what happened?" Farragut demanded as *Merrimack* dropped out of FTL at the perimeter of the solar system twenty-four hours after the first alarm.

The controller on Triton base responded by giving *Merrimack* the current vector of the renegade *Horatius*, and ordered *Merrimack* to pursue and secure.

"Is this a hostage situation?" Farragut asked.

"Not precisely," the controller answered.

"Make it precise for me."

"The Dracs took possession of a Long Range Shuttle and beached the crew and passengers on Thaleia. The planetary governor on Thaleia notified us that our people are not in detention. Not in detention, but they have no way off world. Earth traffic is barred from Thaleian space."

Farragut filled in the blanks. "The governor of Thaleia didn't actively aid the Dracs but didn't do anything to prevent their getaway."

"Precisely."

"Where does Romulus stand on this?"

"Romulus isn't talking to us," said Triton Control. "He answered President Johnson—just to say that Rome had not declared war. His aide indicated to us that our failure to control military vessels wasn't any fault of Rome's and that the U.S. should handle its own affairs."

"Squid feet!" said Farragut.

"The JC are giving this to you, *Merrimack*. If we are to treat this as a mutiny, no one wants the JC to issue direct orders to *Horatius* and be ignored. Commodore Farragut, you have orders to secure the *Horatius* and Legion Draconis by any means necessary."

"Fine," said Farragut, with the com off. Clicked on: "Acknowledged, Triton Control."

Merrimack could run down just about anything near her size, and *Horatius* was not running. Not precisely.

Augustus, released from self-confinement, watched in grim amusement as *Merrimack* closed on *Horatius*. Not that Augustus found the imminent death of Romans entertaining, but he took a vicious satisfaction in the hole Farragut had dug for himself. The Subjugation had given Farragut authority to command Roman troops. Roman troops had mutinied.

How are you going to get out this, John Farragut?

Kill your own?

He had to.

As *Merrimack* closed the range between ships, *Horatius* opened fire.

All ordnance slid off *Mack*'s formidable forward distortion field.

When *Merrimack* drew very close, a mere 100 klicks separating the two ships, Farragut requested the harmonic of *Horatius*' verbal com.

A cluster of bombs detonated on *Mack*'s bow, dimming all the viewports. Farragut took up the caller. "Well, darlin', you can slap my face all night, but I'm still fixin' to walk you home from this dance. Care to talk?"

No response. *Horatius* continued at speed.

Clicked on the caller again, "You can't put in at any port anywhere ever again in this lifetime unless you talk to me. So what do you have to say?"

Herius Asinius' voice sounded thick: "We do not recognize U.S. authority. We fight for Roma Eterna."

Consternation visibly washed off Farragut's face, replaced by a calm, almost smiling expression. He might have been coaching Little League, the game in the bag, and no one else could see it.

"Well, I ain't Caesar—" Farragut began.

"Thank you for acknowledging that, Captain Farragut."

"But I made some assumptions that I thought were kinda obvious. Now I know Rome isn't the United States—"

"Thank you for acknowledging that, Captain Farragut."

"But where I come from, the government doesn't fall just because an office holder dies. Before the surrender, a Roman warship had the right, under Roman rule, to commandeer any United States vessel it could. So all this would have been legal back then. But this is after the surrender now, son, and Magnus' death did not overthrow Rome or its treaties or truces."

"The law according to Captain Farragut," said Herius Asinius. "*We* serve Roma Eterna."

"Then how 'bout we ask Roma Eterna about that?" And with the com open for the Dracs to hear, Farragut told his com tech, "Mr. Hicks, hail Caesar."

Merrimack dropped out of FTL to place the resonant call.

While waiting for a response, Farragut advised Tactical, "Let me know when *Horatius* drops."

The com tech tried to get Romulus on the com, but was informed by a prickly gatekeeper that Romulus did not heel to the summons of American Naval officers. If this were a matter of State, the gatekeeper was certain that Romulus would hear of it from President Johnson.

Tactical reported quietly that the *Horatius* had dropped out of FTL and was very likely listening to the exchange. Probably smirking.

Farragut had experience dealing with stubborn, powerful people. His father was galactic champion of the I'm-too-important-to-take-your-call game.

"I'm sorry," Farragut apologized to the gatekeeper. "I negotiated the peace with Caesar Magnus, and Magnus is not there. In the absence of Magnus, Magnus' successor shall have to answer. But y'all haven't ratified anyone as Caesar. Would the qualified authority be then the Senate? Connect me with Senator Gaius Americanus."

There was a short silence and then, "Please stand by for Caesar Romulus."

Farragut knew that Romulus was already listening, so Farragut did not stand by, just started right in: "I made the truce with Rome, so I know the terms did not alter Rome's internal government. But I'm not real clear on Lex Romana, and I've got a shipload of folks on an open channel here who don't seem clear on the order of the Empire either. I need someone like a Caesar—"

"I *am* Caesar," Romulus broke his silence.

Good. "—to confirm that the Empire still stands and that the truce of Caesar Magnus holds with the full force of Rome behind it. Does it?"

So there was Romulus, backed against the wall. The least uncertainty, hesitation, or hair-splitting in this moment would destroy him. For Romulus to disavow the surrender would be a declaration of war. And Romulus had just told President Marissa Johnson that Rome had not declared war.

Romulus snapped, "Yes, of course it does."

There was a collective exhalation on *Merrimack*'s command deck.

Roma Eterna had just put the Dracs under U.S. command.

"And just so I understand Roman law, were a combat unit to refuse a lawful order, under Roman law the penalty would be death to the soldiers and death to their kin. Even suicide would not spare their mothers, fathers, spouses, and children. Under Roman law. Is that still true?"

Farragut had the authority to command Roman troops, but Roman disobedience put them subject to the penalties of Roman law. Any executions would not be at U.S. hands.

An instant dread chill clutched the command deck.

Horatius, over the com, was deathly silent.

No one had seen that one coming.

Least of all Romulus. He answered in cold fury, "Roman law has not changed." And terminated the connection before he could be trapped into anything else.

Farragut spoke into the com, "All right, Mister Asinius. Come back here. Drop your distortion fields except for your asteroid deflector and follow me to Thaleia."

"We are to be put to death?" Herius asked, stoic.

"Why? You fixin' to break a law?"

Wordless confusion read over the com.

Farragut said, "You didn't understand the chain of command. Now you do. Now follow me to Thaleia, and tell your buddies who have my LRS to meet us there with my people, or so help me God I won't stop at their mothers and fathers and kids. I'll have their grammies, their sisters, their brothers, their dogs, and their goldfish crucified." He clicked off. Ordered *Merrimack* to turn heel.

In a moment he asked his tactical specialist, "Is *Horatius* behind us?"

"Yes, sir."

"Lining up a shot on my ass?"

"No, sir."

Farragut nodded.

Felt Augustus' eyes on him. Asked, "What?"

The patterner answered, "Not what I would have predicted."

Farragut, who had a reputation as being trigger happy—a well deserved reputation—had won this crisis without firing a shot.

"You know, it woulda been real helpful if *your* emperor

had made the status of the surrender clear from the get go. He left that point just fuzzy enough for a proud, hard-headed young Roman to get creative."

"Romulus is not emperor yet. I think Romulus was rather counting on your slaughtering the Dracs."

Jolted Farragut. "Why would Romulus want the Dracs dead?"

"Wasn't the effect on the Dracs he would have wanted. It would be the effect on you. And on Romulus. The more detestable the enemy leader, the more popular your own leader."

If Farragut had done what everyone expected and secured *Horatius* the old-fashioned way, that might have caused the Romans to rally even more strongly round their new unratified Caesar, who had denounced John Farragut's Subjugation of Rome and had denied John Farragut his Triumphal crown.

"Really?" It was too much bloody political maneuvering for Farragut. "Then I'm happy to disappoint him. And you, Augustus? Are you disappointed?"

"I think too little of you for you to disappoint me. Permission to withdraw."

"Granted."

A tittering about the command deck followed Augustus' departure.

Marcander Vincent snarled into his readouts. "Caesar sent him to serve you, my Aunt Fanny."

"Be all kinds of real fine to have him on our side," said Farragut.

"Yeah, that would be fine if it ever happened," said Vincent. "Sir."

"What was that man thinking?" Farragut thought out loud to his exec as *Merrimack* approached the planet Thaleia with *Horatius* heeling like a dog. "Herius Asinius, I mean. Was he trying to start a war?"

"Maybe," Gypsy considered it. "Make a first strike and hope Rome followed his lead?"

"Yeah," said Farragut. "But it would be a strategic disaster with the Hive out there."

"You called it, sir. A proud, hotheaded young Roman. Didn't Calli say: what Rome can afford to do and what Rome will do for pride are two different things?"

Pride was the deadliest of Roman sins. And Herius Asinius' pride had taken a bloody beating.

"Or maybe he didn't want a war," Farragut searched for another motive. "He just wanted to give America a bloody nose and expected Romulus to shelter him. Romulus did give the Dracs reason to expect some kind of support. Romulus has publicly expressed disgust at the surrender without ever repudiating it."

"Hit and run?" said Gypsy. "Herius didn't run. He didn't leave the area. He let *Merrimack* get close. You got called into the street for a gunfight, Marshal. Herius wanted either to destroy the *Merrimack* or have you send him and the Dracs gloriously to the Corindahlor Bridge in hopeless battle."

Gypsy glanced up to the monitor screens as *Merrimack* approached Thaleia. Said: "In fact, it was definitely you he wanted, sir. Look."

The image of the captive LRS came into view on the screen.

"Oh, for Jesus."

Steele saw the identification numbers on the LRS and went rigid.

One of the guards at the hatch, normally mute as a statue, spoke, "Can we still string up their grannies?"

Farragut answered sympathetically, "No, son."

Steele found his voice. Asked hoarsely, "Three casualties? Marines?"

Farragut nodded.

Merrimack collected the Long Range Shuttle, its crew, cargo, passengers, and three bodies. Set the LRS back on course to Earth.

The crew and Legion of *Horatius* had orders to assemble in their cargo hold and wait with their small arms piled on the deck.

Merrimack docked with *Horatius*.

Farragut boarded *Horatius* in person, armed, but without

a Marine guard, his only attendant the Roman patterner, Augustus.

As commanded, no Dracs met him at the dock.

It would have been an easy thing to go to the *Horatius*' control room and purge the cargo hold into the vacuum.

Farragut marched into the cargo hold, took a stand before the assembled Romans and did not order them to ease. Caesar's patterner stood motionless at his flank.

Commodore Farragut announced, "I am pressing this vessel into service in Attack Group One. I will beach whoever does not want to come with me. I need folks to man this boat, so I'll give y'all first shot. Do I have volunteers?"

Mumbles, with sniggers interspersed, rippled through the rigid ranks.

Farragut's voice started soft and got louder. "I am going to the Deep to kill gorgons. Not everyone is made of the same stuff as the Tenth at Corindahlor, and I don't want anyone with me who doesn't want to be there. So if you're not coming, *get off my boat*. And now that we're clear on who you're supposed to be taking orders from and that you still have a duty to defend Rome, choose a place—on the ground safe in Near Space or on board this ship in the Deep End—pick up your weapons, and *do your goddamn duty!*"

Augustus absorbed the final verbal blast with small flinches that were more like half blinks in his otherwise basilisk face.

"DISMISSED!" Farragut ended with a roar, motioned Augustus to fall in, and stalked back to *Merrimack* without waiting for anyone's decision.

The commodore was an idiot. Naive, bright-eyed, energetic, and way too optimistic to be the man in charge of so many men of war. He led by personality. Had a face people trusted instantly. And why? Just because he was good-looking, had bright blue eyes and that glad-to-see-you smile? Or because he remembered your name and every damn thing you ever told him about yourself?

Augustus hated a fraud, and John Farragut had to be a fraud. John Farragut appeared to be the kind of man everyone wanted to exist. And they would willingly follow that image to hell.

"Permission to speak freely," said Farragut.

Augustus' brow furrowed very slightly. "I did not request it."

"Nevertheless, you have it."

"You should not have invoked Corindahlor back there," said Augustus.

"Do I sully the memory of the heroes of the Roman Tenth by speaking of them?"

"The Tenth? No, they're not sullied. And they're hardly heroes. Only an idiot enlists for ground duty in a unit of three hundred."

"What's wrong with three hundred?"

"It's a heroic number. Nations make their honor cadres in three hundreds, so when they are obliterated in hopeless battle, they are heroes. Thermopylae, the Sacred Band of Thebes at Chaironeia, the three hundred at Masada. Never join an outfit that numbers three hundred. Or a multiple of three hundred, unless you want to ride in the valley of death. Invoking Corindahlor was a cheap way to manipulate the Dracs."

"The only one I manipulated was Romulus, and he asked for it," said Farragut. "Herius and his boys just got caught in a rundown while trying to steal a base."

"A stalwart Roman Legion." Augustus' voice dripped scorn. "Their hearts changed in less than a beat."

"Sure they changed quick! Once you kick folks off the fence, it gets real clear real quick which side everyone is on, and decisions get real simple."

"Oh, the insulting, monumental arrogance of the completely dominant. You have no idea why we resent the offered help, even if we need it. Especially if we need it. You saved Rome's planetary ass. You cannot imagine how demeaning it is to be tucked under your protective wing. If not for the Hive, the United States and Rome would be enemies; and I and John Farragut would be staring down each other's guns. And maybe I would be magnanimous in your defeat, but I don't think so. I step on the weak, and that includes idiots."

And Augustus stood back, in a *so there* stance. Waited for comment or execution. When neither came, Augustus said, "Any free speaking coming back at me?"

Farragut shook his head. "Just wanted to know what was on your mind."

Carly Delgado had a scream that could detonate warheads. Did not help at all that the KIAs were getting medals.

"She didn't want no medal! She wanted to be an engineer! A *civilian* engineer!"

Kerry Blue bounced off the bulks like a caged rat. "Let me out! Let me out! I'll kill 'em all!"

"Blue! Delgado! Team Alpha! Stand down!" Steele thundered.

"No!" Carly cried.

Steele bodily took hold of Carly and slammed her up against the bulk. "Only proves you are out of control, Delgado. You're a menace to everyone. *Stand down!*" Let her drop.

She kept dropping. Kind of crumpled to sit on the deck, sobbing over her crossed legs.

Girl Marines crying tore Steele's guts out.

Echo and Delta were taking it just as hard. They had lost a man each, supposed to be on leave. Tad and Enzo. Outstanding soldiers. They were not coming back.

And Reg Monroe, going home for good. Happy as a bride.

Kerry Blue was on the deck now, next to Carly, looking like a mama bitch who lost her puppies and won't believe they're really gone. Looked up to Steele with bewildered forlorn eyes as if he could bring them back.

Kerry's tears. That face. And he could not do what she needed him to do. Never felt worse or less of a man than now.

TR Steele was going to rip the guts out of whoever killed his two big mutts and that happy little she-dog.

"*I* am *not* flying with those bastards!" Cole Darby declared.

The crew and company of *Horatius* had, to a man, volunteered to serve under Commodore Farragut in Attack Group One.

Steele had been ordered to head off talk like that. Been waiting for it. Roared at Darb, "You *are*, or you're going home with a dishonorable!" The words burned him coming out. His dogs were only saying what Steele felt. "You are *not* the only dog soldiers who ever lost mates to the wolves!"

"During a surrender we are!" Kerry cried.

Steele inhaled to bellow at her. Lost all his air.

Steele's solid shoulders slumped. He could not argue with her. Rested his hands on his hips, let his head drop forward. Spoke into the deck, "Gordy already asked Farragut if we could crucify their grannies."

Dak Shepard lifted his teary face from his hands, hopeful. "Yeah? What'd Farragut say?"

17

FORT THEODORE ROOSEVELT had been built in the star system Beta Aurigae aka Mankib Dhi-al-'Inan, The Shoulder of the Charioteer. The ancient Greeks looked up and
saw a charioteer in the stars, but most American children
looked up and connected those five dots into a child-drawn
house. Fort Ted was at the peak of the roof, eighty-two light-
years from Earth in the opposite direction from the Wolf
Star.

Mankib Dhi-al-'Inan was actually three stars, two of
them white subgiants that had wandered off the main sequence hand in hand. They had worked up nice helium
cores but were still very hot, their photospheres still very
white, not ready to blow up just yet. It would take another
million years for them to become dangerous. For now they
were just plain spectacular.

The two white stars swung round each other in a tight
dance, eclipsing each other just about every two Earth days.
So the starlight in Fort Ted varied between bright and
brighter.

A third star in the system, a red dwarf, circled the other
two way the hell out there at eight times the distance of
Pluto to Sol. Between the two main stars and the lights of
Fort Ted, the red dwarf went pretty much unseen.

Merrimack approached Theodore Roosevelt with its

flag, and all the flags in the spaceport, at half staff for the death of a head of state.

The space cav charged out to escort the Roman warship *Horatius* directly round the outskirts of the Fort to quarantine, where dwelled things infectious, explosive, suspicious, or the Roman murderers of three U.S. Marines. The snub-nosed Rattlers of the U.S. space cav always looked smoked. The Rattlers darted in close enough to set off *Horatius'* prox alarms, and ordered the Romans to shut down their distortion field and park.

A maintenance platform closed round *Horatius* and clanked against the hull. The platform generated a distortion field round the ship, and pumped an atmosphere in. The ship's hull iced over in the heated air. The platform powered up an artificial grav, and *Horatius* received orders to pop her hatches.

The maintenance platform kept a U.S. atmosphere—fifteen psi—so it made for an ear-popping moment when the Roman seventeen psi hissed loose from *Horatius*.

The platform uprights turned on the swamplights. Swamps did not cast the hard shadows of floods. The swamps gave an overall illumination like daylight for technicians to work in.

Herius Asinius, in company of his cousin Marcus, stepped outside under a weird starry black sky.

A platoon of U.S. erks stood ready to board, equipped to rip the ship to razor blades. Herius and Marcus almost called the Legion to arms, but on the platform also stood John Farragut, who announced to the erks, "This is *my* ship. These are *my* men. Treat them so."

The erks looked dubious. Farragut added, "And post this."

The erks reverently received the U.S. flag from the commodore. Farragut turned to Herius Asinius. As if waiting for an objection.

There was no way around it this time. That flag was going on Herius' ship. "Don't take down our standards," said Herius.

"No," Farragut agreed. He waved the erks in.

Big men with heavy boots stomped aboard like a wrecking crew. Herius was pretty sure they *were* a wrecking crew.

The astrarch, Marcus, asked, unsettled, "What are you doing to my ship?"

"Nothing that I didn't have done to my *Merrimack*."

Herius and Marcus still cringed at the sudden *brrrrack!* of big drills on the bulkheads. Like undergoing surgery without an anesthetic.

"She'll live," said Farragut. "Herius, your boys are good with swords and y'all know what you're doing in front of a bunch of tentacles by now. What you don't have behind you is what it's like when the light goes out in outer space. The Hive will do that. You're getting chemical and mechanical and manual backups. And you're getting blister turrets with projectile cannon with mechanical loads. When the erks are done in there, we're going out to play with guns that go boom and shells that shred things. We've got some fiend-ishly realistic mock gorgons we can set loose for y'all to shoot to shingles."

Neither Roman was accustomed to such casual flippant talk from a Triumphalis. But guns that went boom did sound like fun.

Herius had known John Farragut had a sunny disposition. Had also seen that sun could burn your skin off. Farragut had blazed at him. Gave him and his Dracs a wrath-of-God thunder-and-lightning kind of talking to. And the hell of it was, Herius Asinius could not argue with a single thing the American had said. So when the moment of decision came, Herius had no choice but to pick up his hand cannon and join Commodore Farragut. He was not happy with how eagerly his men had followed his lead, in glassy-eyed hero worship of the American. All of them were here to a man.

"I mean it about the mock gorgons," said Farragut. "You will swear they're real. And you better hit all of 'em because if you miss any, they'll have you swearing a *lot*."

"Are we getting fire breathers?" Marcus asked.

As if the alternative never occurred to him, Farragut said, "You think I'd take you out there naked? You'll have what I have."

"I don't want your Marines teaching us," said Herius.

Farragut pressed his lips together, eyes to the platform.

Herius sensed a refusal coming, but at last Farragut nodded. "This here is what we call a shotgun wedding. I guess I might oughta better find somebody else to teach y'all. I can keep my Marines off your ship. *But.*"

Herius steeled himself against the *but.*

"Because I need y'all to know what you're doing, and I'm not confident that you can really know something until you teach it, *you* are going to show Bambi and Twinkletoes over there how it's done after you've learned it." He gestured across an expanse of blackness to where another oasis of swamplights illuminated another maintenance platform enclosing two League of Earth Nations ships.

The LEN had added two ships to Farragut's Attack Group One. *Windward Isles* and *Sunlit Meadows.* The LEN were always naming-convention challenged.

In the war between the U.S. and Rome, the LEN had been staunchly noncommittal. In the middle was always a good place to get yourself shot. Americans and Romans regarded their delared enemies more highly than their lukewarm allies.

"I am charging you, Herius Asinius, with making sure they can hold up their end."

"Aye, Commodore," said Herius Asinius.

"Permission to come aboard."

"Good God Almighty, Dallas McDaniels. What the Sam Hill are you doing this side of the Big Dark?" Farragut crossed *Merrimack*'s starboard dock with huge strides to seize Captain McDaniels and thump him on the back, pull back beaming, and hug him and thump him again. Had expected to join up with Captain McDaniels and *Rio Grande* on the other side of the Shotgun. "Last time I saw you, you were saving Mama Farragut's favorite son from a pile of gorgons."

"John, old son, we got chewed."

"Someone I know once told me never ever let 'em aboard."

"And I was right, wasn't I?"

Dallas McDaniels, Captain of the *Rio Grande*, looked like he ought to be on a cattle drive. A tall, spare man all rawhide and whipcord, steel nerves and an easy drawl. Had a seamed, leathery face, dusty-colored hair, and keen eyes locked in a permanent squint.

"They got all the king's horses and all the king's men putting my poor *Rio* back together again. And next thing I know I'm reporting to a *junior* officer. After I saved your ass, too. You want to tell me what's fair about that?"

"Yeah, about that," said Farragut. "The ass saving. I never did get a chance to thank you."

"Well, I'm just going to hold it over your head for the rest of your natural-born days."

"That's fair, *compadre*."

"So now tell me, old son, do I salute or do I bow?"

Farragut flipped him a one-digit salute and ushered Dallas aboard, arm round his shoulders. "Come on in, I'll have Chef Zack cook up something for you."

An odd sound made Dallas lift his eyes. Dallas McDaniels thought he knew all the sounds a space battleship could make. "What is that? Sounds like a cow in labor."

"A cow in labor," Farragut answered. "We carry some livestock in case we get stranded."

"Let's not get stranded."

"Not my first, second, or third choice," said Farragut, as the cow gave a particularly painful moo.

"Are they supposed to do that?"

"Technically, no. I think someone's been screwing around in the livestock compartment."

"Sounds like that would be the cow. I think I'll pass on the veal selection."

The rhythmic thump thump thump of joggers on the track sounded from above decks. A sudden grav burble brought stomachs to throats, bent the knees, and made the steady thump thump thump dissolve into a stagger/bumble/roll.

Dallas' eyes crinkled at the corners. "Now there's a homey sound. I'd have thought a ship of *Merrimack*'s class to have smoother artificial gravity than the rest of us peons."

"Nah," said Farragut. "My *Mack*. She has her moods."

"Don't have to tell me. *Rio*'s brought me to my knees."

"Don't they all?" said Farragut.

"Yes, sir, they do. So where's your crown, Triumphalis?"

"I didn't get it. It was grass anyway."

"Yeah?" Dallas drawled. "What kind of grass?"

John Farragut paid a visit to the Roman maintenance platform. Asked Herius Asinius, "How are the *Mountain Oyster* and the *Kumbaya* coming along?"

"We didn't name the ships," a female voice sounded from behind.

Farragut turned. A hard, thin woman smiled politely. Perhaps fifty years old, her hair a hard shade of blonde. She wore the uniform of a League of Earth Nations captain.

Farragut actually blushed, caught with a mouth full of foot. Gave a chagrined grin. "Yeah, I really said that."

He took the LEN captain's offered hand as she introduced herself and her dark companion with the wide, shiny face, "Fredrika Freiheit of the *Minnow* and this is Captain Ram Singh of the *Nightcrawler*."

"Bait," said Farragut, clueing in to the names. "You're not bait."

"And we're not LEN golf balls, Commodore," said Fredrika. "Don't judge us by the stupid names. *Sunlit Meadows* and *Windward Isles* are police ships, and we make dead with the best of them."

Farragut looked to Herius Asinius. "How are they doing?"

"Very well," said Herius formally. "I would trust the LEN ships at my back."

Farragut turned to Fredrika and Ram. "Then I'm pleased to blue peaches to have y'all in my attack group." He called past them to the erks. Motioned at the LEN ships, "Flag 'em."

Fredrika recited blandly, "LEN convention forbids a League ship from taking on the flag of any individual nation."

The erks paused, looking to Farragut for direction.

"You have your orders," said Farragut. Where his ships were going there could be only one undisputed master.

"Oh, look at the view from here," Fredrika said, turning

to face the spectacular double star Mankib Dhi-al-'Inan, her back toward her ship as the Stars and Stripes were posted on her *Sunlit Meadows*.

Captain Ram Singh, a middle-sized man, well muscled, very black, stood beside her, his arms crossed. "Yes. Very nice," said Ram, as *Windward Isles* received the U.S. flag.

All space farers had ultraviolet filters implanted in their eyes, so Fred and Ram could gaze at the swollen white suns as long as it took for them not to see their ships being re-flagged.

Neither LEN ship was very big. Farragut asked, "What kind of soldiers do y'all have on board?"

"Engineers," said Ram Singh. "All of us."

"You're getting Marines or Dracs," said Farragut.

"We don't fight hand-to-hand, Commodore," Fredrika Freiheit explained. "We don't board pirates. We blow them out of the vacuum."

"You're getting Marines or Dracs," Farragut said again. "We go against the Hive, you *will* be boarded. I don't care how good you make dead. There are just too many of them out there to make."

When Romulus hailed the *Merrimack*, Commodore Farragut took the call immediately. There was no waiting. John Farragut was never one to play tit for tat.

"You have the mutineers with you," Romulus said, aghast, accusing.

"The Dracs?" said Farragut. "They're not mutineers. They were confused."

"Did they pledge loyalty to me?"

"They pledged to Rome."

"They have shown their disregard for orders," said Romulus. "And you put them in your service?"

"They're all straight now."

"Could they have had a hand in my father's assassination?"

"Caesar, that's just plain dumb."

Romulus pulled back from the vid screen, offended.

"It's true and you know it," said Farragut, his voice easy, coaxing. "Those boys are loyal to Rome. If—*IF*—Herius

Asinius had been mad enough over the Subjugation and my Triumph to kill your father, he would have charged up shouting 'Death to the Tyrant,' not stood there and watched a Julian do it for him."

"Commodore Farragut, we need to understand each other."

"I agree, sir."

Romulus held up to the vid screen a court document giving Romulus authority to retrieve Augustus from U.S. custody.

"That again," said Farragut. "The long arm of your law does not reach into my ship." And more conciliatory, "Your daddy gave that patterner to me, and I need him. If I don't use talent like that to stop the Hive, then I deserve to be eaten by gorgons."

"I do not question the importance of your mission, Commodore Farragut, so don't try to wave that around as the excuse for everything you want to do. This man, this *cyborg*, has been implicated in the death of a Caesar!"

Farragut had to laugh. "*Qui bono* wasn't Augustus!"

"Are you accusing *me* of my father's murder?"

"*I* was talking about Augustus," said Farragut. "Don't know why you tried the shoe on."

Romulus drew back, eyes flaring, outraged.

Farragut realized he had been too flippant. "Your father was murdered before your eyes. I don't see how *bono* that is for you either. I'm sorry for your loss."

Romulus lowered his eyes, nodded, appeared to be grieving. Lifted his gaze, his voice abruptly reasonable. "Does it not strike you as odd that Augustus was conveniently absent from Fortress Aeyrie when my father was murdered?"

"No, sir. Not strange at all. Magnus could *only* have been murdered in Augustus' absence. Augustus can connect dots parsecs apart, and I've met Rottweilers less protective than Magnus' patterner."

"What has he told you about me?"

"I did not have the chance to talk with your father all that long."

"I meant Augustus. What has he told you?"

"Nothing that I can remember."

"*Truly?*" said Romulus, somewhere between skeptical and complete disbelief.

"I can tell you lots of things he's had to say about *me*." Farragut offered.

"And does he suspect you of killing Caesar?"

"No, not *suspect*. He came right out and told me I was guilty. By keeping him away from Caesar."

"Then you know not to trust him."

"Sir, with respect, it sounds like you don't know who to trust. And in your situation, I guess I wouldn't either. If you would let us, I could enlist Naval Intelligence to help sort this out—"

"No! You have no business in the rule of our Empire. And if you will not surrender the Roman patterner by reason or law or right or justice, then know this: you may have an assassin on board your ship, and he is at best unreliable. Excuse me now, I have a funeral to attend."

Maybe it was an overdose of paranoia, but as the call terminated, Farragut suddenly wondered if *Horatius*' attack on the LRS had not been executed under someone's orders after all.

"Romulus demanded I turn you over to him," said Farragut. Waited for the patterner's reaction.

The face did not so much as ripple. "I will go."

"No, you won't."

"If I return to Rome," said Augustus, "I will know who was behind Caesar's assassin."

"If you go back to Rome, the only thing you'll know is a bullet in the brain. Romulus is ready to kill just about anybody. You, in particular."

"That is his right."

"Got a terminal death wish, don't you, Augustus?"

"You figured that out?"

"All by myself. And you're not going."

Augustus glared at him like the Rottweiler, Farragut standing between him and his master.

Farragut held his gaze. Finally observed, curious, "Augustus, you're not refusing my order. Why?"

"I cannot. Caesar gave me to you. Damn him. Damn you."

"You want to know who killed Caesar? Well, sacrificing you to Romulus won't get the job done. Won't destroy the Hive either. Magnus gave me a powerful weapon to use, and I've thoroughly bollixed that plan to date—"

"Yes, you have."

"That'll do, Augustus. I ain't fixing to keep squandering what Magnus gave me. He gave you to me to destroy the Hive, and that's what we're doing first. So whatever you and Romulus have going on, keep it out of my way. *And* I'm giving you standing orders: Do not kill yourself so long as you are under my command."

Augustus' gaze turned murderous. He spoke slowly, "And the moment we return to a hot war?"

"Then you can go jump off a bridge."

Made Augustus blink.

18

UPON LEARNING THAT Captain Fredrika Freiheit and Captain Ram Singh had never been through the Fort Theodore Roosevelt/Fort Dwight David Eisenhower Shotgun, Commodore Farragut advised them, "Brace yourself for the biggest letdown of your life."

"Why? What's it like?" said Fredrika.

"Nothing," said Farragut. "I mean really. Nothing. They'll tell you not to move a muscle. Moose gills. It happens in an instant, and you don't even know which instant unless you're looking at the monitors. Then you'll see the stars change faster than the flip of a vid channel. Your ship is here. Then your ship is there in literal no time."

"Beats a three-month flight through the Abyss," said Ram Singh.

"Amen and hallelujah. The Shotgun has saved me a few years of my life," said Farragut. "Just didn't want y'all to go expecting a thrill ride."

Fort Eisenhower in the Deep End was smaller than Fort Theodore Roosevelt in Near Space. Fort Ike had fewer stations, but more starlight, being 2000 parsecs closer to the galactic hub. Fort Ike was wild as befit a frontier town. Gases and all the station's lights made the space fort a bright gaudy oasis in the night.

The last two ships of Attack Group One, the Roman behemoth *Gladiator* and the old U.S.S. *Wolfhound* orbited the main station.

Fort Ike's main station was a ten mile in diameter, ten-story disk, with smaller and smaller concentric disks above and below, so that it looked like a gargantuan Christmas tree ornament.

A young woman accosted John Farragut upon his entry into the main station. Not unusual. Even before John Farragut had taken the surrender of the Roman Empire, women came on to him. He was a good-looking man in commodore's stars, and station women were particularly aggressive.

This was a pert, fit, sunshine blonde, with a neat angular little blonde beard. "Caesar Romulus sent me."

"That's a new one," said Farragut, and strode on by quickly so he wouldn't let slip something rude about the beard.

A signal from Colonel Steele caused a cadre of Fleet Marines to block the young woman's pursuit.

She was very quick, and cornered like a chipmunk. Almost got round the Marines, and Nev had to fire a splinter into her ass to make her stop.

Even at that, she turned and stared down the shooter, daring, a feral near-smile on her face, as if gauging whether he would really detonate the charge. Nev's stony return gaze told her he would, so she finally gave up.

The Marines offered to take the splinter out, but she carried her own extractor. She had been shot before.

A crowd had gathered on the main concourse.

Across a small table set up in the middle of the concourse, Captain Calli Carmel of the U.S. ship *Wolfhound* faced off with General Numa Pompeii of the Roman ship *Gladiator*.

Rows of half shots of vodka were lined up on the table, along with a glass bowl of water, and another glass bowl stacked with little red gel balls that looked like soft marbles.

All around them a crowd thickened. Lots of money was changing lots of hands. Bets made and markers given.

Kerry Blue blurted, "O Gawd! Captain Carmel's doing

hopper shots with Numa Pompeii!" And immediately shoved out a path to the front.

Numa Pompeii. General. Triumphalis. Legend.

A supremely confident and disdainful hulk. Powerfully built, big-boned, brawny. A voice big and heavy as the man. They said if Numa Pompeii, instead of the *Titanic,* had hit the iceberg, the iceberg would have gone down.

Fort Ike was a U.S. installation, and the station authorities did not allow Romans in by the pack, so there was no throng of legionaries behind him. The people behind him chanting, "*NU*ma! *NU*ma! *NU*ma!" were internationals.

Calli Carmel sat tall, a slender gazelle to Numa's water buffalo, cool and elegant. Not for long. No one looked elegant doing hopper shots.

Self-appointed guards kept a small ring clear around the table. So when someone moved close to Calli's shoulder, she glanced up startled. Did a double take. Started to rise.

John Farragut motioned her to stay where she was.

"Commodore?" said Calli. "Are you calling this off?"

"No, I'm lookin' for a bookie here."

"The smart money is on Numa," someone in the crowd advised Farragut.

Someone else countered that, "Numa to win won't pay gurzn gas. The real money is on the number of rounds. You *know* she's going down."

"Mister Carmel!" The shout in the crowd made Calli look. Marines of the 89th, the Bull Mastiffs, raised fists, gave a thunderous double woof and a Hoo ra.

Calli broke a smile, a thousand-ship-wrecking smile that caused men to walk into solid objects, each other, their own feet.

When the man running this circus signaled the betting closed, Numa and Calli each selected one red ball from the first bowl. At a mutual nod, they tossed the red balls into their mouths, clinked shot glasses, washed down the hoppers with the half shot of vodka, rapped the empty glasses upside down on the table, and shouted at each other, "Come on!"

Waited, glowering at each other. A chant started low in the crowd, "Hop. Hop. Hop. Hop."

Calli's head reared, her throat convulsed. She leaned forward and spat a little red frog into her hand. She dropped the hopper into the bowl of water, shouted "Clear!" to cheers from the crowd.

Numa spat out his little red froglet, dunked it. "Clear!" he announced to louder cheers. More of the onlookers had money on Numa for an early win.

Flight Leader Ranza Espinoza's thick brows twisted, dubious, at Calli. "They ain't gonna be calling her Empress ever again."

Flight Sergeant Cain Salvador leaned his head sideways to ask Kerry Blue, under his arm, "What are the rules?"

Cain Salvador was the new guy. Sort of new. Cain had already done two tours. Had tried the civilian gig. Not for him. So he was back. Fit in well with Team Alpha. Kerry Blue made him feel welcome. Hoo ra. Only Cain had done something to make Colonel Steele hate his guts. Had no idea what.

"The hopper has to come *up*," Kerry answered, eyes focused on the action. "You have to drink the glass empty. You're not allowed to dry swallow the hopper. If the hopper sticks in your throat, you can wash it down, but it has to be with vodka. And you have to make it go down. You're allowed to make yourself throw up or go to the head between rounds. But if you run to the head with a hopper still down, you lose. You pass out any time, you lose. You don't match a shot, you lose."

"What if the hopper dies?"

"Oh, honey, this never kills 'em. They get *out*. But if it ain't through the front gate —"

"You lose," Cain finished.

"Who made up this game?" Cole Darby yelped, truly rattled.

"I think it might've been Cowboy," said Kerry Blue.

It was really a sport as old as humankind, down there with geeks biting the heads off chickens and gladiators killing each other in the coliseum.

Calli Carmel at a table with a Roman general swallowing live animals with a crowd of hyenas egging them on.

At the table Calli was making an odd face, as if she had

an ice cream headache. Eyes watering. A tiny red webbed foot flailed out one nostril of her narrow, gracefully shaped nose. She took the little foot between her thumb and forefinger and pulled the hopper out—to a huge crowd roar of delighted disgust—tossed it in the water bowl. Rather congested, she declared, "Clear!"

Darb shook his head, astonished. Like observing a baboon troop. His baboon troop. This was a U.S. Naval Captain and a Roman Triumphalis. Apparently these two had traded shots before—the kind that can kill you.

The crowd was getting thicker, more boisterous.

"Stay in there, Mister Carmel!" Carly Delgado yelled.

Cain asked in dazzled disbelief, "Carmel used to be XO of the *Mack?*"

"Yeah."

"Wish I'd been aboard then!" said Cain with a suggestive chuckle.

Got an elbow in his broad abdomen for that. Kerry Blue took Cain's thick arm from round her shoulders, and shoved it back at him.

"What?" said Cain. "What'd I do?"

"I know Carmel looks good even with a hopper hanging out her nose, but you don't ogle someone else when you're with *me.*"

Numa and Calli had taken to trying to aim their hoppers instead of spitting them into their palms. Calli got Numa a good one off his broad forehead.

Numa, in time-honored Roman tradition, availed himself of the vomitorium between rounds to get rid of some excess alcohol.

Calli, a third Numa's mass, should have and didn't. She was too proud. She looked regal in between coughing up hoppers. But her eyes were getting misty, her lips lusciously full and pouting. Fine chestnut hairs stuck to her moist brow.

"I've never seen Mister Carmel like this," said Dak, marveling.

"Who has?"

"She can't win!" Ranza murmured. "He's a building!"

From the table came the double roar: "Come *on!*"

Numa and Calli had just thrown back number fifteen.

Numa quickly coughed his up, shouted, "Clear!" Dunked his hopper in the water bowl that was now swimming with a couple dozen red hoppers. He waited on Calli. "Trouble, Callista?"

Calli interlaced her long fingers prettily on the table. "Would it kill you to call me *Mister* Carmel?"

"Would it kill you to call me *Domnus*?"

"Yes. I think it would," said Calli. Her midriff flexed. She stuck out her tongue. On it, briefly, sat a red froglet that instantly hopped a mighty hop that cleared the table.

"Clear!" Calli plucked up another red ball. "Put it up, General."

Numa took up a red ball. "Shut up and do it."

They popped their hoppers. Clinked glasses. Threw back the half shots. Swallowed. Slammed the glasses down. Snarled across the table at each other, "Come on!"

Shortly, Numa opened his mouth, let the hopper jump out toward Calli.

Calli, sitting tall, rather primly, waited.

The crowd chant started again, very low, almost a whisper, but a lot of voices, so it was almost ominous: "Hop! Hop! Hop! Hop!"

Made Calli's stomach surge. She swallowed down nausea. Should not have done that.

Hop! Hop! Hop! Hop!

Felt the twist in her gut. She looked concerned.

Numa smirked. Ever so solicitously and kindly he asked, "Are you well, Callista?"

Calli's expression turned peculiar.

"Callista?"

Abruptly Calli kicked back her chair, pushed away from the table, setting the bowls to sloshing, and ran. The crowd made way for her. The big noise in her wake was a simultaneous descending "AWWW!" and a cheering roar, with Numa's big voice behind it all: "We have a winner!"

Only after the crowds had dispersed did Calli emerge from the head. Found Farragut waiting for her.

She leaned her forehead on his shoulder. "How many rounds did you have me for, John?"

"I didn't go for rounds, I had you to win."

She tried to walk, missed her step and wove back in to him. She sniggered. Patted his chest. "Sorry I lost you your shekels."

"Not a problem."

Farragut came from money. Could watch it ebb and flow without concern. "Nice of you to let Numa win one." Winked.

Calli had won the battles that mattered. "Oh, yeah, I planned it that way," she said with heavy insincerity. "For the unity of the Attack Group."

A Marine, Flight Sergeant Dakota Shepard, approached reverently. Advised, "Take the bilge bowl next time, Mister Carmel. I think that's what did you in."

Calli smiled wanly, an alcohol shine to her face. "Oh Flight Sergeant, there isn't going to be a next time. That has got to rank in the top two hundred dumbest things I've ever done."

"Sir?" said Dak. "You were *outstanding*."

Rob Roy Buchanan stared into his drink at a solitary table in Mad Bear O's space bar in the main station at Fort Eisenhower.

Mad Bear O's was a human bar. There was very little social mixing of species in any of the many bars inside the stations of Fort Eisenhower. Different species had different notions of what made for pleasant background sounds, what was drinkable, what was edible, what was breathable, and what temperatures and furniture were comfortable. Many aliens wore environmental suits in the main station because the partial pressures of the gases in that mix humans called "air" were toxic to them at the station's ambient pressure of fifteen psi. Then there were bodily emanations and slime trails, the acceptability of which did not transcend species.

There were no nonhumans in Mad Bear O's. Not because they were not allowed. They just didn't like it. The exceptions were the Sargassons in the aquariums. The large seaweedy aliens assumed brilliant colors that humans found beautiful, and they made soothing, languid motions in the water, which won them safe clean homes and caused humankind to spread their kind across the human-settled portion of the galaxy.

Rob Roy Buchanan was a Navy lawyer in his late thirties, though his face was utterly boyish. He was very slender, very tall, even with his boyish slouch. He'd had a hearing earlier that circadian cycle before the Admiralty, so his chin was not as scruffy as it usually was, and his face looked even younger than it usually did.

A woman wove into the bar, slid into the seat next to him. "Buy a lady a soberant?"

Rob Roy lifted his brown eyes. Stared at a vision. A drunk vision. He signaled to the bartender, who had seen her come in for her landing. Returned that flick of the eyes that said: Coming right up.

"I stink," said Calli.

"You smell flammable," said Rob Roy.

The soberant arrived promptly. Rob Roy and Calli sat a long time, not speaking. The music was American cool jazz.

Rob Roy said at last, "You know, you even look fetching with frogs crawling out your nose."

"You saw that?" Calli asked, wincing.

"I won forty shekels."

"Farragut had me to win."

Rob Roy's expression became very wry, almost bitter.

"You are still the prettiest woman I've ever seen," said Rob Roy not looking at her. "The strongest. The most courageous."

"Then why did you give me the push?"

Rob Roy opened his hands, kind of helpless. "I'm out of my depth here. You're out there going head to head with a gorilla. You beat him in battle—twice. You know you two are becoming like Patton and Rommel out here. Then you've got your John-had-me-to-win-Farragut. And last time I was with you, I watched Numa slam you against a wall and I didn't do a damn thing about it. John Farragut called him out—which is what I was supposed to do and never could. Makes a man feel pretty darn studly. AND you've got your Caesar Romulus, Empress Calli. What am I?"

"You're really stupid, Robbie. Sweet. Cute. Really intelligent, but God Bless America, are you ever dumb."

"Are you saying I have a shot here?"

Calli lightly beat her forehead against the table. It was a nod.

Sargassons have no gender.

This seaweed decided *he* wanted to be John Wayne, the twentieth century cowboy. But, just to avoid confusion with the real John Wayne, the Sargasson decided to be John Wayne's brother Steve instead.

No one knew that John Wayne was not the actor's real name, or if he ever had a brother. That was neither here nor there. The seaweed was tripping anyway. The members of Attack Group One consented to call the thing Steve "to avoid confusion."

"Thoughtful of it to clarify that," said Commander Gypsy Dent.

"Careful," Steve's handler warned. "He will be able to tell you are being sarcastic if he hears you."

"Then I'd better steer wide," said Gypsy, watching the tank float in on its hover platform, with a great length of peacock-colored vegetation undulating in the water.

Gypsy's brown eyes rolled to the commodore. "John Wayne's brother?"

Farragut kept his mouth tight shut. Nodded. If he spoke, the Sargasson would know he was laughing.

The Sargasson had been added to Attack Group One at the insistence of Naval Intelligence, with the backing of the xenos, as a secret weapon of sorts.

The idea had merits. Of sorts.

Sargassons were known for their hyperaccurate sense of physical incongruity even in alien beings. Medical examiners employed them in autopsies, because Sargassons had an uncanny talent for detecting what did not belong in a human body, or any other alien body, down to the cellular level. In a limited sense they were patterners. They could find rogue cells, but could not say what they were. They could only tell you, through a translator, what was out of place in a body.

They also looked good in a fish tank.

The Sargasson Steve Wayne was added to Attack Group One in hopes he would be able to detect physiological changes in insects when the insects were brought into proximity to the Hive. Given that the insects had to be detecting Hive resonance, the hope was that the insects' physical changes would indicate the Hive's harmonic.

"Dang," said Dallas McDaniels, staring at the tank in the commodore's Mess. "I was afraid that was the salad."

All cultures everywhere had in common one universal sign of unity, the sharing of food. So Commodore Farragut gathered the commanders of his Attack Group aboard *Merrimack* for dinner.

Chef Zack had gone into Fort Ike to the market for Deep End delicacies, so he was ready to show off.

There were no veal dishes on the menu.

The guests were still arriving when a Marine brought Commodore Farragut a message. "Some white greta with a beard gave me this to show you, sir."

The message had the Roman imperial seal on it.

"Persistent," Farragut commented. Did not take the message. "Nil it. Ask TR to come see me after dinner."

"Aye, sir."

Herius Asinius sat stiffly. Reluctant to eat or drink anything in hell. Had to eat. It was, after all, dinner. But he drank only water, because you could not drink a toast with water. And it was impolite to push alcohol on anyone who did not request it. Herius would not have to raise his glass to anything Farragut proposed.

Calli looked imperial and sober. She drank iced mnomsadian tea. Kept a wineglass in reserve at her place for toasts.

Farragut got merry. Had most of them laughing. Exchanged tall tales with Fred and Ram.

"So we're leaving Thaleia and we didn't want to take anything Thaleian with us. You've heard of the kudzu effect?"

They all had. The danger of alien imports was not alien disease. Diseases did not jump genetic codes, so Earth life was not susceptible to alien pathogens.

The danger was the kudzu effect—where an invasive species was hardier and more aggressive than native stock, overwhelmed the ecosystem, and pushed the native life out.

"Thaleian life makes kudzu look like Gypsy's potted plants."

Commander Gypsy Dent could not keep a plant alive for love or money. Gypsy claimed that her plants were sensitive.

"So we're leaving Thaleia and we have to sanitize the ship because Lord knows what kind of Thaleian slime mold we've tracked on board. You were there, Herius."

Herius Asinius nodded, mutely.

"So we evac. Everyone. Everything. The ship's dogs, the livestock, the houseplants—except Gypsy's houseplants; they're dead anyway—the lab insects, the telltales, the hydroponic gardens, everything living.

"Now I have this chief who is— What is the word for the Og?"

"Unique," Calli supplied diplomatically.

"Oh, no, the Og is completely crackers," said Farragut. "So the chief of my boat has these two goldfish, James and Dolley. Og enlisted them. Rated them. There are erks on board *Merrimack* outranked by James and Dolley.

"Og forgot to evacuate the goldfish. And the engineers take a neutron hose to *Merrimack*."

Lifted his eyes to the overhead. "Well." Nodded. "We killed James and Dolley.

"I am down planetside squaring away all our equipment, and the Og is up here on my boat using TR Steele's Fleet Marines to hold a full military funeral for James and Dolley. Dress whites. Drum corps."

"Caskets?" Fredrika asked.

"They were this big," said Farragut, thumb and forefinger a goldfish length apart.

Fred, Ram, and Dallas were laughing themselves to tears. The alcohol helped.

"The gun salute got everyone's attention. Sure got mine."

Even Numa Pompeii was snorting guffaws. "What happened to the Og?"

"I managed to keep TR from killing him."

Herius Asinius would not even smile. Asked, "Why is this Og still in your Navy?"

Farragut's eyes sparkled as he gushed, "Oh, hell if I know!"

The commanders recovered by the time the coffee and soberants came around, and the briefing board took over one side of the Mess.

"All right, gentlemen." Farragut stood up. "Why we're here and where we're going. The capsule version.

"First task, before we cross the frontier, we're fixin' to give Steve Wayne a chance to find out what the insects are detecting."

The Sargasson in its tank spread its brilliant blue and green and gold fronds.

"*Merrimack* will approach a Hive swarm close enough for the ship's telltales to react. Steve will work his Sargasson analysis magic on the telltales. Best scenario has Augustus figuring out the Hive harmonic from analyzing Steve's impressions of the insects. We use this information to kill all the gorgons, and we all go home and start shooting at each other again."

Numa Pompeii and Dallas McDaniels thumped the table in support of that plan.

"If Augustus can't pull the information together, or if we do get the harmonic and the gorgons fail to die, we proceed to the next scenario. Attack Group One goes to find Constantine.

"Now Contantine is in a star system we're calling Sagittarius Zero. From Earth, it lies a straight shot through the Lagoon Nebula and NGC Sixty-Five Thirty, but twice the distance. That puts it thirty-five hundred light-years from here at Fort Ike, in the general direction of the galactic hub."

Dallas McDaniels gave a low whistle, and the commanders exchanged murmurs. "How in blazes did Constantine find this world?"

"PanGalactic automated scout ships, we're guessing," said Farragut.

"It would take forever for his automatons just to get there from Thaleia," said Herius.

Farragut nodded. "Six months best speed. One year round trip. The man is apparently as patient as a trapdoor spider, and he always has one eye on the escape hatch.

"Sagittarius Zero is a single formed G Two star, nearly a twin to Sol, and Planet Zero lies one astronomical unit from it in a nearly circular orbit."

"Home away from home," said Dallas.

"Way away from home. Once Attack Group One passes the frontier, we are looking at a good month's journey in total res silence. So prepare your messages home before we fly off the map, because you won't be talking with your loved ones for two months. Any messages during the dark time will be by courier missile relayed through the repeater.

"Our ships will be flying in a five hundred klick spread, connected by com filaments. We will be towing boxcars of explosives and extra ordnance."

Calli knew John Farragut liked overkill, but this seemed excessive even for him. "Sir, among the six of us, we have enough ordnance to destroy several worlds."

"There are gorgons equivalent to the masses of *many* worlds in the Sagittarius Zero system."

At the end of the buzz of whispers, Dallas McDaniels asked, "You sure we got enough box cars?"

"Fortunately, space makes us all a mote in God's eye. We can get to Sagittarius Zero without coming within five light years of a gorgon, and we won't attract notice provided we don't resonate and we keep the running lights off. At the frontier we will shut down all our displacement chambers. Ship-visiting will be by shuttle only.

"Once we reach Constantine's solar system, we will need the patterner to plot us a course in to the planet."

Caused some murmurs. Fredrika asked aloud, "The gorgons are that thick inside the solar system?"

"Best we can tell from one thousand parsecs, they're that thick. Just hope we don't need to use the boxcars to get out.

"What we do once we get to Planet Zero will depend on what we find on Planet Zero."

"A trapdoor spider?" Ram Singh suggested.

"We need to assume that Constantine will see us coming. And even with as impregnable a location as he's got, I have to expect Planet Zero also has PanGalactic sentinels in orbit, just like he had at Thaleia. I'm hoping he doesn't die before we get there. He's fairly old, even for a rejuv. Our mission objective is to find out how he has managed to live within a Hive presence."

"What? So we can learn to live among them?" Fredrika's tone betrayed her disgust with the usual LEN line of live and let live.

"No," said Farragut. "So we can kill them all."

Met with amens, hear-hears, and a Hoo ra.

"We depart Fort Ike at eight bells. You've got the rest of this evening to get your ships in order, watch Magnus' funeral on the res feed, let your crew go into Fort Ike, or do what you need to do."

At the meeting's end, Commodore Farragut and Jose Maria de Cordillera walked Herius Asinius and Marcus Asinius to *Merrimack*'s displacement chamber. Caught furtive expressions of the Marine guards flanking the hatch. Some harassment that didn't happen because Farragut was there.

Jose Maria waited until the Romans were safely away and he and Farragut were out of earshot of anyone to speak. "Is it not asking much of your Marines to serve side by side with the killers of their comrades, young Commodore?"

"Hang it, Jose Maria, about all I do out here is ask folks to give more than they got! And I got no room for eyes for eyes and teeth for teeth!"

Jose Maria lowered his eyes, penitent. "I am out of line."

"No. No, you're not, Jose Maria." Punched his own palm. "If you weren't right, you couldn't have torqued me off."

Saw him in the main concourse on the eve of her leaving. Calli had heard he was here. Come to Fort Ike directly Magnus had been assassinated. Ostensibly to tour the battlefront in this time of crisis.

Calli knew it was really to avoid the long knives.

Gaius Bruccius Eleutherius Americanus.

He had brought his wife and his children.

During the last peace, Gaius had been an instructor at the Imperial Military Institute. Like Numa Pompeii, Gaius Americanus had been one of Calli's instructors. Unlike

Numa, Gaius had given Calli every chance to succeed, gave her his wisdom, gave her his respect.

Calli wished she were John Farragut that she could run up and throw her arms around her old mentor in an unbridled hello. But Captain Carmel kept the bridle on. "Gaius."

Gaius looked for the source of the voice. Caught sight of Calli with a warm sad smile. Crossed to her. Took her hand in both of his. "Callista." He glanced at her uniform, its insignia. "What are we now? *Captain* Carmel?" No surprise in his voice. Entirely expected.

"Numa told me you were here," said Calli.

What Numa had actually said was, "Your patron is here." And had commented that Caesar Magnus was not even cold and here's Gaius Americanus suddenly seized of an urgent need to observe the Deep End.

Calli had refrained from commenting back that it was telling in the Roman Empire when it was safer to be closer to the Hive than to Palatine.

Gaius' face looked old, pinched with tight lines. Maybe he was even ill. "Gaius, what's wrong?"

Gaius spoke sadly, "Caesar is dead. Gorgons are mauling our ships. Roman worlds in the Deep End are being evacuated. That is not enough?"

"I would have thought you would stay in Roma Nova."

"I won't be discussing internal affairs with you, Captain Carmel," he said to be overheard. Then, for her to read between the lines: "You were always a quick study."

She nodded.

What he actually meant was that it was more difficult to arrange a Roman hit in an American space fort than to arrange one on the Roman home world.

But no more difficult than arranging a Roman hit in Fortress Aeyrie. There was no such thing as a safe place.

Gaius had been Magnus' right hand. Rumors had it that Gaius Americanus' name was written in Caesar's sealed testament, which Romulus had not opened. If Magnus had enemies, then Gaius Americanus had the same enemies.

He had fallen back to regroup, recon, collect allies, form a plan, then act. Calli knew Gaius was not one to go charging across a minefield without a map. Perhaps he meant to establish a government in exile here in the Deep. He would not be able to tell the U.S. Naval captain any of that.

Gaius studied Calli, troubled. Finally it came out, pained, "Why were you on Romulus' arm when Caesar died?"

Calli answered, "Keep your friends close."

Everyone knew the other part of that saying: Keep your enemies closer.

"Is that why you play drinking games with Numa Pompeii?"

Calli's almond eyes shut in embarrassment. "I was hoping you hadn't seen that."

Gaius could not say he hadn't.

"Do you think less of me?" Calli asked.

"Does it matter what I think?"

"Yes!" she cried in earnest.

"Why?" Gaius asked, like a Socratic teacher might.

"Because *you* matter."

"It was disappointing," Gaius confessed.

"That hurts."

"I cannot change the truth."

"I know. That's why I have always loved you."

His brindled brows moved upward. "Keeping your enemies closer?"

"We're standing at arm's length, Gaius."

He smiled. "You and your Attack Group have a safe and successful journey, Captain."

They parted. Calli called softly after him, "Gaius."

He turned.

Very softly, "Keep Romulus much, much closer."

Calli walked away from Gaius, and suddenly there was Numa Pompeii. A mountain in her way, with that all too familiar supercilious smile. "Teacher's pet."

Calli walked past him. Tried to ignore him. There was a lot of Numa to ignore.

"A lay for an A, Callista?"

Stopped her.

She had always done well in Gaius' classes.

She turned round.

Numa's presence daunted. An adamantly sexual power.

The way Numa looked through her. Difficult to maintain a Naval officer's dignity under that penetrating, demeaning gaze.

Numa smiled at her. "There's a reason that saying doesn't rhyme in Latin, American girl."

Calli stalked up to Numa. Gave her nose a kittenish wrinkle right in his face. "Numa? I'd have gone down on Gaius Americanus for an F."

As Fort Eisenhower Control gave *Merrimack* an exit route to depart, an urgent res signal came in from Fortress Aeyrie.

Farragut muttered, "Romulus had better not be insisting I surrender Augustus."

Not.

Farragut took the call, clicked off. His eyes rolled toward the putative heavens. "Oh, for Jesus."

"Sir?" Gypsy inquired.

Farragut groaned, "Romulus really did send her."

"Who?" said Gypsy.

Colonel Steele reared back, appalled, disbelieving. "The *beard?*"

Farragut nodded. Motioned. Not happy. "TR, go get her."

19

H ER NAME WAS AMADEA. No surname. Just Amadea.
She was a mercenary, sent by Romulus to assist the Attack Group in getting to Constantine.

She was one hundred years old. She had known Constantine before his supposed death.

Amadea used to be a professional quarry in the Most Dangerous Game—a typically Roman sublegal pastime for extremely wealthy and ruthless Romans, the idea lifted directly from Richard Connell's short story, "The Most Dangerous Game." The hunters hunted human beings for sport.

Quarry in the game were ranked by the number of games they survived against hunters of a certain skill level. Quarry were never armed. "White tiger" was the rank of an unarmed quarry who had killed or taken the surrender of an armed expert hunter. Technically, the quarry was not supposed to kill the hunter, but sometimes they got angry.

Constantine had enjoyed the game. Was an expert.

Amadea had forced Constantine's surrender. Had pressed his own gun to his forehead.

She was a white tiger.

She boarded *Merrimack* under a Marine watch the whole way.

"What was *that?*" Cain Salvador cried after Amadea was escorted off the dock.

"White tiger," said Ranza Espinoza.

"I mean on her *chin*!"

"That would be a beard," said Ranza.

"Looks cute on her," said Carly, fingers tracing her own chin, speculative.

"No, it don't!" Dak cried.

"The fashion started in Rome," said Ranza.

"They can just keep it!" said Dak.

"It's really an Egyptian fashion," said Darb. "A female pharaoh would strap on a beard so she would be taken seriously."

"If she wants to be taken seriously, then why'd she make herself so darn cute?" said Cain. "I mean, except for that—that thing."

"She's messing with you," said Kerry Blue, giving Cain a push with her whole body. "It's workin', ain't it?"

Physically Amadea had a superficial resemblance to Maryann about her. Farragut's late wife Maryann. Petite. Sunshine blonde. Had what they called an American smile—teeth all perfectly shaped and in perfect alignment and too white. Cute little figure. Young. Maryann would be forever young.

But substantially, this creature was not Maryann at all. Hard, jaded, knowing, old. Refurbished to springy youth. And there was that belligerent beard—blonde, neat, smaller than a shot glass, but about the same shape. A dare, the beard. May as well have glued a penis on her chin.

"Captain Farragut."

Amadea's rejuvenators had not taken enough of the slack out of aging vocal cords. The voice was thin, with a harsh edge. "We got off to a bad start." She thrust out a confident hand.

Farragut, very unFarragutly, kept his fists on his hips. "Ma'am, I don't carry mercs on *Merrimack*, but since Caesar sent you, as a courtesy to Caesar, you'll be traveling with us on board one of Caesar's ships. General Pompeii has agreed to take you aboard *Gladiator*. You will not get in the way of military operations."

Amadea gave a perky nod, with a smile. "Caesar sent me because I know Constantine. I can be useful."

"I don't doubt you knew Constantine sixty years ago. Your information is a little stale. And why should Constantine remember or care about you?"

"I'm the one that got away. Big egos remember that sort of thing. I'm also probably the only person who knew Constantine was still alive. I have known for the last sixty years. But—" with a lifting of wheat-blonde eyebrows, "no one listens to me." And switching her gaze past Farragut to Augustus, she said, "*You* knew, I bet. I look forward to hearing what you make of what I have to tell you, Augustus."

"Look elsewhere," said Farragut. "If you have useful information, add it to the database. Augustus will find it. Talking isn't a real efficient way to get data into a patterner, and I won't have you wasting his time."

"Funny. 'Rude' is not a word I've ever heard spoken in connection with John Farragut."

"Neither is 'mercenary,'" said Farragut, and to the Marines, "Get her off my deck."

Merrimack's crew wanted Augustus off-loaded as well. Rumor had gone round that Augustus was a Heraclid. Augustus had obviously had his mind altered, and he had no old personal memories.

Heraclids were the modern bogeymen. But they were real. They looked like anyone else, and dwelled among normal men. You never knew who they were. The whole idea was that you would never know.

Stories went round and round of Heraclids breaking memory and becoming violent again, but those stories were all modern myth. There had never been a real case of a Heraclid remembering who he was, or attacking anyone after he'd had his brain altered.

Farragut had no patience with rumor. Went straight to the suspect. He could always trust Augustus to speak an ugly truth. In fact, Augustus enjoyed ugly truths. Farragut asked him right on the command deck: "Augustus, are you a Heraclid?"

"I am not," said Augustus, and that should have been that. But Augustus, having been given an opening, could not leave it at that. "You do, however, have a Heraclid on board."

Techs stiffened round the command platform, flinched at their crowded stations. The Marine guards at the door exchanged glances. Gypsy turned round to stare.

Farragut looked as if a round had gone off in his face.

"Thanks a heap, Augustus." If the rumors weren't flying before, they were swarming now. Upsetting people was what Augustus did second best.

"You asked," said Augustus.

"I did. I deserved that." Farragut easily owned up to his up screws.

"Who is the Heraclid?" Colonel Steele demanded, but Farragut raised his palm to cut off any answer Augustus might give. "That information is confidential. It does not *ever* need to be known."

"Sir?" the com tech ventured. "May I say something?"

They were all thinking it. Farragut let young Mister Hicks say it. "Let's have it."

"If we have a baby-killing madman on board, is it fair for us not to know who it is?"

Farragut had the answer ready for all of them: "The Heraclids were all cured. No Heraclid has ever reverted. Our Heraclid doesn't even know who he is, and that's the point. They've been given new lives and I'm fixin' to let ours keep his."

Caught Marcander Vincent exchanging a *like hell* glance with the scanner tech.

Farragut ordered Mister Vincent directly, "You will forget about it. I will brig anyone caught trying to dig up the identity of any supposed Heraclid on my ship. Acknowledge."

A chorus of ayes.

Steele said quietly, for only Farragut, "I think I should know, sir."

"And I don't," Farragut answered back.

"Aye, sir."

The Heraclidae were survivors of a LEN colonial disaster, twenty years ago now. A brain malady in the planet's first settlement had caused the adult men to kill the women and children.

"I was seven years old when that came over the news,"

Mr. Hicks commented aside to the cryptotech. "I was *sure* my stepmom was a Heraclid."

Qord Johnson shook his head. "Heraclidism only happened to men."

"Yeah, well I was seven and you never met my stepmom."

The best physicians of all the nations of Earth could do nothing for the violent survivors, other than sedate them and prevent them from killing themselves in remorse.

The Roman Empire was leagues ahead of any Earth nation in the area of brain research, because, unlike any nation of Earth, Rome *would* experiment.

Rome volunteered its medical resources to try to help the Heraclids.

And succeeded. They cured the disease, and altered the memories of the guilt-stricken men. Gave them new identities, with bland histories. The Heraclids kept no memory of ever being a colonist, of ever being married, of ever having children. The LEN allowed the cured Heraclids to be inserted into the populations of various member countries, where they had led quiet, unremarkable lives for the past twenty years. No Heraclid had ever relapsed into violence, or sought psychiatric help for hideous phantom memories.

The project was witness protection taken one step further—protecting the witness from himself.

"No Roman mole has even turned out to be a Heraclid," said Farragut. "Hard as it is to believe, it looks like the creation of the Heraclidae was a genuine humanitarian operation on the part of Rome." And because it was so hard to believe, he asked Augustus, "Was it? Purely humanitarian?"

"Mostly," said Augustus. "Not entirely. You know our researchers seize any chance to experiment on the human brain. In this case, success just happened to benefit everyone."

"It's benefiting the baby-killer," Steele said.

Farragut announced that Commander Dent had the deck, and he withdrew, taking Augustus and Steele with him, leaving the crew to debate whether they would rather remember committing an atrocity or have their brains turned into vanilla.

Marcander Vincent was first. "All respect to the commodore," he did not sound necessarily respectful, "but I don't want anyone who's had his head carved open by a Roman brain butcher serving on this ship. And that sure includes the cyborg. Don't know why we can't just ship 'im over to *Gladiator* with the white tiger."

Chief Medical Officer Mo Shah, lifted large brown eyes at the commodore's entrance in the company of Lieutenant Colonel Steele and the Roman patterner Augustus.

A warm man, but not excitable, not enormously expressive. Mohsen Shah was a Riverite. Measured, patient. Enduring.

Riverism was a philosophy. A religion without dogma. Riverites were seekers of understanding.

Where many religions claimed to have the word of God from prophets—and many of their followers wondered why God never talked directly to them—Riverites held that God did speak directly, to everyone. God's word was the stars, the rain, color and sound, the half-life of elements, the arrow of time. Creation was the firsthand testament of the Creator.

Understanding it was the quest.

The River was a symbol of life. At any point in the river, the water passes through, but the river remains. Motion without end, but not cyclical.

Life flows.

"Mo. Do you know if we have a Heraclid on board?"

Mo Shah took the commodore's question like a rock in the stream. He flowed around it: "Why are you asking, sir?"

"I just want to know if you know if there is a Heraclid aboard the *Mack*."

"I am knowing, yes."

"Do you know his identity?"

"I am knowing," said Mo placidly. "I am not telling without cause."

"Exactly what I wanted to hear, Mo," said Farragut.

And turned toward Augustus and Steele, stern. "This matter is on a need-to-know basis. Mo needs to know. I don't need to know. And TR, you don't need to know. Augustus, it's a crying shame that you know, but I order you not to tell anyone. The witch hunt stops *now*."

Augustus lifted his eyes to the overhead, smiling, as if he had just taken a hit in some kind of game.

Steele stood as rigidly as a man could stand at ease, his jaw locked. His breathing was loud through his flaring nostrils.

Augustus looked down at Steele, smiled. "You are going to be fun."

Augustus' voice exuded the kind of sexual innuendo that makes a man's skin crawl and makes him want nothing touching him, not his clothes, not the air, just get everything off, away, right now. Steele could not stand to be in the same airspace as this creature. Said to Farragut, "Permission to withdraw."

"Go."

The hatch no sooner shut behind Steele when Farragut ordered Augustus, "Leave Colonel Steele alone."

Augustus glared like the cat from whom you've taken a baby rabbit it had just begun to bat around.

"You get out of here, too." Farragut nodded Augustus away.

Alone in the lab with Mo, Farragut sat heavily. "Hell."

Mo brought him a drink. Water. From Mo Shah, it was always water.

"How was it coming to be known that a Heraclid is serving on board *Merrimack*?" Mo asked.

"I stepped in a cow pie Augustus left out for me. The whole thing was just a stupid rumor before I opened my mouth. But a lot of smart people believed it. Mo, why did they think Augustus was a Heraclid? He doesn't even fit the profile."

"He is fitting a misunderstanding of the profile," Mo suggested. "Augustus is having no memories. Heraclids are having false memories. Unless one is being versed in the case of the Heraclidae, then one could easily be confusing a lack of memory with a substitution of memories."

In Heraclids the catastrophic memories had been canceled out with neural white noise. Dreamboxes then gave them dull histories. Altered brain chemistry lowered their aggression and ambition, so none of the Heraclids would become a celebrity or politician or sports hero, which might put him in a position to have his past dredged up by the mass media and falsehoods discovered in it.

"Augustus is having no memories?" Farragut questioned. Heard himself. Shook his head. "I mean, Augustus doesn't have any memories?"

"I asked him where he went to school," said Mo. "He said he was not remembering. Now how, I was asking myself, can one be forgetting school? He is having all the end effects of early learning—speech, socialization (such as it is being)—but the events that created his neural structures, those are being missing from memory. It is as if he has only been existing for less than ten years."

"I'm told he's a sadist."

"He is being so," Mo averred, his face solemn.

One corner of Farragut's mouth pulled up into an ironic smile. "When I heard that, I pictured whips and leather. But that's not it, is it?"

Mo shook his head in agreement. Touched his own temple. "*This* is being his target."

The mind was Augustus' playground. He poked around for suspicions, hypocrisies, something he could stab a psychic knife in and turn slowly.

"Admiral Klein," Farragut murmured.

Augustus had found something to say to Admiral Klein to make it worth Klein's entire career just to connect his fist with Augustus' smug face.

Fighting with your coworkers would get you sacked from just about any employment you could get in the U.S.A. outside your family business. Admiral Klein was Navy. More discipline was expected. He was not allowed to hit a surrendered allied officer under truce.

Augustus had found just the right nonactionable words, and Admiral Klein tossed his own career into the atomizer.

Admiral Klein had probably been fun.

Mo said, encouraging, "I am being fairly certain there is being nothing that anyone could be saying to be making John Farragut be hauling off and hitting him."

Farragut, after he figured out what Mo said, nodded. "I like to think so."

Not that Farragut didn't love a fight. Gunfight, space battle, sword fight, fistfight. He loved it. But it took more than bad words to get him there. Call his mother a whore, and that's just you blowing wind out your face. Didn't change his mother, and just proved you were a drup. No action required. Farragut was not a puppet. No one could pull his strings and make his arms swing.

"But he is playing mind games," Mo warned. "And Augustus is having a highly organized mind. Be watching your ass, Commodore."

The Attack Group was scarcely underway toward the frontier when *Merrimack* received a communication from Amadea on board *Gladiator*. The hail went first through the com tech, then Gypsy Dent, who passed it to the commodore only reluctantly. "I don't know what the beard is saying, sir, but it sounds like something you should know about."

"Farragut!" Barked his own name into the com. Did not turn on the vid. Did not want to look at Amadea's perky bearded face.

"Just wanted to make sure you picked up the tachyon clicker, Captain Farragut," said the mercenary. She sounded a hundred years old. "Have you?"

"I don't even know what one is."

"It's a faster-than-light communication form used by patterners. You need a tachyon receiver to pick it up. Patterners have them implanted. I carry one. Your friend is communicating covertly with another patterner out here."

My friend. Covertly. "So what is he saying?"

"I don't know," said Amadea. "It's all clicks. It's a patterner code. I don't think it can be broken. I know the patterners have been told by Rome not to communicate that way, but just try to stop them."

"Send me what you have," said Farragut.

He was being played and knew it. Yet it would be militarily irresponsible to ignore such a warning from any source.

Found Augustus in his quarters. There were no sleep racks on board *Merrimack* long enough to accommodate the Roman, so the quartermaster had stowed Augustus in torpedo rack room number six with the spare torpedoes.

Farragut had never seen a rack room decorated before. Augustus had moved many of his belongings in. The deck was carpeted, the overhead draped with a Roman canopy. One torpedo rack had been converted into a sleep pod with richly textured bedding. Augustus, who slept half the day, reclined atop all the cushions. Did not rise at the commodore's entrance.

A reproduction Winged Victory like the original one in the Louvre spread her white marble wings over the spare torpedoes. A graceful female figure. "Interesting choice for you," Farragut commented.

"She speaks to me," said Augustus.

More interesting, given that she was missing her head.

Farragut became aware that he was gripping the recording capsule in his fist as if he could crush it. Asked Augustus, "Did you know we passed through a tachyon clicker?"

"Yes," said Augustus, one hand loosely screening one closed eye, two fingers resting on his brow, two on his Roman nose.

"Were you going to report it?"

"No."

"Why not?"

"It's irrelevant."

"Irrelevant to what?"

"Anything."

"You're communicating with someone beyond this ship."

"No."

"You didn't send a signal to someone?"

"No."

Like talking to a two-year-old. With twenty younger siblings, John Farragut had talked to a lot of two-year-olds. "Did you pick up this signal?"

"May have."

"Yes or no."

Augustus finally deigned to open his eyes. Flicked in the direction of Farragut's fist. "I don't know exactly what you have there, so I don't know if I picked that one up."

"Did you pick up a tachyon clicker message within the last day?"

"We passed through one."

"So I hear. Was the message meant for you?"

"I don't know."

"Are you going to continue making me excavate for answers?"

"Ask better questions."

Farragut gazed up at the headless Winged Victory.

One Admiral Klein. Two Admiral Klein. Three Admiral Klein . . . Ten Admiral Klein.

Held the message capsule lengthwise between thumb and middle finger. "Do you know who sent this message?"

And instead of the answer of a two-year-old, he got complete information, thoroughly compressed, Augustus-style: "He's dead. You killed him."

Took Farragut by surprise. He was some moments in assembling the bits and pieces of information contained in those few words. The sender was dead. So the message could not be current. The message must have been sent some time ago at a great distance from here. The sender had to be a patterner.

I killed him.

Augustus had known the sender, and had obliquely given Farragut his name.

The name flew out of Farragut's mouth, "Septimus."

Rome's patterners seemed to be numbered rather than named. The earliest one, created decades ago, had been called Primus—the First—followed by a patterner called Secundus—the Second. Both of those patterners had died before John Farragut was even born. Following them had also been a Tertius, and presumably a Quadrus, Quintus, and Sextus, because John Farragut had done battle with the patterner Septimus just over a year ago.

The patterner Septimus died in a rundown with *Merrimack*—but not before Septimus had shot a pea hole through *Merrimack* stem to stern, distortion field and all, with a shot that singed the hair on top of Farragut's head.

The days-long chase left Septimus comatose, with a brain hemorrhage. Like an overloaded engine burned out. Farragut remembered the dried-out eyes. The smell.

Here, now, was a tachyon clicker from Septimus just arriving from whatever part of space it had been sent sometime while Septimus still lived.

An old signal, from one patterner to another, that Merrimack happened to pass through. Irrelevant as an old letter. Maybe private. Maybe painful. From someone like Augustus.

A message from a dead patterner. Killed by John Farragut.

"There, but for the grace of God, it could have been you?" Farragut asked.

"No. It could not," said Augustus, sitting up. "*I* would have had you."

PART THREE

Heart of Darkness

20

CRICKETS, KEPT IN TINY cages on the command platform, started to chirp, much faster than any temperature would ever warrant. The ship's status lights turned yellow, with a laconic report from the lab: "We have Hive sign."

Tight beams from all ships of the Attack Group confirmed Hive sign. Farragut turned to Marcander Vincent at the tactical station, "Something you want to tell me, Mister Vincent?"

"Target located, Commodore. Thirty by twenty by one hundred seventy. Vector indicates it hasn't noticed us. And it's not a sphere, sir."

Gorgons in space always traveled in frozen spheres. Marcander Vincent was defending his failure to sight them.

"It's kind of a wad," Marcander Vincent added.

The gorgons had apparently scattered to attack a ship, had been outrun, and were now re-forming into a sphere.

"They don't see us."

"Let's poke 'em," said Farragut. "Signals, give me a res ping."

Merrimack emitted a single resonant pulse on a random harmonic.

The gorgon bunch continued to crawl over each other, but the whole wad, as Tactical called it, veered.

Marcander Vincent reported, "Target has changed vector.

Target is now on intercept course with *Merrimack*. Intercept in one hundred twenty seconds."

"Commander Dent, get us on an evasion course—away from Fort Ike. Relay course to the Attack Group. Maintain current distance of separation from the gorgons. Do not engage."

While Gypsy issued orders, Farragut got on the intracom to the lab. "Gentlemen, you may start your experiment."

The Sargasson—Steve Wayne—could now turn his singular sensitivity on the insects in the lab, in an attempt to detect what it was about insects that allowed them to detect a Hive presence.

But after a scant few moments, the lab hailed the command deck. The voice was Patrick Hamilton's. "Commodore Farragut, could you—?" Stopped, started over, "Sir, we have a problem. Can you come down here?"

Farragut exited the command deck, took the ladder down like a firefighter's pole.

First thing he saw upon bursting into the lab was that the xenos had removed the Sargasson from his thousand-gallon tank. Or so it appeared. Farragut had become accustomed to walking in here and seeing the alien's long, long leaves undulating with the water's motion. Blue, green, red, fantastical colors.

The big tank appeared empty. Then he saw it. Had seen it when he first came in but hadn't recognized it. A brown shriveled mass clotted at the bottom corner of the tank, behind a rock, like dead algae. A speaker, mounted outboard the tank to transmit the Sargasson's translated signals, issued a moan.

Farragut nodded at the speaker. "Is that the Sargasson?"

The worried xenos nodded.

"What's he saying? Can you translate that?"

"That *is* the translation," said Patrick Hamilton, the ship's xenolinguist.

Doctor Patrick Hamilton was Lieutenant Commander Glenn Hamilton's husband. A slender, aesthetic man. Handsome in an artistic fashion. Civilian through and through.

Eyed the commodore warily. Knew the reason that the

crew called his Glenn "Mrs. Hamilton" was not because she was Patrick's wife. They called the commodore "Admiral Nelson" in the same breath.

Farragut put his hand to the tank where the ash brown Sargasson cringed. "Is he ill?"

"Not exactly," said Patrick Hamilton. "That is the picture of mindless terror."

Farragut stared at Dr. Hamilton, grasping for a direction. Said, "*Talk* to it!"

"How do you give a pep talk to *mulch*?" Patrick cried.

"Oh, for—can he hear us?"

The xenos gave Farragut a microphone. Farragut clicked the mike on. "Steve?" He clicked off. "I feel like an idiot." Clicked on. "Steve. Don't be afraid. We're two hundred klicks from the gorgons, and we're not fixin' to let them any closer. Just relax, collect yourself."

The plant wilted further. Moaned.

"Saddle up, Mister Wayne! You're making a wreck of yourself here. This is fear itself. The gorgons are way the hell out there. Would it help if we increased our distance?"

Gibbering issued from the speaker.

"Give him some time," Patrick Hamilton suggested.

"No," Farragut slapped the microphone into Patrick's hand. "He looks like hash. There'll be plenty of time and plenty of other gorgons where we're headed." And he signaled the command platform, "Mr. Dent, organize parting shots at the gorgon mass from all ships, then get the fleet out of here."

Merrimack, Gladiator, Rio Grande, Wolfhound, Sunlit Meadows, Windward Isles, and *Horatius* moved through the frontier of defended space. The last outpost of civilization—an automated chain relay station—was here. The Attack Group could send courier missiles to this station. The repeater would relay their messages on from here via resonance. The station could also accept res messages from Earth or Palatine, and send them after the Attack Group via courier missile.

The Attack Group passed the *Monitor* at the edge of nowhere. Exchanged signals and received their last transmission by resonance, the *Monitor*'s "God speed."

"And now we go silent. Mr. Dent, take us dark."

The ships' proud running lights blinked out. The Stars and Stripes came inboard to the sound of Taps. Portholes were masked over with one-way light screens.

Already dark and alone in the vastness of space, the big ships became small. The void, the hugeness pressed inward.

There is no mild space, no rough, no warm. It is all the same. Absolute. Ruthless. It does not rage. It does not becalm. It forgives not.

A ship was a world unto itself. Your light, your air, your pressure, your up, your down, all contained within the ship's bulks, in the middle of literal nothingness. The enormity beyond the metal edges of the world lay completely beyond the grasp of the earthbound. The fragility hits in the middle of the dark watch, and makes a man wake up shaking. And John Farragut becomes your mother, your father, your Earth, your shield, the holder of your light, your water, your breath. The mind turns cultish, removed from what you know, the edge of your world close enough to touch.

Actually touch it, and it is cold.

Easy to deify the one who holds all the power and all the answers.

Out of the blue—or out of the black, as things came here—Augustus told Farragut, "You are an inadequate god."

Farragut glanced behind him in the corridor for some other inadequate god. He was alone with Augustus.

Farragut had come up to the top deck of the *Merrimack*'s fuselage, to stand underneath the outer hull, listening to the clunking over his head. The Marines were out there, hull walking.

Farragut absorbed Augustus' words. Decided he really had heard correctly. Nodded. "Yeah. Damn good thing there's a greater power working out here. And I am for sure not talking about the Hive."

"Have you not heard?" said Augustus. "The Hive is the Rapture. Might this not be the hand of God?"

"Is somebody actually saying that? No. This is not God's will."

"How do you know?"

"By using the brains God gave me! — Oh, now that don't sound right." As an ill-sounding rasp/buzz sounded from the distortion field and something heavy thumped the hull and something else scraped, skittered, bounced.

The Marines were out there practicing with a new weapon, called a scythe by those who could pronounce the word, a grim reaper by everyone else. It was a blade mounted on a long pole, designed for slicing off gorgons' mouths the moment they insinuated through the ship's distortion field. Developed directly following Flight Sergeant Kerry Blue's escapade on Thaleia wherein she buried herself alive with a gorgon in her Swift's distortion field and carved off all its mouths.

The space between *Merrimack*'s hull and distortion field was much wider than in Kerry's Swift. It was awkward going out there, the gravity iffy, the atmosphere minimal, so the Marines were all in suits, the only light from their headlamps.

"Anyway," said Farragut, eyes up as if he could watch his Marines through the solid hull. "This can't be the Rapture, most of the people that got rapt so far have been godless Romans."

He was not taking this seriously.

A man with that much power must lose perspective. And how did a man ever gain that much power without having power lust?

Came a teeth-curling metal on metal sound, and a scream. *Merrimack* was notorious for her training injuries.

"And God Bless America, that for sure doesn't sound right." Farragut was in motion, calling for a medic and charging for the nearest air lock to bring the wounded man in.

The man defied the pattern.

There was a great deal of ship-visiting during the journey to Sagittarius Zero. Early on, Farragut announced his intention to visit first *Gladiator* then *Horatius* in the company of Augustus and Colonel Steele and Captain McDaniels from the *Rio Grande*. Numa countered with an invitation to a formal dinner on board Numa Pompeii's ship.

Gladiator's dining chamber was a grander space than the commodore's Mess on *Merrimack*.

Farragut had been here before. This time he was eating.

And it was Roman style this time, on couches. Eating while reclining was supposed to be better for the digestion. Most Americans found it tough on the elbows and easier to slop their wine. At least the wine did not land in the lap.

Herius Asinius was quiet as a cat. He wore a gray tunic, trimmed in scarlet, but then Herius was a tough enough looking hombre to get away with wearing a dress. The tunic was sleeveless, showing off the SPQR brand on his muscular arm.

Colonel Steele had difficulty breaking bread with the murderer of Reggie, Tad, and Enzo. He would not even look at Herius Asinius. And he was not at all comfortable on the couch. Certain that he looked stupid. At least he'd been allowed Navy blue. Steele had always considered dress whites and food a deadly combination.

Dallas McDaniels, in dress whites, had the couch posture down cold. Looked like he might have been resting by the campfire out on the trail. Should have brought his harmonica.

Augustus coiled easy as a snake on his couch. Maybe because he was currently serving on board a U.S. ship, but he wore trousers instead of a tunic. He was all in black with three blood-red studs. Flavian colors.

Dallas leaned over to Farragut, said for only Farragut to hear, "So, John, old son, what do you think I'd look like with a toe ring?" Nodded ahead.

At Numa Pompeii, arrayed in Roman tunic, toga, oak-leaf crown, and thick bronze bracelets on either thick wrist. He was barefoot but for the toe ring.

"You'd look right purty," Farragut told Dallas. And aloud, to Numa, "Nice crown, Numa. Did Caesar's testament get unsealed before we went silent or something? Should we be expecting an announcement this evening?"

Numa smiled, shook his crowned head. "It doesn't matter whose name is in that testament. The Senate has the last word."

Farragut translated: "Your name's not in there, is it?"

"Not a chance. Magnus and I never saw eye to eye."

"You're a Senator. Who are you voting for?"

"The best man."

"You're voting for yourself."

"Absolutely."

The meat was spiced beyond recognition. So was the wine. "What do I have here?" Farragut asked.

Numa motioned with the pointy end of his spoon, which he had just used to dislodge a snail from its shell. "That is squab. And that there is the dormouse."

Numa Pompeii, Herius Asinius, and Augustus were eating their slugs, pigeon, and rodent, so Farragut followed suit. And Steele followed Farragut.

The honeyed figs were too sweet but not bad. What Farragut really wanted after all that was some black coffee. Got it. Unfortunately, it was also heavily spiced. Cinnamon this time. He pushed his coffee aside. Brought up the reason for his visit.

"The League ships came out here naked," said Farragut. "They're engineers with swords. Just won't keep body and soul together when the gorgons get through their skinny little distortion fields. I'm fixin' to move some real soldiers onto their boats."

"I hope you are not looking to me, Commodore," said Numa. *Gladiator* was an enormous ship with many decks to defend. Numa said he could spare none of her crew or legionaries to defend another vessel.

"In that case, I'm volunteering two cohorts of Heri's Dracs from the *Horatius*," said Farragut. "Herius?"

Herius Asinius carefully measured his words before speaking. "Are your Marines not capable?"

"There are just more of y'all," said Farragut simply.

"My Marines are capable," TR Steele declared. And to Farragut, "We don't need them, sir."

"But do the South Africans and the Malaysians need to know New Jersey quite that well?" said Augustus. Augustus had apparently heard lively stories of a Jersey-born Marine named Kerry Blue.

Became clear that he'd struck farther below the belt

than he'd even intended when Colonel Steele turned a deep shade of murderous crimson.

Numa Pompeii did not know anything about New Jersey, but recognized a barb when it flew from couch to couch even if he did not understand a bit of it. "Commodore Farragut, I am happy to see that our patterner is showing you every respect he has ever shown me."

Farragut nodded, grinning into the table. "Numa, if you're happy, I'm happy."

"Eat shit," said Numa.

"Die," said Farragut.

Numa and Farragut reached across the space between couches to touch wine goblets.

Numa said, "Did you know, *Commodore*, that this Attack Group was my idea? Your Joint Chiefs co-opted it and put me under your command."

"Numa, if you weren't reporting to me, then you'd be reporting to Dallas McDaniels or Calli Carmel."

"I would *not* be reporting to Callista," Numa vowed. "As to chain of command, it would be more efficient and appropriate if *Legion Draconis* reported to you through me. You should be asking me about what cohorts to move aboard the LEN ships."

"Not in this man's Attack Group, Numa. I'm not haggling over command structure."

He did not sound provoked, but his tone invited no argument.

Romans regarded themselves as the natural masters of the universe. Always had. Never stopped. Though their tactics changed to stealth when force was not a viable option.

The Roman Empire never fell. In its supposed fall, Romans achieved a death grip on disciplines of power and influence, and embedded their language into them—law, science, medicine, religion.

Unable to withstand the spread of Christianity, Rome infiltrated its power structure. Imposed the Latin language on the Church—the only Church at the time. Kept their hold on the Catholic Church until the late twentieth century, with the end of the Latin Mass.

Appropriate dinner conversation in a place that had a

vomitorium was wide open. The Romans talked freely of religion and politics, so it was open season on both as far as Dallas McDaniels was concerned.

"If I remember, Roman priests didn't marry under Roman rule," Dallas said. "What the hell was that about?"

"Control," said Numa. "What else? The Christian prophet Paul said, 'It is good for a man not to touch woman.' A peculiar idea, but politically useful. Rome made that law for men in power. So power would pass by merit, not by blood. Romans chose the heirs of their secrets carefully and not necessarily by blood kinship."

Dallas said, "It's not a nation, it's a conspiracy!"

"You would think so. Adoption was always common in Rome. We were open to forming attachments with the like-minded, rather than simply the same genes."

"Most of us find family ties pretty strong," said Farragut. "Like 'em or not."

"It's a natural inclination, for certain," said Numa. "But Rome is more evolved than that. The impulse remains to preserve others like yourself. But like yourself *how?* Physically like yourself? What exactly of yourself most needs preserving? Plato argued that pregnancy of the soul is superior to pregnancy of the body."

"Now here I thought that was an argument for homosexuality," said Farragut.

"That is the flat-minded interpretation. Pregnancy of the soul is a passionate need to pass on the essence of oneself, what is important. To a degree what you value might find safe harbor in like genetics. But if the fruit of your loins is a doorknob, do you vest what you treasure into *that*? Or into a like soul who will protect what you pass down, whether that soul dwells in a female or male house or a white, brown, black, or yellow house? That is how Rome survived. Rome is more a melting pot than the U.S. has ever been. The U.S. remains more mosaic than actual meltdown. Rome is just as varicolored as the U.S. but not multicultural. Absolutely not multicultural. The important thing, what survived the Long Silence, is Rome itself. The American highest state of being is the individual. We are Roma Eterna and we have more right than you to say *e pluribus unum.*"

"Yeah, like to get that off our currency," Dallas drawled. "Aren't you the same boys who brought us the Inquisition?"

"As a matter of fact, we are," said Numa. "For the record however, the Inquisitors tortured and killed seven hundred people, not thirty thousand. The story has been embellished, as if seven hundred were not gory enough. And the targets of the Inquisition were not the openly declared Jews and Moslems. Rome, same as the U.S., reserves the right to seek out and kill moles in its midst—do we not, Commodore Farragut? The Inquisition was a security measure. Those who professed to be Roman and were secretly something else, those we killed."

"The iron maiden wasn't overkill?" said Dallas.

"The iron maiden was not ours. Someone added that to the story to make it more juicy. For those who like that sort of thing."

Dallas leaned over so he could see the patterner. "That wouldn't be *you,* Augustus?"

"Meat screaming," Augustus said dismissively, bored.

"Okay, the Catholic Church gave Rome the shove," said Dallas. "Wasn't your God to begin with. So Rome is back to borrowing other peoples' gods."

"We have to borrow them," Augustus said. "No god ever bothered to approach us directly. Everyone seems to see God except us. Anyone here see a pattern in that?"

"Yes, it means you're going to hell," said Steele.

"There is no going, Colonel," said Augustus. "It's already fact."

Back on *Merrimack,* Steele wanted to get away from Augustus at best speed, but Augustus wouldn't stay out of his footsteps. Steele finally spun on him, "What do you want!"

"I am sensing animosity," said Augustus, disingenuous. "Was it something I said?"

The murderous color returned to Steele's face. There was no mistake.

Steele could muster nothing more clever than, "Drop dead."

"As attractive as that suggestion is, I have orders to the

contrary. I also have orders not to torment you. So now you may report my violation of orders to your commodore."

Steele smoldered. "I can fend for myself."

Augustus stepped away, smiling. "You will wish you had accepted the protection."

Kerry Blue in sick bay. Uncomfortable. The bruising and tearing were two days old.

Mo Shah repaired her, frowning. "Kerry, who did this to you?"

"You never ask me that, Mo," she said, perplexed, then, "Oh!" She curled half up on the examination table. "Did he give me VD? I'll kill him!"

"No, there is being no disease," said Dr. Shah. "Kerry, was this voluntary?"

"Hell, yeah. You thought—? Oh. No." She laughed. "Wasn't like that. He was just a little rough. And a lot big."

Mo Shah remained stern. "I do not want to be seeing this again. You may get dressed."

"Oh, trust me. It won't happen again. It was kind of an experiment."

Mo Shah's usually serene brow kept a fretful pinch in it. "Next time this is happening, I will be needing a name and I will be filing charges."

"Really?" Kerry was amazed. "What charge?"

"Destruction of government property."

Kerry fell back on the table, laughing to tears.

"I am being serious."

Kerry had been charged with destruction of government property once before—for getting a sunburn. So this should not have surprised her, but it did. She wiped away tears, thought she was done, but burst into a fresh gale. Managed to squeak out: *"Uncle Sam owns that, too?"*

The story of what Uncle Sam owned spread through the ship in a hydrogen flash. A laughing hydrogen flash.

Red haze and homicidal wrath. Stalking up the corridor. Sick. The bottom had fallen out of his world.

Someone had been screwed, and it wasn't really Kerry Blue.

Helpless fury, hollow anguish that could only be allayed by blood.

A bulk, a sky-blue uniform blocked the way.

"Game of squash, TR?"

Steele could scarcely focus on the commodore. Scarcely talk. Mumbled, "No, thank you, sir." Made to pass.

"It's an order, actually," said Farragut, moving again into his path.

Steele met his eyes, stunned. The eyes looked straight through him.

An angry Farragut was a quiet Farragut. Said nothing more.

Steele replied, the only thing he could say that would not land him back on Earth without his scrambled eggs, "Aye, sir."

Withdrew into battle stillness. To be in the moment and nothing beyond it. Stay in that cold clarity where nothing exists beyond the range of your own senses.

On the squash court some of it stole back into the disciplined emptiness. He smashed the little green ball about the court as if slashing gorgons. Rammed shots without aim, with such force they had to reach the front wall at some time amid all the mad ricochets. Broke one racquet.

Cracked his head against the wall returning a shot. Touched his head. Looked at his fingers. Blood.

Suspected Farragut might have let him win, though Farragut never let anyone over the age of twelve win anything.

Steele left the court, soaked to his eyelashes, a towel round his neck. Apologized to the commodore for his disrespect in the corridor. Didn't feel any better, but the battle—it hadn't been a game—brought him back to himself.

You are a soldier. You are not the most important thing out here.

Heart, pride, everything was still smeared on the deck by a clueless girl and a soulless monster.

You have your duty.

He had been so quick to fly into action, he hadn't stopped long enough to think that Kerry Blue did not need avenging. Hurting Kerry Blue had never been the objective. Kerry Blue was laughing about it.

Steele was the only one wounded here.

Patterners never miss.

"You could provoke a stone."

"A stone, but not John Farragut."

"Oh, I'm plenty smoked," Farragut moved from the hatchway into Augustus' torpedo rack room. "You disregarded a direct order."

"The Marine refused the protection."

"Colonel Steele cannot countermand any order of mine. You will desist."

"I did nothing to Steele. Anyway, I'm done now."

"You bet you are. You will confine your shots to me."

"I tried. I didn't get any farther with Mrs. Hamilton than you did."

Blue eyes blinked wide.

Hamster. Augustus had gone after his adored Glenn Hamilton.

Farragut blinked again in shock.

And suddenly he was laughing.

"That is not the reaction I was looking for," Augustus admitted.

Still laughing, Farragut turned back to the hatch. Said, "Jesus would've slapped you."

"You are better than your God?"

Farragut shook his head, leaving. "Jesus wasn't Navy."

21

FOR THE SHEER ENORMITY of space, there should have been no difficulty finding a clear path to Sagittarius Zero.

Were a ship to shut down its sensors and fly a straight random vector through the thick of the Milky Way, its chance of colliding with a single star would be remote. The space between stars was vast.

"Hive sign," the lab reported up to the command deck. "We have Hive sign."

"How?" Marcander Vincent beat on his tactical console.

"Evade," Gyspy Dent ordered. "Mister Vincent, who is moving in?"

Marcander Vincent looked at his monitors. "All of them in a ten light-year radius. Nearest sphere is still four light-years galactic north."

Mister Hicks relayed reports from the other ships in the Attack Group. They had Hive sign. "Not sure which ship in the Attack Group caught their attention first, but we have it."

"Someone must have resonated."

Commodore Farragut bounded onto the command deck. Passed the basketball he'd forgotten to let go of to a Marine guard at the hatch. "Where are we?"

"Hive spheres are converging," said Marcander Vincent. "They're making a box."

"Find us a path out of it," said Farragut. And signaled the lab, "Get our Sargasson on the telltales. I want this harmonic identified before we lose this Hive sign."

The Attack Group moved together on an evasion course.

A clatter sounded against *Merrimack*'s distortion field. The ship had plowed through a field of space debris.

A burble disturbed the artificial grav. Bigger than normal.

The ship's distortion field, while protecting the ship and its contents from catastrophic effects of inertia at FTL, still allowed through hints of what was happening outside.

Everyone felt it. A sensation of drag. As if *Merrimack* were running into a head wind, or more as if *Merrimack* were an airplane dropping landing gear in atmosphere. And there was a sound like wind.

Something had attached itself to the distortion field.

"What did we pick up?" Gypsy demanded.

Marcander Vincent hesitated in disbelief. "Gorgons."

Not a sphere. Not a wad. Long strings of the monsters were spread wide, like Herius Asinius' parachuting gorgons at Thaleia.

An individual gorgon was only a meter in diameter. Too small to activate a prox alarm.

Alarms sounded. Lights flashed red.

Gypsy spoke into the loud com: "Prepare to repel boarders!"

Rio Grande jetted hydrogen fire at *Merrimack*.

Gladiator reported boarders, *Horatius* assisting.

Wolfhound tended the smaller *Windward Isles* and *Sunlit Meadows*.

Someone on the com was sounding Mayday.

Farragut looked to the com tech. "Who is that and how is their Day any Mayer than ours?"

"It's the Meadow Muffins," said Mr. Hicks. The League of Earth Nations' ships.

The Mayday went abruptly silent. The LEN ships' coms were out.

"I guess their day *is* Mayer than ours."

*   *   *

Marines clad in atmospheric suits poured out *Merrimack*'s top air lock and fanned out atop the hull. They stood atop the ship, wielding long-poled scythes, dragged the blades against the adamant distortion wall. Sliced off gorgons' heads as they emerged inside the field. Cursed the gore that dripped down on them. Blinked against the lights, weird and confusing—chemical glow from their own headlamps, the bounce back from the distortion field, and the bizarre yellow-white hydrogen blaze from *Rio* striking the other side of the distortion field.

Became very, very dark when the hydrogen fire stopped.

Patrick Hamilton in the lab took the hail from the command deck: "Our Sargasson, Cowboy Wayne, has another chance to be a hero," said Farragut. "What's he make of the telltales?"

The Sargasson guttered in the tank, clutching its rock. Patrick responded: "I think he's speaking Swedish."

Gorgons clotted thicker and thicker on the ship's distortion field. The com failed. Then the lights.

The atmosphere changed. Ears popped. A wind moaned through the corridors.

"Hull breach."

The air inside the ship rushed out to fill the space between the hull and the distortion field. Command dispatched a runner topside to advise the Marines of the breach. But they would already know, having felt the wind, the change in air pressure.

Colonel Steele dispatched two squads of Marines armed with swords to where the gorgons were coming up through the underside of the starboard wing. The monsters had chewed through the air locks and were coming up a flight elevator shaft from the underwing flight deck.

Augustus joined the charge from behind. A Marine turned to see who was behind him. Suddenly not sure which side the monster was on.

The black eyes were not quite there. Not hollow. A wide focus. A terrifying, inhuman expression on the patterner's face. A heavy hand cannon wired into his forearm.

Marines never fired projectile weapons inboard other than a splinter gun, a weapon with which you could change your mind. For the tight quarters and thin bulks, you could never afford to miss, or to shoot through your target.

Augustus opened fire.

Marines swore and hit the deck.

The cannon raked down gorgons, row on row, its projectiles exploding within its targets, and continuing no farther. The shots came close to Marines' ears, shoulders, but did not touch. And the Marines swore at him, even as the gorgons that had been right in front of them dissolved.

Augustus moved to the front, preternaturally swift, and the Marines made way for him, and fell in behind.

Colonel Steele glanced aside at the killing machine now in the fore with him, just as Augustus fired up. Didn't even seem to look. Just turned the cannon up. Fired. And a gorgon splatted down from the overhead.

The masses of gorgons that poured up from the flight elevator were trying to outflank the Marines by climbing up the bulks and skittering along the hangar deck's very high overhead. Augustus picked them off, as Steele and his Marines hacked down the gorgons on the deck.

The cannon fire stopped as abruptly as it had started.

"Colonel Steele!"

Steele fell behind the front line, looked toward the voice.

Found a Marine, several Marines, staring at Augustus who had turned around to face them.

Augustus. Not moving. A vacancy in the black eyes. The hand cannon pointed at the Marines.

It wasn't Augustus anymore. It was a gorgon on two legs with a deadly accurate hand cannon pointed at Steele's Marines. The Marines were hesitating. The man had just a second ago been their comrade-in-arms.

Steele was in motion. Up from behind, he lunged at Augustus, and slashed, a huge stroke, spinning himself off-balance and onto the deck grates.

Two fat, severed cables flopped loose from Augustus' neck.

Augustus' posture slipped. His face changed. Confusion and pain. Awareness.

Seeing someone home, the Marines standing at cannon point lowered their ready swords, and dashed around Augustus to get at the gorgons.

Augustus reached down, pulled Steele to his feet with less effort than lifting a toddler. He unplugged his cannon from his forearm, shrugged out of the straps. Let the cannon drop to the deck. "What else we got?"

Steele gave him his sword. "Do you know how—"

Augustus gave the blade an instantly expert pass, said, "Apparently, I do."

He reached behind his neck, unplugged the severed stalks of cable hanging from base of his skull. He shook the cut ends at Steele. "You *could* have just yanked them out of their sockets."

"I was trying to cut off your damned head!" Steele snarled. Meant it.

"Short again," said Augustus and moved back to the front to hack down gorgons.

Alpha Team patrolled the lower decks, searching for other flanking breaches. Okay, it was necessary duty, but it felt cowardly.

A barking from somewhere deep in the lower sail turned to wild growling and snarling. Ranza Espinoza jerked her head toward the ladder. "Blue, check the mutt."

The sail was one hundred fifty feet down, a narrow shark fin, narrowing all the way down fore and aft, and no wider than six feet wide port to starboard, filled with equipment, most of which was not functioning right now.

Kerry found the miniature shepherd halfway down. Farragut's favorite dog. Snarling and snapping, its hackles raised. Raised hers, too.

The space between the hull and the distortion field was much, much narrower around the ship's upper and lower sails than around the ship's fuselage. No Marines were outside this part of the hull, shaving off gorgon mouths as they insinuated through the distortion field.

The idea was that once the gorgons insinuated through the distortion field, they would not just start gnawing on the nearest section of hull. They would take the path of least resistance to the food—meaning that they would skitter up the hull to the topside where the Marines were waiting for them with scythes and hydrogen torches, where the orientation of gravity favored the defenders.

Kerry shone her chemical light on the bundles of cables and hoses and conduit that ran up and down the sail. The light caught the severed end of a loose hose sticking through the hull. "Holy Mother—"

Hoses don't have teeth.

Started into her wrist com, "We've got a—" The com was out. Kerry faced up and yelled, *"We got a hull breach down here!"*

Steele felt something—maybe that was his soul—drop right out of him.

Post Kerry Blue inside the ship in reserve, and she gets the flanking attack. There was no protecting the woman.

You just can't keep them safe. Commodore Farragut had left his young wife safe on Earth, and she killed herself. You could not win. This kind of thing should just not be allowed to happen.

It was an eternity—probably less than an hour—before Steele could get down into the lower sail where Alpha Team held several breaches, cutting off anything that stuck itself through the hull.

Their voices carried up.

Carly Delgado: "Why is it so hot? How can it be hot? We're in outer space. Open a window."

Cole Darby: "The system is uffed."

Kerry Blue: "What happened to redundance? What happened to redundance? Where is the fox-trotting backup system?"

Darb: "This is the backup system."

Ranza Espinoza: "Colonel on deck."

Steele said, "What do you need down here?"

"Boosters," said Ranza.

Steele had brought them. Intradermal drugs to keep the fighters going. He produced a fistful of them from his pockets.

Glanced over Alphas. They looked good. Shiny. Dragging a little. No serious wounds. "What else?"

Met Kerry Blue's eyes. "If someone could throw some water bottles down here, that would be good," said Kerry. "And something for the dog."

Bloody drool dripped from the dog's mouth. Its muzzle burned from caustic gorgon ooze.

"You'll have it," said Steele. Retreated up the ladder, feeling suddenly stronger, as if he'd taken one of the boosters.

Patrick Hamilton, PhD, was no kind of soldier. He was a xenolinguist. Did not mind playing water boy to Marines and amateur vet to a ship's dog during a gorgon siege. His petite wife, whom they called the Hamster, was a more formidable swordsman than was Doctor Patrick Hamilton.

He'd got that lot in the lower sail taken care of, and returned to his lab. Found the hatch open.

A dog, a Doberman, nearly knocked him over charging out. The bitch plowed into Patrick's legs, then galloped up the corridor, dragging a long gray rag in its mouth.

Took a moment for Patrick Hamilton to realize what he'd just seen. That was not a long gray rag. That was the Sargasson, Steve Wayne. Yelled, "Inga! Bad dog—!"

Spun round at the crashing and thrashing within the lab. Saw the jagged hole torn in the overhead. Water on the deck. The thousand-gallon tank overturned. Gorgons snapping at flying insects loosed from their containers.

Patrick yanked the hatch shut and took off running up the corridor after the dog and the Sargasson.

"We have a second swarm."

"How can you tell one swarm from another?" said Farragut, turning.

Augustus was there, his scalp raked open, a hunk of bone missing from over his right eye, drying blood smeared on his face. "There are soldiers in the galley."

Soldiers. Also called can openers. The second, deadlier form of the Hive. Soldiers were tougher than gorgons, with harder bodies, and giant pincers instead of masses of tentacles.

Farragut shouted for backup and followed Augustus to the galley at a run.

The metal hull overhead the galley angled up, grotesquely curled, peeled back, the shimmer of the distortion field visible through the enormous breach. Pincered aliens jumped down to the deck. A knot of Marines and Chef Zack, blocked from the hatch and backed into a corner, defended a position behind a metal food prep bar with a protective overhang, which kept the soldiers that jumped from the overhead from landing on them.

Chef Zack was there, shoulder to shoulder with the Marines, wild-eyed, grisly, hacking off pincers with his butcher knife.

With all the hand-to-tentacle gore they had witnessed, there were still some blades and some people just more chilling than others. There was Chef Zack, his face spattered with gore, wielding his butcher's knife, howling, nightmarish and barbarous.

Farragut and a team of navvies opened up with hydrogen torches, jetting streams of fire at the overhead to stop any more monsters from dropping in, and trying to burn a path from the hatch to the trapped Marines.

Augustus advanced, plowed into the thick of the soldiers, slashing with two swords, like a walking daisy-cutter. Hacked off a pincer that was tearing his thigh open. The bleeding stopped instantly from the horrendous wound. He continued slashing, limping now, some of the thigh muscles disconnected. He dragged his torn limb, advanced like a zombie, pincers flying off either side. An inhuman monster you want on your side.

He got through the aliens to the Marines and leaped over the metal bar into their refuge with them. Took Chef Zack's knife from him, threw it down. Yelled, "Incoming!" Leaped up onto the bar like a gorgon and bodily threw Chef Zack over the aliens, between the hydrogen jets, and over the navvies' heads.

Zack hit the deck clumsily. Probably broke something, but Zack got to his feet and ran out of the galley even as Augustus was hurling another man up and over. And another.

Augustus paused in his airlift to slice pincers off the nearest aliens snapping at the bar, until there was a layer of maimed aliens in the way of the intact soldiers. He seized up another Marine, stripped his sword from him, and under protest set him flying.

The next Marine Augustus heaved forward but did not let go. The Marine bit his tongue, swore the air purple. As in the space between the bar and Farragut's men, a dozen aliens leaped up to catch a flying man that did not come their way.

"Heads up!" Augustus roared.

As flaming monsters spilled from the overhead, falling into the places Farragut's men just sprinted back from.

No sooner had the aliens dropped, when Augustus hurled two more Marines across the wider space to safety. Heard a bone snap on that landing.

The air roiled now with black caustic smoke. Difficult to breathe. Difficult to see.

When there was no one left behind the bar but Augustus, he stalked back through the jam of soldiers, splitting them open with two swords. The navvies keeping hydrogen jets flaming on either side of him to keep him from being crushed.

A pincer grazed his scalp. Another raked the skin and muscle off his left-side ribs. The bleeding was brief.

When he joined up with the navvies, they executed a controlled retreat from the smoking galley, lobbed fragmentation grenades inside, and sealed the hatch.

In the corridor, the Marines and navvies stared at Augustus, part in awe, part fascination at the open bloody meat and the bared bones and cables.

Farragut eyed the Roman head to sliced-off toe. Said, "If you have anything left in you, I need you."

"I am yours to command."

Farragut told his navvies, "Send Kit Kittering and the Og to the command deck, and somebody find an atmospheric suit big enough for this guy." This guy being Augustus. "Augustus, with me."

"Commodore on deck," Glenn Hamilton announced.

Gypsy's eyes widened briefly at Augustus. Reported to Farragut in the calm, grave voice of someone stating their imminent death, "We have lost navigation."

Chief Engineer Kit Kittering reported quickly to the

command platform. A boyish young woman, square shouldered as a toy soldier with short, blunt-cut, dark hair, large doll eyes, and a foul mouth. She glanced at Augustus. Stared in shock. Said, "You look dead." And, at toy soldier attention to Farragut, "Yes, sir!"

"Here's what we're fixin' to do," said Farragut, making eye contact with Gypsy, Hamster, Kit, and Augustus. "We load the irresistible harmonic into a res chamber and equip it with a chemical fuse to turn it on after it has left this ship. Once we start that fuse, we can't miss any step in this plan or we are gorgon chow.

"We dislodge the safe from my quarters and load it on board a skiff. The skiff gets hand-cranked out to the port wing flight deck and prepped for launch. We nock the gyro so the skiff will fly in a circle. A big circle.

"The res chamber with the delay fuse goes into the safe inside the skiff.

"We take down the distortion field over the flight deck and launch the skiff as fast as it will go. The fuse burns down and the skiff starts resonating the irresistible harmonic. We take *Merrimack*'s distortion field down to minimal to let all the gorgons bale out and go chase the skiff.

"We'll have until they catch up with the skiff, insinuate through its distortion field, eat through the hull, and eat through the safe, and eat the resonator to get out of here."

Kit said, "A Star Sparrow is much faster than a skiff."

"Too fast," said Farragut and Augustus at once.

And Farragut by himself, "If the gorgons don't have a chance of catching it, they won't chase. Same reason I want the circle. I want *this* here bunch of gorgons on board *my* boat to respond to that harmonic. Not the gorgons ten light-years away.

"Mister Dent, find Colonel Steele. Have him get all our hull walkers inboard and either tethered down or locked behind an air lock away from any hull breaches.

"I also need some Marines to keep the gorgons off Kit's crew while they get the skiff loaded and onto the flight deck. Augustus, coordinate with Kit on the fuse."

Kit asked, a tremor in her voice, "How do we launch the skiff? Is this a suicide mission, sir?"

"I've got that part," said Augustus.

"You're not committing suicide, Augustus."

"Don't need to. I'll rig a fused launch for the skiff."

Farragut looked to all of them again. His eyes had that bright blue gleam that made you think you were going to live. "Get everything in the right sequence at the right time. All this has to be happening right now. Og! Turn around."

As Chief Ogden Bannerman appeared in the hatchway.

"Get me some big guys and some equipment to move my safe."

Farragut moved the contents of his safe into Gypsy's safe. An act of optimism. That there would still be things to be kept secret twenty minutes from now.

Og's erks unbolted the commodore's safe from the deck. Without lifts, it was difficult to move. Gypsy ran to the command deck to lessen the ship's gravity to make the transport of the safe from the commodore's quarters out to the port hangar deck easier. Surprised that the ship still had gravity.

Marines coming in through the air locks were redeployed to keep the path from the commodore's quarters to the port hangar deck clear of gorgons.

Kit Kittering brought a resonator to the hangar deck where Augustus prepared a skiff to autostart and to fly on a lame duck course. Kit kept staring at him, pieces of him that ought to be inboard hanging out but not bleeding. Naked tendons moved in the back of his hand.

Without looking, Augustus said, "Am I interesting, Mister Kittering?"

"Hell, yeah."

She readied the irresistible harmonic. Checked it four or five times. Had Augustus check it again.

He would not activate the fuse until the last. Kit already had an irrational dread that the resonator would start itself. And she an engineer.

Gypsy arranged a human com chain to relay shouted messages from the command deck to the hangar deck.

Marines in atmospheric suits brought suits for Farragut and the big walking corpse, along with tethers, scythes, and flamethrowers.

A report came shouted down from the command deck:

soldiers had chewed their way out of the galley and were spreading through the ship.

Erks pushed the skiff into the flight elevator, sealed the hangarside of the air lock behind it. Augustus, Farragut, and a squad of Marines were sealed in with it, flamethrowers at the ready as they opened the flight deck side of the air lock. The erks manually cranked the skiff up the elevator to the flight deck.

Gorgons were sparse on the flight deck, not much up here to eat.

But up above, the distortion field was clotted with gorgon upon gorgon, slowly insinuating in. The Marines took scythes to the emerging mouths. Other Marines pushed the skiff into a launch slot, clamped its gear down.

Farragut observed the gorgon layer overhead. Could be tonnage up there.

Augustus followed his gaze.

"The moment we retract the distortion field for launch, all those gorgons up there will come *down*," said Farragut. Looked at the little skiff underneath the imminent avalanche.

"Need to get rid of the *down*," said Augustus.

"I need to get the order to Gypsy to kill the gravity before the distortion field goes."

Marines, Farragut, and Kit positioned themselves on the lift, ready for retreat.

Augustus set the fuse on the resonator, closed the safe. Set the skiff to autolaunch. Jumped down to the flight deck on his one working leg, shut the skiff's hatch. Ran/hobbled to the lift. "Thirty. Twenty-nine."

Farragut banged out the signal for the erks down below to crank the elevator back down fast. Marines pulled the topside hatch shut over them as the commodore's team came down.

Farragut ordered through the shouted relays: "Kill the ship's gravity! Now!"

Knew it was done before the acknowledgment came back. Farragut's feet left the deck.

"Retract port flight deck distortion field."

Acknowledgment came back through the relay.

Augustus continued the launch countdown: "Nine. Eight.

"Release deck clamps."

"Releasing—" the erk started. Interrupted himself, "They're stuck! Negative clamp release!"

Farragut started forward to climb up and force the clamps open.

Augustus pulled him back with the words: "Five. Four. I suggest everyone evacuate the hangar deck. Now."

Sudden awareness in all of them of the danger. A spaceship was about to take off from the overhead to which it was clamped.

All personnel dashed out the big doors that divided the ramp tunnel from the hangar deck. They hooked their tether ends into the deck grates.

Ignition was thunderous against the overhead. The flight deck groaned.

Suddenly part of the hangar deck overhead ripped up and off. Farragut glimpsed open space as the wind started.

The skiff—and deck plates and the deck clamps—shot away.

Farragut's tether went taut. Knocked the air out of him. The outbound wind howled.

Threw him against someone else. Maybe Kit.

The outrush of atmosphere sucked the big hangar deck doors shut with a boom.

Farragut did not drop back to the deck with the doors' shutting. There was still no gravity. But he was no longer twisting and whipping round on the end of his tether in the hurricane wind.

Heard a crash.

Asked, floating. "What is that?"

"The skiff hit us!"

"Where is it now?"

"It is not on course," was all Augustus could say for sure.

"What if it's snagged on us?" said Kit, entangled in Farragut's tether.

Augustus answered, "Then we are irresistible in five. Four. Three. We have fuse burn. And resonance—*now*."

All eyes turned in the direction that up used to be.

22

I T WAS INSTANTANEOUS.

Gorgons and soldiers lifted away from *Merrimack*'s distortion field. And kept going.

Lights came on. The coms returned to life.

The first order over the com was Farragut calling the command deck: "Commander Dent, restore gravity on a ten count."

Gypsy acknowledged: "Gravity restore initiated."

Crew, Marines, and loose objects returned gradually to the deck. The ten count gave personnel time to find their feet before the weight set in. Made for a better return to the deck than Augustus' evacuation of the galley.

Farragut ran up to the command deck. Announced over the loud com: "All hands. All hands. Secure personnel from any hull breach. Report immediately if unable to comply. We are dropping the distortion field. *Prepare to expel boarders.*"

And he nodded to Gypsy to make it happen.

"In ten, nine, eight—"

The countdown halted for someone to chase a dog.

Resumed.

"Seven, six—"

Halted again for Marines engaged in combat with soldiers. Waited for their retreat behind an air lock.

The count resumed.

On zero, *Merrimack* dropped all but the ship's forward asteroid shield.

Any aliens still insinuating through the ship's distortion field were suddenly released into the vacuum. And immediately hied away. Any alien sucked out a hull breach made no attempt to hold on.

Once free, they all pursued the irresistible harmonic.

"Restore distortion field."

"Restoring field, aye." Then: "Field in place."

"Mister Dent, get us out of here."

Merrimack blazed out of the area, wary now of large fields of small objects.

Marcander Vincent was immediately bucked down from his position at tactical. The kid from the Hamster shift took over the tactical station.

The space battleship executed a wild goose path while the crew and Marines rooted out and killed the remaining gorgons and soldiers on board.

So long as a single gorgon was alive on *Merrimack*, the entire Hive knew where the ship was. Let it see *Merrimack* going in a false direction.

The whole ship knew when the last gorgon died. The telltales stopped chirping and fluttering. And Kerry Blue's euphoric screech filled the ship corridors, because it was her sword stroke that made the telltales go quiet.

Then it was time to search for the wounded and put names to the dead.

The moment that all crew and company were accounted for, Farragut felt all the energy leave him, sudden as a telltale collapsing to rest.

The adrenaline buzz gave way to dead tiredness.

Hamster had taken a booster and told the commodore and the XO that she was good to take the next watch. She dismissed her commanding officers from the command deck.

Farragut made sure Augustus made it to the ship's hospital, then dragged himself to his quarters.

Brain gone muzzy. Not even sure what he was squinting at.

Spoke to no one there: "Why is there a long gray rag in my shower?"

Once upon a time, World War II fighters would get into a melee and suddenly find themselves surrounded by nothing but wide blue sky. The enemy, their comrades would be abruptly nowhere in sight.

Out here, you very quickly became surrounded by absolute nothing.

Merrimack had lost the Attack Group.

Had procedures in place for just such an eventuality. Proceeded to the rendezvous coordinates coded for this leg of the trip.

And found *Rio* already there, scorched but intact.

Dallas McDaniels' voice came over the tight beam: "John, old son! Thought we lost you."

Wolfhound and the LEN ships arrived soon after. Calli came over to *Merrimack* on a skiff. "I don't know what happened. I thought we were dead, and suddenly all the gorgons—" She opened her hands like a magician showing nothing there. "Vanished. Did you do that?"

Calli could not say that the LEN had been disappointing. She hadn't expected much from them to begin with. The LEN had never faced a tentacle before. "But I didn't expect them to be boat anchors!"

"How about the Dracs?" Farragut had stationed two cohorts of Dracs on board the LEN ships.

"What you'd expect from Roman legionaries. The Dracs are the only reason I still have the boat anchors with me."

Gladiator and *Horatius* were not accounted for.

Merrimack, Rio Grande, Wolfhound, Sunlit Meadows, and *Windward Isles* settled in to wait for the Romans.

Circling the rendezvous coordinates in the waiting, the commodore conferred with his senior officers. "How did the gorgons find us?"

"Someone resonated," said Gypsy. "That's the only way."

One of Dallas McDaniels' eyebrows went up, the other went down, and he looked at Gypsy sideways in complete disbelief. *"Who?"*

There was no way to tell for sure. Resonance only existed in the instant. Once the sender stopped sending, the resonance ceased to exist. Resonance left no trail.

Steele said, "None of the watches on *Merrimack* saw anything suspicious around any res chamber."

Captain Carmel and Captain McDaniels reported the same.

"Then if no one confesses, we won't know," said Farragut.

"Had to be someone stone stupid," said Dallas McDaniels. "How can anyone in this man's Navy be that dumb."

Farragut shook his head. "I'd be willing to offer amnesty to anyone who confessed—because I'd really like to know if it was stupidity instead of sabotage—but if someone other than y'all asked to see me in confidence, that would be a dead giveaway to all these folks in my Attack Group who want this stupid man-jack or jane dead, so I'm not expecting anyone to come forward."

"It had to be someone with a death wish," Colonel Steele said. "Do we know anyone like that?"

Mo Shah patched up Augustus as best he could. The Roman's wounds were ghastly. Whole muscles had been stripped away, his cables laid bare, some of them severed.

"Is that not hurting?" Mo Shah asked.

"I am not caring," said Augustus.

The medical officer filled in the deep wounds with temporary gel. New tissue needed to be cultivated. And Mo Shah needed Augustus' assistance making the repairs. Had drugs and nanites brought up from Augustus' quarters in torpedo rack room six.

Mo Shah scowled and became more and more troubled as he set up the tissue cloning tanks. Finally asked, "Colonel Augustus, what is being your mother's name?"

Augustus reclined, coolly serene, pink gel quivering in his hideous wounds. Gouged-out pieces of bone from his left eyebrow and left cheek along a wound that just missed his eye gave him a wicked gaze. "Mary Shelley."

"Father's name?"

"Victor Frankenstein."

"I have been thinking so," said Dr. Shah, not overly surprised. Reassured, more the case, that he had not been mistaken somewhere.

Farragut found Jose Maria in sick bay, playing a Spanish guitar at Augustus' cotside.

Saw that Augustus' cables had been repaired. The flesh was coming along more slowly.

The Sargasson had been moved out of the commodore's shower and into a tank in sick bay. Mo Shah was pretty good with houseplants. A touch of green had returned to Steve Wayne's gray fronds. Still the Sargasson did not look well.

There was a junior medic tending Augustus.

"Where's Mo?" Farragut asked.

"I got the short straw, sir," said the medic.

Augustus said, "The MO was being contemplative of being stabbing me."

"Augustus, how in the hell can you torque off a Riverite?"

Augustus did not answer the question. Or maybe he did. He said, "Ever think that maybe you killed Maryann?"

Jose Maria missed a chord.

Farragut said, "I know I did. I live with it. Hurts. I knew I wouldn't be there for her. Never should have married her."

As if Augustus had pointed a gun at him and Farragut took the gun and emptied all the chambers into himself. Left Augustus with an empty gun.

Augustus looked perplexed and weirdly without anything to say.

Farragut pulled up a seat. "Now. Did you learn anything when you were taken over by the Hive overmind?"

Augustus shook his head, scratched at his new scalp. "There is no mind. There is some awareness of Self. Self as in a kind of Us but without plurality. The Hive does not regard itself as many. There is no sense of individual self. What the Hive does—it's a program. But there is no 'die' command."

"Damn. Then how do they die?"

"They don't die when some overmind says die. When local conditions add up to a state that will no longer support an individual expending the energy to sustain itself, it ceases to be. And because the individual doesn't see itself as an individual, it gets suckered into disintegrating."

"Did you identify the Hive harmonic?"

Augustus gave a wry, nasty smile. Pink gel dripped from his cheek. "What is the frequency of your brain waves?"

Farragut shook his head. "I'm not a patterner."

"Neither was I at the time. I was part of It. It never occurred to me to identify and remember the harmonic. It was I. I was it."

"I don't know what kind of augmentation you've got going on there in your skull, but is there any chance of getting the harmonic off your own equipment?"

"Way ahead of you. Tried that. Resonance leaves no footprints."

Jose Maria paused over his guitar. "Is it true, as it seems to be, that the Hive can locate the origin and reception point of a resonant pulse?"

"Yes. It does. I could sense all of them. All of Us. All of me." He rephrased several times, none of the expressions quite fitting. "And let me tell you, it's a vast universe out there."

"How widespread were You?"

"I am reasonably certain the Hive is extragalactic."

Farragut gave a low whistle.

"Is there any chance that the signals we're picking up from Constantine's planet aren't real? Maybe there is no life on Planet Zero, and all this is really a Hive lure, drawing us into a trap?"

Augustus and Jose Maria both shook their heads.

"I mean, think about it. The Hive could be mimicking signals of human life to draw us in."

The heads kept shaking.

"Why not? Even a fish can learn what a lure is."

Jose Maria tried to explain. "If I understand the beast, as Augustus has described it, the Hive cannot conceive of a separate mind—or shall I say the Hive program cannot process a logic set separate from its own. The if/then decisions of the Hive are the only ones possible. A trap requires empathy. The Hive has no empathy. The elseness is the sticking point."

Augustus rephrased, speaking as the Hive, "If I know it, everyone knows it, because I am everything."

"Well, gentlemen, that all flew straight over me," said Farragut.

"The Hive cannot put out bait or set traps," said Jose Maria. "The Hive has no imagination. It can scarcely be said to think. So it cannot imagine that we are even thinking beings, much less imagine what we think. It assumes— without even going through the act of assuming—it just *knows* that we must know everything it does."

Augustus cut to the conclusion. "The signs of life on Planet Zero are not a trap. At least not a trap set by the Hive. The Hive does not lure. The Hive goes and gets what it wants. The Hive will never surprise you on purpose."

Jose Maria added, "I doubt the signs of life from Planet Zero are a trap set by Constantine either. Constantine's choice of lairs has more the appearance of a fortress than a trap. Everything around it screams at us to stay away. Exactly as it did on Thaleia."

"It screams at *me* to just send a planet killer in there and have done with the bastard. But since Constantine seems to be living there without getting eaten, we need him alive. Because what Constantine knows, *only* he knows."

"About your Roman, Commodore Farragut."

"Which Roman, Mo? I've got two whole Roman warships MIA."

"*Your* Roman."

That had to be Augustus.

Augustus was John Farragut's Roman because no one else could stand him. Except for Jose Maria de Cordillera and Jose Maria was a civilian, and therefore did not count.

Not sure what Augustus had done to piss in Mo Shah's river, but Farragut sensed personal animosity as Mo reported his findings to Commodore Farragut, Commander Dent, and the civilian microbiologist Jose Maria de Cordillera.

"Augustus is having two sets of DNA."

"Is he a chimera?" Gypsy asked.

"No, he is not being so."

Farragut turned aside to Gypsy, "What's a chimera?"

"A fused twin."

Farragut felt his chin back up. "That *happens?*"

"The chimera usually doesn't even know," said Gypsy. "Until the children she knows damn well came out of her own body don't match her DNA. The children are often barren."

Gypsy did not sound happy, and she did not sound disinterested. A frown on those bold features looked forbidding.

Farragut stayed on course. Asked Mo, "Augustus isn't one of those chimeras?"

"The body Augustus inhabits is being twenty-five years old."

"Hardest twenty-five years I ever saw," said Farragut.

"Accelerated aging can be happening when a clone is being made from adult cells."

"Like Dolly the sheep," Jose Maria said.

Mo nodded. "Dolly, the world's first cloned mammal, became old before her time."

"So Augustus is a twenty-five-year-old clone?" said Farragut.

"Augustus is not being entirely twenty-five and not entirely a clone. He is having original parts—the brain in particular is being predominantly original. The age of the brain is being uncertain. But the brain is having the original pituitary gland, which is causing the accelerated aging in the body. The body is being an altered clone. It is having different genes activated than in the original man. Some genes have been altered, some have been engineered. This body is being much taller than the original, and this body is being strung with cables. It is crawling with nanites, the function of which is seeming to be the maintenance of the augmentations and the prevention of the body from rejecting them.

"The augmentations are causing considerable pain to the clone body. The implanted brain is being painfully aware of this.

"The assembled unit of clone body and original brain,

this man we are knowing and loving as Augustus is being approximately eight years old."

"Eight?" said Farragut with a start. "Augustus is eight? Why did the engineers let the body age? Cloning has come a long way since Dolly the sheep."

Jose Maria suggested, "Maybe his makers wanted a more sedate variant of the original."

Farragut remembered Augustus saying once: *Young men die easily in packs.*

The hormonal storm of a young man was probably not a good quality to have in a patterner.

This operative had not been designed for reckless heroics. A forty- or fifty-year-old disposition was what the creators probably wanted. Not what they got, but may have been what they wanted.

"So where is the twenty-five-year-old brain that came with Augustus' body? And why not keep them together?"

"I am not knowing," said Mo.

Jose Maria did. Spoke in sudden insight: "Because the brain was the desired part. Or I should say the mind. A mind cannot be cloned. The vessel—the brain—defines its contents. The experiences of a person, his life, builds his brain and forms the mind. The original brain had the logical inclination and the analytical synapses already formed. The clone body is merely a vehicle manufactured to house that brain. Trauma damages the development of a brain. The clone body developed with embedded cables and painful alterations. The clone brain, scarred by its experiences, was probably not what the engineers were looking for in a patterner."

"Well, somewhere there's a body without a brain and a brain without a body. So what did the Roman Frankensteins do with them? Did they unite the two spare parts?"

"That is a fairly ghastly concept," Jose Maria agreed.

"It's a crime against humanity," said Gypsy.

"Augustus is not the criminal," said Farragut. "He is the crime."

"Are we sure?" said Gypsy.

The grim scenario of brain transplants had been around since before the technology was ever available—body transplants really. The fear had always been that a wealthy egomaniac wanting eternal youth would cultivate a young body, remove the brain that grew with it, and have his own brain moved into the new home.

Any benefit according to that scenario was obviated here in that Augustus did not remember his former self. Augustus knew he had a past life. He had mentioned it once. Farragut hadn't known at the time that Augustus was being literal. But Augustus' memories did not go back more than eight years—which was why the crew had supposed him a Heraclid.

"Why would anyone want that done if he couldn't remember who he was?"

"Maybe the rich bunghole who thought he was buying a powerful new body didn't get what he bargained for," Gypsy suggested.

A voice from behind answered: "That's the thing with coming to life; no one gets to bargain."

Augustus had risen from his cot and come to the MO's office. He stood in the entrance, dripping pink gel and looking very like Frankenstein's monster.

Farragut was the only one who did not give a guilty flinch to be caught talking about Augustus behind his back. Said, "The volunteer rate for becoming a patterner has got to be real, real low."

"No one volunteers to become a patterner," Augustus said.

"I can believe that," Farragut said. "No one—no one in their right mind—would volunteer to have his brain separated from his body."

"Did you commit a crime?" Gypsy asked.

Augustus gave her a withering glare. "I was Caesar's right hand."

"I take that as a no," said Farragut.

"No one would sink that kind of investment into augmenting a criminal mind," said Augustus.

That put to rest any idea at all that Augustus had ever, in any incarnation, been a Heraclid.

"Did you play piano when you were three?" Jose Maria asked.

Farragut and Gypsy darted odd glances at Jose Maria, not sure where that question had come from.

Augustus said, "I was never three."

Jose Maria countered, "Your brain was."

"That person no doubt played piano at an early age," Augustus said.

It had been known for centuries that learning to play the piano when one was three years old greatly improved one's problem solving ability. Roman households may not have a chicken in every pot, but there was a piano in every nursery. It was considered a basic right.

Mo Shah said, "We have been knowing for a long time that Rome is performing prohibited experiments on human beings, but brain transplanting is being far beyond the pale."

"It is only ever done to create patterners," said Augustus. "Opportunities are few and the success rate is very small. Had it failed, I never would have known."

"What happened to the brain that grew up inside the body you're using? The clone whose body you snatched," said Gypsy. "*That* brain had a thought or two."

"I have no first- or secondhand information on the disposition of the clone brain," said Augustus. "But I know the same as you know. They chucked it."

"Maybe they put it in your old body," said Farragut.

"You just won't let anything go, will you, John Farragut?"

"While there's hope," Farragut agreed.

"While there's life," Augustus translated. To John Farragut the words were nearly synonymous. "Then give it up, because that is not what they did. If the 'old body' had been salvageable, then that man would have lived. What you are refusing to grasp here is that the primary prerequisite for becoming a patterner is the quality of being dead."

23

"I'M TOLD HIS NAME was Cyprian Flavius Cassius," said Augustus without emotion. "He was twenty-three when he died."

"Why do you call yourself *he* and not *I*?" said Farragut.

"I don't remember ever being such a person," said Augustus. "I am quite literally a new incarnation. I am not he."

"You are remembering nothing?" Dr. Mo Shah asked.

Augustus seemed to search his memory. Said at last, "I'm pretty sure I got laid a lot."

"Do you remember anything *in between* being Flavius Cassius and Augustus?" Jose Maria asked, and took a step back, as if afraid to hear the answer.

Augustus gave no indication of remembered horrors. Perhaps a little boredom. "Not really."

"I would think you would be in an utter panic!" said Gypsy Dent. "It's—good lord!—it's *unspeakable*."

"You'll have to 'speak' more than that, Commander Dent. I don't know what you're talking about. What panic am I supposed to be in?"

"You were—*disembodied!*"

Augustus considered panic. Apparently, it had never occurred to him.

"Panic how? As you pointed out—I had no body. I couldn't even tell you what sort of container my brain was housed in. Without senses, without mouth to go dry and prickle and sour, without stomach to flutter and wrench, without palms to slick and heart to race, tear ducts to burn— What do you *feel*? Emotion is a biochemical reaction. Without the physical expression of fear to feed back into the brain, where does emotion go? How does one panic without the outward symptoms? Besides which, I think my creators must have suppressed my consciousness. I may as well have been in a womb."

"And nothing came through from your subconscious?" asked Jose Maria.

"Nothing specific. I had no time sense, I know that. Music. I think there was music. Some stimulus that evoked an awareness of music in my occipital lobe, because I certainly had no ears. It was a long dream remembered dimly if at all. And I woke up knowing things this other person, this Cyprian Flavius Cassius, could never have known. I suppose I learned things in my—what to call it?—sleep? Gestation? But I don't remember acquiring the knowledge. I simply *have* it. What the creators did, how they did it, is not information I will ever be given access to."

"You were Cyprian Flavius Cassius," said Farragut. "Now with a clone body and reengineered brain you're Augustus. They gave you only one name this time. Like a slave."

"I am not a slave," said Augustus.

"You are programmed to absolute service to the Empire," said Jose Maria. "How is that not slavery?"

"Who gives a rip! I just came in here to get pain medication," said Augustus. He crossed Mo's office, leaving a trail of pink slime behind him, and took from Mo Shah's supply cabinet what he came for. "I was created. And not by God. Who owns this life if not the Empire?"

Gladiator and *Horatius* showed up at the rendezvous coordinates twenty-three Earth hours later, not badly damaged, or else already repaired. The Roman ships had in tow the boxcars filled with explosives. Minus one.

Numa had some words about *Merrimack*'s navigation skills and their ensnarement by gorgons. Farragut asked in return if *Gladiator* was volunteering to take point.

The white tiger Amadea claimed one hundred twenty gorgon kills in the battle on board *Gladiator*.

Kerry Blue couldn't believe it when she heard it.

"She's *counting?*"

Kerry Blue. Posted under the ship again. Not even sure what she'd done this time, but her timing couldn't be worse.

It was after the services for the dead, and the Group was closing in on Sagittarius Zero. The ship was pretty well patched up, and the erks got the hangar decks put back together. Very important, because the hangar decks were where the Marines played basketball. Kerry could hear the basketball up there, thudding. Feet stampeding back and forth. Everybody bellowing.

Kerry's Alpha Team, eliminated way back in the first rounds, would be cheering for Delta against Echo.

Playing the championship game now had been Farragut's idea. After Tad from Delta and Enzo from Echo were killed on leave, the championship match just kind of went away. Farragut proposed that the championship game go on in their memory, with Farragut and Steele filling in for Tad and Enzo.

Thought it would be good for morale, and it sure sounded like it was working.

There was a big party happening up there that everybody—everybody not on duty—was at. Crew gave up their sleep cycles to be there, stomping and hollering in the hangar deck.

And Kerry was down here. She didn't know why. Just knew she wasn't up there.

She didn't get released until the game was over—huge roaring finish and all—and company and crew were going back to where they should have been, laughing and talking about the game.

Not that Kerry Blue didn't like to see her team happy, but their hilarity in the forecastle just smushed her face into the fact that she'd missed the game of the century.

Her mates could scarcely tell her about it because they kept breaking down into incoherent cackles.

Steele. Steele had done something funny. And Steele was never ever funny.

Steele's side—Echo Team—lost the game. Steele had to drink a beerful of Rafe's shoe.

"A what?" said Kerry.

"A shoe full of Rafe's beer."

"Rafe's shoe, filled with beer."

"Beer. From a shoe. Rafe's shoe. They filled it with beer, and Colonel Steele had to drink it."

"Rafe has the biggest feet on the *Mack*," said Kerry.

She pretty well detonated her team with that one.

"WE KNOW!" they all shouted back at her, and next thing she knew they're on the deck howling and laughing themselves to gasps all over again.

And that wasn't the end of it. Darb recovered first, continued the story, "Well, the Old Man chugs down the shoe, and his face is *red*. I mean he's *red*. He slams down the shoe and demands another. Okay, you had to be there, or I'm not telling it right."

"No, no, it sounds really really funny," said Kerry. "I wish I'd been there."

"Well, why weren't you?" said Cain, wiping his eyes.

"'Cause I got posted under the ship, where else would I be!" Kerry snapped.

Dak explained it to Cain, "What it is, is Colonel Steele hates Kerry Blue. Everybody knows that."

Darb said, in an altogether different voice, "Yeah. Really really hates her."

The change in emphasis the way Darb said it turned a switch in Kerry's head. "Oh, God."

Darb saw her lights go on. "You just now finally noticing that, Blue?"

Kerry met Cole Darby's eyes, rather terrified. Said more faintly still, "Yeah."

The happy baboon, Dak Shepard, blithe and utterly oblivious snorted, "Hell, you gots to be all kinds of real stupid not to know Colonel Steele hates Kerry Blue!"

Kerry sat, numb, "All kinds of real stupid."

Darb patted her shoulder. "Good morning, Sleeping Beauty."

Kerry dropped her head all the way between her knees.
The colonel. He's the damn colonel.

"Oh, *crap.*"

A knock on his hatch. Couldn't really call it a knock. More of a tap. Better not be one of his Marines. It was really a girl sort of knock.

Steele belched. Grimaced.

Nothing like shoe-flavored beer.

"Come in."

And there she was. Kerry Blue.

If she had been at that game, he would have fallen over his own feet. Would have bollixed all his shots. He was supposed to be playing for Enzo. He had done right by Enzo. The game had come down to the last second.

Now he had to face Kerry Blue.

"Sir, I don't want to be posted under the ship anymore."

Steele reacted slowly, smoldering. A disturbed dragon. "Are you questioning my orders, Marine?"

"Yes, sir."

Like being shot. No. He'd been shot. This was worse. Worse than his worst fears. He would rather be shot again.

This must be what it was like to swallow poison. Naked. In front of everybody.

Like talking to a firing squad, he said, "Do you want a transfer?"

"No, sir. You know I don't."

His arms crossed themselves. It was a defensive posture. He could not uncross them now. That would look weak, indecisive. He needed all the barriers he had. Tasted a bitter, stinging sourness in his mouth. Told her, brusque, "Instructions on how to file a charge are in the manual. Look it up."

"Oh, come *on.* I'm not doing that."

Felt the color coming and going from his face like a beacon. No mistake now. They really were talking about what he was afraid they were talking about.

She knew.

She knew, *but she didn't hate him.*

Scarlet, pale, scarlet.

His thoughts whited out. The closest to real panic he had

ever come in his entire life. He retreated behind his rank, "Dismissed."

Kerry Blue looked around her as if she'd missed something. He had not answered her question/demand. "But—"

"Get out."

There might have been a little foot stamp there. And don't she dare do cute girl things, or he would lose all control, dignity, all—whatever he had to lose, he would lose it.

Kerry turned to the hatch. Yanked it open to show how angry she was. She looked back, "I don't want to go anywhere." She stomped out, yanked the hatch closed behind her, trying to make it slam.

The hatch reopened in a moment. Just a crack. Only the voice came in. "I don't want you going anywhere either."

The hatch closed again.

Heat blazed, fell away cold. Blazed.

How does it feel to want, Blue?

Jose Maria de Cordillera came to Commodore Farragut's quarters with Augustus during the middle watch. Apologized for disturbing him. "Something odd," said Jose Maria. "If you please, young Commodore. The behavior is odd."

Augustus agreed; there was odd behavior out there worth observing.

Farragut found his command deck crowded with xenos, observing the oddity on the monitor screens, muttering to each other, or muttering notes into recorders.

Showing in several views on the various screens, two Hive swarms moved in very close proximity to each other, with some overlap between the two, the soldier swarm leading, the gorgons following. Neither of the swarms were formed into a sphere. Each was an amorphous mass.

It looked as if the soldiers were eating the gorgons.

Neither swarm appeared to be taking notice of the Attack Group.

Jose Maria advised the commodore, "These images are two years old. We are not seeing this in real time because we are keeping our distance and this is a passive scan."

The gorgons each swelled obscenely, and, slowly, pushed out a bluish-white gelatinous extrusion that curled back on itself until, when the extrusion was all out, it formed the shape of a pretzel.

The gorgon itself was left shriveled down to an empty sack with dead stalks of tentacles hanging on.

The gelatinous extruded loops coalesced into solid larval blobs. The white bodies developed short stubby leggish appendages, with a single large sucker orifice ringed and ringed with little teeth. The oriface clamped onto the empty gorgon sack that had produced it, and sucked it in, tentacles and all. The stubby teeth were visible through their translucent bodies, chewing.

This was the genesis of horror beyond horror.

"Gluies."

A hail came over the tight beam, "John, old son. You awake?"

Farragut took the com. "No, compadre. I'm having a nightmare. Are you *seeing* this?"

The gluies then turned on the soldiers, which had been eating them while they were in their gorgon form. The roles were reversed now. The gluies attached their orifices to the soldiers' hard bodies and sucked the soldiers' insides out.

Dallas' voice sounded on the com again: "And if that don't scare your balls inboard, you just aren't paying attention."

Farragut turned to Jose Maria. "Does this upset your theory of the Hive being a single coherent entity?"

"It is upsetting on a number of levels," said Jose Maria.

The gluies chewed the empty shells of the soldiers.

Farragut shook his head. Did not understand what he was seeing. "Gluies are *babies?*"

Augustus said, "It might be easy to assume gluies are larvae because they are white and repulsive and pushed out of a gorgon's ass. But they destroy the gorgons and feed on the soldiers."

Jose Maria added to that, "So between the gorgons and the soldiers, we have a net population loss, which does not qualify as reproduction."

Farragut tried again, "So gluies are parasites laid inside a gorgon host. Something that feeds on the Hive? Now there's a switch."

"Drawing from any Earthly reference is certainly tenuous and probably dangerous," Jose Maria warned.

Augustus, speaking like a machine, said, "More data is required."

"Gluies have been observed feeding in concert with both gorgons and soldiers, so I cannot abandon the assumption that gluies are Hive," said Jose Maria. "And there is nothing to eat in this area of space and much of the Hive. Even the human body will digest itself in starvation."

Gluies were the worst, the most feared form of the Hive. The doomsday version.

"We have few hard facts on gluies," said Jose Maria.

"We have one," said Augustus. A very hard fact, very hard to take. "No ship has ever survived contact with gluies."

The yellow sun of the Sagittarius Zero system grew visibly brighter and larger than anything else in the star field. Attack Group One had arrived.

The star system was choked with asteroids, which were assumed to be gorgon spheres.

"Why are they here?" Gypsy stared at all the images, baffled. "Shouldn't they be moving toward food?"

The Attack Group had stepped down from FTL, and approached the Planet Zero from orbital north, coming in perpendicular to the system's orbital plane.

The xenos had expected that the gorgon presence would be thinner up here than in the orbital plane, but this was not so. Gorgons haloed Planet Zero like globular clusters around a galactic hub.

Farragut asked Augustus to plug in to the ship's navigation system and guide the pilot in around the masses of aliens.

The Attack Group had penetrated twenty astronomical units into the Sagittarius Zero system when Augustus bolted straight up, yanked his cables from their connections at the base of his skull and said: "They know we're here."

Crickets chirped.

"Hive sign," Gypsy Dent reported.

Farragut got on the tight beam to his group: "Go FTL.

Exit star system. Use rendezvous coordinates nine. Execute *now*."

A sound like wet snow on a window.

Farragut looked up. "Now what is *that?*"

He turned to Tactical, but Tactical had gone dumb.

His XO stared as if into headlights. "Um."

Gypsy Dent never ummed.

"Gluies, sir," Gyspy said.

As the lights went out.

24

"FIRE ALL JETS. FIRE."

"Firing, aye."

Hydrogen-fueled fire blazed from *Merrimack*'s ports.

"Commander Dent, get another decoy craft organized to resonate the irresistible harmonic and lure the Hive away from the ship."

"Aye, sir."

Crew hastily prepped a new decoy craft as *Merrimack* spewed fire. Fired until the gluies shrouded the ship so thickly that the fire blew back in the barrels and the jets shut down.

The gluies would be oozing through the distortion field next.

"Deploy hull walkers."

Marines clothed in atmo suits and armed with scythes and flamethrowers poured out the topside air locks to take up positions on the hull.

The atmo suits, a glaring international orange, set them apart from the sickly bluish-white aliens that seeped through the distortion field.

The hull walkers had no luck with the scythes. The blades, sharp and smooth as they were, stuck in the gluies' gelatinous bodies. Even when the Yurg managed to slice off a piece of intruding gluie with a swift mighty stroke, the white lump fell to the hull and did not die. It lay there, waiting to be stepped in, corroding the hull.

The Marines fired up their handheld flamethrowers. Carried their fuel in two separate backpacks, one solid hydrogen, another for an oxidizer to make the hydrogen burn.

Gluies did not ignite. They melted, and not quickly. Gave off a lot of smoke. And they kept moving even after you burned a third of their body away. Melt off their feet, and they just kept moving in slow slug fashion.

"Burn off their mouths," Ranza ordered her team. "Try that."

Kerry Blue could not stand to look at those nubbly little teeth. Filled every gaping mouth she saw with fire.

The atmosphere was thin out here between hull and distortion field. Even so, it quickly filled with smoke, roiling thick.

Gluies plopped down from the distortion field to the hull. The hull became coated in gluish white. Left a Marine nowhere to stand. They disintegrated your atmo suit, burned your ankles, let the smoke inside your suit to sting your eyes. You had to clamp your teeth on your rebreather and remember to inhale only through your mouth and out your nose because gluies smelled like death.

When your suit was compromised, you had no choice but to burn out a path to the nearest air lock.

A wind across the hull signaled the first hull breach. The ship's atmosphere exhaled into the space between the distortion field and the hull.

Colonel Steele ordered the rest of his Marines to retreat inside the ship.

Lobbed a grenade out behind him. Paused in the air lock, waiting for the blast. Reopened the hatch to check for effect.

Gluies, peppered with frags, continued to advance.

Steele sealed the hatch.

The ship filling with smoke. The air scrubbers had ceased operating.

Farragut ordered all hands to atmospheric suits.

The order was relayed through the ship by shouts.

A runner came to the command deck to report that the decoy—the wild goose they called it—was partially prepped but that Augustus would not fuse it.

The runner turned, feeling the brush of someone behind him. Gave an involuntary yelp.

Augustus, in chemical light, looked monstrous. The new skin and bone made a slash of lightness across his haggard face behind the face shield of his atmospheric suit.

"What's holding up the fuse, Augustus?" Farragut asked.

"Your wild goose will never leave the flight deck. The moment you open the distortion field for launch, that boat will plow into a solid pack of gluies and stick there and resonate the irresistible harmonic right here."

"Even if I kill the gravity?"

"Won't make a bit of difference. The pressure on the distortion field is immense. The gluies are pushing in. The gluies will fill up any open space instantly, with or without gravity."

"Can something else get through the gluies? Torpedo? Star Sparrow?"

"No."

Farragut accepted the answer. If there were a decoy that could get through gluies, some other ship would have tried this before. And lived.

"Anyone see a way out of this?"

"Go to your God like a soldier," said Augustus.

"I'm not fixin' to roll to my rifle."

The odds of survival weren't long. They were nonexistent.

No ship ever survived gluies.

Augustus waited for some stupid sunshine from Farragut, some there's-always-a-first-time sort of happy dung.

But what Farragut said was, "If this be our Corindahlor, then let's do it right."

And he was giving orders: "Take the fire suppression system down in the sails and the wings and in the compartments abutting the hull. Any blaze high enough to kill a gluie will activate the fire suppressors, and I won't have *Mack* fighting for the other side.

"Close all hatches to ship's interior fuselage."

Closing the interior hatches in effect created a second hull within the hull.

"Another place to retreat?" Augustus asked as the shouted orders echoed through the corridors.

"No, it's a place for the xenos to figure out how to combat gluies. Tell the Sargasson we need to know what harmonic our insects are listening to, and we need it right now."

A runner delivered the message to the lab, where insects were wildly singing and caroming off the sides of their canisters. The Sargasson wallowed in its tank.

The xenos had been trying scans on the insects, painstakingly charting their physical changes down to the molecular level. But the gluie encasement had shut their equipment down. Without their computers, the xenos wallowed like the Sargasson in the dark, listening to gluies drip down from the distortion field and slap onto the hull.

"Commodore."

Farragut looked to where Gypsy was standing by the clearport on the command deck. A white gelatinous mass pressed against the port, like the underside of a slug.

Farragut addressed his deck crew, "Okay, shut down the command deck. Lock it up, gentlemen." Nothing was functioning anyway: tactical, com, fire control, targeting, nav were all down.

The crew secured their stations and took up H packs and flamethrowers to join a battle at a hull breach.

Farragut's hand grasped the shoulder of a shaky young specialist. Advised, "If you're fixin' to heave, you better do it before we get out there, son."

The specialist tore off his helmet and lunged for a waste port.

Wiped his mouth, replaced his helmet.

"You good?" Farragut asked.

Nodded. "I'm good, sir." Exited the command deck with the others. Gypsy secured the hatch after them.

Farragut led them up to the top deck where gorgons were penetrating the hull.

* * *

Some navvies had slapped together sets of mechanical bellows and were pumping them into the vent to clear the interior smoke out to the space between the hull and the distortion field. That sort of worked for a while, but the vents were now clogged with gluies.

"I got this one," said Cain Salvador. Reached up, stuck the nozzle of his flamethrower in the vent.

The blowback of flame sent Cain jumping back into Colonel Steele.

Farther up and down the corridor gluies oozed through the overhead, dropped to the deck. The chemical lamps were going out, or else they were covered by gluies. The Marines of Team Alpha had only the light of their own headlamps.

The light caught on an interior hatch. All eyes followed the light. Considered retreat.

Kerry Blue said, "I ain't dyin' in the dark. I'm gonna go burn shit."

Steele motioned the team to the left and right.

The Bull Mastiffs gave a woof and advanced to face the white death.

On the top deck, Augustus seized the back of Farragut's helmet, swiveled it to force him to look at the passive sensor on his atmo suit. The patch was vivid orange, creeping toward red.

Farragut roared: "Cease fire! Cease fire! Somebody's H pack is leaking! Atmo is almost four percent hydrogen. *Clear the deck!*"

He shepherded his crew down the hatches.

Let the patterner throw the leaking H pack up the hatch with a flash grenade. The hatch slammed shut before the fireball cannoned across the deck.

The defenders huddled under the hatches, listening for the blaze to die.

It died quickly. Farragut put his hand to the ladder to go back up.

"This way," said Augustus.

"I'm not ready to pull back this far."

"This is the quickest route to the port wing."

Farragut was about to ask why he wanted to get to the port wing. Then he became aware of a Morse clanging. He hadn't picked up on the pattern before through all the other din.

Heard it now. "What's it saying?"

"Engine Five's containment field is fluctuating."

Engine Five was affixed under the ship's port wing, inboard of the underwing flight deck.

"Mister Kittering is attempting to isolate the engine."

"Can we eject anything into this crush?"

"No. She won't be able to eject it. Best she can do is get the engine's containment field on the other side of the ship's distortion field before containment collapses."

The most stable functions on board a spaceship were its distortion fields and its engine containment fields. An engine containment field was just another distortion field with a magnetic component to keep the matter and antimatter separate from each other. The magnetic field in Engine Five had become unstable.

Farragut set out at a run through the dark interior of his ship. Knew the shortest route to anywhere.

"The Hive hasn't gone after an engine in a long time," he said, running.

The Hive learns. And the Hive had learned that breaching an engine's containment field destroys the swarm. Or, perhaps equally important to the Hive, breaching an engine destroys the food the swarm wanted to eat.

But these were gluies. The kamikazes of the Hive.

Farragut and Augustus came out of the ship's interior at the portside ramp tunnel. The wide space radiated heat. There must have been a hydrogen flash here, too. Melted globs of gluies without feet or mouths clung to the deck grates. But there were no human skeletons. Company and crew had managed to get clear before the flash. Underneath the deck grates, water sloshed.

Already, another rank of gluies oozed down from the hull onto the flight deck.

Farragut ran to the sound of the Morse clanging.

It came from inside the air lock to Engine Five's compartment.

The inner hatch was ajar. Farragut gave it a tug.

The signalman inside the air lock fell out of it, dropped his spanner. He had been messing up his signals now anyway. His hands shook. His lips were ashen blue. He stood up. "Commodore."

Chief Engineer Kit Kittering stayed inside the lock, swearing.

"Talk to me in English, Kit."

"They—they've—" Kit's hands moved jerkily.

Augustus said, "That hatch will not shut."

Kit huffed. "I can't get this hatch to shut to seal off the engine!" She came out of the lock, gave the hatch a push.

The hatch bounced back open at her.

The hinges and their pins showed heavy corrosion and warping. Gluies had been here.

Augustus seized the hatch, pulled up. The warped pieces groaned. Bent back toward neutral position.

Cracked.

Broken pieces fell through the deck grates.

Kit walked through the hatchway into the air lock. "So we're ground zero for the matter/antimatter annihilation." She leaned against the hatch to the engine compartment and curled up to die.

Augustus said, "This is probably preferable to getting eaten or burned alive."

Farragut turned and faced the advancing mass of gluies.

Kept his eyes open.

And saw gluies retreat like a foaming ocean wave from a beach.

The white mass pulled away, back to the breach by which the horde had entered the wing.

He could see through the jagged breach to the distortion field. Watched the mountainous crush of gluies lift away like a shroud from the distortion field and move away into space.

The gluies that were still inside the ship, bottled against the distortion field, tried to insinuate their way out.

The containment field around Engine Five stabilized.

The ship's lights went on.

The air systems breathed to life, sucked away the smoke and miasma of burned gluie from the compartments and corridors.

Disassociated globs of gluie remaining on the deck, without mouth or feet, dissolved through the deck grates.

Farragut called into the air lock. "Get out of there, Kit. I have things for you to do."

The gluie at Kerry Blue's toes melted. The one at her heels turned and slithered up the bulk and out the breach the way it came.

A touch at her waist made her jump. Then she saw it was Colonel Steele's hand. She slumped a little, laughing. Leaned against him. "Oh, my God."

Heard someone, somewhere, yelling: "Someone else is resonating the irresistible harmonic! *Someone got a decoy out!*"

"Bet it was *Gladiator*," said Carly.

"Bet it was *Rio*." Dak.

"Give me odds and I'll take the Meadow Muffins," said Darb.

All through the ship gluies pulled back, tried to get out. Crew dove out of their way and opened hatches for them.

Farragut's voice sounded on the loud com: "All hands, all hands, get yourself tethered down or into the interior of the ship behind an air lock. I'm fixin' to take down the distortion field to let this trash out."

He had returned to his command deck to find it intact. Without the crew inside it, the gluies had not deemed it worth the effort to breach. The specialists were returning to their stations.

"All decks, report. Are we clear to purge gluies?"

Waited for the decks to lock down, hook down, report in.

"Distortion field down in ten, nine, eight—"

Tactical was organizing the sensor signals into images that made sense to the human eye.

"Seven, six, five—"

The systems monitors read normal for all six engines.

"Four, three, two, one—"

The distortion field blinked out. The gluies trapped within it flew away as if propelled.

The air moaned through the hull breaches.

"Restore distortion field."

"Restoring field, aye."

The wind ceased to moan.

Hive sign had not stopped on board the ship.

Gypsy got on the loud com, "All hands. We have a clinger. Find it. Kill it."

The tactical screens presented images of gluies pouncing on a decoy vessel that was moving away from *Merrimack*.

"I hope to Jesus that's a decoy," said Farragut in a sudden horrid thought. Realized he didn't know what was under that mountain of death. All the Hive swarms within the Sagittarius Zero star system moved toward it. Gorgons, soldiers, gluies. Billions of Hive mouths.

"Where is my Group?"

And over the tight beam: "Farragut to Group. Call in."

Wolfhound called in. Mostly intact. They'd had gorgons.

Gladiator called in from the fifth planet. Reported heavy damage. They had taken on gorgons. Scraped some of them off in the dirt.

Horatius called in. Intact. Gorgons. *Horatius* had spent another boxcar of explosives.

Rio Grande called in. Chewed all to hell. Can openers. Fifty-five deaths that they knew of so far.

Windward Isles. The XO called in. Captain Fred was having her arm reattached and did anyone have any type AB negative blood. The gorgons ate theirs.

Sunlit Meadows called in. Hull damage. One death.

"How'd we rate gluie treatment?" Tactical muttered to navigation.

The Group converged on *Merrimack*'s position.

Rio looked a horror. The hull chewed with enormous gaping rents. You could see people inside on the decks.

But most horrifying to the Group was learning that *Merrimack* had gluies.

"Wouldn't have survived it without the interference," said Farragut. "Which one of y'all got the wild goose out?"

No one answered.

Tactical sounded off: "Commodore, bogeys. We have bogeys. A lot of them. Spaceships. Not ours. No IFF."

"The devil comes to collect his due," said Augustus.

They were small vessels, probably drones from their size. Their design elements were clearly human. Clearly PanGalactic.

On the Group's com a mechanical voice sounded. Familiar. Distorted. But Farragut had heard the voice before. It addressed Commodore Farragut by name. "You shall not resonate. You shall follow your escort. You shall not scan the limpets. Touching the limpets in any way whatsoever will destroy them, and my lord's protection will cease."

Specialists at their stations mouthed silently to each other, *"My lord?"*

"Farragut to Group. Follow *Merrimack*."

And *Merrimack* followed its drone escort on a course toward the fourth planet. The techs looked for the limpets they were not supposed to scan. Found them. Small objects hooked to the distortion field. They had to be resonating the Hive harmonic.

"We need us one of those."

"As soon as we figure out how to scan it without losing *his lordship*'s protection."

Merrimack's fabrication plant was already powered up and at work constructing patches for the hull and the decks. The ship was down to three flight decks, the fourth eaten away. And it looked like *Rio* was going to need a lot of help.

Telltales kept flying through the ship, chittering and crawling. The ants would not go to earth. The Zakan moths fluttered. *Merrimack* received reports—the situation was the same on the other ships. Hive sign without Hive on board.

Jose Maria postulated, "Perhaps there are no Hive elements on board. Perhaps the protection of the limpets causes the panic."

"That's real probable, Jose Maria, but I want this ship searched millimeter by millimeter."

Gypsy acknowledged that.

Farragut said, "I'm going down decks to light a fire under

those xenos. Augustus, you're thinking real loud. Come with me."

En route to the xeno lab, Augustus said, "We passed through another tachyon clicker on approach to the solar system."

Farragut frowned. Tachyon clicker. That was a covert message between patterners.

"Your white tiger didn't tell you?" said Augustus.

"She's not my white tiger," said Farragut. "And no, she didn't. Is this another signal from Septimus?"

"No. This signal originates from the fourth planet of this system. The clicks have the signature code of Secundus."

Secundus. The second patterner ever created.

Secundus had been the patterner Caesar Daisius sent to Thaleia to rein in Constantine sixty-one years ago. Secundus was believed killed in the same blast that killed Constantine.

Apparently, that belief was mistaken if Secundus was out here in the Deep, sending tachyon clickers from Constantine's world.

"Secundus joined the other side," Farragut concluded.

"He did. Not by his own will. This clicker is a repeating warning. A recording transmitted over and over on automatic. It's directional—streaming toward Palatine. It warns any other patterner not to tap into any of Constantine's systems. Secundus says he was infected by a Trojan Horse program which caused him to serve Constantine. He states it in a way that could get around his programming."

"Are you sure this message is genuine? It would be jolly convenient for Constantine if my patterner is afraid to access Constantine's data."

"Crossed my mind. This is real."

"Does this mean we have an ally on Planet Zero?"

"Secundus is dead. Only the warning survives."

Farragut turned in the corridor to face him. "You sure this time? Did Secundus' last message say 'I'm dead?'"

"Patterners have limited life spans. Secundus died a long time ago. And no, we don't come back for a third time. The second time is final."

Farragut remembered Septimus. That patterner's second death had been brain death.

"How limited a life span? When does your warranty expire?"

"Last year," said Augustus.

The fourth planet of the Sagittarius Zero system appeared on the ships' monitors. White clouds scattered over oceans of blue. The land masses showed part barren brown, part green with vegetation.

In addition to the glut of PanGalactic sentinels circling the planet, there was a spaceship in orbit.

Roman.

Farragut was about to hail *Gladiator* to ask Numa Pompeii if he could identify the ship.

Then saw that he did not need to ask a Roman. Jose Maria had turned white, rigid. Stared in unmistakable recognition. Nostrils flared. A quiver started under his chin. His dark eyes held a coal fire burn.

"Jose Maria?"

Jose Maria's voice came out a vibrating rasp: "That is *Sulla*."

25

THE UNKNOWN MACHINE voice on the com addressed Farragut again. This time with a vid to go with it. The image of a man, cabled like a patterner, his expression vacant, gray eyes dull. His voice was flat, mechanical, but still familiar. He invited the ships which were able to land to do so in the protected zone. He invited all ships' personnel to the surface. Said that his lord Constantine would grant Commodore Farragut an audience.

Commander Gypsy Dent saw recognition all around her on the command deck. She had never met the man, but she had seen his picture once. "Is that Sebastian Gray?"

The late Sebastian Gray had been XO of the *Merrimack* in between the service of Calli Carmel and Gypsy Dent.

Farragut answered, his mouth dry, "Looks like."

The patterner who looked and sounded like Sebastian Gray said, "You have seen the power of my lord's invention."

Farragut muted the audio and clicked off the vid. "He's saying Constantine invented the Hive." He looked to Augustus for comment.

"Bullshit," said Augustus.

"I appreciate a concise report. Jose Maria?"

Jose Maria, looking fragile, said, "I concur with Augustus."

Farragut clicked audio and visual back on. "What does your lord want?"

"My lord needs nothing from you. My lord invites you to land your ships and be restored. You have a patterner on board. I would like to interface with him."

Farragut muted the com again, shut off the vid in surprise. Looked to Augustus.

"Of course he would," said Augustus.

"How does he know you're here?"

"Does he?" said Augustus.

Farragut clicked the link back on, spoke, noncommittally, "I have a patterner?"

"His name is Augustus," said Sebastian Gray.

Constantine had more intelligence of the Attack Group than the Group had of him. Farragut did not want to say anything else. "Mister Gray, thank your lord for us. Farragut out." Clicked off. "Damn."

Augustus said, "Right neighborly for a man who claims to have created the Hive; displaced gorgons to Thaleia; and cabled up a patterner. I take it Sebastian Gray *does* meet the primary prerequisite for becoming a patterner?"

"Yeah," said Farragut. Sebastian Gray was dead. "Jose Maria, are you all right?"

Jose Maria was breathing into his hands. Shook his head, no.

Gypsy said, "You're not going down are you, sir?"

"At some point I'll have to. Someone who has his secretary refer to him as my lord will only talk to the top guy. And that's why we're here. I could use you, Augustus."

"So could Constantine. He wants me. He needs a patterner."

"He has one. Are you sure that wasn't Bast instead of Secundus warning you on the tachyon clicker?"

"The clicker has Secundus' signature pattern. That kluged together Sebastian Gray thing is nothing. Constantine just trotted that out because he doesn't want to look like he needs a patterner."

Jose Maria said, "If Constantine has done that to your man, young Commodore, what has he done to the people on *Sulla*?"

Augustus answered that one. "Don't worry, *Don* Cordillera. And I mean this benignly, your wife is dead. He wants me. His patterner Secundus is dead. Constantine needs another patterner. I won't be taken. I would be more secure on my own vessel. Permission to launch Striker."

Steele reinterpreted Augustus' request, "Commodore, he's going down to the planet to join *his lord*."

Farragut spoke to his patterner, "Augustus, go."

In a short time, the little red-and-black Striker launched. And immediately moved toward the planet.

Steele did not speak. Grinding teeth, muscles bulging at his jaw, his glower all shouted silently *I told you so*.

"There he goes," said Gypsy. "Never would have guessed Augustus to be a traitor to the Empire."

Tactical reported, "Sir! The Striker isn't moving under its own power. It's being dragged. That's a hook."

Farragut moved to the tactical station to see the readouts. "Here's the distortion hook. Here's the Striker's output. The Striker's force is working in the opposite direction. Augustus is trying to get away. Constantine is dragging him toward the planet."

Steele blurted, "Why doesn't the Roman cyborg shoot his way free!"

Tactical said, "Why don't *we* shoot him free?"

"We can't afford to shoot," said Farragut. "We could hit Constantine. Or piss him off enough to feed us back to the Hive."

The Striker continued slowly toward the atmosphere. The readings from its engines' output indicated the engines were red lined.

Farragut sent: "Augustus, stand by to shut down engines. We're going to hook you."

It was a command you could only give to a patterner. The engine shutdown needed to be precise. A millisecond too soon, Constantine would reel the Striker to the ground. Too late and the Striker's maxed engines would be bottled, their energy turned inward, and Augustus boiled away.

"Standing by," Augustus answered, laconic.

"Hook him!"

"Deploy hook, aye."

Merrimack threw out an energy field—like a fist closing round Constantine's energy fist closed around the Striker—as Augustus cut engines.

Much slower now, the Striker still moved toward the atmosphere.

"We did tug-of-war with a black hole," Tactical cried against his readouts. "How can we be losing against this guy?"

Someone murmured, "This guy controls everything."

"I don't ever want to hear that," said Farragut.

Gypsy said, "Constantine has the better grip. He has a seamless hold on the Striker. Our distortion hook has a gap in it where it fits around Constantine's hook."

"Then let's close our grip," said John Farragut. "Extend our hook down to the planet to enclose his hook's generator. We'll pull the whole installation right out of the ground."

Smiles broke out on the command deck at the scale of the operation. The smiles faded as it became clear that Commodore Farragut wasn't the only one thinking huge.

Tactical reported reluctantly, "Commodore. Constantine's distortion hook is anchored halfway to the planet's core. If we tug, we'll just move the planet."

Farragut had not expected to be outflanked. And hadn't expected that Augustus wouldn't come up with a better idea.

Augustus' voice sounded on the com: "You must know I have a mandate to self-destruct before allowing myself to fall into enemy hands."

A new voice sounded on the com. John Farragut had never heard it before but could guess immediately who was speaking. "Augustus, I am not your enemy."

Augustus' voice went on: "Self-destruct sequence loaded. Engaged. Ten. Nine."

Farragut shouted, "Augustus, I override your mandate!"

"Six. Five."

The voice of Constantine cajoled, "Give me a moment to reason with—" at the same time that Farragut shouted, "Augustus, abort self-destruct!"

"Three. Two. Hail Caesar."

Farragut looked to Gypsy who instantly ordered, "Drop hook!"

Constantine did not drop his hook. The blaze of bottled fire traveled down the hook to the ground installation that erupted in the shock wave from the Striker exploding within its distortion field.

When the second hook vanished, the glowing debris expanded in a glittering sphere before going completely black.

Farragut stared at the darkening screen from within a numb shield of disbelief. The mind threw up a wall against it. Wasn't real.

Watched in a strange detachment. It was all just something viewed on a screen.

"Tactical," Farragut said. "Current status of the Hive."

"Unchanged, sir."

Farragut hoped Constantine wanted something more from the Attack Group than Augustus.

"Elaborately staged," Constantine's voice came over the com, humor in it. "I suppose the patterner set that one up."

Farragut had only thought he was numb. Sudden fury poured out before he even knew he had it. "You bastard son of a bitch, you killed my officer!"

Constantine's reply sounded less certain. "I had no intention of harming you. If you were listening to his transmissions, then you know that man killed himself. Please note that it was you who acted with hostility, even after I saved you from my legions."

Farragut shouted, "You shipjacked my Striker!"

"Do not shout at me. Do you know who you are talking to?"

"I'm taking a guess here that I'm talking at Constantine Siculus."

"This is my world. You came to me. Land your ships. I will repair them all. My automatons will fabricate anything you want."

"Land where?" Farragut demanded, curt.

Gypsy had words bulging out her eyes, but she would not cross the commodore on his command deck.

"Anywhere in the green zones. Follow my signal to my palace. Bring *Don* Cordillera."

Farragut clicked off. "Now how in blazes does he know about Jose Maria?"

Gypsy said, "Sir, we *aren't* putting down?"

"We are no safer in orbit than on the ground. In fact, the closer to Constantine's palace, the safer. Take him up on his invitation to park some heavy artillery in his backyard. Send *Wolfhound* and *Horatius* down. TR, take the Wing down in their Swifts. The Battery goes down with *Wolfhound*. Set up a field camp. Cozy it right up next to the source of Constantine's transmission. I don't have to tell you this is hostile territory. Secure the perimeter, get a dome up, secure the ground. Accept *nothing* from Constantine. No gifts, no food, no technical assistance. Take *nothing* inside the perimeter. Herius Asinius will report to Colonel Steele on the ground."

He paused to ask Gypsy, "Do we have jammers on?"

"Yes, sir."

Jammers prevented displacement into the ship.

"Does Constantine?"

In a moment, Gypsy answered, "Yes, sir. He does."

Nothing would be displacing either way.

"Don't drop jammers for anything."

Well staged.

Farragut could not believe how angry that remark made him. And the assumption was true, actually. That fiasco had been staged, but not by John Farragut.

Augustus should have been able to get out of that tug-of-war. Should have known how never to get in it.

How many times had Augustus expressed the willingness to die? Even under orders not to commit suicide, he had found a way to get the job done anyway. An honorable excuse. He had to self-destruct so as not to fall into enemy hands.

Damn him.

Farragut felt weirdly directionless. Lost. With Augustus you always knew where you stood. When you lost your up, your down, your horizon, Augustus was there to slam you to the deck and show you *down*.

An indispensable thorn in his side, painful for its absence.

And Jose Maria, his moral compass, had been taken out,

too. The sight of *Sulla* had knocked Jose Maria's world sideways.

Farragut found himself at Augustus' torpedo rack room six. Looked for him here. Something of him. Augustus had not taken his things back to his Striker. As if he had meant to come back here. The carpets were still down, the Roman canopy still up. The tapestries hung from the torpedoes. A cushion, fitted into one torpedo rack, made his bed. The headless Winged Victory marble still loomed over the torpedoes.

Augustus was really gone.

Ad patres.

Farragut did not understand. It was pointless. Unnecessary.

Augustus could have predicted that would happen. That Constantine would hook his Striker. Had he manipulated Farragut and Constantine into sending him into a situation in which he could get himself killed?

Surrounded by Hive, living at the mercy of the enemy, Farragut could not hold a service for Augustus right now, which was just as well because Farragut was the only man in the Group who could stand him, and he was so mad at Augustus he would just tell him to go to hell.

When he came out of the rack room, Gypsy was there in the corridor. She saw his face. "You *can't* be crying for him."

"You're right, Gypsy. You're right. So I don't know what this is." He roughly dried his face with his palm heels. "I am just so almighty *pissed*, GOD BLESS AMERICA!" He shouted back through the hatchway into the rack room.

"Find anything in there, sir?" Gypsy peered through the hatch.

"I wasn't really looking. I was blessing him from here to Gehenna. I have been played. I trusted him."

"That may not have been real smart, sir," Gypsy said gently.

"He was always honest with me. I *thought*. How can you mistrust someone who calls you an idiot to your face? I am so angry with him for not being what I thought he was."

Gyspy listened, lending a sad, calm strength. "What was that, sir."

"Defender of Rome. I thought I could count on him to be that."

Farragut's anger was always fleeting. This anger lodged in his heart and stayed. He turned around and went back into Augustus' compartment. He had more things to call him.

26

A WEEK HAD PASSED since Attack Group One arrived at Sagittarius Zero. The Group ships had assumed a wider orbit around the fourth planet than the ghost ship *Sulla*.

Sulla sent no signals other than its running lights. Jose Maria de Cordillera watched the ship drift underneath *Merrimack* every time around.

Rio still looked hellish. The erks were using *Windward Isles* and *Sunlit Meadows* as platforms to effect repairs on it.

PanGalactic ships moved in to offer assistance. Were told to move away.

The Marines and Dracs had established a field camp on the ground.

Time was coming for Commodore Farragut to face the god of Sagittarius Zero.

First, Farragut took a skiff from *Merrimack* to *Gladiator*.

A giant scarab cricket swooped down on his head as he disembarked on *Gladiator*'s dock. Farragut ducked. "Ho! Numa! Call off your bug!"

Numa Pompeii apologized with a deep chuckle. "We still have a Hive presence, but we can't find it. We're starting to think Constantine's limpets are provoking our crickets."

"Yeah, that's our thought, too," said Farragut, brushing his hair back into place with his hand.

There was a Roman shuttle in the dock. Herius Asinius had come up from the field base to listen in on what the merc had to say about Constantine Siculus.

Amadea had changed her appearance. Still had the beard. A very fine gold chain threaded through it now to make it gleam. Her eyes were now as gold as her hair.

The voice was an old woman's.

"Constantine craves respect and recognition of the powerful," Amadea told the commanders. "If he doesn't get it, he tends to kill them."

She paused, because Farragut and Numa were talking behind their hands.

"Is that what became of Caesar Magnus?" Farragut whispered to Numa Pompeii. "Magnus failed to respect or recognize Constantine?"

Numa shook his head, muttered back, "Magnus never knew Constantine. Caesar Daisius put the hit on Constantine."

Amadea continued, "He thinks he's a great hunter. He isn't. Don't bother lying to him. He'll think you're lying, no matter what you tell him. He cheats at everything. He's not a good chess player. He needs to clear off most of the board before he moves in for checkmate."

"So he's bad with too many variables," Numa said.

"How does he play baseball?" said Farragut.

"He doesn't."

"Football?" said Herius Asinius.

"No. Neither kind. He considers them thuggish."

Thuggish. From a mass murderer who hunts human beings for fun.

"How did you get him to surrender to you in the game?" said Herius Asinius.

"Gun barrel pressed between the eyes," said Amadea. "That usually does it."

Merc talk. Farragut hated it.

"What does he want?" said Farragut. "We know he wanted Augustus. Now that Augustus is dead, why are we still alive?"

"He will want all the technological developments of the last sixty years. And he is thinking that Augustus' death was a show. Was it a show?"

Farragut stared back at her, said harshly, "What is wrong with you?"

Amadea continued, "He may want your ships."

"For what? An invasion?"

"He sees himself as Caesar. All he's missing is the empire. I think Thaleia was meant to get a last minute rescue like we got here. You weren't supposed to win at Thaleia. I think Thaleia was meant to see the Second Coming of Constantine."

Farragut and Numa looked at each other. Farragut lifted his eyebrows. Numa gave a facial shrug.

"I think it was a bad idea to put troops on the ground. Constantine will try to buy your men. And he *will* buy them."

"My men are not for sale," said Farragut. "And Rome has its pride." He exchanged glances with Herius Asinius.

"You have no idea what Constantine can offer," said the white tiger.

"We know you're for sure for sale. That's why you're not going down. How does Constantine know my name? How did he know I had a patterner? How does he know Jose Maria de Cordillera is with us?"

"Moles," said Amadea. "You have them. Romans always use them. Constantine is Roman."

"Are you one?"

"I am Roman."

"Are you a mole?"

"I am working for Caesar Romulus. Put a lie detector on me. Are you going down to meet with Constantine?"

"In time."

"I'm coming with you."

Farragut did not bother to tell her again that she was not setting foot on the planet. As he joined the skiff to return to *Merrimack*, he told Numa Pompeii, "Take the tiger up on that lie detector. Find out who she's really working for."

Caught the edge of a brooding scowl from Herius Asinius, who offered no comment. Herius shared little with anyone except his cousin.

Farragut's demand had made Herius Asinius remember a furtive girl with ash brown hair and matching ash brown eyes—no beard—who clutched a landing disk to her chest back on Thaleia.

Jose Maria de Cordillera did not respond to the tapping at the hatch to his compartment.

The hatch opened.

Jose Maria was kneeling, his back to the hatch, his feet crossed beneath him, backs of his hands resting on his thighs, thumb and middle finger touching. He held his back straight, shoulders wide. His long black hair was held back in its silver clasp. He presented an artistic Zen figure. Still. But there was a terrible tension in the stillness.

"I'm sorry to interrupt your meditation," said John Farragut in the hatch.

The silver clasp moved side to side, no. "There is no interruption. Nothing to apologize for." Jose Maria rose to his feet in a fluid motion. Faced Farragut with red-rimmed eyes. "This man is evil."

"We knew that."

"It is a fraud. I recognize it as such. That ship cannot be *Sulla*. So why do I react with anger when an evil, deceitful man tries to deceive me?"

"I'm just fixin' to take the bastard out as soon as we get his secret."

"Amen."

"Of course that plan is complicated by the possibility that Constantine has the same plan for us."

Jose Maria's voice trembled, "How dare he use the *Sulla?*"

Farragut signaled the command deck. "Get a hold of Sebastian Gray. See if his Supreme Self will grant me that audience now."

Under Constantine's sun, insects flapped and chirped in crazed chaos. Friendly resonance was not friendly. The Hive was here. And while the bugs were a big pain in the face, they were helpful reminders that territory just didn't get any more hostile than this.

Wolfhound and *Horatius* had set down a scant one klick from Constantine's palace. There was a low hill between the camp and the palace, so you couldn't see it. Still, Constantine was real close. Behind the camp, another half klick in the opposite direction from the palace, stretched an open sea.

No one challenged Colonel Steele's choice of sites, so the Marines and the Dracs constructed their field camp here, threw up their energy dome, and placed the big guns, ready to fire in any direction.

The line in between the U.S. side of camp and the Roman side of camp was even hotter than the force field perimeter that divided all of them from Constantine's world.

Inside the Roman half of the camp, the Legion carrier had detached and put down four boxcars in a square, forming a makeshift legionary fortress. It blocked the view from the U.S. side.

Outside the perimeter, even closer than the palace, just across the river from the Roman side of camp, PanGalactic automatons were building, busy as ants and as fast. They threw up structure after structure. Marines paused between watches to see what was going up now.

The automatons were building just about everything except guns and defenses. There was already an amusement park. Several bars for different tastes. A pool room. An elaborate swimming pool with swim up bar. A whorehouse. A stable with pretty horses and a riding trail. A golf course. A casino. And several pedestrian boulevards lined with buildings that looked like shops.

A shuttle had come down from *Merrimack*. Brought Farragut and the beautiful Jose Maria de Cordillera. They had gone outside the perimeter. Steele was really torqued that Farragut would not take a Marine guard with him.

Kerry Blue heard Farragut tell Steele before he left, "Constantine already has us captive. I go unarmed. He'll either take it as sign of trust or a sign of my recognition of his superiority. And, TR, I want you to remind everyone: no one kills Constantine."

Kerry was outside the perimeter with Cole Darby, setting up listening devices meant to pick up sounds and filter out everything but the voices. Problem was nobody out here was talking. A lot of smiling people over there across the river in their fantasy town and not one of them chattering, which was okay because what the Marines really wanted to pick up was Constantine in the palace.

But Constantine and his patterner Sebastian Gray weren't talking either.

And just what was Constantine supposed to say? "As you know, Sebastian, the resonant code I use to control the gorgons is doo dah day." Yeah, that would be great if he said that.

Kerry struggled with the spindly array, snarling.

A robot approached. Kerry and Darb drew weapons. The automaton recognized the gesture, the weapons. Halted. A human voice came out of the machine: "May I assist?"

"No. Move it out, bolt-hole."

The robot apparently understood slang. Inclined its body in a mechanical bow and glided away.

Darb and Kerry got the array set up. "They can try this thing out on Commodore Farragut and *Don* Cordillera. You just know Farragut's gonna be talking."

Batting insects away from their faces, Kerry Blue and Cole Darby requested reentry through the perimeter.

Entry required two checks of identity. One by a human guard, and a confirmation by a handheld identification device. Kerry got a green from the handheld, but the Yurg challenged her:

"How do I know that's really you, Blue?"

Kerry, hot, uncomfortable, impatient, snapped open her jumpsuit, pulled down the top, and tied the sleeves around her waist. She shook down her sweaty hair on her bare shoulders. Glared at Yurg from under sweaty brows.

"Uh, yeah, those look like Blue." Yurg let her in.

But he barred Darb.

Cole Darby shrugged out of his jumpsuit, tied the sleeves around his waist. Did not have the same effect.

"Pleased to say that doesn't help me, my man."

The Yurg did a full scan on Cole Darby before letting him inside the perimeter.

Kerry dragged her sweaty arms back into her sticky sleeves, looked over at the Roman camp. The Dracs had a soccer field staked out and were kicking a ball around.

A voice carried across the camp from the other direction: "Blue! You brought that uffing weed down here!"

Kerry snapped up her jumpsuit, and trotted over quick time to see what she'd done this time.

Found TR Steele, fists on his flanks, his glare fixed on something on the ground. Kerry followed the blue dagger gaze down to a clump of green leaves.

Froggy toes and big eyes peeked out from under the foliage.

A lizard plant.

Kerry owned a lizard plant. Native of the planet Arra in the Myriad.

"That's not mine," said Kerry. She crouched down with her arms outstretched. "C'mere, boogs."

The lizard plant did not reach for her, cooing. This one turned leafy tail and ran for the nearest tree. As there were no trees, it scampered up Colonel Steele and took refuge atop his buzz cut head, one webby foot just above one glaring ice blue eye.

"Looks good on you, sir," said Kerry, standing back up. She grinned at him. Saw through his snarl now. Tried not to laugh at him, but he looked really sweet. She suggested brightly, "I could bring my lizard plant down from the *Mack*. Yours and mine could get together for some wild weed lovin.'"

Steele turned utterly scarlet. Bellowed, "*They will not!*"

The lizard plant snugged down on Steele's head.

Kerry nodded up. "Where'd you get him, sir?"

Commodore John Farragut and Jose Maria de Cordillera walked to the palace slowly, observing the land. The ground was a different color on the hillock than in the camp, yellower here. The trees on the rise were Earth trees, willow, cypress, tamarisk, sumac, the weeds goldenrod and thistle.

Then the flora changed again as they neared the palace. Iron-red earth, with spongy blue, green, and yellow bushes that looked like coral formations.

The palace was like no other building in the world, though there were few enough buildings on the entire planet. Most of those were factories.

The palace was unique. Nothing PanGalactic about it, with its soaring marble pillars, high clerestories, wide graceful stone steps curving up the rise. It was tall, but not so grandiose as something Roman.

Farragut and Jose Maria mounted the wide, wide steps. Guards in Roman regalia did not challenge them.

Open graceful arches led from a wide terrace into a great hall.

Farragut dropped to one knee, hand to the jewel-encrusted floor.

"Are you well, young Commodore?"

Farragut was speechless. Ran his palm over the mosaic of gemstones—precious emerald, ruby, and sapphire, semiprecious opal, zircon, lapis, tourmaline, garnet, topaz—the whole jewel box, all lined in lead.

Without rising, Farragut abruptly turned his eyes up. And there it was, the mural on the ceiling, white gaps in the picture where earthquakes had taken out pieces. The marble columns showed cracks.

And the floor. The floor. Farragut got to his feet, looked for it. Found it.

A U.S. landing disk embedded in the gemstone floor.

He met Jose Maria's concerned gaze, astonished.

Grand interior doors groaned in parting, robes rustled, whispering against the gemstones. A leonine figure swept in, crowned in a golden laurel wreath. He stood before the throne, arrayed in gold and red, and looking half his 120 years. Constantine Siculus, grand as Caesar.

Announced in booming voice, "Commodore Farragut. *Welcome to Arra.*"

Farragut brushed the dust from his hand. He had not recognized the palace from the outside. He had only ever been inside.

In the star cluster known as the Myriad, Farragut had displaced landing disks down to the Archon Donner's throne room. One errant landing disk had come in too low, displaced itself into the floor. And there it was.

At the time that *Merrimack* departed Arra, a radiation storm was approaching and a LEN evacuation of the planet was underway.

Here Constantine claimed to have moved the whole planet Arra almost a thousand light-years across the galaxy, and set it in orbit around a new sun with a survivable rotation deep in Hive space.

Constantine seated himself on Donner's throne. His lion's mane of hair and beard were coppery gold and Zeusly. His forearms were encased in truly gaudy golden gauntlets decorated with gemstones and colored lights. Behind his crowned head rose Donner's monumental black plaque engraved with alien script.

Sebastian Gray entered quietly, cabled, plugged in and vacant-eyed as a patterner. He took up a post at Constantine's flank, exactly as Farragut had seen Augustus stand by Caesar Magnus.

Constantine took pleasure in Farragut's amazement. Terribly casually he said, "You know Sebastian Gray."

"I did," said Farragut. And to Gray, "I got that keettrig out of the attic for your widow."

Gray gave no reaction.

"It is difficult to talk to a patterner when they are connected. But you know that. Is your patterner truly dead?"

Farragut's eyes flared, burned; mouth pulled into a wolfish set of teeth, jaw tight, breath deep and furious. Fought down an eruption of words.

Constantine *caused* Augustus' death. What kind of idiot question was that: *Is your patterner truly dead?*

Constantine pushed on, "But where is the Triumphalis?" Farragut heard irony in it. Sensed rivalry.

General Numa Pompeii was a Triumphalis, crowned, robed, and imperial. Constantine was not except by his own decree.

"Upstairs," said Farragut.

"Your *Rio Grande* wants repair, and I have constructed a cradle for *Merrimack*. Bring your ships down."

Farragut shook his head. "Mighty neighborly, but my birds are better off flying."

"Do not resonate," Constantine warned. "And do not try to analyze the limpets."

Constantine's eyes were now on Jose Maria de Cordillera. Waiting for a question.

Constantine had left *Sulla* in orbit to be seen. And he knew who Jose Maria was. A learned man. A Nobel Laureate. Widower of a passenger on board the long-missing *Sulla*.

Everyone knew that *Sulla* was the first victim of the Hive, though *Sulla* had never been found. Till now.

Jose Maria refused to play this game. Stayed silent, dignified, contained.

Farragut asked, "Constantine, what do you want?"

"I want nothing. I do anything. I move worlds to suit my purpose. Where was the might of Rome when Telecore was dying?"

Got a flinch out of Jose Maria with that one. His wife had helped terraform Telecore.

"*I* am the might of Rome," said Constantine. "I conquer death. Is that not what gods do?"

Farragut felt the muscles of his face move into a peculiar set. He inhaled, did not speak. Thought loudly: *Are you mad?*

Constantine answered the stare, "I have seen that look before."

"Bet you have," said Farragut.

The camp's energy screen opened to receive Farragut and Jose Maria back inside.

"I don't ever want that opened without verification," said Farragut, walking in.

The Yurg started after him, uncertain, "Uh, sir? Is this a test?"

Farragut stopped. "What do you think?"

"Can I scan you, sir?"

"You had better, son."

Scanned and verified, Commodore Farragut met up with his Marine CO, Colonel Steele, who had a plant on his head.

"That's an interesting look for you, TR."

Webbed feet held on to the gunsights fixed on either side of Steele's eyes.

"It's not Flight Sergeant Blue's, sir," said Steele. "It lives here."

"Significance?" Jose Maria asked Farragut, his voice unnaturally soft.

"That lizard's an Arran life-form," Farragut explained. "The Archon Donner had a shelf full of them in his palace."

"Convergent evolution?" Jose Maria speculated.

"It's not a verge," said Flight Sergeant Kerry Blue. "That's the real thing. I have one just like it."

Steele pried the plant off his head. "You don't seem surprised, Commodore."

"Already had that shock, TR."

Steele looked troubled, daunted. Asked, "Is this Arra?"

Farragut shook his head. "I don't know. We're a long way from the Myriad."

Moving worlds. That was a big one to swallow.

"Air pressure's wrong. Show me around the camp."

Steele and Farragut started out along a pond, which was wholly contained within the perimeter. Jose Maria, isolated within himself, walked a few steps behind. Remote, distressed, he took only half notice of their alien surroundings.

In the pond a train of baby fluff balls, gold and brown and cute as ducklings, paddled with tiny webbed feet after a grotesque adult. The Marines called the adults skaterays, or mudskates, or bubblebacks, or wartrays, or flying uglies. The adults were shaped like a skate or a ray, but warty and toad-skinned, blotched a gray-brown sort of green, with tufts of warthoggish hair bristling from their warts. And the warts *pulsed*. Fully grown, they were a yard long with broad wings and a lizard tail. The tiny baby feet must be temporary.

The trees around the pond were breathing. Stout, rubbery growths—also warty—but prune textured. The warts opened to inhale. The tree exhaled out a central stack in its very wide trunk. The branches, gnarled as an ancient oak's, spread wide, with black-green rags for leaves.

Farragut, Jose Maria, and Steele walked along the perimeter. Farragut asked about the detection arrays. There was nothing to report from those.

Farragut entered a text message into his com and showed it to Steele.

Be careful what you say outside of the ships. Constantine is listening to us, too.

"Yes, sir," said Steele. Then, "What's he like?"

Farragut changed the text. Showed Steele:
Barking mad.

They walked on. Came to a trench. Farragut looked across it to the Roman side of the camp. Looked around him for someone playing a joke, but no one was laughing.

"What," Farragut began, not even sure what to say, "is *this*?"

Herius Asinius answered from across the trench. "It's a trench, Commodore. Traditional in a Roman encampment."

"Not down the middle of *your own camp*."

He glowered at Steele for explanation.

"This is new, sir," said Steele. Then, "I should have known about this."

The trench ran the entire width of the camp, dividing the U.S. from the Roman side.

Farragut said, very, very softly, "Fill it in."

And stood at the edge of the trench, and waited.

This was not Have-this-filled-in-by-sundown. Or Fill-it-in-when-it-fits-your-schedule. This was the commodore is waiting for the damned thing to disappear right now.

Equipment appeared. Men and machinery could not have moved faster had they been under gluie attack and making this trench as if it had never existed was the only thing that could save them.

Farragut walked across level ground to the Roman side.

He paused at the far end to observe the new town across the river. A Roman passed him field glasses for a better look.

"Is that a baseball diamond?" said Farragut.

"Yes, *Domni*," said the Roman. "New today."

It even had lights for a night game. "That's really low," said Farragut. Turned around to finish his walkabout.

He had come full circle with Jose Maria and Steele. They were back to the pond with the breathing trees.

In the water, a mud-colored adult skateray chased a fluffy baby with murderous intent, flapping and hissing. The fluff ball keened piteously and paddled frantically with tiny feet in a tight, tight circle, too tight for the adult to turn and line up a bite. A clutch of other babies milled together nearby, cheeping.

A sudden sploosh made the officers look.

Kerry Blue at the water's edge. She had thrown a rock.

Steele thundered, "Blue! What are you doing!"

"It's an orphan! It just wants a mama!" Then "Sorry, sir. Tryin' to help, sir."

Jose Maria noted the scene. The players. An adult with its own brood. An orphan child trying to join the family.

Jose Maria explained to Kerry, "An orphan is competition for that creature's own young. This one has lost its mother. This is survival of the strongest. It is natural selection."

Farragut, also watching the little drama, declared, "*I* am natural. No less than the trees and the stars, I have a right to be here. And *I* select the fuzzy thing. Flight Sergeant Blue, go rescue your . . . thing."

John Farragut despised a bully.

Kerry Blue splashed into the pond. The water came up to her waist. She scooped the keening orphan into her hands, kneed the brute adult in the chin, and trudged ashore. The adult hissed, incensed, flapping its flaps against the water.

Kerry climbed out of the water with a bright smile that left Steele dizzy. Kerry Blue, her clothes clinging to her body, face beaming, hands cuddling something helpless. Steele turned to stone.

Kerry gushed, laughing. "Thank you, sir."

"My pleasure, Flight Sergeant," said Farragut. Because she had charmed a smile out of Jose Maria.

Jose Maria had not said a word about *Sulla*. Had not asked Constantine about survivors. He knew he was being baited. Filled him with a storm of grief and outrage.

A young woman's tender heart under that Marine uniform made him smile.

He warned Kerry gently, "You realize that will grow up into *that*."

He pointed at another adult, this one in full view on the land, humping across the short scrub grass, its flapping body undulating up and down. At the pond bank it launched itself into the air, glided low over the water and landed in a breathing tree, there to drape itself over a low branch to hang like Dak's socks over the water.

"Don't care," said Kerry. She named the baby Barnacle Bob.

"He's not coming with us," Steele commanded, scowling his worst who-let-girls-into-the-Fleet-Marine scowl.

And could not believe he called the thing *he*. The woman made him crazy.

"Aye, sir," said Kerry. "*Don* Cordillera, what do these eat?"

Jose Maria nodded at the other babies in the pond. "Well, the algae look appetizing."

Kerry skimmed a heaping handful of pond scum off the water, and set the green mess with Barnacle Bob in the shelter of some woody reeds.

On his way back to the shuttle with the commodore, Jose Maria glanced toward something beyond the camp perimeter. His glance held, became a stare.

His smile faded. He became very still, except for his chest, which rose and fell with deep, wounded breaths.

No one dared approach him, except Farragut who would approach a snarling musinot if it were one he cared for. Jose Maria cut off anything Farragut might say. "Do *not*."

Farragut followed Jose Maria's hard stare.

To a woman, approaching the camp with a light, dancer's step, her flowing trousers fluttering about her legs like scarves. She was perhaps fifty or sixty years old, naturally aged, her brown skin softly lined over elegant facial bones. Her long, long black hair was threaded with gray. She held one artistic hand over her heavy silver necklace to keep it from bouncing on her chest. A large blue diamond sparkled on the ring finger of her left hand.

A Marine asked Jose Maria, "Will you be going back out, sir?"

All the Marines sir'd Jose Maria, even though he was a civilian.

Jose Maria shook his head, mute. No, he was not going out.

The woman came right up to the energy field, searched past the sentries who refused her entry. She leaned to see around them, caught sight of Jose Maria, and she tilted her head with a gentle smile.

Jose Maria stopped breathing. May as well have turned to stone.

A sentry strode in from the perimeter to Jose Maria. "The lady is asking for you, sir. What should I tell her?"

Jose Maria stared back at the young man blankly. Then made a motion like a shrug. "Shoot it," he said, and walked back to the shuttle.

The shuttle returned to *Merrimack* in thickest silence. Upon arrival, Jose Maria went straight to his quarters without a word.

Gypsy Dent met the commodore at the dock. Informed him quietly, "We have a possible situation, sir. Signals picked up a tight beam from *Gladiator* to the planet surface—*not* directed to the field base."

"To where, then?"

"To the palace. Was that to you, sir?"

Farragut shook his head. "I didn't get a hail from *Gladiator*. When was this?"

Gypsy glanced at her chron. "Twenty minutes ago."

"No. We were back in camp by then." He signaled the command deck. "Hamster. Get Numa on the com for me. Ask him what he's doing."

He was on his way to the command deck, when the ship's alarms went off. He was running anyway. Charged onto the command deck, Gypsy on his heels. "What are y'all doing to my boat?"

"We've been pinged," said Lieutenant Glenn Hamilton. "Res pulse. The gorgons have noticed."

She already had the ship moving out of orbit.

"What idiot—?"

"Caesar Romulus, sir," Glenn answered.

"Oh, for Jesus."

"I wasn't able to contact General Pompeii, Commodore," said Glenn.

"To hell with Numa. Hail *Rio*."

In a moment the com tech said, "I have Captain McDaniels on the tight beam."

Farragut took up the com: "Dallas, we have a problem."

27

Farragut passed the flag to *Rio Grande* and told Captain McDaniels to find out who Numa was talking to on the surface. Turned to his res tech: "Give me Romulus."

Romulus was on the resonator demanding a status report. "Numa Pompeii has already informed me that the Attack Group has made contact with Constantine Siculus, *and* that you managed to lose the patterner Augustus. I expect to hear updates from *you*, Commodore Farragut."

Farragut told Romulus, "I sent my report to the Joint Chiefs on the repeater. You'll have it in a couple weeks. I don't have anything to add to what General Pompeii told you except that it is a military *imperative* that no one resonate on any of our harmonics. Farragut out." He jammed the link off with a "Lord Almighty!"

Said to the res tech: "Disable this thing."

Wondered how in hell Romulus got word of all that so quickly. It could only be that Numa Pompeii had his own repeater—a lot closer than the Group's repeater back on the frontier. Numa's repeater would have to be disposable, because it would be aswarm with gorgons right now, just like *Merrimack*.

To Gypsy he requested, "What are we looking at?"

"Gorgons converging from all directions. Apparently, any other res pulse trumps the protective one. That's why

Constantine told us not to resonate. And those limpets we weren't supposed to touch? Those disintegrated the instant Romulus pinged us. And we are running out of directions to jink, sir."

Farragut nodded. "Take us toward the sun."

The listening station outside the Marine/Drac camp picked up a conversation. From the direction of the palace, very rough, garbled, but the techs on board *Wolfhound* were able to clean it up enough to get the words.

There were two speakers.

One: So you are here after all. Are you here to serve me or to serve me to my enemies?

Two: Before I cross that Rubicon, you must make me a promise.

One: What am I to promise you?

Two: The pretender Romulus' head. Detached from the rest of Romulus.

One: You needn't have insisted. I already intend to do that when I am Caesar.

Two: If he lives, I am destroyed. There's not a corner in the Empire I could go. Your word. Give me your word as Caesar.

One: You have it.

Two: Then you have me.

And that ended the voices. The first speaker was undoubtedly Constantine, but who was the other?

Steele tried to raise Farragut on his wrist com, but got nothing. Stalked on board the groundbase ship *Wolfhound.* Told the XO, "I need to get a message to *Merrimack.*"

Was told: "*Merrimack* has left orbit. We just heard from Captain McDaniels—*Merrimack* has gorgons."

Steele kept a measured calm exiting *Wolfhound.* Found Flight Leader Ranza Espinoza monitoring the perimeter. Demanded, "Who is outside the bead?"

"From our side, only Captain Carmel. From the Roman side, I don't know. I'll need to ask the Dracs."

Acting Commodore Dallas McDaniels hailed *Gladiator.* Requested to speak with General Numa Pompeii.

Gladiator's frosty XO answered instead. "The Triumphalis is not available."

"Get him," said Dallas.

"He is not here," the XO said.

"Not here as in not *where*? If he's not on the command deck, then get him there."

"The Triumphalis is not on board *Gladiator*."

"Where is he?"

"The Triumphalis did not see fit to file an away plan with this officer."

Dallas McDaniels signaled down to *Wolfhound* and *Horatius*, asking if Numa Pompeii were with them. Numa Pompeii was not to be found on either the U.S. or the Roman side. He also learned that Captain Carmel was somewhere outside the bead. At that, Dallas ordered all the ground troops under lockdown.

"I want every man-jack and jane confined within the perimeter until the return of the *Merrimack*. Acknowledge."

"Aye, sir."

Steele marched toward the Roman side of the camp. Sensed someone behind him, and whirled. Almost drew on her.

"Jesus, Marine!"

It was Kerry Blue.

"Mack *left*? Without *us*? How can they do that, sir? They can't do that!"

"They have gorgons," Steele growled at her.

"We have to go with them! Those navvies can't hack their way out of a swarm of butterflies! They don't have more than two sword arms in the whole crew."

"What do you want to do, Marine? Commandeer *Wolfhound* without Captain Carmel, take off, and go rescue *Merrimack*?"

"Yes!" Kerry cried.

One of the things that drew him to this woman—she said what he felt and could not say.

He motioned her to about-face. "Get back to your post, Marine."

On the Roman side, Steele discovered the perimeter not locked down.

"Why not?" Steele roared at Herius Asinius.

"I have men still outside the perimeter," Herius answered, gazing outward, not at his commanding officer, hands clasped behind his back.

"Doing what?"

"Recon," said Herius Asinius, his expression sullen, smoky. Muscles stood out in high definition under his bronze skin. Romans bred their men that way. This one was built like a stallion.

"Recon," said Steele in high disbelief. "I thought Romans did everything by remote."

"Our remote equipment is PanGalactic make," Herius Asinius said silkily. "It makes sense to use PanGalactic products against their inventor—*if* your brain is made of pig iron."

Steele did not credit for a moment that the missing Romans were surveilling anything. They were playing with the toys or dealing with the enemy. He challenged, "Then what have they found out?"

"They have not come back yet," Herius Asinius explained, almost sweetly.

"Bring them in immediately."

Steele waited for Herius Asinius to comply.

Herius moved with surly slowness. Spoke into his com. In Latin. Could have been reciting *Mary Had a Little Lamb* for all Steele knew.

Dark sultry eyes watched Steele watching him. A defiant gleam in the eyes. The Roman knew Steele couldn't understand him. Probably did start reciting *Mary Had a Little Lamb*.

"Report to me."

"I am told I do," said Herius. "Report to you."

"Is General Pompeii with your men?"

The question made Herius blink. "Not to my knowledge, no."

"Is he in your camp?"

"No," said Herius. And the blink made Steele believe him.

"Where is he?"

Herius Asinius said, "The Triumphalis is wherever he has decided to be."

* * *

Calli Carmel had heard a thunderclap under a blue sky. She knew the sound of displacement. She also knew that Constantine had jammers in place, so whoever was displacing was doing so at the pleasure of Constantine.

Calli had immediately informed her XO she was leaving the perimeter.

She left from the Roman side, ran over the new bridge across the river into the new town that had mushroomed up over the last several days.

She prowled the construction sites in the direction from which she had heard the thunder, between the brothel and the beer garden, the pool and the bowling alley. There were many people in the streets, silent people, smiling at her.

She glimpsed a figure different from the rest. Big. Moving with a distinctive commanding stride.

Calli sprinted closer. Hid behind a wall, peered around it.

There was Numa Pompeii, walking with a purpose, straight through the town and out the other side to wild fields of alien grass and black rocks.

She tailed him at a distance. Debated catching up with him, but she wanted to see where he was going first.

Waited while he hiked over a hill.

When he was out of sight, she dashed across the open space up to the summit. Fell down flat in the weeds to spy and to encrypt a text message into her com to her XO.

From here she could see a small PanGalactic transport in the middle of a field. Sebastian Gray peered from the open hatch, and beckoned Numa Pompeii to hurry.

Numa strode at his own pace. Swaggered up the ramp.

Calli sprinted. She ran full out across the scrub weed, and jumped through the transport's hatch as it began to close.

"Whew," she said blithely, guiding her long hair out of her face. She sat in an empty seat. "Where are we going?"

Sebastian Gray, in the pilot's seat, swiveled round. "You will leave your com behind, or I will report myself abducted. If I am caught aiding the enemy, I will be dismantled."

Calli hesitated. She could not be tracked without her com.

In her indecision, Numa seized her wrist, stripped her com off, and pitched it out of the transport. Then put it to Calli: "Coming or staying?" Poised to pitch her out, too.

Calli said, "I'm with you."

Numa double-tapped the back of Sebastian's seat. "Let's go."

The hatch closed.

"John was right not to trust you," Calli said as the engine started up.

"Your commodore trusts me."

"He didn't let you go with him to interview Constantine. In fact, do you have orders?"

"Commodore Farragut did not limit my initiative."

"You don't have orders," Calli translated. She leaned forward to address the pilot, "Sebastian."

The pilot did not respond to the name.

"*Are* you Sebastian?"

"I am told I was," said the pilot, eyes ahead, the small craft moving low to the ground, almost brushing the tops of the weeds.

"Do you remember me?"

"I know who you are, Captain Carmel."

"Where are we going?"

Sebastian did not answer.

Numa answered for him, "To the main resonator, to get the Hive's harmonic."

"Why doesn't *Sebastian* just *tell* us the harmonic?" said Calli.

"You don't know much about patterners, do you?"

Numa Pompeii had been the man who gave Augustus to Farragut.

"I've heard bad things about Augustus," Calli confessed the sum of her knowledge.

"Certain inhibitions are hard coded into a patterner. The man may *want* to help us, but coding prohibits an outright breach of orders. I must ask him for something Constantine hasn't thought to forbid him from doing. Sebastian can't *tell* us the harmonic. But he can show us."

The transport skimmed across a wide desolate region, across the river, and out of the safe zone.

Calli moaned. "This is bullskat." She leaned forward, elbows on her knees. Her head hung forward so the tip of her long ponytail curled on the tops of her boots. "I should brig myself for this."

Merrimack circled the sun on one of the Trojan points of the innermost planet.

Gorgons and soldiers could only approach in spheres. A Hive sphere's nominal distortion field protected its members from the sun's irradiation. The sphere's members could not separate out without burning away.

This close to the sun even the spheres had to rotate to maintain a tolerable inner temperature.

Merrimack's Navy gunners took target practice at them. The gorgon sphere's normal defensive tactic of breaking up before incoming beams was self-destruction here. The navvies played games with them.

The ship was as happy as the goat on the roof. It just could not ever leave the roof.

The xenos had started breeding the miniature cows.

Commodore Farragut seized a moment to confront his civilian adviser in his quarters.

Jose Maria de Cordillera had filled his living compartment with a holoimage of wide, wide sunlit fields. He stood, leaning pensively against a partition, but the partition was eclipsed by the holoimage, so that Jose Maria appeared to be leaning on sunlit air when Farragut let himself in.

Uncharacteristically, Jose Maria did not turn to acknowledge the commodore's entrance. So Farragut got right to the point: "Why did you tell my Marine to shoot your wife back there on the planet?"

Jose Maria straightened from his lean, turned. He looked calmer now, sober. The smoldering fury had burned down to sad ash. "Did you notice her ring?"

"The boulder?" said Farragut. A large blue rock of some fourteen karats had glittered on the woman's left hand. "Couldn't miss it."

Jose Maria reached into his breast pocket, withdrew a ring. The stone was a big pear-shaped blue diamond surrounded with little round white diamonds that made it ignite blue fire in the light. "Mercedes left the boulder home. This is the Blue Empress."

He handed the ring to Farragut. The stone dazzled blue before blue eyes, a natural diamond, one of the named stones from Earth itself.

Doctor Mercedes de Cordillera would not have taken such a ring with her to a secret Roman terraforming project in the Deep End. Jose Maria de Cordillera kept his wife's ring over his heart.

"The silver necklace you saw is still in her jewelry box on Terra Rica. Those dress clothes are in the back of her closet. She took khakis and denim and hiking boots and lab shoes with her on her voyage."

Farragut shook his head, suggested, "Constantine could have replicated her favorite things after he rescued *Sulla*."

"Those clothes are not her favorites. And that smile—"

Jose Maria broke off a moment, the anger welling again. He took a breath. "That was her awards ceremony smile. Mercedes did much philanthropic work. She was often invited to recognition dinners, and she could not bear them. She practiced a gracious smile so she would not look too strained accepting awards she did not want. I told her she looked like a plastic Virgin Mary. But people love the Virgin, and the practiced smile recorded well. That was the smile she used in public when she accepted awards.

"That was the smile that *woman* gave me. That was not my smile."

He put out his palm, and Farragut replaced the diamond ring in it.

The palm closed into a fist over Jose Maria's heart.

"That was not my Mercedes."

Commodore Farragut did not attempt to communicate with his Group, for fear of compromising their safety. He could see them on his monitors—see them as they were eight minutes ago.

"Commodore, the Hive has a new trick," said Tactical, and reported a gorgon sphere hiding in the shadow of the innermost planet. Pushing out glue.

"Fry 'em," Farragut ordered.

Merrimack sent a nuclear warhead into the mass of them. The gluies died in one sun's light or the other.

Navvies barked like Bull Mastiffs.

Xenos noted the precise distance from the sun where a disassociated gorgon could rotate itself to maintain a survivable temperature and where turning just made it into a rotisserie, and *Merrimack* parked herself in orbit there.

The ship's insects calmed.

The crew relaxed.

The stay in the sun gave time to continue repairs, to hold a service for mates lost to the gluies, and to figure out how to get back to Planet Zero, which Farragut refused to call Arra.

Farragut received a request from Jose Maria over the com. "Will the young Commodore join me in torpedo rack room six?"

Farragut told him yes. Announced to the command deck, "Mr. Dent has the com and the watch."

He slid down the ladders, barreled through the corridors. Crew moved out of his way. They were accustomed to the commodore in motion, so his speed did not alarm them.

Farragut hoped that Jose Maria had found something useful among Augustus' things.

As he neared the torpedo rack room that had served as Augustus' quarters, he slowed almost to a stop. Strains of a Spanish guitar sounded from inside the hatch. But Jose Maria was waiting outside in the passageway for Farragut. So who was playing the guitar?

A recording, of course, Farragut realized. Impossible hopes did leap.

Still, *Don* Cordillera had the look of a diabolical cat. "Jose Maria?"

"After you, young Commodore." Jose Maria motioned toward the hatch.

The music stopped as Farragut opened the hatch.

Augustus barely had time to say, "Don't touch me," when he was wearing John Farragut.

"Augustus, I never thought I'd be happy to see you!" Thumped him on the back.

"Get off me."

A man who had no use for affection, Augustus did not appreciate the too-enthusiastic welcome back from the dead, like the zealous greeting of a big dog. At least no licking was involved.

"Ha!" Farragut seized his shoulders, pulled back to beam at him, gave him another bear squeeze and whomp on the back before letting go. Stood back marveling with the brightest of Farragut smiles. "How in the hell?"

"Constantine is not the first or last person to arrange his own death," Augustus said.

"You could have told me!"

"I needed you to sell the truth of it. You're a very bad liar."

"I'll work on that. I mourned you, you bastard!"

"And did an outstanding job."

Now that Farragut thought of it, an annoying number of people, upon learning of Augustus' death, had asked: *Are you sure he's dead?*

"Who *does* know?" Farragut asked.

"You and the *don*. You are the only people I trust other than the flattop, and he is too stupid to be useful. *Don* Cordillera is useful because he is smarter than Constantine. You, because you are unpredictable."

"Your voice came from the Striker. It wasn't a remote relay. We checked."

"As did Constantine, I have no doubt. My voice was a recording. I programmed several messages to be triggered by different situations or prompts. I miss my Striker, but it was necessary for it to be destroyed to convince Constantine of my death."

"Where have you *been?*"

"Here." Augustus motioned to the racks of torpedoes behind the Roman tapestries. "Hugging torpedoes."

"Do you know what's been going on? Constantine has managed to load our bases."

"No," said Augustus. "He hasn't."

Not sure of the basis of that flat "No," but Farragut liked the authoritative sound of it.

"Constantine is not as all mighty as he appears," said Augustus. "He's a puff adder."

"How much is puff and how much is real adder?"

"Equal parts venom and vapor. Constantine is a user, not a creator.

"His planet is not Arra. There is only one transplanted trench of Arra down there, and that is the parcel that included the Archon's palace.

"That ship in orbit is not *Sulla*. It's a reproduction shell. The power output is all wrong and it's not even constructed of the same material as *Sulla*.

"There are no *Sulla* survivors here—"

"Mercedes—" Jose Maria blurted.

"Is not here," said Augustus. "You knew that."

"I did." Jose Maria nodded, placed his hand over his heart. Closed his eyes as if praying. "I do. I thought I had let her go." He opened his eyes, resolute. "She is gone."

"There is more agriculture and animal husbandry on board *Merrimack* than there is on the whole of Constantine's planet. The people in his town are not people. I'm pretty sure that Constantine is the only human being alive in his realm."

"What about Sebastian Gray?" said Farragut.

"That thing?" said Augustus. "That is not Sebastian Gray. That is not a patterner. I don't think that thing is even alive."

28

SEBASTIAN GRAY PILOTED the skimmer over rocky fields of scrub grass that gave way to barren hardpan, then up and over a lush jungle.

At last he brought the skimmer straight down through the jungle trees to land in a tight clearing.

There was a building tucked in the trees. Calli did not see it until the craft was on the ground. A low concrete structure hidden from the air by the jungle canopy.

The skimmer's hatch opened. Moist air rolled in, warm.

Numa unstrapped from his seat and swaggered down the ramp. Jungle calls sounded in the sweet dense air.

His voice carried back into the open hatch of the transport: "Callista, are you waiting to see if I get eaten?"

Calli called out, "I'm waiting for Sebastian to get out before I leave this boat."

Numa's footsteps crunched closer. "What's he doing?"

"Sitting in the pilot's seat," Calli called out. "This is a trap, you idiot."

"Of course it's a trap, you silly American cowgirl. This could be the last foolish thing you ever do."

Numa marched up the ramp, unstrapped the patterner from the pilot's seat, and hauled him bodily down the ramp.

Roman leaders took wild risks. It was expected.

Not the sort of thing someone with Calli's brass was supposed to be doing.

Calli finally climbed out. "I'm not the one who got out of the transport and left the pilot in it."

She followed Numa Pompeii, who kept his hand closed firmly on Sebastian's elbow.

They had not gone more than ten steps toward the hidden building when the skimmer lifted off the ground, ramp still hanging off its side, hatch still open. It ascended above the tree-tops, and flew away, stranding the three of them in the jungle.

Sebastian gazed straight ahead while Calli and Numa watched the transport go.

"Constantine is big on dead man switches," Calli commented.

All PanGalactic products had bomb dates, fail safes, and dead man switches, rigged so that, in the absence of a controller, something happened.

"Constantine is big on dead men," said Numa.

And the jungle began to shiver, snap, and shred. A tree fell. Winged animals rose screeching above the noise of thrashing foliage, savagely consumed.

"The gorgons will eat the evidence," said Numa. "Constantine will make up any story he wants about our disappearance."

Calli pointed at Gray, "But what about him? How does Constantine's patterner get out of this?"

"Apparently, he is expendable."

"Let's spend him," said Calli.

Numa drew his side arm, shot Gray in the head and the chest.

Gray's eyes, already glazed, did not blink. He didn't die so much as he ceased to function, folded into a cumbersome pile on the ground.

Calli started under the trees toward the shelter of the building.

Numa seized her arm, yanked her back hard. "We are meant to go there." He let go of Calli, tossed Gray over his shoulder like a duffel bag, and broke into a run in the direction back toward the barren zone.

The sound was enormous, everywhere. The jungle become voracious, devouring itself. Animals squealed.

A million thoughts whirled within a single moment of decision. Calli could dash into the shelter or follow Numa.

Sebastian Gray had brought them to the building.

Calli plunged into the jungle after Numa.

She quickly ran into advancing gorgons. They were coming from everywhere. Seemed to be closing in a ring toward the building.

She spied Numa, up ahead, throwing Sebastian's carcass at a mass of gorgons in his way.

The gorgons trampled over Sebastian, showing no interest whatsoever in the carcass. They kept coming at Numa, who dodged wide, big as a defensive back, agile as a punt returner.

Calli saw that once Numa got past the advancing gorgons, the gorgons did not turn around to chase. They kept coming toward the building. Toward her.

"Don't turn back!" Numa shouted from somewhere up ahead in the underbrush.

Calli threaded a path between trees, skirting around gorgons where she could, cutting off their mouths with her knife when she couldn't.

It became clear that Numa was on the right course. Just get around the gorgons, and they lost interest. Meet them head on; they try to eat you.

Calli slashed off giant fronds from the trees, pushed them into the many mouths that reached at her, as she leaped, shoved, crashed through the wide waves that she could not sneak around.

Sunlight gleamed ahead through the thinning jungle.

Scratched, bleeding, breathless, Calli broke into bright sunlight.

Wide-open, featureless hardpan stretched away to the horizon, with nowhere to hide. The thrashing and screaming was all behind her in the murky jungle. A small moving dot ahead, wavering in desert heat, was Numa Pompeii.

Calli ran flat out and kept running.

* * *

Calli caught up with Numa in the night. The winds were dead calm, the sky clear. Moonshadows edged heavy Numa Pompeii's heavy footprints into clarity.

She came upon him where he rested, miles from the gorgon-choked jungle they had escaped.

She dropped to sit by him. Lungs burned. Throat stung. "I would have headed into that death trap building."

"Is that a thank you, Callista?"

"No. You knew that Sebastian Gray's offer to bring you out here was a Trojan Horse." And she yelled at him, "*Why are we out here!*"

"The thing with Trojan Horses is to be ready to beat the hell out of whatever comes out of the Horse."

"What would be the point of luring you out here?"

"To kill me, of course."

"Constantine? He can kill all of us at any time."

"Just me. Without alienating my men. Constantine wants followers, not rival leaders. Constantine means to be Caesar. And he knows that will only happen over my dead body." He squinted at her in the moonlight. "Callista, what have you got there?"

Calli had brought with her, miles into the hardpan, a very large pulpy green leaf.

"It's my frond," she said, and lay down for a few minutes with the big leaf over her like a blanket.

The sun was rising. Numa stood up.

Calli pointed ahead, "That way?"

"That way is the palace and field camp. But that way," Numa pointed off to the left, "is the shortest route to the river. How thirsty are you?"

"River," Calli pointed her frond left.

Numa nodded. "River."

They set out toward the river, the rhino and the gazelle, Calli carrying her frond over her head like a parasol.

Eight bells sounded on *Merrimack's* third day in the sun. Navvies had slept soundly without expecting an alarm.

Farragut considered sending a resonant message to the JC. But that might upset a balance. He sent a courier missile instead, wondering if it would make it out of the star system, then turned to his patterner.

"Augustus, can you calculate how many gorgons I can pack onto *Mack*'s shell without losing the helm?"

Kerry at the pond's edge, listened to the trees wheeze, and watched adolescent wartrays pumping up their warts.

"Which one is yours?" Carly asked, joining her at the bank.

"I can't tell."

"What kind of mother are you?"

Kerry lifted her shoulders, let them drop with a sigh. "They grow up so fast."

Darb came up alongside Kerry. Watched the wart creatures. "How long can we live like this?"

Kerry shaded her eyes at the sun, as if she could really see *Merrimack*.

Captain Carmel was MIA. Carmel's XO had heard nothing since Carmel left the perimeter. The Dracs had found her com out in a field on the other side of the new town.

The Dracs also reported that all those black rock formations out there in the scrub grass were piles of dormant gorgons and can openers.

Tandem shouts sounded through the camp:

"Incoming!"

And *"Hold your fire. Do not fire!"*

A fireball in the sky, roaring down, flaming pieces of it flying off, till the fireball became a flaming spearhead.

"That's *Merrimack*!"

Gorgons in burning shreds peeled off the fiery shape. *Merrimack* in a blaze thundered over Constantine's palace, shook the ground, and cracked pieces of the mural off the throne room ceiling.

Got Constantine's attention.

Farragut hailed Constantine, "Could use some assistance here, sir."

Constantine's voice rumbled and quaked: "How *dare* you!"

"I'm just tryin' to get these burrs off my hide. Why'd you let them come after me?"

"You betrayed me!"

"How did I do that, sir?"

"You resonated! You were told not to, and you defied me!"

"No, sir. And no, sir. I did not. Caesar Romulus resonated *me*. Gorgons home in on a receiver same as they home on a sender. Caesar didn't get the order not to resonate and he doesn't much obey me either."

"Caesar? Caesar! Go aloft and see what I can do that your *Caesar* cannot!" Constantine declared.

Merrimack ascended out of the atmosphere. Before the gorgons could close back in on her, limpets attached themselves to the ship's distortion field, and the Hive lost interest again. The ship's protection had been reinstated.

"Well played, sir," said Gypsy when the com was off.

Farragut made a motion of casting out a fishing line and reeling it in. "Not my favorite sport."

And it nearly strangled him to signal Constantine, "Thank you, sir." Shut the com off. Leaned over the arm of his chair and spat on the deck.

"Must you, sir?"

"Ass kissing," said Farragut. "Leaves a taste."

"Commodore" McDaniel hailed *Merrimack*. "Where you been, old son?"

"Hell, Dallas. Just went for a walkabout. Anything happen while we were gone?"

A hesitation. "Red Rover."

"Come on over, compadre."

Dallas took a skiff over to *Merrimack*. Boarded gingerly, expecting the deck to come up and hit him.

Dallas McDaniels brought a recording. Taken from the Marines' listening array on the planet. "I didn't want this out there for anyone to pick up."

One: So you are here after all. Are you here to serve me or to serve me to my enemies?

Two: Before I cross that Rubicon, you must make me a promise.

One: What am I to promise you?

Two: The pretender Romulus' head. Detached from the rest of Romulus.

One: You needn't have insisted. I already intend to do that when I am Caesar.

Two: If he lives, I am destroyed. There's not a corner in the Empire I could go. Your word. Give me your word as Caesar.

One: You have it.

Two: Then you have me.

Farragut started with the obvious question, "Who was outside the perimeter when this recording was taken?"

"Captain Carmel."

"Oh, Cal." Farragut put a hand to his face like a cage.

Gypsy bridled. "Sir, you *don't* suspect—"

"No, I do not," Farragut groaned. "She has a talent—no, it's a gift. Cal has a *gift* for getting herself into compromising positions."

"She does that, sir," Gypsy agreed.

"How long has she been missing?"

"Three days."

"Not good."

Had they not been told: Constantine clears off most of the board before he moves in for checkmate.

Farragut trusted Cal could get herself out of whatever she had got herself into this time. Though historically, that had not always been the case.

"Numa Pompeii is also missing," said Dallas.

"What of the recording?" Gypsy said. "Where's the merc?"

"Amadea is not on the planet," said Farragut.

"Neither, supposedly, is Numa Pompeii. Maybe that's Numa talking?"

Farragut nodded at the recording. "Honestly, I don't think that's anyone. I think Constantine wants us to suspect our own. He wouldn't let us pick up anything he didn't want us to hear." He withdrew the recording bubble from the player, gave it back to Dallas.

"The idea of the Attack Group was so we could support each other. It's not serving this scenario. In this situation it just gives Constantine more hostages. Just as soon as the gorgons and the can openers settle back down and clump back together into their spheres, Dallas, I want you to take *Rio* and the LEN ships and take a walk. Get out of this star system.

"I'm going downstairs to give Constantine something else to look at. Commander Dent, announce me to the Self."

Farragut arrived in camp by shuttle. He summoned TR Steele inside. Told him not to be alarmed if *Wolfhound* or *Horatius* noticed *Rio Grande, Windward Isles,* and *Sunlit Meadows* missing from orbit. "Don't announce it. Just keep it quiet."

Then he left camp, alone, from the Roman side, over the bridge and into the town, through all the forbidden fruits Constantine laid out before his men.

The Marines objected loudly after he was underway. The commodore needed a guard, they said.

Steele barked all of them to attention. "*You want something to do!*" he roared at them.

They didn't. Expected a drill now. They had been drilling evacuation ever since *Horatius* and *Wolfhound* set down.

Instead, Steele picked up a soccer ball and started toward the Roman side of camp. "Fall in!"

The Marines followed the colonel over to the Roman side. Herius Asinius came out to meet the approaching front. His Dracs fell in behind him.

Steele threw the ball, hard, at Herius Asinius, who caught it.

"Put up or shut up," said Steele. "Lupes versus dogs."

Herius Asinius spun the ball on his fingertip. "You are on, Colonel Steele."

Constantine made Commodore Farragut pace a smooth spot into his gemstone floor, waiting. When at last Constantine deigned to appear, he said, "You have come to thank me for sparing your ship yet again." He had arrayed himself in a toga of gold cloth over a tunic of brilliant red this time, but wore the same atrocious golden gauntlets encrusted with gemstones and blinking lights. The wreath on his head was golden oak.

"I have come to demand you stop trying to seduce my men," said Farragut. "I want that amusement park removed from my camp."

"You are accusing me of seduction? If you cannot control your men, that indicates a want of leadership, does it not?"

"I am controlling them," Farragut fired back. "Remove the toys."

"This is my world," said Constantine. "Not yours. You came here. I did not summon you."

"You displaced gorgons to Thaleia!"

"Also my world," said Constantine.

And with a sudden suspicion, Farragut threw out a guess, "And to Telecore!" Telecore, the Deep End planet secretly terraformed by Rome and devoured by the Hive.

"Also my world," said Constantine.

Farragut could not interpret the answer. Had Constantine really sent the gorgons to Telecore? Puff? Or adder. "Telecore wasn't yours."

"It was in my territory. You exist in my domain with my permission. With me, you are safe. Without me—"

Constantine's head jerked back, a red spot suddenly there in the middle of his forehead.

Constantine blinked. Touched the red. Not blood and not from a hole.

Paintball.

Constantine's gaze locked beyond Farragut. He rose from his throne, volcanic. "*Amadea!*"

A second crack appeared in Constantine's almighty calm. This one a roaring fissure. To the automatons in the chamber, he thundered, "Get her!"

The automatons moved with inhuman speed, but by the time Farragut turned, the tiger had vanished.

Constantine growled at Farragut, "You will hand over the white tiger."

"It's not my world," said Farragut. "And she's not my tiger. She belongs to Caesar."

Caesar, and not meaning Constantine.

Farragut turned and strode out, braced for a shot in the back, but he made it outside to the light.

He jogged down the wide steps from the terrace.

Did not want to return to the camp too quickly. He took the route through town.

The automaton guards were darting about like Keystone

Kops. The white tiger had got away. But that was what she was good at.

In his brooding walk through the town, he became aware that he had picked up a shadow.

He halted suddenly. Spoke without looking round, "I hate to say this to a merc, but: good job, gal."

He swore he could hear a smile.

Not sure who threw the first punch—because it was probably really a kick. This *was* soccer, after all. And it was probably Kerry Blue. At Kerry's size, down, dirty, and first was the only way to survive.

It was supposed to be a soccer game, Marines versus Dracs, but when the shouting started, well, Kerry Blue don't shout at big guys. Took one down curled round his family jewels. And now it was an almighty brawl.

The game was gonna be no decision, but the U.S. of A. was gonna win the fight. Do you Romans understand *semper fi*?

Silence descended in a wave. Shouts and thudding fists damped down till there was only one voice shouting.

The Voice of God.

Oh, hell, Commodore Farragut had returned from Constantine's palace. He was back in camp calling down holy Jesus

Marines and Dracs scrabbled up from the dirt. You never saw a bunch of U.S. Marines and Roman legionaries try to look so small.

Farragut prowled the settling dust. Lightning bolts flashing from his blue eyes.

"WHAT IS THIS?"

"Soccer game, sir," someone said. Had to be an American, because the Romans called it football.

Everyone stood at rigid attention. Stomachs drawn way in—expecting to be gutted. Eyes a thousand yards away. Don't make eye contact or you'll burn to a cinder.

The Archangel Farragut stalked the forest of them. Closed on the COs—Colonel Steele and the legate Herius Asinius—neither of whom had dirty knees or bloody knuckles.

"I take responsibility, sir," Steele began. Got cut off.

"No, you won't, Colonel Steele. Shut up."

Never heard the commodore call Steele anything but TR He was mad as hell.

And then, glory hallelujah, the wrath of God fell on the Roman, Herius Asinius.

Raked him up and down and reamed him through the middle, screaming. Struck Herius Asinius dumb. "I should have expected this, Hairy Ass Asinine-us!"

Kerry Blue gasped so hard she thought she'd inhaled her teeth.

Farragut suddenly stopped in mid-roar. His gaze caught on Constantine's spy monitors outside the perimeter.

Farragut drew his side arm, stalked outside the bead, and blasted the monitors more times than were needed to make sure they were dead, dead, dead.

As soon as he'd gone outside the perimeter, Marines had jumped to make sure he could pass back in. In he came, holstering his side arm, thank God, but still roaring at the legate, this time for allowing Constantine to set up monitors outside the camp.

"*With* respect," Herius had reached his limit. "Perimeter security is U.S. reponsibil—"

Farragut had lifted a forefinger. Stopped Herius' voice in mid-word as if there were lasers jetting from that finger.

Farragut's eyes shifted, seemed to become aware of all the stupefied Marines and legionaries.

He rasped to Herius Asinius, "Come with me." He stalked to his shuttle, the Roman legate following stiffly. The shuttle hatch banged shut like the door to the wood-shed.

Colonel Steele commanded everyone back to duty.

The crowds broke up in muted obedience. Resentment emanating from the Romans, worse than in wartime.

29

THE RIVER FLOWED wide, lazy, and clear, showing the color of its rock bed. Calli knelt at the bank to drink. Reared back on her heels. "Fish!"

"You intend to catch one?" said Numa, snide.

"They mean the Hive isn't here! We must be inside the protected zone." She took off her boots and her jumpsuit. Numa blatantly stared at her.

She knotted her jumpsuit and inflated it into makeshift water wings. She waded out to deep water, floated with the current.

The river ran right between Constantine's new town and the camp. The current would carry her there.

In moments, Numa bobbed up beside her, like an elephant seal. Floated on his back, head first. Stayed near Calli so he would not need to look where he was going.

A distance down the river, a cloud of insects blew into them. Numa submerged. When he came up for air, he shouted at Calli, "What the hell are you doing?"

Calli was grabbing at the air, catching insects, popping them into her mouth. She answered with her mouth full, "Eating!"

Numa regarded her like an odd lab experiment. "Do you even know what those are?"

"They're seventeen-year locusts."

"Are you sure?"

"My funeral, right?" She gave him a smile with a bug wing stuck between her teeth.

She was sure. John Farragut had once regaled her with several locust recipes from back home in Kentucky. Any of those now sounded better than live bugs, but Calli carried very little in the way of a fat reserve. She was shivering most of it away in the river. And when she stopped shivering, she would know she had hypothermia. "I don't know where my next meal is coming from."

"I'll skip this one, thank you."

"Not like you couldn't afford to miss a meal or twelve."

Then, after awhile, Numa said, "Damned noisy, your lunch."

"Locusts are always like that. Even without the Hive around."

All insects perceived Hive proximity. Most of a locust's abdomen was a drum, with the drumhead just behind the base of the wings. The internal structures of the males vibrated the drum to make the distinctive noise.

"Why would Constantine bring locusts to his world?" Numa growled.

"Accident," said Calli between bugs, as if it were obvious.

"*Twice?*" said Numa, pulling a powerful sidestroke.

Calli stopped bug-catching to stare at him.

Numa said, "Herius Asinius told me there were locusts on Thaleia."

Calli frowned. "I heard the same thing from the Marines."

Why would Constantine make the same mistake twice? Unless he wanted locusts here.

Come evening, Herius Asinius left the perimeter without notifying anyone or asking anyone's permission, soccer ball under his arm. He crossed the bridge over the river, strode into the forbidden town to the forbidden soccer stadium and turned on the lights.

Kicked the hell out of the soccer ball.

After a time, a hologram flickered onto a team bench. Constantine might have chosen to look realistic, but he chose to appear like a glowing apparition, with a nimbus around his shining form. The voice sounded like it was coming from the apparition: "He had no right."

Herius Asinius snorted. Said in a surly tone, "You saw that?" Gave the ball a hard boot. Farragut had humiliated him in front of everyone. Apparently not just his own camp.

"This is my world. I see everything. I can help you."

Herius glowered at the apparition from under wilted dark locks, his face shining with sweat. "Go plant those lips on someone else's butt." He jogged away to collect his ball and kick it downfield.

The voice followed him, a disembodied spirit. "I don't understand why yours are still attached to that swaggering Yank."

Herius picked up the ball, stalked back to the bench. "I only take orders because—" He didn't really have an end to that sentence. He put the ball through the hologram.

"You don't need to put on a show for the U.S. spy arrays," the hologram spoke. "They cannot detect us here."

Herius shouted at the image. "I know what you're trying to do. You are so obvious! So get this clear: I am not a traitor."

"And Commodore Farragut is not Caesar."

Herius went silent. Stood like a nervous stallion, nostrils flaring. Lips twitched. Had he been a stallion, his ears would be intently forward.

"He is not even Roman," said the image of Constantine.

Herius mumbled something unintelligible, shut his mouth again.

"Would you like to deliver *Merrimack* intact to Rome? Haul it under racked spears to Palatine?"

An inadvertent sound like a moan of hunger escaped Herius. He said nothing. His gaze stayed fastened on the image of Constantine—looking at him from the corners of his eyes, as if he wanted to rip himself away, but he was stuck.

"You came out here to save Rome from the Hive. If you can do that without helping your conquerors, well. You needn't answer me now. Think on it."

Constantine blurred to a glow that brightened, too bright to look at. Rose like a star into the darkening sky.

Steele sent a shuttle up from the surface in the middle of the camp night. He signaled *Merrimack*. Told Hamster to wake up Commodore Farragut and have him personally meet the shuttle. "Tell Commodore Farragut these are authentic."

Farragut woke up like a struck match. Got to the dock before the shuttle arrived.

The hatch opened to Captain Calli Carmel and General Numa Pompeii, wet, but no longer dripping. They had left puddles under the grates on the shuttle deck. The skin of their hands was puckered, as if someone had scrubbed a deck with them. Calli shivered, her lips blue; Numa was sunburned to blisters.

The perimeter guards who had tested them as authentic accompanied them from the shuttle.

Farragut said, "Where's the cat that dragged y'all in?" He quickly got his jacket off and settled it round Calli.

"We're dead, sir."

"Looks like," said Farragut. Got on the com and summoned Doctor Mo Shah to the dock.

Calli held the warmth of the jacket round her. "I'm keeping this this time."

Numa's eyes shifted from Farragut to Farragut's jacket and back. "Marking your territory, Commodore?"

"There are worse ways," said Farragut.

Calli's brows flew up. She didn't add a word to that exchange.

"Where have y'all been?"

Calli answered, teeth chattering audibly, "Numa thought the best way to find the nature of a trap was to step in it."

"And you, Cal?"

"Oh, me? I'm an idiot."

There was an *um-hm*, from Numa.

"Didn't say you weren't," said Calli. "That was not Sebastian Gray. Not even a piece of him. There was not an edible part of his body. Sebastian lured Numa out. I wanted to see who Numa was meeting. And I got caught in the same snare."

"We did not get caught. We are here. Reporting back to the commodore," Numa told her, then told Farragut, "We're dead. I thought it might be helpful to let Constantine go on thinking so."

"Popular tactic these days," said Farragut. "And not that I don't admire independent action and initiative, but cutting our people off from their leadership in the face of an intimidating power just ain't the course of action I would ever approve."

"Calculated risk," said Numa.

"Error in judgment," said Calli.

"Cal, your pocket is whirring."

"Oh." Calli fished in her pocket. Brought out locusts. "I—we—were thinking these might have helped Constantine get the Hive harmonic. He brought them to Thaleia by accident. Then he brought them here. They have a drum behind their heads. Maybe it could be acting as a res chamber."

Farragut nodded to a guard to collect Calli's bugs from her shaking hands. "Take those to the xenos. See what they can detect. Have Augustus look at the data."

Numa's head turned whiplash quick.

Augustus was alive.

Farragut ordered Calli and Numa, "Get cleaned up, patched up, ready for action. We are about to get hairy."

His com sounded an emergency buzz. "But not this soon," he said, concerned, and took the hail. "Talk to me."

Gypsy on the command deck advised, "I have Captain McDaniels for you. Patching through."

Farragut felt a thickness in his throat. *Rio Grande* was supposed to escape. Something had gone wrong. Farragut yelled into the com, "Dallas! You still here?"

"Not for long, old son. We got through the thick of it, passed the last planet, thought we were clear, and got mugged. We've got gluies."

Farragut's throat closed up.

"Power's gonna quit any second. John, old son, look in on Joleen and my boys if you get the time."

"That's a promise, compadre."

"And Meadow Mouse and Sunny Thing won't leave us, so you might better look in on Captain Fred's and Ram's folks too."

All three of them. They were the ones who were meant to get away.

Tried to maintain a strong voice, "I sure will."

"*Vaya con Dios,* pardner."

"See you on the other side."

Didn't know if Dallas heard him. An empty quiet answered back.

PART FOUR

The Corindahlor Bridge

30

WHEN AT LAST CONSTANTINE deigned to respond to the hail, Farragut demanded: *"Help them!"*

The pause that followed was long. Very long.

The answer was spoken slowly, "Commodore Farragut. What exactly would you have me do?" Almost sounded as if he didn't know what Farragut was talking about. But of course he did.

Urgently, frustration bleeding, not too proud to beg, Farragut said, *"Rio Grande, Sunlit Meadows,* and *Windward Isles*! Give them their protection back!"

The following pause was even longer. Finally: "Just what did they think they were about?"

Farragut's eyes crushed shut. *Rio* had gluies, for the love of God. "I'll order them to come back. Just put the protection back on."

"Why?"

Why? What could he say to this monster? "Please."

The god liked pleading from the powerful.

But Constantine answered, "No. I *choose* not to. You must realize I do not brook defiance. Your ships got what you asked for. You cannot change your mind now."

The link severed.

In the silence, Farragut imagined he could hear the gluies chewing on *Rio*'s hull. The screams of the dying.

*   *   *

Kerry Blue on sentry duty. Walked the bead on the U.S. side of the camp with Cain Salvador under the noon sun.

They had been told to stay alert, as if trouble were on the horizon, but no one would give any clue of what exactly they were supposed to be watching for.

The systems monitor called in a perimeter breach. Three hundred yards to the east along the bead. That was Roman country.

"Don't Rome got its own sentries?" said Blue to Cain. She returned systems' call: "Inbound or outbound?"

"Unknown."

"Great."

Cain had his field lenses on. "I got him. Outbound. We got ourselves a Roman walker."

"Yeah, I feel like a walk," said Kerry, starting out after the figure.

"Don't get close, Blue. Do not engage."

"I know. I know. I just want to see if that's who it looks like. And where the hell he thinks he's going."

"Blue!"

"What!"

"Last time anyone saw Captain Carmel, she was following a Roman to see where he was going."

"Yes, Mom."

She gave the walker a wide lead. He never looked around or back. Apparently didn't give a squid's butt who might be watching him. Kerry had a hard time believing this sortie could be authorized.

Constantine's town grew larger and spread closer to the camp every hour. Looked even bigger from inside it. Looked like places you saw in travelogues. It was hard not to gawk, but Kerry kept her attention on the Roman—who wasn't really that hard on the eyes—strong shoulders and a hard sculpted ass that was poetry in motion.

The forest of buildings ended abruptly. Kerry stopped right there. The back side of Constantine's palace was just across another bridge back across the river. It led off to the tree-lined approach to the back steps of Constantine's palace.

The Roman started up the palace steps. Kerry saw the SPQR brand on his arm flash in the sunlight.

Kerry withdrew into shadow. "Alpha Three. This is Alpha Six."

Cain's voice returned: "What'd you get, Blue?"

"I am looking at Hairy Ass Asininus walking up the steps to Constantine's palace."

"Get back here, Kerry!"

"On my way."

She turned around, back through the city. Thought for a moment she had taken a wrong turn because nothing looked familiar.

Looked up at a building, taller than most of the others.

A figure stood outside, on the balcony, gazing in the direction Kerry thought the camp lay.

She knew him.

Had known him well. Tried to call his name, but her voice failed her.

Cowboy.

Android guards flanking the approach to the palace let Herius Asinius pass. He was not terribly surprised to find Constantine on the terrace. Expecting him.

The tunic was saffron yellow. The toga brilliant red. The crown was gilt laurel. The overwrought gauntlets were blinking.

"Ave," said Herius Asinius.

"What do your masters think of this visit?" Constantine greeted him, also in Latin.

"I don't care what the Americans think."

"I knew you would come."

"Don't think you know me," said Herius, sullen.

"I do know you."

From the direction of the camp, sirens wound up, blared.

Herius spun round in a defensive crouch.

Constantine looked in the direction of the sound. "What is the alarm for?"

"That means the camp is under attack," said Herius, on edge. "Are you attacking my men?"

"Not I," said Constantine. Puzzled, curious, but not concerned. "Perhaps your crazed American commodore has launched an attack on your Legion."

"The sirens are American," said Herius dryly.

The com on Herius Asinius' hand was blinking a silent demand for attention. He ignored it.

Constantine's eyes flickered toward the blinks. Ordered Herius, suspicious, "Answer that."

Herius lifted his hand. Snarled into the com, *"What?"*

"Domni! Where are you! We have been ordered aloft. We have gorgons inside the perimeter!"

Herius Asinius turned on Constantine with a look of betrayal. "Why?"

"There are no gorgons in your camp," said Constantine, condescending.

A roaring of engines sounded from the direction of the camp. Clouds of rising dust billowed over the hillock that blocked the view.

Constantine snapped to Herius, "I don't care what the American is doing. Order your ship and your men to stay."

"Not if you're attacking them!" Herius cried, starting down the steps.

"You shall stop!"

Herius froze.

Impatient, annoyed, Constantine said, "Come with me."

Automatons had moved to block the base of the stairs.

Herius turned on the steps, glaring up, fear, anger in his dark eyes.

"Come, come, come," Constantine beckoned him up, with the attitude that all this pother was trivial and Herius was upset over nothing.

Contantine mounted a narrower set of white stairs up to the roof of the palace, from where they would be able to see the camp. As he climbed, Constantine activated his own com and demanded to speak to Commodore Farragut.

A terse answer sounded from his com: "Farragut."

Constantine said, "Remember what happened to your other three ships that tried to run."

"Wolfhound and *Horatius* were *not* trying to run! They were sitting where you invited them! And you set your gorgons loose on them anyway! Why wouldn't they run now!"

Constantine opened his mouth to object. Shut off the com. His authority slipped. He seemed confused.

From the direction of the U.S./Roman camp, a Roman legionary came running, sprinted through the automatons, and up the palace steps to the terrace. He wore a German-made displacement collar and carried a second one along with a landing disk.

He hastily searched about the terrace. Glanced up. Spied Herius Asinius and Constantine on the steps to the roof. And ran up, taking the narrow steps by twos and threes.

"*Domni!* We need to go. I brought these in case the gorgons cut off the way back." He presented the second collar and the landing disk to Herius Asinius.

Herius took the collar from the messenger. Put it on. Then reached to the runner's neck and took the other collar, too.

The runner blanched. "But that one is for m—" Stopped himself. Hand to his neck. Looked like a naked slave thrown to the lions.

"Get out of here," said Herius.

The man flew down the steps.

Herius offered the second collar to Constantine. "If you want."

Constantine declined. "Those will not work here." He continued up the steps to the roof.

"If you will not drop the jammers to let me out, then I would rather displace into oblivion than be eaten by gorgons."

"The gorgons are contained," Constantine snapped peevishly.

Constantine reached the rooftop. Turned toward the encampment.

The serenity fell off his face.

Herius Asinius arrived at the top. Followed Constantine's stare.

The U.S./Roman camp was overrun with gorgons.

Kerry Blue heard the sirens. Took the call on her com. It was Cain: "Kerry! Haul your pretty ass back here! We have gorgons!"

"I'm coming! I'm coming!"

Then she shouted up to the balcony. "Cowboy!"

Cowboy abruptly withdrew from the balcony without answering.

Kerry ran inside the building to meet him at the bottom of the stairs—only to catch sight of him—wayward prick that he had always been—bailing out a back window.

"Cowboy, you ass! We have to scramble! The gorgons are loose. You don't want to stay here!"

Alive. Cowboy was alive. Just like Sebastian Gray and *Sulla*.

But what had Constantine done to Cowboy that Cowboy didn't know her?

Cowboy, that lying, cheating married bastard had probably laid every woman survivor of *Sulla*. Didn't matter right now. Marines don't leave their own behind. Kerry ran out the back door. "Cowboy!"

Other people in the street were acting weirdly normal. Oblivious to the sirens, or to Kerry Blue shouting and chasing Cowboy.

Kerry heard the *Wolfhound* and *Horatius* power up. They had been practicing evac since they first set down. They could all be gone in four minutes.

"Frag it to hell, Cowboy, we're dusting off!"

Cowboy went into the casino.

"Oh, for—!" Kerry stumbled over her own words. Tempted to just leave the bastard here. Then thought: Had Constantine made Cowboy immune to gorgons? If that was true, then she really had to get him back to *Merrimack*. Kerry ran into the casino.

The doorman, who seemed deaf to the sirens, asked her if she felt lucky.

And for all the lights and bells and merry little machine tunes in the key of G, no one seemed to be talking to each other in the casino, though they were drinking a lot and winning a lot.

She picked out Cowboy from among the gamblers. Saw him slipping through a door.

Kerry heaved out a growling snarl. The man wasn't worth it. Had never been worth it.

She charged through the door. Expected to see him with a *linda* back here. But Cowboy was alone in a back room.

"Cowboy, you dick! Do you have the gorgon harmonic?"

He looked at her strangely. The face was Cowboy's. The way the face moved was not.

"You are not Colonel Steele."

Two dozen smart retorts came to mind before reality set in. Kerry Blue felt cold. "And you're not—"

Oh, Kerry Blue, don't ever tell the android imposter you have smoked his cover. Never been accused of being a brain, but this was a depth of dumb she did not know was in her.

She started to back away slowly.

Cowboy's face did not change expression. Quicker than a gorgon, he had her side arm in his hand, aimed at her. Pulled the trigger.

No one had programmed him to know that U.S. weapons were coded to their bearers. The side arm did not fire for him.

Kerry spun for the door, felt herself wrenched short, her left hand caught in a crushing grip. She heard/felt the snap. That was her com crushing under the android thumb. Her sweaty palm slipped from Cowboy's grip, and Kerry Blue was out the door. Slammed it and dashed through the casino.

She yelled into her com, but got no reply.

Burst out to the street at a dead run. The doorman told her better luck next time.

Heard the Cowboy thing coming after her. Faster than human.

Kerry Blue ran for her life, hard as she had ever run. Even knowing that no human could ever outrun a well built android.

"Do not do this," Herius Asinius pleaded. "Make your monsters stop."

Constantine did not seem to hear him. Drifted to the railing, jerkily, in a disbelieving kind of stagger. Staring at the gorgons invading the camp. His lips parted in amazement, denial.

Tentacles snapped. Black bodies rolled, spidered in their blundering, ravenous advance.

Gorgons within the safe zone.

"You must have resonated," Constantine accused. "I told you not to resonate."

"Then it had to be the Americans," said Herius. "Not us!"

The Roman ship *Horatius* lifted from the ground.

Constantine pulled back his broad sleeve, glanced fretfully at the lights on his jeweled gauntlet, then back at the gorgons, entirely at a loss.

Herius gestured with the runner's displacement collar. "If you can't stop them, can you drop the signal jammers? I can have us displaced to my ship."

Constantine shook his head, eyes fixed on the gorgons.

Gorgons tumbled into the pond inside the U.S. camp. Mouthed tentacles snapped at the wartrays and ravaged the breathing trees.

A slow acidic smile spread across Constantine's lips. His shoulders moved with a couple of spasms of suppressed laughter. A malevolent knowing.

Herius Asinius did not know what exactly it was that Constantine saw, but he knew what the smile meant.

Constantine had recognized the gorgons as programmed fakes. And Herius Asinius could forget about living out this day.

Herius made a quick grab for Constantine's gauntlet, got hold of it, and gave a mighty yank.

The gauntlet pulled loose from Constantine's forearm.

As it came free, the glowing lights went instantly dark.

Constantine breathed deep with wrath, spoke with measured, feline patience, "Herius Asinius, do you know what a dead man switch is?"

Constantine was big on dead man switches.

And there was an instant change in the ambient sounds. The sound of a million mouths rose from all around. Birds took to the air, screaming. The forests moved. Black rock formations in the fields uncurled and sprouted legs.

"This is what a real perimeter failure sounds like," said Constantine Siculus.

Like crashing blades of a gargantuan harvester.
"And soon you will see what real gorgons do."

Kerry Blue ran. Air raked her throat. Pulse thundered in her ears. Eyes stung, watered. Footsteps thudded right behind her.

She tripped. Went sailing forward. Grit gouged her palm heels. First chest, then knees hit the ground.

She writhed over onto her back, with her legs cocked. Kerry Blue was going to go out kicking.

31

KERRY BLUE BLINKED grit and tears from her eyes. No Cowboy loomed over her to kick.

She scrambled to her feet. Tried to stop bleating. Turned a three sixty.

The people in the town had all stopped moving. The street was creepy and still.

There was Cowboy, back a few steps, stopped and fallen over like a plastic doll.

Anyone who was not a real human being had stopped. And that was everyone but Kerry Blue.

She laughed a little. Cursed a little.

Tried to brush the grit out of her bleeding palms.

Noises beyond the town were horribly familiar. Sounded like Thaleia used to sound. Like gorgons. Lots of gorgons, eating.

Wolfhound rose above the rooftops into the sky off to her left.

Then a squadron of Swifts shot into the air.

Then another squadron.

"No!" *Oh, no. Oh, God.*

Kerry ran in the direction of the launching spaceships.

Ran to where the damned river and a damned sheer terrace on the other side of the damned river blocked her damned way.

She had to backtrack to get to the bridge.

Another squadron of Swifts streaked overhead.

Kerry Blue screamed.

Told herself Colonel Steele would have left a Swift for her. Alpha Six would be waiting for her where she landed it.

She zigzagged through the town's labyrinthine streets, growing more and more frantic.

Glimpsed it between buildings—the bridge.

She charged across the river.

Ran to the empty camp, over wide patches of flattened grass where the big ships used to sit. She couldn't see for the breathing trees, but she knew there must be a Swift waiting for her on the far side of the pond.

She ran harder, while a mass of gorgons closed in on the pond from the fields behind the abandoned camp.

On the palace rooftop, Constantine put out a demanding palm to Herius Asinius for his gauntlet. "Now give it back."

"You mean without it, you will die?" said Herius Asinius. The gauntlet was Constantine's control panel. The controls were inoperative at the moment, but Herius Asinius knew what he had.

"No. *You* will die. Give it back." The palm waited.

Herius backed several paces away from Constantine on the flat white rooftop.

Constantine snapped his fingers at his guards, enormously annoyed. "Retrieve the gauntlet."

Dead man switches did not apply to Constantine's bodyguard. The guards responded with the empty precision of androids.

Before the androids could get up the steps, Herius clamped one of the displacement collars on the gauntlet and sent it.

The gauntlet/control panel vanished. A thunderclap of air closed on the instant vacuum in its wake.

With only one displacement signal and Constantine's jammers still active, the gauntlet's scattered pieces would arrive irretrievably nowhere.

Herius Asinius said, "Hail, Caesar."

Constantine's breathing heaved up to a roar. "You *idiot!*"

The android guards had halted, finding their orders now impossible to execute.

Constantine ordered, "Get that man!"

Herius tried to run. The androids caught him immediately. Herius was a brawny man, but the machines were heavy and implacable.

"Kill him," Constantine ordered. Then, immediately, "No! *Don't* kill him!"

The androids paused over the conflicting orders. The latest took precedence. The androids kept their grip on Herius, hard.

"Hold him here," said Constantine, gathering up his billowing red robes. "Hold him here until he is eaten!" And to Herius Asinius and anyone monitoring him he pronounced: *"Sic semper malefidelibus!"*

Merrimack's com tech received a hail from Herius Asinius on the surface. Farragut jumped on the com: "Heri! Talk to me, son."

Herius spoke fast. "Constantine smoked us. I'm dead in another hundred ticks. Constantine's control panel was in his left gauntlet. I had to destroy it. But he must have another control center. If you can track him to wherever he is going right now, that should show you the location of his backup controls. Here they come."

Gorgons. He meant gorgons.

Farragut lifted his face, met Gypsy's gaze. "Get a loc on the source of this transmission and *hook him*. Track Constantine."

Targeting worked for a fix on Herius Asinius' com transmission. Gorgons, real ones, had eaten past the fake gorgons and were closing on Herius' position on the palace rooftop.

"Targeting, talk to me."

Targeting was sweating. "Commodore, I think I'm running into Constantine's jammers. His jammers are still operational. I can't get an accurate solution on Herius Asinius."

"Get a messy one. I don't care if you take the whole palace, just get a hook on him!"

The hook was an extension of the ship's force field. It would encase Herius in the ship's defenses.

"Aye, sir," said Targeting. "Ready hook."

"Deploy hook."

"Hook away." Then. "No good. Negative hook. Negative hook."

The hook bounced off a ceiling field which Constantine maintained over the palace.

"God bless America! Fire on the gorgons approaching the palace!"

"Acquire gorgons," Gypsy ordered Targeting.

"Not happening, sir."

Farragut ordered: "Take your best guess and fire."

"Firing, aye."

Beams rained down on the palace grounds. Deflected uselessly off of Constantine's overhead defenses.

Gorgons, well below Constantine's skyward shields, had reached the palace steps.

Herius Asinius' voice came again over the com: "Thank you for that. Get Constantine. It has been an honor, sir."

Farragut kept the com open. Listened to his screams at the end, because he could not leave him to die alone. When nothing sounded over the com but crunching, he turned the com off, his face wet.

He inhaled an angry sniff. "Do we have a loc on that royal bastard?"

"I have a visual." Tactical threw the image of Constantine onto the main screen. The command staff saw Constantine walking—strolling—across his compound. Gorgons moved toward him, but Constantine's mouth moved, speaking orders to his android attendants, and instantly the gorgons lost interest in Constantine, to swarm instead on the inedible androids with a special fury.

Numa Pompeii had come to *Merrimack*'s command deck. Watched the screens. "Apologies, Commodore Farragut, we have seen this behavior before."

"We have," said Farragut. "We sure have."

The androids were resonating the irresistible harmonic. Had to be.

On the monitors, Constantine strolled, fearless. Pointing

to his attendants, who sacrificed themselves to the Hive, suicidally resonating.

Numa said, "Augustus discovered that resonating the complement of a harmonic cancels out both harmonics."

"We found that out the hard way," said Farragut.

Rome had used that information against the U.S.

Farragut said, "Commander Dent, let's share that discovery with Constantine."

"Calculate complement to the irresistible harmonic," Gypsy ordered.

The res tech and the cryptotech started calculations.

"Complement calculated and loaded," the res tech reported.

Farragut looked to Numa. "Is this going to work?"

"If Constantine *is* using what we call the irresistible harmonic, it will work."

"Send it."

Gypsy ordered, "Resonate complement."

"Resonating, aye." Then, "No good. Negative signal."

"It didn't work?"

"I didn't send," said the tech. "I don't have a green."

Tactical spoke up, "It worked. Look."

The gorgons down on the palace grounds lost interest in Constantine's androids as quickly as they had gained it. They turned round to pursue the moving life-form on the walkway.

Constantine glanced aside. Glanced twice. Broke from his haughty stride and ran, chased by demons.

Bitter laughter rippled across the command deck.

Constantine scrabbled and ducked into a concrete bunker.

"Okay, there's his hideout. Constantine's backup controls will be down there."

Gorgons clotted *Merrimack*'s distortion field. Navigation lined up a dive into the atmosphere to burn them off before the ship could lose her helm.

The res tech reported brightly from his station, "Commodore, I know why I didn't get a green light."

"So do I. A harmonic and its complement cancel each other out. When you resonated the complement, neither existed."

The tech deflated. "I wanted to show off, Commodore."

"Sorry, son."

Wolfhound was rising from the atmosphere. Gorgons swarmed on *Wolfhound* as soon as she was spaceborne.

Horatius was still in the atmosphere.

As *Merrimack* porpoised out of the atmosphere, Gypsy ordered the pilot to steady the ship's course to receive the Swifts returning from the planet. It meant collecting gorgons again, but there was no other way. The Swifts could not survive out there on their own.

Navigation tried to calculate a run to the sun. The escape route was closing. A wall of gorgons eclipsed the sun. He tried to figure if the ship could get up enough inertia to carry her through the gorgon wall to the safety of the sun's blaze. *Mack* could accelerate to FTL. So could Hive spheres. And the gorgons had mass on their side. He looked at flanking maneuvers. And the data kept changing. He would not have solid numbers until all the Swifts were back. While gorgons continued to mass between *Merrimack* and the sun.

Gypsy called to the flight decks, "Did we get all Swifts inboard?"

"We are light one," said Colonel Steele.

"We're light *two*," said Chief Ogden Bannerman.

Kerry Blue raced against an oily black-brown wave of gorgons marching in from the field behind the camp. She had to get to her Swift first. Knew her Swift had to be there. Colonel Steele would not strand her.

If Colonel Steele knew she was alive.

Kerry's com was fuzzed. She couldn't tell Steele she was still alive.

If Steele thought she was dead, he could leave her.

The sunlight dimmed, though there wasn't a cloud in the sky.

She made it to the pond. Saw tentacles on the far bank. This was going to be close. She ran along the bank. Heard a roar from above.

A Swift entering atmo. "Here! Here!" Kerry jumped up and down waving her arms. "Colonel, I'm here!"

The Swift passed low, right overhead and sped onward.
"No! No! I'm here! Oh, no! Oh, skagit!"

Stepped wrong on the wet embankment. Foot slid, leg
buckled. She fell sideways. Water surrounded her up to her
shoulders.

Gorgons spilled over the banks.

Kerry splashed, scrambled for footing in the slimy mud.
Tore at the reeds to climb out.

Suddenly her face, her whole head, was enveloped in
slimy wetness. She couldn't see. Couldn't breathe. Her foot
skidded again. Knee dropped in the mud. She fell into the
woody reeds. A whip-hard gorgon tentacle hit her back.
Knew she was dead.

Merrimack dove once more into the atmosphere.

As the shroud of gorgons burned off in the friction, the
ship's sensors returned to life—just in time to detect Constantine's bunker opening, and a small ship launching out of it.

The little craft hit escape velocity and shot past *Merrimack*.

Too late to get off a shot, *Merrimack* signaled any ship in
the Attack Group: "Fire on unidentified craft! Get him!"

Horatius failed to get a lock. Fired anyway. *Horatius'*
shots went wide and wild.

Wolfhound was dark, and did not even receive the order.

Gladiator, clotted with gorgons, could not fire solid ordnance. Could only get out beam shots, and beam shots were
useless shooting from behind a fleeing enemy.

You had to catch an FTL craft coming. Once he was past
you, a ship that small was almost as fast as a Star Sparrow.

As *Merrimack* climbed out of atmosphere, Farragut ordered, "Get a Star Sparrow out there!"

"Launching Star Sparrow, aye."

But Constantine was ready for that. One shot from a
beam cannon out the stern of Constantine's escape craft
detonated the Star Sparrow well short of its target.

Tactical watched Constantine getting away. The small
PanGalactic racing craft showed on the screens. Tactical reported solemnly, "Target will reach the edge of the solar
system in one minute."

Watched it go in a grim vigil, as navigation reran his numbers, because his first calc said *Merrimack* could not reach the sun.

"Constantine is passing the ninth planet. Will clear in fifteen, fourteen—"

The escape craft exploded in a double blast—one on its bow, the other from its engine losing shielding.

Tactical stood right up at his station and crowed, "It's *Rio* and the Meadow Muffins!"

32

THE IMAGE OF *RIO Grande* resolved onto the monitors, riddled with holes, but carrying no gluies, limping between *Sunlit Meadows* and *Windward Isles*.

Dallas McDaniels' voice came over the com. "John, old son, why didn't you kill *all* these buggers while you were at it?"

"*Dallas!* Glory be, Dallas, I thought you had gluies!"

"We did. They melted all to piss. Now here I thought you did something to rescue us."

"It was nothing I did."

"Do not be so sure, young Commodore," said Jose Maria, who normally said nothing on the command deck.

Farragut turned, surprised.

Jose Maria continued, "Remember, *Merrimack* blanked out a harmonic a few minutes ago."

"Oh, my God," someone said. Could have been anyone. Hope leaped across the command deck—

Only to be quickly damped down by a sound they all knew, of gorgons snagging the force field again, clustering impossibly thick.

"Dallas, bag your ass to the sun if you can. Don't come anywhere near us. We are caged here. Circle wide and get yourself in a close orbit to the sun. Then try to shoot a way clear for us from the sun side. Gypsy, take us on another dive into atmo. Jose Maria, keep talking."

"Two events occurred a short time ago. *Merrimack* canceled out the irresistible harmonic, and the gluies on *Rio Grande* died. Did those two events coincide?"

Farragut called into the com, "Dallas, do you have a chron mark on exactly when your gluies quit living?"

"Sure do. Sending."

Merrimack received the chron reading at the moment of the gluies' death. Farragut ordered the res tech: "Match time against the time we resonated."

"It's a match, sir."

"A perfect coincidence," said Jose Maria. "But not a co-incidence, I think. Cause and effect is strongly indicated."

Farragut was not following. "What does this mean? Gluies aren't Hive?"

Gypsy said, "Gluies must be Hive. We saw gluies come out of gorgons."

"Two," said Jose Maria. "There are two Hives. There *were* two Hives."

"*Rio Grande* ran into a rival gang?"

"I believe so. And I believe the Hive produces gluies to kill rival Hive soldiers. I have heard gluies called antibodies. That may not be a bad analogy. The Hive uses gluies to attack foreign bodies within its space. And that is why the irresistible harmonic was irresistible."

Farragut said, "One Hive's resonance is another Hive's 'Die monster die.'"

"Yes, young Commodore. I believe that is the case."

"The irresistible harmonic pissed the holy hell out the first Hive, because it was the signal of the second Hive!"

Jose Maria nodded. "And when you blanked out the irresistible harmonic, the second Hive died."

"Then, God Almighty, we need the harmonic of *this* Hive!"

"How do we get that?" Gypsy asked soberly. "We killed Constantine and blew up his escape ship."

Kerry Blue groped at her face, blinded and suffocating, and trampled by what felt like stampeding sticks. Her fingers found the edges of her shroud. She peeled the wet film off her mouth and nose. Inhaled a cry. Pulled the slithery shroud out of her eyes.

Opened her eyes to a gorgon tentacle. Right in front of her. It moved away. Stepped on her foot. Tentacles walked over her.

Another set of tentacles stepped on her back. She felt each mouth jab and lift away, then saw the whole monster stump up the mud embankment.

Gorgons marched over her, around her, till the shoal of them were all passed. Left her sitting in the reeds, drawing quavering breaths.

As if they could not see her. Or did not care.

The wartray, Barnacle Bob, grown very large, stuck to Kerry Blue, draped over her head and shoulders, his warts pulsing.

More gorgons moved by the pond, ignoring the wartrays, ignoring the reeds, the algae, the breathing trees.

Imported Earth trees were going down as if in a hyperactive sawmill—willows, tamarisks. Gorgons buzzed through the thistles and the goldenrod but left the alien bluish purple stalks and red-orange fronds.

Kerry huddled in the pond with the native life.

She lifted her com. Tried it again, shaking near to convulsions, her body in mutiny. Her voice was not coming out very well. "*Merrimack. Merrimack. Merrimack.* This is Alpha Six. I—I think I got something."

Merrimack did not respond. Kerry saw now that the Cowboy thing had crushed her com.

Kerry Blue got up unsteadily, teetered on her feet. She caught two more of the wartrays. They hissed at her. She balled them up in their own flaps and tucked them under either arm like a pair of footballs, and she tiptoed, cringing, through herds of gorgons. She held her breath, tried not to whimper when she really just wanted to scream her head off. Knew, just knew, that any moment the gorgons would realize she was not one of them.

Or they could decide to take a bite out of her anyway. She had seen gorgons in a feeding frenzy get careless with their mouths.

Revulsion got the better of her, and she had to pause and throw up. Spat.

Had to dart away from that spot, because another gorgon thought she'd found something to eat and wanted it.

She crept to where her Swift, Alpha Six, sat, right where she left it. Knew it would be there.

The gorgons had already pulled the canopy back and fished out the emergency rations and one pair of leather gloves. Everything else looked intact.

Kerry stuffed the two unwilling wartrays into the cockpit, then scrambled in herself. She caught the wartrays as they tried to escape, stuffed them back down, and pulled the canopy forward.

She tried the Swift's com. "*Merrimack. Merrimack. Merrimack.* This is Alpha Six. I think I have something."

The signal went, but no response came back.

They left!

She sat in the cockpit, quaking. Gorgons stalking by. The two wartrays trapped with her, hissed, warts pulsing fit to burst. Barnicle Bob throbbed on her head.

"*Merrimack. Merrimack. Merrimack.* This is Alpha Six."

It was getting steamy in here.

She started her Swift's engine. Did not know where she thought she could go.

Merrimack's com tech reported, startled, "Sir. I have Alpha Six."

Steele's expression, to anyone looking at him at that moment, was a bald confession. He moved to the com, shouted into it, "Alpha Six, what is your situation!"

Farragut muted the com to tell Steele quietly, "I'm sorry, TR. That cannot possibly be your Marine. It has to be one of Constantine's fabrications, like Sebastian Gray."

Farragut clicked the com back on and said warily, "Alpha Six, how are you still alive?"

"Captain! I mean Commodore! Sir! Bob landed on my head. The gorgons don't eat wartrays! Or some of the trees and some of the swamp reeds!"

Farragut muted the com again. "Who the hell is *Bob?*"

Jose Maria supplied, "Barnacle Bob. The little creature Kerry Blue rescued, by your leave. Apparently, it has grown up to be Androcles' lion."

"This can't be real," said Farragut, though the incoherent voice sure sounded true Blue. Into the com, not certain quite what to ask, Farragut said, "Flight Sergeant, you have 'Bob' there with you?"

"No, *no*. I made him shoo on home. I didn't want the xenos poking at him. But I have two other ones. They're mean, but they seem to be keeping the gorgons away."

Farragut confessed to Steele. "That is, without any doubt, Kerry Blue."

Jose Maria nodded. "And what this implies makes sense."

"It *does?*"

"Life emerges to survive conditions present. With the Hive here, life would emerge with natural defenses against the Hive. The natives are resonating—on the Hive harmonic."

Something else made sense. How Constantine had recognized the fake gorgons as fake. The fake gorgons had attacked native life in the pond *which Constantine knew were immune.*

"Alpha Six, you are clear to dock, portside flight deck." And to the flight deck crew, "Get Alpha Six aboard quick and get my ship moving again. I don't think two little wartrays are going to keep the gorgons off the whole space battleship." To the lab: "Get the Sargasson functional. We need him *now*. Have him do whatever it is Sargassons do to detect what harmonic the wartrays are resonating."

The battle had changed. Before now the xenos had only insects to work with, which could detect Hive resonance. Now they had creatures that truly appeared to be *sending* Hive resonance.

"Augustus, report to the lab."

Alpha Six arrived without gorgons. But *Merrimack* picked up a blanket of gorgons on her force field while allowing Alpha Six to dock.

Colonel Steele was waiting on the dock. He jumped up on the icy Swift, slid the canopy back.

Saw Kerry Blue's brown hair, wet and stuck close to her head, looking like a chick just out of the egg.

"Watch it, sir," said Kerry, handing up wartrays. "These guys are really mad."

Steele handed the wartrays down to xenos, who were

also waiting on the dock in dancing impatience. They accepted their hissing charges and ran to the lab.

TR Steele reached down into the cockpit, hauled Kerry up by her armpits. Set her on her feet before him atop the Swift.

She trembled, her heart beating fast between his big hands. She bewildered him with her scared kind of courage. Her maddeningly soft feminine cheek leaned close to his chest. Good thing she stank like hell or he would have kissed her right there.

Her bleeding palms touched him as if making sure he was real. She was smiling and crying.

Steele handed a very unsteady and smelly Kerry Blue down to big Dak Shepard, who said up to Steele, "She's gooey."

"Bob peed down my neck," said Kerry.

Steele snarled.

Two xenos charged into the lab like a pair of running backs with their wartrays. "Where is Steve Wayne!"

"Who?" said the Marine guard.

"The Sargasson!"

"John Wayne's brother!"

One xeno rapped on the Sargasson's tank. "Come on, Mr. Wayne, time to ride! Wake up!"

Doctor Patrick Hamilton hurried in protectively. "Don't—" He put his hands to the tank to keep it from sloshing. He searched the bottom for the unhappy alien. "Steve? *Steve?*"

A lot of short black hairs, like a hundred eyelashes, floated inside the tank. A great deal of water lay splashed outside the tank, standing in puddles on an adjacent worktop and on the deck.

The wetness trailed to where one of the ship's dogs, Inga, the Doberman, lay curled in the corner of the lab compartment, chewing on an old sock.

The xenos became suddenly aware it was not an old sock.

Patrick Hamilton stared at the bulks, which were spattered with tiny droplets as from the shaking of a wet dog. His hands vibrated, open and useless. He mumbled, "I'll shoot her. I'll shoot her."

Farragut hailed the lab demanding status.

"We're dead," said Patrick Hamilton. He habitually left off the "sir" when addressing Farragut.

"Explain that."

"Steve Wayne has been murdered."

"Put Augustus on the com."

"Augustus is not here."

"Didn't he report to the lab?"

"No."

Chief Ogden Bannerman was on the com now, "Commodore, Augustus is not on board *Merrimack*."

"How is that possible?"

"There is a Swift out without leave. Alpha Two."

"Alpha Two didn't come back?"

"Alpha Two came back. I ticked that crate in myself. And Alpha Two's pilot, Flight Sergeant Dak Shepard, is on board. Some time between the return of the Swifts and our last descent into atmo—when all *loyal* hands was manning our swords—Alpha Two disappeared from its slot without leave."

"You can't just exit space dock while all ship systems are down and we are on manual!"

"Well, sir, *you* can't, and *I* can't, but somewhere in the same time period, that half-human piece of Roman spytech stopped registering inside our force field. He is *not* hiding in the torpedo racks."

Farragut sent over the loud com: "Augustus, report to the command deck."

Received no acknowledgment.

"Augustus went to rejoin his master," said Colonel Steele, who had returned to the command deck. "I just hope Augustus was with Constantine when *Rio* blew his escape ship to hell."

33

THIS, *THIS* IS HOW Jehovah felt during the Deluge. Damn them. Damn them all.

Constantine paced his bunker, waiting for all of them to die.

He had watched the plot of his decoy escape ship blink out from his monitor. Somehow the traitors had managed to destroy the decoy. Disturbing. That should not have happened. His decoy should have got away.

Connecting ordnance to a vessel traveling FTL should have been beyond their technology. He needed to get that technology.

He would be able to glean it from their ships' dead carcasses once the traitors were all eaten.

Mean little rodents. All of them. How difficult was it for them to recognize a superior power? His dominance was self-evident. And apparently too much for their little rodent brains to conceive.

He got up to check his resonator. Made dead certain that all the limpets outside his sanctuary had self-destructed. He would not have his protection used by those parasites any longer.

He would need to play this differently next time. Deal with rodents as rodents. The mistake had been offering friendship. Next time he would cut off the heads of the commanders first and in front of everyone, then proceed from there.

He passed from one chamber into another. The lights, which should have automatically illuminated, didn't.

In the dark, something flew into his open mouth, lodged in his throat.

He gagged, instantly afraid. Could not help but swallow. The object felt round and rubbery going down.

He blinked in the dark. Someone was here.

Dread gave way to elation.

Augustus.

Constantine laughed out loud. "You weren't in your ship either! Great minds think alike." He touched his own throat. Still felt the impact of the ball. "What was this?"

"Goodwill insurance," said Augustus. "That could have been a bullet. But it wasn't."

"I'm glad it wasn't a bullet," said Constantine. Swallowed uncomfortably. The bruised sensation was still there. "What was it?"

"You don't know if it's anything at all," said Augustus. "But you can't afford to kill me until it finds its way to the head. It's not a popper, so don't try to cough it up. It expands. It will choke you coming back the way it came in. The other way is merely unpleasant. If you live to see it."

Constantine smiled past the death threat. Chided him, "Augustus, harming you is the last thing I wanted. I need you. I am your best friend. With you, I can rule Rome as it should be ruled."

Augustus had few expressions other than disdain. "What do you know of Caesar Magnus' assassination." It was a demand, not a question.

"*You* weren't behind that?" said Constantine, a little surprised.

Augustus gave no reaction except to repeat, "What do you know?"

Constantine hesitated, irritated, reluctant to confess. But it was not worth spending a lie. "Nothing at all. I'd have got Magnus sooner or later, but this? This was just bad timing. Killing him now opened the door for that weasel Romulus

instead of *me*. It just adds a complication. I will prevail."
Then thought to add Augustus. "*We* will prevail."

"So you are not guilty but not innocent," said Augustus.

Constantine did not really understand the question. Thought he was all done with that Magnus thing. "How is that?"

"You wanted Magnus dead," said Augustus.

Constantine laughed. Bellowed, "Who didn't!"

"Who didn't," Augustus echoed softly. "That information would have been vital for you to have before you started talking."

Augustus moved toward the bunker's second exit.

"What do you want!" Constantine cried. "With me, you can have *anything*! Name it!"

Augustus answered, "Justice."

"You'll have it!"

"I know."

Clawing, breaking, scritching, and shattering sounded behind Constantine, and suddenly he knew he had swallowed a resonator.

Any harmonic would do.

Augustus passed through the second exit.

Constantine cried after him. "Have it your way! I'll do anything!"

"Really?" said Augustus. Shut and bolted the door. "Die horribly."

34

THE HIVE HAD MOVED like a mud slide into the space around Planet Zero. All calculations indicated that gorgons could and would catch *Merrimack* if she tried to return to the sun. Most tricks only worked once against the Hive.

Farragut could not be sure if the other ships of the Attack Group were still alive. He could only make sporadic contact when another ship entered the atmosphere at the same time as *Mack* to shed its latest gorgon coat.

The gorgons had already learned to bail from a ship's distortion field when the ship began its dive. Finding a clear spot to come back up was getting harder and harder. Like an arctic sea icing over. There were not many breathing holes left. The masses of aliens clustered round the tenuous outer layers of atmosphere, thick as pond scum, so ships collected another coating of them the moment they returned to space.

"Figure about a seven-thousand-klick radius for the planet, including atmosphere. Gives a surface area of six-hundred-sixteen-billion meters squared. That's sixteen hundred sixteen billion gorgons to cover the whole sky."

"Darb?" Carly Delgado squinted at him, gorgon gore stinging her eyes under her face shield, her sword and her hair dripping. "Nobody needed to know that."

* * *

Gorgons clotted the distortion field again. The lights failed again. The command deck operated under the lurid chemical glow of the emergency lights.

A white light flashed on and off, falling on the faces of the command deck crew. Most of the faces were very young. So intent on seeing anything at all by any light that at first no one noticed the light itself. One of those things you see but forget to question, because everything else is abnormal.

Became aware of it. It was white and it kept going on and off. And it was coming from *outside*.

A tech squinted at the clearport, it finally occurring to him to wonder how there could be a light in outer space flashing through a solid coat of gorgons. He turned round at his station to stare at Commodore Farragut who noticed it, too, said: "Is that *Morse?*" Gestured at the air. The light. On and off.

The com tech and the cryptotech started counting the blinks. Dit Dit Dah Dit.

Gypsy Dent moved to the clearport, tried to see past the light to the source behind it. Reported, "There is a Striker out there, sir."

"Augustus?" Farragut started forward. But Augustus' Striker had been destroyed.

"It's a Striker," Gypsy repeated. "It's blue and white." Augustus' Striker had been red and black. "It's touching our distortion field." She turned to meet the commodore's gaze. "There are no gorgons on him."

"He has the Hive harmonic."

The command deck stirred.

Calli Carmel was on the command deck now, in borrowed clothes. Farragut asked her instead of Numa Pompeii, "Calli, what *gens* is blue and white?"

"Sempronius," said Calli. "The patterner Secundus was a Sempronius. Secundus is dead."

Numa Pompeii, haunting the command deck like a beached whale, said in heavy irony, "So is Augustus."

"That could be Constantine in Secundus' Striker, for all we know," said Colonel Steele. "Or one of Constantine's androids."

Farragut asked, of the flashing dits and dahs. "Is anyone getting this?"

"Yes, sir," said Qord Johnson, the cryptotech. "It's Morse. Telling us to enable our res chamber and giving us a harmonic to resonate."

Farragut turned to Gypsy. "Make it happen."

Gypsy Dent immediately ordered the res tech to enable the ship's res chamber.

"Enabling res chamber, aye."

"Commodore Farragut, may I speak?"

"General Pompeii?"

"I don't know who that is out there. We can see he *has* the protective harmonic. *Doesn't mean that is what he is giving to you.*"

"Res chamber enabled."

"Load the Striker's harmonic."

"Loading harmonic, aye."

"Sir!" Colonel Steele was unable to restrain himself.

"Let's have it, TR."

"This Roman knows who is out there." Steele would not call Numa Pompeii by name or rank. "He *knows* we're being fed something deadly. He just never intended to be on board *Merrimack* when it happened."

Farragut looked to Numa for reaction. General Pompeii assumed the posture of a serene and lofty mountain. He would not die sniveling. He would not live sniveling. Said, "I cannot tell you what the person in that ship is thinking. The command is yours, Commodore Farragut."

"The thing in that ship is Augustus," said Steele. "He's going to deliver *Merrimack* to his Caesar."

"It is Augustus," said Farragut, certain.

Gypsy noted softly, "Augustus wants you dead, sir."

"Not arguing. But not this way."

"Harmonic loaded."

Calli spoke to Farragut, "We're back at the Myriad."

There had been a moment in the Myriad when *Merrimack* was at the mercy of Augustus' Striker. Augustus could have taken the battleship out right then. Instead he let *Merrimack* escape.

There was a sin that needed atoning.

"You won't get away with this twice, John."

"Resonate harmonic," Farragut ordered.

"Resonating, aye."

Eternity passed in the red emergency lights, the white Morse flashing. Shouts of the crew, battling gorgons, carried up to the command deck.

"It's a garbage harmonic," Tactical concluded.

Just as the lights went on in the command deck and the gorgons peeled off the distortion field around the command deck.

The monsters moved aft, joining the attack on the sail and wings.

Someone realized aloud, with a nervous laugh, "It's a big ship."

"She's a big ship," said Farragut. "Pull the res chambers from all the Swifts, all the launches, everything we have aboard, and disperse them through my big ship with the new harmonic. Make it fast."

The ship's intracom was not working. Steele quit the command deck at a bellowing charge, calling for techs and Marines.

Farragut shielded one side of his face from the incessant flashing from the clearport. "Get Augustus on the com. Make him stop blinking."

"Receiving a signal from the Striker," said the com tech as the Morse stopped.

"Let's have it," said Farragut, gesturing to his own com.

Augustus' voice requested permission to dock his Striker in the cargo deck.

"Permission granted." And to Gypsy, "Let him in as soon as we have power on the cargo deck."

"Aye, sir."

Numa Pompeii spoke. "Commodore. We need to get this harmonic to the other ships. Mine, in particular."

Calli gave a sign like an auction bid that said: Mine first.

The res tech asked, "If *Wolfhound* and *Gladiator* and *Horatius* didn't make it to the sun, then their coms are down right now. How do we get the harmonic to them?"

"We don't," said Farragut.

Numa looked like he'd been shot. The rest of the command crew gave small flinches, sounds and stares of shock.

No one voiced protest, but the stares waited for explanation.

"Mr. Johnson. Calculate the complement to Hive harmonic. Load and resonate."

Shock gave way to murderous enthusiasm. Even some cackles.

Farragut was going to kill the enemy all at once.

"Point of consideration," said the crypto, even as he obeyed, calculating the complement. "We don't have to kill the Hive. We can just stop them and learn how they do what they do."

"I don't want the Hive stopped. I want it dead."

Qord Johnson verified his calculations. Glanced over at the Roman general. There was to be no privacy here, so he just said it to the commodore: "If we're successful here, the secret of how the Hive determines the location of the source of a res pulse dies with the Hive. Does Augustus have that? If he does, when the hot war breaks out, the Romans will have it." Qord looked at Numa "And we won't. Complement calculated. Ready to load."

"Load complement," Farragut ordered.

"Loading resonant complement, aye."

Jose Maria moved in very close to murmur to the commodore. "This is genocide."

"I can live with that."

"As can I," said Jose Maria, stepping back. Reminding him was all.

"I will sleep very well tonight. My only nightmare is right now if this *doesn't* work."

"How could it *not work*?" said Numa.

"The Hive learns. They saw us kill the other Hive with the complement of its resonant harmonic. Is this group ready and waiting for this? When we resonate; they could all switch to channel B. Then we have nothing at all."

"Complement loaded."

An awful silence stretched an eternal second.

"That scenario cannot happen," said Jose Maria. "The Hive is not aware that the Hive harmonic is a secret. It cannot conceive of a secret."

Did not sound convincing.

"Any message, sir?" the res tech asked.

"A ping worked for the gluies. Just a ping."

"Standing by to resonate complement."

"Execute."

"Resonating. Aye."

And waited.

Nothing happened.

"Do we have green?"

"Negative, Commodore," said the res tech. "Resending. Green. I have a green light now. Harmonic sending. We canceled out *something*."

But nothing had changed on the monitors.

The sensors were all clear and functioning. Showed images from space. Gorgons still entombed the *Horatius*. Pretty sure that was *Horatius*. It was a ball of gorgons clotted on something the size of *Horatius*, but it could be *Wolfhound*. The huge ball would be *Gladiator*.

Shouts from the inner decks had changed to outbursts of disgust.

There were still the billions of gorgons in space. Tentacled monsters in chaotic motion.

But there was something different in the motion. Not obvious at first. Gorgons moving in space, but the tentacles were not whipping. The tentacles were breaking off from the bodies. Opening mouths kept opening, breaking off the ends of the tentacles and fanning into tenuous rings of debris.

The gorgons, all of them, had instantly frozen in the perfect cold of space. The inertia of their last motions kept their thrashing limbs moving in many directions at once. They were now dreamily shattering.

The haze of gorgons at the edge of the atmosphere slowly fell, igniting. Would become six hundred billion meteors.

The com burst to life.

"*Merrimack. Merrimack. Merrimack.* This is *Rio Grande*. John, old son, did you do this?"

"Any ship. Any ship. This is *Wolfhound*. Our outboard gorgons have stopped coming in. Inside, we have a mess.

Inboard gorgons melted. Request the location of Captain Carmel."

"*Gladiator* has dead gorgons on board. Request the location of the Triumphalis Numa Pompeii."

Calli got on her hand com, answered her XO.

Numa on his hand com, signaled *Gladiator* that he was on board *Merrimack*.

Marcus Asinius was not requesting the location of his commanding officer. He knew.

"*Merrimack* to *Horatius*, are y'all still with us?"

"We live," said Marcus. Grief suppressed, suffused, in the hollow voice.

"All ships, this is *Merrimack*. Get rid of your gorgon jackets. You look bad. Then annihilate the gorgons round the planet before they hit atmosphere. They'll destroy the climate with all those burning corpses."

He clicked off. Regarded the rest of the images from outside. All the frozen spaceborne corpses. "I don't like seeing them out there." Ordered Steele: "Break 'em up."

Steele gave the order: "Wing. Battery. Secure space junk."

Yelling, crowing, laughter crackled over the com from the Swifts and the gun bays, as explosions lit up all the monitors in a barbaric frenzy.

Gypsy Dent murmured to Farragut, "Isn't that a little . . . unseemly?"

"No, it's not," said Farragut, moving toward the hatch. "I'm fixin' to man me a gun and see if I can still hit a target."

Gypsy gave a wry moue, then said, "When you get back, sir, can I have a go?"

Farragut clambered up the ladder to the ship's gun blisters, eager as Christmas morning. Ran down the corridor. Skidded to a halt.

Augustus stood in his way, in the middle of the corridor, still and expressionless as a sphinx.

Farragut's smile was jubilant. He talked too fast to finish a sentence, "Augustus! You were— I can't even— You did it! God bless America! Come with me. Tell me how you did it. I'm fixin' to take target practice on frozen gorgons. Come on if you want a shot."

Augustus did not move from Farragut's path. With surreal slowness he drew his side arm. Lifted its muzzle toward Farragut.

Farragut asked, uncertain, "Is that a yes?"

Augustus' voice was flat as his expression. "I have a commission to kill you."

"No," said Farragut.

Heard the shot.

Felt the heat singe against his ear.

Heard a body slump and drop to the deck behind him.

Farragut turned round.

The white tiger Amadea lay dead on the deck, gold eyes open and staring, a burn hole in her forehead.

She had moved so quietly, Farragut had not heard her come up behind him. She gripped a gun in her dead hand.

Augustus spoke, "She offered me half."

Farragut cried, bewildered, "Half of what? Who put a hit on me?"

"In order: half of nothing, and probably no one."

"Do you want to explain that?"

"No."

"Do anyway."

Augustus stalked back to the body, kicked the weapon out of the corpse hand. "I don't think you were the end target. Your death was incidental."

"Not to *me*."

"You were a means to an end. I believe our mercenary set me up to kill you in order to give her an excuse to kill me without facing prosecution." And with false innocence: "Who could want me dead?"

"A lot of people, Augustus. But there's only one who demanded that Amadea be attached to my Attack Group."

Romulus wanted Augustus dead. Romulus sent the white tiger with the Attack Group. Amadea would not have collected payment for Augustus' death unless she did the killing. And Augustus said, "She was even happier than you were to see me alive."

"How did she get on my ship?"

"Did you search every craft *Merrimack* took aboard during the planetary evacuation?"

He hadn't. Of course he hadn't.

"You need to tell me how you got the Hive harmonic."

"From Constantine."

That jolted Farragut. "Constantine is still *alive?*"

"No. I'm ninety-nine percent sure, not. Request permission to go to the surface to look for his teeth."

Didn't even ask what Constantine's teeth would be doing on the surface. "I'm coming with you." Farragut started back down the corridor, talking into his com. Called for a shuttle and called for security to collect Amadea's body.

Farragut then looked up at Augustus with a huge shaky smile, about to speak. Augustus cut him off. "You know I took an oath to goddam Caesar. Do *not* thank me."

35

CONSTANTINE'S RES CHAMBER was still resonating the Hive harmonic when Augustus returned with Commodore Farragut to the bunker to look for Constantine's teeth.

Farragut turned the resonator off.

Contantine's teeth lay scattered, mostly on top of the res chamber. Constantine had been hugging it, trying to be one with the source of the friendly harmonic. But the resonator that Augustus had forced inside him was sending another harmonic. Any other harmonic trumped the friendly harmonic.

Constantine's polymer shoe soles were here, with some torn polymer clothing. Bloodstains darkened the concrete floor.

The small resonator he had swallowed was still here, on the floor, without its spongy covering. Still resonating in a wide pool of melted gorgon residue.

Augustus crushed it under heel. *"Sic semper malefidelibus."*

"Ever thus to the faithless," Farragut said.

He climbed out of the bunker and up to the palace roof to find Herius Asinius' teeth.

Merrimack's technicians were copying Constantine's database onto an independent device, where it could not corrupt any of *Merrimack*'s own data. Numa Pompeii's people were doing the same.

Victory was perilous. Now that the threat which united the U.S. and Rome was dead, no one was quite sure where anyone stood.

Debate had begun over who owned the world and the factories on it. Rome, the U.S., and the LEN each planted a flag in the soil and made their declarations.

"It won't be long before we stick our gluies on each other," said Farragut. "But I don't want it to be here."

Intelligence officers from several ships, picking over Constantine's database, discovered that the attempt by *Rio Grande* and the LEN ships to leave the Sagittarius Zero system without Constantine's notice had actually succeeded.

Constantine had *not* known that the three ships were gone until Farragut begged him to restore the protective harmonic to save them from the attacking gluies.

Constantine's refusal to help had not been his own choice. Constantine could not restore the protective harmonic to *Rio* and the LEN ships because he had never removed it.

Rio's limpets never stopped resonating Constantine's harmonic. Upon leaving the solar system, *Rio* and the LEN ran into the rival Hive. The harmonic that was friendly on Constantine's world made the rival Hive want the three ships dead.

Constantine had not been above painting events out of his control to look like the result of his own conscious will.

So, too, he had claimed responsibility for the Hive's destruction of the planet Telecore. His database spoke otherwise. Constantine had not even known of the existence of Telecore until Rome surrendered to the United States and the catastrophic events at Telecore became public knowledge.

The puff adder had been puffing.

Displacement equipment was found in Constantine's bunker. PanGalactic of course. And there were records of messages from Amadea to Constantine, going back decades.

"Amadea was working for Constantine," the Naval intelligence officer reported. "She planted the landing disks on Thaleia."

Farragut put that one to Augustus. "I thought you said Amadea was working for Romulus."

"She was," said Augustus. "On and off. She worked for whoever was on top at the moment. And always for Amadea."

Amadea had been Constantine's source of information from Near Space. She had sent him the story of the disappearance of *Sulla*, and a picture of it, from which he manufactured a replica. There was also a recording in the database of Doctor Mercedes de Cordillera, taken before her fateful journey on board *Sulla*, receiving an award for advancements in medicinal botany. Her flowing trousers fluttered as she climbed the steps to the podium. The Blue Empress glittered on the hand that accepted the plaque. Doctor Cordillera smiled beatifically for the recorders.

When Attack Group One mustered at Fort Theodore Roosevelt for an unspecified destination deep in the Deep End, Amadea knew exactly where they were going.

Because Romulus wanted Augustus dead, it was easy for Amadea to get Romulus to attach her to the Attack Group. From there, she could either take credit for delivering Augustus to Constantine, or she could kill Augustus for Romulus, depending on how events turned.

Hers was the voice on the garbled surveillance recording insisting that Constantine kill Romulus. She could not afford to have both of them alive in the end to compare notes and find that she had been playing them both.

Amadea had sent Constantine public records of personnel in the Attack Group—John Farragut, Jose Maria de Cordillera, Numa Pompeii, along with obituaries of personnel killed on *Merrimack* during battles with the Hive. Commander Sebastian Gray was one. Flight Sergeant Cowboy Carver was another. Cowboy had been a colorful, popular man. For some reason, Constantine thought that would have made Cowboy special to the commander of the Marines on board *Merrimack*.

"Cowboy wasn't even killed by the Hive. He got himself

blown up," said Farragut. "Rank that scheme down there with my fake gorgons taking a bite out of a wartray."

"And your lame tirade at Herius Asinius at the soccer brawl?" Augustus suggested.

"Lame?" Farragut pulled back. "My tirade *worked*. Constantine believed it. And you said I wasn't a good liar."

"You're not. You're wretched. That charade only worked because you were dealing with an opponent who did not—would not—know you. John Farragut never castigates his men in public, and he never messes up a name. Hairy Ass Asinine-us? That was way under the bottom. You were strident and nervous, two states in which I have never seen you. Luckily, you were putting on a show for a blind man. But I will admit the brawl looked real."

"That *was* real. I gave TR orders to pick a fight with the Dracs, and I wanted a full scale melee by the time I got back from Constantine."

"Insults don't normally break a Roman's discipline," said Augustus.

"TR challenged Herius' men to a soccer game. The fight broke out by itself."

Augustus muttered in self-irony, something that sounded like: *too stupid to be useful.*

"*Heri believed me*. Heri didn't know my lame tirade was a sham until I took him into my shuttle away from Constantine's surveillance equipment and told him what I was about. Heri did what he had to do. Even after everything went to hell." Farragut became solemn, lips pressed together hard. Said, "We call that uncommon valor where I come from."

Commodore Farragut sent his report to the Joint Chiefs by res pulse, proposing that the Attack Group continue on to Telecore, the first human outpost destroyed by the Hive, to make certain the Hive threat had been neutralized.

General Numa Pompeii requested to separate from the Attack Group. "I should like to be back in Near Space for the Senate vote on the new Caesar."

John Farragut's blue eyes went completely blank for a moment. Information was not getting where it needed to go. Or had this disconnect been intentional? Farragut said, hesitant, "Numa, you'll need a time machine for that one."

The Triumphalis seemed to grow larger in affront.

The Roman Senate had held the vote without him. Numa had been in contact with Rome. He, the Senator, the great Triumphalis Numa Pompeii, and no one had thought to tell him.

More likely his contacts had been told not to tell him.

Numa sounded betrayed. "Romulus was not to unseal his father's testament until after our victory." He darted an accusatory look at Augustus.

Augustus said flatly, "You told Romulus I'm dead. No one is sending *me* messages. I know less than you."

Numa, in umbrage, said, "Apparently there was some sudden need for haste. And apparently there was a quorum. And apparently there was a clear majority. And *I* need to ask an *American*: who am I to hail as Caesar now?"

"Same guy as before," said Farragut. "Romulus."

Numa looked disgusted.

It was Augustus who stood straight up and vibrated like a spear just stabbed into the deck.

From that, Numa's expression turned to mixed surprise, suspicion, and realization.

Numa and Augustus weren't talking—not in front of an American—but Farragut could connect some of these dots.

Romulus had not waited for a victory against the Hive to unseal his father's testament.

Romulus had waited until he knew Augustus was dead and not a moment longer.

Augustus had sealed Magnus' testament. Augustus knew what was in it.

And Farragut had a fair idea that the document Augustus sealed probably wasn't the document Romulus presented to the Senate before the vote.

Farragut looked from Numa to Augustus, their silence saying all that needed saying. "Glory be, y'all have got yourselves an Almighty coup."

Celebrations broke out all across the human-settled portion of the galaxy upon news of the destruction of the Hive.

Romulus planned an enormous festival for his coronation. On that subject, Numa and Augustus remained as secretive as only Romans could be.

And on Planet Zero, the Dracs and Marines were finally allowed to play with all the toys.

Roman legionaries were using the soccer field. U.S Marines used the football field and the baseball diamond. They had to be day games. The lights weren't working. Constantine's dead man switches had shut off most of the power. Most of the automatons had ceased functioning, and Constantine's personal guards were unresponsive.

Insectoids were quiet for the first time in forever.

On the last day on Planet Zero, Farragut held a feast in the open air.

The ships in orbit ran on skeleton crews with guards. Everyone else was down at the party. And everyone was allotted time downstairs at one time or another.

Merrimack's Chef Zack entered into competition with *Rio*'s Mama Beau and *Wolfhound*'s Minister of Foodage for the favor of the celebrants. And all hands partied like they had just saved the universe.

You could hear Numa Pompeii holding court at his end of the party. His booming voice carried the length of the clearing. The Americans couldn't understand what he was saying because he was speaking in Latin, but all the Roman men around him roared with laughter.

Calli Carmel stopped by Numa's table. "I brought you dessert." She left a locust on his plate.

Inga the Doberman had been stripped of her rank and her dog tags, and drummed out of the Navy. Jose Maria de Cordillera, down on the planet, walked his new pet dog.

Dak Shepard was reunited with his Swift, Alpha Two, which Augustus had parked near Constantine's bunker.

"Hey, who ate all my pretzels?"

Cole Darby told Kerry Blue, "Good thing Bob thought you were his mama."

Cain and Dak looked at each other, suppressing snickers.

"Uh," Cain said. "Bob didn't think Kerry was his ma."

Kerry curled her lip. "Well, why do you think he saved my life, bozon?"

"Uh," said Dak. "Your hair was really slimy when you came back, Kerry."

"Bob peed down my neck."

"Kerry, the xenos say that wasn't pee."

"Oh. Oh. *Oh.* Aw, no. Eeyeew!" Kerry got up, brushed herself off as if she had ants, and stalked away.

The demoted tactical specialist Marcander Vincent approached Commodore Farragut, requesting a transfer.

"You got a reprimand and a demotion, Mister Vincent. You deserved it. Transferring to another ship won't help anything."

"That's not it, sir. You're allowing a Heraclid to serve on your ship, fine." His eyes flickered to Augustus with suspicion and hatred. "Let me serve elsewhere. I just can't serve on board with a baby killer."

"Denied. Learn to live with it. Unless you are giving me your resignation."

Marcander Vincent looked shocked sick. Had not expected that at all.

"But I wish you wouldn't," Farragut went on. "I need you where you are, Marcander."

"Yes, sir. Thank you, sir."

Marcander withdrew, rattled.

Augustus wore a crocodilian smile. "You asked Mo Shah."

Farragut shook his head. "Didn't have to."

An unremarkable man, Marcander Vincent was older than Farragut and advancing nowhere. "He can't outrun this one. If I transfer him, he'll find out wherever he goes, there will be a Heraclid on board. I won't let that happen. And *you* aren't going to tell him."

"Me?" Augustus wore innocence like a cobra in a tutu.

"You're a sadistic bastard, Augustus."

Augustus nodded; this was so.

Kerry wandered away from the party. She had brought her pet lizard plant down to the planet to visit its own kind, and now wasn't sure where it had gone off to. She walked along the river, through a thin forest of native trees, where couples were trysting.

Came to where the river fed into open water, and she walked along the sea strand, the yellow sun glancing with diamond brilliance off the wide-open blue.

Something odd moved ahead. Closer, it resolved into a mast rocking side to side.

Kerry came to a sailing boat tied to a dock.

Had to be one of the toys Constantine had built to tempt the Marines and the Dracs.

Kerry walked out to the end of the dock. In her Marine boots she gingerly stepped from the dock, over the gunwale to a polished wood deck. Sounds rose from below. She called down tentatively, "Ahoy?"

Up the steps from the cabin rose a buzz cut white-blond head. Arctic blue eyes lifted. Steele's big hand motioned. "Take in that line."

Kerry looked where Steele gestured. The rope was probably "that line." She unwound it from its brass cleat on the dock, and pulled it on board.

Steele used a deck hook to push off from the dock. The sloop drifted out.

Kerry helped Steele haul up the white sail. It filled, billowed. The deck canted. Kerry kept her footing easily. She'd had much worse from the *Mack*.

The wind carried them out to the deep water.

Kerry Blue didn't know a boom from a broomstick, but it was clear that Steele had done this before. He handled the craft with masterful ease. Kerry felt as if she had stepped out of her own life into someone else's.

They sailed over shining water under an alien sky.

Kerry mostly watched Steele move. Nothing prettier than a man who knew what he was doing.

He was wearing shorts so she could see the muscles in his hard legs flex, the blond hairs gleam in the sunshine.

She felt an expectancy. Waiting for something to happen. Afraid to breathe on the moment.

Steele had secured a couple of beers from the party. He

brought the bottles up from the cooler in the cabin, gave one to Kerry, and they sat on the deck watching the sun paint the sky as it sank toward the water.

Kerry asked, "How do you know how to do all this?"

Steele did not look at her. His eyes fixed into a squint at some faraway point on the horizon. "Some rich man got a tax write-off on his little yacht if he took underprivileged kids out of the Midwest—who would never *ever* have a need to know any of this—took them out to the Atlantic and taught them how to sail." He sounded angry.

"Sounds like fun," Kerry said.

"I *loved* it. I didn't know whether to thank him or hit him. So what was the point of it all if I would never ever get to touch another yacht in my life?"

"Guess you better thank him," said Kerry.

Blond brows lifted like a shrug. "I decked him. Waiting for the shuttle to pick us up and take us back to Oklahoma. Laid him right out."

Kerry laughed, leaned her cheek against his hard, hard upper arm.

Steele stood up. Turned the sloop around toward land.

The sky turned deep velvet. There ought to have been stars, but there were probably too many dead gorgons out there for that. One of the moons rose bright and swollen on the horizon. Solid ground felt odd underfoot after being on the water. Kerry walked back upriver with Steele toward the camp, where the party was still in full rev.

Passing through the trees, Kerry saw moving shadows and heard giggles in the dark. Made her wistful. Steele was not pausing here. And she'd thought maybe he might.

They approached the lights and noise. Kerry got in front of him and stopped short, faced him, palm to his chest. "I had the best time."

Steele grunted.

Kerry searched his face. "Do I have a great big wart on my forehead, 'cause you're not looking me in the eyes."

"Big wart," said Steele. "You need to get that looked at."

"Colonel—"

A rustling in the underbrush made him look.

A cluster of green leaves scampered out of the dark, scrambled up the tree that was TR Steele, and perched atop his head.

Steele gruffly pulled the lizard plant off him, set it down snarling with a bullying bluster, but he didn't crease a single leaf.

"I'm taking the next watch topside," said Steele and left Kerry there.

Kerry took a step after him, started to call.

Another rustling of leaves and patter of quick feet neared. Kerry's lizard plant galloping toward her, joyous to see her.

Kerry crouched down with open arms.

Her lizard plant jumped on Steele's lizard plant and the two twined into a single leaf ball, tails entwined, trilling.

Kerry stood back up, hands on hips. "Oh, now that's just not *fair*."

In the morning, *Merrimack, Rio Grande, Wolfhound, Gladiator* and *Horatius* left Sagittarius Zero in the custody of the two LEN police ships.

Farragut had embraced Ram Singh in parting, gave him a kiss on both cheeks. Kissed Captain Fred on the mouth. Fredrika bid all of them, "Don't shoot each other on the way home."

36

THE ATTACK GROUP was underway to the dead world
Telecore. A tense journey. A lot of things not being said.

In a briefing room on board *Merrimack*, Farragut
watched the stand of the Roman Tenth at Corindahlor.

The bridge spanned two miles across the Corindahlor
Channel, a choke point between land masses. U.S. forces
held either side and hemmed in the Tenth Cohort of the
Praetorian Guard on the bridge. The Guard could have
withdrawn, lowered their dome, and displaced out. They did
not have to die. But they would not go. Kept launching ordnance at the surrounding enemy.

One of the three centuries of the famous 300 was Flavian. You could spot them by their black-and-red colors.

Unfortunately for the victors, who made this recording,
the record showed the Romans at their most tenacious,
their most valiant. The damned thing was a more stirring
piece of propaganda than the Romans themselves could
ever have staged.

In the end, the U.S. won the bridge but lost the planet.

Came to the famous scene. The U.S. troops had penetrated the dome. Facing certain death now, the defenders
refused to surrender.

A young Flavian stud, very like Cowboy—even had his
shirt open like Cowboy in the icy air—leaped onto the

bridge railing with a savage smile, fired his weapon, roaring at the oncoming troops.

His field armor flickered out.

And he laughed. Fighting to the death. Ferociously alive.

Projectiles tore into his chest and he fell over the rail into darkness. Below would be the icy water of the Corindahlor Channel.

"There ought to be a legal limit on the number of times anyone can play back that damn thing."

Farragut turned to Augustus. "You really can't tolerate national heroes, can you?" Nobody ever disparaged the Roman Tenth.

And then suddenly the dawning. Obvious now that he saw it. How could he not have seen it. "You were there."

"*I* was not."

Farragut asked the computer if there was a Cyprian Flavius Cassius in this record. The recording backed up to the cowboy making his stand on the rail, laughing. Froze on his image.

Farragut looked from him to Augustus. The only man alive with a right to scorn these men.

No wonder he was so angry. The others were in Elysium. He was here, serving the enemy.

Cyprian Flavius Cassius on the bridge, eternally young, laughing at death.

"Why didn't you keep your name?"

"It is not my name. I know of this the same way you do— from seeing that recording."

"You don't remember this? It's not possible. How can they erase a memory that vivid? Neurons in the brain talk to each other."

"It is not I. I was not there," Augustus said, dispassionate, detached. Dead inside. Nothing left of the life that was.

Telecore still had its atmosphere. There was still nitrogen fixed in the soil. The radiation from the neutron hose had long since decayed. There was free water. The planet could be terraformed again.

The Marines set down a field base. Checked the former settlement sites for residual Hive presence. There were no buildings. The Romans had destroyed everything that the Hive did not.

The Dracs pulled the dead man switches from some Pan-Galactic builder equipment and set it to constructing a stone mausoleum on Telecore, undisputed Roman ground, for their legate Herius Asinius.

It was a handsome building, built like a temple, of local limestone and marble, big but not overweening.

There was nothing left of the Legion commander but his teeth. His men put them in a small urn of pure gold. The purity made the urn soft, but it would hold its luster for the best part of eternity.

Dracs in full regalia carried the urn on a bier to the mausoleum under the scarlet-and-gray legion standard and the silver eagle. They laid the urn in a vault under the floor.

John Farragut made his formal public apology to Herius Asinius at his funeral in front of God and everyone.

He placed a grass crown and a bottle of bourbon over Herius' resting place.

"You don't have authority to bestow a crown," said Augustus. "A crown is a Roman award. It doesn't mean anything coming from you."

"It means I think he should have it. And I am more legitimate than your Caesar."

"Thomas Ryder."

Thomas Ryder Steele glared at Kerry Blue as she joined him behind the windbreak he was setting up.

Without trees or grass to slow them, the winds of Telecore swept dirt and sand into the field camp with an unrelenting clatter.

Thomas Ryder Steele seldom heard his own name. "How in the hell'd you find that out?"

"Augustus told me."

The thought of Kerry Blue with Augustus turned like a bullet lodged under a bone a long time ago and forgotten. Something he lived with until it moved.

His emotions must have read on his face because Kerry said, "Augustus never really wanted me. That was really a cheap shot at you, wasn't it?"

She knew. She knew he could be got at through Kerry Blue. Cornered, his voice dropped. "It wasn't cheap. That *cost*."

She had never seen a look like those cold-hot blue eyes. Stopped the breath in her throat.

She had hurt him.

"You're still mad at me for that, aren't you?" She felt the dizzying abyss here between them.

He shook his head. Wanted Augustus dead again, yes. But Kerry didn't love Augustus, so to hell with all that. He croaked, "No."

"But you *are* mad at me."

Blond brows lowered, eyes narrowed, mouth turned down, chin pushed forward. Steele nodded. Had no intention of ever saying it, but it was coming out of his mouth, "Cowboy! You almost got yourself killed *chasing fucking Cowboy!*"

Kerry flinched, startled. Then smiled. Her shoulders shook.

"*Don't* laugh at me."

She did laugh. Not a mocking laugh. A nervous giddy laugh. "We're having a lovers' quarrel!"

"No. That would mean we—" Couldn't finish that sentence. "That you—" Definitely couldn't finish that one either.

"I do," said Kerry. One of them had to jump first into the abyss; guessed it was gonna be Kerry. "I love you. I've always adored you. You're so far above me I never ever thought we would ever ever even have this conversation."

Steele fought like a drowning man. "This conversation is not happening."

Her voice quavered with fear. "Yes, it is." She felt cold. Cold like alone in a space suit in deep space with no ship in sight. He was hanging her out here alone. Her voice shook. "Yes, it is happening, Thomas Ryder. Yes, it is. Don't do this to me again."

"I am your commanding officer. I have a duty not to abuse my rank."

"I ain't being abused."

"You don't get it."

"Got that right, sir."

He drew himself up before her, forbidding, commanding. Duty was his life. "There is a line I can't cross."

"You were pushed," said Kerry. She jumped. Her arms were round his broad shoulders, her mouth on his, one leg round his waist. If not for their clothes, she presented point-blank.

The line dissolved. Rational thought AWOL.

Steele caught her to him. Shoved his tongue into her mouth. Wasn't romantic. Wasn't art. It was naked need, raw passion breaking. His hands were in her hair, on her ass, pressing her to him. Trying to feel every part of her at once. Felt her arms holding tight, heard the passion in her breath, caught the gleam of tears at the corners of her almost-shut eyes.

A frantic insect whine with a patter of wings made Kerry convulse, jerk free. Shut Steele down cold.

Kerry swayed. Laughed weakly. "Sorry." The reaction was reflex now.

Zakan moths.

"No," said Steele glancing around, alert, guarded, grim.

The Zakan moths in the canister at Steele's belt were fluttering madly, keening.

"The Hive's all dead." Kerry traced a finger down his arm, wanting to get back to where they'd been.

Steele shook his head, his big hand warm and firm on her waist. He began slowly, "Marine—"

The ground around them pocked, moved. Crumbling dirt gave way to living holes, ringed with teeth.

A tentacle lashed free into the air.

"Run!" Steele pushed Kerry toward camp as he roared into his wrist com: *"Hive sign! Hive!"*

Merrimack signaled Planet Zero, ordered Ram and Fredrika to get their people spaceborne. *Yesterday!*

Fred and Ram reported back from a safe orbit that Hive elements were emerging from the ground of Planet Zero.

Merrimack also sent the alarm to Thaleia, which so far showed no Hive sign. But the alerts threw the entire area of Near Space into panic. No one knew where the Hive would erupt next.

"Are these galactic seventeen-year locusts?" said Farragut.

Jose Maria de Cordillera answered, "I do not believe this could be a cycle. It may be that when the parent Hive goes silent, that silence provides the trigger for the rise of the next Hive. Why would something so vast, so ravenous, need to reproduce unless it were dead?"

Marines during dust off shot at the gorgons and observed that the gorgons did not dodge. This was a brand-new Hive—born yesterday. They didn't know a damn thing. There was no jamming of weapons. No avoiding shots. Neither former Hive harmonic meant anything to these.

But insects knew what they were.

There was nothing to eat down there on Telecore. The new Hive hadn't figured out how to fly yet to chase the resonance in the sky, but you saw tentacles straining upward in the direction of ships in orbit.

The impulse was to take another neutron hose to the planet and scour them off. But that would not kill the entire Hive, and Farragut did not want to teach the new monsters anything before he turned all their lights out.

"And we thought genocide was going to be easy."

On the screen in the briefing room was the image of Herius Asinius' mausoleum.

Farragut was standing before the screen, brooding, his arms crossed, when Augustus entered the compartment.

Farragut did not move his gaze from the lonely image. "They ate the crown and drank his bourbon."

"He doesn't know," said Augustus.

"*I* do. We will take this world back. For good."

"It's Roman ground."

"Don't care. It's human ground. They can't have it."

Augustus regarded him strangely. "How did you know to come here?"

"I didn't," said Farragut.

Augustus disagreed. "There are patterns you see that I don't." He paused. "I hit the water backward."

Farragut got lost on that turn. And abruptly caught up to where Augustus had gone.

The Corindahlor Bridge.

Stopped the air in Farragut's lungs. He did not even dare move.

What had happened to Cyprian Flavius Cassius after he went over the side of the bridge was not in the recording.

"I remember getting water in my ears."

Farragut turned slowly to face him.

"You know that last stretch of your ear canal when the water threads up to your eardrum? It's only this far." He pinched the distance between his fingernails. "Felt like a bloody yard. I remember that."

"What happens to you now, Augustus?" said Farragut. "When the Attack Group disbands. I really don't want to send you back. Romulus charged you with the murder of Caesar."

"I did not murder Caesar," said Augustus. "But I am going to."

"Augustus, did I ever apologize to you for all that crap I called you in the torpedo room when I thought you self-destructed?"

Augustus shook his head, not important. "Commodore Farragut."

Farragut could not remember Augustus ever addressing him as that. "Augustus?"

Tried to read the gaunt face, the lined brow. As imperially proud, remote, and bitter as on Thaleia. Head high, the dark eyes looking down on him.

Augustus spoke as from a great hollow.

"You have the respect of the dead."

STRENGTH AND HONOR

TO JIM.

Prologue

CAESAR MAGNUS DESERVED to die.

Caesar Magnus was dead. The assassin was dead.

So did anyone really give a rat's aft if someone else may have been involved in the killing of Caesar?

Even if that *someone* might have been Caesar's own son?

Even if that son had assumed the role of the new Caesar?

Either the thought of a patricide leading an interstellar empire did not horribly unsettle the Senate and People of Rome or else denial simply served them better, because the Senate did not challenge the legitimacy of the new Caesar, and the People loved him.

Suspicion was after all only suspicion.

Other than possibly murdering his own father, the new Caesar was a damn fine Caesar.

In his very new reign, young Caesar Romulus had already beaten down the monstrous Hive threat to a shred of its former terror. Only a whimpering presence of Hive remained deep in the Deep End of the galaxy. Hundreds of light-years and many American settlements stood between the remains of the Hive and the nearest Roman target. It would be a long, long time before the Hive threatened a Roman outpost again.

Caesar Romulus summoned home all Roman forces that were serving under U.S. command. Let the Americans deal with what remained of the Hive. It was no longer a Roman concern.

Caesar Romulus renounced Rome's surrender to the United States.

Caesar Romulus expelled the Americans from the Roman planet Thaleia, and reinstalled Thaleia's orbiting sentinels. He staged a spectacular bombing of the Triumphal Arch which his father, Caesar Magnus, had constructed on Thaleia in honor of the American John Farragut, Captain of the U.S. space battleship *Merrimack*.

On the Roman capital world of Palatine, Caesar Romulus redesigned the Monument to the Conciliation. The original monument featured an enormous golden eagle soaring wingtip to wingtip with a bald eagle, like two great powers flying in perfect accord.

In Romulus' reworked monument, the bald eagle cowered on its back under the claws of the diving golden eagle. "Here," said Romulus, "let all humanity know that the Conciliation was a fraud. Here is what Rome really thinks of Pax Americana."

On an interstellar broadcast, for all the known region of the galaxy to witness, Caesar Romulus broke the spears of Subjugation under his own heel.

For that alone, many Romans called for Romulus' deification.

Too savvy a politician to accept divine honors, Romulus expressed gratitude at the depth of his People's regard, but said, "You cannot vote someone to godhood." And that only increased his popularity.

Romulus could do no wrong.

Magnus had already done it all.

Back in the desperate days when the Hive decimated Rome's mighty legions, desperation led Caesar Magnus to surrender to the United States. The surviving remnants of the Roman armed forces were placed under U.S. command.

With Rome's second worst enemy engaged against Rome's most pressing threat, Rome found a chance to rebuild its shattered forces in secret.

While the U.S. carried the greater weight of the common defense against the Hive, Romulus organized the rebuilding of Rome's armed forces on the empire's most distant worlds that lay in the opposite direction from the Hive incursion. He'd started that even before the assassination of Caesar Magnus.

Upon declaration of victory against the Hive, Romulus, now Caesar, unveiled his empire's new battleships.

He paraded his new legions up the Via Triumphalis on Palatine. The legions were very new. Many of the legionaries' voices had not changed yet. They were full of youthful fire, rabid to reclaim Rome's crushed pride, eager and ruthless as only children could be.

Lost on the proud new warriors was that Rome could not have achieved all this had Magnus not surrendered Rome to the U.S. No one would thank him for it.

Romulus had also organized the manufacture of a new generation of killer bots. Automated factories on far worlds in the Perseid arm of the galaxy had been churning out killer bots by the hundred thousand per earthly month.

The Americans never suspected it was happening. Automated weapons were worse than useless against the Hive. Machine minds could be turned against their makers. There was no reason to think Rome could be rebuilding its fleets of killer bots.

Romulus had been looking to the future.

Because of his foresight, Romulus' empire could face the Americans from a position of power, not subservience, when the common enemy collapsed.

There were vicious, jealous whispers that Romulus had killed his father.

Well, he hadn't. There was a recording of the event. Everyone saw the deed. That was not Romulus' hand you saw holding the pen that plunged into Caesar's eye. Whispers said Romulus drove the assassin to it. But no true Roman needed any pushing to kill Magnus.

There was scarcely a citizen in Rome's interstellar empire willing to look too closely for bones in the closet of a Caesar who accomplished everything Romulus had done for them.

But there was one. A Roman who could not allow Magnus Caesar's death to go unavenged for any reason.

He was programmed not to.

Magnus' patterner had a deeply encoded imperative to defend Rome to his last breath and beyond that. To the patterner, Caesar was Rome. And Magnus was his Caesar.

Patterners were dangerous creations, short-lived and difficult. Difficult to create, difficult to maintain, tricky to control. It was dangerous to put that much power into a thing with a mostly human brain.

Only nine of them had ever been successfully assembled.

Caesar Romulus did not know it, but the last patterner was still alive.

The patterner Augustus had belonged to Caesar Magnus.

Augustus was out there. And he did not suspect Romulus of involvement in his father's murder.

He *knew*.

PART ONE

Off the Deep End

If anything's gonna happen,
it'll happen on the Hamster watch.

—proverb on board *Merrimack*

1

LIEUTENANT GLENN (HAMSTER) Hamilton was Officer of the Watch when the Emergency Action Message came in.

She passed the EAM to the cryptotech for confirmation, and immediately paged John Farragut on his personal com. "Captain's presence requested on the command deck."

Captain Farragut's voice came back, "What's this about?"

An instant's blank panic showed on Hamster's face. The captain was often in Roman company. Hamster could not afford to explain. She answered quickly, "Gypsy's hair." And immediately clicked off.

She stood over the com, feeling the eyes of the command deck upon her. With her eyes set dead ahead, she spoke to anyone in range of her quiet voice, "If what I just said gets back to Commander Dent, every man jack and jane on this deck will walk the plank." And she took the com back up, "Commander Dent, your presence is requested on the command deck."

The lieutenant had not requested speed from either the captain or the exec. She did not want to sound alarmed.

And the captain was going to arrive like a missile anyway.

John Farragut blew through the hatch to the command deck like a gust of fair wind, wearing the sky blue uniform of ship's captain.

One of the Marine guards at the hatch announced, "Captain on deck."

Farragut's presence announced itself. He was a big man, fair-haired, blue-eyed, an irresistible force. Energy radiated from him. Nearly forty years old now, he kept the bright enthusiasm of a boy.

Captain John Farragut had lately been Commodore Farragut, but that had been a field promotion and temporary. His Attack Group One had disbanded after fulfilling its purpose. The two League of Earth Nations ships of the Attack Group had stayed behind at Planet Zero. The U.S. ships *Rio Grande* and *Wolfhound* were headed back to Fort Eisenhower. And the two Roman ships *Gladiator* and *Horatius* that had been under Farragut's command separated out on orders from Caesar Romulus.

The space battleship *Merrimack* remained alone in very deep space, in orbit around the dead world Telecore.

Telecore had begun life as a Roman colony. Before anyone had ever heard of the Hive, the Romans built a secret outpost on the planet to outflank American expansion in the Sagittarian arm of the galaxy.

Telecore had ended life consumed by the Hive. The Hive was a great soulless evil that existed only to eat. What the Romans planted on Telecore, the Hive came to reap.

The Romans were gone. The Hive was still there.

Captain Farragut liked to know his enemy. He had been in *Merrimack*'s lab with the xenoscientists, observing how newly emerged gorgons behaved, when he received Hamster's summons.

Farragut spoke before anyone could tell him; "The balloon went up?"

Specialists at their close-packed stations on the command deck traded looks. Somehow, from what Hamster said, John Farragut had figured out that the United States was at war.

"Looks like it, sir." Lieutenant Glenn Hamilton nodded toward the forward communications shack, where the cryptotech had cloistered himself with the EAM. "Waiting on confirmation."

Commander Egypt "Gypsy" Dent entered the deck. She had left her ferocious hair in her cabin. Her head was smooth. Her brown eyes were narrowed into a squint, half-asleep. Strong-boned, tall and frowning, Gypsy scanned the monitors for some sign of the emergency that had roused her here. Hamster advised her softly, "It's war, sir."

The eyes opened at once. Gypsy was awake now.

"Who declared?" said Farragut. "I'm fixin' to be almighty unhappy if it was us."

He could not believe the Joint Chiefs would strand him out here in the deepest end of the Deep End, sitting on the biggest warship in the U.S. Naval Fleet, while the U.S. declared war without so much as a stand-by-for-heavy-rolls to warn him.

But Hamster answered, "*They* did, sir."

They. Rome.

The Imperial Government of Rome establishes the following facts:

Although Rome on her part has strictly adhered to the rules of international law in her relations with the United States during every period of the recent Emergency in the common defense against the Hive, the Government of the United States has used the Emergency to abridge the right of Rome to its own government, and continues to usurp the lawful authority of Rome over her own armed forces under pretext of a common defense against a threat that has been diminished to inconsequence in order to perpetuate oppression and to enforce a treaty coerced under most extreme circumstances. The United States violates Roman borders at will, and denies Rome the autonomy and security to which every nation is entitled, in actions more consistent with an organized crime racket rather than a civilized nation.

Pledges extracted upon threat of being fed to monsters cannot be bound by law.

The Government of the United States has thereby virtually created a state of war.

The Imperial Government of Rome, consequently, discontinues diplomatic relations with the United States of America and declares that Rome considers herself as being in a state of war with the United States of America.

VIII.xiii.MMCDXLVI

CAESAR ROMULUS.

––––––––––––

"And you are all rotten people and don't deserve to live no more," Tactical added in a low mutter into his console.

"Thank you, Mister Vincent," said Farragut, a warning in his voice. Loose comments were what got Marcander Vincent bucked down to the Hamster Watch in the first place.

Farragut asked Lieutenant Hamilton, "Where do we stand?"

"We have the text of the President's request to Congress to declare back at 'em," said Hamster, and fed the text to his station.

––––––––––––

To the Congress of the United States:

On the morning of August 13, the Imperial Government of Palatine, pursuant to its course of galactic conquest, declared war against the United States.

The long known and the long expected has thus taken place. The forces endeavoring to enslave the entire galaxy now are moving into free space.

Delay invites greater danger. Rapid and united effort by all free peoples who are determined to remain free will insure a victory of the forces of justice and of righteousness over the forces of inhumanity and of totalitarianism.

I, therefore, request the Congress to recognize a state of war between the United States and the Imperial Government of Palatine.

MARISSA JANE JOHNSON.

––––––––––––

"Congressional recognition is 'imminent,' " Hamster added.

Farragut looked to the com tech, "Nothing from Congress yet?"

"Not yet, sir."

" 'Kay." Farragut drew alongside Commander Dent, his hand between her shoulder blades. He spoke low, "If approval comes in before I get back, keep it quiet. There's something I have to do first."

"Understood, sir." Their heads were close together. Gypsy's brown eyes flicked, her focus shifting across his face, assessing.

There was a time, during the last hostilities, when Farragut had standing orders: Should *Merrimack* ever fall into enemy hands, Captain Farragut must kill his cryptotech. During that time, *Merrimack* had in fact been captured by Romans. Yet the cryptotech, Qord Johnson, was still alive to this day and authenticating the EAM in *Merrimack*'s communication shack right now.

Someone *else* had orders regarding the cryptotech in case of capture now.

You never could trust John Farragut to kill his own people.

Farragut still had his orders regarding the Roman patterner, whom *Merrimack* carried on board.

In case of war, the captain's first task—to be carried out immediately and without question—was to take Augustus down. The Roman patterner was the single biggest threat to U.S. security. Farragut's order was clear. Neutralize the threat. Do not try to capture Augustus or to salvage information from him. As Admiral Mishindi said, "Just drop him."

Qord Johnson emerged from the communications shack. He looked to the captain and the XO. "Sir. Sir." He passed the EAM to Farragut. "Emergency Action Message confirmed. Rome declared war. President Johnson presented her declaration to Congress."

Then it was real. War.

Gypsy studied the captain's eyes. She asked quietly, "Do you want me to do it, sir?"

Farragut shook his head. "If Augustus hears anyone but me coming to visit him, he'll know something's up."

That was true. Normally the crew and Marines on board

Merrimack went out of their way to avoid crossing Augustus' path.

Most men on board would *like* to have these orders.

Captain Farragut could not ever delegate something like this. The day he delegated because he could not carry out an order for himself was the day he delegated command of his ship.

He motioned to one of the Marines who flanked the hatch. "Do you have a single stage piece on you?"

The sergeant fished a small backup weapon from his boot pocket. Surrendered it, grip first.

Farragut checked the load. Head busters. Low velocity projectiles, only meant to pierce a human body, not tear through and through. The point detonated only upon abrupt contact with human DNA.

The sergeant reminded Farragut uneasily, "That piece is coded to me, sir." He felt stupid saying that to the captain. Would feel stupider if he hung the captain out there pulling the trigger of a gun that wouldn't fire for him.

Weapons on board a space battleship were coded to their proper users. A weapon would not fire for anyone other than its coded owner.

But everyone on board *Merrimack*, company and crew alike, belonged to Captain John Farragut.

Farragut assured the Marine benevolently, "Son, there's nothing on this boat I can't shoot."

Even so, he depressed the trigger halfway. A green light confirmed recognition. He let up the trigger, clicked the safety off, cocked the piece, and slipped it into his jacket pocket like a street thug.

"Do you want a Marine guard?" his XO asked.

Farragut shook his head no. "Gypsy, he can hear a gnat spit."

"He'll hear *you*," said Gypsy.

"Good bet," Farragut agreed. "He'll hear me coming. But that's okay. He likes to pretend I don't exist."

Augustus never stood up when the captain entered his compartment. Most times Augustus did not even bother to look at him at all.

"I'll be right back."

Farragut moved out fast. He did not try to soften his footsteps. He needed to sound normal.

This task had to be done. He saw the wisdom and necessity of it. And he knew how to kill—and not just at a distance. Farragut had beheaded the Roman Captain Sejanus on the command deck of his own ship with a sword. He knew how to do this.

This was just another Roman.

The most abrasive, off-pissing, caustic, sadistic son of a Roman bitch he had ever known.

The most loyal. With a courage beyond question.

He was having a son of a hard time with this one.

Farragut would get only one shot, if that. He would not be able to say anything. No regrets. No good-bye. He could not even look him in the eyes. Augustus could read Farragut's eyes. And Augustus was extremely fast.

No one outdraws a patterner.

Just shoot him. A shot in the back if Augustus' back presented first.

A prickle like fear stung his mouth. He tried to blank out his thoughts. Stop thinking and just move.

Sounds of his ship around him were all normal. Booted footsteps on eight decks. Voices through thin partitions— fewer voices at this hour of the mid watch. The steady low hum of six mammoth engines. The sharp thunk of rubber balls in the squash court. Air rushing in the vents. Water moving through conduits. Hiss of hydraulics. Clicking of a dog that needed its nails cut.

His ship was an industrial beauty. Spare. Utilitarian. Thin partitions were only in place to keep things from passing compartment to compartment. Any equipment that might be tucked within walls on a passenger ship—conduits, pipes, struts—was all on view here. There were no ceilings, only the undersides of the upper decks along with more of the ship's inner workings clustered up there in the overhead. You could see what this ship was made of. Except for things dangerous, secret, private, or requiring heavy containment, *Merrimack* was right there for you to see.

Farragut slid down the ladder to the corridor that accessed the torpedo rack room. At six foot eight in height,

Augustus was difficult to billet. A torpedo rack was the only place he could fit horizontally.

Farragut made a conscious effort not to slow his stride. He wondered if Augustus could read deadly intent in a man's footsteps.

He hoped Augustus would not look when the hatch opened. He couldn't remember a time when Augustus ever did look. Augustus' pattern of disdain for Farragut's authority would serve now.

The patterner slept most of the day and all the mid watch. There was a good chance Farragut would catch him sleeping. He was probably going to murder Augustus in his rack.

Farragut kept his right hand in his pocket, gripping the sidearm.

Don't even show the piece, he decided. Just point and shoot through his pocket. The interior space beyond the hatch was tight. The instant that hatch opened, Farragut would be very close to his target. Point-blank, in fact.

His throat tightened up as he neared the hatch. He fought off the personal reaction. *To hell with it.*

Big breath. Hold it.

His left arm was supposed to be reaching to pull the hatch open, but he suddenly could not move it.

He hadn't heard a thing.

Two invincible, cable-reinforced arms had locked around him from behind, pinning his left arm across his chest, his right arm locked against his side. A large hand closed over Farragut's right hand, the one gripping the sidearm inside his pocket.

Squeezed.

The weapon discharged.

The bullet lodged in Farragut's deck boot. The head did not detonate.

The shot itself had made barely a pop. No one was going to come running to investigate.

The rough cheek pressing hard against Farragut's temple pushed his head to an unnatural turn, forced his chin into his own shoulder, immobile.

Augustus' breath puffed against his ear in a whispered growl. "I have the same orders."

2

MINUTES GREW LONG for those who waited on the command deck.

The deep scowl on the XO's bold features made her look frightening.

Commander Dent was already an imposing figure, very tall, heavy-boned, hard-muscled, her head shaved. She had a smooth alto voice that she never needed to raise. Gypsy Dent commanded respect on sight.

Lieutenant Hamilton's size did not command respect, but *she* did. Once you'd been dressed down by the Hamster, you never tested her authority again.

At five foot one with a dainty frame, Glenn Hamilton held her own among the tall, muscular people who surrounded her.

That the captain had an eye for pretty Glenn Hamilton was a badly kept secret. Farragut was the only one who didn't think his affection was obvious.

The commander and the lieutenant maintained straight-ahead stoic gazes, scarcely moving.

Captain Farragut should have reported in by now. Augustus should be dead.

The command deck was quiet. Time suspended.

Com silence broke. Several sharp intakes of breath met the hail to the command deck.

But the incoming signal was not an internal transmission. The hail was resonant, and it originated from Earth.

Congress had recognized the U.S. declaration of war.

Qord Johnson, the cryptotech, asked Commander Dent, "Commence Divorce Protocol, sir?"

"Not until we hear from the captain," said Gypsy. Her scowl took on gargoyle depths.

Glenn Hamilton blurted, "Something's wrong."

The words were scarcely out when an alarm sounded.

From somewhere in the ship, dogs barked.

Merrimack's dogs seldom barked except in case of fire.

"Fire," the systems tech of the mid watch reported. Systems on the mid watch was a young man named Klaus Nordsen. "Fire in the port flight hangar," Nordsen said, then, immediately, "Hull access hatch opening. Flight deck."

The hull access would be someone trapped by the fire in the flight hangar making his escape out to the flight deck.

"Fire crew to port flight hangar," Commander Gypsy Dent ordered.

"Hull access hatch closing," Nordsen reported.

The atmosphere out there between the hull and the ship's surrounding force field was thin and cold. A man did not last long out there without an atmospheric suit. And soon enough, young Nordsen announced, "Hull access hatch opening. Cargo bay."

It seemed obvious that whoever had just fled the fire in the flight hangar was reentering the ship through the cargo bay's man hatch.

But Nordsen then reported, "Cargo doors opening."

Gypsy moved to Systems' console to see the readouts for herself.

Nordsen was right. The hatch in question was not the man hatch, which had shut again. What was opening now were the big doors which admitted the passage of cargo. Even over here in the ship's fuselage on an upper deck, the command crew could feel the pressure change with the big doors' opening. Atmosphere bled out to the space between hull and force field.

Nordsen shook his head at his console, still trying to

make his readouts fit the actions of men fleeing a fire. "Why would they do that?"

Gypsy spoke, coldly certain, "That's Augustus."

The cargo bay was where the Roman Striker was stowed.

The Striker was a Roman ship, small, long range. Fast, heavily armed. A Striker was custom built to house a patterner.

A Roman patterner inside his Striker was a nearly unstoppable force.

Augustus had destroyed his own Striker back on the planet Sagittarius Zero.

It was the Striker of an earlier patterner that was clamped down in *Merrimack*'s cargo bay now.

The fire in the flight hangar was undoubtedly a diversion for Augustus to get at the Striker in the cargo bay and launch himself to freedom.

"Lockdown. Lockdown," Gypsy commanded.

The command deck jolted. Crew felt/heard muffled explosions, probably in the flight hangar. More diversions. Or Augustus destroying the *Merrimack*.

"Lockdown not happening, sir," Systems reported. "I'm showing a command override here." Nordsen turned to Commander Dent. "Override on Captain Farragut's authorization."

Commander Dent looked venomous. "He wouldn't. Override that!" Gypsy ordered. "Set force field to adamant." She pounced on the com, "Captain Farragut, please respond!" And to the com tech, "Why isn't he answering?"

"Sir!" the com tech acknowledged. "The captain's personal com is not registering."

It wasn't off. It was not registering at all, which meant the captain's personal com had been damaged or destroyed.

Farragut's personal com was implanted in his wrist.

Gypsy spoke into the loud com. Her voice resounded through the ship: "All hands. All hands. This is the commander. Set Condition Watch One. Siege stations. Siege stations. Hostile in the cargo bay. Secure cargo bay. Eliminate Colonel Augustus."

Systems reported, "Striker is clearing the cargo bay. Cargo doors closing."

Just because Augustus was outside the hull did not mean he was free of the ship yet.

"He is *not* getting through the force field," said Gypsy.

The ship's force field, rather than her hull, was the ship's true line of containment, what really stood between the ship's atmosphere and vacuum. The low-pressure space between the force field and the hull acted as a kind of air lock.

With the call to siege stations, *Merrimack*'s gun barrels retracted, and the ship's force field solidified over the gunports and torpedo tubes and missile launchers. Nothing but layered engine vents broke *Merrimack*'s energy barrier.

Nevertheless, Nordsen reported, "Force field breach."

This could not be happening.

"Where?" Gypsy demanded, looming over the console. She already knew.

"Cargo bay egress. He's got himself an opening."

Augustus the patterner had found a pattern in *Mack*'s command codes to let him out.

"Seal force field!" Gypsy ordered.

Nordsen attempted to obey even as he voiced concern, "Not sure how good an idea that is, sir. If we manage to trap Augustus in here, can't he just blow himself up and gut the *Mack* with him? Hail Caesar and good night *Merrimack*?"

Gypsy waved off the objection. "He could have done that by now if that's all he wanted. Augustus wants *out*."

Once Augustus was outside *Merrimack*'s force field, then he could still shoot back through the breach and ream *Merrimack*'s insides out. Gypsy would not allow that. "If he guts us, he's coming with us. Get that field sealed *now*."

Even if Gypsy had to sacrifice *Mack* to a Roman suicide, she could not let a Roman patterner in possession of a Striker loose on the galaxy. Because there were bigger targets out there than *Merrimack*.

There was the Fort Eisenhower/Fort Roosevelt Shotgun.

And there was Earth.

"Striker is clear of force field!"

"Damn!"

Nothing to do now but survive him.

"Seal force field!" Gypsy ordered as someone, probably Marcander Vincent at Tactical, murmured, "He's going to wax us."

Nordsen reported, shouting with relief, "Force field sealed, aye!"

Gypsy darted the young systems tech a withering glower to tell him it was a little late.

She heard the com tech dressing down some baboon on his link, "Stay off the intracom if you don't have anything to report!"

Marcander Vincent at Tactical announced, "Striker coming round."

Gypsy ordered, "Change field pattern. Random seed."

Augustus' knowledge of *Merrimack*'s codes would enable him to pierce the constantly changing force field unless *Mack* jumped to an unexpected point in the pattern.

The Striker came round.

And kept going without firing a shot.

"Striker away!" Marcander Vincent reported, surprised. "All speed."

"Track him!" Gypsy ordered. "Mister Vincent, don't lose him! Helm! Pursue hostile! I want that bastard. Lieutenant Hamilton! Find the captain. Find out if he's still on board. Get hold of Colonel Steele. Tell him we may have a hostage situation—"

Movement at the hatch caught her eye. "*Captain!*"

"*John!*" flew out of Hamster's mouth.

Farragut appeared in the hatchway, propped up by the great white rock that was Lieutenant Colonel TR Steele, commander of the two Fleet Marine companies on board *Merrimack*.

A red welt colored Farragut's forehead over a forming lump.

Farragut gestured at his bruised throat, his mouth opening and shutting like a grouper's. He couldn't talk.

His larynx had been crushed. He entered limping, leaning heavily on the Marine CO.

A burn hole showed through the captain's jacket pocket.

Lieutenant Colonel TR Steele of the Fleet Marines was six feet tall and solid, a couple of years younger than Far-

ragut. Steele was a man of enormous courage and loyalty—
not a great intellect—not lacking by any means, just not
packing any to spare. Steele was as down-to-earth as a man
in space could be.

Steele piloted the captain to a seat. Farragut slid down
from Steele's rock hard shoulder to sit heavily.

Farragut gingerly pulled off his right boot, the one with
an undetonated head buster round lodged in it.

Steele hovered over him, his whole head an enraged
shade of scarlet underneath his white-blond buzz-cut hair.

Steele hated the Roman Augustus more than anyone on
board *Merrimack*. It was killing him not to be able to kill
Augustus.

Gypsy's eyes raked Farragut from reddening lump to
bare foot. "Captain, I'm ordering you to the hospital."

Farragut nodded. The motion pained his throat and he
winced. He held up a forefinger to say: *Yes, but first*. He
motioned toward the loud com and mouthed the words,
"Call it."

Gypsy took up the loud com. "Now hear this. Now hear
this." And she read the Congressional resolution to the four
hundred and twenty-five crew of the *Merrimack* and seven
hundred and twenty Marines of the 89th Battalion of the
Fleet Marine:

"Whereas the Imperial Government of Palatine has formally declared war against the Government and the People
of the United States of America: Therefore be it Resolved,
that the state of war between the United States and the
Imperial Government of Palatine which has thus been
thrust upon the United States is hereby formally declared;
and the President is hereby authorized and directed to
employ the entire military forces of the United States and
the resources of the Government to carry on war against
the Imperial Government of Palatine; and, to bring the
conflict to a successful termination, all of the resources of
the country are hereby pledged by the Congress of the
United States."

Even on a ship built for just this purpose, the words had a deep impact.

Gypsy Dent had a husband and two sons back on Earth.

John Farragut had mother, father, twenty brothers and sisters and all of their offspring back in the U.S.

Glenn Hamilton's family—herself and Dr. Patrick Hamilton, ship's xenolinguist—were both here on *Merrimack*.

Colonel TR Steele's Marines were his pack. He lived to fight for the United States. Hated Rome. War was good news.

Gypsy turned to Farragut, who wasn't making any moves toward the hospital yet.

Farragut tapped on the arm of his seat. Gypsy recognized Morse code. When you served on *Merrimack* you learned Morse. It was the favorite communication system of last resort on board ship.

Farragut's dits and dahs ordered: *Initiate Divorce Protocol.*

Gypsy gave the command deck over to the lieutenant so Gypsy could retrieve the Divorce procedure codes from the safe in her cabin. She retrieved Farragut's codes as well, because Farragut's codes were in Gypsy's safe. The captain's own safe had been destroyed earlier during a battle with the Hive.

The cryptotech Qord Johnson ducked into his forward compartment to get his codes from his safe.

Farragut, through pantomime which only Hamster could figure out, ordered a blast bag brought to the command deck to remove Farragut's boot with the unexploded head buster in it.

Hamster also ordered the stores admin to get the captain a new right boot, a new wrist com, and a new sky blue captain's jacket. It was a thing an efficient officer or a close personal friend would think to do. Even so, the knowing glances passed among command deck personnel.

Farragut gave his sidearm back to the Marine guard at the hatch.

Only when Gypsy returned to the command deck and the procedures of the Divorce Protocol were underway did Captain Farragut surrender himself to the medics.

* * *

The United States armed forces had been ready for the eventuality of a violent split with Rome. They were not expecting it to come like this, but such things never go down as expected.

Reality was that the crew and company of *Merrimack* had been sharing living space on a space battleship with a Roman patterner. They had planned to kill him first thing the conflict went hot.

But the Roman patterner got away.

The authors of the protocol recognized that such a thing could happen. Things go wrong. That was an unwritten law of military tactics. Commanders failed to account for it at their peril.

The U.S. needed to operate under the absolute worst case scenario.

They needed to assume that Rome had *all* the U.S. codes.

Access codes, recognition codes, res harmonics, authorization codes, systems codes, targeting/tracking codes, detonation codes, ops codes, com codes, displacement codes, firing codes for every cannon in the battery, every handgun, every Swift, every long range shuttle, every space patrol transport.

And so *Merrimack* and the entirety of the United States armed forces had to change all of them.

It was a complicated routine, which could not follow any pattern. Certain changes were designed to be subject to human whim.

The trick then was the synch up of random decisions with random decisions made in other systems thousands of light-years away.

Resonance allowed instant communication across any distance, but Augustus had been in *Merrimack*'s database, so Augustus possessed all the resonant harmonics currently in Navy use. The harmonics had to be changed and communicated to the Pentagon without Augustus picking up the communication.

The Divorce Protocol had been in place ever since Caesar Magnus gave Augustus to Captain Farragut at the time of Rome's surrender.

The procedures for code changes were not stored in

any database. They resided in a lot of printed text and antique code-wheels stored in the physical safes of key personnel. Even then the text was not complete, providing another circuit breaker against information leaks. There were blanks to be filled in at the time of the Divorce. The more unexpected the method of blank-filling, the better. There was dice rolling, coin flipping, blindfolded pointing, playing basketball games and using the score to pick numbers.

One of first procedures in the Protocol was to organize a nano scrub of the entire ship, starting with Captain Farragut, who had been in contact with Augustus.

The patterner's body was rife with medical nanobots. Augustus may have left some nanomachines behind. And those might not be medical devices he left on *Merrimack*.

Merrimack's hospital was bigger than most city hospitals.

The medical officer, Mohsen Shah, was waiting for the captain when he arrived from the command deck to the ship's hospital on a levitated stretcher.

Doctor Mo Shah was an ageless man, placid, with warm, sad puppy eyes. A Riverite by creed, Mo took things as they came. "Be allowing yourself to be relaxing," he instructed his patient.

To a Riverite, everything was a process. "The River is flowing," he told Captain Farragut serenely.

The River was talking to a salmon.

Lying still was not Farragut's natural state. When he lay back and closed his eyes, he was right back there in that chilling moment, in Augustus' grip, unable to move, locked in the control of a malign strength.

The sensation of being held so still, so helpless, hurtled him back into a childhood memory, when his father used to pin him down in a choke hold and tell him he had to see if he could take it. *You have to know you can take it*. John Farragut never wanted to go back there.

The ordeal had brought back the same helpless feeling all over again. He could not move.

He kicked.

"The River is flowing," came Mo's pacific voice.

Fortunately Farragut didn't have a voice with which to tell Mo what he could do in his River.

Mo turned up the gas.

Farragut's eyes closed themselves. The gas did not relax him. It threw him into twilight.

Augustus' voice came to him once again, speaking against his ear in soft menace: *I have the same orders you do.*

Farragut had been certain in that moment that he was about to die. Knew it and could do nothing about it. But the voice had continued:

"Fortunately for you, only one of us has his orders from a legitimate government. I need you to let me out."

The strained angle at which Augustus had trapped Farragut's head restricted his air, and Farragut could barely squeak out, "I can't do that."

"Oh, I wasn't asking you," Augustus said, and his thumb smashed the com on Farragut's wrist. Then a quick fist to Farragut's throat crushed his larynx.

Farragut could not breathe, could not inhale or exhale. His throat was completely closed.

Farragut felt his own face turning purple, his lungs burning, trying to expand.

Augustus hauled him up, facing him. Red and green blotches swam in the air between Farragut's fading sight and the gaunt face of the patterner.

Augustus' fingers gripped Farragut's throat and yanked his trachea back open.

Farragut inhaled in blinding pain. He tasted blood and tried to cry out. He made no sound louder than a heaving breath.

Farragut was thewed like a bull and loved to fight. He hadn't lost a match in a long time. But Augustus was six foot eight and reinforced with steel and synthetics. Farragut struggled with all the effect of an infant throwing an almighty tantrum. His attempts to get free only annoyed Augustus.

At some point Augustus had enough, and he struck Farragut hard on both sides of the neck, interrupting the blood flow to his head and folding him to the deck.

Farragut had some awareness of being tossed over Augustus' angular shoulder and carried. Somewhere along the way, Augustus had lobbed an incendiary through a hatch, and climbed a ladder. The deck swam away from Farragut's watering eyes.

A top hatch opened. Wind fluttered up around him into the lesser atmosphere of the hull. And then he was on the hull.

Cold. He was upside down and having trouble breathing. Could not draw enough oxygen.

And then he was down another hatch, another ladder.

Augustus let him drop in a heap on the deck like a hunter's kill. But he was breathing.

No one else was here. He heard the fire alarm, heard shouts and stampeding feet passing by on the other side of the partition.

And then he saw the Striker.

It took a moment to register what he was looking at because the colors were wrong. This Striker was blue and white. John Farragut had become accustomed to seeing Augustus' own Striker painted red and black, Flavian colors. Augustus' Striker had been destroyed.

Augustus recently liberated this blue-and-white Striker from a madman who got it from another dead patterner.

Augustus had not been able to enlist any of *Merrimack*'s crew to repaint the Striker for him.

This Striker had the same evil lines as his own. But there was no hard ordnance left on the hard points. Those had been spent over a half century ago by its original owner. Still, the Striker had its energy weapons.

Augustus used Captain Farragut's biometrics—his retina print, his fingerprint, his DNA—to authorize a launch window through *Merrimack*'s force field, and to override attempts from the command deck to lock him in.

He didn't need Farragut's voice print. Voices were too easy to duplicate.

The cargo doors opened.

The higher pressure air of *Mack*'s atmosphere rushed out with a moan through the wide doors to the layer of thinner air held between the hull and the force field.

Now, Farragut thought, now will he kill me?

Augustus should have killed him long ago and always regretted not doing it when he first had the chance.

He ought to now.

Augustus climbed onto his Striker, rode it up the lift through the cargo doors.

The cargo doors were shutting. The outrush of air sped up through the narrowing egress. Augustus' black clothes fluttered in the wind. He looked down like a perverse angel. He was not aiming a weapon at Farragut down there, lying flat on his back, looking up from the deck.

Augustus was not going to kill him.

Augustus had already told him why:

Only one of us has his orders from a legitimate government.

Augustus did not recognize Romulus. To Augustus, no legitimate authority had declared this war.

Without a war, blowing up *Merrimack* or killing Captain John Farragut would be acts of piracy and murder. Augustus was not a pirate.

Augustus, now and always, served Rome.

"John Farragut."

Augustus the battered warrior looked down on him from atop his Striker. His face looked like seamed granite carved into the semblance of perfect Roman features. Cables in his forearms and behind his neck hung loose, unplugged.

"When we cross paths again, know that I will not hesitate to kill you."

Farragut whispered, all breath, no voice, "Yes, you will."

Maybe Augustus heard him, maybe he read his lips, but Augustus blinked. He said something obscene in Latin, dropped into his cockpit, and the cargo doors banged shut between them.

Farragut stagger-crawled across the cargo bay to an authorization pad. He fumbled to cancel all authorizations that would permit opening the force field. He could not speak the instructions and he could not key fast enough.

He heard the breach forming in the field, heard the Striker power up and push off the hull.

The force field resealed.

Captain Farragut heard himself being paged.

He crawled to an intracom, rose up to his knees and hit the intracom. He hailed the command deck, whispering.

The intracom would not register the shape of his voiceless breaths.

The com tech on the command deck scolded him to get off the intracom if he wasn't going to say anything.

Farragut charged into the briefing room, trying out his restored voice box on his assembled officers, "Do I look like a pork butt? Because I sure feel like one."

Colonel Steele stood at one end of the table. He flushed dark, mortified. He would not sit. The Marines who policed *Merrimack* were Steele's men. One Roman had turned the proud Fleet Marines of the 89th into cartoon tail-chasers.

Sitting at the table was the ship's Naval Intelligence officer, Colonel Bradley Zolman. Colonel Z was a darkhaired man of middle height, lean as a ferret. His face might have been attractive if he ever smiled, but that theory had never been tested as far as anyone on *Merrimack* knew. Captain Farragut could not call him humorless, but Colonel Z was definitely humor deficient.

Commander Gypsy Dent was also here, stony, embarrassed at her own failure to contain the patterner.

Two xenos, Doctor Weng and Doctor Sidowski, held down the far end of the table. Weng's and Ski's uniforms were so pristine that the two men might have been CIA incognito. Scientists' uniforms got unfolded from their original bags about as often as CIA pretenders' uniforms did. Anything other than a lab coat made a xeno feel like a dog dressed up for a tea party. Weng and Ski had neglected to add their proper insignia to their uniforms, so they looked as badly dressed as they felt.

Also in the briefing room was *Merrimack*'s chief engineer, Kit Kittering, a little doll of an officer, boy slender, with short dark hair, big round baby doll eyes, and the foulest mouth on board ship. Apparently just about everything in Kit's world was capable of fornication.

"Where do we stand now?" said Farragut, roving the length of the briefing room, too agitated to sit.

"At war," said the IO in the most compact of nutshells. Colonel Z elaborated as best he could. "The exact nature of the war is not clear. Romulus never presented us with an ultimatum."

"Has Rome attacked anyone?"

"Not so far," said Colonel Z. "So far as we know."

There was a lot the *Merrimack* might not know from out here in the Deep, orbiting a planet that lay off the edge of all the maps.

"Word is that Romulus is expelling Americans from Roman ground and Roman space," the IO continued. "Romulus is confiscating all U.S. equipment on Roman soil. He already recalled Roman soldiers from U.S. territories before he declared war. We knew this was coming. We just expected quite a few more steps between that and this."

"Do we know what Romulus expects to get out of the war?" Gypsy asked. "What it will take to finish it?"

"We don't know," said the IO. "And strategy is not our business. This is the Navy, not the Executive Office."

"It's our business to know what *we're* doing out here," Farragut told Colonel Z. "I haven't received orders. You?" Farragut would not put it past the Intelligence community to angle around him.

"Not yet," said Colonel Z. "I have my hands full executing the Divorce Protocol."

It sounded like an excuse but Farragut recognized that the Divorce was a huge task. "We're knocked blind and sideways out here."

"With the Hive," Doctor Weng reminded him.

"We're out here with the Hive," said Doctor Sidowski.

"I know that, gentlemen," Farragut acknowledged.

A new Hive swarm had emerged right down there on the planet Telecore below them.

At the moment, the gorgons of Telecore were stranded on Telecore. The new gorgons seemed to be as inept as one might expect of any newly hatched thing. But Hives could learn—faster than people learned evidently, because the first Hive had driven Rome's armed forces to the brink of extinction.

These new gorgons had not figured out that they could

fly. And no one knew how long it would take them to learn that they could not only fly, but they could escape the planet's gravity, survive in a vacuum, retain mobility in the deepest cold of space and achieve faster-than-light travel when collected together in a sphere. It could take years, centuries, even millennia, for them to learn. Or they could be chasing *Merrimack* tomorrow.

The xenos had known little enough about the earlier Hive. This new Hive presented a whole different set of unknowns. First among those, Farragut put to the xenos: "Why aren't they dead? There's nothing to eat down there."

The Hive was polymorphic. The cells on Telecore were the gorgon type—the eating form. A gorgon appeared as a large dark shapeless sac covered all over in hoselike tentacles, any one of which could take a good bite out of you, because all the tentacles terminated in mouths. The moment the new gorgons erupted out of the Telecore ground, they snapped up everything edible.

The planet's meager food was swiftly exhausted and the gorgons were looking for more.

"We think—" said Ski.

"Maybe—" Weng hedged.

"We have an idea—"

"A hypothesis—"

Farragut could see his exec, Gypsy Dent, on the edge of her chair, glaring at the two scientists as if she might reach down the table and smack them upside the head to make one of them finish a sentence.

Doctor Sidowski must have seen her, because he blurted without qualifiers, "They're powered by resonance."

Faces around the briefing table wore stunned expressions. Captain Farragut was not shocked. The suggestion had been made to him a long time ago that the Hive was a single vast interstellar organism cohered by resonance.

The theory had since been supported by the manner in which the previous Hive perished. Commodore Farragut's Attack Group One had exterminated the original Hive by disrupting its intergalactic nervous system with a single resonant pulse.

As a unified resonant being, the Hive whole might subsist on energy consumed by any of its cosmically scattered units. It was rather preposterous to think on, but the only theory that fit the preposterous facts.

One thing humankind had learned from the first Hive: you can't starve a gorgon.

As long as some part of the Hive somewhere in the universe had enough to eat, the gorgons of Telecore might realistically wait the best part of forever for their next meal.

"Probably," Farragut allowed the resonance-sharing premise. "But we've seen swarms drop below some magic number where they're not worth maintaining. That lot down on Telecore isn't bringing in any energy to the whole. Why doesn't the Hive cut its losses? I want to see spontaneous disintegration down there. Why isn't it happening?"

"Because we're here?" Weng suggested and instantly looked as if he'd shot the captain.

Farragut blanched. *Merrimack* was a resonance source and receiver. Gorgons sensed the *Mack*'s presence. Perhaps resonance promised food, and the proximity of resonance made the Telecore swarm valuable to the Hive whole.

John Farragut was keeping the swarm alive.

"Oh, for Jesus."

Dealing with a Hive was like navigating a minefield. Farragut hated mines.

He shook off his blunder and pushed ahead. "I can't leave those monsters down there unsecured. Any solutions for me, gentlemen?"

"Quick and dirty fix," said Weng. "We could nuke the whole world and take out the local swarm—"

"—But then the rest of the Hive will learn about us from that," said Ski.

"I don't like that idea," said Farragut.

"Neither do we," said Weng, then turned to his colleague to make sure. "Do we?"

"No," said Ski. "We do not."

From battling the last Hive, the xenos knew that any experience of a swarm member was an experience immediately shared by the interstellar whole. You shoot one gorgon with a beam gun, then you must assume that all the Hive members across the universe now knew what a beam gun could do to them—though "knowing" was too elevated a term to attribute to Hive impulses. Augustus had once likened the Hive to a gut. A gut processed input, but it couldn't be said to "know" its own processes.

Nevertheless, the Hive whole would have an awareness of what happened at Telecore. They would be aware if the gorgons of Telecore died, and maybe from their dying glean "knowledge" of what killed them.

Knowledge was power. Farragut wanted to keep the new Hives as powerless as possible.

"I need a plan," Farragut told the xenos. "A viable plan for dealing with the Hive swarms on Telecore in the event we need to leave the planet—because we *will* be leaving the planet. I can't see the Joint Chiefs parking the *Mack* out here watching baby monsters while Near Space is at war."

"A plan, sir. Aye, sir," said Weng.

"Several proposals, sir," said Ski. "For your approval."

The effort to maintain Hive ignorance might be futile. The range of the Hive entirety was incalculable, and God alone knew what other beings elsewhere in the universe were teaching the new Hives even at this moment. But John Farragut was never one to stop running until the umpire called him out.

He did recognize that he could expect no help from Rome. Rome lost most of its Deep End colonies to the first Hive.

Hives. There had been two.

Presumably there were two again. It was only a guess—a good guess, but still a guess—that the new monsters were offspring of the old Hives, because the new monsters were popping up in places the old Hives had been like recurrences of Ebola.

That made for a lot of new gorgons on a lot of old Roman colonies in the Deep End of the galaxy.

But the Empire had withdrawn its remaining populations from the Deep End. Rome ceded all their liabilities to their enemy.

Except one.

There had only ever been one occurrence of the Hive in Near Space. That had been on the Roman colony of Thaleia.

No new generation of Hive had erupted on planet Thaleia.

So the new Hive threat was confined to the Deep End. Rome counted on the United States' self-interest to hold it there.

The Hive was a U.S. problem now.

That placed the United States in a two-front war—fighting the Hive in the Deep and Rome in Near Space.

Captain Farragut turned to his XO and his IO at the briefing table. "We've got two Roman ships of war out here in the Deep End and unaccounted for. Do we have anything on their heading?"

Colonel Z shook his head. "Wherever *Gladiator* and *Horatius* are, they're running dark. They may be headed back to Palatine, but who knows? We can't ignore the possibility that they could be lining up a strike on Fort Ike. In the first scenario, we don't need to worry about them for another three months. The other scenario would be ugly."

Numa Pompeii's warship *Gladiator* and the legion carrier *Horatius* had been members of Commodore Farragut's Attack Group One. His comrades in arms were suddenly enemy combatants.

General Numa Pompeii had been a powerful man during the reign of Caesar Magnus.

Caesar Romulus had sent Numa to the Deep to get him out of sight and out of popular mind.

Marcus Asinius, astrarch of the *Horatius*, was cousin to the late Legion Commander Herius Asinius, whose teeth were interred down below on the planet Telecore. Legion Draconis was not a favorite of Caesar Romulus either.

Neither Numa Pompeii nor Marcus Asinius were fervent Romulus supporters, but they were staunch Romans. Marcus would not question authority, like it or not. But Farragut would not put it past Numa to play Lucifer and storm the gates of Roman heaven.

Numa was a cagey political animal, arrogant, popular. Farragut could not guess what Numa's plans were.

Farragut ordered, "Gypsy, contact Fort Ike. Make sure the Fort's on Condition Watch Two. Advise them to be on the alert for *Gladiator* and *Horatius*. *And* let them know there is a rogue patterner armed with a Striker out here who could take the left antenna off a mayfly from five light-minutes away."

Kit Kittering lifted a finger to insert a comment. "Captain, I kinda doubt Augustus' shooting is gonna be that good. That old Striker was built for someone else and it's sixty years old. Strikers are custom jobs. He's just not gonna run as well in someone else's custom shoes. Patterners don't just *pilot* Strikers. They kind of *wear* them."

Kit had crawled through both Strikers. She knew each machine as well as she knew *Merrimack*.

"It's not gonna to be like our last fight with a patterner." Kit's hand found its way to her midriff as if she could still feel the hole.

A patterner named Septimus, piloting his own Striker, had fired a shot straight through *Merrimack*, through her force field, through Kit Kittering, and out the stern.

"Can you calculate the best speed of this Striker to make it across the Abyss?" Farragut asked his engineer.

The Abyss was two thousand parsecs of relative dark that separated galactic arms of the Milky Way. The Abyss lay between the Deep End and Near Space.

"Seventy standard days," Kit said with a head tilt to either side to indicate some give or take. "He might even get there sooner if he pushes it, but then he would arrive dead. Or vegetablized. Can we suggest it to him?"

"He may not live to see the other side of the Abyss anyway," said Farragut. "He shouldn't be alive now."

Life expectancy of a patterner was limited. When Caesar Magnus gave Augustus to Captain Farragut, Augustus had already outlived his expiration date. He had not been expected to live long enough to become the loose cannon he was now.

"Something else to consider," Colonel Z said. "That Striker Augustus took belonged to Secundus."

Secundus had been the second patterner ever assembled.

"Kit already went through that," said Farragut.

"Mister Kittering was talking about engines and weapons," said Colonel Z. "I'm talking about data. Augustus has

Secundus' data bank. Secundus identified the Hive harmonics using that database. When that Striker hits Near Space, Rome will have the secret of how to identify a single harmonic out of infinite possibilities."

"If Augustus has that information, then we have it," said Farragut. "Don't we have a copy of Secundus' database on *Merrimack*?"

"We do," said Colonel Z. "The secret of isolating harmonics per se is not in the database. Neither is Secundus' methodology. Secundus didn't make notes. But some combination of facts in the database together with a patterner's ability to synthesize data adds up to deep sewage for the United States of America. When Augustus shares that secret with his masters, we have a severe tactical disadvantage."

"I know. I'm the one who brought the bastard aboard," said Farragut. "We couldn't have exterminated the old Hive without Augustus. We needed him."

"Now we need him dead," said Colonel Z. Insinuation there. *Someone* had not done his job.

Kit came to Farragut's defense, "Augustus won't give Romulus skat. And if Augustus doesn't recognize Romulus as Caesar, then who gives a rat's ass? To hell with him."

Farragut gave Kit's shoulder a squeeze as his pacing took him past her, appreciating the loyalty. "Can't afford to get quite that comfortable, Kit," Farragut said. "Augustus is still Roman. When it comes down to Us versus Them, he is definitely a Them." And to the misgivings he saw in his officers' faces, he answered, "And don't anyone think that if I get a shot, I won't take it."

3

"MY CRATE!"

That was Kerry Blue circling her Swift in the flight hangar. The Swift's cockpit was charred black, the compressed air tanks blown, shrapnel stuck in the overhead and stabbed deep into the deck.

She lifted her arms up in the air, her fingers curled into claws calling witness to her beloved Alpha's carnage. "Shit! Oh crap. Oh fugger."

She glared up at a severed air hose flapping every which way twenty-five feet up in the overhead and she yowled, "Will someone shut that thing off!"

Up went an erk to the catwalk to clamp off the hose.

Kerry Blue was an ordinary sort of unretouched rough-pretty. Her race was purebred mutt. The melting pot had melted right here. Kerry Blue stood on the tall side, slim, loose jointed, with just enough padding on the bow and the stern to know you had a woman under those coveralls. Her easy loose walk really let you know.

She was battle seasoned but never hardened. She rolled with every hit and just got back up. Kerry Blue had a natural ability to ignore anything that didn't matter at the moment. She was not a deep thinker, which meant she never thought herself into a hole. She was going to be a lifer, and would probably still be a flight sergeant when they pulled her wings off.

Her wings were everywhere at the moment. Pieces of Alpha Six lay scattered all across the flight hangar.

Her Swift's magnetic antimatter containment field had held fast anyway, the only thing that had. But that thing was real important.

Flight Sergeant Cole Darby was down on the deck, wedged underneath Cain Salvador's Swift with Cain Salvador, trying to pry pieces of Alpha Six out of Alpha Three's undercarriage.

Came the roar. It was loud and it echoed round in the hangar: *"What'd you do to your spacecraft, Marine?"*

The Old Man. TR Steele.

Colonel Steele stopped in the hatchway, fists on his hips, eyes glowering ice blue fire.

Darb sniggered. Someone else cackled.

Colonel Steele was always roaring at Kerry Blue. But her Swift's mess on the deck was so clearly not Kerry Blue's fault that this roar had to be TR Steele impersonating himself.

Doing a good job too. Because if he'd been serious, Kerry Blue would be in the brig for kicking him in the butt.

Cain Salvador whispered aside to Cole Darby, lying on the creeper next to his underneath Cain's Swift. "Did I just see Kerry Blue kick the Old Man in the butt?"

"Nope." Darb kept his eyes on his work. "Didn't happen. You saw nothing. Gimme the torch."

"Colonel's here," Cain whispered. "Do we stand up?"

"Keep welding."

It had taken Kerry Blue over two years to see what Darb had noticed in his first months on board *Merrimack*. Colonel Steele was always an ogre to Kerry Blue, always yelling at her. She noticed that part. The colonel did everything he could to keep her out of his sight, like he couldn't stand the sight of her.

Well, he really *really* couldn't stand the sight of her.

Blue never figured that part out until Darb hit her in the head with it: *He can't stand to be near you.*

That had woken her up.

She'd been wide awake ever since.

Steele came stalking around the husk of Kerry's Swift,

his eyes hard as arctic ice, as if looking for something to criticize in the heap.

Darb cringed in hiding under Cain's Swift. It felt like the whole hangar could just go up in flames right now.

A small movement broke up the Old Man's frown, like a flicker in an image that quickly repairs itself. There was some kind of strong current in here. A sparking. Something was going to ignite. Smelled like someone's career.

Darb heard Kerry Blue talking too fast, too loud: "Look what he did! Augustus torched my crate! Why mine? I was nice to that son of a bitch!"

Kerry Blue had been nice to men beyond count.

Steele's face turned blood red.

Kerry railed on, "Why couldn't he torch *your* crate instead?"

Steele said, "He knew the way to get at me."

Darb tried to reel his legs in all the way under the Swift, cringing.

Kerry brought her voice way down quiet for just Steele — and the two guys trying to disappear under Alpha Three — to hear. "Yeah?"

Darb tried to will his ears shut.

I'm not hearing this. I am not hearing this. Anyone asks, I got no idea. La la la la la —

And praise the Lord, Steele growled at Kerry, "Clean up this mess." He stalked away.

Kerry Blue's voice sailed after him, too cheery: "Aye, aye, sir."

Colonel TR Steele turned his back on Kerry Blue and retreated to his side of that vast chasm that separated officer from enlisted man. *Man*, for Kerry Blue was a man by military definition. A she-man instead of a he-man, but a man as far as the Navy was concerned.

Except that was all bullskat to Colonel Steele, and Kerry Blue was all woman and what the hell was she doing on his battleship? *Enlisted!*

He could not have her. He could not breathe without her. He got all tongue-tied and stupid around her. He could not afford to mess this up.

What *this?* He caught himself thinking. There was no *this*. *This* could not happen. There could be no *this!*

Steele prowled across the hangar to Flight Leader Ranza Espinoza, a big woman, with broad shoulders, boy hips, and fine gray eyes. Her fat shock of coarse, light brown hair was tied back into a ponytail as thick as Steele's fist.

Ranza was a tough soldier, but she was not terrific with details. Unfortunately, the Divorce Protocol was nothing but details.

Steele looked over Ranza's rounded shoulder at the instructions which she kept reading and rereading. "Got it in hand, Flight Leader?"

"No, sir," said Ranza. "This has got me by the short hairs. And I thought I knew everything there was to know about divorce too."

Ranza had three children with three different last names, all back home on Earth with their maternal grandmother.

"You have a brain, Flight Leader," said Colonel Steele. "Use it."

Ranza anguished over the instructions that may as well have been written in Turkish. "Sir, I'm tryin'—"

Steele snatched the instructions from her. "Cole Darby!"

"Sir!" Darb's voice sounded along with a clunk. That was Flight Sergeant Cole Darby bumping his head on the belly of Cain Salvador's crate.

Cole Darby was an overeducated white suburban boy, who enlisted in the Fleet Marine looking for purpose in his life.

The Darb wanted a purpose? Colonel Steele would give him a foxtrotting purpose. He jammed the instructions for the Divorce Protocol into Cole Darby's hands. "Make this happen." *Find your meaning in that.*

"Aye, sir," said Cole Darby.

Steele had expected Darb to bail a long time ago. But the Darb had hung in, fit in. Not that the Darb wasn't still an odd duck in this company. Steele didn't know if Cole Darby had found whatever he was looking for, but he was still here and he was useful most of the time.

Steele watched Cole Darby read the Protocol. Darb's

eyes did not glass over. You could see the cylinders turning and the tumblers falling into position.

Steele returned to Ranza, gestured back with a jerk of his thick thumb. "There."

"Oh," said Ranza on an arcing note, everything becoming clear. "*That* brain."

"Allocate your resources, Flight Leader." Steele tapped her shoulder with the bottom of his fist.

Ranza smiled a gap-toothed smile. "Got it, sir. Thank you, sir."

Steele surveyed the hangar. His gaze fell on a pair of booted feet, sticking out from under the Swift next to Kerry Blue's.

Steele advanced. Let his shadow fall across the boots. "You got a girlfriend under there, Salvador?"

Clunk. Head on the belly. Cain Salvador scrabbled to vertical. "No, sir."

Flight Sergeant Cain Salvador looked like a Marine. Cain was sleek and powerful as a seal. Could have been a real afthole but he respected authority and stood before Steele at stiff attention.

"As you were."

Cain Salvador rubbed his head and crawled back under his Swift, Alpha Three.

Tromping across the deck grates and making a lot of noise operating a maintenance bot to suck the debris and soot from Kerry Blue's exploding crate was Dak Shepard, Alpha Two. Hard not to like Dak Shepard. All heart, guts, brawn, and dick. No brain. Dak was solid.

Flight Sergeant Twitch Fuentes was changing out the canopy of his Swift, Alpha Five. Steele did not ask Twitch Fuentes anything. Steele really didn't want to know how much English Twitch didn't know. Twitch was a good fighter, always ready.

Carly Delgado regularly flew Alpha Four. She had pried up a deck grate and was summoning Dak over to help her with the soggy mess underneath it with a wave of her stick-thin arm. All bone and whip muscle. Carly was a hard soldier. Her small pyramidal breasts looked hard too. Mean.

Too lean. She was looking particularly skinny right now. Steele ordered her, "Bulk up, Delgado."

"I feel better when I'm hungry," Carly answered back.

Steele told her, "I don't care if you eat or not, I want to see more Delgado."

Dak whispered, "Carly! Take your shirt off!"

"Shut up, Dak."

This mess was all Augustus' fault as far as Steele could see. The Roman man-machine was just plain easy to hate.

The war had gone hot and *Merrimack* was stuck in the Deep, snarled up in the Divorce Protocol, tripping over minutia and that was Augustus' fault too. The boffins were afraid Augustus had left rogue nanites.

Merrimack segregated all her systems. Took them down one by one, searched for signs of tampering and scoured for nanites. The crew ran test scenarios designed by the crypto-tech and validated by the systems' normal users and their maintenance personnel.

All programs were reencrypted and reseeded.

Chief Engineer Kit Kittering took down each of the fornicating ship's six fornicating engines one at a time, exiling the fornicating antimatter into space, while she purged the fornicating system, rehoused the fornicating components, recoded the fornicating containment field, recaptured the antimatter (really fornicating on the way back in) and restarted the damned engine.

Codes needed changing on all spacecraft *Merrimack* carried, starting with the Swifts, their force fields, their engine containment shields. Same with the long-range shuttles and the space patrol torpedo boats.

All personnel reported to the hospital in rotation for full nano scans. That included the ship's dogs.

Also to be scanned were the houseplants, the livestock, the hydroponic gardens. Innocuous systems—air, light, emergency light, the lifts—were all refitted with virgin programs. Decks were evacuated and sealed off one by one, opened to vacuum and sanitized.

Scrubbing for nanoparticles, you got to know how really big the *Mack* was.

She measured four hundred feet red light to green light,

eighty-four feet of that across the beam. She was four hundred feet topsail tip to bottom sail tip; five hundred and seventy feet nose to engines, then add another ninety feet onto that for the engines.

"What's that in nanometers?"

"Shut up, Dak."

Steele began to wonder if those instruments couldn't read his thoughts. Absolutely nothing else was private. Steele thanked God he'd never stashed away any images of Kerry Blue in his quarters. Nothing was left unscrutinized down to the nano level.

Harvard educated xenolinguist Patrick Hamilton apparently wasn't smart enough to purge his stash before the searchers hit his quarters. Something turned up in his quarters not meant for wifely eyes. Whatever it was, it didn't cause the security team any concern, but Doctor Pat's wife was the Hamster, third in command of the space battleship *Merrimack*. Those were her quarters too. If Patrick Hamilton didn't think a find like that wouldn't get back to her there must have been a stupid contest running.

Made Steele feel like a fog frucking genius.

Captain Farragut took a walkabout of his giant ship. Not that he could see nanoparticles, but if anything were out of place on his *Merrimack* he could sense it.

The tap tap tap of a basketball drew him to the maintenance hangar. He recognized the cadence of the dribble. The ball's bounces had a feminine sound. The footsteps following the ball were barely audible above the other ship sounds.

As Farragut entered the cavernous compartment, the lone player circled under the basket with a light tread. She jumped. Landed lightly and corralled the ball that bounced off the rim.

She was five foot one and light boned.

Hamster was just plain light.

She played one-on-herself in the maintenance hangar. John Farragut would have joined her, but it was probably not a good idea for him to play one-on-one of any game with Mrs. Hamilton.

Glenn Hamilton wore her auburn hair pulled back in a ponytail. She dribbled the basketball, jumped, and shot. And missed again. Caught the rebound.

"You know there is something ridiculous about you with a basketball."

Hamster glared toward the hatch. Saw John Farragut leaning in the entranceway. "Shut up," she said. "Sir."

Farragut strode in. He beckoned for the ball. She passed it to him, rather strongly.

He bounced the ball twice, took a shot. Missed.

Hamster collected the rebound, jumped and made the shot.

"Gypsy wasn't on deck when you called me to the command deck, was she?" said Farragut.

Hamster had to think back to the declaration of war. It seemed like a year ago since the balloon went up, even though it was scarcely enough time to count in days. More like hours.

She remembered the words she'd used to summon Farragut to the command deck in the middle of ship's night without mentioning war.

Gypsy's hair.

"Hell no, sir!" she answered.

Commander Gypsy Dent's hair was an elaborate nest of serpentine dreadlocks detached from Gypsy's head and exiled to her cabin until Gypsy got off duty, when she reattached it to her head hair by hair.

Gypsy was very proud of her hair, and she had given Captain Farragut an order: "Speak not of the hair."

No one else would have made the connection, even if they had heard Farragut once describe Gypsy's hair as "a war zone." But Glenn Hamilton and John Farragut operated on the same harmonic. He figured it out instantly.

"Don't tell Commander Dent I said that," said Hamster. "She'll sic her hair on me."

She bounced the basketball.

It was the middle of Glenn Hamilton's night. She ought to be in bed, with her husband.

"All not happy in the rose garden?" Farragut guessed.

"*Plant* the rose garden!" said Hamster. She took another shot. Bounced off the rim. "I am *not* going to sleep with *that*."

She flipped the bird at her absent sweetheart.

Farragut seized her impudent digit in his fist and walked Glenn by the finger over to a data terminal. He pressed her fingertip to an authorization pad. Her hand was dainty and tiny in his big paw. Her fingernail formed a neat little oval peeking out the bottom of his fist. He let go of her finger.

The authorization pad showed green. He'd given her access to the captain's quarters.

"You can rack out at my place," Farragut told her. "Be out of there by eight bells."

Glenn collected the basketball. She tossed it from hand to hand, agitated, considering the offer.

Farragut intercepted the ball, kept it. He nodded sideways out the hatch. "Get some rest."

Glenn let her chin drop to her collarbone, suddenly very sleepy. "Thank you, sir."

She left the deck, her little red ponytail swinging side to side.

Farragut forgot about the encounter until mid watch, ship's night, which everyone called the Hamster watch. The delicate smell of someone else, someone female, lingered on his pillow.

Had the damnedest dreams.

"Word is Lady Hamilton spent the day in the captain's rack," Carly arrived in the forecastle with the latest gossip. Gossip had already got there ahead of her, and Darb said back, "Yeah, she did but the cap'n didn't. He was on duty."

"Crap," said Kerry Blue, disappointed. "Hamster should dump Doctor Pat and make the captain happy."

"Never happen, *chica linda*," said Carly. "They're officers. Officers take that skat serious."

"It's not like officers' zippers don't go down like everyone else's," said Cain Salvador.

"Yeah," said Dak Shepard and added with a snigger, "They just make a real loud sound when they get caught."

Kerry Blue's stomach fluttered. That was exactly nothing she wanted to hear.

"Hamster ain't right for the captain," said Ranza Espinoza.

"You think?" said Kerry Blue.

Ranza lifted a sneering lip. "Nah. She's not for him. She's just *here.* Farragut needs a hen, and that chick don't lay eggs."

"Somebody told me Farragut had a wife," said Cain Salvador.

"Yeah," said Dak. "Named Maryann."

"So Farragut *is* married?" said Cain, surprised.

"Was," said Dak.

"A while ago," said Kerry Blue.

"She offed herself," said Carly.

"Really?" said Cain. "Damn, I never found him that tough to be around."

"That's the point," said Carly. "He wasn't around."

"She did it because he wasn't *around*?" Suicide was alien to Kerry Blue and she made a face, looking around for anyone else who thought that was weird.

"Seems a little drastic," said Cole Darby to her frown. "Couldn't she just have an affair with the stable boy?"

"I wouldn't," said Kerry Blue.

"Wouldn't what?"

"Kill myself," said Kerry.

"We know that, *chica*," said Carly.

"Kerry would do the stable boy," said Dak.

Kerry didn't ever want to know what she would do.

Merrimack looked down from the observation deck at the devastated world of Telecore. It was getting time to leave.

Captain Farragut loathed giving ground to the enemy. As a soldier, he wanted to kill them.

It galled him to know that exterminating an entire Hive was as easy as flipping a switch. He had destroyed the two original Hives with two resonant pulses. They died in an instant.

It was pathetically easy.

And impossible at the moment.

Repeating that feat required identifying the specific harmonic that held this new Hive together.

There were infinite harmonics.

John Farragut had been given the first two. Xenos were working on recreating the methodology but if isolating a harmonic were not so damnably difficult then some intelligent entity would have stopped the original Hives long before now.

The Hive was so alien to organic life, so improbable, so contrary to ordinary laws of nature that worlds died before they could realize the nature of the beast.

John Farragut was sure to holy hell that no one would be giving him harmonics this time.

The neutron hose option was tempting. But tactical victory could lead to strategic disaster.

John Farragut would not be the one to teach this Hive what a neutron hose was. But neither could he trust the gorgons of Telecore to stay on Telecore once *Merrimack* left orbit.

The xenos could not tell him what part of a Hive's "knowledge" was learned and what was instinct.

Attraction to a resonant source was probably instinctive. Hive ability to hone in on a source and a reception point of resonance appeared to be an inborn skill as well.

Even now the gorgons of Telecore leaned up, yearning like sunflowers at *Merrimack*'s every orbital pass.

If this Hive behaved like its predecessor, then as soon as these gorgons became spaceborne they would immediately head to the closest resonant source. Assuming *Merrimack* was no longer here, that would make the swarm's target the U.S. Space Fortress Dwight David Eisenhower. A space fort was a stationary target.

Farragut quit the observation deck and swung into the lab. "Doctor Weng! Doctor Sidowski! Show me what you've got!"

"I think we have come up with a workable solution—" said Weng.

"More of a stopgap than a solution—" said Ski.

"—to handle the resident swarm in the absence of human oversight," said Weng.

The xenos presented to Captain Farragut a collection of small drones.

Farragut picked one up. It was lightweight, roughly spherical, larger than a softball, smaller than a basketball. He turned it over and over. "They look like Roman rovers."

Weng nodded. "We nicked the design."

Ski: "They're programmed to resonate on different harmonics. This is the first set—"

"We're calling it Toto."

"Toto is engineered to run around on the surface of Telecore, resonating."

"Gorgons chase resonant sources."

"The gorgons will chase them," said Weng.

"Toto is faster than the gorgons," said Ski.

"According to current data," said Weng.

"We're basically giving the gorgons a little exercise," said Ski.

"Let them burn energy."

"Keeps them occupied."

"What if the gorgons catch Toto?" Farragut asked.

"We want them to."

"Eventually."

"After a while."

"Why?"

"For one thing, the gorgons will learn that a resonant source isn't edible. We want them to think that."

"So in the best case scenario they'll conclude that chasing something resonant is a waste of energy," said Ski.

"We never get the best case scenario," said Farragut. He passed the rover of Toto One back to Doctor Sidowski.

"Aye, Captain. That brings us to Toto Two," said Weng.

Toto Two wasn't in the lab. Ski brought up an image of Toto Two.

Farragut blinked. "Toto Two's a long-range shuttle."

"Toto Two will be orbiting Telecore. If the gorgons achieve escape velocity and leave atmosphere, Toto Two is programmed to commence resonating on a new harmonic," said Ski.

"A new harmonic in case the swarms guess that the first harmonic was a dry hustle," Weng noted.

"Not like we don't have enough harmonics to work with."

"Toto Two is programmed to leave orbit and lead the gorgons off in a direction away from Fort Eisenhower."

"They're wild geese," said Farragut.

Merrimack had used wild geese many times to draw the Hive off a vulnerable target.

"Except that Toto Two will be moving at a velocity calculated to let the gorgons gain on it in small increments," said Ski.

"So the gorgons don't lose interest," said Weng.

"We want to keep them chasing," said Ski.

"That *should*—" Weng began.

"*should*—" Ski emphasized.

"—keep the gorgons off course and unfed for at least a year," Weng concluded.

"What do you think?" Ski asked.

They both looked expectantly to the captain.

"I like it, guys," said Farragut. "Make it work. And hope the gorgons of Telecore get hungry enough to eat each other before we're forced to deal with them again."

4

A BITCH NAMED INGA greeted Captain Farragut at the hatch to the only civilian compartment on the space battleship. The Doberman was former crew. Drummed out of the Navy in disgrace, Inga had become pet to the only man on board permitted to own a pet, *Merrimack*'s civilian adviser *Don* Jose Maria de Cordillera.

Inga sat on Farragut's command, her stubby tail wagging, shaking her whole stern with it, a big sharp white smile on her clueless face.

The creation of smart dogs was an idea that came and went and came and went over the centuries, and met with disaster every time it came, and always went chased by dogs.

It seemed natural for Man to want his best friend to be better. The idea of a genetically engineered canine with enhanced intelligence held irresistible promise.

The results had been the meanest, most unpredictable, most undoglike breeds ever conceived.

Smart dogs had personalities a lot like Augustus' in fact.

With self-awareness came willful disobedience.

Smart dogs were cunning, self-serving, skulking, sulking, depressive, disloyal, mutinous, thieving curs with delusions of grandeur. A dog that would just as soon bite you in the face as submit to a human being's dominance.

Having eaten of the fruit of the tree of knowledge, Man's creations questioned the imperative of unquestioned devotion.

Cadres of dogs trained for fearless service to humankind, loyal unto death, decided to stuff this for a game of soldiers and go their own way. A dog named Bravo, popularly known as Spartacus, led a massacre of his unit's handlers. That fubar ended the last attempt at improving Dog almost a hundred years ago.

The remaining smart dogs had been castrated by their creator and heaved out of the garden.

The Fall of the enhanced Dog was Dog's failure to bow to the Alpha.

Merrimack's contingent of fourteen unenhanced canines was comprised of the three rat terriers—Godzilla, Kong, and Dragon; five miniature shepherds; two golden retrievers in the medical service; Nose and Sweet Lips, the miniature bloodhounds; and Pooh the standard poodle whom the chief considered *his* dog.

Inga the Doberman had been sacked for killing a crewmate. The crew had been seaweed, and may have been dead before Inga started chewing on it, but Inga's behavior was unacceptable for a member of the U.S. Navy nonetheless.

Inga was not a smart dog.

John Farragut gave the now-civilian Inga an ear scratch as he entered the compartment.

At one time holograms of wide open pastures with running horses and deep blue skies had graced the confines of Jose Maria's cabin. The space was bare now, its true small dimensions clear. In it was only a bed surrounded by stacks of crates. One crate served as a chair, another two as a writing desk. Everything else was in the crates.

Jose Maria was already packed. He knew what a declaration of war meant.

"Young Commodore." Jose Maria rose from his chair-crate and turned from his desk-crates to greet Farragut with a smile and a continental bow. He was dressed simply in a charcoal gray tunic and black trousers of elegant weave.

"It's Captain again," said Farragut. The Attack Group

had disintegrated and so had Farragut's temporarily elevated title.

"Young Captain," Jose Maria corrected himself.

A Terra Rican aristocrat, Jose Maria de Cordillera looked refined no matter what he did. Even when he'd been wielding a sword and wading ankle-deep in dying gorgons, he was a mesmerizing figure.

He was an older man, greyhound slender, his long black hair held back in a silver clasp. The silvering blaze at his temples had grown wider in the last year. He had truly beautiful hands, his neat nails shaped very short on the left hand; squared off and somewhat longer on the right. Fingernails of a man who played Spanish guitar.

John Farragut glanced over all of Jose Maria's crates. "Where's your guitar?"

"He took it," said Jose Maria, tranquil.

He. Augustus.

Farragut reacted with a start. "Augustus was *here*?"

Jose Maria had known that Augustus was jumping ship.

John Farragut spoke, a little betrayed. "You didn't warn me."

"I had no idea you were unaware," said Jose Maria. "As it was, I gave him my blessing."

Not the way Farragut had been blessing Augustus.

"I'm sure Augustus appreciated that," said Farragut.

"He swore at me," Jose Maria said with a philosophical shrug.

Captain Farragut could not delay the sour news that brought him here. "I'm sorry I have to beach you at first port of call, which is fixing to be Fort Eisenhower. Under the Divorce Protocol I can't carry a neutral anymore."

Jose Maria showed no offense. "I understand, young Captain."

Farragut continued, apologetic, "I can't even take you through the Shotgun. And I know civilian shuttle schedules have got to be hashed, so I can't even guess how long a layover you've got ahead of you before you can get back to Near Space."

"I know the rules for neutrals in wartime," said Jose Maria, unconcerned. "I have had my eye on that pretty little new-styled Star Racer. I saw them for sale at Portrillo station in the fortress on our last time through. I could never justify buying such a toy before." His dark eyes became impish, "This is a sign, do you not think?"

Farragut smiled, picturing Jose Maria with a sassy space yacht. Jose Maria could easily afford it. He was enormously wealthy, a moral man who felt some guilt at the indulgence. But the war did provide an excuse.

Farragut said, "Do I need to ask what you will christen her?"

"No, young Captain, you do not."

There was soon to be a quick little racing yacht named *Mercedes* dashing among the stars.

Jose Maria's wife Mercedes had been a xenobotanist. She had gone to the Deep End with Romans several years ago on a secret terraforming project beyond U.S. settled space.

Everything about the planet was perfect for terraforming when the Roman explorers found it—its irradiation, its gravitation, its revolution, its rotation, its tilt, its orbital eccentricity, the pressure and composition of its atmosphere, its soil, its water, its sun. It was perfect. Better than perfect—because, despite its ideal conditions, there was no native life to compete with Roman imports.

Soon there was a balanced, thriving ecosystem on the distant colonial world. The Romans named the planet Telecore.

Mercedes Cordillera started homeward on board the Roman ship *Sulla*.

Sulla never arrived.

For a long time no one would speak of *Sulla*'s existence. Voices dropped to a hush at mention of the name. No one would talk to Jose Maria.

With nearly limitless financial resources, Jose Maria set himself on a quest to find his wife. His quest brought him to *Merrimack*.

Jose Maria's home was the unified nation-world of Terra Rica. Terra Rica was neutral in the U.S./Roman conflict. Jose Maria had come on board *Merrimack* as a sword master. The sword was not a recognized weapon of war at the time, so Captain Farragut did not call Jose Maria an arms instructor.

A semantic cheat, but it got the Terra Rican neutral on board a United States space battleship without breaking his neutrality.

In their journey to the far reaches of the Deep End of the galaxy *Merrimack* uncovered a terrible secret.

There really were monsters at the edge of the map.

It turned out that the crew and passengers of *Sulla* were the first human victims of the Hive. The planet Telecore was close behind.

Someone might have wondered why a planet perfect for life had none. Rome had only found Telecore devoid of all life because the Hive had already been there once, eaten it clean, and moved on. And came back.

The Hive ate the terraformed world clean one more time.

The Hive was ancient, resilient, a veteran of countless attempts to destroy it. Swarms could outmaneuver, overpower, and turn high-tech weaponry on its owners. Yet despite all the Hive's collective adaptations and tricks, the individual members could still be cut with a sharp edge. A ship equipped with swords was the first to survive an encounter with the Hive.

Jose Maria had assisted in destroying the original enemy, but failed in his quest to bring his wife home. He knew Mercedes was dead. He would have liked to lay her to rest on Terra Rica.

Sulla had never been found.

Jose Maria was going home alone.

"I must give you something of mine," Jose Maria told John Farragut. "There may not be time later. I gave Augustus my guitar."

Well, Augustus had taken it.

Jose Maria gave John Farragut his Spanish sword.

The elegant sword, its elaborate hilt fashioned like El Cid's colada, bore nicks and scratches of honorable service. The cord that kept it in hand through many battles was frayed. "Hell of a gift," said Farragut, profoundly moved. "Thank you."

He asked Jose Maria if he was going home now to Terra Rica.

"Earth first," said Jose Maria. "I have an audience with the Pope."

"What'd that cost you?"

Eyelids lowered, brows went up. "You are channeling Augustus, young Captain," Jose Maria scolded gently. "That was unkind."

"That was unforgivably rude," said Farragut, surprised that the words even came out of him.

"Forgivable." Jose Maria made the sign of the cross over him. "*Te absolvo.*"

Jose Maria's standing as philanthropist and as a Catholic would make him welcome at the Vatican, seat of the archaic Earth religion which had long since parted ways with the Roman Empire.

"We'll need to delouse you and all your things before we get to Fort Ike," said Farragut.

The crew had come to referring to nanites as lice.

Neither the term nor the requirement surprised Jose Maria. He was aware of all the sanitization happening around him.

Farragut promised him, "I'll have the crew repack your crates when they're done."

Jose Maria demurred, "Young Captain, I have a set of personal nano-machines I should very much like to preserve."

"I'll get you a capsule. We can tow your nanites outboard with the oxygen bricks. You'll need to park them outside the Fort and pick them up on your way out."

"That will suffice. Thank you for accommodating me."

"Are you taking the Shotgun home or are you and *Mercedes* touring the galaxy?"

"I have not decided," he said, thoughtful.

The Shotgun could displace Jose Maria and *Mercedes* across the two thousand parsecs that separated Fort Dwight David Eisenhower from Fort Theodore Roosevelt in an instant. A ship existed in the Fort Ike terminus of the Shotgun one moment, and then in the Fort Ted terminus the next. Never in between.

From Fort Ted, Earth was only eighty-two light-years away. Terra Rica was not much farther but in a different direction.

A hefty tariff accompanied nonmilitary use of the Shotgun. That would not be an issue for Jose Maria if he decided to use the Shotgun.

The alternative to the Shotgun was a three-month voyage across the Abyss—the lightly starred space between galactic arms. Maybe less than three months if Jose Maria tried to set a record in his new Star Racer.

"Fort Ike and Fort Ted are both military targets," John Farragut advised Jose Maria. "Unless the Pope is drumming his fingers, I'd take the long way home. The farther you stay from us, the safer you will be."

"Perhaps then I should pick up a guitar in Fort Eisenhower," said Jose Maria, contemplating the long journey across empty space. "One way or the other, I shall see you on the other side." Jose Maria drew Farragut in for a hug and a kiss on both cheeks, and one more on his forehead, as he would one of his sons. "Vaya con Dios, young Captain."

The ship was nearly cleansed and most of the new communications links established, when the com tech reported, "Captain, I've got a hail on our old res harmonic."

Specialists on the command deck tensed at their stations.

This far into the protocol, no one should be using the old harmonics.

Anyone using an old harmonic had to be hostile, no matter what kind of excuse they tried to give.

Captain Farragut moved over to the com station. "Who is it claiming to be?"

"Numa Pompeii in *Gladiator*."

"Well, he better not have the new harmonic," said Farragut.

Farragut relaxed, but only a degree. Numa was a devil he knew. Made sense for Numa to be on the Attack Group's old harmonic. Did not make sense that a Roman general would be contacting *Merrimack* during a state of war.

Captain Farragut motioned the com tech to put the call on speaker, and he said into the com, "Numa. Maybe I can help you find your way into the nearest black hole. Where are you?"

"Not far from you."

Farragut reared back from the com, motioning the com tech to mute it.

Not good. *Not* good.

Farragut ordered Targeting: "Find him." And to Gypsy, "Are we tight?" He meant the ship's force field.

"We're tight, sir," Commander Dent affirmed. The ship's condition watch had been elevated ever since the declaration, just for this sort of surprise.

Lately an ally, Numa knew where the *Mack* was headed when they parted ways. *Merrimack* hadn't moved from that known destination.

Numa's *Gladiator* was like a hippopotamus submerged in the muddy river water. Hidden. Deadly. Powerful. Territorial.

"Should I move us?" Gypsy suggested.

"Stand by. Just because he says he's here doesn't necessarily mean he's here." Farragut motioned the com back on. "State your intentions, Numa."

Farragut had expected Numa to be long gone. He would be, if his destination really was Near Space.

And if he was not headed for Near Space, what the hell was he doing?

"Permission to approach," Numa Pompeii requested, his voice a rumble as from the volcano.

"You've got my permission to proceed to the Elysian Fields, Numa. Tell me where you are." Farragut muted the com and barked aside at Targeting, "Do we have him?"

"No, sir. Trying, sir." The needle was fat but the haystack was vast. Targeting muttered into his instruments. "Wish I were a gorgon right now so I could home in on the source of a res pulse."

"We have gorgons right downstairs," Gypsy said. "Are any of *them* pointing somewhere besides at us?"

Horrified that he hadn't thought of it, Targeting hastened to check out the idea.

Gypsy then suggested very low to Tactical, who was not helping in the hunt, "Do you know that Mister Vincent would really like to come back on days?"

Tactical could pick up a hint when it exploded on his

bow. Murmured back, "Aye, sir." And set to helping Targeting find *Gladiator*.

Gypsy moved to the captain, where he stood glaring at the com, waiting for Numa's response. Again, she spoke very low. "I don't believe the Roman, sir. He wouldn't still be here. He's got a three-month journey home."

Numa's voice sounded from the com, "I would like to come over under a white flag."

Farragut felt his own eyes go wide. Heard Gypsy whisper, "Bullskat."

Numa Pompeii had not been Caesar Magnus' man.

He was even less Caesar Romulus' man.

Numa Pompeii had not been on Palatine for the Senate vote that elected the new Caesar.

Worse, Numa had not been there to make his own bid for the job.

Maybe Augustus wasn't the only rogue Roman out there.

Making sure the mute was still on, Farragut told Targeting and Tactical, "Bring your search in tight, boys. He's real close."

Gypsy said, still in a whisper, "He's playing us, sir."

Farragut nodded. Numa might betray the current Roman leadership, but he would never betray Rome. He had friends.

Numa Pompeii was an enormously influential man.

And an enormous man. Built like a small mountain, Numa Pompeii moved with surprising speed and agility for his mass and age. He was nearly fifty Earth years old, though doubtless getting muscle rejuvenations for a decade or more.

Farragut nodded for the com tech to take the com off mute. "Are you seeking amnesty, Numa?"

"No," said Numa Pompeii. "A truce. I want to talk."

"You are *not* coming aboard," Farragut declared. He had already cleared *Mack* of nanites. The last thing he needed was a wily—possibly infested—Roman general on board.

"You would come aboard *Gladiator*?" Numa said, incredulous.

"Are you nuts?" Farragut said back. Numa knew Americanese well enough to understand that. "I'll meet you outside. Park the gunboat—and keep it parked. Approach in a small craft to coordinates we send you, then you step outside. If I get sight of your gunship, I start shooting. If *Gladiator* moves, I start shooting." He clicked off. "Send him coordinates. Someplace close to nowhere. We'll see if he shows."

Gypsy asked, "Do you trust him, sir?"

" 'Bout as far as a Planck length," said Farragut.

Gypsy's graceful brows twisted into dubious lines. "That far?"

Insects on shipboard went silent as *Merrimack* left Telecore's orbit. Insects were standard issue on Navy ships in the Deep End. Their sensitivity to Hive presence made them invaluable. Also made them annoying.

The insects had been a nuisance as long as *Merrimack* orbited Telecore, sounding over and over again what everyone already knew, the Hive was here, the Hive was here.

The insects had been banished to the lab to heckle the xenos.

With the return to insect peace, tiny cricket cages were brought back to the command deck of *Merrimack* to resume their function as early warnings.

Merrimack headed out to a place near nowhere.

Numa Pompeii made the rendezvous in a light courier type vessel, all lit up, no armament hanging off it, white flags stiff in the windless nothing of space.

Tactical was able to back trace the location of *Gladiator* to a point two light-years out.

"Keep a bead on him," said Farragut. "If *Gladiator* moves from that position, shoot Numa."

At the appointed galactic coordinates, a large space-suited figure emerged from the Roman courier and floated into the deepest of oceans.

Farragut suited up. Drifted out an air lock.

Space was raw, absolute, stark, beautiful, merciless.

Farragut got a little lost gazing at the overwhelming vastness. Finally he engaged the small jets that propelled him to rendezvous with the other microbe out here in this eternal sea. They braked in front of each other and clasped gloved hands.

The meeting of unequal masses set them on a slight drift, backward for Farragut. They grasped each other's sleeves and touched helmets.

Sound conducted through their faceplates.

"Ave," said Numa. His voice reverberated in Farragut's helmet.

"Hey," said Farragut, an Appalachian hello. Farragut was American blueblood, but he tended to speak like just folks.

They were face to face. So close that Farragut could see very little other than Numa's face, but not so close that Numa would have three eyes.

Numa's face was unretouched and not good-looking. A face like an assembly of stones. Numa had wealth, power, a big personality, and energy second only to Farragut's, so you didn't notice the homeliness of the face unless you were inches from it.

"I can't see Romulus authorizing this meeting," said Farragut. "You're not doing anything treasonous, are you?"

"Not yet," said Numa.

Farragut guessed: "You haven't pledged to Romulus."

"I have the luxury of time."

Kissing Romulus' ring would have to wait until Numa achieved Near Space. That would not be happening for at least three months.

So Numa Pompeii, the General, the Senator, the Triumphalis, had a three-month window in which to decide a loyalty, or to figure out what kind of base of power he might organize.

Numa Pompeii was one of only three Romans other than Romulus who knew that the Roman Senate's vote for Romulus to the position of Caesar had been based on an incomplete last testament of Caesar Magnus.

Romulus had unsealed his father's testament only after he received word—from Numa Pompeii—that the patterner who sealed Magnus' testament was dead.

The patterner was not dead.

Perhaps Numa wanted to get back to Near Space before he could be expected.

"You're not getting near the Shotgun, if that's what this is about," Farragut told Numa up front.

"No. I do not want passage through your Shotgun. It would not look good to accept favors from Americans."

"So what favor can I do for you?"

"I need to talk to Gaius."

The other man who knew that Romulus falsified Caesar's testament was Gaius Bruccius Eleutherius Americanus—the man whom Magnus actually named as his successor in his true testament.

Gaius Americanus was currently at the U.S. Space Fort Eisenhower in the Deep End.

The reported death of the testament's witness, Augustus, crippled any claim to power Gaius could make that Magnus chose him.

Gaius Americanus did not know that Augustus lived.

And Numa could not tell him. With all the U.S. com channels changed, Numa could not contact Gaius in Fort Eisenhower.

"Gaius Americanus is safe in Fort Eisenhower," said Farragut.

"The Senator does not live to be safe," said Numa. "He lives for Rome. As do I."

"Caesar is not Rome?"

"Depends on whether Caesar is actually Caesar."

"Are y'all proposing to set up a government in exile at Fort Ike?"

"A Roman government within a U.S. fortress? That will not fly. If Gaius wants to do anything for Rome—the true Rome—he will need to come out of that fortress."

The suggestion set Farragut on guard. He was accustomed to taking men at their word, but Numa Pompeii was an opportunist.

Until Numa declared a loyalty, God knew where he stood. And God might oughta better check his sources at that.

Farragut spoke, suspicious, "Last time I looked, you and Gaius Americanus were not the best of buds."

"We never had so much in common before."

The commonality would be the knowledge that Caesar Romulus was a patricidal fraud. That was a tie that could bind political adversaries.

"Tell him I want to talk to him," said Numa. "Let Gaius decide if he wants to talk to me."

"I will give him the message," said Farragut.

"And I want the patterner."

Farragut did not have the patterner to give. Apparently Augustus had not bothered to contact Numa upon parting company with *Merrimack*.

Not to give anything away, Farragut sidestepped truthfully, "I won't hand him over."

"You can't hold him," Numa said.

You got that right, Farragut thought. He was not a good liar, so he said nothing.

"Let me talk to him," Numa pressed.

Farragut did not address the demand. Let Numa continue thinking that the U.S. had custody and control of the patterner. Captain Farragut did not come out here to give information to Romans. He took the offensive, "Do you have capability to home in on the origination point of a res pulse?"

"Would I tell you?" Numa parried.

The answer was obvious: *No.*

Farragut said, "I'll let Gaius know you want to see him."

"I need a little more than that, Captain Farragut," said Numa. "If Gaius says yes to the meeting, he will need a way out here."

Farragut agreed to deliver the invitation to Gaius and to arrange transportation for Gaius if he consented to leave Fort Eisenhower.

"Choose someone of unquestionable reliability," said Numa. "I came to you because you are honorable, Captain John Farragut. Most Americans are rabid Roman haters. I do know the American definition of a good Roman. How can I be certain that the transportation you provide won't seize at a chance to turn Gaius into a good Roman even under a white flag?"

"I have just the man for the job," Farragut assured him. "She doesn't hate Romans. She only hates you."

THE OUTER DARKNESS DIALOGS
(Being a series of conversations among Jose Maria de Cordillera, Augustus, and John Farragut on board the flagship of Attack Group One en route to Sagittarius Zero)

A.D. 2445

The dialogs. I.

A: The Hive is entropy incarnate. Entropy is a fundamental condition of the universe.

JF: Well, entropy is an enemy of the United States, so it is my sworn duty to combat entropy.

A: Leave it to John Farragut to simplify the matter down to a one-brain-cell level. Fact is the universe is falling into disarray. The Hive just accelerates it. The universe's ultimate perfect form is destined to be a vast spread of attenuated atoms quivering in the eternal night forever and ever amen. So what is any of it for? Life is a cosmic waste of consciousness.

JMdeC: Stated that way, yes, it would be.

A: The Catholic speaks. Catholic arguments don't count, *Don* Cordillera. When logic fails, you can't just resort to magic.

5

"**J**OHN FARRAGUT, YOU KNOW Numa Pompeii is my least favorite sapient being in the known galaxy."

"I know that, Cal."

Calli Carmel, captain of the wolfhunter class spaceship *Wolfhound*, received the secure message from Captain Farragut on one of the new channels.

She could not believe what he told her. Captain John Farragut expected her to ask her adored former teacher Gaius Americanus to come out of the safety of Fort Ike to meet with the man she called Numa Pompous Ass.

"Do you *trust* him?" Calli asked, all but crawling into the com, as if she could take hold of him and shake some sense into him.

"Glory, no! I'm just delivering the message. It's not an endorsement. Though an insurgency against Romulus' rule would not be a bad thing."

"*If* that's really what this is about." Calli smelled something else.

"It's not your decision, Cal. Deliver the message to Gaius Americanus." The flatness in his voice said he was pulling seniority on her. *Do it, Cal.*

She could probably appeal to Admiral Mishindi, but Mishindi would tell her to follow Farragut on this one. This was the Deep End and it was war. Challenging John Farragut just to keep her favorite Roman safe would be an extraordinarily bad idea.

"It's Gaius' decision," said Farragut. "If Gaius decides to come out of hiding to meet with Numa, give him safe passage out of the Fort and give them a meeting space."

Calli could not argue with that. Hated it. "Can I bug the space?"

"I'd be real disappointed if you didn't."

Captain Calli Carmel was a minor celebrity. Most of her fame was not for her heroism in battle, though she had planned and executed a couple of high impact missions, both as executive officer of the *Merrimack* and later as captain of her own ship, *Wolfhound*.

But what Calli Carmel was known for was her beauty. A stupid thing to be known for by her own reckoning. Anyone could look like anything these days. Calli had the indefinable something *else* that pushed her above and beyond physical beauty. Didn't make it any less stupid.

Calli Carmel had gained notoriety across the settled part of the galaxy when she attended a public ceremony on the arm of Romulus not-yet-Caesar. That ceremony saw the assassination of Romulus' father, Caesar Magnus. So the image of Calli at Romulus' side was witnessed over and over on interstellar media. Ever since then, the media called her Empress Calli.

Nearly two decades earlier, during peacetime, Calli had attended the prestigious Imperial Military Institute on Palatine. Numa Pompeii had been one of her instructors—a belittling, scornful bastard of a non-instructive instructor.

Calli had since used Pompeii's overweening pride and disdain against him. She had embarrassed the Triumphalis more than once in battle.

Another of her instructors at the Imperial Military Institute had been Gaius Bruccius Eleutherius Americanus. Gaius was not a native Roman. He had been born on Earth, christened Dante Porter, an impoverished, illeducated U.S. citizen. He had attended a school system that passed students out like bilge water. It had scandalized and mortified the U.S. when an American citizen renounced his citizenship to sell himself into slavery in the Roman Empire just to get an education.

"Property rights" on Palatine often referred to rights of the property. Dante the slave had the right to food, shelter, and a Roman education.

Roman education was uniformly excellent. Dante earned his education, his freedom, and his Roman citizenship.

Renamed Gaius by the Bruccius family who adopted him, he rose from the bottom of society's birdcage to become a Senator, Consul, and right hand to Caesar Magnus.

Gaius Americanus had been young Calli's mentor at the Institute. He had seen in her a sharp intellect and a fellow outsider. He had been willing to help someone driven to learn.

Calli never stopped adoring him.

She wished like hell she could just lose this message. She would have, except she had been entrusted by John Farragut to deliver it. Farragut's trust had a nearly magical force that made people risk anything not to disappoint him.

She could only pray that Gaius would refuse Numa Pompeii's invitation.

Gaius Americanus had not come to Fort Eisenhower for his own safety. Gaius came to the Deep to keep his family out of reach of Romulus' long knives.

Gaius knew that a man who would kill his own father would not hesitate to do the same to the wife and children of his chief rival if it served him.

Coming out here had been a political mistake. But Gaius valued his family above all else. If he had to do it over again, his decision would be the same.

He recognized immediately—even before Magnus was declared dead—that Romulus had been ready and waiting to seize control out of the chaos. Romulus had anticipated the chaos.

Gaius immediately knew he was the next target, and he moved his family out of Romulus' range. He tried to keep in mind the words of Philip II, upon a retreat: *I fall back like the ram, to charge again harder.* But this ram was finding the footing too slippery to mount any kind of charge.

It did not help that Romulus was an effective leader.

Gaius had been asked, "If he's a good leader, why would you want to overthrow him?"

The question amazed him. How could a patricide be a good leader? Foul was foul. Was Hitler a good leader except for the Holocaust?

He had also been told, "If it ain't broke, don't fix it." To which he tried to explain, "It's broke."

No one wanted to hear that. The expedience of evil allowed decent citizens to turn blind and deaf when it served them.

"What does it make you when you allow a man without morals, without ethics, to lead you?" Gaius said.

"Roman." That was the American answer.

The report of Augustus' death came as a blow to Gaius' efforts to assemble a power base. Without Magnus, without Augustus, Gaius was the sole witness that Magnus named a successor in his last testament. That Gaius was the named successor made him an unconvincing witness.

Then came the invitation to leave the shelter of the U.S. fortress to go out and talk with Numa Pompeii.

The Triumphalis had never been Gaius' political ally. Numa Pompeii was a hawk, a grandiose, bread-and-circuses sort of Roman. A charismatic politician, an opportunist. A bully. But Numa Pompeii was loyal to the empire—his own vision of the empire—but still his loyalty lay with Rome.

Trust him, Gaius did not.

Gaius could not risk his family. But he could risk his own life.

He accepted Numa Pompeii's invitation to come out and talk.

Even before the declaration of war, big ships never docked directly with the main station of Fort Eisenhower. And displacement in or out of the station had never been permitted. Jammers made sure it never happened.

Fort Eisenhower encompassed an assemblage of space stations in a volume of space roughly the size of a small planet. Lights refracted off the exhaust gases from ships and stations, turning the fortress into a manmade nebula, colorful and shining.

At the heart of it, heavily protected, sat one terminus of the Shotgun. Either end of the Fort Roosevelt/Fort Eisenhower Shotgun was a prime target in wartime.

Smuggling Gaius out of Fort Ike required a balance between secrecy and the need not to be mistaken for a bogey by the trigger-happy fortress defenses.

The plan called for a small craft to ferry Gaius Americanus from the main station out of Fort Eisenhower to Calli's heavily armed ship, *Wolfhound*. *Wolfhound* would then carry him to the meeting site.

Calli Carmel came into the main station in person to collect Gaius. Calli was one of few people permitted to carry a sidearm here. She escorted the Roman Senator to the dock.

She wanted to tell Gaius that Augustus lived. But giving information to the enemy was the act of a traitor. Gaius was Roman. She was American. They were at war.

Let Numa tell him.

Security had cleared the corridors of all extraneous personnel. No tourists, no workers, no military personnel except those who needed to be there were there. They had cleared the receptacles of all confiscated goods, emptied the trash, chased off the vendors. Military dogs gave the path a good sniff, then security cleared away the dogs.

Calli and Gaius were scanned and analyzed and verified one more time.

They walked through a semirigid tunnel to the hatch of the Space Patrol Torpedo boat—SPT or Spit boat, as it was known in the Navy.

Gaius halted, looked inside the craft, suddenly wary. "Where is the pilot?"

"I'm the pilot," said Calli. Saw his face. "What? You don't trust me?"

"They used to call you Crash Carmel."

"They still do," said Calli.

"Is there a reason for that?"

"I wrinkled a couple of ships," Calli admitted. "There was some shooting and fire involved."

Gaius looked hesitant, which was fine with Calli. She offered, hopeful, "You can still call this off."

Gaius stepped through the hatch to board the Spit boat.

This was the weakest link of the journey. Calli told him, "If we get hit, it will be here."

Gaius nodded. He strapped himself into the copilot's seat beside Calli.

The Spit boat had a rhino hull. Most ships relied on their energy fields rather than their physical hulls to keep the vacuum out. A rhino hull could survive in space even without a distortion shell around it.

"No weaponry?" Gaius noted.

"We'll be inside a hook for all but a few seconds," said Calli. "Inside the hook, we wouldn't be able to launch a torpedo even if we had one."

Fort Ike was secure, but it hung in the ocean of infinity. *Wolfhound* waited, as close as she was allowed.

A treacherous gulf stretched between them.

Calli was not even really piloting the boat. The Spit boat would be first pushed by the station hook, then pulled by *Wolfhound*'s hook.

There would be a precarious instant in which the station gave up its hook and *Wolfhound* replaced it with its own force field.

Calli heard the controllers exchanging messages over the com. The instruction came from *Wolfhound* to the station, "Cut hook, Ike."

The instruction resonated on the proper harmonic. Calli recognized the voice and inflection of her lieutenant, Amina Patel, on *Wolfhound*.

Fort Eisenhower responded, "Cutting hook, aye. Your boat, *Wolfhound*."

The Spit boat was now naked to the stars.

In the next instant the boat was surrounded by a new energy bubble. *Wolfhound* had thrown out a hook, bringing the Spit boat into her protection.

Wolfhound commenced reeling the craft in. Calli sat back in her seat and exhaled. She cast Gaius a fleeting little smile that was a confession of nervousness just passed. They were both feeling better now.

"That was the naked part," Calli told Gaius.

Then lights appeared, flashing off *Wolfhound*. Someone

was hitting her with beam fire from the direction of outer space.

Because beams traveled at light speed, you never see them coming until they're hitting you or passing you through gaseous matter.

Because the attacker was actually hitting a moving target with a light speed weapon, that meant he had to be close.

Calli clicked on the com, "*Wolfhound!* This is Captain Carmel. Lieutenant Patel, give me a status!"

The reply came from the com tech, with a lot of earnest voices audible in the background, "Unknown attacker, Captain. At indeterminate distance. Possibly retreating."

Retreating, but still firing. There were a lot of flashes. *Wolfhound*'s force field sparkled like blown glass.

The aging *Wolfhound* did not generate as adamant an energy field as *Merrimack*'s, which allowed *Mack* to stand closer to a black hole than any solid object had a right to.

Still, the *Hound*'s field was stout enough to weather this barrage. It was not a convincing attack in Calli's judgment. The beams were having no effect except to light up the ship's bow. Some of the shots were going wide, which meant the attacker was taking aim from a distance of over several light-seconds. It was not an efficient attack at all.

Flights of Rattlers, launched from the space fort, streaked out in the direction of the beam weapon. The brute, snub-nosed, bulky gunships of the space cavalry bristled with heavy ordinance, itching for a fight.

Beams continued to light up the *Wolfhound*.

"Has the look of a diversion," Calli murmured.

"I concur," said Gaius.

The two of them might have been back at the Institute discussing an interesting scenario. Except for the sensation of death tightening Calli's throat.

"So where *aren't* we supposed to be looking?" Calli said, checking the Tac readouts.

Wolfhound's defensive systems would automatically arrange her force field to present the thickest part of her field toward the source of the attack.

Wolfhound, like any ship, was most vulnerable through her engine vents in her stern.

Calli slammed on the com. "Lieutenant Patel! Never mind the beam fire! Cover the *Hound*'s ass!"

A projectile rocketed up *Wolfhound*'s engine vent. The missile did not penetrate but it made the force field grow tenuous. Made the slender energy hook that held the Spit boat flicker.

"Numa, you bastard—!"

In that instant, an incendiary round from somewhere very close and astern pierced the Spit boat.

A flash of fire filled the cabin.

The dialogs. II.

JMdeC: I admit that I find the open-ended, negatively
curved model of the universe philosophically
disappointing. I wanted to see a positive
curve. At the end of the Big Bang, I rather like
the idea of the Big Crunch, in which everything compresses back down to an infinite
point and bangs anew. It reflects the nature of
the universe as I observe it around me—death
and rebirth. Plants going to seed, dying, born
again in their progeny. Instead of a second
bang we seem to be doomed to a whimper. It
disappoints my sense of what ought to be—
cycles of seasons, cycles of procreation. The
negatively curved universe ends in eternal
night. The Biblical Outer Darkness, where lost
souls go in the end.

A: Well, hell, *Don* Cordillera.

JMdeC: Yes. Hell. I reject the medieval, sadistically
conceived vision of hell. Hell is the absence of
God. If you reject God, then you simply die. If
you put yourself into the hands of God, you
transcend this physical reality to be with God.
After everything else is gone, something lives,
while the physical universe of attenuated atoms becomes the Outer Darkness.

A: That's where I'm going. And I have news, so
are you.

JMdeC: The corporeal me, yes. The part of me that
transcends the physical house, no.

A: And where do you propose to go?

JMdeC: Elsewhere.

6

YOU CAN'T DO BATTLE in space with an enemy who won't stand. *Merrimack* raced out to the source point of the diversionary fire that had hammered *Wolfhound* but that shooter was long gone.

Captain Farragut tried to hail *Gladiator* on the old harmonic, but *Gladiator* was not responding.

Anyone listening on the official harmonic had heard Calli's last words: "Numa, you bastard—"

Some doubted her ID of her assailant. But it was not necessarily a *reasonable* doubt.

Numa Pompeii had not stayed in the area to explain, deny, or take credit for the attack, or to find out if Gaius survived it.

Likely Numa was on his way to Palatine. Numa Pompeii had something to offer Romulus now. He had the death of Gaius Americanus.

Still, there were other Romans in the Deep End who could have hit *Wolfhound*.

The Roman Legion carrier *Horatius* was out here somewhere. Marcus Asinius was in command of the ship if not the Legion.

Marcus Asinius and his Legion Draconis had no love for Romulus. They respected John Farragut, but their loyalty lay absolutely with Rome.

Farragut could not see Marcus Asinius participating in an assassination of a Roman Senator. But Marcus could have hit *Wolfhound* without knowing there was a target beyond *Wolfhound* or without knowing the identity of the passenger in the Spit boat.

And Augustus was out there.

"That wasn't Augustus," said Farragut, fact.

"Sir?" said Commander Dent, less certain. The Augustus she knew was a first magnitude prick.

"Augustus is still devoted to Magnus. Gaius was Magnus' chosen heir. If Augustus were anywhere near this neighborhood, Gaius would have made it where he was going."

Augustus had to be on a spearline to either Palatine or to Caesar's mobile palace Fortress Aeyrie to kill Romulus.

The U.S. Rattlers of Fort Eisenhower had caught the second shooter immediately, the one who fired the kill shot on the Spit boat—a lone man in a small craft, not a patterner's Striker. The Rattlers killed him. Killed him a bunch of times. Kept killing him because they could not undo what he did to Captain Carmel.

The burn unit in the main station of Fort Ike smelled like medical gel.

"Is Calli—?" Farragut was about to say *all right*, but he knew she was not all right. "—alive?"

The doctor hesitated, looked thoughtful.

"She's *dead?*" Farragut filled in the silence.

"Those are interesting questions," said the doctor. Too detached for Farragut's liking. Doctor Emil Embry. Older guy, not some kid who joined the Navy to learn the trade. Cool and steady. Almost callous. "She lost a major organ. We are regrowing one for her."

"Which organ?"

"Her skin."

Farragut knew that Calli had been burned. "How bad?"

"One hundred percent BSA," said Dr. Embry.

"I'm used to Naval acronyms, Doc. I don't know your alphabet clumps."

"BSA. Body Surface Area. She has no skin. It was all

necrotic, so we had to remove it. We are oxygenating her through medical gel."

"Will she—?"

Live?

Dr. Embry heard the unspoken word. "If I have anything to say about it, Captain Farragut. And, if may I say so, that counts for a hell of a lot."

Confidence was a good thing in a physician. Farragut felt the muscles in his neck relax a little. He held his head higher. "What about internal damage?"

"The fire damage was mostly on the surface. She did not inhale, which is a blessing. It was a flash fry. It left her muscles in decent shape. Only the outer layer got cooked. Like fried ice cream."

Farragut muffled a sound of startled disgust that rose in his throat.

"Or baked Alaska."

"Oh, for Jesus."

"Her internal organs are getting assistance. So she's in remarkably good condition—for a woman without skin."

Farragut cast a glance upward. *God? Sir? Thank you.*

And back to the doctor: "What about the Roman Senator, Gaius Americanus?"

"I'm less certain about the prognosis for the Roman. He is a strong man, but he's working too hard. He won't come down from the hyperdynamic phase. We're watching him for acidosis, burn encephalopathy, and renal failure. Mister Carmel's body is behaving more sensibly."

"Can I see her?"

"She may not want anyone to see her."

"Let me see her."

Dr. Embry admitted the captain to Calli's chamber in the secure area of the burn unit. Even though the doctor had warned him, John Farragut was not quite ready for the sight.

Removal of her skin left her as a piece of Calli-shaped meat suspended in pink gel in a tank. With her drastically reduced vascular volume, she was kept in a literal blood bath. Medical gel supplied the tissues with oxygen and fluids. There were entubated auxiliary organs working outboard of her body to lessen the stress on her own. Farragut recognized a kidney and a liver.

There was a breathing tube down her throat. They must have blocked her nostrils—wherever those were.

Farragut squinted through the gel from several angles.

"Where's—? Does she—? Does she have a jaw?"

Dr. Embry spoke very softly, "No. Shattered."

Farragut had a replacement jaw himself, so he supposed the jawbone was the least of her worries.

No jaw. That meant she had taken a blow to the face. "How's her brain?"

"In good condition," Dr. Embry answered softly. "That's a hardheaded woman."

"I can testify to that, sir," said Captain Farragut.

Over the speakers Pachelbel's "Canon in D" played soft joy. It made Farragut feel like he ought to be standing at an altar waiting for a bride.

The music and Dr. Embry's abrupt switch from callous jackass to a soft-spoken bedside manner made Farragut wonder, "Can she hear me?"

"Possibly," said Dr. Embry. "She's in an induced coma, but her brain is functioning on the subconscious level and she still has her eardrums. So I thought—" He gave a shrug at the lilting music from the speakers. "Why not?"

Farragut was a tactile person. He would have held Calli's hand, but she was entirely inside the antiseptic tank, encased with medical gel. And she had no skin. He put his palm to the transparent barrier.

He spoke to her. "Well, hell, Crash. You bent another boat. Gaius is alive." She would need to know that. "And so are you, just in case you're wondering. They've got you in the pink medical slime. And I gotta tell you it's not your best color."

He kept his voice buoyant. Did not want to sound like he was attending her funeral. She looked ghastly.

"Gypsy's coming in to see you after I get back. You know we can't both leave the boat at the same time."

Gypsy Dent had been Calli's XO on the *Wolfhound* before Gypsy came to *Merrimack*. Calli and Gypsy were tight as sisters.

"They got the guy who flamed you. They're still picking

pieces of him out of the vacuum with a sieve. You know him. I'll tell you who it was when you get out of there."

The kill shot on the Spit boat had come from a small Roman sleeper vessel, which had been trolling in the dark outside Fort Eisenhower for a very long time. It housed a single pilot—a disgraced Roman sent to redeem himself with a long, long, lonely vigil, waiting for a suicide task.

The second shooter's identity tended to support the idea of Numa Pompeii as the shooter of the diversionary fire.

Farragut quit the chamber, shaken.

He clasped Embry's hand firmly in leaving. "Take care of her, Doc."

"I have every faith in Mister Carmel," said Dr. Embry. "And in me."

"That's what I need to hear."

"Captain," Dr. Embry caught him on an afterthought. "There is a space lawyer who keeps trying to get in here. I find the persistence of lawyers offensive. I don't need hyenas and jackals in my hospital. He's Navy and keeps quoting code at me. I confess I know as much law as he knows medicine, so I have no idea if he's making a valid legal point or not, and I don't care. Can you arrange a restraining order on him?"

Farragut was about to agree but hesitated on a second thought. "Is he this tall," Farragut asked, his hand over his own six-foot-one head, "This big around?" He made a circle with his fingers. "Looks about fifteen years old, and I'm told he's cute?"

"That about describes him, yes."

"Make sure his DNA checks to Rob Roy Buchanan and let him in. He's not her lawyer." He used to be her lawyer, but Calli had fired him a while back. "Oh, and tell him to get a shave."

Captain Farragut proceeded from the secure burn unit to the stationmaster's office.

General Aniston Weld was long past harried. Long past trying to hold everything together. By now he was just watching the pieces fall and adding another note to his list of things that needed addressing.

Things that had been Priority One just a day ago were

now somewhere around number eighty-four with a twelve-ton sinker.

The man in putative control of Fort Eisenhower was not even sure what he was dealing with—an act of war or an internal assassination within the Roman Empire. He knew it happened in his fort and it took out a U.S. Navy captain with it. Captain Carmel may have been the real target for all General Weld knew.

General Weld listened in an odd state of defeated calm as an animated Captain Farragut rattled off rapid fire:

"The Romans have someone inside Fort Eisenhower. He's probably inside the main station. *Someone* had to let the shooters know that Gaius Americanus was leaving the station, *when* he was leaving, and which ship he was on. The mole is likely communicating to the outside by resonance. Resonance leaves no trace. This is a huge fort here, so instead of screening everyone, we should pull the recordings from the surveillance monitors on the burn unit. The mole will follow up to see if Gaius lives. Identify all visitors or loiterers at the burn unit since the attack. Our mole might be one of them."

The stationmaster listened until Farragut came up for a breath, then watched him for another minute like he was observing some energetic alien creature. Weld spoke at last, "You a control addict, Captain Farragut?"

"Yes, sir."

"Hm." It was a satisfied hm. The admission was disarming. "I suppose you'll want all those 'visitors and loiterers' smelled too."

"Please," said Farragut. He wanted them all investigated. "Sniff hard."

"I suppose that's reasonable," General Weld said, riffling through his contact list. "I'll hand it over to my Intelligence unit."

"How's your intelligence here?"

"Not as good as I thought, now, is it?" Weld said dryly. He paged his Chief Intelligence officer and gave him the burn unit surveillance assignment.

General Weld clicked off the com, returned to Farragut. "Interesting that you bring up the burn unit visitors. There has already been one suspicious character in and out of the burn unit. He hasn't been able to get in, but I've been told—repeatedly—that he's persistent. Space lawyer, name—" He snapped his fingers, couldn't place it, leafed through his handwritten notes for something way down below eighty-fourth on the priority list.

"Rob Roy Buchanan," said Farragut.

"That's the one. Your man?"

"No. But I'd bet my eyeteeth he's clean. Go ahead and check him anyway. We can't overlook anything."

"Oh we *can*," Weld sighed. "We just *mustn't*."

John Farragut strode through the station to the shuttle dock for his return to *Merrimack*. Security was tight on all shuttles now. There used to be dozens of them launching any given minute throughout the space fort. Now interstation traffic was a backlogged mess.

Someone is pulling off my wings. Farragut was not thinking about the shuttles.

Thinking of Calli in the bloody tank.

Missing Jose Maria, his father figure. The kind and wise way his father had never been. Jose Maria was gone, homeward bound on a space yacht named *Mercedes*.

And Augustus. Missing—of all people to miss—Augustus. And that thought almost made him laugh.

Alarms sounded. Hatches shut. Red lights flashed. A lot of sounds rose from the travelers—gasps, murmurs, shouts, demands, cries, questions.

A soothing female voice over the loud com announced that the dock was under lockdown and thanked the travelers, some of them shrieking now, for their patience.

The bells sounded an unfamiliar alarm sequence. Farragut knew all of Ike's codes, and he had never heard this particular one.

It had never happened.

Fort Ike was under attack.

Roman attack craft winked in, on all sides of the space fortress, as they dropped from FTL. One of them was the Legion carrier *Horatius*.

Perimeter sentinels had detected the unauthorized approach to the fortress. Barriers went up, energized grids meshed and locked tight, enclosing all the stations of the fortress in a planetary-sized energy shell. No ships, no ordnance could pass in or out without the controller creating an opening.

Nothing was getting through right now.

Roman fire, Roman drones, a Roman destroyer, all caromed off the adamant barrier.

You could see the Roman barrage visually from here, through the wide viewports—flash after flash against their solid sky.

People rushed around Farragut, who stood at the dock with a finger in one ear to block out the noise as he shouted into his wrist com: "Gypsy, I'm not getting out of here. She's your boat." And to let Gypsy get on with her job, he said, "Let me talk to Hamster."

Lieutenant Hamilton took over com contact with the captain. "Hamilton, aye."

"Where are y'all? In or out?"

"We're inside the grid," Hamster answered.

That was more bad than good. Good that *Merrimack* was safe, but very much not good that she could not fire on the attackers unless the controller made a window in the titanic energy shell—or if the attackers breached the perimeter.

The grid defenses heaved out energy bolts, space javelins, chaser rounds, and beams, to put on a dizzying show. John Farragut could not tell from here if they were having any effect.

"Number and nature of hostiles?" he asked Hamster.

"*Horatius* for one. Those will be your boarders if they can get close to a station to throw a corvus."

"Won't happen. They have to get through the grid first. Then a station field."

"Eight cruisers and eleven destroyers are their pounders," Hamster continued. "No *Gladiator*. No *Striker*."

The attackers banged at the joints in the grid. Auto-gunnery sprayed beams at them. Missile silos hurled out hard ordnance.

"These ships are new designs," said Hamster. "We don't

have their specs in our data bank. How can there be this many Roman ships?"

"It means Romulus started executing this attack at least three months before he declared war," said Farragut.

It took three months to cross the Abyss. This attack force launched from Roman territory a while ago.

"There are drones everywhere," Hamster reported. "Can't give you a good count. We think we've been double and triple counting them. They jump to FTL and come back." Then as if she had just been passed a note, "We have IDs on some of these ships." She read off the ship names and their commanders.

Gens names like Trogus, Quirinius, Umbrius—

"This reads like a list of everyone Romulus wants dead," said Hamster.

"The psychotic bastard isn't stupid," said Farragut.

Romulus had sent his political opponents to a very hard target to field-test the new weaponry.

"This is nobody I want to kill," said Hamster.

Romulus no doubt sent them out with standard Spartan orders: With your shield or on it. Victorious or dead. Romulus could not lose either way.

The legion carrier *Horatius* charged at the grid and immediately glanced off the energy barrier as if making too steep an approach to a planet's atmosphere. The big ship spun out to space, winked out, gone FTL.

A pack of U.S. Rattlers that were outside the grid jumped past the light barrier to give chase. It was nearly impossible to chase an FTL target, but Rattlers had high threshold velocities and were probably hoping that *Horatius* had winked out because she was wounded.

As soon as the lockdown lifted from the dock to let the trapped travelers retreat back into the station, Farragut ran to the stationmaster's office.

General Weld was not there. A cadre of Marines told him where the general had gone. Two of the Marines escorted him to the Fort Ike command center. They ushered him through a crush of reporters who were camped outside the command center hatch.

The reporters reacted with a horrified frenzy to see Captain John Farragut here, away from mighty *Merrimack*, in this time of crisis. Recorders followed him. He heard his name reported in voices of alarm and doom, talking about him like Samson without hair. *Merrimack* without her Captain Farragut. A mortal blow to station defenses. They transmitted their apocalyptic reports to Earth under huge banners: UNDER SIEGE!

Farragut made it through the hatch into the command center, where all the voices were low, quick, clear, and efficient.

General Weld was organizing his forces, taking in tactical reports. He glanced up. Double-took. Eyed Farragut up and down. Much calmer than the reporters, he said, "Well, this is unsettling."

General Weld had the most formidable battleship in the United States on hand—except that its head was cut off. Figured.

"Commander Dent doesn't play in the farm league, sir," Captain Farragut defended his exec.

Weld returned to his com, demanding of someone: "Where's the Striker? Anyone pick up the Striker yet?" It was a tired sort of demand.

Weld clicked off and gave his attention to Farragut. "If you have any suggestions, I'll listen to them."

Farragut jumped at the invitation. "You've got Rattlers outside searching for *Horatius*. Don't let them get suckered into a chase. Marcus will just draw them out, turn around and eat them. If your boys and girls want to shoot at *Horatius*, don't worry, he'll come back. He's not going to stay out there with nothing to shoot at. He has orders to take the fort or die trying."

"*Horatius*," Weld echoed. "That was one of yours."

"Yes, sir."

Horatius had been a member of Commodore Farragut's Attack Group One.

Weld issued the recall to the pursuing Rattlers.

Farragut heard someone else in the command center signaling Fort Ted. "Fort Roosevelt. This is Fort Eisenhower. Are you under attack?"

The answer came back negative. There had been no attack on the Near Space terminus of the Shotgun. Damaging one end was all it took to disable the Shotgun. With one end out, the other was useless.

Tactical reported: "Roman drones inside the containment zone."

Weld put off any exclamation of shock and impossibility that came to mind. He told the controller to put *Merrimack* on the interior drones.

The controller complied. "*Merrimack. Merrimack. Merrimack.* This is Fort Eisenhower Control. I have trade for you. Seek and destroy enemy hostiles within the containment zone."

Only then did Weld say to one of his officers, "How in bloody hell did they get inside the grid? Locate the breach."

"Grid holding solid, sir," Tactical advised. "Nothing came through the containment field."

Closer flashes appeared now, clearer without the distortion barrier in between. The new lights would be *Merrimack* annihilating Roman rovers inside the fortress' energy sphere.

Farragut turned his com to the Marine harmonic so he could listen to the Swift pilots' excited chatter, shooting skeet.

"Mine mine mine mine— Oh, you hog!"

"Don't polish that cannonball, Darb! Take the fox-trotting shot!"

"Ho! Shitska! Didja see that!" That was the voice of Alpha Six, Kerry Blue.

"See what?"

The station controller evidently saw what Alpha Six saw. Reported: "Drones appear to be getting inside the containment zone by displacement."

"How?" Weld demanded. "Are they jamming our jammers?"

"No, sir. We don't have any jammers outside the stations. The station jammers are all functioning. We just never put jammers in the empty space between the stations."

"We have a fifth column," Weld concluded. "Who planted displacement receivers in *space*?"

It had been known to happen before—the placement of

Roman landing disks (LDs) in space. No bigger than dinner plates, LDs looked like space debris. This attack had been three months in the approach. The local mole had three months to figure out how to sneak LDs out there between the many stations of the space fort.

"*Merrimack. Merrimack. Merrimack.* This is Fort Eisenhower Control. Seek and destroy displacement equipment in the vacuum."

"Fort Eisenhower. This is *Merrimack*. Already on it. Aye."

The voices coming over the Marine channel sounded like kids on a coin hunt, calling out their victories.

One Swift fired on a displacement disk at the precise instant that a Drone flashed into existence on the disk. Vaporized both of them. "Yahtzee!"

"Didja see that! Didja see that!"

A boom tremored the deck of the command center. The sound came from a com, not from an explosion within the station, but so loud they all felt it. Six more explosions in chain reaction followed.

"Not encouraging," said Weld. "What was that?"

A missile silo on the perimeter had taken a shot up the nose. And its magazine had an insufficient firewall to contain the eruption of its contents.

Because of the distortion shroud, the command center was having trouble assessing the damage.

Tactical reported: "*Horatius* back in range."

Weld's graying brows gave a little lift, marking Farragut's successful prediction.

The command center was receiving feeds from various U.S. media transmitting from Near Space. One featured interviews with anxious families at Fort Ted waiting for their loved ones stranded in the Deep End. The reports lamented in dire tones the inability of the U.S. to send reinforcements to the besieged Fort Eisenhower while the Shotgun was shut down. They forecast what destruction of the Shotgun could mean to the U.S., its people, its economy.

President Marissa Johnson made an appearance, decrying the attack. Her staff had immediately figured out that this attack began before the declaration of war. She called on the League of Earth Nations to break its neutrality and take a stand against the belligerent Roman Empire.

General Weld glanced up at one of the monitors. Saw the Near Space media feed cut over to visuals of the missile silo at the perimeter exploding. "Are we on broadcast?" Weld asked, then answered himself, wearily, "Of course we're on broadcast."

The perimeter explosions were out there for the whole galaxy to see. Then rerun, because they were spectacular — the initial blast, six more explosions, the anxious voice of the reporter with background screams inside the station.

"That's it," said Farragut.

Fire ships clustered round the Shotgun, spewing blue fire suppressant onto the piers. The sensor stations were coated with the stuff. The displacement equipment belched enormous plumes of smoke into space. The dirty clouds spread, curled inward at the energy grid. Bottled inside the energy barrier, the thick clouds made Fort Eisenhower look like a gargantuan murky crystal ball portending an ominous future.

The media picked up the images, sent them across the known galaxy in an instant on resonant feed with the news:

———————

FORT EISENHOWER SHOTGUN DESTROYED

———————

The dialogs. III.

A: There is no elsewhere. This is the universe.

JMdeC: If there is no "elsewhere," then whence the original Bang? It is terribly parochial to think that this is the only everything there is. The Greek word cosmos meant universe. It also meant world. Because the world was their entire universe at the time the word was coined. But there is more to the universe than planet Earth. Can we assume this cosmos, the one that we can observe now, is the only one? You must admit the possibility of universes other than this putative everything. Admit that something beyond our conception and perception could exist.

A: I allow the theoretical existence of alternate brane worlds in higher dimensional space, but I reject out of hand your implication that you are going to evade the entropy of this universe by faith.

PART TWO

The Return

7

ROMAN RECONNAISSANCE DRONES skimmed the rock surface on the night side of the world. All was dark, airless, silent, dead. At less than twenty light-years from Earth the planet would make a good platform from which to stage an invasion. But this solar system was League of Earth Nations territory, which made its planets neutral worlds.

That made the world off-limits to the U.S. military as well as to Rome. But Caesar Romulus was certain he could trust the U.S. to cheat.

If Roman drones could find a U.S. military installation on the planet, Rome could contest the world's neutrality and build its own base on it without bringing the LEN into the war.

Allegedly there was nothing on the planet except an ancient archaeological site.

The Milky Way galaxy was fifteen billion years old.

In the beginning, the universe consisted of nothing but hydrogen.

All other elements were created within stars from the primordial hydrogen.

Those first stars began to form nearly twelve billion years ago.

The lifetime of a star ranges from as short as a few million years to as long as a few trillion years, depending on the mass of the star.

The biggest stars lived fast. After a few million years of existence, the mammoth stars blew up.

Not one of the smallest stars had died yet. The universe was not old enough. The smallest stars burned slow and long and would eventually fade out.

The color of stars varied by mass, appearing in nearly the same order as the colors of the rainbow—red, orange, yellow, white, blue, indigo, violet—from lightweight star to heavyweight star.

Mid-weight, where logic suggested the stars ought to appear green, the stars shone white instead.

The light produced by middleweight normal stars peaks in the green wavelength. But all stars emit all wavelengths to some degree along with their strong suit. In stars strongest in the middle green wavelength, the short blue wavelengths and the long red wavelengths meet in the middle with equal strength, so the star shines a balanced full visible spectrum. The full visible spectrum appears as white light.

There are no green stars.

The biggest, heaviest violet-blue stars burned very fast, spun very fast, blew up very fast. Habitable planets were never to be found orbiting a violet, indigo, or blue star. A few million years was not time enough for matter to cool and for life to evolve around them. The biggest stars tended not to form planets at all. They spun so fast that they kept all their mass close to themselves rather than trailing some out in an orbital plane to form worlds. Metal ionized in the hellish internal furnace of a blue end star. Even helium, which holds onto its electrons more tightly than any other atom, ionized inside a violet star.

A supernova was a gargantuan star in its spectacular death throes. Supernovae scattered their newly created heavy elements far and wide.

The element-rich debris then coalesced into new stars.

Once upon a time, supernovae were common. These days, a supernova appeared once in a hundred years in the skies over Earth or Palatine.

Most habitable planets orbited second generation, middleweight stars—those stars which inherited the heavy elements ejected from the early supernovae.

In first generation stars any element heavier than iron was extremely scarce, including the precious metals of gold, silver, and platinum, as well as some elements that were extremely precious if you didn't have them, like iodine and zinc.

82 Eridani was an old disk star, born eleven billion years ago. It was a yellow star, G type, superficially like Sol, close to Sol in size but over twice its age and less luminous. For a star born so early, 82 Eridani had a lot of metal. It was element-poor compared to second-generation stars. Sol had twice as much iron as did 82 Eridani.

Even so, 82 Eridani managed to spawn planets solid enough to walk on. The earliest evidence of sapient life in the known galaxy had been found on 82 Eridani's third planet. Humans had only explored an eighth of the Milky Way galaxy, so they had only a small sampling of possible worlds, but an age of ten billion years for sapient life was looking like a hard record to beat.

Life on 82 Eridani III died ten billion years ago. With the elements available at the time, the aboriginal inhabitants could not have been robust, so there were no physical remains of the beings themselves. Ten billion years was a lot of time for lightweight remains to turn to dust. The artifacts which human explorers found on the planet were few and often suspected of having been planted there, though challenges to their age held up against any test.

A near pass of something large had swept away the atmosphere of the third planet of 82 Eridani aeons ago. Its surface was mostly bedrock.

The star system's rotation had slowed over the last billion years, and the third planet's orbit had widened out of the habitable zone. The planet's rotation had slowed so that its days lasted longer than an Earthly year.

Terraforming had never been attempted. With inadequate raw materials in the star system, the planet would never be self-supporting. In human hands it had only ever been a scientific outpost, unprofitable and abandoned.

Born before the Milky Way galaxy settled into its spiral shape, 82 Eridani had been around the galaxy a couple of times on a highly eccentric orbit, moving very fast.

82 Eridani had seen it all.

Romans called the third planet 82 Eridani III.

American archaeologists called it Planet Xi.

It had been dead a long, long time.

Roman drones circled in, skimming the rocky surface. The star 82 Eridani shone as a small, cold, orange-yellow disk in the skyless night. The drones transmitted images back by res pulse on a harmonic specific to their mission. Passive scans of ambient radiation were translated to digital images at the drone's controlling station within Fortress Aeyrie, which lurked in the wide-open vastness of space.

The watchers searched for something. Anything. Finding nothing.

Nothing might be a good thing. If no one had any interest in 82 Eridani III, then Rome could smuggle a missile site down there—and paint it red, white, and blue just in case the LEN authorities spotted it and wanted to sanction someone.

The remote pilots located a level site and set down their drones.

The pilots themselves sat light-hours away in a clear, uncluttered compartment inside Fortress Aeyrie, underneath the palace proper. Their displays moved with their heads.

"Motion!" a remote pilot reported, too loud, too excited, wholly unexpected. "The instruments detect motion."

The pilot flinched at the sound of someone else's hand slapping against a console, like an *ah-ha*! Someone crowed, "Got them!"

Another pilot confirmed, "I have motion."

The curator moved in closer to the spotters. "Naturally occurring motion?" Lollius Lunaris requested guardedly. He needed to be absolutely certain of his facts before reporting anything to Caesar.

"Can't be," said one of the remote pilots who had yet to detect anything. "Not on this rock. No seismic activity. The core has gone cold."

"This motion is localized," said the first spotter.

The curator put out the wanted conclusion: "The Americans have an underground installation!"

The first pilot shook his head. "I don't see how. Our rovers put down on bedrock."

"I know that," said the curator. "Tell me, how else does bedrock move?"

"*Domni*, I just drive and shoot." The first pilot magnified his holographic display to fill half the compartment. Scans from the cold distant rock were enhanced to give visual images of what existed in total darkness.

As the curator viewed the barren image from Planet Xi, a smooth tentacle broke free of the planet bedrock, reached toward the camera, looped around it.

The image went dark.

Fortress Aeyrie was a Caesar's spaceborne mobile palace.

The Fortress Aeyrie of Caesar Magnus had been designed to fill the visitor with wonder.

The Fortress Aeryie of Caesar Romulus was meant to scare the crap out of him.

Magnus' fortress had been wrapped in mist. Inside the glistening mist, space opened to brilliant clouds where winged creatures cavorted in the light.

Romulus' fortress was shrouded in dark fog. Inside was a pillar of fire. The visitor must fly into the Inferno to dock with the fortress.

The smart pilot kept his viewports dark and flew in by instrument readings only.

The audience hall of Caesar Romulus was a black sky filled with auroras and lightning flashes. The music was loud and moody, underscored with a heavy percussion line.

Romulus also had a chamber in each of his palaces called the Caligula Room, each an indulgent piece of work for only Caesar and his closest friends to enjoy. The programmers had great fun designing and generating all those women, and testing the sensory virtual masks that made the illusions interactive.

Lollius Lunaris, the curator of the remote reconnaissance force, was never invited to the Caligula Room.

The curator approached Caesar's audience hall. He steeled himself against Caesar's sense of humor.

Lollius Lunaris was admitted through doors that could dwarf a blue whale. He looked across a chasm to where Romulus was seated on his lightning throne.

Romulus looked a natural thirty-seven, his athletic build in perfect proportion. Romulus favored clothes that showed off his physique. You seldom saw the man in a toga—not the easiest thing to drape or to wear well. Lunaris did not own one.

Romulus was here in black close-fitting trousers, a short, sleeveless scarlet tunic, and a short, jaunty scarlet cape over one shoulder, secured with a golden chain that ran under his muscular right arm.

A gold oak crown sat on his thick dark locks, the gold nearly lost in his loose curls. He had the dark indulgent features of a god of love—sultry dark eyes with heavy dark lashes; pouting lips seductively shaped.

The space between Lunaris and the throne looked like a bottomless pit.

Caesar beckoned.

Lunaris must trust Caesar that the floor, against all appearances, was in fact solid under the illusion.

He took a breath for courage. Took a step over the edge. Plummeted *down*.

Oh gods—

And slammed into an invisible deck less than two meters down.

Lunaris lifted himself to hands and knees in seeming midair, looking down into the abyss, sure he saw his stomach down there, continuing on down and down.

"You need not bow quite so low," said Romulus.

"Yes, Caesar." Lunaris got up, trying to show a game smile. Refrained from rubbing his wrists, which hurt like hell.

"Have you seen this?" Caesar gestured toward an illusion that began to take shape on one wall. It appeared like a huge window opening to a scene two thousand parsecs away.

The Fort Eisenhower Shotgun churned out gray smoke into its own protective energy sphere.

"Yes, Caesar," Lunaris answered, feeling round for the edges of his pit to pull himself out.

"Your Deep End counterparts accomplished this."

Caesar was pitting Lunaris against the curator of the remotes in the Deep.

"Did they confirm the damage, Caesar?" Lunaris asked.

"What does this look like?" said Romulus, enjoying the scene.

"Looks like an image taken from outside the American perimeter," said Lunaris.

"Well, yes. The Americans destroyed all the drones inside the perimeter," said Caesar, then added with a smile, "*After* they did this."

"With respect, that is not good confirmation, Caesar."

"Don't be jealous, Lunaris."

Lollius Lunaris was not a high level Intelligence officer but he knew that Imperial Intelligence had a paid informant within Fort Eisenhower—an American, a midlevel agent in the fort's own Naval Intelligence service. That informant ought to be able to confirm or deny the damage to the Shotgun. It disturbed Lunaris that Caesar had not invoked better confirmation than pictures of smoke.

But Lunaris could see he was vexing Caesar. He proceeded cautiously. "Does Caesar know what submarines subject to bombardment by depth charges did during World War Two?"

"I have little interest in ancient history that is not Roman," said Romulus, losing his good mood. "You asked for this audience. What do you have for me?"

"Gorgons, Caesar."

"I have no interest in those either."

"The Hive is on 82 Eridani III."

"No."

"*No*, Caesar?" Lunaris was reporting fact, not a selection of options.

"No, it is not possible," said Caesar.

"Please come see what we are looking at," Lunaris started quickly.

"*You* are summoning *me*?"

"Caesar may check our sources and point out where we misinterpreted the data," said Lunaris.

Romulus rose spryly and jogged down from his dais. He crossed the abyss, appearing to stride on nothing. He halted at the edge of the trap Lunaris had fallen into. "Get out of that hole," he ordered.

Lunaris scrambled out of the pit. Romulus took him by the arm, steered him around the trap to the mammoth doors and pushed him out ahead of him. "Show me."

The six remote pilots rose at their stations and stood at stiff attention upon Caesar's entrance.

"I'm not causing a prang, am I?" Caesar asked, jovially, seeing all the pilots abandoning their controls.

"No, Caesar," Lunaris answered for them.

The reconnaissance drones were equipped with survival backups in case of loss of their resonant control signal.

Lunaris presented Caesar with live images transmitted from the rovers on 82 Eridani III. Luckily there continued to stream images of tentacles breaking out of solid rock for Caesar to witness.

Romulus watched for several moments, then said, "This is a 'scarecrow.' " He used the American word. "We know for a fact that John Farragut's Attack Group used to carry mock gorgons with them. This is one of those. Don't believe all you see." Romulus patted Lollius Lunaris on the back and smiled at him, "You know better."

Then one rover's transmitter showed tentacles disassembling another rover.

Romulus nodded at that image. "You see? Real gorgons would just ignore the rovers because the rovers are not edible. Gorgons only attack metal or polymers if something organic is inside the inedible shell."

"With respect, Caesar," said Lunaris, "would a newly hatched gorgon know what is edible and what is not? Wouldn't they think if it moves itself and resonates, then it must be alive?"

"It is not Descartes," said Romulus. "It does not *think*."

"I advise that we inform the League of Earth Nations of this and advise them to sanitize the world with a neutron hose," said Lollius Lunaris.

"No."

Lunaris sputtered. "This puts gorgons within a year of Palatine!"

Top speed of the old Hive clocked out at 200 times the speed of light. If these gorgons achieved spaceflight, they could be on Earth even sooner than they hit Palatine.

Romulus ignored him. "Recall those rovers."

"Caesar! Gorgons have attached themselves to several of the rovers!"

"Good," Romulus said. "Bring them in. Let us take a look at the American scarecrows. We can trace their manufacture back to the United States, and that will give us legitimate access to the planet. This is exactly what we were looking for. You have done well, Lunaris. Be happy."

"And if they are real gorgons, Caesar?"

"Then John Farragut is not the only man in the galaxy who can use a sword," said Caesar. And on second thought, his hands on either hip where one might wear a scabbard, "Do we have a sword in the palace?"

It took the Roman drones two hours to make rendezvous with Fortress Aeyrie. The palace defenses scanned them for explosives and unauthorized devices. Finding none, the drones were allowed inside the fortress' energy barrier.

"Now we shall see what our gorgons are really made of," said Romulus.

As the drones passed through Fortress Aeyrie's protective field, scarab crickets left their heraldic poses on either side of monumental archways in the palace.

Caesar watched the large insectoids detach from their posts and fly. He had never seen them move, much less fly. "I thought those were bronze ornaments!"

"I think this is what they call Hive sign," said Lollius Lunaris nervously.

"I think you're right," said Romulus, intrigued.

"We need to get you to safety, Caesar."

"I *am* safe! I'm going to kill a gorgon. Where's my sword?"

This was not Magnus' palace any more. Romulus kept weapons in Fortress Aeyrie. An attendant ordered a sharp sword brought down to the rover bay in the lowest level of the fortress.

The returning recon drones slid home into their allotted tubes, which were thirty centimeters in diameter.

Two of the outside caps would not shut.

An inside cap swelled, popped off like a projectile, narrowly missing Caesar's attendant as it bulleted across the compartment and pierced the rear partition.

And something bulged out from the uncapped rover tube, growing, like a hideously distended bowel, diseased, black and oily looking, inflating.

Then a shock of tentacles bloomed free and inflated into hose shapes. Rings and rings of teeth terminated each hose, so the thing looked like a nest of grasping moray eels.

Romulus danced in close with his sword and swung a mighty stroke that mowed off the toothed ends in a swathe. The tips fell to the floor, teeth still gnashing like razor blades. In moments they dissolved in a caustic pool.

The cut stumps of tentacles, still attached to the oily body, emerged from the tube, spurting gore. They splashed Romulus' hand. Romulus studied his hand with interest, the palm, the back, the palm again. "That stings."

He regripped his sword and slashed again to take off the next bundle of stalks that flowered obscenely from the rover tube.

The black balloon of the body sputtered itself empty and dissolved.

The attendant backed away, the neck of his tunic pulled up around his nose and mouth against the caustic stench.

Lollius Lunaris just stared with watery eyes.

Romulus prowled over the gore. "That was easy."

Caesar thought, but did not say: *we lost sixty-four Legions to this?* Not to disparage the might of Rome before anyone.

It ought to have been obvious that there was more to the Hive than he had seen, but he was too elated with himself to go that way.

"So there are gorgons here. So much for America's victory against the Hive!"

"They did warn us it was not finished, Caesar," Lunaris said.

Another tube cap popped, shot across the compartment and dented the rear wall. Tentacles sprouted in a grotesque nest.

"Leave it! Mine!" Romulus dashed in.

The tentacles reeled in like a startled sea anemone, back into the rover tube.

The Hive was already learning.

Romulus stabbed his sword into the tube up to the hilt. He turned his face away from the ooze that jetted out. He pushed deeper, up to his elbow, into the tube. Flinched. Turned the sword, stabbed several times.

He pulled his sword out and revealed a star-shaped wound bitten into his hand.

"Ha!" He regarded his wound from all angles. Rather proud of it. He was going to let it scar. "Any more?" he asked, hopeful.

But the scarab crickets had gone silent.

Romulus tossed his sword to the floor. Let someone else retrieve it and clean it. He passed verdict: "Not nearly as diabolical as the Americans would have us believe."

No one dared remind Caesar that this Hive was born yesterday. Not even yesterday. Today. These creatures had not been around for countless millennia, consuming and learning from every encounter with every alien it ate.

Caesar made eye contact with the men in the chamber, the curator, his attendant. "You are not to tell anyone about this. Not anyone."

Lunaris' face showed bald horror. "They're so close! Should we not call for help from the United States?"

"Oh, is that not what they wish!" Caesar cried. "They planted these monsters in Near Space so they can demand Subjugation again."

"These gorgons hatched out of bedrock, Caesar. How could they possibly be imported?"

"How could the Hive have planted them in solid rock!" Caesar countered. "If gorgons hatch upon the death of their parents, what have these been waiting for?"

"Something to eat?" Lunaris suggested. "The League of Earth Nations should be warned. Earth is not the enemy. The United States is the enemy. Earth is the home world.

We intend to retake Earth. We do not want it eaten, Caesar."

"And I have told you the Earthlings will know when they need to know," said Caesar, and softly, "Did you ever hear the old saying 'two people can keep a secret if one of them is dead?' "

Lunaris felt every muscle in his face just let go, his expression gone stupidly slack. He stared as he would up the barrel of a gun.

Caesar broke a smile. "I never placed much store by that saying. You—and you," he turned to his attendant, "will swear yourselves to secrecy and we shall leave it at that."

They swore.

The human media was filled with images from Fort Ike. The U.S. broadcasts concentrated on the worry and grief of separated families and the interruption of trade between Near Space and the Deep End. Roman broadcasts reran the smoking images of the Shotgun.

The League of Earth Nations protested the Roman attack on Fort Eisenhower on grounds that it was launched three months prior to the declaration of war.

Romulus disingenuously explained that he had deployed a portion of Rome's forces to the Deep for defensive purposes. Rome, he assured the LEN, had no intention of mounting an attack at the time of the ships' launch. But, "sensitive to the LEN protest," Romulus declared he would recall his warships at once.

Romulus had already achieved his objective of shutting down the Shotgun. The LEN protest now allowed Romulus to call his warships back with all possible speed and be thanked for it.

He had cut off U.S. access to the Deep. He had stranded John Farragut's *Merrimack* in the Deep End. And the *Monitor* was deeper still. And *Wolfhound*. Those warships were now three months away from Palatine and Earth.

So were *Gladiator* and Numa Pompeii.

Numa would just need to deal with that. Romulus thought he might leave some crumbs for Numa to sweep up by the time he got here.

"What became of Gaius?" Romulus asked as he strode through his mobile fortress. He did not address the question to anyone. He need only speak to air, and an answer would come to him.

"Dead, Caesar."

"Pity," said Romulus. "Launch Operation Homeland."

Horses bolted across the Kentucky field. A pregnant mare kicked up her heels.

Chief Justice John K. Farragut had just sat down at the head of the table for breakfast, his wife seated at the foot, daughter Lily and the children in between. Lily had re-named all her children Farragut after moving back in with her parents. Could not have too many Farraguts.

A roar from the sky shook the house, shook the ground. Shook great-great grandma's crystal.

Horses whinnied, stampeded.

Through the window His Honor saw the pregnant mare hauling herself away in lumbering panic. "What *idiot*—!"

His Honor rose from the table, seized his revolver, and stormed out of the house, napkin still tucked into his collar. He brandished his Colt at the sky where ranks of Roman missiles passed over, just above the treetops, in his Kentucky sky.

8

T HE CONTINENTAL U.S. had a porous border.
Roman missiles entered Earth's atmosphere high
over international waters, then dropped to sea level and
cruised one hundred feet over the surface to enter U.S. airspace. Those missiles that survived the coastal defenses continued on the deck to terrorize all they passed. They flew
between tall buildings, through mountain passes. They
would seem to be headed straight at a metropolis, then
abruptly lift up and skip over civilian skyscrapers.

Missiles cruised over Kentucky, passing one hundred
feet over the house of Justice John K. Farragut.

Missiles drove into the defensive shields of military in-
stallations at Fort Campbell, Kentucky; Vance, Oklahoma;
Oaxaca, Oaxaca; Tacoma, Washington; Fort Bliss and White
Sands in Texas and New Mexico.

U.S. defenses could not just shoot the missiles down.
Once the missiles hit atmosphere, they caused less damage
if allowed to slam into their heavily shielded military targets than if shot down elsewhere.

Attempts to deflect the missiles had little effect. The missiles course-corrected and pursued their targets with a singular will. Someone was driving them.

Interceptors in space caught many of the missiles before
they reached Earth, detonating them in the vacuum.

Many more got through.

U.S. Space Patrol Torpedo Boats hunted for the missile carriers in space. The missiles could be traced back to their launch points, but the Roman carriers moved away faster than light immediately upon launching their missiles, so the Spit boats found nothing at trail's end.

Five days into the attacks, a Roman armada of five great gunships dropped down from FTL just inside the orbit of Jupiter. They showed themselves silhouetted against the bright lights of the Jupiter Monument so they could be seen and feared on their approach. Their force fields repelled all ordnance, and the Romans wanted that to be seen too.

Roman camera ships broadcast the images everywhere, just in case the United States failed to do it.

Caesar Romulus picked up the scene from his distant, hidden Fortress Aeyrie. His attendants arranged for him to have a wide, wide vista of space, as if he were right there, watching the armada like Xerxes from his throne at the Battle of Salamis.

"Salamis was a disaster," Romulus said. "You might have invoked something better than that."

"Thermopylae then," the attendant revised quickly.

"So was Thermopylae."

The attendant sputtered. Romulus cut him off, "Please do not try again." He settled, mildly disgruntled, into his throne to watch the show.

Saw beam flashes glancing off the five juggernauts.

Saw the five massive ships closing on the fragile blue-white jewel that was Earth.

Saw the five on approach, belching fire at their attackers.

Saw a titanic spearhead shape lower into his view between the leading camera and the five.

Romulus said, "What is that?"

"That—" his personal guard started, leaving a long, long space between the subject and verb, "appears to be *Merrimack*."

"It does, doesn't it?" said Romulus.

"*Merrimack* is in the Deep," another attendant said.

"It could be *Monitor*," said Caesar's guard.

"*Monitor* is also in the Deep."

Romulus commanded, "Get some data weasels up here and get an identity using something other than visuals."

The answer he wanted was not the one he got: "Remote surveillance confirms this is not an illusion. The plots are solid."

"But is it *Merrimack* or *Monitor*?"

"It is *Merrimack* and *Monitor*."

Romulus' head whip-turned toward the vista.

Two. There were two.

"Did anyone bother to confirm the damage to the Shotgun?" Caesar asked.

Silence told him that that particular ball had been dropped and was rolling around under the deck.

"And what does our informant in Fort Eisenhower say?" Romulus tried again.

"Our informant went silent before the Shotgun was destroyed," said an attendant, then revised, "Before the Shotgun appeared to be destroyed."

"Ah," said Caesar. He sat back in his throne. "Let's watch the show."

The five Roman gunships powered up their weapons. Their enormous barrels jutted through their thick hulls, just breaking the surface of their stout force fields, ready to hurl their load of smart shells.

Monitor and *Merrimack* swept in on either side of the lead ship, banged into it with body checks, squeezing it between their own force fields as the Roman ship fired.

The ordnance had nowhere to go. All the force fields were adamant. The only path of irresolute resistance was in the guns themselves.

Unable to come out, the charges blew back.

The lead Roman gunship blew up. Its engine shields lost integrity, and the antimatter reservoirs blew up like minor suns.

Merrimack and *Monitor* had anticipated that, and were away in time, but one of the flanking Roman gunships took a matter/antimatter blast on its bow that flickered its shields.

Romulus watched from his throne. Said, "Who made that Xerxes remark? I want his throat slit."

An attendant asked shakily, "Truly, Caesar?"

Romulus answered, cross, "Of course not. I am angry. I am not mad."

Fort Eisenhower had been blowing smoke.

Few antique submarine movies were ever made that did not feature the submarine, under siege from depth charges, spilling out oil and air and clothing to give evidence of its own destruction. So the odds on success using only smoke clouds to give the appearance of the Shotgun's demise had seemed very small. And it was really the shrill news reports that sold the disaster, the agonized voices of the reporters, the dramatic images of roiling smoke photographed so lovingly and aired over and over. Images of sobbing relatives back home, not knowing the fate of their loved ones. Those people more than the smoke turned back the Roman warships from Fort Eisenhower.

So *Merrimack* was able to return to Near Space in just the time it took to clear the smoke out of the Shotgun.

She arrived at Fort Roosevelt in less than a blink, less than a heartbeat. In literally no time, space tenders had been unwrapping the foil shroud from the ship two thousand light-years from where she existed a moment ago.

From inside the ship, the lifting of the shroud revealed the spectacular twin white stars of Beta Aurigae through the viewports on one side, and the lights of Fort Theodore Roosevelt on the other.

Bigger than Fort Ike, Fort Ted covered a volume of space nearly one light-minute in diameter. Fort Ted held the largest human population not situated on a solid world.

Monitor arrived at Fort Eisenhower from her Deep End patrol right on her sister ship's heels and followed her through the Shotgun to Fort Roosevelt.

Once they cleared the fort the two space battleships blazed out of the Beta Aurigae system, charging the eighty-two light years toward Earth at threshold velocity.

They expected some anger and resentment upon their surprise appearance. But the people of the United States were so joyous to find the Shotgun working, and so profoundly relieved to be connected to the Deep End, and so utterly enraged over the Roman attack on Earth soil, that most people forgave the deception. Red-blooded citizens were willing to support anything that would strike back at Rome.

Marine Swifts from *Merrimack* dove into Earth's atmosphere. They intercepted Roman missiles and herded them like stray doggies, up and up. The missiles tried to turn around, back toward their targets, but the Swifts bounced them higher and kept knocking them, until they were high enough to vaporize safely.

"YeeeHAW, git along little doggie! Oh no no no no no, not that way!" That was Kerry Blue on the com. Her missile had slipped out of her control and had slid under her Swift. "Somebody pick me up!"

"I got your doggie, Alpha Six," That was Ranza Espinoza. She gave the escaping missile a rough nudge. "Take my wing."

Kerry Blue fell in on Ranza's flank, watching her missile get bounced higher and higher. "Can I space that?"

Ranza replied: "No, you lost it. I get to kill this one."

"Are we high enough?" Dak Shepard sent. "I wanna roast this weenie."

Ranza: "Keep going, Alpha Two. You are still in atmo. Alpha Seven, what the hell are you doing?"

"Uh, fugging myself," Cole Darby replied, who was absolutely no good at herding missiles. This was a new scenario for him. It was new for all of them, but Darb did not pick up physical games quickly.

Ranza: "Cain, pick up the Darb."

Cain Salvador, Alpha Three, was good at everything. He collected Cole Darby's diving missile and booted it spaceward again.

Twitch Fuentes, Alpha Five, intercepted a diving missile head on, attempted to duck just under its nose to bump it up at the last instant.

At the last instant the missile also dipped to avoid the head-on collision and so the two collided so hard the missile detonated.

"*Twitch!*" Carly Delgado's shriek filled all the headsets.

Cain: "Yo ho, hombre, you there?"

Kerry Blue: "Twitch!"

Ranza: "Alpha Five, what is your status?"

Twitch: "Hot hot *hot!*" And Alpha Five streaked toward the ionosphere.

The Swifts' cooling systems were not really made for operations within an atmosphere.

"Carly, spot Twitch." That was Ranza. But Carly did not need telling. She was already on her way, flanking Twitch's climb to colder altitudes.

Dak: "Heads up, the Old Man is in atmo."

Cain Salvador: "Flight risk." That was the term for a colonel at the controls of a fighter craft.

Steele: "I heard that, Salvador."

"Oh, fug." Cain fumbled his missile. It turned on its back and dove.

"Did you think you were on a private channel, Marine?" Steele punted Cain's missile back up.

Cain gave the missile a final kick to escape velocity and opened fire.

Upon Ranza's command all the Swifts of Alpha Flight rose to cool off in the way high. They collected Twitch and Carly, then dove back down to round up another batch of Roman missiles out of the U.S. skies.

Kerry Blue thought she would turn all thumbs with Colonel Steele flying with her. Instead she was brilliant. She dropped none of her missiles and picked up one of Darb's.

Steele pretended to ignore her, except once to ask, "The boffins get your crate put back together right, Alpha Six?"

"Yes, sir." This was an open channel. And he was not asking about her crate. "She's okay," said Kerry Blue, afraid everyone could hear the silly grin in her voice.

Thinking the Shotgun destroyed, Romulus had launched his attack on the Continental U.S. before *Merrimack* and *Monitor* were actually cut off from Earth. As Marcander Vincent at Tactical put it: "We got Rom to jack early again."

"We did that," Farragut had to agree.

Gypsy Dent said, "But what if the Roman warships turn around in the Abyss and go back to Fort Eisenhower?"

"A concern, but not a disaster," said Farragut. "Playing dead wasn't our last-ditch effort to save the Shotgun. I just wanted to make the Romans go away the easiest way possible."

"And we did not want to fight *Horatius*," said Gypsy.

"*We* did not," Farragut confessed. Captain John Farragut had a very soft spot for Legion Draconis. "We erased all the rovers inside the perimeter shield and Weld's people caught Rome's inside man, so I really don't think Fort Eisenhower is in serious danger anymore. Thank God I told General Weld not to exempt Rob Roy from questioning."

Gypsy's eyes appeared white all around. "You mean Calli's young man?" she said, astonished, horrified. "He *wasn't!*"

"No, no, Rob Roy wasn't the spy," said Farragut quickly.

"Who was it?"

"One of the station Intelligence officers."

"Oh, my God."

Farragut nodded.

"How can that happen?" Gypsy's own loyalty was unshakable, so the crime was unthinkable.

Farragut shrugged. "Frontier greed." That was the name of the syndrome. Bribery cases were twice as common in the Deep End as in Near Space. "It was actually the Intelligence agent General Weld charged with investigating visitors to the main station burn unit."

"Weld handed the flock over to the wolf!" said Gypsy.

"He did. He didn't know it—how could he? But that's exactly what he did."

And the wolf had eagerly questioned the sheep.

Among the subjects of his inquiry he found the perfect patsy on whom to pin his own crimes. He needed to identify *someone* as the Roman traitor if he ever hoped to stop the hunt for himself.

He found a guileless lawyer, who looked young as a boy, and who had made a pest of himself trying to get into the burn unit where security was tight around the American captain and the Roman Senator.

Rob Roy Buchanan looked like the perfect mark.

But the interrogation had gone horribly wrong. The interrogator found his own verbal maneuvers fed back to him by this junior lawyer, and then he committed a fatal error.

"He told Rob Roy to shut up."

"An Intelligence officer never ever tells the subject of an interrogation to shut up," said Gypsy.

"And not while the fort is under siege and the subject is supposedly a suspected traitor."

The first rule of interrogation was to keep the subject talking.

While Rob Roy Buchanan kept his interrogator talking, other Intelligence officers dug into the interrogator's business transactions and searched his living compartment. They found a million dollars in very cold cash in the freezer, data pointers to a numbered account in his private records, and some unsatisfactory explanations for solo trips through the fort that provided opportunity to disperse Roman landing disks between the fortress stations.

The image in the final report made Rob Roy Buchanan look even younger than usual. His eyelashes were very faint so his eyes appeared to be just the two brown disks of his irises. He had shaved. He looked fifteen years old, except that he stood between six-two and six-five depending on his posture. He looked utterly disarming.

And Farragut had almost, *almost* told General Weld that Rob Roy did not need interrogating.

"That's a good man," said Gypsy. "Calli should keep him."

Many of the Roman missiles and drones hitting the Continental United States were coming from carriers, cloaked in distortion and ready to flee faster than light as soon as they were sighted. But U.S. scanners picked up some other possible sources, moving in plain sight—registered internationals, flagged as cargo vessels.

Some nations would flag a paper airplane if the fee were paid.

Scanners located a suspicious hulk—claimed to be an Eastern Alliance trader—bearing a Freelander flag. Roman missile trails led back to this cargo ship.

Traders normally earned premiums for early delivery.

The Freelander's course led back on itself in a wide circle around nothing, in a hurry to get nowhere.

Merrimack was riding in its shadow now.

"Want to shoot it?" Gypsy asked, standing next to Farragut on the command deck.

"I do," said Captain Farragut. They were so close they could hit the cargo ship with their lights and actually *see* it.

The neutral Freelander flag was posted all over it.

"If this goes bad, it will fall on your head," Gypsy gave a dutiful warning. "Hard."

"Oh, my head's used to it. I have identified the plot as an enemy hostile. Commander Dent, destroy the Freelander."

"Aye, sir. Targeting, acquire the Freelander."

"Target acquired and tagged, aye," said Targeting. He turned around at his station. "It's right *there*. Should we get some space between us if that thing's carrying what we think it's carrying?"

Targeting was still speaking as the com tech reported, "Freelander is screaming that he's neutral."

"Advise personnel aboard the cargo ship to take to their lifeboats and get behind us. Helm, make a few hundred klicks between *Mack* and the target."

Helm responded: "Adjusting separation, aye."

Tactical: "Target is showing life craft."

Helm: "Separation achieved."

The cargo ship was no longer in visual range. But the tags would assure that any ordnance from *Merrimack* would connect with the target.

Gypsy looked to Farragut, "What kind of chaser do you think?"

"I think if we could light a match in there it might do the trick," said Farragut.

"Fire Control. Single torpedo, standard load," Gypsy ordered.

"Torpedo ready, aye. Fire Control standing by."

"Fire torpedo," said Gypsy Dent.

"Torpedo away, aye."

The torpedo hissed upon leaving the ship. It instantly disappeared into the dark in search of the cargo ship.

The damn thing turned out to be a space munitions

dump. The cargo ship became visible like a supernova. All *Merrimack*'s viewports dimmed under the intense light.

Marcander Vincent stood right up at his station and shouted as if across the vacuum: "Hey, Caesar! This is what real up-blowing looks like!"

A haze hung in the atmosphere over the United States. Dark clouds rolled across the continent, visible from space, and rains fell like after a volcano. Winds swept the skies clear to brilliant sunsets.

There was a lull in the missile strikes, but no peace in the silence. America waited for the next wave of attacks.

Captain Farragut received a message from his father.

The judge wanted to move the family to the outer colonies.

"No, sir," said Captain Farragut, an order. And to the judge's outraged bluster, he asked the old hunter, "What's more likely to get shot—a pheasant lying low in the field or a pheasant taking to the air? Stay low!"

"There are missiles over my house. OVER MY HOUSE!"

"Then go up the road and stay with the Lees or the Wilkens," Captain Farragut answered. "Just keep to the ground and do not get into anything that looks like a government vehicle."

"They're doing this to get at you, you know!" the elder Farragut accused.

The missile flights directly over the Farragut house—yes, those probably had been aimed to get the younger Farragut's attention. "Yes, sir."

"Then *you* make them stop!"

"Aye, aye, sir," said Captain Farragut.

The attacks had already stopped. For this moment. That was part of the terror. The not knowing when they would start again.

It was unclear what Romulus had hoped to achieve. The three surviving giant Roman gunships had vanished faster than light. Those could be anywhere.

The attacks on U.S. military installations had not made a single penetration.

So far there had been no strikes on utilities or on civilian transports.

"If he's not going after utilities, that strongly suggests his intent is occupation," Farragut observed.

The Pentagon was adding up the damage, and keeping watch for the next strike, and expressing indignation.

"I suppose this means we'll be bombing Palatine," Gypsy said.

"I think we might oughta better," said Farragut.

"Ya ha and hoo ra!" a Marine guard at the hatchway let loose. Shut himself up, looking contrite.

There came no rebuke for the outburst.

"Can't we hit Fortress Aeyrie too?" Tactical asked.

"Would," said Farragut. "If we knew where it was."

"Palatine is the better target, sir," said Gypsy. "Especially if Caesar is not there."

That would let the Roman populace see the might of Caesar, hiding in his mobile fortress while U.S. ships were bombing Palatine.

Farragut nodded, but warned, "They'll be ready for us. They must know the Yanks are coming."

"Lunaris, tell me about World War Two submarines," said Romulus with a voice of silk.

Lollius Lunaris explained, "There was a tactic—it may even have been a fiction, but it was recounted so often that every American knows it. A submarine under attack would crash dive and jettison debris and an oil slick to make it appear dead to the hunter ships on the surface."

Caesar said, "You had information that the destruction of the Shotgun was likely a ruse and you failed to pass it on."

Lunaris opened his mouth. *I tried to tell you.*

The words went unspoken, but Caesar heard them anyway. "This is the Imperial Palace. There are no half measures. It is your job to make certain that vital information gets where it needs to go. There is no excuse for doing half a job." He swept his hand at the space vista that took up one enormous wall of the audience hall—the scene of a crippled

Roman gunship drifting amid the widely scattered wreckage of another.

"You killed those ships, Lunaris. You are dismissed."

Lunaris tottered out of the throne room, not sure how he managed to stay vertical.

He ordered a sword and fell on it.

President Marissa Johnson dispatched an official protest of Rome's violation of the articles of surrender and of Caesar's groundless declaration of war.

Caesar Romulus opened a visual communication with the American leader. Marissa Johnson had the jowls of a second term President. They were expected, almost required.

In Rome, a man of wealth was expected to be beautiful, whether the wealth was inherited or manufactured. Visually, Caesar was a beautiful man, with those lush brown curls, his petulant lips, his deep brown eyes, and his nose perfectly Roman. His voice was a masculine baritone. Caesar Romulus answered President Johnson serenely. He was much less paranoid and strident since the Roman Senate had ratified his position. "With respect, Madame President, violating the surrender is rather the point."

"The terms were lenient," said President Johnson. "Unreasonably lenient."

Rome's armed forces had come under U.S. command in order to mount a concentrated offense against the Hive. Rome had been permitted to keep its internal government and all its laws.

"We were joined for the common good," said President Johnson. "And the alien threat is still here. Your obligation is not fulfilled."

"The alien threat is in your yard, Madame President. Clean it up yourself. Rome has no obligation to you. I am not a pirate or a thug. Here is how it is: when you pry pledges out of a drowning man as you dangle the lifeline over his head, do you expect the pledges he makes to be binding? Not in any court, Madame President of the United States of America. Not even yours."

"We came to Rome's aid in the Empire's hour of need!"

"America's aid to Rome was entirely self-serving. The defense of Rome was the defense of America. But the defense of America is not the defense of Rome."

And Romulus outlined his demands for a lasting peace. The demands included annexation of the United States of America into the Empire as a province of Rome.

Marissa Johnson replied publicly that the United States would be formulating an appropriate response to Rome's demands. Though she was rumored to have turned directly to her Secretary of Defense and said: "Bomb their ass."

9

I T WAS A WEEK'S JOURNEY for a space battleship from Earth to Palatine. *Monitor* stayed behind at Earth, pretending to be both *Merrimack* and herself. Other attack ships also pretended to be more than they were as their twins stole toward the Roman capital, two hundred light-years away.

Merrimack kept her Swifts inboard to minimize the chance of detection. Chances of being detected at FTL normally ranged between remote and impossible, but any approach to heavily patrolled and monitored Palatine was an exception.

"They know we're coming, so what's the point of hiding?" Carly said, kicking a soccer ball foot to foot on the hangar deck, stir crazy. "And just what are *you* grinning at?"

Kerry Blue and the Darb had just come into the hangar, grinning and sniggering.

Kerry darted in and stole the ball from Carly.

Kerry Blue had not been herself lately. She hadn't been yab yumming anyone. And Kerry Blue had yab yummed just about every man on board. She passed the ball to Darb, who missed it completely. "Darb showed me a Greek play."

Twitch corralled the loose ball as Carly said, "A *what?* Yuk! How cultured! Doesn't everybody die?"

"That's a Greek tragedy," said Darb. "This was a comedy. Everyone gets married at the end of a comedy."

Dak's face rolled up as if smelling mold, "So was it *funny*?"

"Yeah," said Kerry Blue, still laughing at some of the lines. "Lots of sex jokes. It was updated, wasn't it, Darb?"

"No," Cole Darby sighed. "Sex was funny back then too."

Cain reached in a foot and stole the ball from Twitch. "I don't know, my man. Sounds way too Roman for me."

"Me too." Ranza threw her weight into Cain and snagged the ball. " 'Kay, Darb. Tell me how the lupes kept their society secret for two thousand fox-trotting years."

The ship's gravity gave one of its random burbles. Ranza lost her step and the ball. She let her arms slap her sides, watching the ball escape. "Millions of lupes. All over the world. Big fat secret. I can't keep my birth date secret. How'd they do that?"

"In plain sight," said Darb.

During the Long Silence the Roman cloak of secrecy had leaked like the *Titanic*. But anyone who tried to reveal the secret empire came off as a raving dwit. A secret Roman Empire was just another conspiracy theory.

Romans concocted a lot of different conspiracy theories just to keep their real one hidden in the stack. There was competition among them to see who could get the most followers for the wildest idea.

Romans passed down their secret traditions generation to generation, though not necessarily by blood. They did not hesitate to adopt worthy persons, bestow upon them their own *gens* name—their secret true name—and make them part of their tribe.

Romans preserved their language in the disciplines of law, medicine, religion, science, and higher education. Latin infested the English language. The Roman mythos was taught in schools. Roman symbols were ubiquitous—the caduceus, the scales, the symbols for male and female, for the planets.

Roman culture was not buried very deep. Non-Romans would trip over an exposed root and think nothing of it.

Heirs, whether by blood or adoption, blended into local

society. They rose to positions of prominence, whether as research scientist or judge or Pope.

The World Wide Web was the beginning of the empire's resurrection. Global communication made a united organization possible. Race and nationality mattered less and less as globalization progressed. Rome, long accustomed to annexing foreigners, folded the worthy in. Strength and Honor were what mattered.

With the advent of faster than light travel, the secret empire conceived a plan for a mass exodus from Earth, to be deployed once a suitable destination was found.

A U.S. corporation—wholly owned by a secret society of Romans—terraformed and colonized a nearby world, two hundred light years away, in the Lambda Coronae Australis system. The corporation christened the colony Palatine.

In A.D. 2290 the Romans of Palatine raised their standards and their eagles, and declared independence from the United States. The call went out Earthwide to all their secret kind to come. And the Exodus was on.

The result was a severe talent drain from all of Earth, not just from the United States. Romans were everywhere, and they left in tribes. Earth lost, if not the best and brightest, then at least the extremely talented and very, very smart. Romans had cultivated fine minds. They were highly educated and technically adept. Motivated. With a proud—arrogant—history.

There followed a short, embarrassing war of independence. The United States tried to hold onto the colony built under their flag. The League of Earth Nations came out in favor of colonial independence, and promised to lend military support to Palatine if the United States continued to press its claim by violent means.

Next came the attempted embargo. The U.S. cut off all assistance to Palatine and all trade. If Palatine wanted to stand alone, let it stand alone and languish.

Palatine flourished. Romans had designed their new home world to be self-sustaining. Romans used a great deal of automation.

The new Rome started out without a human underclass. Automatons performed menial, repetitive, or dangerous tasks. Wherever there was a problem, there was a programmable solution. Rome had the minds. Palatine had the natural resources. They lacked population, but resolved that by mass reproduction, using in vitro conception and ranks and ranks of incubators to supplement a limited number of wombs. Roman civilization rapidly spread into an interstellar empire. Palatine colonized new worlds faster even than the United States—because Rome did not care if a world had a resident civilization or not. As long as an Earth nation hadn't got to it first, the world was theirs.

Upon arriving in the Lambda Coronae Australis star system, *Merrimack* let loose the dogs of war by launching her Wing. Sprung from a week's confinement, the Marines were rabid to shoot Romans. The Swifts strafed Palatine.

The results were unexpected.

Alpha Seven reported first over the com: "I don't know what the target's transmitting, but I can't get a tone on my own foot."

Alpha Three: "Try taking it out of your mouth, Darb."

"I don't hear a whole lot of hoo ras out of anyone else!" Darb sent. "Are *you* hitting anything?"

Dak offered: "I bit my tongue."

Alpha Flight circled the target for a second pass, but computer-guided sighting went AWOL in the Roman distortion. Shots from the hip rebounded from Roman energy shields.

The Marines then discovered why the lupes had come in low when they attacked the U.S.—Palatine's planetary defenses could not hit a crate on the deck. The Swifts decided to try the Roman tactic against them. They dropped fast and fired low.

But come in too low, you didn't get shot but your shots and you rebounded off the Roman energy shield. Kerry Blue heard Cain sailing away on a high bounce: "WA-hooooooooooo!"

Kerry Blue touched right down on the ground and tried to send a shot in the front door of her target.

The shot came straight back at her. It hit her on the fat

part of the distortion field, so she survived it. She passed verdict on the tactic as she climbed: "That's a DDT."

Don't Do Twice.

None of the attack craft had any joy. Whether shooting in atmosphere or from space, no one could land a significant shot on a Roman military installation.

No one was accustomed to missing.

Cain: "Something is uffing my targeting system here!"

Darb: "You are not alone."

Cain: "That gives me no comfort!"

Alpha Flight was operating near Roma Nova, the daylight side of the world, and they were all overheating.

Ranza Espinoza bellowed: "Alpha Flight! Come on yous! On the roof! Pattern Zulu Tango. Now!"

The Swifts of Alpha Flight rocketed out of the atmosphere on an evasion path to avoid intercepts during ascent.

In the cooling darkness, Kerry Blue sent: "We aren't going home yet, are we? I don't want to go back with gots."

Dak: "Me neither."

Twitch: "Yo."

Cain: "You can leave me here. I am *not* going back to *Merrimack* empty-handed."

Ranza: " 'Kay. Let's go get the chicken. Let's go get the chicken." And she dove into atmo.

Dak rolled over and dove after her. Then Carly, Twitch, Darby, and Kerry Blue.

"Chicken?" Cain asked, falling in behind everyone else.

"A chicken is a yellow bird," said Carly.

Technically speaking most chickens were white. But even Darb could figure out that Ranza meant yellow in the chickenly sense of the word—cowardly.

The Alphas were over Roma Nova. Ranza had her Flight on the deck on a direct line with the Monument to the Conciliation.

A golden eagle was a yellow bird.

The monument had been redone so that the bald eagle cowered on its back with the golden eagle positioned high over it, diving at it, claws outstretched.

"We're not allowed to hit the palace!" Kerry cried as they neared the Capitoline.

"We're not hitting the palace," said Ranza. "We're hitting the chicken."

"We're not allowed to hit the Capitoline!" said Kerry.

"The monument is not on the Capitoline." Darb, that time. "It's at the *foot* of the Capitoline."

"See? Some of the skat Darb knows *is* useful. *Chicken sighted off the starboard bow!*" Ranza veered up the Via Triumphalis. The others followed in a long chain just above the ground traffic.

Citizenry dodged out of the buildings lining the Via to look at the roaring spacecraft, then skittered back inside.

"I can't get a bead," Carly reported on approach, worried. "Ranza, I can't get a bead. The monument's got distortion around it."

"Okay let's do this the old-fashioned way. Line it up by eyeball. We're gonna make a mess. Follow me. Nobody hit the palace or we're all chucked."

"I'm showing hostiles headed in," Darb reported. "Lots. Thirty seconds out."

"Then get this done in twenty-nine seconds!"

"We're gonna get atomized."

Ranza held to her kill course. Closed fast on the monument, lobbed a shot on the golden eagle and veered *up*.

A miss.

Next in was Dak. "Gotcha, gotcha, gotcha—oh!" Looked back, climbing. "Winged it!"

He had taken off the very tip of the golden eagle's portside wing.

Darb made a big hole next to the monument's base.

Carly, Twitch, and Kerry scored clean misses.

Twenty-five seconds down. No time left. "Bad guys are hording in. Whole bunches. Don't seem happy," said Darb. Only thing protecting them from long-distance fire was the close proximity of the Imperial Palace and the grand buildings in this neighborhood. The Roman ships charging in now were bound to be harpies. They would snatch the Swifts out of the sky and haul them off elsewhere to crush them.

"Take your shot, Cain!"

Cain came riding in just topside of a Roman hoverbus.

"Cain, it's up to you now. Bring it home!"

"Cain! Cain! Cain!"

On the deck. On level. Cain's clearsceen filled with golden feathers.

"Hoorah!"

Took his shot and veered straight up. "Mama, get me outta here!" Cain yelled, a whole fleet of pissed off and ugly coming after him.

Covering fire was coming from above as Alpha Flight climbed away from Roma Nova, chased by an angry mob.

"Alpha Flight. Alpha Flight. This is *Merrimack*. You are clear to approach portside flight deck, hot as you need to."

The Alphas cleared atmo and came in at a near crash atop *Merrimack*'s port wing. *Mack*'s force field clapped down over the Swifts.

Merrimack's force field lit up and sparkled under a rain of fire.

Clamps rose up from the flight deck, clamped the Swifts down. The elevators carried the fighters down inside the ship to the hangar deck.

At the green light, the Alphas popped canopies.

The whole hangar deck was filled and chanting, "Cain! Cain! Cain! Cain!"

Anyone who could be here was here.

Merrimack must have jumped to FTL to have this many people free to crowd the hangar.

Kerry climbed out of her Swift, jumped down to the deck and joined in the chant. "Cain! Cain! Cain!"

The man of the hour climbed out of his cockpit to stand atop his Swift. Cain Salvador gave a sheepish shrug of his big shoulders, and an "aw shucks" kind of nod. He gave his admirers a thumb's up.

And suddenly the deck went silent.

You knew who was here without looking.

Colonel Steele. Stalking through the crowd.

Flight Leader Ranza Espinoza stepped forward, talking before the colonel could reach the front, "Sir, this was my idea, my responsibili—"

"Shut up."

Ranza shut.

Steele stalked up the line of Alphas.

"I thought that kind of crap died with Cowboy Carver."

Ranza started, "Sir, I—"

"Shut up."

"Hm," Ranza made a sound, uncertain whether she should verbally acknowledge that order or just obey it.

"That stunt was extremely dangerous. Not only was the target unauthorized but it was within range of civilians and the palace which are absolutely off-limits. Your actions were not on any list of contingency plans. It was freelance bullskat."

Steele paced, his head red, fit to steam out his ears.

"Here is where I tell you how deep a hole you've dug for us. Unfortunately, I can't reprimand any of you."

Pacing. Teeth grinding.

The Alphas' gazes remained fixed stiffly forward but all of them just wanted to exchange glances and say, "Huh?"

Steele was mad as hell. And not just at them. Someone wearing a lot of brass had got hold of that bullmastiff's leash and yanked.

Words came out of TR Steele like he was performing his own appendectomy: "They are dancing in the streets back home. I have orders from our C in C to buy each of you a beer."

And to the cheer about to erupt, his forefinger jerked up in the air to silence it, and he warned all on deck, "You can sit on that till I leave."

He spun on Ranza. "Espinoza, this doesn't ever happen again."

"Aye, sir. And I agree. I should never—"

"I don't give a skat if you agree, soldier. You just do."

"Aye, sir."

Steele stalked back through the ranks. A navvy, not in Steele's chain of command, spoke over his clanging march toward the doors, "The beer order is coming from *President Johnson*?"

Steele looked at the navvy and snarled. He had just said that. "*I* wouldn't."

He nearly collided with Chef Zack come marching into the hangar deck with a six-pack in either hand. Zack had appointed himself to the task of hand delivering the President's order.

Someone else brought in the recordings to show the Alphas what had caused the Presidential hallelujah.

Cain hadn't just knocked the golden eagle off its perch. He had knocked the monument base over sideways so that the bald eagle, which used to be cowering on its back, now looked for all the world like it was rolling over to get up.

That's what they were roaring about Stateside.

"Wow," Cain looked at his work. No wonder the beer got here before his Swift even dried off.

"That's my hole," said Cole Darby. He pointed at the hole that allowed the monument to cant over. "That's my hole."

"Nice hole," said Cain.

"A *real* sharpshooter would have picked off the chicken without breaking the bald eagle's left toe," said Cole Darby.

Cain swaggered over, hooked his arm round Darb's neck, snugged him in close for a side-by-side hug, nearly strangling him in the crook of his elbow. "And here's my man, Darb. I love him like a brother."

Darb's voice came out strained, muffled by a face full of muscular arm. "I'd feel much better about this if someone other than a guy named Cain were talkin'."

The handle to the hatch of Steele's private compartment clicked, turned.

Steele watched it, scowling. Could not quite believe what he was seeing. Someone was letting himself into Steele's quarters without knock or permission.

The hatch opened to Kerry Blue, holding beer for two.

Steele looked away. "Flight Sergeant, you do not want to be here."

She let herself in. The hatch shut behind her. "That was crappy what they did."

They? He was plenty pissed with her too. It wasn't as if she hadn't been flying with Alpha Flight. Kerry Blue had been as much a part of it as Cain Salvador.

"I am not happy with any of you." Steele rested his chin on his fist, not looking at her.

"Huh? Oh, I wasn't talking about the Alphas. We did

what we did and I really expected to be in the lower sail right now guarding a box of donuts for it. They shouldn't be giving you different orders from two hundred light-years away about your Marine Flight."

They. He lifted his head. She was talking about President Johnson and the DC brass holes.

Kerry finished, "I thought the chain of command went both ways."

"So did I," Steele said into his fist. Still pissed, but amazed that she understood why he was pissed.

She offered, "I can go to the lower sail if it'd make you feel better."

She had already made him feel better. She got it. She *got* it. He just wanted someone to recognize that he had been undercut from on high. And of all people, it was Kerry Blue who got it.

If he felt any better Kerry Blue would be on her back on the deck right here, right now.

"Give me those beers and get out of here," he said.

"You can handle these by yourself?" Kerry put her lips to the mouth of one bottle before surrendering it. "Sure you don't need reinforcements?"

"Out!"

10

THE MEDIA WERE CALLING IT the Doolittle Raid, after an air strike nearly a half millennium ago. That operation had not taken out a single military target either.

The strike on Palatine had rattled a lot of windows and cracked a few foundations, made the Romans dive like prairie dogs, and rolled over the chicken. That was about the sum of it.

But U.S. morale soared, and that had probably been the real mission objective anyway, because *Merrimack* was ordered home. The crew were not told if other ships were being left behind at Palatine, but everyone on board wondered why they couldn't stay in the enemy system to do some real damage.

Titus Vitruvius lay in his sleep chamber in the city of Antipolis on the planet Thaleia, not sleeping.

His tiny chamber in the ziggurat had once been clothed in the illusion of a tree fort. That was too babyish for him now. Now his chamber was rigged to appear like a Legion commander's quarters aboard a ship of war.

While he was in his room he was not in a self-contained city on an automated factory world. He was on board the Legion carrier *Horatius*. In his world, he had taken over command of *Horatius* upon the death of Herius Asinius.

On a shelf of gods he prayed to, he had Mars and Bellus and Minerva and Virtus and Honorus. No one really quite believed in gods but it never hurt to ask them for favors.

Also on the shelf was an image of Herius Asinius. Rome did not officially deify people anymore, but Titus did.

Titus belonged to *gens* Vitruvius, but the standards and the grey and scarlet legion colors in his room were *gens* Asinius.

Because Thaleia was the home of PanGalactic Industries, the patron god of the planet Thaleia was Vulcan, the craftsman. Outside of the self-contained city's pleasant illusions, the world was bleak, harsh. But it had an atmosphere, free-flowing water, sun, wind, and minerals. Thaleia's settlements existed to serve its factories.

Titus Vitruvius wanted nothing more than to get off of Thaleia. Vulcan had no place on Titus' shelf.

Titus preferred Mars to Vulcan, Achilles to Odysseus. Brawn and courage to industry and cunning.

Thaleia's factories were largely automated and self run, so the population of Thaleia was small as planetary populations were reckoned. The factories churned out killer bots. PanGalactic Industries' killer bots had been redesigned so they could not all be commanded to self-destruct by a single signal as the first generation of killer bots had been. There used to be millions of them, and soon would be again.

Thaleian factories manufactured the missiles and the drones that were terrorizing America, and they assembled the carrier craft which transported the missiles and drones to within striking distance of Earth.

Thaleia's factories had also rebuilt the planet's orbiting defenses. At a distance of seventy-one light-years, Thaleia was the closest Roman planet to Earth and to the hated United States of America.

The heavy defenses kept the enemy away from Thaleia. Titus had expected the Americans to make their strike here instead of Palatine. But Thaleia sat out that action, and Titus was disappointed.

If he must be on a planet instead of on a warship, Titus wished he could be on Palatine, shooting Americans out of the Roman sky.

His mother wouldn't let him go anywhere.

He was at the age where your mother is a boat anchor. And he was unfortunate enough actually to have a mother. His friends had been born from incubators. Lucky them. Oh, they knew where their maternal DNA came from, but *Jupiter!* You get pushed out between a woman's thighs, she thinks she owns you and does not let go. Ever. His mother just did not understand. Titus had fought against the Hive. He had helped Herius Asinius defend the Roman fortress! He was a combat veteran! He was twelve years old!

Upon his final parting, Herius Asinius had given Titus an order to protect his mother. Titus knew that legionaries often got orders they didn't like and they were expected to obey. But things had changed since then. If Herius Asinius were alive, he would give Titus new orders. Titus just knew it.

Titus still kept his ant farm and his jar of zakan moths with him. They used to give warnings of any Hive presence. The moths only ever did anything if Hive monsters were very, very close.

The Hive in Near Space was dead. It was completely gone from Thaleia.

The last Hive stragglers were thousands of light-years away in the next arm of the galaxy, across the Abyss in the Deep End. Titus kept his telltales because they had been a gift from Herius Asinius, whom he adored. And they had saved his life once.

Midnight. Titus was awake, and not sure why. His eyes were open, watching the ants.

They crawled out of their tunnels as if someone had kicked their container.

The zakan moths began to chirp.

"Mater! Mater!" Titus Vitruvius ran into his mother's chamber. "Hive! Hive sign!"

Verina Vitruvia stirred sleepily. Her compartment smelled like flowers. She smelled like flowers. She moved her long hair from her face. She groaned at the chronometer. Mumbled, "It must be something else." Her head fell back into her pillow.

"No. They are here." He tried to shake the bed, but it wouldn't shake.

Verina's voice came from the pillow. "Go back to bed, dearest."

Titus stomped into the corridor and pulled the city alarm. Flashing lights flared to life, and the clangor rose up and up the spiral corridors of the ziggurat.

Verina was up as if catapulted. She ran into the corridor and shut the alarm back off. She hissed at her son to keep herself from shrieking, "What are you doing!"

Screams rose from somewhere. Male voices.

"You've started a panic," Verina scolded, trying to usher Titus back inside their chambers. "We will be fined for this."

"Romans do not panic," said Titus.

"What?"

The screams. He meant that men were not screaming just because the alarm sounded.

The screams sounded like men on fire, and they were coming from way down in the lowest level of the ziggurat.

Then the alarm reactivated. The lights were flashing, the clangor blaring. Someone else had pulled it this time.

Verina turned Titus around, started to herd him down the ramp to the exit. Titus planted his heels and seized her night cloak to make her stop.

"Don't go this way. The gorgons are under the city. That's where they came from the first time. This way." He took his mother by the hand and tugged for her to come up the ramp.

He bellowed—as deep as a boy's soprano voice could bellow—to everyone they met stampeding down the spiral corridor to turn around and go to the roofs. He shouted for someone to contact the home guard to order an airlift to take them off of the rooftops.

A voice responded from somewhere in adult baritone, a military acknowledgment, "It shall be done."

And Titus at last understood why Herius Asinius, the god, had ordered him to stay in Antipolis.

Romulus returned to the Imperial palace on Palatine, abandoning the safety of his mobile palace Fortress Aeyrie to be with his people. He publicly regretted that he had not been here during the raid.

The U.S. ships had already withdrawn from Palatine by the time Romulus took up residence again.

Upon his return, Romulus found rumors of Hive appearances in Near Space circulating on Palatine. Romulus could not believe how quickly the word of the Hive spread from his own trusted people on Fortress Aeyrie to Palatine—even after he swore them to silence. Caesar was going to crucify someone for this.

But the rumors going round Palatine were not of gorgons on 82 Eridani III.

These rumors were of gorgons on Thaleia.

"Kill the rumors and find out what is really happening on Thaleia," Caesar ordered. "It's all U.S. propaganda."

A top adviser lingered behind after the others had left. The aging general Julius Zosimus was not close enough to be a confidant. Romulus did not have those. But Zosimus was given as much trust as one could expect from a man who had seen his father murdered by a top adviser.

The two were alone. Zosimus knew there were anti-surveillance jammers here. Still he drew close and kept his voice low. His lips barely moved in case anyone had a camera on him. "Caesar, there appears to be a real gorgon presence on Thaleia. Not large, but it's—"

"Rumor," Caesar finished for him. "Listen to what I am telling you. *Kill* the *rumors*. Everyone is to understand that the gorgons in Near Space were only ever U.S. propaganda, and that we are too clever to swallow any dung they try to feed us."

"Understood, Caesar."

At the base of the Capitoline a wide swathe of new grass sprouted where the Monument to the Conciliation used to stand. Of the Monument itself nothing remained. The wreckage had been removed quickly after the American attack.

General Numa Pompeii stood on the new grass, too late to the dance.

There had been U.S. ships over Palatine, and Numa Pompeii had not been here to turn them away.

Numa Pompeii had spent the last three months slogging across the two thousand light-years of the Abyss. Caesar might have waited until *Gladiator* could pass through the U.S. Shotgun before he decided to declare his war.

Romulus had known exactly what he was doing.

The palace guards admitted Numa readily enough. A servant offered him the traditional refreshment, which Numa declined. Another servant showed him to a chamber, there to wait.

The Imperial Palace that Numa Pompeii remembered was built of blue and white marble, with stately Ionic pillars holding up coffered ceilings.

The circular chamber in which the returning Triumphalis was left cooling his heels had been redone in holoimages, so he was standing inside a storm cloud.

Lightning flickered. Thunder rolled. The short, graying hairs on the back of Numa's thick neck stood up with the electricity.

Numa Pompeii had dressed for an audience with the Self, not as a Senator, but as a general. His polished bronze cuirass was inlaid with gold and silver across his vast chest. Greek style leather tabs skirted his short tunic. Bronze greaves sheathed his shins. The formal military garb left his powerful arms and legs in view.

He wore his siege crown.

"About bloody time, Pompeii." Caesar Romulus strode into the chamber with a lightning flash.

Romulus sported an old style Roman cloak draped over black clothes of a modern cut. A small gold oak wreath sat on his lush curls.

Numa was certain that others found the lightning distracting, but he did not flinch at the bolts. He kept his eyes on Romulus. The young man had gotten very comfortable in his role since Numa last saw him. All his stridency was gone. There was a sure, easy set to his posture.

"Whose side are you on?" Caesar asked.

"You stuck me in the Deep," said Numa. "Blindsided me with that declaration of war. Held your confirmation vote without me. I am on your side of course."

Romulus grinned at him. "You always land on your feet,

Pompeii." He nodded like a rival recognizing a superior player. "I am told you killed our Gaius Americanus and Captain Callista Carmel."

Numa did not bother telling Romulus that the attack on Gaius and Calli Carmel was not his doing. Caesar already knew that. Denial would just make Numa sound weak. He asked in turn, "Are they dead then?"

"I'm asking you," said Caesar.

"I cannot confirm the report. I *saw* the attack. I did not stay around for the result. A lot of American ships were out for my blood and there was a very large U.S. space fort within quick striking distance of the scene."

"That part jibes with what I have heard. I remember listening to a recording of Captain Farragut calling off the chase. I think he said, 'Let him go. Numa's gotta be flying out of U.S. space faster than a turkey in November.' "

"Faster than light, actually," said Numa.

Caesar's voice went soft with a venomous undercurrent. "I am told that the reason Gaius left the fortress, and the reason the Americans think you killed him, is that you invited Gaius out."

"True," said Numa, looking Caesar in the eyes.

Caesar blinked. "You killed him?"

"I invited him out," Numa said.

"Why did you want to meet with Gaius? What did the two of you have to talk about?"

"I did not want to meet with Gaius. I wanted to offer him transportation home. You do know that you marooned two senior Senators out there without access to the Shotgun."

"*You* found your way home."

"I did." Numa let the sourness bleed into his voice. That trip had been a monumental waste of time. "A ship can run a lot of drills in three months. It is a very long journey when your world is at war. Longer still when your world is under attack."

"We survived," said Caesar. "Without you."

"I rejoice," said Numa.

Romulus was suddenly cheerful. "I'm glad to see you, Pompeii. I am. I have work for you to do. But first."

Caesar Romulus stepped back, held his ring hand before him, downward, so that one needed to kneel in order to kiss it.

The dialogs. IV.

A: Do you not, *Don* Cordillera, have a problem being Catholic even knowing that your Church was created as a Roman power lever?

JMdeC: The secret Roman imperialists lost their grip on the Church in the twentieth century.

A: We did not lose our grip. We let go. Yet Catholic priests still learn Latin. Why is that?

JMdeC: The idea of Latin in the Church was not to be a vehicle for your language. It was so the faithful might go to any church in the world and hear the same Mass. The idea was to make the church catholic.

A: It served to unify the Roman Empire.

JMdeC: The Church still stands without Romans.

A: In Vatican City. Within Old Rome.

JMdeC: You abandoned the Vatican.

A: Rome left a lot of valuable crap behind if you noticed. A fortune.

JF: That means something?

A: We're coming back, don't you know?

11

BASE SIRIUS WAS A U.S. outpost, critical for its location within nine light-years of Earth.

The main star in the system, Sirius A, was just over twice the mass of Sol, and twenty-six times as bright. That and its closeness made Sirius the brightest star in Earth's sky.

But Sirius A was not the Dog Star of ancient Greece.

It was the companion star, the Pup, Sirius B, that had caused wonder in the ancient heavens.

Two millennia ago, Sirius B left the main sequence and swelled up to red gianthood. It ballooned so large and bright that it was visible from Earth in the light of day. The Greeks thought the heat from that giant red star made the Dog Days so hot. But the Dog Days were only hot because Sirius appeared closest to the sun when it just happened to be summer in the northern hemisphere.

The Dog Days of August continued to be hot for millennia after the red giant shrank down to a planet-sized white dwarf, dense, dim, invisible in Earth daylight like any other star—leaving later Earthlings to wonder what was so special about the Dog Star, and how could anyone possibly imagine that Sirius added heat to Earth's northern summers.

The U.S. space station Base Sirius orbited the bright primary star at four times the distance from Earth to Sol. Even at that, the station's muscular solar filters were needed to keep Base Sirius from burning up.

And these days there was also the Pup to consider. The orbit of Sirius A and Sirius B around each other was highly eccentric. At the moment, the two stars were just widening from periastro, putting Base Sirius almost the same distance from one as from the other. From the station there was no confusing the two—the main star was several times bigger and ten thousand times brighter than the Pup.

The station orbited the main star on a slight oblique so that its view to Earth was never occluded.

"Occultation, ninety by ninety by three," Station Watch sang out. "Incoming hostile. It's a big one. Nothing stealthy about this one."

"Call the station to invasion alert," the stationmaster ordered, then hailed Jupiter Control to advise them that Base Sirius was about to come under attack.

"We see him, Sirius," Jupiter Control answered on a resonant link. "*Wolfhound* will respond."

"Send more ships," Sirius sent. "My lookout is telling me the incoming hostile is big."

"It's very big," Jupiter Control acknowledged. No comfort there. "It's *Gladiator*. Tell your people to stand by for heavy rolls."

The station immediately hailed its rescuer: "*Wolfhound, Wolfhound, Wolfhound*. This is Base Sirius. What is your location?"

A wolfhunter class spaceship appeared from behind the ferociously bright primary star. "Base Sirius, this is *Wolfhound*. We are here."

"Thank God," Sirius responded, watching the enormous plot that was *Gladiator* closing on the system.

Base Sirius received *Wolfhound* into its energy field and established hard dock. The ship essentially became part of the station and added its strength to the force field.

Gladiator approached, brute, daunting, nearly the size of the space station.

Wolfhound kept up continuous fire on *Gladiator* as the Roman massif approached. The station itself was poorly armed, its defenses designed to repel pirates.

The gigantic *Gladiator* jammed a force field hook through the station's force field, and pried it wide. *Wolfhound* had to instantly cease fire.

Gladiator stabbed a corvus into the station hull and drew alongside with deafening booms.

Then sounds of metal tearing and shearing carried throughout all three vessels.

The stationmaster sent a nervous message to the adjacent *Wolfhound*, "You're not leaving us are you, *Wolfhound*?"

Wolfhound could cut and run. An orbital station could not.

"No," *Wolfound* answered. "*Gladiator* will not take this station."

Metal tore. Romans cut a wide opening in the station's bulkhead to create their own dock.

Air pressed in on the sinuses and the ears with the addition of *Gladiator*'s heavier Roman atmosphere.

Roman soldiers stood in the rough dock, prepared to board the station.

They hesitated at the sight of tendrils racing along the deck, in through the breach, into *Gladiator*, quick as snakes. The tendrils wedged themselves under hatches, through vents, all through the ship.

The Roman boarding party cut the tendrils. The tendrils immediately re-formed, re-fused, became whole again.

"Sever those," Numa Pompeii ordered from his command deck as the tendrils stretched into the compartment.

"The men are trying," *Gladiator*'s exec answered very quickly, with something more urgent to tell him: "*Domni*, there is an autodestruct rigged and counting down. Ground point is *Wolfhound*."

"Isolate *Wolfhound* from the station," Numa ordered.

"Unable to comply, *Domni*. These—*tendrils*—are all through the station. And now they are in *Gladiator* and they are preventing our interior partitions from sealing."

A Roman ship was built like a chambered nautilus. The tendrils caused this nautilus to leak through every chamber.

On a Roman ship, the partitions were fire walls.

The Triumphalis made an impatient sound. "What is their intent?"

"We have no message from *Wolfhound*, *Domni*. The countdown is at two minutes." The exec tried to sound pragmatic. Was not succeeding. "Earth minutes. They're shorter."

Even Numa Pompeii was a little disconcerted, confused. A bluff was no good without a warning.

The count was down to one minute forty seconds. No ultimatums were coming.

"I don't believe this," Numa snarled to himself, and aloud: "Recall our boarders. Quickly. Hail *Wolfhound*."

In a moment the communications specialist presented the com: "*Wolfhound*, *Domni*."

Before he opened the com to speak, Numa Pompeii paused to check: "Who is captain of *Wolfhound*?"

"Callista Carmel."

"I mean who is captain *now*."

"The captain of record is still Carmel."

Numa muttered, impatient. He had seconds here. "*Wolfhound*, this is Numa Pompeii of the Imperial warship *Gladiator*. What is your intention?"

"To blow your ass to kingdom come if you don't release this station."

Numa Pompeii took a physical step away from the com as if it had reached up and bit him.

The voice sounded again on the com, "You like fire, Numa? You can give it, let's see how you can take it."

General Pompeii immediately recovered himself. Spoke into the com, "Callista, there is no need for this."

An unfamiliar female face appeared on the video. Unfamiliar lips moved to the sound of Calli Carmel's voice: "Back it off, Triumphalis, or you're coming with me."

It was without a doubt Callista. With a new face. Still he knew her.

There was no time for grappling with the disconnect between the unfamiliar face and the familiar voice and the all too familiar attitude. Numa said, "This is pure hysteria."

"*Hysteria*?" Calli echoed, surprised at the distinctly female word. "That's Greek for 'womb,' isn't it? Do you mean you can't stand losing to *any* woman? Here I thought it was just me."

"I am not losing!" Numa thundered.

"What do you call dying with all hands on board? Oh, that's right, *I'm* about to call that winning. You will have to call it losing, because Rome is not taking this station."

Irritated, impatient, with that damn countdown grating on him, Numa scolded, "Callista, this is not how battles are fought."

"It's my ship, my station, my battle. We're doing it my way. This is my pyre, and those snares make sure you're in it. The ties that bind. If you're still here in sixty seconds, you die."

"So do you," he reminded her. She had to know. But she wasn't getting it.

"I'm small coinage," said Calli. "You always tell me so. But I am taking out the great Numa Pompeii and the *Gladiator*. My tombstone will look good with a silver star on it. And I spent enough time on Palatine that that actually matters to me. *I can't lose.*"

"Your crew and the station personnel would rather live."

"But I pretty much want you dead, and I would really love for you to know what it feels like to burn alive, so I can't decide what I hope you do here. I'm all in. Call or fold."

Weary, exasperated, Numa jerked his head to signal the specialist to cut the com link.

Numa turned to his exec: "Is everyone on board?"

"At once, *Domni*. But you do not think she is bluffing?"

"I *know* she is not! Seal the ship the instant everyone is on board. Break those damned snares, tendrils, whatever they are!"

Twenty-two. Twenty-one. Twenty.

"She would take out her own ship and an entire American station?"

"Move! Move!"

Thirteen. Twelve.

The last Romans clattered back aboard. Hatches shut. Tendrils severed.

But the tendrils immediately eeled through the seals to re-form themselves, leaving a small breach in the Roman hull.

"The seals are imperfect!"

Nine. Eight.

"Get some space between us!"

Gladiator separated. The tendrils stretched, snapped. The ship's seals closed. The force field solidified.

Five. Four.

Gladiator wore away faster than light.

"Abort! Abort!" Calli ordered. "Shut down destruct sequence!"

Three. Two.

"Destruct sequence terminated, aye."

Calli took no moment to relax, already barking, "Load Star Sparrow! Target *Gladiator!* Hit him!"

"Star Sparrow loaded, aye. Acquiring firing solution."

"Fire when ready!"

"Star Sparrow away."

Gladiator launched a missile rearward to meet the Star Sparrow and detonate its warhead before it could catch up.

Numa Pompeii ceded Sirius Base to the Americans.

Captain Calli Carmel boarded Base Sirius. She was a tall woman, thinner than she had been, and she had always been slender. Her new scalp produced an uneven thatch of something that passed for hair. The new hair was thinner and several shades lighter than her former luxurious chestnut locks. She cut her new hair very short because it would not grow right and she did not have time to screw with it.

She asked after the wounded and after any damage to the station.

Snapped ends of *Wolfhound*'s snares hung out the large breach which the Romans had cut in the station's bulkhead. The force field had resealed upon *Gladiator*'s separation and kept everything inside intact. The stationmaster had already summoned a patch crew.

"You sounded dead serious back there, Captain Carmel," the stationmaster said, shaky with relief.

Calli's dead silence said how dead and how serious she had been.

"How did you know he would back off, Captain?"

"He left," said Calli.

"I mean, how did you know he *would* leave?"

"That's when I knew."

The stationmaster grew angry. "You would have—?"

Calli cut him off. "You can't go into a game of Russian roulette without accepting that one of those chambers *does* have a round in it."

Outraged, the stationmaster asked, "You play?"

"Only when the stakes are worth dying for," said Calli.

Base Sirius sent a request to the Department of Defense: Next time we signal for help, don't send *Wolfhound*.

There was not going to be a next time. The showdown at Base Sirius had proved the vulnerability of these lone outposts.

The Department of Defense ordered the immediate evacuation, dismantlement, and booby-trapping of all space stations outside of a fortress. Solo orbital stations were all hostages waiting to be taken.

"I will be accepting requests for transfer in my cabin," said Captain Carmel, preparing to leave the command deck of her ship, *Wolfhound*, which had just disconnected from Base Sirius.

A round of snorts circled the command deck, and a chorus of raspberries sounded over the intracom from engineering—what her crew thought of her offer to take their transfers.

There was a stark sincerity to the juvenile noises. They left no doubt that Calli's men were still her men, every man jack and jane of them.

A proto-smile jerked at her lips. "That's so sweet," said Calli, struggling to keep her eyes from puddling up.

"The name of this boat ain't *Lapdog*, Captain," said Lieutenant Amina Patel.

According to Amina, anyone who did not know what the captain was about after the battle at the Citadel musta gotten a legal separation from his brain. *Wolfhound* already had a berserker reputation, and her captain was called Crash Carmel for some reason or other.

Her com tech gloated, "Did you see the look on Pompeii's face when he saw you, Captain?"

It hadn't occurred to Calli that Numa might not have known what she looked like after his attack on her shuttle. She had quickly gotten used to being behind this face.

"Yeah," said Calli softly.

She gave the watch over to her lieutenant and left the command platform because she thought she was about to throw up.

Calli returned to her cabin. Looked in the mirror.

Is that what it took? she wondered. Get your face flamed off to get respect? Or did Numa Pompeii think she became "hysterical" because he ruined her looks? Is that what it came down to?

She turned the mirror over. Did not care what Numa Pompous Ass thought of her. Just glad he had believed her.

She had cared very much which choice Numa made. Even though she had wanted him dead, he made the choice she really wanted.

There was a buzzing in her hands, as if her pulse had sped up a hundred times. She swallowed down nausea. She had come very close to killing a lot of people today, half of them friendly.

Watched her hands shake.

She lay down, closed her eyes. Weathering the aftershocks. She had won.

She could kill Numa later.

12

ROMAN ATTACK CRAFT HAD returned to the American skies, nagging as wasps.

Romulus' three surviving new gunships had not been sighted again in the Solar system. They had not just dissolved, so they must be somewhere the U.S. truly did not want them.

Monitor patrolled the Solar system, actively hunting for them.

Plagues of unmanned fighter craft in Earth's atmosphere harried U.S. military installations. The Roman craft could not penetrate the military base's force fields, but they interfered with deliveries of supplies, and with personnel coming and going.

Defenders destroyed them, but others arrived from hidden carriers to take their places without delay.

John Farragut arrived at Fort Carolina under a swarm of them. It had required his entire Marine Wing to get him inside the force field dome.

He had come to hear the admiralty discussing the status of the conflict.

This war had been nothing but unconventional. Romans always knew how to reinvent war. Hiding one's true objective was not new, but Romulus was inscrutable—though a lot of people expressed a desire to scrut him.

Rome had not been able to stop U.S. imports and exports. The United States was a member of the League of Earth Nations. Anything could enter or exit the United States as long as a ship of a League of Earth Nation member carried it.

There were constant alarms from U.S. colonies across Near Space. None amounted to more than a cry of wolf, probably started by the wolf. Rome was trying to make the Americans scatter their resources.

As for Romulus' objective in declaring this war, he was keeping that to himself. Unless he was hiding in plain sight.

"Could Caesar seriously—seriously—mean to annex the United States to the Roman Empire?" the Secretary of Defense put it to the admiralty.

"He would be mad," said one.

"So was Hitler," said Admiral Mishindi. "Did not make him less dangerous."

The Secretary recognized Captain Farragut who wanted to speak. Farragut stood up, said, "Augustus told me America was a Roman colony."

"Not seriously," said the Secretary.

"Augustus," said Farragut, "was serious."

"Is the patterner still alive, Captain Farragut?"

"He was way too alive last I saw him, sir."

"But now?"

Farragut shook his head. "I don't know." A Striker had a higher threshold velocity than *Gladiator*. "He should have arrived in Near Space before Numa Pompeii if he were coming." *So I guess it's starting to look like not.*

Captain Farragut walked under a sky of Carolina blue streaked with contrails. Sunlight shimmered slightly through the distortion field.

He sighted a tall willow walking with an easy stride under the Carolina dome, a veteran certainty in her gait. Her strong slender figure made even dressdown khakis look good. Her face tended toward the elfin. Her skin was baby smooth, but she couldn't be that young, not with a walk like that. Her short hair was a sassy mess of nothing but cowlicks.

Farragut moved in to stride beside her. "I feel like I should know you." He reached across himself to offer his hand. "John Farragut."

Her long-fingered, baby-smooth hand slid into his grasp. "Hi John. I'm Calli Carmel."

His blue eyes grew huge. He pulled her into him with a great bear hug, held onto her. "Oh, for Jesus!" Rocked her. "Oh, for Jesus."

"I guess I look awful," said Calli over his broad shoulder.

"No," he choked.

She caught the chagrin in his voice. "Right." She pulled back to look at him. "John, you look like you've been hit in the face with a wet cat."

"Well, I might. It's like I just got caught flirting with my sister!"

She had been in his chain of command so long he could not think of her as anything but one of his sisters.

She blinked in delighted surprise. Spoke, tickled, "You were flirting with me?"

His face turned an honest pink. He fished about for a subject to change to. "How do you like the Yankees' chances in the Series this year?"

"Don't you try to take it back, John Farragut. I don't look in mirrors much."

"It's not bad at all, Cal. It's cute. It's just really, *really* different."

The face was heart shaped, less symmetrical than it used to be when she had been Helen of Troy. The jawline was altogether different. The nose shorter, pert. Eyes light brown. An attractive face with a powerful life force behind it.

"It's a field job," said Calli. "Uncle Sam special. They were talking about six weeks to get me into a specialized clinic and re-create what I used to look like, and lots of over the budget money that I am not spending on a *face*. I told 'em gimme the off-the-shelf jaw, stick in whatever eyeballs you got on hand, slap a nose on me and get me back in service. There's a war on."

John Farragut held her hands in his. They were her same full-sized hands but with no lines whatsoever, and her nails were thin — the pliant nails of a little girl. Calli said, "Aren't they ridiculous?"

"It's good to see you with skin on, Cal." He kissed her ridiculous fingertips. Took her face, kissed both her baby soft cheeks, her brow, her mouth. Pulled back, ran his hand over the fuzzy top of her head. "What's with the hair?"

"I don't know, John. I think it's on strike. I never realized how *heavy* all that was. I may never grow it back."

"I heard your buddy Numa finally made it back to Near Space."

"You heard that," said Calli wryly.

"Just a little almighty furball at Base Sirius."

"No furball," said Calli. "I told him to leave and he left."

Farragut had heard the details. "Dumb, Cal. Don't do that again."

"I probably won't have to. Apparently I've established myself as a real DNFW."

Do Not Foxtrot With.

"I don't guess nobody's fixin' to be asking you to dance this war," said Farragut.

"I hope not," said Calli. "Between you, me, and the brick wall, I don't have another one of those stunts in me. I just hope I've built up enough psycho capital to carry me through to the end."

"I'm sorry about Gaius Americanus," Farragut told her. He had heard the news of her mentor's passing.

Calli's new face fell, more reflective than mournful. Her eyes were down, her brow pinched. She did not seem sad. "I was sorry to hear that too." Spoken too carefully.

He picked up her intonation. "What do you know, Cal?"

"I don't—" she started, paused very long. Lifted her head. "—*know*."

He listened carefully to what she was not telling him. They had both seen too many dead people walking around on their hind legs these days to trust an obit. Unless you saw the body, you did not really *know*. And even then you checked it for DNA.

Calli said, "I want Numa dead. And I don't even care who does it. Romulus can plant him on a pike and that would be good for me."

"The guy who actually flamed you and Gaius was Prae-fect Rubius Siculus."

Calli nodded. She had been told. "I uffed him over pretty good," she said with some regret.

"You saved his life."

She remembered that moment with stinging clarity. "I didn't do him a favor."

She had saved Rubius Siculus from a disaster of her own making, and she had killed Romans under his command in the process.

Rubius Siculus hated her. Had a right to. He had prob-ably died happy thinking he had killed her. And that was okay with Calli. She had never hated him. He had just been there.

But it could not have been Rubius Siculus' private ven-detta that brought him to Fort Eisenhower, a voyage of months, to lurk there in the darkness outside the fortress, alone, for time without measure, waiting for someone at long last to come out. Rubius Siculus had to be under orders.

"We never did catch the ship that executed the diver-sion," Farragut told her, apologetic.

"Oh, I know who that was," Calli said. "Rubius Siculus was always under Numa Pompeii's command. This is Numa Pompeii's work."

Farragut signed time out. "If it was Numa, why didn't he just let Gaius come aboard *Gladiator* and slit his throat?"

"He wanted to take me out too," said Calli.

"You weren't the target, Cal."

She seemed insulted. "My being there was a *coinci-dence*?"

"It would be an odd universe without coincidences. Yes. You were collateral and you know it."

That stopped her.

She did know it.

Organizing a hit on Calli did not fit Numa Pompeii's practiced disdain. Numa was her nemesis, but she had never been hated by him. She was too far beneath him ever to be a rival, or worthy of a plot of any sort.

Numa did not give her any more thought than to toss an insult her way if she crossed his path.

"He could have killed you way back at Planet Zero," said Farragut.

"But it was Numa who called Gaius out of the fort." Calli gave her last best argument.

"Gaius could have said no to Numa. But sooner or later Gaius was coming out. And however he came out, whenever he came out, someone would still be camped out and waiting for him. It just happened to be Numa who gave the opening. Whoever ordered the hit had the money to buy off a station Intelligence officer who could tell him exactly when and how Gaius was leaving the fort. He had military resources to deploy at least two ships in the Deep End to make sure the deed got done."

"Numa has power and money," said Calli, but she did not sound convinced anymore. Numa had been with her at Planet Zero.

"Seems to me the person who had motive and means to set up the assassination of Gaius Americanus would be the same person who had motive and means to order the siege of Fort Eisenhower," said Farragut, and almost as an afterthought, "and the motive and means to set up the assassination of Caesar Magnus."

The dialogs. V.

JF: We hold these truths to be self-evident. That
        all men are created equal.
A: While we of the Empire recognize your self-
        evident truth to be buzzard vomit.

13

THE ROMAN SENATE HAD convened in the Curia. Neither
consul was present, not an odd thing in wartime. *Those*
men had real work to do, thought Romulus.

The poet had called Romans *masters of the world, the
People who wear the toga,* so the toga would be with Rome
forever though it could be a bitch to wear. All Senators
wore them, white with deep crimson bands of strictly pre-
scribed width. The crimson boots came in and out of fashion. Currently out. The poet had said nothing about Romans
being the People who wear the crimson boots.

It seemed some opposition Senators had brought a guest
to the Curia today. And Romulus had to wonder what those
ferrets were up to. No coincidence that "Senate" and "senile"
stem from the same word.

At last a messenger arrived at the palace. He bowed very
low before the throne. Caesar's attendance was requested
in the Curia.

"Yes, I was wondering when they were going to let me in
on their plot," Romulus murmured.

Romulus deigned to appear. He draped a toga of solid
blood red over his short black tunic and trousers.

The colors of his own *gens,* Julius, were black and gold,
but Romulus considered black and red the most dramatic

combination, and wondered how the damned Flavians had secured those colors.

The stone building of the Curia sat in counter position to the palace on the Capitoline. The Curia had been constructed circular this time, like a theater—rather fitting given the shows put on here.

When Caesar arrived, a young black man was on the Senate floor with Senator Trogus.

Trogus was a weasel—lean, aesthetic, pinched-faced. A suspicious, heel-biting, garbage-picking rodent. Trogus questioned everything put before him. For a man in a position of public trust Trogus showed a singular lack of trust in anyone else, even his emperor.

Trogus had proved himself in battle all right, but he had not supported Caesar's declaration of war. He opposed it actually, remarkably lacking in vision of *Empire*.

Trogus had been one of a handful of Senators who had opposed confirming Romulus in his father's position. That was to be expected. The five percent rule said that five percent of any population will oppose any given proposal just for the hell of it.

Romulus made a show of tolerating Trogus. It made Romulus look good to be so forbearing of the Senator's open animosity.

The young man whom Trogus and his troglodytes had trotted in for this show looked to be kin to the late Gaius Americanus. His features and his posture were the same, just younger. This could be nothing but kin to Gaius. Romulus had thought all of Gaius' family was hiding in the American Fort Eisenhower in the Deep End.

The visitor had been thoroughly screened by security. Trogus gave the young man's name as Dante Porter, born on Earth in the United States. Security found a birth record of such a Dante Porter, but it was far older than this man appeared. This looked like a younger version of Gaius Americanus. But anyone could appear like anyone these days, so a DNA test had been done.

Romulus entered the chamber quietly, unannounced. He stood next to Senator Ventor who hated to sit for so long, and was standing against the back wall. Romulus muttered aside to Ventor, "Gaius' bastard?"

"Clone, I should think," Ventor murmured back. "His DNA is nearly a match to Gaius. Has only the variations you would expect in a clone."

Romulus did not think that Gaius had ever been cloned. "Just what the Empire needs," Romulus muttered. "Another Gaius."

The chamber had gone silent.

Romulus had been noticed.

The Praetor paused the proceedings to welcome Caesar to the Curia.

Caesar Romulus strode down the steps to take command of the Senate floor. He turned round at the center of the open space and looked round to see who was attending this circus.

Quirinius, of course. And Umbrius and Opsius, men of inaction, existing only to lie down in Caesar's way.

Romulus came back round to the young man, Dante Porter of planet Earth.

No toga. This Dante Porter was not a Senator. He wore trousers and a black single-breasted jacket of midthigh length. A white shirt with stand-up collar made him look vaguely like an old-fashioned priest. His hair was very short and lay close-crimped against his dark head.

Romulus walked half round him, sizing him up. The young man let himself be studied. Did not become unsettled.

Caesar spoke at last, aloud, for everyone to hear: "Am I to understand you are Gaius' bastard?"

"No, sir," said Dante Porter. The voice was not the voice of a young man. It was elderly and shockingly familiar. "I am that bastard, Gaius."

Romulus immediately looked to Senator Trogus. As expected, Trogus was enjoying his triumph. Trogus collected the desired shock and murmurs with a superior smile. The Senate chamber stirred with the rustling of togas, the rush of whispers.

Romulus would not be thrown. He had been ready for some attempt to unbalance him.

When the chamber hushed, Romulus spoke mildly to the Gaius-thing, "I have been told you are a clone."

"The outer centimeter is all cloned material," Gaius explained, pinching his own baby soft cheek. "But my beauty is only skin deep. I earned those sags and wrinkles and spots. I lost them in the fire. And I want them back. Alas, they are ash, and here I am with new skin." And then, as if reading Caesar's mind, "Yes, Romulus, like a snake."

The floor seemed to be moving. Romulus fought for balance.

The voices swept all around him in the chamber like wind rushing.

Gaius . . . Gaius . . . Gaius.

Romulus declared loud enough to silence all the whispers. "Gaius is dead. This is an American creation."

The security guard who had performed the original verification moved down to the floor, brandishing a DNA probe. "With permission," he solicited Senate's indulgence. And to Gaius, "May I, *Domni*?"

Far from objecting, Gaius opened his arms. "I insist." He offered all of himself. Let the guard pick a place. Any place.

It was a nanoprobe this time. Too small to see or feel. The nanoprobe could reach deep. The guard extracted random cells from several places within the young-looking man.

The deep cells were not the same as the first sampling. This time they were perfect matches in both DNA and age to Gaius Bruccius Eleutherius Americanus.

Senators fired questions at Gaius—questions to which only Gaius would know the answers. The man on the Senate floor remembered Gaius' private conversations. He correctly failed to remember any imaginary incidents laid out to trap him.

When the Senators were satisfied, Caesar Romulus had a question for Gaius: "What was the name of your street gang?"

Romulus dredged up Gaius' squalid past in front of the Senate. Not that any one of them did not know, but Romulus thought they needed reminding.

Dante Porter, as he was called at his birth, had risen up through slime. "East Street Pirates," Gaius answered frankly, pushing up his sleeve to bare his forearm. He remembered only then with apparent chagrin that his gang leader tattoo had been burned off too. Under his sleeve now was only unmarked young skin.

"Ah. The albatross has fallen off," he said in slight surprise. "My bones were tattooed here." His gangland tattoo, the mark of an old sin, had been a garish mark on his forearm. Something he lived with and could not remove for himself, like the ancient mariner's albatross.

Fate had intervened to take the stain away.

"I can start wearing short sleeves," he said, a little bit astonished, as if he had been absolved.

At the end of the grilling, no one doubted that this young-looking man was the elder statesman, Senator Gaius Bruccius Eleutherius Americanus.

The Praetor asked formally, "What has Senator Gaius to say to the Senate?"

"I am here to tell you that the testament which was read here before this Senate, the document purported to be the last testament of Caesar Magnus, suffered an elision. A line was deleted from Magnus' true will."

All eyes turned to Caesar. Waited for Caesar to speak. Waited long. The Praetor finally had to ask, "Have you any answer to that, Caesar?"

"No, of course I have not!" said Romulus. "I have *questions*. *Does* the testament have an elision? How could it? I read the testament of Caesar Magnus to this Senate. I broke the seal right here in this chamber."

Senator Trogus spoke out of turn, "No one tested the security of that seal before Caesar allegedly broke it for the first time."

"*I* did," said Caesar. "I tested it. I wanted to be sure I had my father's will. Why did *you* not test it? I shall tell you why. So you could come back later and throw doubt on its authenticity, just in case my father's final word contained something you did not like!"

Gaius said, "Romulus, I thought I left that twisted brand of leadership behind on East Street."

"All your insinuations are built on vapor," said Romulus. "Because the author of the testament, *my father*, Caesar Magnus, is dead."

"There is also the word of the patterner who sealed the testament," said Gaius.

"We don't have Augustus' word. Augustus is dead."

"You have *my* word, a witness," said Gaius. "Who was almost dead. Am I vapor?"

"Tell us again, who put you back together, Gaius?"

"The Americans," Gaius admitted without hesitation.

"And how did you get back from your hiding in the Deep, Gaius?"

"An American military transport through the U.S. Shotgun," said Gaius frankly.

"You took aid from the enemy. In wartime. I accuse you of treason, and of colluding with the enemy in time of war." He signaled to the guards. "Take this man to a cell."

Gaius answered back, "Sir, I accuse you of treason and attempted assassination."

Romulus reeled back as if shot in the chest, "You dare accuse me of my father's murder!"

"No," said Gaius. "The assassination *attempt* was on *me*. The assassination of your father was rather a success."

Guards moved in to flank Gaius, hesitant yet to touch him.

Gaius spoke to the assembled Senators in the rising rows. "Examine the testament. You will find the gap."

"A gap," said Romulus, derisive. "Lack of evidence is no evidence. Have *Augustus* come in and testify."

A shadow eclipsed the sunlight that had streamed through the round window at the top of the dome.

Something was moving up there, very close.

Nothing was allowed to fly over the Capitoline.

There followed the deep heavy clunk of something substantial making contact with the stone roof.

"What *is* that?"

Sunlight glinted around sharp-edged metal landing gear supporting a small spacecraft with lines of a wasp, in red and black.

It was a patterner's Striker.

14

"**A**UGUSTUS!"

The entire Senate stared up to the top of the dome.

"What is he doing?"

"Testifying?" Gaius suggested.

The round window at the center of the dome cracked. A metal leg of the Striker's landing gear jutted through the circular opening with a rain of pelleted glass. Senators fanned out toward the surrounding wall. There was nowhere to run with a Striker out there. There was a bunker deep beneath the Curia, but no one wanted to go underground.

A brass tube struck down from the dome like a bullet in the center of the floor, taking a chip out of the red marble. Bits of tempered glass clattered down around it.

The Senators shied from the canister on the floor as if it were a grenade.

Once the glass stopped raining, they saw the canister was the shape and style of a formal container for a parchment roll, delivered more harshly than usual.

The shadow of the Striker lifted away from the broken window.

Romulus bellowed for the home defense.

Already the hiss of outbound missiles could be heard through the opening in the dome.

A cadre of guards trooped into the Curia to surround Caesar. They brought a personal force field for him.

"A little late," Caesar said, but strapped on the mechanism and activated it. He motioned the guards away from him. They took up stations at the exits.

Senator Ventor was standing at the wall with one finger to his ear in order to listen to a phone in his other ear. He called across the Curia: "Caesar, I am getting word from Imperial Intelligence. That is not Augustus' Striker."

"I knew it!" said Romulus. "This is a hoax."

Ventor demurred, "One moment, Caesar." He listened some more, then spoke. "They are telling me that could very well be Augustus *inside* the Striker. But the Striker is not the one built for Augustus."

"What? He *borrowed* one?" Caesar said, losing patience.

"The chirp from the vessel identifies it as a Striker that disappeared sixty years ago. It belonged to the patterner Secundus. It was blue and white. These new colors make Intelligence think that Augustus could be at the controls."

The Striker up there was red and black. Flavian colors. Augustus was Flavian.

"And it's certainly not Secundus."

Romulus' gaze fell on Numa Pompeii seated in the front row. Numa had held his position rather than scurrying to the wall with most of the others. He was now conferring with someone on his com, appearing discontented.

Caesar strolled across the floor, leaned on the railing that separated them. Caesar asked faintly, casually, looking up through the broken skylight. "Pompeii, what was that?"

Numa Pompeii clicked off his com. "They're telling me it is Augustus."

"Not dead, is he," Romulus observed.

Numa, unapologetic, said, "My information on that *did* come from the Americans."

Romulus turned from the rail.

"Senator Gaius, make Augustus come in."

"I do not control him," said Gaius. "I never have. I never supported patterner technology. Augustus already knows the truth of it, and he has made the judgment. He only needs to execute the sentence."

Caesar's eyes widened. He pointed, the full length of his arm extended toward Gaius, imperious. "Now *that* is a threat."

Caesar's guards did not hesitate to lay hands on Gaius this time and take him to a secure cell under the nearby Coliseum.

There were no prisons for punishing criminals in Rome. Imprisonment was not a sentence in the Empire. Cells were only for holding the accused for investigation and trial. And for holding slaves likely to flee.

Of the canister lying on the Senate floor in a scatter of glass bits, Caesar commanded: "Have a bomb squad destroy that!"

"No!" Senator Quirinius shouted, moving between the guards and the canister. "In the name of the Senate and the People of Rome, no! That was delivered to the Senate! The Senate must be allowed to view the message inside!"

Many other Senators shouted, murmured, grunted agreement. Even some of Caesar's followers added their voices, curious to see what the patterner sent them.

The guards hesitated, torn between Caesar and the Senate.

Caesar clearly feared what was inside the canister, which made even more Senators want to see it.

Romulus abruptly reversed himself. He waved off the guard. Told Senator Quirinius, "Go ahead. Take it. See what the traitor fed you through your roof before he ran away."

Quirinius moved around Romulus to get at the canister.

Romulus spoke as Quirinius stooped to pick it up. "Clean it first. I would not want you to come down with something lethal and incurable."

Imperial Intelligence opened the message canister before a room full of witnesses, and withdrew from it a document that turned out to be a copy of Magnus' testament, date-sealed with a chemical tag. The seal's molecules came from a specific numbered batch created for just this purpose. The molecular decay gave the document an indisputable time stamp.

"It is the testament of Caesar Magnus," said the Intelligence magister. "The authentication copy."

"Authentication copy?" said Caesar. "There is such a thing?"

"Yes, Caesar."

"How would Augustus just happen to have it?" Caesar asked with heavy scorn.

The magister dropped his voice. "As the witness who sealed the original document, he is supposed to have it, Caesar."

The document proved identical to the testament Romulus had unsealed before the Senate. Except this one had one more provision.

This one named Gaius Bruccius Eleutherius Americanus as heir to Caesar's position.

Caesar's choice of his own successor was not binding. But Caesar's choice was always due heavy consideration.

Caesar Magnus' nomination of Gaius had received none.

Gaius, brought before the assembled Senators in old-fashioned chains, was allowed to speak. "Romulus deleted the line," said Gaius. "That is the reason Romulus waited until he believed Augustus was dead before he unsealed Magnus' testament. Then I, as the only other witness, became target of an assassination attempt ordered by Romulus—Caesar Pretender."

Gaius was returned to his cell while the Senate ordered data experts to make a close analysis of the testament Romulus had first presented to them.

Upon analysis, the experts concluded: Yes, there was evidence of an elision.

Romulus was then called to speak.

"Gentlemen," said Romulus. "I am irritated. I am insulted. Know that this pains me deeply. I don't deserve this. It is demeaning for me to have to explain this. Very well. Let us play this charade to the end. Let us assume, to argue on behalf of the devil, that someone may have deleted a line from my father's testament. May not that someone have been *Augustus*, who is more than capable of perjury and data manipulation? The same Augustus who orchestrated my father's murder? May not that someone have been *my father?* Could my father not have had second thoughts on naming an heir? And Gaius? My father named *Gaius?*

"We have a story—from Gaius and the Americans—that someone made an attempt on the life of Gaius Bruccius Eleutherius Americanus. We have no proof that this attack ever occurred.

"Oh, yes, I know we have Gaius' new skin as evidence of *something*. Is it not interesting that this purported attempt on Gaius' life left Gaius in much better condition than he was in when he ran away? Better than when he ran away from Rome directly after *my father was murdered!*

"Yet you look at me with suspicion. Was *I* ever a gang leader? *If* my father's testament was altered, why are you assuming it was done by me? *I* wasn't named Caesar's heir. If I changed the testament, *why did I not put my own name down as heir!*"

"Because it would be too obvious," said Senator Trogus. "Because this way you can use the absence of your name as a sign of your innocence."

"That is pathetic," said Romulus. "That is so—never mind. The Senate confirmed me as Caesar based on my competence. But since you think you need to, go ahead. Retake your confirmation vote. I will abide by the decision of the Senate and the People of Rome. Do it. On *belief* that a rogue cyborg and a runaway *American* Senator—beneficiary of this fraud—have uncovered *my* father's true—nonbinding—testament. Take your vote."

There had been no Roman strikes on American soil for days, while rumors of political turmoil on Palatine made the rounds. With both *Merrimack* and *Wolfhound* orbiting Earth, Captain Farragut seized on the relative quiet to invite Captain Carmel to his Mess for dinner.

"Permission to come aboard," Captain Carmel requested in *Merrimack's* shuttle dock.

"Come on in, Cal," Farragut welcomed her in with a huge wave of his arm.

At Farragut's side, his normally sedate XO, Commander Gypsy Dent, saw Calli and cried, "Your *hair!*"

Gypsy and Calli embraced, Gypsy crying, "Your *hair!*"

Calli laughed, "What about my *face?*"

"The face is fine," said Gypsy. "It's a face. But, oh, honey, we need to do something about this." Gypsy fluffed up a brown tuft on Calli's head.

"Cal, don't take help from Gypsy," said Farragut.

Gypsy held up a warning forefinger. Didn't say it, but the words were in her flashing eyes, *Speak not of the hair*.

Gypsy's own elaborate and carnivorous-looking hair was still banished to her cabin.

The three officers proceeded to the Captain's Mess. They were on appetizers when Lieutenant Hamilton appeared in the hatchway. She motioned down their looks of alarm and told them all to stay seated. "Nothing wrong with the boat, Captain," she anticipated Farragut's first question. "I just wanted to tell you this in person as soon as we heard it. Augustus is back."

Farragut knocked over his champagne glass. Gypsy pushed away from the table to avoid the spill over the edge.

A small maintenance bot unobtrusively saw to the cleanup as Farragut demanded, "Where!" His heart leaped in eighteen different directions.

"On Palatine. Over Roma Nova."

"Romulus is dead then," Farragut concluded.

"No. Augustus dropped Magnus' complete testament on the Senate floor."

"And the Senate turned on Romulus like a pack of wolves," Farragut wrote the end of that scene.

Lieutenant Glenn Hamilton hesitated on distasteful reality. "The Roman Senate reconfirmed Romulus as Caesar."

Farragut could not stay in his seat. "They have proof that he's a liar, probably a patricide, and—!"

"They don't care," said Hamster.

"Romans don't back down, John," Calli said. "It's a proven fact that even Americans tend not to back down once they've taken a public stand, even in the face of compelling argument or new facts. Changing your mind makes you look indecisive. It's a sign of weakness."

"I thought—" Farragut strode to one end of the table. "I knew—I mean I *knew*—" To the other end of the table. "Once the truth came out, the Senate would toss their original vote. What the Senate did was—" Farragut sat back down, stunned. "I don't believe it."

"Welcome to the real world, sir," said Gypsy, with a hand on his broad shoulder. She sounded rather sad. She liked John Farragut's version of the world. "I hear you were an Eagle Scout."

"I *am* an Eagle Scout," said Farragut. You never stopped being an Eagle.

"Strength and Honor are worshiped in adjoining temples," said Calli. "Rome's been hitting the Strength pretty hard, a little light on the Honor."

"It gets worse," said Hamster. "On behalf of these United States, President Marissa Johnson recognized Romulus as head of state of the Empire of Rome."

"What?" Farragut and Gypsy spoke as one.

Only Calli was not surprised. "I have to guess Johnson doesn't want to look like she's undermining a foreign country's legitimate government."

"The CIA has been in that business for centuries," said Farragut. "What's different now?"

"Opposition to Romulus only reinforces popular support for him. Johnson's recognizing Romulus defangs him. He can't keep calling us lying, scheming tyrants if we're saying hail Caesar."

"Hope I didn't ruin dinner," said Hamster, taking a backward step, preparing to return to the command deck.

"No. Good call, Hamster," said Farragut. "That was definitely a need-to-know." He detained her with one more question, "Where is Augustus?"

"On the loose," said Hamster. "With a price on his head."

Chef Zack had peered into the Mess. He sent in the salad of Centaurian greens, broiled ostrich, and tussah fruit with a stronger bottle of wine.

Farragut speared one of the lavender-colored fruits. "So Romulus got Marissa to salute. The man can get anyone to do *anything*. I'm still wondering how Romulus got Magnus' own friend to kill Magnus."

"Money is the usual tool," said Gypsy.

Assassinating a Caesar was clearly a suicide mission, so any money would be paid to a survivor. Though Imperial Intelligence would follow that money trail to the beneficiary, who would not remain a survivor for long.

And the assassin—his name was Urbicus—was an old friend of Magnus. He belonged to *gens* Julius same as Magnus and Romulus.

"This was not a work for hire," said Calli.

Farragut tried another angle. "If someone were leaning on Urbicus, why wouldn't Urbicus have just reported the threat to Imperial Intelligence? Does that mean it was Imperial Intelligence who was doing the leaning?"

"No. It means it had to do with sex," said Gypsy.

"Of course it had to do with sex," said Calli.

Farragut could not argue. What else could make a man so thoroughly misplace his brain?

There was someone out there whom Urbicus had no business loving.

After both Caesar and the assassin were dead, Imperial Investigators recovering the assassin's purged data files had found too too many pictures of a girl. A sloe-eyed bambi with long coltish legs. She was flat-chested and slender as a reed. But she was clothed in all the pictures.

It was obsession at a distance. Julius Urbicus had never actually crossed the last line with her. The girl did not even know him. Urbicus had a collection of images of her in the gymnasium, in the pool, at picnics, laying flowers in a temple, dancing in a school play, riding in a transport, sleeping in the sun.

"Think of Hadrian and Antinous," said Calli.

Gypsy blinked away that image. "I'd rather not."

"I have a sister her age," said Farragut.

Calli said, "Would you rather be known as Caesar's assassin or a pedophile?"

"Caesar's assassin," Farragut and Gypsy spoke as one.

Then Farragut alone, "But Urbicus never touched that girl. He was just creepy, not criminal. How could Romulus get him to kill his friend Caesar Magnus and die over a secret like that?"

"Someone promised to cut up Pretty Girl if he didn't kill Caesar," Gypsy guessed. "That's why Urbicus couldn't take it to Imperial Intelligence. The double I's would have killed her themselves to remove the lever."

"Well, whoever was making the actual threats, it wasn't Romulus," said Calli. "Not directly. Romulus had no contact with Urbicus in the months before the assassination. Romulus' enemies checked that."

"Hell, I wouldn't want contact with him either," said Farragut.

"The *capita* always distances himself from the crime," said Gypsy. "He gets someone else to tell someone else to walk and talk for him."

"So Romulus would have had someone he trusted threaten Urbicus," said Farragut, then echoed himself, "Someone Romulus trusted. That narrows it way down. Cal?"

A very odd look had fallen across Calli's new face.

She said, "That narrows it down to one."

"Rom?"

That was her innocent, wheedling voice. She wanted something.

Romulus responded, "Hm?"

She came into the study barefoot, her dress a jewel-colored assembly of strategically tied scarves. Maybe there had been seven at one time, but now there were five.

"Who programmed that raunchy redhead in the Caligula room?" She flounced down to sit at his feet in a billow of silk where he sat at his reading desk.

"I don't know," said Romulus, eyes on his documents. "I have not seen her recently."

"I deleted her."

"That explains why I haven't seen her."

"She was rude to me."

Romulus made a small noise like a partial laugh. "She's just a bunch of code."

"Not any more."

Romulus' brows lifted. "I suppose you showed her."

"Well that is the point—I haven't." She stood up, came round to the front of his desk, braced her palms on the edge of it and leaned over so he had to look at her. "Whoever programmed her wants a lesson in respect."

"I shall talk to the programmers." He sat back, stretched out his legs. Looked up at his sister. "I don't want to rein them in too hard. There really have been some fun surprises in that room."

Claudia made a small moue. She had to allow that.

She circled behind him, looped her arms round his neck, lay her cheek on his hair. "You are distracted."

"I am." He put his hand over her hands on his chest.

"Is it the re-vote?"

"No. That is behind us now. It's Augustus. I commanded him dead, and he is not dead."

"He is Flavian. Make the Flavians turn him in," said Claudia. "Start executing their children until you have the rogue Flavian in custody or dead."

Romulus patted her hands. "Efficient, Claudia. But not in our best interest."

"You are irrevocably Caesar now. Do what you want. Marry me. I want to be Empress."

"We can't."

"*Why?* The prohibition is prehistoric. There is no danger of idiot offspring anymore. As if you and I would leave the construction of our sons and daughters to chance. We would get the best of both of us. Not that we have a single idiot gene between us."

"Oh, we do," said Romulus with an unhappy chuckle. "Don't fool yourself, dear. Look who sired us."

He had her there. She gave a *hmmm*. "Well then, eliminate *those* genes for certain. Marry me."

"Claudia, you know appearances matter." He reached up to touch her beautiful face. "It would not be popular."

"You are extraordinarily popular."

"Crowds are fickle."

"It is what I want. No one is more devoted. Who better to be at your side?"

It was true. There was no one more constant. No one he could trust. He held her perfumed hands. "It will happen. But not just now."

"When?" she demanded.

"When I am sitting on the Papal throne in the Vatican in old Rome, and America is annexed into the Empire, and I am giving my address *Urbi et Orbi et Cosmi*. Then the People and the Senate will deny us nothing."

15

WITH ROMULUS FIRMLY reestablished at the helm of the Roman Empire, Roman missiles resumed their attacks on the Continental United States.

So did Roman drone fighters.

Both weapons were renewable and persistent as gorgons. Unlike gorgons, the drone fighters numbered only in the dozens at any one time. The drone fighters were adaptable, elusive, almost creative. Sometimes they acted in concerted packs. Other times not. Their behavior evidenced programming far more advanced than anything the United States had ever developed. Naval Intelligence badly wanted a drone fighter's central processing unit for analysis.

"Catch it! Catch it! Catch it!" Carly Delgado cried over the com. "There's money in it! I got your topside, Twitch, just catch it!"

The rest of the Alphas kept the other drones off Twitch's back as he drove his Swift down on a drone he had cut out of a pack.

He rode it all the way down and mashed it into the ground, pinning it under his belly shield. He had the stoutest part of his force field down there, trusting his mates with his ceiling.

He and the drone were still intact, on the ground, in the middle of a cornfield.

The fight had started in Kansas. Coordinates said Twitch was in Nebraska now. The drone struggled to get out from under his Swift. Twitch kept it pinned.

The drone blew up under him.

Fluent Anglo-Saxon from Twitch.

"What'd you do?" Ranza sent.

"Catched it," said Twitch.

Drone fighters always scuttled themselves when crippled. That was why there was money in a capture.

Thwarted, frustrated, Alpha Flight raced to the roof to let off heat and much foul language.

Twitch, who had cooked something in his undercarriage, returned to *Merrimack*. Alpha Flight returned to atmo without him.

There was a lot of yelling on the com from Echo Flight. Roman drones had ganged up on the new guy in Echo, who was screaming.

Kerry Blue would have screamed too. It was a horrible sight. A mob of Roman drone fighters hit Echo Six and hit him again, shooting, ramming, bouncing. They could have killed him by now, but it looked like they were saving that part.

Kerry loosed her guns. Nailed one drone. "Hoo ra!" Turned wide.

Roman drone fighters were built for maneuvers in atmo. Swifts were not. Kerry's kill hadn't turned any of the rest of them from their game of beating up Echo Six.

Cain and Delta Four disintegrated another drone. Both pilots claimed, "Mine!"

Steele was ordering Echo to the roof before they burned up.

Echo Six, the new guy, tried to climb with his Flight. The drones slammed him down and down.

Too many drones, too close to Echo Six.

Echo Six went down in a stream of smoke.

Immediately a U.S. evac rig rose from the ground. It was necessary to remove the crippled Swift out to vacuum in case its magnetic antimatter chamber lost integrity.

If the drones meant to cause havoc, they should have gone after the evac rig next. They didn't.

The drone that had killed Echo Six was busy turning a victory roll.

After a quick cool-off, the surviving Echoes returned from the vacuum in a pack and erased the gloating killer drone from the sky. No slamming, no games. They just executed him. All of them could claim that kill.

The surviving Roman drones scattered. They bounced up and down in the air. Looked like they were laughing.

Alphas and Deltas chased and killed them all.

And a fresh round of drones entered atmosphere, while the Marine Swifts had to head topside again. The new drones prowled for ground targets.

TR Steele ordered the entire Wing back to *Merrimack*. His dogs howled loud protests but all obeyed.

Locked down on the hangar deck, the Swifts slammed their canopies back.

Hot, angry Marines climbed out of their Swifts.

No one angrier than Colonel Steele.

"Sir!" the Marines appealed to him, like pet dogs looking to their master, as if he could make it stop raining.

Steele's jaw was set, blue eyes ice hard.

A helmet rocketed across the hangar, bashed into the bulk. Steele's.

He stalked out of the hangar.

The bullmastiffs settled a little. Good to see the Old Man angry. TR Steele was going to make it stop raining.

Captain Farragut heard Colonel Steele coming before he saw him. Met him outside the command deck and redirected him to the briefing room. Asked Commander Dent to join them. Hailed the IO, Colonel Z, on his com and requested his presence as well.

Gypsy Dent arranged for recordings of the drone encounter to be piped to the briefing room.

The officers watched the debacle play back.

"This is whaleskat," Farragut told the Intelligence officer. "Steele's dogs don't need to catch one of those things to know what's driving them!"

The spontaneity. The end-zone gloat. The gang mentality. The victory roll.

"Those aren't machines driving," said Steele.

The Intelligence officer, Colonel Z, agreed. "The behavior argues against an onboard artificial intelligence. We're still certain that the missiles are automatons, but the drone fighters do appear too smart. They apparently have remote human drivers using a resonant signal."

Virtual jockeys. V-jocks, they were called on *Merrimack*.

Naval Intelligence had insisted all along that the Romans were using sophisticated onboard computers.

"How could anyone ever think these were artificial intelligences?" said Farragut throwing an arm wide across the deadly playful images. "Computer brains *cost*, and Rome spends these things like trash. They're not afraid of dying. And they're snotty."

Steele was incensed. V-jocks brought to mind an image of someone lounging in a comfortable chair, his feet up, drink and snacks at his elbow, playing games.

They had played games with Echo Six.

"They laughed. They *laughed!*" Steele roared, red in the face.

The playback had come to the bouncing drones.

"Could be interpreted that way," said Colonel Z, studying the image.

"We'll never defeat them like this," said Farragut. "Steele's dogs kill a drone, a new one comes down from the carrier, and the pilot is right back in it."

"Kill the pilots," said Colonel Steele.

"The pilots could be anywhere," said the IO, like the last word in an argument.

"They could be anywhere, but they're *not*," said Farragut. He was not going to be stonewalled. "They are *some-where*. Some places are more likely than others. I wouldn't look for zebras in the wardroom—I'd look in a zoo. And zoos are in major population areas. *Narrow it down!* Where would you put V-pilots?"

"We have V-jocks here on *Merrimack*," said Colonel Z. "The Roman V-jocks could be on a ship as well. Which means they could be, I beg your pardon, anywhere."

"Our V-jocks are on board to give options to this mobile battle platform. Why would the Roman V-jocks be on a *ship* for an invasion of *Earth*? Earth isn't going anywhere! A shipboard base gives them no advantage and it makes them vulnerable. If I were a Roman commander, I would keep my remote pilots on the ground and shielded."

"And scattered for greater security," said Colonel Z. "Which means they could be in Asia for all we know."

Asia was the popular term for the Perseus Arm of the galaxy, in the opposite direction from the Deep End and just as far away.

Farragut blinked. "You think they're in Asia?"

"There is no solid reason to think the remote pilots are precisely *there*," said Colonel Z. "My point is the search area is inconceivably vast. The V-pilots could be separated by light-years. We'll never ferret them out. We don't know that they're all in one place."

"But we do," said Gypsy.

She had been watching the recordings, still playing on the monitor. She pointed. "Can you stop that and replay that last segment?"

The recording was set back. Farragut, Steele, Colonel Z, and Gypsy Dent watched a drone on an attack run. The drone fighter inexplicably lost concentration, jinked, and shot wide of anything like a target. Another drone suffered the same malfunction immediately afterward. Then the first drone shot at the second drone.

The IO was mystified. "What could cause that kind of malfunction?"

Gypsy kept her eyes on the playback. "I know exactly what's causing that." And she asked that the officers move the discussion into *Merrimack*'s own remote pilot center. She commanded one of *Merrimack*'s V-jocks to join them there.

Merrimack's remote control center was a small bullpen with a half dozen stations.

Steele stood against the wall, muscular arms crossed in front of his wide chest. V-jocks. Steele didn't like 'em. Marines called them gamers. And the word was not used kindly when spoken by a Marine.

Gypsy cranked up the simulator and loaded a ground strike program.

Commander Gypsy Dent took a seat at a console next to

the gangly V-jock everyone called Wraith. Gypsy put on a V-helmet and told Wraith, "Take an attack run with me. Race you to first kill."

"You're on, sir."

Wraith was an expert. He immediately located a target in the simulation, moved into position, and was locking in for the kill.

Gypsy—the person, not the remote craft—physically reached over from her station and shoved Wraith. Wraith's simulated craft jinked and his shot went wild.

"Hey!" Wraith cried, and, in instant retaliation, he shoved her back and took a virtual shot at her craft.

Wraith and Gypsy took off their V-helmets and looked up at their audience.

Farragut said: "All the remote pilots are in the same room."

Commander Gypsy Dent turned to Wraith. "Push me again, I'll pull your ears off, soldier."

"Yes, ma'am."

"And don't you ma'am me. I'm not your mama."

"Yes, sir."

"Thank you for your help, soldier," said Gypsy.

Farragut was absorbing the import. Could the Roman pilots be in the same room, reaching over and shoving each other? Sniping at each other? "It sure fits," said Farragut. "But I just always pictured a lot more discipline from Rome."

"They're kids," said Gypsy. She had two of them.

"Not necessarily, sir," said Wraith, ducking his head between his bony shoulders, sheepish.

The IO added, "I seem to recall *Merrimack* once had a casualty in its own Marine Wing, a Swift flying backward into an explosive, I believe? And another pilot tunneled a Swift twenty feet into a planet?"

"Yes, we did," Steele said tightly. That second one had been Kerry Blue. His Kerry Blue.

"Our Fleet Marines are a boisterous group," said John Farragut.

"So the Roman V-jocks aren't as disciplined as the Legions. Where does that get us?" said Z.

"It gets us looking for one concentrated installation," said Farragut. "Possibly a bunker."

"Which could still be anywhere in the galaxy," Z repeated wearily.

Gypsy shook her head. "They're kids and they're close to home."

"*All* Roman soldiers are young these days, Commander Dent," said Colonel Z. "Children are mass produced and mass schooled."

"They don't mass teach remote piloting," said Gypsy. "It's not regarded as real warfare. It's useful, but there's no honor in it. A remote is the weapon of a coward."

"Or of someone you want to keep safe," Farragut boarded Gypsy's train of thought.

"Remote work would be choice duty for a child who actually has *parents* instead of genetic donors," said Gypsy. "The parents could keep their child safe and still have him serve the Empire. I would look on Palatine for their bullpen. Maybe Thaleia. In fact, look at Thaleia first. Putting the pilots on Thaleia would keep the whole project together. Thaleia's population is all engineers. What's an engineer's child going to do in wartime?"

The IO allowed, "Thaleia has a small population. That does make for a search with small enough parameters to be reasonable. If we come up empty, then we haven't squandered a lot of time and resources on this goose chase."

"Do it," said Captain Farragut.

Colonel Z set his intelligence analysis programs to sift through Department of Defense surveillance recordings of the planet Thaleia. He was looking for traffic patterns, materials movements, and energy emanations from underground.

Colonel Z located a likely site, within a military base, underground, with high security. Traffic surveillance recorded adults arriving with a child and departing the site without the child.

Farragut had Z go back to look at surveillance from the time of the bunker's construction. The foundation gave a picture of its layout. It was the sort of place the spooks called a Land Sub—a self-contained twenty-four-hour operation with dormitory, dining, and operations facilities like a submarine, except that this facility was subterranean. Colonel Z estimated one hundred and eighty personnel inside.

Armed with enough certainty, Farragut took the proposal to Admiral Mishindi.

"I don't need to tell you, John, that anything on Thaleia is a hard target," Mishindi warned.

"We need this target," said Farragut. "The remote attack drones are replaceable. We shoot down the drones, the pilots come right back in with a new machine fresh out of a carrier. But if we take out the pilots, that's a victory."

Mishindi nodded, "And so much for Rome's much vaunted one hundred percent survivability for their remote pilots. That would wake them up to the realities of war."

Farragut added, reluctant, "The reality of war is that we are gunning for children on this one."

Mishindi nodded, grave. "Most of Rome's fighting force is of an age that has kept me up in the middle of many a night. We can't let them continue killing Americans. Enemy combatants are righteous targets."

"Yes, sir."

"John, do you want to be excused when we move on the Gameroom?"

Gameroom was the spooks' name for the site of the Roman V-jocks' bullpen.

And Mishindi had apparently agreed to the attack.

The offer tempted. Farragut's voice hitched as he tried to answer. Had to clear his throat before he could push ahead, "No, sir. I wouldn't send someone else to do what I wouldn't do."

"You're not sending anyone, Captain Farragut. I am."

"That's sophistry, sir. If you need the *Mack* to hit enemy combatants, *Mack* will hit enemy combatants."

Mishindi dismissed him. Farragut started to go, turned at the hatch. "Sir?"

"Captain?" Mishindi answered, quizzical.

"What if, instead of a space strike, we take the Gameroom."

"Take the Gameroom," Mishindi repeated slowly, rolling the absurdity of those words around his mouth. "You can't hold a Roman installation on a Roman planet."

"We don't need to hold it longer than it takes to get the pilots out. We penetrate the planetary defense, penetrate the installation, nap the kids, and run like hell. That's Plan A."

"John, I can't remember last time a Plan A ever worked."

"Then we go to B."

"What's plan B?"

"That will be determined on the ground. I'll bet my ass Rome's not expecting ground troops."

"Is your ass going in?"

"Yes, sir."

"I like the general concept. But Captain Farragut, your ass is not going into the installation. Send Marines. That's what they do."

"Sir—"

"That's an order. The United States does not need Captain John Farragut in Roman captivity. Send another ass."

16

MERRIMACK HAD BEEN TO Thaleia before, on a mission to destroy the only Hive presence ever recorded in Near Space. Rome had never wanted Americans on its manufacturing capital, but had no choice then.

Rome's fears regarding Americans exploring Thaleia and probing into all its facilities back then were validated now. The U.S. space battleship *Merrimack* was able to penetrate Thaleia's impenetrable orbital defense system.

The planet's topmost shields allowed for sunlight and air movement through it. A spacecraft could get through if it moved slow enough to make itself an easy target.

Merrimack moved slow. She absorbed all the hits Thaleia's orbiting sentinels had to give.

Underneath the top shields, any given point in Thaleia's atmosphere was in range of at least two emplaced guns on the ground.

In the atmosphere *Merrimack* unleashed a myriad of Wild Weaselets — tiny unmanned decoy craft which showed false profiles to make the Thaleian defenses give chase.

At low altitude *Merrimack* deployed one genuine craft, a Lander, amid another cluster of Weaselets.

The space battleship itself stayed as a top shield over the Lander until the Lander set down on top of the target installation. Then *Merrimack* moved away to distract the planetary defenses from the landing site.

Merrimack crossed to another continent to attack a secondary target—the rebuilt Ephesian munitions factory—as if that were what she'd come for.

The Lander plunged an auger through the top entry hatch to the bunker, which jutted up like a submarine's sail.

The opening revealed a steel ladder, extending down into a concrete shaft.

Flight Leader Ranza Espinoza reminded the Marines, "After yous get in there, if someone draws on yous, drop 'im. I don't care if she's a ten-year-old with pigtails. If her hands ain't empty you drop her."

The Marines sent a camera scope down the hole first. It showed a cross tunnel, which was clear of people, but there were beam sentinels at every ceiling corner. Those opened fire and took out the camera.

The camera's death gave the Marines a measure of the sentinels' beam strength. The Marines' personal fields would protect them.

Marines climbed, slid, jumped down the ladder, and fanned out in the corridors.

Beam fire from the auto sentinels glanced off them.

"C'mon, yous. Get in. Get in! Stop gawking at the flashy lights."

Doors opened. Four Roman guards armed with beam cannons came running out. Ranza dashed in close to one guard, like jamming up a boxer, pushed the barrel of her head buster into his face, and fired.

The round penetrated, but did not explode as it should have. It had not encountered DNA.

The guard, with a neat bullet hole just below his nose, closed a crushing hand on Ranza's throat. She fired into the guard's midriff. That round did not detonate either, but it penetrated the guard's CPU. Motion ceased. Ranza pried the polymer hand off her throat. Coughed. Rasped, "Pan-Galactic products, boys and girls. Hit 'em under the ribs!"

Other Marines took down the remaining three automaton guards. Kerry Blue was shooting the beam sentinels out of the ceiling.

"Whatcha doin', Blue?"

"They bother me," said Kerry Blue. She hit another one.

Carly with a now-that-you-mention-it look said, "Me too." She shot out another sentinel.

When there were no hostiles left standing in the corridors, and the sentinels no longer flashed, the Marines faced five locked doors.

Ranza retrieved a projection of the bunker's layout from her wrist com. She sent Green and White Squads to the dormitory sections of the installation. Teams Alpha and Baker of Red Squad, and Charlie and Delta of Blue Squad each took a door to one the four operations rooms.

"I hear adult voices in there," said Cole Darby with his ear against the door to Gameroom One. "I hear kids, too. But there are adults in there."

Guards. They hadn't expected human guards. Internal guards were always light at Roman installations, so human guards seemed excessive in such a well-defended place.

But the adults were probably here more as guardians than as guards. Because children had less developed brains, they tended to try to get away with things they shouldn't and failed to weigh the consequences of their attempts. The region of the brain that governed impulse control and moral judgment was last to mature.

Ranza ordered down the auger and drilled the lock on Gameroom One. She tossed the auger over to Team Baker, who had broken theirs.

High voices sounded within the Gameroom, all shouting at once. Some screaming. Sounds of scuffling, ducking and covering.

Ranza sent a camera scope through the hole in the door. She counted up the people in the room before the camera was caught and stomped on.

Ranza signaled back to her team: Five adult guards armed with beam cannons. Twenty-five underage V-pilots hiding under their stations.

The pilots themselves had no firearms as far as the camera detected. There would be no reason to have firearms on home ground among friends. High spirits and live rounds would only make the young pilots a menace to each other.

On Ranza's signal the Alphas turned on headlamps. They could expect the lights to be out in the wolf's lair.

Cain Salvador hauled the door open. Ranza Espinoza and Dak Shepard charged in first, low. Beam shots flashed off of their personal fields. Carly Delgado darted in, thrust her knife into the kidney of the guard who sprang out from beside the doorjamb to jump Dak from behind.

Real blood darkened Carly's blade. The Roman contorted, squeaking. Carly jabbed again, higher.

"These aren't PanGalactic guards in here, *hermanos!*" Carly shouted. "They die better!" And she darted aside to let the others in.

Dak was locked in a sparring match with a guard, both of them wielding their beam cannons as if they were staffs. The guard got Dak pinned up against the wall, choking him with his weapon. Dak let go one of his hands from his cannon to rabbit punch the snarling face in front of him. He brought a knee up into the man's groin as the guard sagged from the punch, and gave him a cannon butt on the back of his neck on his way down. He stuck a knife in the Roman to make sure he stayed there.

Beam fire crisscrossed the chamber. Children shrieked under their consoles. They seemed about eleven or twelve years old.

There was a rack of swords on the wall. One boy dashed out of hiding, went for the rack, took down a sword. Twitch Fuentes folded him over, his big fist in the boy's diaphragm. The boy withered to the deck, trying to breathe. Twitch tossed the sword to Ranza, because energy bolts and head busters weren't doing the job here.

A Roman guard intercepted the toss. He raised the sword at Ranza.

Kerry's foot in the back of the guard's knee brought him to a sudden begging posture before Ranza. Ranza drove her heel into his chin, sent him reeling backward. Kerry jumped clear of the falling sword. Ranza stomped on the Roman's throat.

Another guard scuttled out from under one of the consoles where he'd been hiding like a child. Cain seized the dropped sword, took a mighty swing at the man's head.

Something came off with a spurt of blood—a piece of

skull—flying with a rag of bloody hair and spray of gray matter.

Kerry felt a sharp crack on the side of her head with a wet slap. She blinked, spat. A shard of skull, not hers, slid, dropped from her head. She had to peel the scalp with its bloody hair off her. Gray gore stuck to her skin, her hair, her uniform. "Oh. Oh." She was perilously close to heaving up breakfast. She retreated into a detached persona, like a remote control robot. Emotionless. Wrapped in stillness.

Wiped blood from her eyes. Saw no more guards standing. There were only bleating children cowering under their battle stations.

Cole Darby, who wore a language module, informed the children in halting Latin that they would be unharmed if they obeyed. Told them to come up with their hands out.

The Romans came out mewling, crying. A couple emerged dry-eyed, with fiercely protruding lower lips.

"Pick your brain, Kerry?"

A white-hot haze fell before Kerry Blue, and she was suddenly back into her empty place. Her voice came out in a weird cat hiss: "Shut up, Dak."

"Move 'em out!" Ranza shouted. "Darb, don't bother pulling the res chambers. You know they're just gonna change all the harmonics."

The prisoners shuffled through the door in a line out to the corridor.

Cole Darby said, "Uh, there's a countdown happening in here."

"Oh, beat yourself dead!" Ranza cried.

The bunker was counting down an auto-destruct sequence. The system had probably been demanding verification and not gotten a proper response from anyone.

"The bunker knows it's in hostile hands," said Darb. "It's going to self-destruct."

"Or it's just going to flush us out with a false countdown," Cain suggested.

"Hell, I'm not going to bet the barroom on that," said Ranza. "Get everybody out within the count!"

"What countdown!" said Dak. "I don't hear a countdown. What kind of word is *quinquaginta?*"

"It's a countdown in Latin, you bozon!" said Darb, getting a little panicked. "Isn't anyone else wearing a language module?"

Carly shrugged. "I ain't here to negotiate."

Ranza: "And I ain't here to die! Move! Move! Move!"

Team Alpha herded the children toward the doorway, except for the one Twitch hit. Twitch ended up carrying that one.

The other three Gamerooms had been secured. Teams Baker, Delta, and Echo were already marshaling their children out and up the ladder, Yurg carrying two of them.

The last child in Gameroom One decided to block the exit, his hands and feet braced on the doorjambs for a suicidal stand. *"Virtus et Honus!"*

Ranza hunkered down and charged, rammed him through the opening, almost to a first down.

"Gameroom One, clear!"

The Marines tossed timed explosives behind them into each Gameroom, just in case the countdown was a bluff. They did not want to leave the equipment in Roman hands for new recruits. Whether by Rome or by the U.S. this installation was in for a good up-blowing.

Redundance was good. Redundance was good.

Marines scrambled up the ladder through the top hatch into the Lander, pushing little butts up as fast as they could go. Colonel Steele was up there seizing wrists and hauling children up and over to Cain, who loaded them into the Lander's hold.

With all the Roman prisoners in the hold, Cain slammed the rear hatch shut. The remaining Marines were coming up much faster, strapping themselves into their seats as fast as they boarded.

Steele's hands slipped on Kerry Blue's gory wrists. He grabbed her upper arms hard, lifted her up and passed her over to Dak. Ranza shouting from below, "Go! Go! Go! It's gonna blow!"

Ranza was the last one up. "Clear!"

Steele secured the bottom hatch of the Lander.

Darb, buckling in. "Is it going to implode or explode?"

"Now what kind of Darb question is *that!*" Ranza there,

dropping into the seat next to him. "Honey, it's gonna 'plode! Don't give a frog's tit about the details!"

Steele shouted to the pilot, "Get us airborne *now!*"

The engine whined.

The bunker 'ploded.

The concussion slammed into the Lander's force field, heaved the stomach into the throat. And suddenly reversed. The Lander waddled *up*. The Marines could feel the motion and shouldn't.

The lights dimmed to dark.

"Ex," said Darb.

"Huh?"

Lights back up.

"'Plosion. Wasn't very big. Only enough to scuttle the bunker."

"How'd you know it wasn't a big explosion?"

Darb stomped at the deck with one heel. " 'Cause these S-Nine Landers aren't shielded for crap."

Ranza turned to Steele, "Next sortie, leave this guy. He is full of too much skat I don't never need to know."

Steele looked to Darby. Said at last, quietly, "We probably shouldn't have set down the Lander on top of the bunker?"

Darb nodded, reluctant to agree. "Sir." It was a dumbish mistake.

Steele looked to Kerry. She seemed to be in one piece. Unhappy. A slime of repulsive stuff on her. He could not see a wound on her. Wished he could take her into his shower and clean her off. He could still see a pretty woman under that revolting mess. He was a dead man and knew it.

Ranza was speaking, "So what's the difference if it's an implosion or an explosion? If it was a big one, either way we're swimming with the sushi."

"An implosion would have impeded the liftoff," said Darb.

"Impede," Ranza echoed. "Who uses that word? What's an impede?"

"Really small pede." Darb put his forefinger and thumb close together. "Like a centipede. Less legs."

Kerry was looking out a viewport as the Lander rose. Murmured, "Here's the interesting part."

She pictured what Calli Carmel looked like trying to get from Fort Ike to *Wolfhound*.

We got in. We woke them up.

Getting away from Thaleia involved a lot of Stingers which had not been out there on the inbound leg of this journey.

Shots from the Stingers battered the Lander.

Kerry Blue did not need to know that these Landers weren't shielded for crap.

A shadow fell over them.

It was *Merrimack*. Descending. The great ship formed a top shield over them. The Lander was still vulnerable on the horizons. Stingers swarmed on every horizon.

A distinctive boom reverberated through the bulkheads. The Lander had been hit by a sounder, making way for something large.

"Good night," said someone. The end.

They were about to be Carmelized.

Kerry closed her eyes. *This is gonna hurt*.

She heard the whoosh. Orange lights of fire flickered behind her eyelids.

Did not feel the bone deep agony.

Opened her eyes. The Lander stopped rocking and booming. The fire was on the other side of the force field.

"*Mack*'s got us."

The Lander was inside *Merrimack*'s distortion field.

Merrimack rose straight up with the Lander in tow, Stinger strikes flashing off the force field in useless pretty sprays.

Safe. Kerry sat back. Listened to her head pound.

Dak on one side, sweating like a cold beer.

Carly on the other side. A lot of blood on her, none of it hers.

The prisoners in the hold started to make noise, yelling and stomping and banging on the bulks like a cageful of bad-tempered monkeys.

"Oh, you know what?" Kerry Blue unstrapped, getting up, wincing. "I've been hit in the head. I'm icky. I'm not in a good mood. This is not happening." She stalked back to the rioting hold. Wrenched open the hatch.

She stood in the hatchway, her eyes wild, chin forward. Felt the blood and brains drying on her face. Hair wet with it. She was a grotesque vision and knew it.

The children silenced at once.

"We need to lighten the load," Kerry rasped. "Who wants to walk?"

They all stared at her, became very still.

She glared wildly over every last one of them. Spoke crisply, " 'Kay then. I'll get the straws." Kerry slammed the hatch.

She sat back down, head still throbbing. But the hold was quiet.

"How'd you do that, Blue?" Carly asked.

"Easy," said Dak. "Kerry Blue has all the brains."

Kerry whispered, "That is so not funny." Looked as if she would cry.

Started to laugh like a lunatic till she thought her head would split.

Kerry unloosed her straps so she could lean over her knees. Her head ached so bad it pushed tears into her eyes.

Her blurry gaze fell upon an object on the deck. The sword that had got all this junk on her. It took her thoughts a moment to catch up with what happened back there in the bunker.

She sniffled. That hurt. Mumbled into the deck, the sword swimming before her eyes.

"Why'd they have swords in a bunker on Thaleia?"

17

CAPTAIN JOHN FARRAGUT recognized the boy. He had seen him on his first mission to Thaleia—a young boy with his arms clasped around the legate of Legion Draconis as the city of Antipolis smoldered after a gorgon attack. He remembered the dark eyes. The boy had grown, as boys will, and cut his curls very short since then.

Farragut entered the briefing room on his ship. He wore a language module. John Farragut liked to try to speak to people in their own tongue. People usually appreciated the attempt, though Augustus had forbade him to ever speak Latin in his presence.

Farragut took a seat opposite the boy at the table. "Are you Herius Asinius' son?"

The boy's eyes widened. He stayed silent.

"Convention says you can give me your name, soldier," said Farragut.

"Titus Vitruvius," the boy announced, and added his rank. "Pilot."

Farragut nodded. He recognized the name.

"Why did y'all have swords down there, son?"

Latin was one of those languages that actually had a good translation for the word "y'all."

A child's idea of not talking was flexible. Titus sneered. "As if you did not know."

Farragut was the man who first put swords on a space battleship. Swords were used to kill gorgons.

Farragut was instantly on his com. Spoke in American: "Farragut to command deck. Gypsy, get a message to the JC. Hive presence on Thaleia."

He sent Titus back to the brig and returned to the command deck.

Gypsy turned, searched his face in hope there was some mistake. "The Hive is in Near Space? We're certain?"

Farragut nodded, his mouth tight, massively not happy.

The first Hive presence on Thaleia had been brief—a duration of mere months. Romans, Americans, the League of Earth Nations, and nearby alien species had all ganged together to exterminate the monsters. And until now everyone had supposed that the planet Thaleia had escaped an eruption of a second generation Hive. Rome had reported Thaleia clear while new swarms were springing up in the Deep End.

"The boy couldn't have lied?" Gypsy made a last grasp for a better answer.

"No. He didn't even mean to tell me," said Farragut, in motion. He wasn't really pacing the command deck. He was stalking. "Interrogating children is like shooting fish in a barrel."

"Who shoots fish in a barrel, sir?"

He shook his head. He didn't know. "Had to been some 'billy's idea of a good time."

The United States released the news that Rome was covering up the presence of the Hive on the Near Space planet Thaleia. The broadcasts reached Palatine under headlines like: WHAT YOUR GOVERNMENT WILL NOT TELL YOU!

Both the U.S. and Rome had repeater stations that made sure that the other nation's homeworld received its propaganda.

Roman broadcasts in turn showed images of dead children, purportedly killed in a U.S. raid on Thaleia. They also unveiled "secret U.S. recordings" of Roman children being tortured and killed in U.S. detention. The images were certain to shock, sicken and outrage anyone and everyone.

According to Rome the United States was using their fiction of a Near Space Hive presence as a pretext for their invasion of Thaleia, while committing atrocities on Roman children there.

The real captive children from Thaleia—one hundred of them—were on board John Farragut's space battleship. Three of them had been banged up during capture, treated in the ship's hospital, and were currently housed in the brig.

Analysis of the Roman broadcasts revealed the images of dead and tortured children to be digital fiction. "No children were harmed in the making of this propaganda feature," said Colonel Z when he brought his report to the command deck.

"This is dirty combat," said Farragut.

"No, this is dirty politics," said Colonel Z. "Rome's better at it than we are."

"I never saw this coming," said Farragut, stunned.

Gypsy Dent touched his shoulder, said gently, "You wouldn't, sir."

Farragut's own claims of gorgons on Thaleia were meeting with more skepticism than Rome's claims of child torture.

Unlike on the Deep End colony of Telecore, there was plenty to eat on the Near Space world of Thaleia—a vicious plenty that would fight back against the Hive—but plenty. Yet there were no vast swarms of gorgons to be seen from space, chewing across Thaleia's fields of razor grasses and whipthorn.

If Rome was covering up a Hive presence, they were covering very well, and making a liar out of Captain Farragut.

Merrimack's Intelligence officer offered to produce some visuals to prop up the U.S. story.

"No," said Farragut. "I'll go back to my source."

"I shall conduct the interrogation," said Colonel Z.

"No, I've got him," said Farragut.

"Sir," Colonel Z objected. "You are not trained in interrogating children."

"I'm *not?*" said Farragut, almost laughing. "Do you know how many kid brothers I have?"

*   *   *

Titus Vitruvius was escorted back to *Merrimack*'s briefing room again. He told his guard that he was not talking, so she should just take him back to the brig right now.

When the guard delivered the boy to the briefing room, Captain Farragut was already seated at the table, popping back oqib nuts. He offered the open bag to Titus. "Nut?"

Titus Vitruvius refused with a big shake of his head, his chin up, arms crossed.

"Sit," said Farragut.

Titus sat, stiff as a Roman standard.

"Do you know why we're at war, son?"

The child did not even register the question. He answered what was on his mind. "You're just mad because we tore down your arch. You should never have got that."

Accustomed to hearing non sequiturs out of children, Farragut followed the leap. Titus was talking about the Triumphal Arch erected on Thaleia to mark the human victory over the Hive in Near Space. Caesar Magnus had dedicated the arch to John Farragut.

Romulus destroyed it.

Farragut sat back. "I never really liked the damned thing."

The boy stayed rigid. His whole being shouted: I am not talking. See me not talking.

"Heri said you were a brave soldier, Titus Vitruvius."

"Don't care what any American said."

Negative declarations apparently did not count as talking.

"Heri," Farragut explained, "was Herius Asinius, legate of Legion Draconis."

A gasp escaped Titus.

"Heri said you defended the Roman fortress at his side. That's why I'm surprised to find you in a Gameroom, Titus. I thought you were bound for a Legion."

Titus' fortress of attempted silence crumbled. "I wanted to join a Legion!" he cried. "They posted me with the gamers!"

"Have a nut."

Titus shook his head a vigorous no.

"Diomede Silva dined with me after we took the *Valerius*.

And I dined with Numa Pompeii when he took my *Merrimack*. You're allowed to have a nut." Farragut tossed one at him. The boy caught it by reflex.

Titus stared at Farragut. He asked, awed, "You met the great Numa Pompeii?" He nibbled cautiously on the edge of the nut.

"Met?" said Farragut with a big laugh, and regaled Titus with war stories.

The boy listened wide-eyed, enthralled. Farragut had him fighting very hard not to smile at a story about Herius Asinius and a trench.

And Farragut told him how the brave Herius Asinius died.

The tale had the boy in tears—soldier tears, so they were allowed. Titus Vitruvius was profoundly moved, and proud to have been associated with a man like Legion Commander Herius Asinius.

"You and I have the same mission," Farragut told the boy. "The same duty to Herius Asinius. Now I don't expect you to tell me anything about Rome. Tell me about our enemy, the Hive."

Titus sniffled. He sat up imperially straight. "Like what?"

"Gorgons came back to Thaleia again, didn't they?"

"They're all gone," Titus said, unconvincingly.

"You had swords in the Gameroom," Farragut said.

Titus looked at him straight and spoke like a miniature adult, not a question, "You're never sure they're gone, are you?"

Farragut stopped breathing for a moment. It had been one of the worst moments of his career the day the gorgons came back to Antipolis the first time.

"No, sir," Farragut answered the child gravely. "You're never sure."

And he got Titus to tell him about the night the Hive returned to Antipolis the second time. Titus gave him the exact Roman date.

"You don't have a big population on Thaleia," said Farragut. "Why hasn't the Hive overrun the planet by now?"

"We are Roman," said Titus proudly.

"Y'all were Roman the first time round, and y'all needed help then."

Titus admitted, "They're not that smart this time." He meant the gorgons, not the Romans. "They don't turn our automatons on us. They don't make it hard to breathe. They're easier to kill."

But the Hive learned. From each and every encounter. The new Hive would have learned quite a lot from the deaths of the gorgons of Thaleia.

"They're all gone now," said Titus. A loud unspoken *maybe* on the end of that. "There weren't that many anyway. Not like last time. Someone said they didn't have time to plant a lot of seeds."

"Seeds?"

Titus shrugged. "They come out of the ground."

"Hell of a thing to keep quiet," said Farragut.

"We were afraid you'd invade," Titus defended.

"I did that anyway."

Titus seemed to remember then that John Farragut was the enemy. But he couldn't seem to get the right hate up.

Before Farragut returned Titus to his fellow prisoners, he told him, "You're right, you know. Heri should have got the arch."

A journey of three days brought *Merrimack* back to Earth where she dropped off prisoners, picked up equipment, and walked some dogs.

The drone fighter raids over the U.S. had stopped immediately after the raid on Thaleia, so the skies were quiet.

TR Steele sat on the edge of a pier on the waterfront at sunset. Actually he was more like propped against the pier, his legs out in front of him at an angle, beer in hand.

Sun on his broad shoulders threw his very long shadow out before him.

He looked out to the water. A wide sky. Seagulls. Sails.

Sighted her off the port beam. A young female approaching up the sea strand. Loose build. Rangy walk. Tank top showed her wide shoulders. Shorts of girene green. Hard-toned legs. The only soft parts on her were what separated her from the boys.

She strolled to him. Let her head tilt. Her hair was loose.

She guided a windblown lock to behind her ear. "Come here often, soldier?"

"Only when I'm taking time out from maiming children." Roman propaganda had lodged under TR Steele's skin, and stayed there crawling and biting.

"Romans talk," she shrugged. "Their lips move but it still smells like it's coming out the other end."

Steele snorted. A real woman of refinement, his Kerry Blue.

Steele was uncomfortable around refinement. Kerry Blue always managed to say what he was not allowed to.

"Thanks," he said. Her take on it knocked things into perspective.

A piper ran across the sand at the waterline on its little stilt legs. A gull squalled.

Kerry Blue lifted her leg over his, like mounting a horse, to sit straddling him, face-to-face, hips to hips. Warm.

She propped her forearms atop his broad shoulders, her wrists crossed behind his head. Her fingers toyed with the short hairs behind his neck. Her brown eyes looked into his.

He gazed back. "What are you doing, Marine?"

Her body rocked a little.

"Sir? Nobody's fooling anybody here."

The rough palms of his big hands cradled her head, fingers laced in her hair. He had no idea what had become of the beer. He agreed, "No."

"Just another man and another woman on the waterfront," said Kerry looking round at the sunset couples. "We're just harder than the civilians."

"One of us is a lot harder."

"Thomas?" His name in her voice set all his common sense free on holiday. "Can we go somewhere?"

It was a career wrecker.

Thomas Ryder Steele could not even spell career at the moment.

He unwound her arms from round his neck, stood up, enclosed her hand in his to take her somewhere.

*   *   *

Lying on his back. Morning sun in the window of the little room. She'd fallen asleep on top of him. Steele with his arms wrapped round Kerry Blue. All the way around, to hold her, all of her, contain her, protect her. That could not happen. Kerry Blue would not be contained or protected.

She stirred.

She'd gotten maybe an hour's sleep. He none. He did not want to lose a moment.

He felt her breathing. She lifted her head. Her hair fell in her face. She focused on him. Smiled. "Hi."

Her sleep-swollen face looked amazing. She. She. The heaven-break-open, lightning-strike, star-shattering sex had nothing to do with her skill, though God knew she had gobs of experience he never wanted to think about.

It was this woman he had lived with for several years now. Courageous in her own way. She would be screaming her head off in fear, but still fighting in the front line, right there for you.

Her muscles were cute, girl-hard under smooth skin. Scars flecked her arms and legs. She lived rough.

She parked her chin on his sternum, eyes looking up at his face. "You still gonna be mean to me?"

"Meaner."

He ran his palms down her back. Her skin was slightly damp.

He had thought (and that would teach him to try thinking!) that once he gave in, the need would be finished. Get it out of his system. He'd been wrong seven times now. And deep down he'd known it. He had tried so hard to resist. Because now he was—knew he would be—utterly lost. There was no getting over this woman, ever.

And she. What did she think?

He brushed a grain of sleep out of the corner of her eye. Her eyelashes caressed his thumb.

He said, "The rat on you around ship is that you haven't been yourself lately."

She knew what he was talking about. She tugged on his blond chest hairs. "Been holding out," said Kerry.

"Never heard you could do that."

"Never nothing worth holding out for."

What he wanted to hear. Amazed to actually hear it. Made him want to go out and bring down a buffalo or something with his bare hands.

"Was I worth it?"

"Oh, yeah."

She nipped his nose and got up to take another shower.

He listened to her patter around in there. Could get used to hearing that every morning.

He ought to marry her. For a lot of reasons. Mostly because he wanted to.

Not that it would allow her to splash around in his shower on board *Merrimack*. They still could not get caught together.

He couldn't ask her to marry him. She could laugh. Oh, you thought? How could you be so dumb?

Chilled him to the bone to think she might not be as serious as he was. She got what she was holding out for. All done? Game over?

He called into the bath, kept his voice nonchalant: "Ever been to Vegas?"

"I got no money! What am I gonna do in Vegas?"

We could walk down the glittery streets, stroll by a tacky chapel and hope she says, "Hey, Thomas, let's get married."

A sudden signal on Steele's com broke the perfect morning. He had turned that damn thing off.

The com turned itself on, as it could in dire emergency.

And then there was Kerry Blue dashing out of the shower, dripping wet, grabbing up her clothes, calling down abominations. Her com was awake too.

SpaceCraft One had been shot down. President Johnson was dead.

18

"**H**OW COULD THAT HAPPEN!" Farragut tried to keep his voice down, talking to his admiral.

Admiral Mishindi on video from Base Carolina looked haggard. He shook his head, completely in sympathy with Captain Farragut. "Tranquility Base got pounded last week. The President decided she had to make an appearance on the Moon for morale. It was unscheduled. Quiet. No media. We had Secret Service thick as Hive around her. Everything was fine until she tried to come back to Earth. Rome had someone on Tranquility."

"A mole!" Farragut cried, astonished.

"A deep seeded mole. Just when we think we got them all." Mishindi pushed his lower jaw forward, frustrated past words. "The mole obtained the field codes for SpaceCraft One. And all those Roman warships we stranded at Fort Ike? Those dropped out of FTL right here. They opened fire on the President's ship. *All* of them, including your old friend, the *Horatius*. The President did not have a prayer. Not a solitary prayer."

"Did we get the mole?"

Mishindi closed his eyes and nodded grim satisfaction. "Our people on Tranquility showed great restraint in taking him alive. I cannot guarantee that his interrogation will strictly abide by convention."

"Where are the Roman warships now?"

"Oh, they're still here. Punching the hell out of Washington. The state, not DC. Ground defenses are taking hell. *Monitor*, *Wolfhound*, and *Rio Grande* are already there. *Merrimack* is to engage the Roman warships as soon as you get your people aboard."

Farragut knew there were a lot of military bases in Washington, but: "Why Washington?"

"Fault lines. It's a disaster, John. Rome's not even targeting the military bases. Those are too well shielded. And they're not shooting at the cities, which would be an obvious crime. They're shooting into Puget Sound, which is not as obvious but still criminal. Tacoma, Whidbey Island, and Seattle are built on top of shallow faults. The shallow ones make the surface rock."

Gypsy already had *Merrimack* curving shots around the horizon, tagging Roman ships over Washington, and shooting missiles out to chase the tags.

As soon as Colonel Steele reported on board, *Merrimack* charged in to take an interceptor position over Seattle.

The Swifts were bottled up in the hangars, their force fields inadequate against the kind of firepower let loose in the brawl over Washington. The Marines were all at their gun blisters.

"Have fun on leave, Kerry Blue?" Ranza said as Kerry swung into her gun seat. As if the rest of her team had been waiting for her.

Kerry took up the controls and started shooting at missile ports of enemy ships.

"Yeah, I did." Her hair was still damp. "You're it!" she crowed as she nailed a missile just emerging from its chute. "You're it!" Got two.

Dak craned his head around. "What got into Blue?"

"I'm saving the world," said Kerry Blue.

There was no lack of targets. They were just all very very fast, and the big ones were shielded. Targeting was all by instrument. Visually all you saw were the flashes in the dark above, the gray clouds of smoke rising from the blue planet below. The tactical plot looked like a three-dimensional scribble. The Marines had only two orders: stop the enemy from shooting at the ground, and shoot the enemy.

"So who's in charge now?" said Kerry. "Not Sampson Reed?"

"Well, uh-yuh," said Cole Darby. "That is how the chain of command works."

Sampson Reed?

The chin. Himself. A great shock of thick honey-colored hair, pearly white teeth, vast slab of dimpled chin, lantern jaw, mind like large curd cottage cheese.

"Why weren't we escorting SpaceCraft One?" said Carly. Then, to a target, "Gotcha!"

"She had Secret Service."

"When's the last time you saw the Secret Service take out a Roman ship of war?" said Cain. "She shoulda had *us*."

"They said the head of state should not be a legitimate target," said Darby. And to his target, "Oh, come on, stand still."

"Who's they? They who?" said Cain Salvador. "What p-brane said that? And please say it wasn't Vice President—I mean President Reed."

"It was. He did," said Darb. "Oh, for—! I hit you, you Roman ace in the hole! Stop moving!"

"SpaceCraft One was a military transport!" said Cain. "MARISSA JOHNSON WAS THE COMMANDER IN CHIEF OF THE UNITED STATES ARMED FORCES!"

That kind of sort of made her a military target.

"Yes," said Darb. "I'm just telling you what our new Commander in Chief said."

"We're doomed," said Dak.

"Yep."

Kerry sang out, "You're it!" and another, "You're it!"

Carly: "Ho, *chica!*" She bumped forearms with Kerry Blue.

"Gotta be the R and R," said Dak. "I want me some R and R."

Carly leaned over to Kerry. "Was he that good?"

Kerry jerked, startled. Prickling fear tingled her throat. Carly knew? Kerry Blue turned her head to stare at Carly's foxy grin.

Kerry could see that Carly knew *what*, but Carly didn't know *who* with. Carly had recognized the Look. Left Kerry nowhere to hide but behind the truth. "Uh, yeah. He was that good."

"Civilian?" Ranza was in it now.

"No." Kerry tried to concentrate hard on a target. Said quickly, "Can't talk about it. He's wrong branch of the service. Wrong. Wrong. Wrong."

Wasn't quite a lie. Carly and Ranza let her off with sly winks.

Kerry's face felt to be some color of flame. Needed to shoot at a target.

And suddenly there weren't any. "Hey! Where'd they go?" She stood up in her seat. Dak declared his instruments had gone dead.

But nothing was wrong with the instruments. The Romans were just gone.

Middle of the melee, all the enemy ships vanished.

They had jumped to FTL and did not reappear.

Merrimack jumped to FTL to pursue, but lost the Romans in the scrambled trails leading off from the heavily traveled space between Earth and the Moon.

A ship in space could not do battle with an enemy who won't stand.

Merrimack returned to orbit Earth, waiting for the enemy to come back.

They didn't.

The reason behind the disappearing act came later, with the news that the League of Earth Nations had stepped in.

The Roman attacks on the shallow American faults had caused tremblers in Canada, Japan, and the Pacific Rim.

The LEN demanded Rome stop its attacks at once or consider itself at war with all of Earth and her colonies.

And Rome did cease fire. Even apologized to the LEN, excluding the U.S. per se.

Rome offered to send in planetary engineers to settle the tremblers. Rome had colonized many a restless world. Roman engineers could calculate where to drill vents to bleed off pressure under the Earth's crust and control the movement of the disturbed plates.

The Romans only caused such chaos because they were capable of undoing much of it. Romans had always been as gifted at building as they were at destroying. They could put the world back better than they found it. Only let them come in to fix it, they asked.

Of course that would mean allowing Roman engineers in to the U.S. Northwest.

The LEN relayed the offer to its member nation. The American response ran along the lines of: "We'll consider that while we check the weather forecast in hell."

The nations on the other side of the Pacific rim also declined Rome's generous offer of engineers. Those nations would engage their own repair crews. They only needed to know where to send the invoices for restitution.

As the faults under the Pacific Northwest lay close to the surface, the Roman strikes had caused—and continued to cause—intense shaking. The Romans may as well have been shooting at the civilian centers for the fire, upheaval, chaos, injury, and death they caused in the state of Washington.

Civilians in the area had died by the thousands. Rome could not bring them back to life. More civilians by the millions had been left homeless. Seattle's airport and spaceport were down. Commerce was at a stop, and the military bases suffered ruptures.

The U.S. Secretary of State told the Roman Praetor Peregrinus, "This isn't war. It's terrorism."

The Roman response was frosty. "And what do you call kidnapping, torturing, and murdering children?"

"Propaganda," said the Secretary. "You *do* realize you are reciting your own propaganda, don't you?"

"No. It's not." The Roman Praetor stood by the official line. But analysis of his vocals and his body language said that he had inwardly blinked. The State Department considered that progress, however small, to get someone of Peregrinus' station in the Empire to question his own information.

This was not the Rome of Caesar Magnus. Magnus flew with eagles. Romulus crawled with termites.

*　　*　　*

Senator Ventor and Senator Philadelphus joined Caesar in the bath. The baths in Roma Nova were patterned after those in ancient Bath in England, though the new baths were not lined in lead and the frisky frescoes here had been lifted not from Bath but from ancient Pompeii.

Men spoke more freely in the soothing waters, naked, with a glass of wine at the side, and pictures of uninhibited men, women, and goats on the walls.

Romulus knew a lot of Senators had begun to question his leadership and the direction of the war.

These two, Ventor and Philadelphus, were counted among Caesar's allies. But Romulus was always sensitive to changes in the current. It was time to get these two in the water and see which way they floated.

Ventor propped himself at the edge of the long pool. "Is it true there are gorgons on Thaleia," he asked, pseudo-casual. "Or is that U.S. propaganda?"

"A bit of both," Caesar answered, sounding unconcerned. "There have been gorgons seen on Thaleia. That much is fact. The Americans have puffed up the numbers. The gorgons' numbers are few and Intelligence suspects they were planted."

"Planted!" Philadelphus sputtered. His hand gestures made a splash. Caesar's casual attitude was no comfort at all. "Who could have planted gorgons on Thaleia!"

"The United States," Caesar suggested. "Or Augustus."

Philadelphus had investments on Thaleia. "Where can I get the names of the children whom the Americans killed and the ones they are holding prisoner?"

Romulus brushed the question aside. He was Caesar, not a directory. "Where is Augustus?" Caesar looked from one Senator to the other. "I am unhappy knowing he is out there. No one claims to see him. Did he defect to the Americans?"

"Don't know, Caesar," Ventor said.

"Does Augustus not have a kill switch?" Romulus said.

"No, Caesar," said Philadelphus. "He is not a PanGalactic product."

"Shall we then fight fire with fire?" said Romulus. "Where is the next generation patterner? Send *that* after the rogue!"

"There are no more," said Ventor. "Augustus is the last."

"Your father killed the project, Caesar," said Philadelphus.

"Damn him," said Romulus.

The Senators went rigid with a start.

Romulus met their stares. "Why should I not damn Augustus?"

"Oh. I—" Philadelphus started. "Sorry, Caesar."

"The patterner project has always been too costly," said Ventor. "Huge overruns are the usual. Too many failures, not enough good candidates. And the final product is short-lived and dangerous. It's just too much power to put in a single being. The patterner Secundus was turned to work for the enemy. And now we have Augustus out there apparently acting for Augustus. That should not be happening. A patterner is programmed to serve Rome absolutely, unquestionably, even to his death."

"And when the hell is that going to happen? His death?"

"He could already be dead for all we know," said Ventor. "We do know there will be no others."

Imperial Intelligence received a recording from an anonymous source. Anonymity was rare in the modern age, and the message did not stay anonymous long.

At first the message was assumed to be from Augustus. But Imperial Intelligence traced the message back to Caesar Magnus' dead assassin, Julius Urbicus.

Until now the death of Caesar Magnus had been a murder without motive. A lot of men had wanted Magnus dead, but Julius Urbicus was not one of them.

Julius Urbicus had been a longtime associate of Magnus. He had served with distinction in the earlier wars. He had lost his sons in those wars. His wife left him. Julius Urbicus had not remarried. He had been entirely too interested in young girls—one in particular, though he never acted on those impulses. He was always a quiet, tightly contained, disciplined man. Magnus had trusted his steady statesmanship.

Few people knew about Urbicus' fascination with girls until he killed Caesar. Julius Urbicus had less than nothing to gain by killing Magnus.

The message from the late assassin originated from a secret cache. Its posthumous release had been triggered by an obituary.

A young girl had died.

Lilia.

She was the object of Julius Urbicus' obsession. Pictures of young Lilia clogged his database. Images of ten-year-old Lilia moved around the walls of his bedchamber. Lilia's innocent smile, her deep brown eyes.

Lilia had died earlier today. An accidental drowning.

The message arrived at Imperial Intelligence seconds after Lilia's death notice was posted.

Imperial Intelligence summoned Caesar's sister Claudia to their center.

She answered the call peevishly. She had a public appearance this evening and must get her hair done. That probably meant her face, too, which changed according to the fashion of the day.

Imperial Intelligence headquarters was away from the Forum, mostly underground, constructed like a catacomb. It exuded a creeping dread—all without illusions. It was cut from unpainted weathered stone, like a ruin.

Ancient Rome had been full of color. As was modern Roma Nova. Everything was tinted.

Intelligence headquarters had no color. It stood naked as if bleached by age. Going down into it gave you a sense of walking into your own tomb. And that you had died a very long time ago.

Claudia paused in the corridor to touch a carved limestone figure, a muscular male haunch. She ran her fingers along its solid sinews. Claudia liked male bodies. That was no secret. Nor should it be. Romans prided themselves on living at full throttle.

Over a decade and half ago, Claudia had attended the Imperial Military Institute in the same class as her brother Romulus and the young American woman Calli Carmel. Claudia had never intended a military career. Claudia was there for the men. Officially Claudia had withdrawn to pursue other interests. Actually she was sacked for a plethora

of disciplinary infractions. She had only been admitted to
the Institute out of deference to Caesar Magnus. Magnus,
who never expected anyone but himself to put up with
Claudia, was not upset or surprised by her sacking.

Claudia was only ever prepared for a career as imperial
brat. At the Institute, all the attention given to Calli's beauty
set Claudia to fury. Claudia made a point to sleep with anyone Calli did. Calli was selective, so she was pitiably easy to
keep up with on that score. The looks were more difficult.
Claudia, accustomed to being the center of all attention,
was determined to be the most beautiful woman in the
world, something Calli never worked at. Calli just had
beauty. At one point Claudia was physically identical to
Calli, and still everyone could tell them apart. They said
Calli was the prettier one.

Calli claimed looks were not that important.

"Then you shan't mind if I take a razor blade to your
face," Claudia said.

"I should mind that a lot," Calli had replied.

Claudia made her entrance at Imperial Intelligence
briskly, as if she had only a few moments to spare for the
curiosi.

Dour agents took her to a secure area, and played a recording for her.

It was a bad amateur work. Audio and video only. Flat.
No enhancements. Obviously done in secret by a nonpro-
fessional.

It opened to the sound of pounding, as of fists on a
closed door, and the visual of a figure recognizable as Julius
Urbicus scurrying toward the camera. You saw his fingers,
huge in the frame, adjusting the position of the tiny camera.
Then he drew back.

Julius Urbicus' seamed face frowned into the camera. He
threw a piece of gauze over it, very thin, something that
would hide the camera from view without opaquing the recording. The image softened, became slightly fuzzy.

A woman's sharp shout sounded from off camera, "Urbicus! Open up, you pervert!"

Julius Urbicus left the frame. He returned with a woman
following him. He sat at the edge of the frame, and anx-

iously watched the woman approach. His posture tensed as if he were mentally guiding the woman to sit in a chair positioned at center focus of the camera.

She sat. And her face came into the picture.

One of the many incarnations of Claudia Julia. Long chestnut hair. Brown almond eyes. Long gown with a loosely draped bodice. Evening gloves up over her elbows. "Here." Claudia threw a static photograph at Urbicus. "I brought you a present. Bet you don't have this view of her."

Urbicus bent over the photo. He did not present it toward the hidden recorder. A groan found its way out of him, of some extreme emotion. Could have been fear, anguish, lust. It was impossible to tell.

Claudia produced a fistful of cartridges from her glittering handbag. They were ink cartridges for antique style pens.

"Load *all* the pens so you don't need to worry about getting them mixed up," she instructed. "I promise it will be a fast death. *Hers* won't be if you fail."

Urbicus could not tear himself away from the photograph.

Claudia held out the cartridges in her gloved fist. "Her fate is in your hands."

Urbicus received the cartridges into trembling hands. One of them would kill Caesar. And Julius Urbicus would die shortly after.

He begged, abject, "Promise you won't hurt her."

She flashed a brief eye roll. "Oh, I *swear*."

She rose, bending forward to flash her breasts at him. Might have been a cow flashing her udder for his reaction. She let herself out.

When she was thoroughly gone, Julius Urbicus tottered to the camera. The image became nothing but his palm reaching toward it. The picture went black.

No message had accompanied the delivery of the recording to Imperial Intelligence.

How would one compose a cover message like that? Julius Urbicus was barely holding himself together, and he was about to murder Caesar. How would he say he was killing Caesar because of a girl? Betraying his country, himself, his friend, for her? What could he say: If you are seeing this recording, Lilia is dead and I have killed Caesar for nothing. You are seeing this because I, the lying treacherous assassin pedophile, have been betrayed.

No, there could not have been a message to go with this record.

Claudia looked to the Intelligence officers who were looking at her, waiting.

She waited. They waited.

Then finally, irritated, Claudia said, "Why do you show this little horror show to me?"

They were not expecting her to say that. Behind their stony masks they were reeling. They waited for something more.

And Claudia waited back.

They stayed silent.

She became agitated. "Why am I here?" She stood up, pointed toward the door as if to dispatch them. *"Go get her!"*

An agent, confounded, explained to her, "Claudia, you are under arrest."

She gave a shrill little laugh at something so very not funny. "Who do you think that is, you *coiens asine* who pass for Intelligence!"

They were not seeing what she was seeing.

One prompted politely, *"Domna?"*

Claudia said, as if the picture ought to be clear even to the blind and the dead, "That is the American spy, Calli Carmel!"

19

"**I**T LOOKS LIKE YOU."

Claudia coughed, drew her chin inward, affronted. "She can only try!"

The *curiosi* looked from the image in the recording to Claudia. It was not an exact match, but Claudia was a work of art and the work was constantly in progress.

Claudia had, during her days at the Imperial Military Institute, looked nearly identical to Calli Carmel.

To hear Claudia tell it, it was Calli who mimicked Claudia in those days, not the other way around, and Claudia changed her own looks because Calli's mimicry struck her as too weird.

"Just why do you suppose Calli cut all her hair off and changed her face again!" Claudia challenged the stunned Intelligence agents. "Bit of a mutt face now, isn't she?"

One of the *agentes* told her, "Captain Carmel's face was recently burned in an attack outside Fort Eisenhower."

"Of course it was," Claudia said, patronizing, nodding in nostril-deep sarcasm. "The same attack that made Gaius Americanus change his face and pretend to be dead. Where is the intelligence that is supposed to be down here? *There was no attack on Gaius Americanus and Calli Carmel!* It was a story made up by the American CIA! So there you have it—the Americans and their spy Calli Carmel killed my father. And Gaius Americanus was in on it!" She stood up to go. *"Do something!"*

Merrimack's hospital was filled past capacity with casualties from the Northwestern military bases. The ship's Marine companies were on the ground assisting with disaster relief.

Cain Salvador strapped a wounded man onto a backboard for evac to *Merrimack*'s hospital. He brushed dirty sweat off the top of his lip with the dust-covered back of his wrist. Gave himself a mud mustache.

"I need to quickly go to my office," the man protested weakly, scarcely able to move. "I was supposed to soon be in a meeting."

"Take it easy, sir," said Cain. "I'm sure your meeting was canceled."

"Where am I to now be taken?"

"*Merrimack*, sir. Just relax."

The man did seem to relax.

"I've got this one," said Cole Darby, taking over for Cain. Darb strapped the man down tight and hailed *Merrimack*. He asked for the Intelligence officer instead of the hospital.

"Colonel Z? This is Flight Sergeant Cole Darby down on the planet. I think I have a Roman here."

The man, immobile on the backboard, rolled his now enormous eyes toward Darb. Darb crouched next to the man, gave him a reassuring pat on the restraints as he spoke into his com, "What do you want me to do with him?"

Wolfhound sat on a rubble hillock and pumped out drinking water as fast as she could make it.

"I feel like a milk cow," said Captain Carmel standing in the shade of her beached ship as John Farragut hiked up the rise, stepping over the hoses running out from *Wolfhound*.

The water synthesizing system on board the wolfhunter class ship was overkill for servicing a single midsized ship. It had been designed for a situation just like this.

Actually the wolfhunter was designed to fight her way

into a site under siege and provide drinking water to the population.

Captain Farragut joined Captain Carmel in the shade. They surveyed the scene around the waterfront. Saw nothing not wrecked, broken open, upended. Lost count of the sources of belching black smoke. *Merrimack*'s dogs were down here, searching the collapsed buildings for trapped survivors.

The sky up high was merciless blue.

Farragut spoke in a very odd voice, not quite believing what he was telling her, "Calli, you're wanted for the assassination of Caesar Magnus. They have a cross ready at the base of the Capitoline for your execution."

Calli absorbed this news, then said, "I don't rate a sword?"

Roman *honestiores* had to be executed by the sword.

"Don't be flippant, Cal."

She nodded. "I've been warned about that. Can't seem to help myself." The news was so utterly absurd. She asked, "I killed Magnus?"

John Farragut nodded. "You and your lover, Gaius."

"I begin to like this story."

"Cal."

"You know I can't speak a man's name without rumors flying."

"According to rumor, you and Gaius have been flying."

"Even now that I've lost my looks?" She ruffled all her cowlicks. Concrete dust fell to her shoulders.

The Roman public was ferociously in love with the news story. They loved Calli's new face—especially the way the Roman media retouched the shadows to make her look haggish. They relished the sight of a proud American beauty brought low. It validated their belief that the Americans had been behind Caesar's assassination. They knew it all along.

"Sampson Reed is suggesting they hold a trial in The Hague," said Farragut. "Get it cleared in the international arena."

"I am not going to kangaroo court."

"I don't think The Hague hops."

"I am not going to court," said Calli. "It'd be a waste of time and prove nothing. Rome will say America bought off The Hague when I'm exonerated. If Rome can't already see this is a pile of squid muffins, no trial will make it more obvious. They know the United States had no motive to kill Magnus. Magnus surrendered to us and submitted to the Subjugation. We *liked* Magnus. We had nothing to gain by his death."

"But you did."

"I did?"

Farragut pulled up a headline posted in the American media directly after Magnus' assassination: EMPRESS CALLI.

She had acquired that nickname because beautiful Calli had attended the event (which was not meant to be an assassination) on the arm of Romulus.

"So why am I not empress?"

"Romulus turned you down, you presumptuous slut. Their words."

"They called me a slut?"

"A presumptuous slut."

"Oh, when a Roman calls you a slut, you've gotta be the whore of Babylon. Can someone explain to Reed this is an obvious farce?"

"Reed likes the idea of international cooperation. Says innocence can breathe in the open air."

"My Commander in Chief is a dwit. Does he realize that the person who can testify to my whereabouts on Palatine before the assassination was *Romulus?* Honest to God, John, if I could get a hold of Augustus I'd tell him to pick me up right now."

"That would look sublime."

"It is sublime! In that corner I've got a sociopath hailed as Caesar and in *my* corner I've got a Commander in Chief with the IQ of birdseed."

A miniature shepherd dog, head hanging, tongue hanging, coat gray with dust, padded up to the captains and flopped down on the tops of Farragut's boots, panting. Farragut looked to Calli. "Know where I can get some water?"

*　　*　　*

"Darb's getting a bong!" Flight Leader Ranza Espinoza announced. Her bright grin showed the gap between her front teeth.

"No bullsh?" The more massive Cain bumped into Darb with his shoulder, making him stagger. "What for?"

"Our Darb bagged a Roman spy trying to sneak on board *Merrimack* as a med-evac case," said Ranza. "So he's getting a cute little piece of hardware to hang on his dress jacket."

Kerry Blue crouched on a cinder block to stretch her back muscles. She smiled up. "How'd you manage that, Darb?"

"The guy was splitting infinitives."

"Everyone does that," said Carly, surprised she remembered what an infinitive was.

"I don't even know what that means," said Cain.

"It's something impossible to do in Latin," said Darb. "Or Spanish. It used to be improper English to split 'em but that rule got flushed because the only reason it was ever improper to split an infinitive in English was because you *can't* do it in Latin. Well, English isn't Latin and this isn't the Roman Empire, so everyone splits infinitives now. Well, this guy, to absolutely prove that he was *not* a native Latin speaker, used an infinitive in every sentence so he could proceed to then split the hell out of every one no matter how bad he had to completely mangle the language to always do it."

"Darb, I'm glad you understood what you just said."

"You can kiss my bong, Dak."

"That is not Callista."

Numa Pompeii watched the recording in the cheerless underground chamber of Imperial Intelligence Headquarters. Twice.

It was not just the features and the voice, which anyone could alter, but the way the woman moved, the nuances of her voice, the words she chose. There was nothing of Calli Carmel in that woman who pushed poison ink cartridges at Julius Urbicus.

Numa Pompeii saw that Imperial Intelligence already

knew that. They were just fishing for corroboration of Claudia's story where they thought they could get it.

Imperial Intelligence had closed ranks around their leader. The woman in the video *must* not be Claudia. That was the fact. Now they needed to find or create proof.

One of the *agentes* prompted, "Remember this is a disguise, Triumphalis. You need to look through the surface."

"I would know Callista anywhere," said Numa. "And that is not she."

"You don't suppose the recording could have been tampered with?" another suggested.

"Suppose whatever you like," said Numa, who could read a battleground. "I am not an expert in data tampering."

Romulus had his *curiosi* trying to make Numa confirm his sister's wild story, even when it was obvious that the person in the recording was Claudia. It was every inch, every gesture, every word Claudia. It was the soulless soul of Claudia. And it was the quick, cagey, psychotic mind of Claudia to claim it was Calli instead. Just like her brother.

It was Claudia. But Numa was not going to champion the truth when it could get him stabbed in the night.

The *curiosi* did not intimidate Numa Pompeii. But Numa was smart enough to be wary.

He was not trusted, Numa knew that. He was not let in on Caesar's strategy in the war—if Romulus even had a strategy.

The strikes on the Washington coast had been Rome's first substantive hit on the United States in this war. And it brought out all the negative effects of battle on Earth. The United States shared an atmosphere with a lot of neutral nations Rome did not want entering the conflict on the wrong side. Romulus pushed his limit on that one.

Romulus had demanded the U.S. surrender, but that was bluff and posture. If serious, it was unrealistic at best. Romulus hadn't the background in either statesmanship or warfare to be Caesar, and it was beginning to show.

It would catch up with him sooner or later. Numa needed to survive until later.

He told the *curiosi*, "If the recording has been altered, then that could be anyone."

"Calli Carmel?" they pressed.

"If you need it to be."

"Why did the little girl need to die?"

Claudia pouted, vexed. "Why are you asking me?"

"It was a needless death," said Romulus. "And it has turned out unfortunate."

"Who knew the old sod had a sleeper message? I took care of it, did I not? It was an accident anyway."

"Was it?"

"Of course."

A camera shoved its way in front of Calli Carmel's face, her new face streaked with mud, dust, and sweat. Calli was ready to answer questions about her ship's water synthesizing system and the relief effort here in Seattle, but the reporter asked Calli, *inter nos*, if that figure talking to Caesar's assassin in the assassin's secret recording wasn't really Calli after all.

Calli glared into the camera, looking cross. "Yes, that was I. I was in Rome as guest of Romulus. I was on his arm at his father's assassination. Romulus had charge of my comings and goings, and you know I could not have got my face changed or gone to Urbicus' house without Romulus providing access. I delivered the poison pens to Urbicus to force him to kill Magnus. Romulus promised I would be empress if I helped him. But he ballasted me after he was done with me. I destroyed my looks in a fit of self-hatred." She presented her new face to the cameras. "I have found Jesus now. I forgive Romulus for using me. But for his arranging his father's murder, that is between Romulus and our Lord Jesus Christ."

The recording went straight to broadcast through the civilized part of the galaxy.

The entire crew of *Merrimack* gawked at the image of their former XO confessing to Magnus' assassination.

It was playing on the monitors of the command deck.

"She didn't say that!" Hamster cried, on the verge of laughter.

"Oh, I bet she did." Farragut said, hiding an amazed smile behind his hand, his eyebrows lifted so high they were stuck somewhere in the overhead.

He had never heard a higher, more suspiciously scented pile of moon cheese in his life. Yet the media were picking it over as if it were real news.

Calli had already learned that the best way to fight lies was not always with the truth. No matter what she said in answer to that question, no one was ready to believe her. So she fed them a bigger, fatter, juicier, sizzling lie. Let the public choose between Romulus' sister forcing the assassin's hand or Romulus' lover doing it with help from Romulus. Romulus came out smelling either way.

Gypsy shook her head at the monitors. Murmured, "Oh, Cal, honey, you spent too much time in Rome."

Doctor Weng and Doctor Sidowski had bad news for Captain Farragut.

"Toto Two has been activated," said Weng.

"Toto . . . ?" Farragut started, hadn't located the brain cell that housed the meaning of that name yet.

"Two," said Ski.

"Telecore!" Farragut had it now. "The decoys."

Merrimack had left two sets of decoys behind in the Deep End to draw the gorgons of Telecore away from human settlements.

"The gorgons acquired escape velocity—" said Weng.

"—and FTL capability," said Ski.

"So fast!" It had taken the new Hive only months to discover they could survive in vacuum and attain faster than light speed travel. Farragut was dismayed. He had hoped for more time—something measured in decades.

"Like ducks to water," said Weng.

"Woke up Toto Two," said Ski.

"Are the gorgons at least following the bait?"

"Yes, sir."

That was a break. "Are they gaining on Toto Two?"

"Yes, sir," said Weng.

"At the proper speed, sir," said Ski.

"Should give us more time, sir." Weng.

"We hope, sir." Ski.

"Thank you, gentlemen."

"Captain?"

"Yes, Doctor Sidowski?"

Ski, with a self-conscious glance down at his own shuffling feet: "Is Captain Carmel seeing anyone?"

The dialogs. VI.

JMdeC: I see patterns. I can tell you a snowflake under normal circumstances will have six symmetrical arms. I can tell you a tiger will have stripes. Can you do better than that?

A: I can do better if you tell me the temperature and the species of the tiger. I can do even better if you tell me the air pressure and show me all the tiger's ancestors.

JMdeC: So chaos comes into consideration with how fine you split the hair.

A: All depends on how fine you need the hair.

JMdeC: If you know all the variables, you can predict the result.

A: Yes.

JMdeC: Of course my *if* statement there is clearly an impossibility so even a patterner can forget about one hundred percent accurate predictions.

A: [nodding] Only uncertainty is certain.

20

BEFORE DAWN IN ROMA NOVA on the planet Palatine the city was cloaked in deep gray. The stars were fading. The companion star of the Wolf was still visible, bright as a big planet, twinkling. Two of the planet's six insignificant moons hung low over the western hills.

The air scarcely stirred. From the Palace on the Capitoline Hill the river appeared as a black glassy ribbon winding underneath the graceful arches of the viaducts between the Forum and the Coliseum. Birds sounded a few notes from the tiled rooftops. Silhouettes of the Kwindaqqin spires soared into the soft darkness, their gaudy colors yet to appear.

Caesar had not slept. Dressed in black, he walked the loggia like a brooding Hamlet.

For over a week Romulus had been fighting the ghost of the assassin. Romulus told his people that the assassin's recording was a CIA fiction. The woman wasn't Calli. Neither was it Claudia. It was a fabrication. The scene never happened.

Mist hung over the river.

Sirens woke up in an eerie wail.

Caesar met his guards bursting into his chamber, asked, gesturing at the noise, "Is that real?"

The first guardsman gave a breathless nod. "Yes, Caesar. U.S. space fleet. Invasion strength. One hour out."

A second guard added, "They're approaching from the galactic southeast, under heavy distortion."

Romulus turned to look through the archway at the lightening sky as if there would be something to see.

On the ground, across the cityscape, lights appeared in many windows.

"I thought the Yanks were busy with their earthquakes," said Caesar.

"The American military role in the rescue effort was somewhat overstated."

"Somewhat?" said Romulus. Glanced toward the sky. "Invasion strength?"

All week long the American media had been showing images of their space battleships in orbit around Earth, their flags at half staff for President Johnson's funeral— images of ships which must have left the Solar system a week ago because they were almost *here*.

"What things do you wish moved to your bunker, Caesar?" an attendant asked.

Romulus started to answer. Froze.

They're coming for me.

This full-scale U.S. invasion was revenge for their President Johnson.

Possibly they knew the location of Caesar's bunker.

"I want to be with my people," Romulus declared suddenly, and he went down into the mass City shelter with the civilians.

The first wave appeared, winking into real space as the ships dropped down from FTL speed. Between the false plots and the double appearances, the American ships numbered somewhere between a thousand and eight thousand.

The fleet made a horrific image.

"I'm glad we're the invaders," said Ian Markham at Tactical. "I wouldn't want to see us coming."

Still the fleet was not an overwhelming force on a planetary scale. The terror would be in the wondering if the Americans had come to drop nukes.

Tactical scanned for antimatter in the planetary system

in case Rome had salted the approach. Ian Markham pronounced the path clear.

Roman sentinels orbiting Palatine opened fiery eyes. Missiles streaked out to meet the invaders.

U.S. beam fire detonated the missiles before they could reach their targets. The fleet advanced through clouds of debris.

Ships of the Roman home guard turned out to form a feeble blockade. It was nearly impossible to block ships in space. All the defenders were outflanked, leaving the Roman ships to chase the Americans toward the planet.

The fleet's biggest ships descended, the ones that did not care what hit them. *Merrimack*, *Monitor*. The space battleships were nearly invincible when locked inside a seamless distortion field.

Roman destroyers opened fire on *Merrimack* and *Monitor*, while other Americans ships fired on the destroyers.

The big ships ignored them. Descending.

Inside the atmosphere, the barrage from space ceased.

Roman beam fire could too easily glance off an American distortion field and stab into a civilian population. Exploding warheads could radiate the atmosphere. And a successful shot on any one of *Merrimack* and *Monitor*'s combined twelve engines would unleash an apocalyptic amount of antimatter into the air.

The invaders, unconcerned with littering the landscape, lobbed shots on enemy spaceports below them. Nothing penetrated a Roman base's stout energy dome, but the fire kept anything inside there locked in.

Merrimack proceeded to a northern continent. The mammoth spearhead shape descended over thinly populated ground, sending bulky pad-footed animals running. Flying snakes sprang and glided away in glittery flocks. The battleship sank down gently over an open field, so low the branching antler weed scratched at the force field round *Merrimack*'s bottom sail.

"Set the roaches free," Commander Gypsy Dent ordered.

Systems created a breach in the ship's lower force field. Container hatches opened to drop thousands of small mechs—reconnaissance robots—that skittered through the alien weeds toward a Roman spaceport. The mechs were small and moved at a pace which made them indistinguishable from resident insectoid life, and would allow them to penetrate the same kind of shields that allowed personnel to walk through. The official designation was Automated Recon Mech, ARM, and they looked more like beetles, but no one loved them and they were difficult to crush, so they were better known as roaches.

As *Merrimack* rose, robotic air-to-air gunships launched from the spaceport on the horizon. Waiting for that, *Merrimack* punched the base through its launch windows with beam fire. Black pillars of smoke spouted from the dome.

Merrimack moved away from the drop site, her scanners looking back to see if anything else came out to stomp on their roaches, which had already dispersed themselves over ten acres.

"Got away with that one," Cole Darby remarked, waiting in the crowded Lander for the Marines' turn.

"The first one is free," said Ranza.

The roaches had been a trial balloon, testing the resistance to objects on the ground. Any reconnaissance the ARMs gathered would be extra.

"Coulda sent us down on that drop," said Cain, wistful.

"You thought this was a cruise ship, sweet baby?" said Darb.

Merrimack brushed down again, a thousand miles away from the first drop site. Aircraft met her approach this time. *Merrimack* fired small projectiles at them. The unmanned Roman airplanes went down easily, plowing up the Roman ground.

"Drop horses," Gypsy Dent ordered.

Merrimack dropped vehicles, small two- or three-man hovercraft. Silver Horses they were called, after some old time cowboy hero who would whistle and his horse would come. The Silver Horses scattered as *Merrimack* rose into the air.

More Roman aircraft came over the horizon. Left smoking trails going down.

Still nothing was shooting down at *Mack* from orbit.

"It's true," Ian Markham remarked, looking up from his

tactical readouts to see the blue sky through a clearport. "Rome is scant on the inward pointing weapons."

And it made sense. Palatine was one nation. Ground to ground shots were not in the Romans' home game playbook. They hadn't had home game since their war of independence a century and a half ago.

And the orbital platforms which Rome built for making space-to-ground assaults were all in Earth's Solar system right now.

"Enemy aircraft sighted."

"Erase the birds," said Gypsy. "Fire at will."

When the air was clear again of intact Roman craft, *Merrimack* moved to another drop zone a scant thirty miles from the drop site of the Silver Horses. The space battleship bent low to ground. Her lower sail divided a field of feathery red grasses as tall as trees.

"Drop the dogs," said Gypsy.

This time *Merrimack* put troops on the ground—seven hundred and twenty Fleet Marines—in between the clumps of soaring red plumes. Roaches skittered out at their feet in all directions.

"Hang onto your goolies, boys," said Cain, moving out.

"Kerry Blue, you can hang onto mine."

"Shut up, Dak."

Ranza drew her weapon at the soft hiss of something coming in fast through the red plumage.

Almost shot her Silver Horse.

Merrimack rose away, moved across the continent, clearing the sky of everything in it. She touched sail to drop roaches on a communications tower.

Moved off to a military installation where Roman Legions were stationed. Robot aircraft rose in black clouds around the base. Came down in black hailstorms.

A ring of missile emplacements guarded the site outside the installation's force field perimenter, so the missile launchers could fire without breaching the base's shield. *Merrimack* punched out all the outboard missile launchers, then pounded at the base itself with a few experimental energy blasts. The base was well shielded even at ground level, and nothing got inside.

Tactical took a sounding of the surrounding ground. Got the plot of the underground cargo tunnels by which equipment was transported into the base. *Merrimack* dropped bombs into the ground over the top of the tunnels until several sections caved in.

Taking a cue from the Roman attackers at Washington, *Merrimack* shot beams underneath the Roman installation to loosen the ground. Shook the shielded emplacement like a snow globe. Didn't think the LEN would be objecting this time.

Merrimack moved on to a Roman training camp. Found it not shielded and not currently occupied. *Merrimack* left it a crater.

Tactical back-traced the underground tunnels to a central transfer station. Drilled a hole with beam fire to where several tunnels converged. Opened up with the hydrogen hose down the hole.

The space battleship continued her cross continent rampage, hitting every power plant she saw, punched solar collectors and dams. Shot torpedoes into rivers to change their courses. Roared out to sea to mow down wind turbines.

"We have someone's attention, Captain."

"About time." Captain Farragut took the alert in stride. "How many?"

"It's *Gladiator*."

"That's enough. Fire on *Gladiator*. Continuous fire. And take us back to the party on the roof."

Merrimack fired up at *Gladiator*. The beams glanced off *Gladiator*'s force field in all directions. That was to remind Numa that he did not want to get into a brawl down here.

And Farrgut did not want Numa sniffing around for *Merrimack*'s dogs.

"Keep firing," said Farragut. "I don't want a nanosecond to go by that something's not hitting *Gladiator*."

"Aye, sir. With respect, sir, what can he do?"

"He can smother us."

Gypsy clarified, "He could hook us in his force field."

"But then if we die, he dies," said Targeting.

"If that's what Caesar told him to do, that's what he'll do — and Romulus will consider it a better-than-even trade."

Merrimack ascended into the darkness of space.

"*Gladiator* is moving out of range," Targeting reported. "Far side of the planet, still in atmo."

"Hail *Monitor*," Farragut ordered the com tech. And when Mr. Hicks had *Monitor* on the com, Farragut took up the caller: "Martin, you still down there?"

"That I am, John," Captain Martin Washington of the *Monitor* replied.

"Numa's headed your way. I think he means to snuff you in a suicide cocoon."

"Sounds uncomfortable. Are you on the roof?"

"Yes, sir."

"Coming up. Thanks for the heads."

The battle in the vacuum was largely around Palatine's main power stations. No world ever liked to keep antimatter in atmosphere. The matter-antimatter power plants in orbit fed energy to the planet surface by beam.

Unlike the power plants orbiting Earth, none of the power plants here served neutral nations. Many American energy companies served other countries, and many American energy companies were partly or wholly owned by neutral nations. Rome had not been able to turn out the lights in America. Palatine's power stations were all fair game.

The energy stations were all well shielded, but the attacking ships didn't need to destroy them. They need only punt them out of orbit to render them useless.

Rio Grande was embroiled in a slug fest with *Trajan*, who was putting up a fanatical defense of a power plant. *Monitor*, rising out of the atmosphere, added a punch at *Trajan* with a planet killer.

Trajan choked. Her force field wavered, blinked out.

Rio took the power plant for a ride.

Admiral Burk directed another ship, the cruiser *Edmonton*, which hadn't yet deployed its Marines, to board *Trajan*.

Ian Markham at Tactical reported: "Something odd happening out there."

"Something more specific, please," said Commander Gypsy Dent, irritated.

"There's a plot out there drawing a lot of Roman fire, and it's not one of ours."

"Augustus," said Farragut just before Tactical cried, "It's a Striker!"

"Whose side is he on?" said Gypsy.

"Not ours," said Captain Farragut.

The Striker was a slippery target, evading or destroying any shot directed toward it, U.S. or Roman.

A beam shot from the Striker crippled the U.S. cruiser *Guadalajara*.

Roman ships converged to bang away at the wounded ship.

"Fire at the jackals!" Farragut ordered.

But the Roman ships opened the cruiser up to vacuum.

Monitor slung a hook out to surround *Guadalajara*, stretching her own force field fearfully thin, and hurtled up to FTL, vanishing from the battlefield.

No one tried to pursue.

Chief Engineer Kit Kittering, watching the Striker on the monitors, observed out loud, "That old Striker doesn't have any solid ordnance." Just as the Striker sent a cluster of pencil missiles up the gunports of the U.S. Landing Command Ship *Chimney Rock*.

"Yes, he does."

Chimney Rock's force field flickered out, leaving her naked in space. A single beam sliced her in two. Ships from both sides moved in to save/destroy what was left.

When Augustus had taken the old Striker from *Merrimack* months ago, its magazines were empty. Augustus had found someplace to reload since then.

The Striker started down into the atmosphere. Farragut immediately barked, "Target the Striker!"

He could not let Augustus down there to pick off his ground troops.

"Lost him," said Tactical.

"How can you lose him in the atmosphere?" Gypsy's voice came out brittle, as if about to dismiss Markham from the deck.

Targeting came to Tactical's rescue, "Striker has submerged into the ocean off the coast of Roma Nova. We're just not very good underwater, sir."

Gypsy looked to Captain Farragut, astonished. As if only

John Farragut could know what Augustus was doing under the sea.

Farragut shook his head. "We are not following that cobra into its hole."

"We should find him and hit him while he's underwater," said Kit. "That Striker's not built for undersea ops."

"Neither are our weapons," said Farragut, but not to give up, he ordered, "Send down the V-jocks. Let them take their shot."

The remote fighter craft launched. The V-jock named Wraith, safe in his compartment within *Merrimack*, declared that his remotes would win the war.

A sudden blast like a small nova filled the viewports. A concussion rocked the ship. Someone's antimatter had escaped containment. "Jesus Christmas!"

And another nova immediately after the first.

"Ours?" Farragut demanded.

Tactical responded, "No and yes. *Trajan* did not want to be boarded."

"Norris," Farragut whispered like a prayer. The other nova would have been *Edmonton*. Captain Norris of the *Edmonton* had been charged with taking *Trajan*.

Mr. Hicks on the com reported that *Monitor* had returned to the battle zone. *Monitor* had with her the survivors from *Guadalajara*. There were very few. Captain Washington communicated *Guadalajara*'s FTL vector to other ships in the fleet. Just in case *Monitor* did not survive the battle, someone else would know where to collect the dead later. The wreck of the *Guadalajara* would not just vanish into history like the Roman *Sulla*.

Wraith sent his report from the remote control chamber. The remotes had got as far as the water. They submerged where the Striker had gone in, then lost contact. Wraith could not even say what hit them.

Merrimack's force field lit up with a boom and shudder.

"*Shit!*" That might have been anyone.

"Striker," said Tactical. Had not seen him coming. "On the Sixes."

"The number of the beast," said Systems.

The Helm was jinking. Another shot landed. The distortion field dispelled most of the shock. The deck still started into a roll, abruptly stopped and did not settle back as the inertial system stabilized.

"He's after *Merrimack* now!" said Tactical.

Gypsy looked to Farragut, "Does this mean Romulus is dead?"

Farragut shook his head, couldn't tell. He was taking a message from Admiral Burk: "The Striker is your responsibility, *Merrimack*. Take it out."

Farragut heard the subtext in the admiral's voice: *Don't let the patterner go this time*.

Helm was steering a wild random course. And, knowing that his own randomness had a pattern to it, switched hands.

Tactical advised, "I'm counting at least six Roman ships firing on the Striker."

"Is the Striker returning fire?"

"No, sir. We're his only target."

The Helm had run out of hands, so Farragut took a turn driving the boat in a weird scribble path as he spoke, "The only certain shot we have will be up the Striker's barrel. We need to jam a shot up his nose. Here, take this."

He gave the helm to Kit. She bobbled and wobbled. "You're going to jam up a patterner?"

Gypsy took a hand at the helm. Graceful lines with sudden turns. "You know he's going to do the same thing—jam something up one of our barrels. And Augustus has actually *done it before*."

"I remember," Farragut assured her. "It's not his Striker. It's sixty years old and built for someone else. Systems, clam us up!"

The ship's gun barrels reeled in. Klaus Nordsen at Systems took the ship's force field to adamant.

Merrimack was almost safe, but quite useless in this mode.

Roman ships swarmed around the Striker like sharks to blood in the water.

Captain Farragut picked up the caller, told the com tech, "Put me on the old Attack Group code."

"Aye, sir. You're set to resonate, sir."

Farragut opened the com and spoke: "Augustus. Looks

like a one-sided friendship out there." He did not identify himself. Did not need to. "Why do your friends want you that dead?"

The familiar laconic voice on the com returned: "There's money in it."

Romulus had put a bounty on the patterner's head.

In space there is no up and down, but the Striker's orientation in space was the same as *Mack*'s, as if the two were standing on the same floor facing each other.

With the com on mute, Farragut spoke aside to Gypsy, "Get a line up his cannon barrel. When you've got it, make a window and take him out. Make it happen." And on the com, Farragut started up a chat, "Augustus, you're fighting for an evil government that wants you dead. Do you see anything wrong with that?"

"Got a line up my barrel yet?"

Farragut's startled inhalation through his nose was probably audible over the com. Augustus knew what Farragut was doing.

"You couldn't dissemble your way to a surprise birthday party, John Farragut."

The Striker suddenly jinked wildly, and darted away from the planet.

"Stay with him!" Farragut ordered.

The Striker led *Merrimack* on a chase that took them around Palatine's outermost moon. It was a small moon that could sit inside the Gulf of Mexico. Sunlight reflected bright off its face.

Merrimack circled once around. "Where is he?"

"He's on the far side," said Tactical. "Mirroring us. Maintaining distance."

They circled. *Merrimack* came round to the dark side of the moon. "Stop all progress."

"Stopping, aye."

The ship stood still, waiting for Augustus to come around. He didn't.

"Where is he?"

"Opposite us."

Tactical showed no incoming ordnance curving round the moon. No tags. Augustus was waiting too.

"Ready all torpedoes, ready all forward beams, and stand by to open our field and fire everything we've got."

"Torpedoes ready, aye. Beam cannon ready, aye. Standing by, aye."

The patterner had already destroyed a U.S. cruiser and a U.S. command craft and a hail of Roman missiles. Patterners did not miss.

"Stand by to clear the moon. At my command, take the *Mack* straight up, open the gunports and hit him straight on."

Gypsy would not question orders. She arranged all stations to readiness for everything to happen at the captain's single command.

"Ready, aye. Standing by, aye."

Gypsy stood aside, hands clasped behind her back, at ease.

John Farragut was a straight shooter.

Augustus knew that.

Gypsy could only obey. Mentally she said good-bye to her husband. Her sons. She and the proud ship were about to die in this showdown.

Captain John Farragut and Augustus out in the street, guns ready, waiting for one to say *Draw*.

"Fire."

PART THREE

The Janus Gate

21

BRIGHTNESS FILLED ALL PORTS, overloaded all the monitors, bright as if plunging into the sun, with a thunderclap and roar, shudder, and crackling hiss.

Saw it. Heard it. Which meant, *We're still here!*

A shout from Targeting: *"Got him!"*

Specialists jumped to their feet at their stations. *"Yeah!"*

Brightness dying away, the main monitor showed the Striker, spinning in space, its force field flickering.

Commander Gypsy Dent shouted orders over the noise. "Targeting! Tag the Striker!"

Dead. Augustus had to be dead. But the U.S. could not let the Striker or the contents of Augustus' data bank fall into Roman hands.

"Fire Control! Stand by to fire torpedo on the Striker!"

Gladiator's great hulk moved in between *Merrimack* and the Striker.

Targeting: "Tags—No good! I—I've tagged *Gladiator*."

"Fire!" said Gypsy, not to leave money on the table. "Fire on *Gladiator*! Targeting. Get a tag on that Striker!"

Lights of *Merrimack*'s torpedo detonations flared against *Gladiator* to no effect other than the lights.

Targeting reported, "I have tags on *Gladiator* again. *Gladiator* has the Striker inside a hook."

The Romans wanted Augustus' machine memory. Gypsy would not give it to them.

"Fire on *Gladiator*. Continuous fire."

From somewhere in the melee around the planet a Roman was spitting out killer bots like hornets from a nest, and they were swarming here to the outer moon. *Merrimack* threw off a wall of energy to detonate a mass of them short of the ship.

"Targeting. Get a firing solution on the thinnest part of *Gladiator*'s hook."

"Targeting, aye. Solution acquired, aye."

"Fire Control. Fire all beams."

"Firing, aye."

The tendril of energy that connected *Gladiator* to the captive Striker lost integrity.

"Hook the Striker!"

But too quickly, a flight of Roman fighters had swarmed in, surrounded the Striker in a tight box formation, and locked their force fields together into a solid shell. The tortoise was an old Roman tactic.

Captain Farragut was peripherally aware of the rest of the battle around the planet, of a fireball in Palatine's atmosphere. Someone had slid into the planet's gravity well. Romans were responding. It was their planet. They could not let any ship's antimatter containment fail in their atmosphere.

Farragut said, "I want an ID on that ship. Friend or foe?"

A Roman salvage craft was rising from the ground to meet the falling wreck.

"Foe," said Tactical. "Roman."

Captain Farragut had Mr. Hicks open a tight beam communication link with Captain Dallas McDaniels of *Rio Grande*. "Need a favor, compadre."

"Name it, John, old son."

"Hook the tortoise. Keep a drag on it. I don't want the lupes escaping to FTL with the Striker."

Immediately an energy hook shot out from *Rio Grande* and lassoed the Roman tortoise formation. It was an energy loop instead of the sort of hook that takes the target object within the ship's force field. Not as secure a hold, but a lot safer in case the target decided to blow itself up.

The tortoise dragged *Rio Grande* like an anchor.

"Done," said Captain McDaniels. "What do you want me to do with this slow tortoise now?"

"Try to angle him away from anyone friendly. Keep a hold on him, until I tell you, then drop him and run for your life."

"John, old son, do you mean to tell me you're about to throw that dead Roman ship down there at me?"

There was an imminent matter/antimatter explosion coming up from the planet Palatine in the body of the crippled Roman ship.

"Yes, sir."

"Send it," said Captain McDaniels.

Captain Farragut looked to Commander Dent. "Got that?"

"Aye, aye, sir." Gypsy quickly issued orders to the various stations to set up the delivery of the ship-bomb to the target Roman tortoise.

The actions and calculations, based on ever shifting input, would be too complex and come in too fast for voice commands to execute the firing sequence. The decision algorithms and resultant action triggers were loaded into the fire control program.

Merrimack moved in close to the planet as the Roman salvage craft seized the falling spaceship and swung it spaceward at better than escape velocity.

The wreck came flying back into vacuum.

Merrimack hit the Roman wreck with a repulsive force to redirect it toward the Striker.

Rio dropped its hold on the Roman tortoise and sprinted away.

The tortoise, abruptly free of Rio's drag, hurtled away in the opposite direction—on an intercept course with the wreck which was going rapidly critical.

The redirection pulse had been enough to shake the last coherence from the antimatter containment system of the ruined craft. Antimatter met matter short of interception with the tortoise. Detonated.

"Miss!" Tactical cried.

"Close enough," said Targeting.

The pure white nova expanded and kept traveling into the assembled ships of the Roman tortoise. The blast shook the box formation of Roman fighters. Their combined force field wavered.

"Fire on the tortoise!" Gypsy ordered, and missiles arrowed into the unstable formation.

The tortoise shell broke apart. The Roman fighter ships staggered, naked to the vacuum. Beams from *Rio Grande* picked them off.

"Lasso Striker!" Farragut ordered. He did not want to bring the Striker inside *Merrimack*'s own protective field in a hook. There was no telling what the tug-of-war over the Striker's carcass had done to its own magnetic containment fields. Farragut would not risk *Merrimack* swallowing an antimatter blast from the Striker.

"Got him!" Engineering reported.

"Oh, hell, Numa's going to sit on us," said Farragut. "Helm, take us somewhere."

The Roman Legion carrier *Horatius* moved in to cut across the hook, but Helm changed course, avoiding the cross.

"Can we go FTL and still hold a lasso hook?" Farragut asked anyone who might have an answer.

"Chances are against it," Kit Kittering replied. "We're more likely to drop the Striker."

"We don't dare reel him in, and Rome's not fixin' to let us keep him," said Farragut. He made the decision he had been avoiding. "Scuttle the Striker."

Gypsy immediately ordered, "Tag the Striker."

"Tagging Striker, aye. Striker tagged, aye."

"Launch torpedo."

"Launching torpedo, aye."

The torpedo screeched out from its tube below decks— detonated.

No pronouncement came from Tactical. Just a gasp.

"Hit?" Gypsy inquired.

"No!" Tactical cried, just now making sense of his readings. "*Gladiator* intercepted the torpedo! He's got a hook on the Striker. A whole hook."

"Hook over hook," Farragut ordered.

Merrimack's energy hook clapped over the top of *Gladiator*'s, like a fist over a fist, and pulled. "Let's arm wrestle."

Merrimack's hook was not solid. The secondary grip kept threatening to slip.

"Oh, for Jesus." Farragut got on the fleet com: "Any ship! Any ship. This is *Merrimack*. *Gladiator* is stretched! *Hit him!*"

Admiral Burk returned on the com, "Not your fleet, Captain Farragut."

Farragut leaned straight-armed over the com. Turned his head, appalled and amazed. Met Gypsy's brown eyes. She spoke low, "Missing Calli, sir?"

He nodded. "Real bad."

If Cal were here, she wouldn't need asking to kick Numa around.

But *Rio* was here. Captain Dallas McDaniels slammed a planet killer up *Gladiator*'s stern.

Which should have done something but didn't. Numa had been braced for the blow.

Beam bursts flashing on *Mack*'s force field were from the Legion carrier *Horatius*.

Gladiator got a firm hold on the Striker, yanked.

"Lost hook!"

Targeting spoke, "Sure hope Augustus has that Striker on self-destruct mode, because there he goes."

The Striker, with whatever was left of Augustus, disappeared inside *Gladiator*'s dark maw.

Admiral Burk sounded the order for the fleet to retreat to FTL.

22

U.S. SPACECRAFT HAD VANISHED from the Lambda Coronae Australis solar system.

The lights were on in the capital city of Roma Nova. The skies were clear, the city untouched.

"Did our Legions crush their ground troops?" Caesar Romulus asked, coming up from the city bunker with a throng of people after him. He wore a crown of bright paper loops on his dark curls. The children of Roma Nova had taken to decorating him down in the shelter.

"There were no enemy ground troops, Caesar," a military adviser informed him.

"No one can win a war without ground troops," said Caesar, incredulous.

"They cannot put troops down without air-space superiority and they don't have it."

"The United States has been denied!" Romulus pronounced to the delighted throng around him. They escorted him from the city bunker to the palace.

Inside the palace, one of Caesar's most devoted attendants appeared distraught. The older man looked up and beheld Romulus as if beholding great Caesar's ghost.

"Caesar!" Atticus cried in shock and relief. "I looked inside your bunker! I feared—" His hands shook in the presence of a miracle. As if Romulus had returned from the dead. The man's knees buckled under him, as he was crushed with relief, in tears and groveling for joy.

Adoration was good, but this was embarrassing and overdone.

Roma Nova had not been hit. This sort of shock at Caesar's survival was a bit theatrical. Romulus pushed Atticus away with his foot. "I'm fine. Get up."

"I saw your bunker—"

"I wasn't there," Caesar said, annoyed. "I wanted to be with my people."

Romulus shed his fawning servant at the door to his informal business office. An Intelligence officer waited there. A more seemly sort of man, this one saluted, fist to chest. "Caesar."

Romulus did not greet him. Couldn't remember his name. "Where is Augustus?" Caesar demanded.

"Dead, Caesar. Inside the Striker."

"Where is the Striker?"

"In our possession."

Romulus inhaled, drinking in the sweet bitterness of the moment. "So then, do you have something for me?"

Romulus had demanded Augustus' head on a platter.

"In quarantine, Caesar. There is a lot of nanoactivity in the Striker. The men are being cautious. I understand they will be making up a plate for you when it's safe."

"Wise." Caesar controlled his impatience. "I thank you."

He turned a control to open the windows.

Romulus' satisfaction was colored by voices of people in the street. They were not calling Romulus. They were calling Numa Pompeii.

Romulus crossed to a tall window, pulled back the scarlet curtain.

Pompeii colors were out in force—bronze and steel—through the streets.

Numa Pompeii was the hero of the hour. Numa Pompeii had defeated the renegade patterner. Numa Pompeii had battled back *Merrimack* and set the U.S. fleet to rout.

"Come with me," Caesar bade the Intelligence officer.

Caesar Romulus found Numa Pompeii waiting in Caesar's audience hall, preening. None of the holoimages were powered up, so the chamber appeared as it truly was, a stately space, its high ceiling held up by pillars, its walls painted with frescoes of serene landscapes, mountains and vineyards. There were no storm clouds. No lightning.

"Pompeii!" Romulus entered at a jaunty strut, not to show the least sign of weakness in front of the massif that was General Numa Pompeii.

The big man's smile looked smug, his salute felt ironic.

Romulus told him, "I suppose you'll be expecting another Triumph for this." And Caesar quickly stepped up to his dais, to get his head above Pompeii's.

Numa Pompeii shrugged a great shoulder. "The people seem to expect it."

"Yes, the people." Those fickle people.

"But I don't," Numa continued.

"How modest of you," said Romulus, wondering if he ought not to demand a DNA check on this person.

"Because the Yanks have not retreated," said Numa. "Not really. They have only gone FTL. They are minutes away."

"You have seen this?"

"Some things you know without seeing. I have seen that half the world is in blackout. There are areas without public water."

"Yet our defenses here held!" Romulus opened his arms to his light-filled palace and the happy people outside who did not seem to be wanting for water.

"Roma Nova held because Roma Nova was not hit," said Numa. "The primary power plant for this continent was destroyed. You are running off your local backups now. All the orbital power stations are off-line. We've lost several spaceports and underground terminals, and all the communications satellites. Foreign tourists and business travelers are clamoring to get out. I will have a full report for you when all the damage assessments are in, Caesar." Numa strode for the doors, turned, and added as if in afterthought, "But Augustus really is dead this time."

Romulus brightened. "You've seen him?"

Numa Pompeii nodded down.

Romulus snapped his fingers at the Intelligence officer. "I want those remains verified."

"It shall be done, Caesar," the Intelligence officer inclined a bow.

Numa Pompeii left the presence at a swagger, threw wide the tall doors of the palace. Let in the chants from outside: "NU MA! NU MA! NU MA!"

After the third servant gawked at Romulus with an expression of utter shock that could have nothing to do with his paper crown, Romulus ventured down to his bunker alone.

The imperial bunker was a large warren of rooms like a small palace, complete with bedchamber, servants' quarters, kitchen, and throne room.

He found the small hole that had been burned through miles of dirt, through the bunker's massive concrete stone and concrete foundation, up through the seat of Caesar's throne and out through the back of the throne at head level.

A shot. A Striker shot. From outside. From under the sea.

Romulus started to shake. He crouched, dizzy, glad he was alone.

Oh, shit. Oh, crap.

A patterner's shot, clean through all the palace defenses into his place of safety, and twice through his throne.

That would have been my head! He shot at my head!

He sat on the oriental carpet. Brought his breathing under control. Recovering.

Stared at the hole.

His breaths came deep with bitter defiance and triumph.

You missed. YOU MISSED!

He allowed himself a laugh. It sounded maniacal even to his ears, but he was alone and he had to laugh. *You're dead, damn you, patterner, and you missed!*

The invasion fleet lurked just beyond the orbit of the Wolf Star's companion star. All the U.S. troop carriers were out here too, waiting their turn.

Signals from a plethora of roaches on the planet surface did not indicate that Rome was aware that the Fleet had set a couple thousand Marines down on Palatine. The guerrilla strikes could go forward.

Ships of neutral nations were rising from Rome's civilian ports. Members of the League of Earth Nations—Italian, Chinese, Brazilian ships—as well as alien ships.

No ships were coming in at the moment, though the Fleet kept watch for the possible approach of Colonial reinforcements. The Roman Empire was vast. But surveillance had yet to indicate that the capital world had called for help from its hundreds of colonies, except for nearby Thaleia. Those ships would never reach Palatine.

Merrimack felt big and empty without her Marines.

The ship smelled like popcorn. The captain and off-duty crew assembled in the maintenance hangar to watch the resonant broadcast from Earth. The news included a Presidential address—or the News from the Continental Shelf, as Sampson Reed was known, in reference to his vast chin. Farragut had ordered popcorn brought in from the galley for his crew.

Reed's speech was largely a justification of the attack on Palatine. He spent a lot of verbiage trying to appease the League of Earth Nations, which apparently was furious that it had no warning of the attack, as many League nations had people doing business on Palatine.

"No warning!" someone in the maintenance hangar yelled at the video. "What does the League think a declaration of war is!"

Someone else: "They wanted us to give them the date of our surprise attack."

"Oh. Got it."

When the President of the LEN came on video, the audience in the space battleship's hangar yelled at the image and threw popcorn through him.

"If you can't stand the bombs, stay off of Palatine!"

The U.S. Secretary of Defense got a cheer when he gave warning to the LEN not to send ships to Palatine because they would be turned away. Those League ships that were already on Palatine could leave, but don't try to come in. The U.S. would not be responsible for whatever happened to any ships that got through.

Then they got to see Caesar on national broadcast. Rome was calling the battle a victory.

Jeers and catcalls drowned out much of Romulus' speech. The ship's dogs were running through the video images picking up all the thrown popcorn.

Farragut studied the image of Romulus.

It looked like Romulus. Moved like Romulus. Spoke like Romulus—not that Farragut could hear much of what he was saying over his crew's enthusiastic abuse. This Romulus did not have the subtle flaws of an automaton. It was not an imposter. It was far too *Romulus*. Alive.

Romulus was alive. And Augustus was dead.

This is not right.

It had taken a while for a sense of reality to catch up with Farragut. *I killed Augustus.*

After the news show, Captain Farragut returned to the command deck. His arrival startled the Officer of the Watch, Lieutenant Hamilton and the rest of the Hamster Watch crew. "Something wrong, Captain?"

Farragut shook his head. He left Hamster in charge of the deck. He dropped into a seat at one of the day crew's stations. Told Hamster, "Not sleeping."

Hamster made a head motion in the direction of the now quiet maintenance hangar. "Sounded like fun over there."

"I think they had a good time," said Farragut, unusually subdued. He fell silent.

I killed Augustus.

Not sure he believed it. Seemed a fact. He knew by now never to trust the report of a death unless you actually see the body. This one felt real.

He asked Hamster, "Did we get any readings on the Striker during the time we had it?"

Hamster checked the records log. "Yes, we did. Looking for something specific?"

"Any life signs?"

"None. When we got hold of it, the Striker was colder than the grave." She looked at Farragut. "We knew that."

"We did," he said. " 'We're just having a hard time believing it."

He had outdrawn a patterner.

That should never ever have happened.

A patterner's brain was augmented to allow it to interface with a data bank and analyze the whole of its contents. The patterner was designed to use the human brain's natural inclination to detect patterns and to order data on a level that machines could not do. Human *insight* was necessary to conceive of the need or to realize the impact of a data set before a machine intelligence could recognize it.

If, while pursuing an inquiry, the human mind encounters an unexpected pattern the human suspects could be critically important, the human mind—some of them—will chase that pattern. A program will carry out its task, then stop. A machine, when asked a question, answers with the facts within its programmed parameters. A human, asked a question, can sense something odd in the apparent responsive facts—something relevant but not conceived of when the question was first asked—and the human will look for more facts.

Telling a machine to look for "something that could be critically important" was just not specific enough criteria for a machine mind to retrieve all relevant data and then order it. Machines overlooked targets of opportunity. Because a programmer had to consciously see the opportunity and program for it before the machine could know opportunity when opportunity presented.

When creating the patterner mind—in a case of scope creep run utterly amok—the engineers gave patterners enhanced physical strength as well and then tailored a spaceborne weapon around them—the Striker.

Augustus had always rejected the term cyborg. He did not fit the definition. He was not a human being enabled to survive an extraterrestrial environment by means of artificial implants.

Augustus' alterations did not enable him to survive. They gave him a very, very short life span.

But Augustus should have killed Romulus before he died. He should not have come up from the planet while Romulus still lived.

Farragut was missing something here. Had to be.

The pattern was all wrong.

23

THE AIR PRESSURE WAS higher, but after your first nose blow you didn't even notice that it was any different from Earth pressure. The alien plants didn't seem to smell much. Darb said that probably meant the native proteins had a different orientation, whatever that meant. Everything felt a little heavy here, including Kerry Blue's own feet. The sun was too white.

Alpha Team got the go-ahead to proceed to their first target. "Rome don't even know we're here," said Ranza, packing her gear onto her Silver Horse. "Move it out."

There had not been enemy troops on Palatine since the war of independence one hundred and fifty years ago. All wars since then had been fought on colonial worlds or in space over stations, convoys, and outposts, never the home worlds.

Still Rome had not let down its guard. The target of the day was nearly impregnable.

Alpha Team had been inserted on the planet surface to hit a manufacturing facility.

The site had not been vulnerable from the air. It was contained in a double energy barrier that excluded everything except slow-moving objects at certain points at ground level.

Inside the energy barriers were the compound's solid polymer walls.

The factory made res chambers—one of three such manufacturing facilities on Palatine.

Security sensors on the rooftop watched for any unauthorized approach. Defensive weapons lay dormant in underground pits.

So far the place was matching up to the information Recon had given the Marines. The little spy bots had done their duty.

"Gotta love roaches."

"Darb?" said Kerry Blue. "You don't never want to say that around me."

The facility was also protected by its isolation. It was set in a prairie, convenient to nothing.

The team put on shaggy, tawny yellow camouflage gear and approached to the perimeter of the facility's surveillance area. They joined in with a vast shambling herd of tawny yellow herbivores that were grazing on the high tawny yellow grasses. The Marines moved in at a grazing gait among the three-toed yaks. The shaggy hooded cloaks disguised their own human shapes. Recon had advised them that detection of a human shape or human motion would trigger the installation's auto-defenses.

Closer to the facility the approach was blocked by a wide barrier of imported tanglethorn, planted round the factory like a corn maze—without any pathways. It was a solid barricade of vicious vegetation. Rip you to ribbons sure as razor wire. Unless you had a cool torch on hand.

Someone had not been thinking when he put up this barrier instead of razor wire. The tanglethorn grew tall and dense enough to obscure the Marines from the roof monitors' view when they got close enough. And the stuff was easy to tunnel through. The cool torch broke down the woven thorny stems into component molecules that then formed a soft layer of litter at the Marines' feet as they hollowed out a man-sized tunnel through the tanglethorn. The operation left enough of the tightly woven branches intact overhead as a ceiling to shield their work.

"Nice of the lupes to plant this shit," Cain whispered.

Recon hadn't mentioned any Roman listening devices. The hiss of their cold torch hadn't attracted any gunfire. They easily reached the factory's outer wall.

Perhaps razor wire would have announced too loudly that there was something of critical importance inside the lonely building.

The installation was self-contained. Power generators and water synthesizers were all inside. The air in there did not need to be pleasant because there were no human workers. But the equipment did need cooling.

There were no dedicated air vents. Air came in with the raw materials deliveries that came in via deep underground tunnels. Sneaking in with a delivery had not been a viable option. Entries were heavily monitored and measured. Even the air intake was metered.

Exits less so.

The Romans could have closed in the waste water system too, but a decision had been made somewhere along the line to draw the line somewhere. There was a point where an excess of caution was truly excessive, not cost effective, and just served pork to some contractor.

The place was protected by spatial barriers, energy barriers, physical barriers, continuous monitoring, and exact measurement of all deliveries. That ought to be enough.

The Marines found the pipe where Recon said it would be. A large pipe that carried out industrial water, heat, and liquefied manufacturing waste. One-way valves kept the water from back flushing, and stopped the odd water rat from swimming up the pipe and getting itself dead in the filtration system.

Dak Shepard widened a pressure relief hole in the top of the pipe with an awl.

Alpha Team had come armed with robotic eels the boffins had ginned up in between games of Moebius chess on *Merrimack*. The eels were thin as minnows. While the rest of the team was already in retreat, Cain Salvador, the fastest runner of the Alphas, fed the eels into the pipe. Had to feed them in one at a time so no sensor could detect a potential clog.

The eels raced up current, as programmed, negotiating

the valves and turns, seeking air, but programmed to avoid their point of launch. You didn't want one of those coming back at you. The eels were programmed to jump out of the water at their first chance.

And to detonate when dry again.

At the last eel drop, the rest of the Alphas were already at the tunnel entrance in the shadow of the tanglethorn, picking up their tawny yellow hoods where they left them, and waiting for Cain to come charging out of the tunnel like a cannon shot.

Don't really care if the roof surveillance picks you up at this point. The installation and its monitors were not long for this world. By the time it identifies you as intruders and warns you to stop your approach, you're already pelting a retreat through the yellow grass. Or mounting a yak if you can catch one. Or getting your mates almost trampled by stampeding yaks, thank you for that, Cain Salvador.

Meet up at pre-set coordinates. Cain the last to arrive, because there's no steering a yak.

Summon your Silver Horses outside the area of the factory's vigilance. Beyond the surveillance equipment's programmed scope of interest, you just don't exist. And off you go, close to the ground on your Silver Horse, listening for the kaboom.

Silver Horses left no tracks, except for a faint heat trail that was quickly carried away and dispersed in the prevailing winds.

The initial space battle had taken out any satellite that could have picked up a visual image of the fleeing Alphas on their ground skimming horses.

Somewhere along the way Twitch Fuentes steered around and pointed. *"Mira!"*

All the Alphas turned to look. Saw it before they heard it. The pillar of fire, straight up, sky high, blue and orange with transparent swirls of superheated air curling off of it.

"Wooly Bully!" said Dak.

"Ausgesichnett!"

Kerry Blue leaned forward around Cole Darby seated in front of her on the Silver Horse. "You German, Darb?"

"No, I just like the sound of the word."

The factory going up in flames was one of just three factories on Palatine which produced Roman res chambers.

Romans were as big on redundance as the Americans were. Which meant Teams Baker and Charlie were doing the same thing to the backup plant and the backup's backup half a world away.

Any new res chambers would need to come in from the planet Thaleia—but only if the Thaleian ships could get past the U.S. Fleet lying in wait outside the solar system.

The Silver Horses drew a snaking path cross-country, avoiding all cities and settlements.

They crossed a narrow sea in darkness under a chill rainfall.

Got themselves to the designated hideout area for a short rest. A place with tawny yellow grass where they could sleep under their shaggy cloaks. It was not raining here.

Woke before dawn for the next raid. "Would be a hell of a lot easier if we could just displace," said Carly, a little saddle sore. Wiry Carly Delgado didn't have much upholstery on her butt.

Seemed like the whole planet was under displacement jammers. All the ships in space were. No one wanted to be on the receiving end of a displaced bomb.

Dak checked his landing disk and displacement collar for correspondence. "Hey! I got a green light!"

"Dak, you boon!" Kerry cried, scared for his life. "They changed the color codes!"

For the siege of Palatine, all U.S. displacement equipment had been coded in reverse of international standard. Red was green and green was red. Green was not a good thing to see on U.S. displacement equipment down here. Green meant stop. Wrong. No go.

"Oh," said Dak, disappointed. "Yeah. It just looked so friendly. It's green."

"Think of green gobs of goo gushing from your gut," Darb suggested.

"Okay. Yeah. That works," said Dak. "I think I got it straight now."

"All yous!" Ranza commanded. "Forget about displacing! There ain't gonna be no shooting up a flare to get displaced out of here, 'kay? Ground don't get more hostile than this, 'kay? You step in sushi, there ain't gonna be no dust off. There ain't no cavalry. It's just us. Got that?"

"Why'd they give us these?" Kerry Blue flipped the displacement collar hanging off her Silver Horse.

"Shit if I know," said Ranza.

"So why aren't the Roman jammers on our target list?" Darb asked.

"That's a lot of targets, Darb. Jammers are everywhere. Saddle up, boys and girls. And just so yous all know, the lupes got a real good idea we're here now."

The Alphas' next target was Palatine's data relay station.

The Romans had sensors orbiting all their colonial worlds throughout their vast Empire and around any other world they could manage to deploy a spy satellite. The sensors picked up enormous amounts of various kinds of data. Information from the sensors came in to Palatine via resonance.

There was no stopping a res pulse without knowing the exact harmonic. If you knew the harmonic, you could white out the pulse with its complement harmonic. But State harmonics were closely guarded secrets, and there was no taking a guess. Harmonics were infinite.

There were hundreds—thousands—countless—satellite eyes sending data to Palatine on unknown harmonics. The Americans could not punch out all those eyes, and could not stop the satellites from transmitting their data.

But the Marines could take out Palatine's receiver station.

The eyes would still be staring but the optic tracts would be gone. All that information from all those distant eyeballs would not arrive at Palatine.

No doubt another relay station elsewhere (redundance being good and all) was receiving the data, but it wasn't getting to this planet now.

Speeding away from their victory on Silver Horses, the Alphas were jubilant. Kerry Blue shared a horse with Cole

Darby. Cole Darby felt her behind him. Kerry Blue's hands resting on his hips. Maddening.

A man makes a big score, he wants to celebrate with a lady. But Darb knew who Kerry Blue belonged to. Pretty damn obvious. Some of the guys back on *Mack*, confused by the sudden drought, had gone to the MO to ask if Kerry Blue were not dying of some strange space ailment. Darb knew better than to try to celebrate with Kerry Blue.

Ranza Espinoza was female. Sort of. Ranza was off-limits because of her rank, and that was a good thing, because Ranza scared him.

Carly was kind of pretty in a lean hard kind of way. But she and Twitch were real close friends. Twitch was shorter than Darb, but wider and brawny. Twitch didn't say nothing, but you didn't want to be on wrong side of that hombre.

That left Darb dating Hot Trixi Allnight in the dream boxes on *Merrimack*. Trixi wasn't real but she was better than a real shiv between the ribs.

Trixi wasn't here now.

Still Darb could ride the high of their demolition, feel the wind in his face, Kerry Blue back there laughing.

Cain sideswiped them. Kerry Blue licked her middle finger and waggled it over at Cain.

Darb wanted to be Cain when he grew up. Except that Cain was younger than Darb. Cain was one of the top picks in anybody's choose up game. Korean / Hispanic / white / black / yellow / brown mutt. Hell, there was probably some Cherokee in there too. Cain didn't have much of anything in the way of body hair and he shaved off what was on his head. If Darb did that he was pretty sure he would look like a penis.

Kerry Blue's laughing voice. "Darb, what are you *doing!*"

"Singing! Can't you tell?"

Kerry Blue's giggle. "No."

Felt/heard the jarring bang underneath them. Kerry Blue's grunt. Cold spot on his back where she had just been. Him sailing through the air without his Silver Horse. Hit the ground hard. Heard a snap. No pain. Real bad sign.

Heard words he only understood because he was wearing a language module: *"Don't move."*

24

THE PROVINCE AROUND THE ROMAN capital city maintained a facade of normality. By now Caesar was aware there were enemy vermin on the planet, but refused to acknowledge they were of any consequence. As for the power, water, and communications problems elsewhere, well, some inconveniences were to be expected.

He also knew that U.S. ships were somewhere outside the star system turning merchant vessels away from Palatine. He would just see how long the League of Earth Nations tolerated *that*. If the Americans could use the LEN as a lever, so could he.

There had been a few minor surprises, but Caesar Romulus knew he was winning this war.

Today the Magister of Imperial Intelligence, in person, carried the head of Augustus to Caesar.

It was not actually the head. That would be too grisly. Too psychotic. Rome was a modern civilization.

What Munda brought to Caesar was Augustus' black box—the data bank that had been implanted inside the patterner's head—on a covered silver platter.

The Magister of Imperial Intelligence was tall, severe, his face thin and hard like something carved in stone with razor blades. Munda had no ability to smile, not even an evil smile. His sense of drama was limited. He did not carry the silver platter over his head, balanced on one palm, or even have a servant do it for him.

Munda brought the platter to the palace in the company of three of his *curiosi*, agents of the secret police. They were admitted to a reception hall.

No holoimages shrouded this room. No illusions. No lightning strikes, of which Romulus was notoriously fond. Munda did not like holos around him when he was not the one controlling them.

This room was only what it appeared to be. The walls enclosed a wide and tall space in the palace annex, with tall Ionic columns, beautiful frescoes of gardens and villas and aqueducts, olive trees and grape vines. Sedate paintings, all of them. The frisky frescoes were in the bathhouse. The floor of mosaic tile featured animal portraits within geometric borders. Overhead soared a coffered, painted and gilt ceiling. Clerestories let in the daylight.

Caesar did not make the magister wait long, did not take the throne when he entered. Munda appreciated Romulus not playing intimidation games with his own Intelligence *agentes*.

"Munda!" Caesar strode in smiling. Senator Ventor heeled at Caesar's flank, clad in a toga that reflected his rank. Caesar and Munda were both simply dressed. They had nothing to prove. "You have something for me."

"Per your desire, Caesar," said Munda. "I give you—"

Munda lifted the polished silver lid.

"—Augustus."

Caesar's eyes widened despite himself. Ventor, standing a few respectful paces back, craned his head to see around Caesar.

"It's huge," said Romulus.

The data receptacle was two inches in diameter, not entirely round because it was not entirely rigid. Its surface was a smooth gray. It was the biggest data storage unit Caesar had ever seen.

"It is a big one," Munda allowed. "Sixteen exabyte capacity."

Romulus stepped closer. Shied back again on a sudden thought.

"Is it clean?"

"Any cleaner and the data would be erased," said Munda. "We need the data. But we're certain this is infected with a lethal virus."

Romulus shrank away farther, backed into Senator Ventor and stepped on the hem of his toga.

"Lethal to data," Munda clarified. "A data virus. We are setting up a discrete system in which to analyze the data, entirely isolated from any other system."

"We know this is infected?" Romulus asked in a voice that clearly said, *Why they hell did you bring this in here?*

"We cannot afford to assume otherwise, Caesar. Nanites have eaten out the data banks of the Striker, and left no data tracks to be recovered."

"Nanites." Caesar looked round as if he could see the infinitesimally small machines crawling.

Palace guards at the doors glanced down at their feet. The *curiosi* did not blink.

"Are they on the loose?" Romulus asked.

"The nanites on the Striker were self-limiting. They executed their tasks, then ceased to function. Then housekeeper nanites erased even those from existence. It was a precision process. Typical of a patterner."

Romulus put on black kid leather gloves. He had expected to need gloves to keep the data bank pristine. Now it was his hands, not the data bank, which he felt needed the protective barrier. He took a step closer, tentative as a wild animal lured by an offering of food. He peered over the edge of the platter. Glanced up from the silvery black box to Munda's stone face.

"Are there any nanites in there?"

"We detected no nanoactivity. Does not mean there are no nanites in there. There are nanoparticles all through the patterner's remains. Nanites kept his body from rejecting the augmentations. Some of his bionanites are trying to keep his remains alive even now."

Nanotechnology had been known for over four hundred years now. Machines worked faster as their size decreased. Machines with walls one atom thick worked very fast and required miniscule amounts of energy to operate.

The first nanoscale devices counted specific molecules in a chemical sample. The next natural task was to have them identify pathogens in a blood sample. Then to diagnose disease. Then more advanced nanomachines were used to seek out and destroy pathogens in the human body.

The CIA and Imperial Intelligence had come up with less benevolent tasks for them. Nanomachines could modify physical materials at a molecular level. They could be programmed to replicate themselves, or to build or destroy structures one atom at a time.

No one could say what use a malevolent patterner might put them to.

"Most of the nanites in Augustus' body stopped functioning at the patterner's death," said Munda.

"Most." Romulus took another step back, snugging his gloves on tighter. He nodded up at Munda. "Touch it."

Munda shifted, uneasy. "Really?" More uneasily still under Romulus' blinkless stare. No one was offering Munda gloves. "Caesar?"

The magister's stone face turned chalky, as if he'd been asked to set himself on fire.

Senator Ventor stared. The *curiosi* were very still. The guards held their breaths.

Romulus broke into laughter. "Of course not." He gave a boyish grin.

Munda did not laugh.

Senator Ventor stepped forward. He had brought polymer gloves with him and he put them on. His hand hovered over the silvery receptacle. "Is it fragile?"

"No. Not at all," said Munda, but added, "I wouldn't step on it."

Ventor inhaled. Boldly done, if to be done at all. He closed his hand around the ball and lifted it.

"Has some weight to it," he said, feeling his hand still intact, no spikes driving into his palm, no explosions, no sudden itches.

"Yes." Munda was glad enough to be able to let the platter drop to his side.

Sounds of disturbance carried through the monumental wood doors of the chamber. Then the doors themselves parted. Palace guards were challenging a knot of Senators who would not be turned away. They wore their togas with the crimson stripes to impress their rank on Caesar's minions.

These men were too high-ranking to be manhandled without further word from Caesar. As the doors parted, the guards looked to Caesar, searching for permission to club these men.

Caesar lifted his hand high, beckoned to the intruders like visitors. "Enter."

The guards let the four Senators through, but closed ranks behind them, blocking the attempted entry of the Senators' attendants. The guards shut the doors on the attendants with some shoving and scuffling.

Munda's *curiosi* took several steps forward from the wall where they had been standing at ease. They crossed their arms now and fixed their basilisk gazes on the Senators in silent warning.

Senators Trogus, Umbrius, Quirinius, and Opsius stalked in with long strides, chests puffed out, eyes and nostrils flaring, mouths twitching in umbrage.

Trogus, leader of this rat pack, shouted, "This is an outrage!"

"It is certainly disrespectful," Caesar allowed in a civil voice with a whisper of a smile.

Two of the Senators had the sense to be abashed.

Quirinius had, in the days of Caesar Magnus, been considered the third man in the Empire. His rank was now closer to two thousand and fifty-first. Still he was a seemly person. Dignified. Quirinius gave a nod of apology toward Caesar.

Trogus would not be shamed off course. His voice was thin and irritating. "That is the most valuable data reservoir in the Empire! It is not a ball to amuse Caesar! You shall surrender the patterner's data bank to the Senate immediately!"

"You want it?" said Caesar faintly. He met Ventor's eyes, tilted his head toward Trogus.

Ventor took up the cue, tossed the silvery black box to Senator Trogus.

On reflex, Trogus caught it bare-handed. Was immediately aghast at the thing in his hands. He took note of the gloves on Ventor and Romulus. A tremolo infected Trogus' voice, "Caesar?"

Umbrius, Quirinius and Opsius drifted backward.

The palace guards leaned attentively inward. The *curiosi* looked curious.

They all watched Trogus in silence for several extended, loudly ticking seconds.

"Well, there he is," said Caesar. "The formidable Augustus."

Senator Trogus tried to recover his dignity and control. His voice came out pitched too high to have any semblance of courage. "Of course any sabotage will be in the *data*."

"Yes, we all know that," Romulus said, impatient. "What you really came here looking for is something to use against me. Augustus' own version of my father's testament will be in there."

Trogus sought the high ground. "What we are really looking for are the Hive harmonics. The menace has returned to Near Space. There are gorgons on Thaleia."

"And you suppose I am not looking for Hive harmonics? I am not so petty and irresponsible as to use my position for personal spite."

"Your decisions have been questionable, Caesar, and I have a duty to question them. This data bank belongs to the people of Rome. It is not to be kept by one man or tossed about like a toy!"

An inner door opened. The guards held their stations. This was an intruder not to be denied. She was allowed through like a swallow through the rafters.

Claudia entered with a swish of silks and billow of patchouli and dark spice.

"Is he here?" she said, her dark exotic eyes alight.

She danced to the center of the knot of men. She faced Trogus. Her fingers lifted with a glitter of emeralds. "So here is the dreaded Augustus."

"Claudia, don't —"

Claudia plucked the data receptacle from Trogus' hand.

"What? This?" She turned her wrist as if holding a faceted bauble to the light. Augustus' data bank was plain and gray no matter which way she held it.

"It's harmless," said Trogus.

Claudia spoke to the black box in silken spite, "Did you see this moment coming, *patterner*?"

Senator Ventor deftly snatched the data receptacle from Claudia's fingers before she could decide to punish it.

The Intelligence Magister, Munda, growing agitated watching the valuable data passing hand-to-hand, held up the tray and urged Ventor, "Kindly replace the black box on the tray, Senator. We have a segregated system set up to analyze it and control any data surprises."

"What? What?"

The sudden screech made everyone start, and Ventor nearly bobbled the silvery ball.

"Why are you here!"

Claudia went rigid, her hands clenched into glittering fists, her eyes staring at air with fear, fury, and hatred.

Romulus opened his hands solicitously to his sister. "Claudia?"

Claudia shouted at someone not there, *"Shut up! Shut up! Go away!"*

Caesar's guards and the Intelligence *agentes* hastily scanned the chamber for light benders and pinpoint sound packets. They found nothing in the chamber that could be causing false images.

A murmur came from someone, "Seems Banquo's ghost is in the room."

Romulus detonated. "I *heard* that!" He rounded on Senator Umbrius. Caesar commanded his guards, "Slay him!"

Caesar's guards look alarmed, but started forward, drawing their swords, for *honestiores* required a sword.

Umbrius' eyes grew huge. The rest of the man visibly shrank.

Romulus held up his hand. Said quickly, "I rescind the order. I am enraged is all."

Banquo's ghost. As if his sister were here confronted by the ghost of someone she had conspired to murder.

Romulus spoke in deadly calm to Umbrius, "You impugned my sister's honor and I reacted as any man would. But I am not *any* man, I am your Caesar and you will apologize to me and to my sister."

Umbrius did, earnestly, on bended knee before Caesar.

Claudia was taking backsteps. "Get that thing out of here!" She might have been talking about Umbrius, but she was looking at empty space. "It's not real!" she screeched. At least part of her knew that.

"What do you see, Claudia?" Romulus moved toward her.

She whirled on him. "Don't you dare try to make me sound stupid!"

Romulus flinched back from her rage. He made to put his arms around her. Stopped. His mouth burned. He backed away carefully. Talked soothingly, "Well, Claudia, obviously it has light benders on it. None of us can see it. You need to tell me what is there."

Munda marked Caesar's deft wording. Most other people would have said, *Tell me what you think you see.* Caesar's *Tell me what is there* sounded as if he believed her entirely.

But Claudia's attention was now on her own hands. She tried to rub something off them. She beheld her hands in advancing horror, as if they were covered in something hideous.

Munda covered the data receptacle on the platter and whisked it away, his *curiosi* in his wake, back to the catacombs of Imperial Intelligence.

25

"**D**ON'T MOVE!" ROMAN legionaries bellowed. A lot of them. Large boots tromping, and a barrel of some projectile weapon in Cole Darby's face.

Okay, thought Darb cooperatively. On the ground, not sure if he was lying on his back or his front. Getting the idea his neck was broken. Not moving was not a problem. If the lupes ordered him to move he was screwed. Didn't feel his own breath from his nostrils against his upper lip and wondered if he was breathing. If not, he ought to be blacking out soon.

Heard grunts of the others. Ranza. Cain. Dak. Carly. Twitch. There was some kicking going on.

Kerry Blue's cry sounded frightened. *"Darb!"*

A voice in Latin: "This one's dead."

A lupe may have kicked him because Darby's head rocked slightly against the grass and he felt his cheek move against the dirt.

The pitiful cry, *"No!"*

I love you, Kerry Blue.

Strange face loomed close to his. No pity there. Very young. Perfect Roman. Cole Darby moved his eyes to tell the face he was not dead.

"He's alive!" Kerry cried.

The face rose away.

The Latin pronouncement, "No, he's not."

Barrel in his ear. Kerry Blue's screech. The leading edge of a blast.

Claudia cried for days, racked by headaches. Blisters, real ones, appeared on her hands. She scratched at them until her hands were bloody. Specialists tried to block the reception of the nerve endings to her brain, but it didn't help. As if the itching was not in her hands but all in her head.

She screamed from a stabbing pain in her eye.

Medici sedated her.

More than once she bolted up from what should have been deep sedation to scream: *"Pater!"*

Attending *medici* looked up as Caesar Romulus entered Claudia's room in the private clinic. He had brought fresh flowers.

One of the attendants took the flowers and put them into a vase at Claudia's bedside.

Claudia was unconscious, twitching, moving, her face pale against the pillow, her thick eyelashes quivering, noises coming from her throat.

"You cut off her hair," said Romulus, shocked. It brought to mind Calli Carmel, and he had to wonder if Calli were not behind this monstrous attack.

"She was tearing at it," said a *medicus*. "We have it here." She indicated a side table where Claudia's long dark locks lay cleaned, combed, and bagged next to her emeralds. Hair was easily reattached, and Claudia looked in no state to be missing it.

Her hands were covered in gauze, her wrists bound in soft restraints at her side.

"She has been calling for your father, Caesar," a medical attendant advised, insinuation in his voice.

"She is calling God, you idiot," said Romulus.

Chastised, the attendant said, "She is in terrible pain."

"Then stop the pain! What is wrong with you?"

The senior *medicus*, Pontius Placidus, moved in, took over.

"We have shut off the neural pathways from the nerve

endings to her brain, Caesar. We cannot stop the pain. The nanites are *inside* her brain."

"Nanites!" Caesar recoiled. "From the patterner's black box?"

"Yes, Caesar."

"Other people have touched the black box with their bare hands," said Romulus. "Why isn't Trogus scratching *his* hands off?"

"The nanites are programmed to activate upon a trigger event."

"What trigger?"

Pontius Placidus said quietly, "Caesar, may we talk in private?" and showed Caesar to a door. Opened it for him and let Romulus precede him through it to the kind of room where they tell you, "I'm so sorry."

The room was chock-full of potted plants, crowded with life, green and flowering. Tiny jewel birds uttered soft fluttering notes, not their characteristic hard banging chirps. The light through the false windows was soft as Earthlight. The chairs were overstuffed to hug you when you sat in one. The hearth held an eternal flame.

Romulus refused the chair. He was dressed all in black, even to his gloves, which had become part of his usual garb. He held his arms crossed so hard that he was hugging himself. Struggled not to bite the hand that tried to heal. He just wanted to execute the lot of these quacks and bring in someone competent.

Pontius Placidus was the best neurologist in the Empire.

"There are several specialized types of nanomachines at work here," Pontius Placidus explained. "The syndrome is activated by a combination trigger. The recognition molecules react with a specific target biologic. In this case the recognition molecules are reacting to a near DNA match to Magnus. A filial match."

"Augustus targeted *me*," Romulus translated.

The medicus seemed to hedge. Continued, "DNA is not enough. It is a combination trigger. Contact with DNA having filial commonality with Magnus is the first thing the nanite looks for. That contact triggers the nanite to construct a second set of recognition molecules, which are dispatched to the hippocampus and the frontal lobe to troll for electrical pulse patterns within the central nervous system that equate to patricidal memory and guilt."

"Stop!" Caesar cried. "You cannot possibly read a mind from electrical pulses."

"In a limited sense, yes, we can," said Placidus. "A patricidal experience alters the map of the human brain. Crime leaves physical tracks. The recognition molecules look for the shape of a memory. Killing one's father is a major event. The experience leaves an impression—a characteristic brain pattern."

"The nanite cannot have found that in my sister," Romulus declared.

"It thinks it did," the medicus said diplomatically. "That event triggers the creation of yet another recognition molecule which looks for a guilt reaction associated with the memory. Guilt dwells in the frontal lobe—guilt as in the fear of being caught. The nanites do not look for remorse, which is a separate pattern. Finding a filial match for Magnus' DNA, patricidal memory, and guilt, the nanites then construct other nanites to inject information into the brain. They bring the patricidal memory to the fore cortex and create visual, auditory, and olfactory electrical pulses. Electromagnetic pulses trigger the release of the brain's own neurotransmitters to create a synthetic reality—pain, visions, stench, itching. Other nanites create the physical blisters."

"You are implying that my sister is guilty of something and I know that is not true. She is high-spirited and self-indulgent. That is all. Very well, she is a brat. I know that. Augustus was a murderous renegade. He killed our father and tried to divert his own guilt to a high, high target. Augustus and Gaius Americanus and the American Callista Carmel are all in this."

Pontius Placidus could see that familial loyalty was blinding young Romulus to the obvious guilt of his sister. A difficult thing to explain to a Caesar. "The recognition molecules—"

Romulus cut him off. "*If* Claudia has a memory of killing our father, then Augustus' nanites *created that too*. He just had his nanites destroy the evidence of that part of the scheme before he let you find the 'recognition molecules.' He was a patterner! He could create and hide evidence at will! Claudia did not kill our father. I know she did not."

The medicus had not considered the possibility of the patterner planting a false memory first, then sending his recognition molecules out to find it. "I apologize, Caesar. I fell for it. You are correct. It would not be beyond the ability of a patterner."

"Where would Augustus get the raw data to find the pattern to do that? He had American help, didn't he?" Romulus guessed the answer he wanted to hear.

The medicus was reluctant to follow that leap. "Nanotechology has been around for hundreds of years. We have it. The Americans have it. Brain alterations? I'm afraid those are Roman advances, Caesar. Augustus had Secundus' Striker. Strikers carry extensive data banks already installed. You are correct, patterners don't normally construct things. But this particular patterner, Secundus, worked under Constantine Siculus. That means both Secundus and Augustus had Constantine's database."

"PanGalactic Industries," Romulus gave a horrified murmur.

Constantine Siculus was the founder of PanGalactic Industries. The father of modern manufacturing. Tell the PanGalactic program what you want with great specificity, and PanGalactic will figure out how to get it made. Augustus must have asked for very specific nanites.

"Augustus knew I wanted his head!" said Romulus, agitated. "Those nanites were meant for me!"

"I believe you may have it, Caesar."

"How do those nanites travel? Are they loose in my palace?"

"They are only mobile within a human body. But they may pass by contact like dust. If you are the nanites' true target, then you are in danger, Caesar. The nanites could be on your gloves if you touched the black box even with your gloves on."

"I didn't touch the black box at all."

"Claudia. If you touched your sister after she touched the black box, you are certainly already exposed."

"I haven't." A chill passed through Caesar's body. He had started to touch her many times, but always stopped himself.

"Myself," said the medicus. "I have touched the black box extensively."

Pontius Placidus could tell by the look on Romulus' face that Caesar would love to throw the medicus into the nearest annihilator. Caesar instead commanded soberly, "Kindly confine yourself to a quarantined area."

"Yes, Caesar. Anything Claudia touched may carry these nanites. With your permission I shall organize a cleansing of this site, and the reception area where she first contacted the black box. We can sanitize your shoe soles on the way out."

"Good man," said Romulus. "I have noted your initiative, your thoroughness, and your discretion in this affair."

Pontius Placidus nodded, accepting the recognition. He could expect tangible gratitude for his service. Caesar Romulus could be wildly generous.

"Make her comfortable," Caesar commanded. "And *get those things out of her brain!*"

"I will do my best, Caesar."

Romulus breathed a big angry inhalation, about to shout at Placidus that best wasn't good enough. Forced himself down from boiling wrath. Tried to find words to impress the urgency on this intelligent ape. "Pontius Placidus, she is your sister. She is your daughter. She is your wife. She is your mother. You understand how important she is?"

"Everything possible will be done," said Pontius Placidus.

Romulus left the clinic, quaking to the foundation of his being.

Romulus contacted his chief of palace security with orders that Senators Umbrius, Trogus, Quirinius and Opsius be expelled from the palace and denied future access, by force if necessary. Then he added Numa Pompeii to that list. He thought about ordering Gaius Americanus killed or quarantined, but Gaius was confined under the Coliseum, so there was no point dredging him up.

Romulus considered having an arsonist torch the palace annex.

Damned Augustus again.

He had wondered about the shot through his throne in his bunker. He wondered what made Augustus so sure Romulus would be on the throne when he took the shot.

Obviously Romulus had not been on the throne, and obviously Augustus hadn't been sure.

But Augustus knew—for sure—that Romulus wanted his head.

Augustus had left this trap for him.

Claudia sprang it instead.

It was meant for me. It was meant for me.

I survived you again, you mechanical zombie abortion. I am Caesar and you are dead!

Romulus was filled with a sudden sense of elation, an amazing freedom. The air felt clean and pure in his lungs. He was alive, and he felt like celebrating.

Merrimack ghosted a French merchant ship that was not where it was supposed to be, on a stealthy approach to Palatine.

Captain Farragut did not like to shoot at civilians, even French ones. But he did not intend to let the ship pass. The decision was between gentle ramming and terminal blasting.

"Let's show ourselves," said Farragut.

"He could run, sir," Tactical advised.

"Then we'll catch him again when he drops to sublight at the planet. We know where he's going."

Merrimack moved in close enough to read the name on the hull, *Pharaon*.

Merrimack swept in front of the freighter. Hailed on the international channel and commanded the ship to turn back.

The freighter *Pharaon* did not respond. Maintained course.

Merrimack's Intelligence officer, Colonel Z, suspected the freighter was not the French craft it appeared to be.

Thaleia was the more likely point of origin.

Farragut looked to his exec. "Anything, Gypsy?"

Gypsy Dent had sent a res inquiry to Earth upon first sighting the freighter, to verify the ship's authenticity.

"Waiting for something back from France," said Gypsy.

"Bumper cars," said Farragut.

Helm made two gleeful fists. "Aye, aye, Captain!"

"Go easy," said Farragut. "Don't hurt him yet. See if he has anything to say now."

Merrimack moved in like a killer whale trying to balance a baby seal on its nose, while the com tech held his headset away from his ear.

"What do you have?" Farragut asked.

"He's squawking," said the com tech.

"What's he saying."

"It's in French."

"Aren't you wearing a module?"

"It's real bad French. I got the words 'outrage' and 'my government.' "

"We can wait and see what his government has to say."

"Can I keep bumping him, sir?"

"Oh, sure. Carry on."

Reports from Palatine indicated that *Mack*'s Fleet Marines had some success on the ground. But Farragut was beginning to suspect they had paid dearly for it. Several teams had dropped out of contact. He could only pray they were on the run.

Intelligence had been sifting through ground chatter within the Roman populace. The scandal of the hour was that Caesar's sister Claudia was calling for her father and sprouting blisters on her hands.

"What was Lady Macbeth's first name?" Gypsy mused.

"I don't know," said Farragut. "Was it Claudia?"

Romulus had accused the patterner of poisoning his sister. John Farragut never took Romulus' accusations at face value. But there were rumors about Augustus' head on a platter and programmed nanites that made it sound like Augustus really had committed this attack.

But it also sounded like the nanites had been meant for Romulus.

Augustus meant for his head to go to Caesar on that platter.

But he miscalculated who would touch it. Augustus got Claudia instead of Romulus.

Farragut guessed Augustus would want to get Claudia too, but Romulus had slipped the snare entirely.

And it seemed a pretty precarious snare with a number of tenuous links, all of which must be connected in order for the nanites to find their target.

Augustus was a patterner. He could calculate patterns too intricate for the human mind to hold. Still, "Wouldn't you think he would have some more direct, more certain way to get Romulus?"

"Maybe he was long past his life expectancy and he was just *missing* at the end," Gypsy suggested.

Hamster: "Maybe he's counting on you to finish it, John."

"Oh, if that's the case he really did lose it at the end. Not that I wouldn't love to set Rom's soul free. I'm not a political assassin. Unless I meet Romulus in battle, that just can't happen."

And anything that Farragut could do to Romulus just wouldn't be bad enough. Clearly Augustus missed his target.

"Captain, we have trade."

France had failed to acknowledge the freighter out there.

"*Pharaon* is not French?"

"Not French."

"And the not-French ship has friends," Tactical reported. "Roman gunboats, three of them, not disguised as anything."

"Not-French ship is running," said the helm.

Captain Farragut stood up at his station, a hunter's gleam in his blue eyes.

"Tally ho."

The dialogs. VII.

A: *Don* Cordillera, does your Church still have those thrones and dominations, and those sixteen-headed, eight-winged seraphim no one can look at? So how do you know what they look like anyway?

JMdeC: That is the apple talking. It was the choice of the apple that caused Man to leave the Garden. It is the willingness to let go the apple that takes us home. You cannot find God by logic.

A: And there is the supreme cheat, damn you. Knowledge got Adam kicked out of the Garden and you can't find God through knowledge. There's a double bind. How bloody convenient. When your game doesn't make sense, make the first rule of the game that you need to turn off your God-given brain as a prerequisite of playing. Now that explains John Farragut, but you, *Don* Cordillera, you have eaten way too many apples to sucker yourself into discarding all you know. I'll bet your soul there are no seraphim.

JMdeC: *My* soul? Not yours?

A: I don't have one. I was created by man.

26

ALL AROUND PUGET SOUND heavy lifters hauled pieces of bridges and streets and buildings out of the water. Tremors continued to hamper attempts to make order out of the chaos in the Pacific Northwest.

But the cities had drinking water systems working now.

The wolfhunter class ship *Wolfhound* lifted off the uneasy ground and returned to space, taking up a vigilant orbit around Earth.

She had gone from milk cow to traffic cop. *Wolfhound* routinely stopped incoming vessels to demand identification.

"Wear off, *Wolfhound*. We are French nationals," the latest object of interest declared, and kept going forward toward Earth's atmosphere.

"Cease forward progress, *Bertrand*," Captain Carmel of the *Wolfhound* commanded the French ship. "Please wait while we confirm your identify."

"I have already told you who were are."

"You will wait until France agrees with you, *Bertrand*."

The French merchant ship did not slow or alter course.

"Hook the Frenchman," Calli ordered.

"Hooking the Frenchman, aye."

Wolfhound threw out an energy net to snag *Bertrand* and stop the ship from getting any closer to Earth.

"This is piracy!" *Bertrand* declared. "The United States cannot board a vessel of any League signatory!"

"We are not boarding you, *Bertrand*. You and I are waiting together for confirmation from France. Then you may be about your business."

"I will be about my business *now*!"

"You are—allegedly—our ally, and Rome declared war on us. You have given us no assistance. Is it too much to ask you to wait while we make sure you are who you say you are? What happened to all for one and one for all? Wasn't that a French saying?"

"You derive great protection from our neutrality! See how we lifted siege from your Pacific coast? As long as Rome is not at war with the whole world, *you* are sheltered by *our* peace. Would you have us open the whole world to nuclear fire? Do you not have laws against illegal search and seizure?"

"We are not searching you, *Bertrand*. And we'll let you go, if you prove to be French."

"I need not prove anything to you! This is not our war. You will let us go now."

"How is it not your war?"

"Rome does not fight us, and we do not wish to fight Rome."

"You don't? Didn't you just say you were a member of the League of Earth Nations?"

"You know that we are. And the League of Earth Nations shall hear about this!"

"As we are part of the League, that means the League is hearing about this right now. And *this* member of the League has a war on its hands, like it or not. War was declared on us, and the rest of Earth goes about business as usual."

"You are talking in circles. You have not been listening to a word I say—"

And he was right. Calli Carmel hadn't been listening. She was just letting the Frenchman rail while she waited for the report from France. As long as they were talking, the Frenchman wasn't doing anything dangerous.

The hand signals from her com tech on the other channel caught her attention. Thumbs up. The Frenchman's identity was confirmed.

"Release hook," Calli ordered.

"Hook released, aye," Engineering responded.

Calli took her com off mute to interrupt the Frenchman, who had been scolding her without taking a breath. "Okay, you're free. I'm glad we had this time to talk. Have a good day."

She needed some polite words to show on the transcript, which was certain to be attached to the Frenchman's complaint to the LEN.

The com tech reported: "Captain! The Frenchman is calling back."

"Don't take the call," said Calli.

The red-haired kid at the com, Red Dorset, happily clicked the Frenchman off. "That one was nasty."

"They're all nasty," said the cryptotech.

Tactical reported, "Italian transport coming in. Lord, Italy has a lot of traffic."

"At least the Italians *wait*," said Calli, moving around the close-packed deck to the tactical station to see the plot's attitude. "They moan, but they wait." She reached over Tactical's shoulder. Her long finger with its baby-thin nail pointed at the Italian plot. "Check this one out."

"Aye, aye, Captain."

The Italian vessel stopped upon request.

Red Dorset at the com station issued a verification inquiry to his Italian contact, Guglielmo Baptista in Old Rome. Red and Guglielmo were on a first name basis by now.

International traffic to and from Earth had continued as if everything were normal. If anything, traffic had increased. To the rest of the world, the conflict was "the American war." Palatine was America's enemy, not theirs.

Red Dorset drummed his fingers at his station, waiting to hear back from his Italian buddy. He thought out loud, "I wonder if the Frenchman didn't have a point back there. These other countries do sort of protect us by continuing trade."

"He had *a* point," said Captain Carmel. "One. But those ships can still damn well stop for an ID check."

Red was young and talked a lot. Calli could picture a redheaded toddler driving his mother up the wall with a constant "Why? Why? Why?"

"It's surprising—" said Red. "Well, *I* think it's surprising—Rome hasn't been hitting our infrastructure while we're sabotaging theirs. Not complaining, mind you. But why isn't Rome hitting our infrastructure?"

"Because Romulus thinks America's infrastructure is *his* infrastructure. That's the Province of America down there, and we're just infesting it."

Rome had hammered just one small part of the United States. The upper left-hand corner. Romulus would not want to ravage the entire countryside. He did not want to take possession of a disaster area. Romulus wanted a fat productive province.

Red Dorset sat suddenly straight, hand to his earpiece. He spoke into the com, "*Grazzi*, Guglielmo!" And turned to the captain. "The Italian checks out."

Calli took up her com to officially thank the Italian pilot for his patience and gave him leave to continue to Earth.

And Red was asking questions again. "How can Romulus think he can take over America? He can't get air space superiority. Is he just going to walk in and plant his Eagles on the Mall in DC and everyone will just hail Caesar?"

Calli nodded. *It'll be something like that.*

Captain Farragut had lost contact with two of his Marine units who were down on Palatine. No one else was sharing information on how many other Marine units from other battalions were down there or how many of those were now missing. And Farragut did not have good data on how the softening up of the battlefield was progressing.

Ship noises had a hollow ring without his seven hundred and twenty Marines. A lot of heavy feet were not thumping round the raised jogging track at all hours. Spirited games were not played against the navvies in the squash courts or in the basketball court that was actually the maintenance hangar.

The crew were slightly older, more measured men and women, with advanced engineering degrees and less brawn than the Marine companies. The crew played less. Shouted less.

Merrimack was quiet, circling Roman space like a shark, waiting for swimmers to dare cross her waters.

Captain Farragut spent a lot of time in the squash court.

Playing squash with his XO was to remember just how very long her arms were. And hard. In Greek myth the woman Daphne turned into a tree. Farragut was convinced that Egypt Dent was that very tree turned back into a woman. She was moderately fast. Very fast for a tree. More strong than agile. She didn't change direction quickly but she could smash that little green ball as hard as any Marine. Gave a loud *"Uh!"* with every smash, like a tennis player's grunt or a martial artist's *kiap*.

Swinging hard at a fast-moving target with a comrade close by had been good training for using swords to cut down gorgons.

Gypsy missed a return, and the hard little ball hit her in the thigh. Hard. "Gorgon bite!" she cried, limping off the pain. She growled at herself. "Out of practice."

"As are we all," said Farragut, lining up a serve.

Gypsy spun her racquet in her hand and crouched ready for another volley.

Farragut served.

Gypsy returned. "Are we—*uh!*—getting any updates—*uh!*—on the new Hives? *Ha!* My serve."

"If there are any reports, I'm not getting them." Farragut tossed the traitorous ball to her and crouched ready for the serve.

"*Uh!* Ace!"

Farragut retrieved the ball and tossed it back to her again. "I really don't think anyone is compiling reports on the Hive."

Gypsy frowned. Her frowns were frightening. "Do they think if they pull the sheets up over their heads, the gorgons can't bite them?"

"I guess." A mighty return. *"Cowabunga!"*

The little ball thudded at Gypsy's feet. She scowled at the captain. "What kind of word is that?"

"No idea." He tossed his racquet up and caught it by the grip.

"We don't have any shortage of Thaleian supply ships trying to run the blockade," said Gypsy.

And some of them were succeeding. It was a high-risk run, but if the ship was coming from Thaleia, odds were high that it was unmanned, so anything on board was replaceable.

"If the Thaleians can send supplies off world that means the Hive presence on Thaleia hasn't gotten critical."

"Yet," said Farragut.

"Any updates on Toto Two?"

Last she heard the decoy drone flock dubbed "Toto Two" had been leading the gorgons of Telecore away from Fort Eisenhower.

"Gorgons are still chasing." Farragut slammed a shot off the rear wall. It sailed to the front wall where Gypsy crowded it back into the front wall. Scored.

"But," said Farragut.

"With Weng and Ski, there's always a but," said Gypsy.

"Always. And Weng and Ski tell me they have evidence from a monitor on the planet that *other* gorgons have lifted off the surface of Telecore and *those* headed off in the opposite direction."

"Toward Fort Ike."

"Toward Fort Ike."

Gypsy lost her serve.

"Can Weng and Ski confirm that?"

"Nope." Farragut aced his serve with a mighty blow. "The gorgons ate the monitor."

Gorgons from Telecore would be several years getting to Fort Eisenhower. But years had a way of evaporating in time of war. Farragut would rather do something about the gorgons some time *before* they were eating through his hull and chewing on his boots.

No one was ready for another battle with the Hive.

And, if these had been swords instead of squash racquets right now, Gypsy woulda just cut his arm off.

*   *   *

"Romulus has announced he will be holding games in the Coliseum," Mr. Hicks reported from the com station.

Farragut gave his head a small shake. Not sure what made that remarkable. "That's what the Coliseum was built for."

"I mean with gladiators, sir. Fighting to the death."

"You have got to be shagging me."

"How can Romulus announce anything?" the systems tech asked. "I thought the Marines took out Palatine's relay station."

"That was the resonant receiver station," said Hicks. "That took out their reception of galactic surveillance. The local network is fine and Romulus can still send his pronouncements *out* on the capital harmonic."

"And he's going to hold games," said Captain Farragut. "Glad to see he has his priorities in order."

Lieutenant Glenn Hamilton, looking over Tactical's shoulder, not terribly sure of herself, said, "Captain, we have trade."

Farragut turned to Ian Markham at Tactical, brows very high and questioning why Tactical had said nothing.

"It's *Wolfhound!*" said Markham, hands up, defensive.

"Moving sublight," said Hamster watching the plot. "Approaching the planet. Lots of Romans around and no one's shooting at her."

"She's giving all the recognition signals," said Tactical, his face growing hot. Wanted to say he didn't need the captain's girlfriend looking over his shoulder. Hamster should stick to the mid watch.

Farragut looked to Gypsy. "Did you know Cal was coming?"

Gypsy shook her head, as surprised as anyone. "No, sir."

Mr. Hicks had *Wolfhound*'s harmonic on the resonator before the captain could demand it.

"Calli, where are you?" Farragut sent without a preface of any sort.

There would be a moment while the *Wolfhound*'s mystified com tech passed him over to *Wolfhound*'s captain. Calli answered, "John?" her voice very surprised. Then uneasily, "Do you want to verify yourself?"

"Cal, I'm lookin' at your ship entering Palatine's star system."

"My *Wolfhound?*"

"Your *Wolfhound*."

"Blow it up," said Calli.

"Roger that. Farragut out. Helm! Get us between *Wolfhound* and the planet, yesterday!"

"Aye, sir." Engine sounds crescendoed. "We're there, sir."

"Punt."

Merrimack rammed the Roman backward before the Roman could register *Merrimack* in the area.

Merrimack opened up with beam fire, and sent tags to the false *Wolfhound*'s stern in prep for torpedoes.

Mr. Hicks put his current communication on the speaker. "Captain, this is what's coming over the fleet channel."

The voice on the speaker sounded like Calli Carmel's, requesting assistance, claiming *Merrimack* was in Roman hands and firing on her ship.

But Admiral Burk was not the old woman who lived in a shoe, and knew for damned certain that *Wolfhound* was not assigned to his Fleet. Burk opened a tight beam to *Merrimack*, "Captain Farragut, I assume you confirmed that the ship is not *Wolfhound*."

"Yes, sir," said Farragut, his ship not pausing in its fusillade on the Roman imposter. "I just talked to Cal seconds ago. Looks like the lupes have infiltrated our Fleet channel."

"Very well. Carry on."

Lieutenant Colonel TR Steele stood straddling his Silver Horse in the tundra dusted with snow. Windblown ice crystals hit the Silver Horses with a thin tinny clatter. The Marines, the Silver Horses, and their gear were camouflaged black and white as volcanic rock and snow. Curtains of auroras waved in the weird sky that was neither night nor day. TR Steele felt like a ghost.

He had died inside when he received the signal from Flight Leader Ranza Espinoza. Ranza had hit the panic button and there had been no further word after that. No information. It had been sudden whatever it had been.

Kerry Blue was in Ranza's unit.

Steele's team had stopped here to check their bearings.

A Marine known as the Yurg stood with his ear pressed to his com, listening to the Fleet channel. Yelled, "*Merrimack*'s shooting at *Wolfhound*."

Steele scowled, confused. "*Wolfhound* is here?"

The Yurg paused. "No. Guess that's why the Cap'n's shooting."

A shower of big red meteors, which may have been the end of the Roman imposter, drew wide fiery streaks across the dark sky. The men grunted some hoo ras.

It was warming to know *Merrimack* was nearby.

"Fleet's switching over to Channel B," the Yurg advised.

Steele nodded. Switched his own com over. He looked to Icky Iverson, who had been a damn long time getting a read on their present location.

At long last Icky announced, "We're here."

The Marines dismounted their Silver Horses.

Their footsteps made harsh sounds in the brittle air.

The Marines had navigated to a weapons depot. One of the fleet's big ships had buried supplies here in preparation for the team's next guerrilla attack.

Steele's men found the place by global coordinates. There were no physical markers at all to distinguish it from the surrounding tundra.

Icky found the edges of the lid, which melded perfectly into the landscape.

The Yurg pried up the top. Shone a light inside the underground cache.

"*Shit!*"

"Everything's gone!"

"Drop that!" Steele yelled, of the cover. "Mount up. Run!"

Marines ran to their Silver Horses, Steele shouting into his com, "Gabriel. Gabriel. This is King Rat. Are you up there? Depot's been smoked and we're about to be bounced. Can we get a dust off?"

"King Rat, this is Gabriel. That is affirmative. Keep running. We'll catch you."

Marines mounting their Silver Horses. Lifting from the

ground. Icky, in the rear, slipped. Landed on his face. Steele turned a circle with his horse. He bellowed at Icky, "Get on!"

Icky got himself up. Took a step. Lost his balance again. The ground was moving.

In the dark sky, out of the moving curtains of red lights, a mammoth spearhead shape descended, growing larger.

Merrimack.

The motion in the ground was all around the Marines.

Suddenly Romans poured out of camouflaged pits, too dark, too many to count. Steele slashed wide with his field knife, sliced one Roman's throat open. To no effect.

Androids.

You only get one shot with an android. Immediately the knife flew out of Steele's hand; his cannon and his sidearm lifted away. He lost contact with his saddle. No idea what became of his Silver Horse. His wrists immobilized in a superhuman grip.

Two Silver Horses sped away in icy clouds.

And immediately plowed into black nets. Metal screeched against volcanic rock.

A swarm of androids crowded around *Merrimack*'s lowering sail.

While, black on black, a low flying sheet of killer bots moved in fast.

Merrimack opened up like a dragon, spouting hydrogen fire at the advancing bots.

The androids stormed the sail as *Merrimack*'s hatch opened. Navy sharpshooters on a platform picked off androids one by one, trying to weed them out from their Marines. The ship could not just scoop up the whole skirmish and spit out the bad ones—a Roman android in captivity tended to go off like a bomb.

Steele struggled. The android held him fast. He could not even wave at the sharpshooters to tell them to nail this thing.

The androids were thick around the sail. If *Mack* had her Fleet Marines on board, *they* could fight these things off, Steele thought.

He lost sight of his men in the throng of androids.

Merrimack's force field had solidified. It glittered under the auroras. The hatch to the lower sail was still open.

Steele could see Captain Farragut hanging from a ladder like a pirate in the rigging of an ancient ship, weapon at the ready, searching all round. Steele could not hear him through the force field, but could see his mouth moving, clearly yelling: *TR! TR!*

As TR Steele fought uselessly against the machines that dragged him. He was pulled down, kept going down.

Underground. Lost sight of Farragut. Of *Merrimack*. Of anything.

From the subterranean blackness he heard the space battleship rising, the searing shriek of outbound fire following after her.

27

FARRAGUT CAME UP THE LADDER from the lower sail like a missile launch. He charged onto the command deck, bellowing: "Tracking! Do we have him? Where is he?"

"I can tell you where we lost them, sir," said Tracking. "The lupes must have killed all the coms and the tracking units. The colonel's disappeared from the grid."

The coms and the tracking units were dead. And what of the Marines wearing them?

Farragut stalked the confines of the crowded deck with a ready fist. Nothing safe to hit, and it was all his equipment anyway. "What was Steele's next target?"

"Space control relay tower, five clicks from where the lupes grabbed them."

"Let's go get it."

"It's shielded top to bottom, Captain," Gypsy advised, only after giving the orders to put *Merrimack* on course to the target.

Merrimack descended back into Palatine's atmosphere. Because the ship and her shields were designed to deflect anything she met head on, she plowed sideways into the relay tower.

The enemy shields held, but the tower canted over, its foundations uprooted.

Merrimack rose out of the atmosphere to massing Roman warships, avid as piranha, *Gladiator* in the thick of them.

The command crew could tell that the captain wanted to get into a street fight with Numa Pompeii. The better part of valor ordered, "Dodge and run. FTL."

Farragut took some verbal fire from Admiral Burk for free-lancing.

"I support the men under my command, sir," Farragut sent back.

Expected to catch hell for that remark, but no more hell was forthcoming. His next communication was Admiral Burk ordering the Fleet to switch communications to Channel C.

Roma Nova, the second eternal city, lay tranquil, beautiful and impressive in the morning light. Romans loved to impress. The city had been built on the premise that human beings *need* beauty. Only observe the amount of work and money spent on art and music, and one must recognize the need for beauty as a basic hunger.

Opponents of Caesar expected some backlash at Romulus' proposal of holding games in Roma Nova. Especially from areas of the planet suffering the effects of the U.S. military strikes.

But the backlash was limited. Places still struggling without power were feeling patriotic and defiant. Let the Americans see Rome unbowed. Households with independent generators invited neighbors and stranded travelers in to watch the games from there.

The Senate and the Roman intelligentsia were appalled at the very idea of gladiatorial contests. Appalled at the public interest in them, at the distraction from things of importance.

Senator Trogus, who was not permitted into the Presence since his contact with Augustus' black box, appeared before Caesar as a projected holoimage, ugly in his anger. "This is outrageous. It's prehistoric!"

"No, games lie squarely in the historical era," said Caesar smoothly. "There is written documentation of them."

Trogus sputtered. Caesar had taken a convenient turn down a semantic detour and had not addressed the point. "We are an enlightened society! You make us into cartoon barbarians! Caesar, you humiliate us in front of the civilized galaxy!"

"Gladiatorial contests are the farthest thing from barbarism," said Romulus, composed, sober.

He was seated very casually, both feet on the seat of his throne, one folded leg resting flat, the other up at a right angle. He was all in black but for the gold of his oak leaf crown. Black and gold. Julian colors. "I honor our fathers. I do not disavow them as some men will. I remember where we came from. The games give a man who is without honor a chance to restore his dignity, his status as a man, by blood and courage. A last chance at honorable death. This is a *privilege*. What could be more elemental? More Roman?"

"I suppose Caesar intends to have an old-fashioned spectacle of animals tearing at each other as well!"

Romulus drew himself up straight in his throne, astonished and offended. Feet on the floor and palm to his chest as if stabbed to the heart. "No. What kind of sick mind could suppose that? Animals are innocent and without honor. What have you against animals, Trogus?"

Left Trogus tangled in his own argument. One must choose words with extraordinary care when talking to Caesar. No one was better at stabbing you with your own blade than Caesar Romulus.

Let Trogus feel idiotic for bringing up the subject of animal fights.

Romulus did not mention that there could be some animal *feeding* at the games.

The lifting of the hood revealed an underground passageway, wide, high, all stone. Stone archways led off to chambers on either side blocked by metal bars. Cages. Prisoners crowded the cages. Animal snarls and scuffling sounded from farther down the brooding corridor.

"Colonel!"

The voice came from down the corridor where TR Steele was headed. He saw his Marines. Behind bars.

Cain Salvador. Dak Shepard. Twitch Fuentes. Carly Delgado. Ranza Espinoza.

Steele's heart stood still, leaped into sunlight. Kerry Blue.

The Marines crowded at the bars, thrilled and dismayed to see their CO down here.

Steele's own team was in there too, arrived ahead of him. Icky Iverson. The Yurg. Big Richard. Taher. Menendez.

Androids ordered the American prisoners against the back wall, then opened the cage to push Steele in.

No one rushed the door. No human ever won a hand-to-hand with an android.

"Fresh meat," the prisoners in the opposite cage announced.

The barred door clanked shut behind Steele, locked. His Marines rushed forward. Kerry Blue seized the excuse to get her arms round Steele. Everyone else was mugging him too. The Yurg reaching over the rest of them to pat Steele on his buzz cut blond head.

"Do that again, Marine, I'll brig you," Steele snarled.

Yurg grinned. Colonel never made too many jokes. "Yes, sir."

Kerry Blue pressed against Steele's side like a missing piece restored. Nothing looked too grim anymore.

He had to let go of her to clasp other hands and knock fists with his men.

The Marines bombarded him with news. Darb was dead. They killed Darb.

Steele hushed them. "Save it. Don't talk."

He turned round to see all the Roman eyes across the corridor, watching them. Listening.

Steele tried to take in all of what was here. He had twelve Marines with him, men and women together in one roughly ten- by twenty-foot cage.

He noted that the lupes had let the Marines keep their language modules, and their gunsights still bracketed their eyes. But no one had a com on him.

There were Romans down here too, behind bars, separate from the Americans. The group in the cage opposite the Marines were bigger men, healthier, and better kept than the shabby collection crowded into the cage at the intersection of the next corridor.

A heavy weight dropping on the overhead made a loud dull thump and sent sawdust sprinkling down from the wooden ceiling.

The oddity of this place caught up with Steele. He spoke out loud, incredulous. "Where the hell are we?"

"Roma Nova, sir," said Icky Iverson.

More to the point, Ranza Espinoza said: "Under the Coliseum, sir."

A Roman prisoner in the cage across the corridor offered, "If they fit you for armor, you're going up there." He nodded up at the ceiling.

"Don't listen to them, sir," said Ranza. "Those guys've been torquing us around with that skat since we got here."

"If it's skat, why are you here?" the Roman called. "This is Death Row."

" 'Cause they don't got nowhere else to put us," Ranza shot back. "Rome don't got prisons."

The prisoner smiled ironically, gave the heavy metal bar a flick with his finger. "Hm. Verily."

Steele turned to grip the bars. He watched the Romans watching him from behind their bars. "I thought Rome didn't keep prisoners."

"We're not prisoners." The man grinned and spat. Didn't quite make the distance across the corridor to the American cage. "We're gladiators."

Steele gestured down the corridor at the other cage of sorrier Romans. "What are they?"

The gladiator gave a disparaging glance toward the shabbier men. "Dead," he answered.

"Scum," said another gladiator.

"Crabs," said another.

A flat surly voice from the slum answered, "You're exciting me, O Big Strong Gladiators."

"Those are criminals," Ranza told Steele. "Bottom of the birdcage."

Steele looked at the gladiators in their cage, then at the scum of Palatine in their cage. "What's the difference?"

"Gladiators fight each other. The scum get fed to something."

The animal noises from somewhere in these catacombs pressed to the fore of Steele's attention.

"Gladiators take an oath," said a gladiator.

"Yeah," said Ranza. "To endure burning, beating, killing, bludgeoning, buggering—"

"Ho!"

"Okay, I added that last one," Ranza admitted.

"They swear to take that all?" said Steele.

Ranza nodded.

Steele shrugged. Those were all good things to happen to Romans.

The duty of a prisoner was to escape. Ranza had been taking note of things about their surroundings. One of the first things she noticed was there were no cameras down here.

Steele didn't believe it. "There have to be cameras."

The Romans chuckled at him. "This place does not exist."

Steele could not see any sound recorders but could not afford to think there were none. There had to be listening devices with American POWs down here. He asked if the Marines had been interrogated.

"No, sir."

That sealed it. "They're listening," Steele told her.

After that, Ranza and Steele conferred under cover of a cloak. Gladiators hooted and offered to pay to watch what he and she were doing under there.

While the Marines tapped a cover of Morse garbage. Any Roman surveillance would think there might be embedded messages in all the junk. At least Rome could not afford to leave the cryptic messages unanalyzed.

Tapped nonstop nonsense:

Claudia is a cow.

Claudia is a sow.

Claudia is a bowwow.

Claudia is a meow.

It would give the Roman cryptos something to chew on while Steele and Ranza plotted an escape. The code was all

crap and the Alphas could keep it up till the Claudias came
home.

. . . slut.

. . . mutt.

. . . butt.

Under the cloak Ranza and Steele communicated silently in a combination of signs and lipreading. Steele did
not trust whispers.

Ranza told Steele about the guards. They were almost all
automatons. Not many human guards. Ranza had seen one
or two.

She told him that the human guards never approached
close enough to the cages to be grabbed. The guards carried
shockers—contact-type shockers—in case some klutz of a
guard dropped his shocker and it fell into a prisoner's
hands, it couldn't be used against the guard. Unless he was
idiot enough to come within arm's length of the cage.

A guard had been grabbed by the scum while the Marines were down here. Automatons had come to the rescue
real quick for that. But if a brawl broke out, no one would
come.

Automatons were stationed at all the outer doors. There
were no patrols. Automatons did the feeding. Automatons
emptied the crappers. Ranza told him the criminals had a
deader in their cage. He lay dead in there all day. Automatons
fed and emptied the cage but left the stiff. A human guard
came later. Didn't notice the body till the inmates demanded
it be removed. The guards made the prisoners stand against
the far wall, and they brought down more automatons before
they opened the cage and dragged out the corpse.

How does the automaton know who is guard? Steele
asked.

Ranza shrugged, guessed, *Signals from an implant?*

Steele considered what could be worked around that
piece of information. He pressed his fingers to his ears to
keep out the tapping so he could think.

. . . hag.

. . . rag.

. . . bag.

. . . drag.

. . . gag.

On top of the Morse, other Marines kept up a cover of whispers for Roman surveillance to pick up. The Roman spooks would eventually sift out the whispers from the Morse and all the other noises, and figure out what the Americans were saying in secret.

Then the Roman cryptographers' next task would be to decipher what "My dog has fleas" was code for. And how much wood would a woodchuck really chuck.

At night—at what the Marines assumed was night—the lights went out. No warning. Just sudden darkness. It ended any covert conversations under the cloak.

Bioluminescent mold or lichen on the ceiling gave off the faintest pale green glow so the underground chambers were not totally black once the eyes dilated.

The jailers had provided mattresses for the POWs to sleep on. The Marines kept their mats stacked against the back wall when not in use. They dragged the mats out to the floor as soon as their eyes adjusted to the dark.

Carly shared a mat with Twitch. Ranza kept to herself, and no one bothered Ranza. The men beckoned Kerry Blue as she tiptoed through the reclining bodies. Most of them knew her too well. There was an assumption that being with her once conferred a lifetime membership. She picked her way through them, dropped down on a mattress near the wall, to lie back to back with Colonel Steele. All the men sounded a disappointed, "Awww."

Steele snarled low into the wall, his back to her. "Not a bright idea, Marine."

She stayed where she was, back to broad back. Whispered, "Sir? It's a *cage* full of *men*."

"They're Marines."

"So are you."

The colonel had no business ever touching her. Ever. And that had not stopped him.

He growled, "As you were."

28

THE WORDS *VIRTUS ET HONUS* were chiseled into the back wall of the gladiators' cell.

Strength and Honor.

Ranza had found a small stone which had crumbled out of the floor, and decided she wanted to write *Quantum coiens pignus* on her cell wall with it.

Big deal.

"Tell me how to draw that," Ranza asked anyone.

Cain started spelling, "Q—U—"

Ranza interrupted, "But how do you write that in Roman?"

Cain was confused. "*Quantum coiens pignus* IS Latin."

"I mean the letters," said Ranza. "Don't they write in those squiggles?"

"No. Just use Roman characters."

"I don't *know* Roman characters," Ranza tried to tell him again.

"Um," said Cain. "They write the same as us."

"No shit?" Her silver-gray eyes blinked surprise. "Romans use our alphabet?"

"Uh," Cain started, changed his mind about what he was about to say. Said, "Yeah. Q—U—A—"

Ranza scribed the letters with her stone into the wall as Cain dictated. She muttered, "Dang, those lupes stoled everything from us, didn't they."

*   *   *

Every day the gladiators were let out for exercise in small numbers in the company of automatons. POWs were not.

The Marines traded taunts with the gladiators. In spite of the insults, you could tell the gladiators regarded the American POWs as several steps above the Roman scum in the other cage. *Those* were something you scrape off the sole of your sandal. The POWs were soldiers, and therefore honorable. They were just on the wrong side of the war.

The noises from above started early this day, sounds of lots of people climbing bleachers. Festive voices. Music. Vendors hawking goods.

All the sounds funneled down here.

The prisoners watched a giant lizard float past on a heavy lifter through the corridor that divided the Americans from the Romans. The beast was fourteen feet long not counting its eternal tail. The great expanse of its rough skin was mottled green, brown, and dark red. A thick squat horn topped its nose like a small pyramid. Its wide feet were three-toed like a dinosaur's.

The lizard was chained to its platform, but so lethargic it didn't seem to need restraints. It took no interest in the humans. The Marines could not see its teeth. Didn't want to. The thing looked smelly and wasn't.

"Local life has an opposite thing going," said Kerry Blue. "Opposite *orientation*. To its protein. That's why the lizard doesn't stink to us and we don't smell tasty to him."

Her cellmates looked at her strangely. "How'd you know that, Blue?"

"Something Darb told me." Tears sprang suddenly to her eyes. She dashed them away before they could escape. "That's why on some planets we can't eat anything." Her face wrinkled up. She did cry.

"Darb?" said Steele. Jealousy in the name.

Kerry's arms hung uselessly at her sides. "He was like everybody's weird brother. Came out with these strange bits of information. Like in comedy everyone gets married. Tragedy everybody dies." She wiped her face with her sleeves. "I'm gonna miss him for a while."

Ranza said, "*I'm* gonna miss him." Cole Darby was her outboard brain.

Soon automatons, more of them than usual, trooped down to the dungeon. They passed the Americans by and stopped at the criminals' cage and ordered the prisoners against the back wall.

An automaton opened their cage.

The dirty Romans—and these were, literally, dirty—cringed.

You didn't like those guys. They were Roman and they were slime. Still something moved in the gut, made the breath come shallow, drummed at the nerves to hear the names of human beings called forward for execution.

An automaton called a name. Terror showed in all the men's eyes. No one answered.

Then you noticed, because an automaton was picking one up, the tiny capsules on the stone floor in the passageway.

The automaton that picked up the capsule walked into the cage and down the line of prisoners. Some of the men had bloody ears.

Apparently the prisoners had dug the thin capsules from their earlobes and pitched them out to the corridor.

The automaton found a match, perhaps to the blood. The machine being seized the prisoner and dragged him out screaming and thrashing.

A gladiator cupped his hands around his mouth and scolded, embarrassed, from his cage, "Not in front of the Yanks!"

Five other prisoners either came as their names were called or got forcefully collected.

One of the damned let himself sail away into a euphoric hysteria. He smiled and blew kisses back to the ones left behind, his eyes glassy. Another vomited. His cellmates offered comfort: "Don't do that in here! Who's going to clean that up!"

The automatons shut the cage and took the condemned away.

When the automatons came back for the gladiators, the chosen stepped forward proudly when called. Those were led out in chains rather than in the grip of automatons.

When they were gone, the underground cell blocks took on the quiet sullenness of a death watch.

Ceremonial trumpets blared from above.

A tumultuous cheer, and thunderous chanting: "CAE-SAR CAE-SAR CAE-SAR."

Steele's artic blue eyes lifted. "Is that prick up there?"

A little later, raucous jeering signaled the appearance of one or more of the condemned criminals in the ring.

Then, not from above, but from somewhere in the underground corridors, sounded the clanking of stout chains, a tremendous roar, a pounding and splintering of massive wooden doors.

Kerry whispered, "That thing's down *here!*"

The noise was coming from the direction the lizard had gone. Not lethargic anymore. It sounded enraged.

Angry huffing and puffing and hissing built up to another roar.

Then came the sudden sound of chains rattling out. A huge door opening. Great limbs thrashing, claws gouging, the beast launching itself up a ramp and out.

Shrieks and cries from the crowd, the voices full of fear, awe, and blood thirst. Drumming pandemonium reverberated down below. Noises of horror and disgust carried downward, followed by cheers and fervent applause.

There was a smaller sound amid the din, very close. A voice of a single someone right above the Marines' heads. Whimpering against their ceiling became a soul-curdling scream. Then a roof-shaking thwomp!

A rain of splintered sawdust and sand filtered down from the ceiling.

Kerry Blue shook the grit out of her brown hair. The lupes had taken her hair band away from her for some reason. She moved over to crouch next to Steele, who was blinking sand from his eyes.

And it went on.

You couldn't talk. Because you couldn't think. Just listen to the sounds.

After a while, the giant lizard floated back through the corridor the way it had come, lazy on its lift, breathing deep and slow. Its yellow eyes showed no interest in the aliens behind the bars.

Much later, after all the noise had died away, automatons returned some of the gladiators to their common cell. The men were clean, shaved, and dressed in fresh tunics. They collected nods of recognition from their cellmates. Apparently you got taken care of if you won.

Some time in the middle of the night Steele became aware of Kerry Blue tapping Morse against his hip with her forefinger.

Kerry tended to get her d's and her u's mixed up, so she ended up telling him: *I love yod.*

He had no choice but to tap on her hand: *I love yod too.*

Two nights later, a screaming and howling and banging carried up from the dungeons to the guards' chamber on the ground level.

The brawl down in the cages sounded like a hoax. The human night guard was too smart for that. He waited an hour or more after the sounds died away to wander down to see if anyone had been killed. If the deader was someone scheduled to die in the morning, he would need to pick a replacement.

He did not turn on the underground lights, as he did not want to disturb the animals. He carried a lamp to review the cages.

He found the body. It was fish-belly white, in the Americans' cage, lying against the bars.

And there was a skinny American woman, all the way *through* the bars so she was standing in the corridor— except that her head was caught between the bars.

The large male body lay right where she could spit down on it. There was a long gash in his head, crusted with blood, and a bloodstain on the stone floor under him.

No problem with him. Someone else could clean that mess up on the next watch.

The woman was a problem. She turned her head at the guard's approach. Friendly as a badger, that one. She cocked a leg, ready to kick.

The guard brandished his shocker. He ordered the American prisoners to get back against the far wall. Then told the woman to squeeze her skinny ass back inside.

She gave a feral snarl. The bars prevented her from angling her face around to look at him, and her dark hair was in her eyes. She kept her heel up and ready to clock him if he came up behind her.

The Romans caged farther down the corridor told him to leave her like that. They goaded him: Take her! Take her!

The guard was not getting snared in this. He was smarter than that.

He tried to keep his distance and still get a better look at the woman. He was not altogether convinced that she couldn't get her head the rest of the way through those bars. Maybe if she left her ears behind.

From the look of her, he guessed she might do just that.

He touched his shocker to the bars at the edge of the cell, hoping that would carry through and stun her. But the weapon didn't activate against metal.

He wished he could just kill her. Unfortunately he did not have the authority to kill U.S. POWs. And explaining the need for deadly force against a female that size would not advance his career.

"Call for reinforcements!" the prisoners cackled.

"You need automatons! *Lots* of them!"

"Help! Help!" someone called in falsetto.

There were dogs bigger than she was. He was twice her size.

He made sure the other Americans were still against the back wall, before he quickly, gingerly darted in from the side, near the bars, out of the striking line of her waiting heel, and jabbed her with his shocker.

Even before she dropped, he felt a very large hand close on his ankle and *pull*.

He fell harder.

The Romans prisoners howled and clamored like baboons, calling for guards, in earnest this time.

The Marines reached through the bars and pulled the guard's body close. They'd got very lucky. The guard's head had smacked the stone floor hard. He was unconscious or dead.

The Yurg's body had cushioned Carly's face-first drop straight down.

Kerry supported Carly's head as the Yurg got out from under Carly and rose to his feet.

They had chosen the Yurg to be the deader because he was a very pale guy and he had the longest arms. His head wound was only a slice which he had cut with his own thick thumbnail, sharpened against the stone wall. It was a shallow gash, but a scalp wound bled like a son of a bitch, and he had looked frightening.

Steele gouged the recognition capsule out of the guard's earlobe.

The guard's blood on Steele's hands, the guard's capsule, and the guard's control unit won him an amazing green light on the lock of their cell door. The Marines stared at the miracle.

There was a moment of breath-holding before the opening of the door.

Everyone tensed. This next move would trigger the alarms. Had to. This scheme could not be working this well.

Steele pushed.

The cell door swung open with a tired creak.

There could be silent alarms, but the Marines wouldn't know that unless automatons came marching down.

The gladiators yelled bloody murder. The criminals beckoned sweetly with crocodilian smiles for the Americans to let them out. They could help, they said. They could show the Americans the way out, they said.

The Marines ignored them except to stay beyond grabbing distance from any of them.

Dak pulled out the rope they had made from braided strips of mattress covers. It had been stowed under one of the mattresses. The Marines had been careful to stack the mattresses good-side-out during the day.

Kerry Blue and Twitch Fuentes gently maneuvered Carly back through the bars. Twitch carried Carly out of the cell, Ranza seized up the guard's lamp and they all ran.

"Wrong way!" the Romans tried to tell them.

It was the wrong way if the Marines intended to get to a door. But they knew there were automatons by all the doors.

The Marines were going out the death gate.

Kerry Blue had always been good at getting men to brag. At a stray mention of a "death gate," Kerry's expression of repugnance got the Romans to pile detail upon gross detail, with vivid descriptions of what went through the death gate, and exactly where the death gate was.

The Romans talked enough for the Marines to kluge together a rough layout of this subterranean labyrinth. And the Romans had volunteered information like, "You can't escape from the arena. It's not like old Rome. The lowest boxes are seven meters up."

Okay, that means we need the rope to be longer than twenty-one feet. Thank you very much.

Ranza covered the lamp with her shirt to dampen the beacon as they moved stealthily through the labyrinth. The other prisoners kept up their clamor, but apparently no one believed them.

Twitch hissed, *"Mira!"*

Ranza turned the light to a dark alcove where, piled like trash, was a collection of things taken from prisoners upon capture. There were U.S. landing disks and displacement collars in the pile.

For certain there would be displacement jammers in effect here, and there were no coms in the pile with which to signal the *Mack* anyway.

The Marines did not want to be weighed down by something they probably would not be able to use. Still they grabbed a few displacement sets just in case God and the *Merrimack* smiled on them.

They proceeded to a primitive lift made of wood and operated by chains and a pulley. Ranza doused the light entirely. The Marines hauled themselves up to ground level, and stepped out to another wide tunnel. This passage smelled of chlorine.

The Romans had cleaned the stones with bleach.

Kerry whispered, "This is it."

A lot of horrible stuff came this way. The Romans dragged the dead out of the arena through here.

The Marines dashed out the death gate into moonlight. They stood in the wide bowl of the Coliseum, a vast pit open to the sky. Insects, night birds, and bats flitted in and out of the high archways. Pennants stood listless in the idle wind. Underfoot was sand. *Arena* was Latin for sand.

Two moons gave the Marines double shadows. They moved back to the wall and proceeded like a line of rats out of moonlight into deep shadow.

Dak tied their braided rope onto two of the displacement collars to weight the end. He passed the line to Cain.

Cain swung the weighted end in circles to gather momentum for his toss. He let the rope fly at a high column in the first row of boxes seven meters up.

The line struck the side of the column. The weight of the landing disks caused the end of the line to loop several turns around the column.

Perfect.

"Quick!" Ranza sent Kerry Blue up the rope first. It was supposed to have been Carly, who was lightest and quickest, but Carly was still unconscious. Kerry scrambled up as if all their lives depended on it, and pulled herself over the knee wall. She got hold of the rope's counterweights and kept them in place so the rope would not unwrap from the column.

With the top secured, Steele held down the bottom of the line and sent the Marines up one at a time.

The rope was amazing. They never should have got away with making it. No guard ever searched their cell. Romans continually fell into the trap of relying on automatons. Their disdain for low tech was unforgivable in a people who lost sixty-four Legions to the Hive because of that disdain.

The Marines were feeling extraordinarily forgiving just now.

Cain and Yurg were next up, so they could help others get over the top. The Yurg carried the lamp between his teeth.

Twitch, wearing Carly Delgado draped across his shoulders, came up next. Cain hauled Carly up from Twitch's shoulders, then the Yurg helped Twitch over.

Twitch immediately gathered up Carly again, took the

lamp, and set off through the rows and aisles of the amphitheater, scouting a way out.

He was not looking for a door. There were seventy-six of them. He could expect automatons and alarms at every one of the seventy-six.

On the second level at the outer wall on the moon-shadowed side of the Coliseum, Twitch chose one of the many open archways that framed large statues. This one looked like the goddess Diana.

Twitch turned off the lamp as he drew close. He gently settled Carly on the floor between Diana and the arch, then traced his route back so he could show the others the way.

All but four of the Marines were already over the knee wall by the time Twitch returned. Icky Iverson was climbing the rope.

Down in the arena, Colonel Steele glanced up. He noticed Kerry Blue up there at the knee wall still holding the counterweight down. He growled low at Cain, "What is she still doing here? Get her out of here!"

Cain turned his head aside, whispered, "Beat it, Kerry, I got this."

Twitch beckoned Kerry to come with.

"Behind you!" the Yurg shouted, making everyone jump.

Down in the arena, Steele turned. The shot tore into his chest.

Kerry's screech tore the night sky, *"Thomas!"*

Steele spun round, one hand still clutching the rope. Lost his grip. Fell on his back.

Kerry's face appeared over the knee wall, screaming.

Ranza dropped to her knees at Steele's side.

Icky rotated on the anchorless rope, skinned his knuckles on the wall, slipped. Avoided landing on Steele, and fell into Dak Shepard.

Steele's blue eyes were round in shock or death. Steele's hand lifted, zombielike, from the sand to point at Kerry Blue, the eyes staring at Cain behind her, bloody mouth moving. Repeating his last order.

Romans charged across the arena. Dak hurled the dangling end of the rope up and over the wall, out of Roman reach. Yelled at the Marines up there: "Go! Go! Go!"

Twitch reeled in the rope faster than he thought he could move. He unwound its weighted end from the column. Cain pried Kerry Blue away from the knee wall, and dragged her at a run behind Twitch with the others into darkness.

29

C OULD NOT SEE A DAMNED THING for her tears and the dark. Kerry Blue just kept hold of Cain's hand and ran the way he pulled her. Twitch was out in front, leading them up steps and through the black passageways of the Coliseum.

The blackness broke to a patch of midnight sky through an open archway.

Framed by the arch was the hard silhouette of a woman, larger than life, holding a bow and arrow. Statue.

Kerry glimpsed movement around the statue's plinth, of people hiding there. She almost cried out a warning, but then recognized the figures as Marines.

Carly was on the floor, stirring, holding her head.

Twitch never slowed down. He charged up to the statue and quickly tied the rope around giant Diana's marble legs, while the waiting Marines whispered to Kerry and Cain, "Where's the Old Man?" And Kerry couldn't talk.

Twitch threw the free end of the rope out through the arch. He gave the rope a good tug to test its strength, then motioned for the first climber.

Cain ordered in a whisper, "Kerry, go!"

She hesitated.

"You ain't going back," Cain told her, hauling her toward the rope. "I got orders. Move your ass."

And Kerry would not hold up everyone else with a balk. She scrambled over the edge. Twitch and Cain kept hold of her until she got a grip on the rope and whispered, "Okay okay okay."

When they released her, she slithered down as fast as she could without tearing her palms off.

The rope was too short. She had to cling to the bottom end and let herself drop the last yard or two.

Landed on her feet, felt the jarring in her shins. Rolled on hard paving stones.

She rolled up to a crouch. Looked up. Did not move. Saw that the arch through which she had just escaped was positioned directly above one of the seventy-six arched doorways to the Coliseum.

And behind the bars of that arched doorway a human silhouette moved, turning outward to face her with the silhouette of a weapon.

Fear leaped inside her like iced daggers. The breath stopped in her chest. She froze in her crouch, staring. Did he see her?

Trying not to move anything more than her eyes, she lifted her gaze upward. Someone else was clinging to the rope up there, waiting for her to move. She hoped the others could see her wide wide eyes. The climber had stopped on the rope. Sensed something desperately wrong down below.

A motion behind the bars drew Kerry's gaze forward again.

The figure inside the arch raised the weapon toward her, taking aim.

The planet stood still.

The end of the rope swayed over Kerry's head.

I'm right behind you, Thomas Ryder Steele.

The loud voice from the dark commanded, "Stand away from the door. Do not approach."

Automaton.

Kerry heard a small gasp up above, faint as a rush of air, though there was no wind.

Then there were no more whispers. No sound but night traffic in the city.

Kerry's breaths came shallow. She stood up carefully. Turned around slowly. Took several tentative steps away from the door, nothing exploding, nothing stabbing into her back.

She kept walking stiffly away.

Didn't dare look back. But heard seven more times a drop and a roll, and the automaton voice commanding someone to stand away from the door.

Night turned to day, and the day was half gone before the Coliseum's Vigil of the night watch was summoned before his superior, the Sub-praefect of Roma Nova.

The Vigil had spent the last hours in helpless, useless waiting, goaded by a sense of dire urgency. Time was of the essence and he had been commanded to stay put, do nothing, and talk to no one. He listened for a public broadcast, for sirens. Still heard utterly nothing of the prison break.

When at last he was summoned, the Vigil reported to his superior's office and blurted at once: "American soldiers are loose in Roma Nova. The populace must be warned."

The Sub-praefect left that declaration out there an inordinately long time before he gave his slow measured answer, "*You* shall not tell me what *must* be."

On the floor next to the Sub-praefect's pearwood desk lay the rope the Vigil had untied from Diana's legs and reeled up from the second floor archway. Now that he could see it by proper light, the Vigil could identify the material. Strips of mattress covering. The fabric had been judged too thin to hold anyone's weight, so the Americans had braided it.

"I accept responsibility," the Vigil announced at rigid attention.

"No," said the Sub-praefect, much as he would like to toss this person into the criminals' pen. "You are *not* taking responsibility because there is *no* prison underneath the Coliseum, we are *not* holding POWs there, and this fiasco *never happened*."

All the brilliant people in this empire, and the Sub-praefect got a Vigil who signaled a lockdown that locked the automaton guards safely away from the escaping prisoners.

And he had shot their only captive officer.

Caesar had actually taken that news with a strange serenity.

There could be no recriminations, because none of that had happened.

"That kind of news does not get out," said the Subpraefect. "Ever."

"But they're out there!" said the Vigil. "The Americans!"

"And you are going to apprehend them," the Subpraefect assured him. "And when you do apprehend the American soldiers, your captives will be freshly landed troops."

"But they are—"

"*Freshly landed troops*. You have never seen them before in your life."

"I—"

"Have never seen them before in your possibly severely foreshortened life. Put your ears on, listen closely, and repeat this back to me, so I know you understand: There are no escaped POWs loose in Roma Nova."

Automatons took Ranza Espinoza, Dak Shepard, and Icky Iverson back to their cell under the Coliseum. Two automatons for each of them, though one would have done. All the mattresses had been gathered up and taken away. Ranza's writing stone had been removed from the cell. The words QUANTUM COIENS PIGNUS remained etched in the wall.

A gladiator, seeing only three of the escapees returning to captivity, remarked in utter disbelief, "They *made* it?"

"Don't answer that," Ranza quickly ordered Dak and Icky.

Big Dak's face was wet with tears.

The gladiator guessed, "Well, not all of them anyway."

A U.S. patrol picked up an FTL plot moving from the direction of Thaleia toward Palatine's star system.

"Fat PanGalactic supply ship moving your way," the patrol notified Fleet and gave the vector.

"Take it, *Merrimack*," Admiral Burk ordered.

"Get me a Star Sparrow out there," Farragut told Gypsy.

A Star Sparrow was really the only thing for intercepting an FTL target.

Gypsy ordered up a T541 Star Sparrow with a shipkiller load, then ordered Targeting, "Tag the Thaleian."

"Targeting, aye. Tag away."

"Fire Control. You have permission to launch Star Sparrow on general vector forward of the Thaleian."

"Firing Star Sparrow, aye." Fire Control responded.

Energy coiled within the ship. A metallic scream rose from the launch tube with the missile's leaving. The recoil carried through the deck, and the ship sang.

"Star Sparrow away," Fire Control reported.

Targeting: "Tag has locked on target. We have a green."

"Transmit tag signature to Star Sparrow," said Gypsy.

"Transmitting tag sig, aye." In a moment, "Star Sparrow has a lock. Time to intercept eleven seconds."

"Is the target evading?"

"No, sir. Target holding course. He's on the rails. Coming in hot. Contact in three. Two."

Waited.

None of the ship's stations said anything.

No flash appeared on the Tac screen.

Farragut turned to his silent tactical. "Report."

Marcander Vincent shook his head, at a loss, "Nothing happened."

Fire Control reported, "Shipkiller did not detonate. Repeat, the warhead did not detonate."

"Old ordnance?" Tracking suggested.

"Ordnance never gets that old on this boat." Farragut moved quickly round to look at the tactical screen. Demanded, "Tag status!"

"Gone," said Targeting. "We have lost contact with the tag. The lupes may have erased it."

"Where is my Star Sparrow?"

Gypsy sent to Fire Control: "Ping the Star Sparrow."

"No return ping, sir," Fire Control responded. "We lost it."

Farragut said, "*Lost* as in it's a runaway, or *lost* as in it's joining the other side?"

"Lost as in we have no signal and no idea," said Tactical.

"Find it! I don't want to eat this one." And to Mr. Hicks at the com station. "Get me Fleet."

Mister Hicks immediately raised the flagship. "I have Admiral Burk, Captain."

Farragut took up the com. "Fleet, this is *Merrimack*. We have a Star Sparrow that failed to detonate and now we've lost track of it."

He braced for Burk's hand to come right out of the com and rip the stars off his collar.

But Burk's voice came back resigned, tired, and grim, "You're not the first one, *Merrimack*."

The admiral told him that the Romans had apparently foxed the U.S. tracking system for hard ordnance. He was advising all ships to adjust tactics until a solution was found.

"No hard ordnance? That leaves us basically with beams," said Farragut.

"Yes," was the hard answer.

At least Marcander Vincent waited until the com was closed before he opened his mouth. "That's bullsh! Intercept an FTL target with beams? That don't happen."

It didn't happen. The Roman supply ship from Thaleia made it into Palatine's star system, where Roman ships flocked around it to escort it at sublight speed to the planet's atmosphere.

Harsh words passed back and forth over the com among members of the U.S. Fleet.

A direct hail to *Merrimack* carried the ironic voice of Captain Washington of *Monitor*:

"*Merrimack*, I found your Star Sparrow."

Farragut seized up the com. "Marty! Thank God!"

"Not what I've been saying here," said Martin Washington. "Your Sparrow was the one with the shipkiller?"

John Farragut was all but singing hallelujah. Laughing with relief. "If my bird had found any other ship but yours, that warhead would have lived up to its name."

"That is true. You owe me. And I'm going to collect on this one, John. I'll make a list."

"Marty, I'm ready to kiss your feet!"

"Foot-kissing will not be on the list."

Admiral Burk directed both captains to a separate channel on which to give them instructions.

"A U.S. light cruiser will be arriving from Earth carrying commandos. *Merrimack* and *Monitor* will provide distraction strikes while the commandos are inserted on the ground near their targets," said Burk. "We need to get a lot more aggressive here, gentlemen. The softening up process has got to proceed faster. We need to get our invasion forces on the ground with all possible speed."

"Without getting our invasion force massacred," Marty Washington added.

"I do realize that, Captain Washington," said Burk, offended.

"Something is happening on Earth," Farragut suddenly realized.

Burk seemed to shrink. All at once he looked old. The admiral admitted, "We think Romulus is making an end run."

"Should we even be here?" said Farragut, alarmed.

"We absolutely must be here," said Burk. "We need to make something happen here before Romulus makes his move there. Your battleships would be of no use on Earth right now."

"Why?" Martin Washington asked.

Farragut and Washington could tell that Burk did not want to explain. But he had to. "The population of Earth has, over the last several months, increased by as many as a million Roman tourists."

"Tourists," Captain Farragut echoed.

"A million," said Admiral Burk.

"Where?" said Captain Washington.

"Just about everywhere except the United States. The biggest concentrations are in the European nations. They are residents of Roman colonies."

Rome had over four hundred colonies in its Empire.

"The Romans have been coming in by way of LEN colonial worlds on board civilian ships owned by LEN member nations. The Roman tourists are mixed in with League civilian passengers. We can't shoot them, we can't stop them, we can't board them, we can't even turn them back."

"What are the 'tourists' doing when they get to Earth?" Captain Washington asked. "Massing armies?"

"Not that we have detected yet. And our allies *are* keeping an eye on them."

"Then what are they doing!" Farragut cried.

"Right now?" said Burk like a man waiting to wake up from an awful and absurd dream. "They're sightseeing."

PART FOUR

Gladiator

30

TR STEELE CAME TO CONSCIOUSNESS on his hands and knees, expelling liquid from his lungs. Wet. Naked. The floor was hard and slithery under him. Lamplight felt warm on his skin. He saw the light from behind his closed eyelids. Heard words he could not understand. They sounded Latin. That meant he was in hell.

He blinked slime from his eyes.

Heard rushing water, then felt the tepid rush hitting him in a strong stream. Pink water swirled off him to the white floor between his palms. They were hosing pink medical gel off him.

But who were *they*?

He shielded his eyes from the spray, trying to see who *they* were.

They looked like medics from their white coats, gloves, eye protection, and face masks. Two of them. Looked like zoo keepers from the elephant pikes they used to make sure he stayed in place.

The water stopped, replaced by a rush of warm air from above, drying him off.

Off to one side there was a tank filled with pink medical gel, draining now. He had been in there.

A pallet floated over beside him. A medic rolled him

onto it, strapped him down. He might have overpowered the two right there, had he his wits about him.

The medics left him alone in the room.

Physical straps on his wrists and ankles held him in place. He was still naked, no cover on him. A lamp kept him at body temperature.

He saw now that his chest was whole. There wasn't even a scar. His coarse golden chest hair was a little finer in the place where the shot had blasted through him.

He tested his bonds, found them all too secure. He determined to jump the medics when they loosened the straps.

That idea evaporated. When one of the medics returned, it was in the company of an automaton. Steele's bonds were not loosened until the automaton had a good grip on him. The medic fit a rough tunic over Steele's head. No belt came with it.

The lock on the door opened to the medic's touch. The verification must be in the medic's ear.

The automaton kept hold of Steele through the door. The medics stayed inside the white room.

The automaton took Steele down the corridor at a walk for sixteen feet to a set of steps. A human guard joined them there and down the steps to another passageway.

Coming to a turn in the corridor, Steele had to wonder where the hell he was.

He had gone from a sterile medical facility to—

I'm still under the Coliseum.

He was back in the familiar dungeon corridor, just not approaching from any direction he had ever come unhooded. The automaton walked him past an alcove where weapons lay stacked in haphazard piles like trash—swords, morning stars, double axes, maces, elephant pikes, and U.S. beam cannons. A U.S cannon was not useful to anyone until it was recoded to its bearer.

Because his hands were held fast in the automaton's grip, Steele had to lean his head to the automaton and brush his temple against the android shoulder so he could find out if his sighting bracket was still attached there, outside his eye socket. It was.

The human guard noticed the motion. Said something snide to him in Latin.

"Huh?" said Steele.

The guard pushed an American language module into his language port at the base of his skull and said again, "Good luck trying to find your own weapon in that heap."

As Steele approached his cell, he saw with a dull and sinking sensation that there were more people in it. Almost a dozen. Had no one escaped?

Immediately he looked for Kerry Blue.

When he got closer he saw that, besides Dak Shepard, Ranza Espinoza, and Icky Iverson, the other Marines were not the same ones who had been here before. These were from Echo Team.

"Ah, hell," said Steele.

The Marines looked round at the sound of his voice. Acted like he'd returned from the dead.

On *Merrimack*, Mister Hicks at the com had been monitoring public Roman com channels. He reported: "The Romans are going to pit an American against a gladiator in the Coliseum."

Farragut erupted. "They can't!"

"They say they can. They say he died trying to escape capture. They revived him for a proper execution."

"I don't give a damn what they say or if that makes any legal sense. That's bullskat."

"And you know it won't be a real fight," said Hicks. "It's going to be an execution, because the American is untrained. But he's a legate so he deserves the sword."

"He's a *what?*" Farragut suddenly felt very cold, a suspicion creeping up his spine.

"They claim they have an American legate. A Legion Commander. What is that in American?"

Gypsy looked to Farragut, "A Legion equates to what? A battalion?"

Hicks said, "They're saying they have the Legate of the U.S. Legio LXXXIX Bullmastiff."

"Oh, for Jesus."

* * *

Under the Coliseum, the criminals were taken out early in the morning on game day, so they could be put to death first. You heard the monsters roaring as they were prepped for the feeding.

Guards in full regalia came for the gladiators later. At the same time, Steele was also taken out of his cage. "Where am I going?"

A guard nodded up, "Arena."

"The lowlife get the animals," a gladiator told Steele. "You will actually face a Roman gladiator. That is a sign of respect, Yank."

Farragut played these honor games, but to Steele the enemy existed to be destroyed. He spat on the floor of the corridor. "Animal's an animal."

The gladiators girded for battle. Steele was left barefoot in his unbelted tunic.

The gladiators were instructed to swear their oath before Caesar.

"I'm not swearing that," said Steele.

"Neither do the animals," said a gladiator.

Ranza yelled through the bars. "They can't do this! You can't do this! There are rules for treatment of POWs."

A Roman guard spoke to Steele instead of Ranza, "You died. You're ours."

A lift carried Steele up in chains between two guards.

Stout gates parted to sunlight and universal booing.

The two heavily armed men in ceremonial armor walked Steele out to the center of the arena in chains.

Steele craned his head around to look behind him. They had left the automatons behind at the lift. Those did not enter the ring.

The enormity of sound hit him like an ocean wave. Mass emotion sparked the air like a physical current.

The space seemed all the grander for being walled in. The shape gave it a sense of moment, focus, energy, like a stadium or a diamond or a cathedral. The tiers of seats, the crowd took on the presence of a single Roman monster.

Steele blinked in the sunlight at things he had not seen in the dark during the escape. All the bright colors, the painted stucco and statues, the black and red marble walls.

The fabulous buntings flying. Caesar's gleaming golden eagles. And there was the head prick himself ensconced in his gilded box. No Claudia at his side.

At the center of the arena, one of Steele's ceremonial guards unlocked his chains. The heavy cuffs fell away from his wrists. The other guard dropped a short sword at his feet, and the two backed away, their shields locked. They were not his opponents.

Steele stood alone and amazed. Unchained. Life was suddenly possible.

He picked up the sword, put it through a few experimental passes to heckles from the spectators. They weren't there. The blade was everything.

The gladiator sword was shorter than he was used to, better suited to stabbing than slashing. Steele was a slasher. He would need to get closer to his opponent.

A trumpet blare sounded from a rank of long thin *cornu*, heralding something.

A massive gate opened. A gladiator advanced from shadow.

Big guy. *Big* guy. The way Rome bred them. Tall as Augustus with a lot more meat on him. He held a short sword, the *gladius*, same as Steele's, in his right hand. He held a rectangular shield, a stout one, on his left arm.

He had a helmet. That would limit the Roman's peripheral vision, if Steele could ever get to his periphery. He wore full armor, a cuirass of metal-clad leather round his chest, front, and back, a tabbed leather skirt round his thighs and nads, and metal shin guards.

All that equipment ought to slow him down, but Steele couldn't count on that. That was a big damn Roman.

The gladiator lifted his sword to Caesar and the crowd. Too much space between them for Steele to dash in with a surprise stroke.

Steele, in his rough tunic with only a sword, probably ought to run, but there was nowhere to go. And Steele was not inclined to run from anything. Certainly not from a Roman.

He eyed the shield. The gladiator would use it. It made him feel safe. He would try to feel out his opponent before striking. The Roman had the time. He was not naked.

As Farragut would put it, *he's not going to swing at the first pitch. He's going to take one to see what you've got.*

Steele charged in high, at a slight angle, eyes on the man's sword side. Made the gladiator commit the shield across himself, and lift his sword up for a counterstrike across his own shield.

While Steele shifted at the last instant, lunged instead toward the gladiator's shield side and down low.

Steele's left knee hit the sand as a pivot on which to swing himself round with the sword under the Roman's shield, slashing from the back. He sliced the gladiator's Achilles' tendons through to his anklebones.

Steele rolled away as the big man went down in a howling heap. The crowd rose in a tsunami. The great sea of Romans erupted booing. Caesar was booing.

Steele scrambled to his feet, gingerly danced in to stab the gladiator under his helmet, up under his jawbone to finish him. The crowd cheered that. Even Caesar clapped his hands wryly.

Steele tugged the shield off the heavy, rubbery left arm. He found the sword which the gladiator had dropped, and kicked that behind him. He looked round to see if anything were running at him from behind. Clear, he picked up everything—the shield, his sword and the gladiator's sword—and he retreated to the far side of the arena.

From another gate strode not another gladiator but a man dressed like the grim reaper carrying a spear instead of a scythe. This was supposed to be Hades. The figure proceeded out slowly. Steele waited for him, but Hades did not come for Steele.

Hades strode out to the fallen gladiator. He poked the body with his spear to make sure he was thoroughly dead. Hades wore skeletal gloves, which made his fingers appear very long and bony. He gestured to a slave to take the body away.

The slave was dressed like Steele in a rough tunic except that the slave had a belt. The slave came out with a meat hook, which he plunged up into the gladiator's rib cage and dragged him off the arena floor by a rope through a tall gate.

The sign over the gate read *Portia Libitinensis*.

The death gate. Steele recognized it now. It had been dark when he had come out that way.

He dropped his shield, sprinted across the sand behind retreating Hades, to an alarmed wave of sound from the crowd, and snatched the spear clean out of Death's hands.

He could have killed Hades right there, but Steele darted away again. He got what he wanted from him. The crowd was laughing.

Steele returned to his little arsenal. Now he had a spear, a shield, and two short swords.

The crowd sounds subsided to confused muddled noise. Steele sensed a quandary here. That was not supposed to have happened. It was meant to have been Steele going out on the meat hook.

Now they had a dead executioner and a still living victim standing in the way of the next act of this circus.

Caesar gave a shrug and an impatient gesture to someone else in his box, who relayed instructions over a com, perhaps to backstage. Or under stage as it was here.

Steele picked up the spear, tried to get a feel for it and gauge a distance from which he could get a realistic shot at Romulus.

The sand in center stage heaved, fell back in a cloud of dust. A screeling sound of sand in a winch set the teeth on edge. The sand lifted, spilled from the great wooden trap door in the arena floor as it opened. Out from the depths burst an alien thing.

Like a cross between a prehistoric wild boar, a buffalo, and an angelfish, with a short thick coat of violet-gray hair and black bristles. A stand-up mane lined its highly arched, narrow back from head to broom tail. The Romans had tipped its four tusks in polished copper, filed dagger sharp. Angry little yellow eyes gleamed in the sides of its massive head. The tiny eyes squinted against the flying grit on the wind. The pig didn't like the sand either. It sneezed, then folded its enormous head back to rub first one eye against its bristly side, then the other eye on the other side. It blinked. Teary eyes found Steele.

Steele crept forward, jabbing with spear and sword, circling round the snorting animal, which turned with him, keeping its tusks toward him, until Steele felt the wind at his back. He dropped the sword, reached down, grabbed a fistful of sand and threw it into the little piggy eyes.

The head folded back with a sound between a squeal and a roar, as the creature tried to clear an eye.

Steele snatched up the sword again and charged at the blinded beast with both weapons. He buried the spear into the high crest of the neck, then slashed down the slab side of it with the sword.

Blood, red and warm, gushed free. Then Steele was airborne without his weapons. The beast's dying convulsion threw Steele high.

He landed in a hard roll, quickly scrabbling away from the creature's thrashing final throes.

Steele got to his feet and walked—because nothing was chasing him—back to his little arsenal, which consisted now of the gladiator's sword and shield.

The man with Caesar in Caesar's box, possibly the ringmaster of this show, was looking nervous and perplexed. Caesar gave another shrug. His gesture seemed to say: What else you got?

While the Romans were prepping another opponent, Steele dragged his sword and shield over to the shade at one edge of the arena under a box of women, the kind who, in collective, you call a bevy.

You would never find Kerry Blue in a bevy.

Steele had learned back in his hellion youth that women who decorated their eyes like that liked bad men. He reached up a thickly sinewed, bloody arm and beckoned, demanding in American, "Give me your water."

And down into his hand dropped a water bottle. He drank. Poured some in his eyes, rinsing away blood and sand.

Heard the gates open with a collective gasp from the sea of spectators.

A long fat eel, big around as a Swift's fuselage and three times as long, glided on finlike membranes that lined its either side. Pale, translucent, some color of flesh, it glided low across the arena, spitting sand clouds out underneath it in fans. The crowd was shrieking in terror, the lower boxes pulling back in their seats.

Steele dropped his water bottle.

The thing didn't seem to see him, and Steele couldn't see its eyes. Couldn't tell how it was moving itself. Seemed to be sucking up sand and jetting air and sand out its underside gills.

He watched it float across the arena, glimpsed its underside. Saw a slit like a manta's mouth, filtering, grazing. The eel happened over the dead pig. Paused there, but passed over. Too big.

Still the eel managed to rake the top layer of hide off it in passing, then it turned, trolling for something closer to bite-sized.

Steele dropped his shield and ran all out toward a gate.

The eel in languid pursuit passed over the tall shield where Steele had left it in the sand.

The monster seemed to hiccup with a grinding sound, and glided onward, leaving the shield behind, its surface scraped.

The gate was locked of course. Steele flattened himself against the gate set within its slight recess, which at least got him off the grazing field.

But the eel, frustrated with the pickings in the sandy arena, turned itself over sideways and came gliding around the curved wall, making a circuit, its mouth sucking.

Steele's hiding place was fast looking like a deadly mistake. His recess in the wall was turning into a vertical food trough.

As the eel swept round the wall, Steele dashed back into the center of the arena, to roaring laughter. Wished to hell he had the spear back. The damned gladiator sword was too short.

Steele ran behind the eel to collect the shield.

The eel reacted to the movement, turned round.

Steele huddled down, holding the shield over him like a shroud with both hands. He waited for the eel. Heard its advancing intake of air and sand. As it came over him, he rammed the tall shield into the slit mouth, hard.

The beast bowled him off his feet. Steele felt the gills sandblast him as they passed over.

Then the eel turned over belly up like an attacking shark. Steele ran out of the way of its mad thrashing, as it tried to dislodge the shield from its mouth.

The bottom rows of box seats had backed up into the second tier. Romulus was laughing.

Spearmen posted in the audience moved down to the first row, ready to repel the eel in case it came up.

Steele staggered to the arena's edge, caught his balance against the wall. He'd lost his sword. It had to be buried in the sand under the convulsing eel. He roared up at one of the guards. "Give me your spear!"

The man stared down at him as if he were mad.

"Give me the fucking spear!"

The guard looked across to Romulus, who appeared amazed, delighted, and he motioned for the guard to give Steele the spear.

The eel flipped back over, coughed out the shield, spitting yellow fluid on the sand. Might have been eel blood. Its sides rippled in wrath or pain.

Steele approached it, spear at the ready.

The eel backed away from him—the crowd laughing uproariously—the monster retreating from the mouse.

Ain't funny down here.

The eel rippled backward. Its tail touched the wall, and it turned its head with a start. Steele ran in, stabbed the spear into a nexus of dark conduits visible through the eel's translucent skin just behind its head. He could only hope those were blood vessels or something critical in a nervous system.

May as well have been an off switch. The thing collapsed instantly, motionless, yellow stuff leaking from its mouth.

Steele staggered away from it, breathing hard. Not sure why he had chased the thing. Something the Romans had said down in the dungeon. If you bore the crowd, they'll kill you themselves.

The crowd was not sounding murderous. They were happy with the show, chattering excitedly, laughing.

Steele cast about for his sword. It was nowhere to be seen.

The pig-buffalo had finally stopped twitching. Steele retrieved the other short sword from its carcass. Like yanking something out of a stone.

Steele's muscles were losing their strength.

The front rows were refilling.

Steele looked around to see if he could find where he'd dropped his water bottle.

The crowd had taken up a chant: A-da-mas! A-da-mas!

Caesar was looking somewhere between amused and bemused, and now just musing what to do.

Those animals had been meant to kill some of the scum from the criminals' cage. Steele guessed the lupes were going to keep bringing out shit till something got him dead.

Soldiers in full armor came out next. Bunch of them. This was it. Steele just didn't have anything left in him. He faced them, gory sword in hand.

The lead soldier shouted something at him in Latin. Sounded like a command.

Another said in American: "Drop your weapon."

Steele let the sword drop.

The soldiers surrounded him, poked him to make him walk back through an arch, into a caged lift. Not the way he came in, and not the death gate. The crowd was on its feet, cheering him as he descended.

The guards prodded him down an unfamiliar corridor where automatons took custody of him and forced him into a shower.

He expected gas for sure, but he got water. Cold, but clear drinkable water. Under the flow he found he had taken the skin off his left knee and one elbow. His shoulders were scraped. There was a big knot on his shin he didn't remember getting, and another scratch from who the hell knew what. A million stinging points from the sand blasting he'd got from the eel.

A clean tunic waited for him when he came out. Still no belt. Food.

An intradermic injection took away some of the ache that was setting into his muscles.

The Romans had removed his language module when they sent him into the arena. They plugged it back in now, and punched a capsule into his earlobe.

Automatons took him back to his cell. He took note of all the doors, all the corridors along the way, who or what was on guard where.

As he came in sight of the cell, the Marines gasped and rose to their feet. "Colonel!"

"I knew it," said Dak. "I knew it!" Dak had absolute faith in the Old Man. Dumb, but Steele appreciated the faith. Steele knocked forearms with Dak and accepted the *hoo ra!*

The Roman gladiators in the opposite cell rose slowly too, clapping ironically.

"You were meant to die, you know," a Roman told him.

"Got that," said Steele. "Gives real meaning to getting the hook."

He shuddered at the afterimage of the big gladiator being hauled away like zoo meat. Then he became aware of animals roaring from their cages. And suddenly wondered what actually became of the defeated gladiator's body.

Another Roman remarked, "You must have done well, *Adamas*. They like you."

Must have. With a language module plugged in, he could now understand the chant that had followed him out of the ring.

A-da-mas! A-da-mas!

It was his name in translation. Steel.

He actually owed these gladiators for that remark about not wanting to bore the crowd. But he was not about to thank them.

Ever in escape mode, Steele asked the Romans, "Why didn't they send automatons out to get me?"

The gladiators recoiled. "Not in the arena!" A shudder in it, as if Steele had suggested blasphemy. "It is not *done*."

Munda, the Magister of Imperial Intelligence, requested a private meeting with Caesar Romulus. Munda claimed to be free of nanites but Caesar did not permit him in the palace. Caesar came to Imperial Intelligence wearing an exosuit as if he were in outer space.

Munda received him in a secure chamber. Caesar would not sit, would not touch anything. Munda remarked on none of it.

"I wanted to alert you before I informed the Senate, Caesar. It seems the patterner Augustus isolated the harmonics of both of the new Hives."

Caesar inhaled in cautious wonder. Stopped short of a smile. "Are you sure?"

"We won't know for absolute fact until we resonate the complements and both Hives die, but it seems real, because we have the method by which he derived them."

This was Power. Ultimate Power.

"Who else knows?" Romulus asked.

"Only the team I have assigned to this project in Imperial Intelligence."

"The Senate has this?"

"No," said Munda.

"But they'll find it for themselves. The have a copy of Augustus' data bank," said Romulus, testing.

"But they don't have the Striker," said Munda. "They didn't ask for it and we didn't volunteer it. It's a sixty-year-old vessel. But half the key is in the old Striker."

Caesar was hard pressed not to laugh. "Then we can keep this secret!"

"We could, but why would we do that?"

"The Hive will arrive at Earth before it reaches Palatine."

Munda looked disapproving. On Munda's face that counted as horrorstruck. The man was expressive as rock. "The Hive knows no nations. It is not a weapon," said Munda.

"Can you not see it?" said Romulus. "Earth on the eve of destruction, the United States on its knees, and Rome delivers—Passover."

"An enjoyable fantasy," Munda allowed. "Please be serious now. The Hive cannot be contained. This is not a matter of war, but a question of humanity."

Caesar nodded gravely. "Of course it is. Thank you for your outstanding handling of this project."

Magister Munda died in his sleep.

31

THE EARTHLY ORIGIN of the escaped Marines forced them to stay near the city and its surrounding terraformed cultivation. Being human they could not forage off the alien land. They could not digest any of the native growth.

Neither could they go into the city in daylight. Their clothing was U.S. issue arctic black and white camouflage, out of place in Roma Nova in the spring.

At least their clothes were frictionless. Nothing adhered to the fabric. Their bodies might get ripe but their clothes never smelled of anything.

They had been hiding in an olive grove since their escape from the Coliseum. Unfortunately it was springtime and there was no fruit on the trees.

There were ducks on the pond, but getting one was the trick. The birds' presence did indicate that there were edible things in the pond. However in this season the edible aquatics were still tadpoles, not even full frogs.

There were violets to be found in the shade, but there was not a Marine born who could survive on violets. In the forest beyond the olive grove there were last fall's acorns. The white oak acorns. The ones from the red oaks gave you cramps.

Farms covered the beautiful landscape, but they all had security systems.

There was one picturesque little farm on a hillside with sheep and spring lambs, guarded by a dog.

"What happened to the dog?" Kerry Blue asked over a lamb supper in the forest.

"Don't ask," said Cain.

The meal was more of a breakfast, because it had taken the better part of the night to get a fire going, then to prepare the meat without proper tools.

The next night Carly managed to snag a woman's tunic that had been left out on a deck, and the Marines sent Kerry Blue into town foraging for food in daylight.

She came back with five pizzas and a lighter for making a fire, which she pitched to Taher, their designated chef.

"How'd you get that?" Taher wondered at the gift of fire.

"I asked," said Kerry.

"You *talked* to Romans?" said Big Richard. "Now how didn't that give you away?"

"I told them I was a Russian student and my language module was an American piece of shit."

"Kerry does better than Cain at food duty," said Menendez, tearing into the pizza.

"Yeah, what she brings isn't still walking or clucking."

"Hey, I killed it and skinned it, and it was good," said Cain.

Carly gave a goatly bleat and opened another pizza box.

"Blue still gets better stuff," said Menendez just before he plunged an entire slice of pizza into his mouth.

"That's 'cause Blue has a marketable commodity," said the Yurg.

Kerry Blue threw dirt in his face.

The Yurg wiped off his face, picked dirt off his pizza. "That sucked, what I said, Blue."

"Yeah," said Kerry.

Night was closing in. They took stock of their displacement collars and landing disks in the last light. They had only five sets of displacement equipment. The escaped Marines numbered eight.

"Fine, then we send five, and they send their collars back for everyone else," said Cain.

"Fine, but is there any chance in the known universe that

we can find an area not covered by Roman jammers?" said Big Richard.

Carly checked a displacement set for correspondence. "Uh, a really good chance."

Heads whipped round. Carly held up her LD and collar. The lights were all red. "We're here."

"We just need a destination correspondence now," said Cain.

"How do we do that?" said Big Richard. "We don't have a com. Makes these things about twelve shades of useless."

"We have a com." Kerry Blue produced a Roman-made universal com she'd got on her last foraging mission. "If anyone knows a U.S. channel, see if you can raise the *Mack*."

Cain seized the com. The Yurg kissed Kerry's hands. "Kerry Blue, I am sorry for what I said. I am not worthy to be in your company. I am mud. I am garbage. I am rat feces."

"Eyeew." Kerry pulled her hands away from his.

"Forgive me?" Yurg asked.

"Yeah. Forget it, Ratcrap."

"*Mack Mack Mack.* This is Alpha Three drinking wild whiskey. Can we get a dust off?"

Mister Hicks literally jumped out of his seat on the command deck. He turned to the captain. "Sir! I have evaders calling on the emergency channel on a nonstandard com."

The captain and the XO both moved to the com station, motioned for Hicks to continue the communication.

Hicks put the call on the speaker as he answered, "Alpha Three, this is *Merrimack*, please authenticate."

"We're in the pit of fubarosity here, how would you like us to do that?"

"What's your name, son?"

"*Captain!*" Cain recognized the voice. "This is Flight Sergeant Cain Salvador, sir!"

"What color is the exec's hair?"

"Never seen it, sir. Her eyebrows are black."

Gypsy scowled at Farragut. Her dark eyes warned: *Speak not of the hair.*

Gypsy asked a question of her own: "What is the mid watch called?"

"Hamster watch, Commander Dent, sir." Cain knew her voice too.

"What is redundance?" said Farragut.

"What is—?" that stumped him. Then, "Oh! *Oh!* It's good! It's good! It's good! It's good!"

Farragut turned to Gypsy, "Authentic enough for me."

"I agree," said Gypsy.

Farragut said, "Get us in range and get them out of there."

Gypsy spoke into the com, "We are showing five displacement signatures, Flight Sergeant."

"That's all the displacement equipment we have," Cain returned. "There are eight of us."

"Then gear up five and stand by to displace. We will advise you when we are in range."

She could hear Cain barking, "Blue, Big Richard, Yurg, Taher, Menendez. Collars! Disks!"

Kerry Blue could not say how scary it was to stand by for displacement while wearing red lights. At least if this went south, she would never know it.

Cain lifted the com.

A black figure out of the dark came over Cain. Black-gloved hand sealed over his mouth and the com flew out of his hand. Immediately, Kerry Blue was bowled off her LD. A black-clad figure landed on her, held her down.

Romans were coming out of the trees. She couldn't count them, could hardly see them. They moved like humans. Kerry saw guns, and that was enough to take the fight out of her.

When chaos resolved out of thrashing black figures, Kerry counted ten Romans, and still eight of the good guys. No one had managed to get away.

The Romans acted like humans. They taped the Marines' mouths shut.

Kerry guessed the lupes weren't trusting automatons' decision-making skills on this mission.

Kerry recognized one man when the black mask came off his face. That one used to be the night Vigil under the Coliseum.

Gypsy Dent's voice was sounding on the com. "We are in range, Flight Sergeant. Take your disks."

Romans stared at each other in amazement. You could see the whites of their eyes get real big.

They had clearance to displace five people onto *Merrimack*.

The Vigil muted Cain's com. Another Roman said, "What can only five of us do on a space battleship?"

The Vigil said, "Five of us, armed, with a chance to board *Merrimack*? We have the element of surprise."

"It's an enormous risk."

The Vigil took Kerry Blue's displacement collar roughly from her neck and closed it round his own neck. "Who else wants the honor?"

Four others unsnapped collars from the other Marines, and snapped them round their own necks. The five Romans who were staying behind kept weapons trained on the Marines.

"We'll never get another chance like this!" said the Vigil. "We have green lights! Fortune favors the bold!"

Cain moaned on reflex. His shock was genuine, staring at green lights that had been red just moments before.

The Romans stood on the disks.

"All greens."

The Romans must have brought jammers into range with them. Did they not realize that?

"Tell your ship to bring us." A Roman shoved a weapon into Cain's face and made to take the gag from his mouth.

"No! Don't trust him on the com," said another Roman. "He'll just give a warning. Don't wait for *Merrimack* to bring us. Initiate send."

The five Romans touched the controls on their collars.

In a thunderclap, they vanished, lights showing green on the LDs.

The remaining Romans looked smug.

The Marines looked appropriately horror-struck.

"We have boarders on *Merrimack*," one Roman told another in crowing disbelief.

He should have paid attention to that disbelief. The U.S. boffins had switched all the red and green lights that came down to the planet, just to confuse the Romans. The switch confused Marines too. Kerry Blue silently recited *Red is right. Green is . . .* She tried to remember what Darb said about green lights. *Think great green gobs of gushing goo?*

Merrimack had gone silent. Commander Dent must have figured out something had gone wrong down here. Not that any piece of the displacing Romans could possibly have arrived, gooey or otherwise. But *Mack*'s displacement techs knew the difference between a red light and a green light.

A Roman, still imagining that the boarding of *Merrimack* was a success, ordered his technician, "Quick, restore displacement jammers to this area!"

The technician was checking his equipment. Trying to comprehend what he was looking at. "Jammers are showing already on . . ." Slow horror just making itself felt. The Romans stared at the green lights on the U.S. equipment. Starting to suspect they had made an assumption they should not have made. They hadn't even thought to question the meaning of a green light. Green was simply the universal go.

There were only five Romans left now. In the Roman confusion, the Marines jumped them. Fought hand to hand. Or boot to chin—Kerry Blue's favored method, as her hands just weren't that strong.

The Marines took the Roman weapons, quietly shot their owners with them, cut the capsules from their ears, hid the bodies in the woods, and threw the capsules into the river.

Watching the moons' light on the river, Kerry clawed the tape from her mouth. "Who's got the com?"

They all looked at each other. No one spoke.

"Well, who had it last?" said Kerry.

"One of the Romans?" Taher suggested.

"Fubarosity," said Cain.

Steele was taken out of the cage again. He was given no armor. That meant it was feeding time for the animals.

"Good-bye, Adamas," said a gladiator.

The ceremonial guards unlocked his chains and dropped a short sword at his feet as they left him in the ring.

This time there were two men already out there. One

wore a metal half-collar of sorts and a thickly padded sleeve on one arm. He wielded a heavy net, which he flourished like a matador's cape. The other gladiator, who wore a helmet, had a short blade sheathed in his belt, and carried a trident. Steele was calling him the picador.

Steele supposed he himself was the bull.

But he wasn't.

The two gladiators saw Steele enter, then turned their attention toward another gate with an attitude of anticipating something big and deadly to come charging out.

Steele wasn't waiting.

Steele darted across the arena, came up behind the picador, the crowd shrieking a warning. Steele got there just as the man was turning. Steele slashed down on his shoulder right where the helmet left off. The picador fell to the ground, spouting blood, that ghastly shade of arterial red, in a strong pulsing stream.

Steele seized up the trident, raised it high and threw it downward through the other gladiator's swirling net, pinning the net's edge down through the sand to the wooden floor. Steele crouched to launch himself into a charge at the gladiator, when the gates burst open. The giant lizard bolted out with a metallic screaming growl.

Not the lethargic thing Steele had seen float past his cell on a lift. This beast was gnashing and snapping in a crazed fury, its giant tail lashing. The spectators all drew back in their seats.

The lizard bugled and roared as if in pain, and came straight at Steele.

This is not right.

Steele dodged behind the gladiator who was trying to get his net free from the trident. The lizard ignored the gladiator and tracked Steele's motions. It wanted him and only him.

Kerry had told him that humans did not smell tasty to the giant lizards. Humans were not edible.

And the lizard did not appear to be hungry. The only thing Steele could think of was the object the medic had punched into his earlobe. Steele bet his life it was a transmitter.

Galloping dinosaur feet shook the floor. Spectators

laughed, feeling the jarring in their seats. The lizard tossed its head, ramming its pyramidal nose horn into the wall. A great scream rose from the crowd, descending in nervous laughter.

Steele was running, dodging, shifting directions, letting the momentum of the lizard's great mass carry it past its mark, tumbling nose over tail, and getting up roaring. Like a rhino chasing a chipmunk. One skid on the sand and Steele would be done.

He couldn't find a still moment to lift his sword close to his neck without cutting his own throat, so he dug at the capsule in his earlobe with his fingernails.

And *turn!*

The lethal tail swept past.

The capsule came out, a small rod, no bigger than a ten-gauge wire, between his blood-sticky fingers.

The surviving gladiator had his net free by now. He swirled it over his head, either to net Steele or to drive him toward the beast.

Steele pitched his capsule at the gladiator.

The lizard instantly lost interest in Steele, and followed the capsule's arc through the air. The giant head bowed down and plowed through the gladiator's net. Metal fabric tore before the pyramidal horn. Lizard jaws closed on the gladiator's middle, and the beast gave him a backbreaking dog shake before hurling him aside. The beast then pounced on a spot in the arena, scrabbled in the sand with its three-toed feet, and stomped.

The stomp must have crushed the tiny transmitter, because the lizard lay down in a sudden flump, relieved and panting. A shred of metal netting still hung off its face. Its giant sides moved with its pain-free breaths.

The lizard's yellow eye focused on Steele, then shut. Didn't care about him.

And Steele didn't care about it anymore.

The chant started: *A-da-mas! A-da-mas!*

Steele collected the gladiator's short blade from its sheath at the corpse's waist, and the trident from the sand. He tested the weight of the trident in his hand.

He moved close to Caesar's box. Looked up.

And damn everything to hell, Romulus wasn't there.

32

"I'VE LOST CONTACT with the Marines," Mister Hicks announced from the com station.

"We've lost correspondence," *Merrimack*'s displacement tech reported to the command deck. "Roman jammers are in effect down below."

"Clam us up," Gypsy told the displacement tech. "Restore our jammers."

"Jammers activating, aye."

Gypsy ordered the com tech, "Stop hailing. Go silent."

"Gone silent, aye," said Mister Hicks, somber. They had been so close. He had just talked to Flight Sergeant Cain Salvador. They had come within seconds of getting five of their own out of there.

Captain Farragut prowled station to station, helpless. Five Marines just within grasp, and suddenly gone. He could not give up.

"Did we get the coordinates of the displacement equipment?" Farragut asked. "We can take the *Mack* down and pick them up."

"Forty-one degrees, twelve minutes, fifty-nine seconds north latitude, eighty-nine degrees, two minutes, fifteen seconds west longitude." Marcander Vincent looked up from his tactical station to Captain Farragut. "They're in Roma Nova, sir."

"God bless America!" Farragut shouted, frustrated to hell.

He had orders—strict orders—not to enter space over Roma Nova. "Get us out of here. Fire something at Numa's ship on the way out."

Marcander Vincent noted: "I have a ship rising out of planetary atmosphere. Italian signature. Has the appearance of an Earth civilian craft."

"Check that one!" Farragut ordered, wanting badly to shoot something.

Upon leaving atmosphere, the Italian ship jumped to FTL. *Merrimack* followed and easily picked it up again on a predictable course toward Earth. The ship executed no evasive maneuvers. No Roman ships accompanied it in escort.

Merrimack took up a parallel course. Mister Hicks hailed the ship. "Italian vessel, this is the U.S.S. *Merrimack*. Identify yourself."

The pilot begged, "Don't shoot. We have children on board! They are children!"

"We're not going to shoot," Captain Farragut told him. "We'll probably hook you if you don't check out. And contrary to Roman propaganda we don't torture children."

"We will 'check out.' This is a school bus!" the pilot cried. He recited his school district's identification and the ship's identification numbers.

Mister Hicks sent the confirmation request to Italy via res pulse. He received back confirmation that the vessel really was a school bus from a suburb of Old Rome, carrying a group of young students. The Italian added a plea not to hurt the children.

Everything checked, yet something was odd. John Farragut picked up a subliminal sense of something not quite fitting. But it was nothing he could bring into focus.

Most of the viewports were masked, but Marcander Vincent angled a scanner beam through one to reveal children. They were in the ten-year-old range, acting like kids with some adults in the back. The pilot was sweating like a smuggler, but then he had a space battleship menacing off his port quarter.

There was something wrong.

"He's smuggling," said Farragut.

"What do you want to do, sir?" Gypsy asked.

Farragut shook his head. Enough that there were children on board and it was an Italian vessel.

"Wear off. Notify Jupiter Control. I want this bus checked again next week when it's coming in to Earth."

A Roman guard, a human one, came down to the dungeon underneath the Coliseum with a contingent of automatons to the POWs' cage. The man sent an automaton into the American cell.

The automaton knew which prisoner was Steele. "Here, try this on," the automaton told him.

This was a gladiator's helmet.

Ranza Espinoza moved to the bars and shouted at the human, "This is a violation of conventions of war!"

"And I'm sure we'll hear about it," said the man outside the bars. He was standing carefully on the corridor's center line, out of arm's reach from either side.

"What pinhead was this made for?" Steele tossed the helmet back at the automaton.

The automaton turned to face the Roman. "He rejected it."

"I see that," said the human and gave orders to another automaton in his ranks. "Find a bigger one."

"A bigger helmet?" the automaton requested clarification.

"Yes, a bigger helmet," the man said, irritably. "Go." Then thought to add, "Find a bigger one and bring it back here!"

Steele recognized the man now. He was not a guard. He was the one Steele called the ringmaster of the games. The Romans called him a *lanista*.

In the arena the *lanista*'s tunic glittered. Here he was wearing blue jeans. He had a mane of flowing yellow hair, chiseled features, and manicured hands.

"You have become a popular villain, *Adamas*," said the *lanista*.

Steele said nothing. Stared like a bull.

When the automaton returned with another helmet, someone from the gladiator's cage called, "You're going against one of *us!*"

Steele looked around the *lanista*, across to the gladiator. "I never had a problem killing Romans."

The second automaton entered the cage, offered the helmet to Steele. "Here, try this on."

Steele did. Felt like wearing a bucket with eyeholes. There was metal around his head, but he wouldn't be able to see a blow to avoid it, so it didn't strike him as a gain. Steele was an offensive fighter. He didn't win hiding behind armor.

He took the helmet off. Tossed it at the automaton. "I'm not wearing that one either."

"He rejected it," the automaton told the *lanista*.

The *lanista* nodded wearily to the automaton. To Steele he said, "Nevertheless, it is yours to wear or not to wear. I am tired of you and I hope you die."

"Same," said Steele.

After the *lanista* collected his automatons and left the dungeon, the gladiator pointed across to Steele. "I hope it is you and I."

This time Steele couldn't say the same. The man was another big one, a black-haired, bronze titan. The others called him Xeno.

Xeno informed him with a grin, "To yield you lift a finger."

"This one?" Steele asked.

"No."

It occurred to Steele that he hadn't seen this one in a while. Xeno had gone out to the ring one day and had not come back. Steele asked him, "Aren't you dead?"

The gladiator Xeno shrugged massive shoulders. "They like me."

One of society's dregs called over from the death cage, "*Adamas!* Don't use your sword for blocking."

Two others added at once. "Especially not against an ax."

"Yes. Not against the ax. Don't use *anything* to block an ax."

Xeno's head turned with a wolfish snap at the criminals. "You're aiding the enemy, traitor!"

The criminals smiled. "Yes, we are!" said one.

Another of the condemned said, "What are you going to do to me?" And he cackled, as if he were fatally funny.

Steele doubted how sound the advice could be coming from a piece of crap. He asked the criminal, "Have you been out there?"

The condemned man grinned. "I've seen the vid casts from the colonies. They haven't held games up *there* in a long time." He pointed at the ceiling.

"They fix the fight?" Steele asked. Not really a question. His fight against the lizard had certainly been fixed.

So the answer surprised him. "You would think," said the condemned man. "But in front of this crowd? If this crowd spots anything fake, you will both be tied to a bull's horns. When I go out there, they will want to see groveling and pissing and my insides spilling out. From gladiators they want to see a *fight*."

"I'm not a gladiator," said Steele.

All the expressions changed. The prisoner narrowed his eyes. "You think not, *Adamas*?"

Steele's armor arrived in the morning. A leather cuirass with leather shoulder pieces. There was no metal on his such as he had seen on the Romans' armor. Good. He didn't need the weight. Gravity was slightly stronger here already.

He received one of those stout leather oblong shields his guards carried. He bashed it against the cage bars to see if it would really hold up against a pounding.

From across the corridor someone called, "Ah, you out with the real gladiators, *Adamas*. Today you die."

He left the helmet behind in the cell when the guards came to get him. Automatons kept the Marines against the back wall, while human beings in full armor shackled Steele. One carried a short sword for him. Another picked up his shield and the discarded helmet and brought that along too.

When the gates opened and the sunlight hit Steele's white-blond hair, the noise swelled to a riot of cheers and catcalls and roars. The stands drummed with stamping feet.

Steele's surrounding wall of guards expanded away, leaving his sword, his shield, and his helmet in the sand.

Steele immediately seized up the sword and the shield, and moved from the spot, just so not to leave himself where the Romans planted him.

He looked up for surprises, glanced around the arena for trapdoors threatening to open.

Gates opened, one on either side. One gladiator strode out from each gate.

Steele knew them from the cage.

On the left was a big guy—as if they weren't all fox-trotting huge—wielding an ax. Didn't know his name. Steele was calling him the Ax now. From the right came a bulky black man armed like Steele except that he wore a helmet—a helmet not as bad as the metal shroud with eyeholes they had given Steele. This gladiator's eyeholes were big and insectoid-looking because of the metal mesh which protected the cutouts.

The gladiators closed in with measured steps from either side. When they were far enough into the ring, Steele sprinted to the wall and made a flanking run back around the Ax.

First thing you learned in sparring two opponents was to get them both on one side.

Steele chose the side with the Ax because that was the more dangerous. If Steele didn't take the Ax down first, he was never getting him down.

Don't try to block an ax with a sword, the condemned men had said. Looking at the weapon, Steele believed it. Don't use *anything* to block an ax, they had said.

The ax looked like it could cleave iron bars.

They don't fix the fights, my ass, he thought.

But the guys may have been right about the crowd recognizing fight-fixing when they saw it. There was an awful lot of contempt in the crowd noise as the two gladiators stalked toward him, and the derision didn't all feel directed toward him.

The Ax took the point position as the two closed in. This was going to be like boxing a bigger man with a longer reach. Steele was only six feet, so he had done that often. The only way to box a man with arms like an orangutan was to jam him up. Steele dropped his shield and edged forward with just his sword.

An enormous gasp sounded from all round, punctuated by titters and jeers. He had given up his shield.

The shield would slow him down.

The heavy ax was rising up for a killing stroke. Steele barreled in like a fastball. In before the blade came down. The long ax handle hit his shoulder as he ran into the holder. He bodily collided with the Ax full length, jarring his teeth. Felt the crunch of flesh and bone against his blade as his sword drove in low. Steele rolled off to the side, wrenching his sword out with him.

The ax fell limply from the gladiator's grip. Steele jumped aside to get clear of the wounded man, who was tottering and trying to hold his guts inside the horrible wound.

Sounds of delicious revulsion oozed from the crowd. Groans, deeply felt, rose from their own intact guts. They loved it. Intoxicating, to be so close to death and to take their next breaths without pain, exhilarated to be alive.

Steele was busy locating the shield he'd dropped and keeping an eye on the other gladiator.

He kept the tottering, mortally wounded Ax between himself and his fresh opponent. When the Ax fell in the sand with a ghastly spill, Steele bounded over him, landed low to snatch up the ax and jabbed it toward the other gladiator to back him away.

The gladiator danced out of the long weapon's reach. He tapped the ax blade with his sword, testing, watching for his opening.

Steele stalked forward, jabbing, keeping his opponent at bay until he was standing over his shield.

The ax was too heavy to be of use to him beyond poking his opponent away. If he tried to wield it in earnest, he would die like the man behind him.

He chucked the ax forward. The startled gladiator made a huge leap backward from the enormous blade as Steele took up his shield and lunged forward. He roared on a furious high, "Come on! Come on!"

The crowd rose in a wave, roaring.

Two men with swords and shields clashed. The spectators liked this much better than two against one. All of them screamed at their chosen fighter.

The gladiator smashed his shield at Steele. Steele met it with his own shield. Mistake. If his shield was engaged—

The sword was coming in low. Steele deflected it at the last instant with his own blade, not quite in time. He felt its edge draw a line of fire across his thigh.

A second blow from the gladiator's shield knocked Steele on his back.

Steele kicked the man's ankles. As the gladiator stumbled and caught his footing, Steele sprang to his feet.

The noise swelled. A bizarre current he could feed off of. The burn in his thigh was nothing. The noise pushed him into an adrenaline high, too hot to care about the pain.

The two circled round the ax. The gladiator kept glancing down at it. He had to move his whole head to do it because of the limited field of vision his helmet gave him.

To Steele seeing was life.

He would not be lured into moving his shield too far from center, because that was apparently what the gladiator wanted him to do.

At a wild overhead strike, Steele jumped back. At a sword swing coming in from the side, Steele dodged to the other side.

The gladiator tried slamming his shield into Steele's shield again; Steele was ready to take the hit—and not straight on this time, but at an angle that blocked the gladiator's sword arm. Steele was already reaching around him with his sword for the man's hamstring. Got the back of his knee instead. The gladiator folded hard onto the knee and pitched backward, unable to hold himself upright. His helmet hit the arena floor, and sat askew on his head, blinding him.

Steele dashed in, stabbed into the crease of his groin. Arterial spray and sounds of enthusiastic disgust from the crowd answered him.

As the spectators relished the sickening horror, a whole cadre of fully armed soldiers came out of a gate. One commanded Steele to drop his sword.

The sword dropped from his hand of its own accord. The guards surrounded him in their box formation.

Heat was leaving with the end of danger. Steele was feeling his wound now. He saw his leg coated with blood.

The guards held ranks around him, while all eyes turned to Caesar's box.

Romulus of late appeared only for the games' commencement, then gave his seat over to some picturesque damsel while he tended to weighty affairs of state and war.

The yellow-haired *lanista* walked out in his sparkling robe to the fallen Ax, whose guts had fallen from his abdomen.

The designated sweet of the day in Caesar's box stood up. She came to the gilded rail and spread her bangled arms to the crowd, soliciting their opinion.

The enormity of sound swelled, most of the thumbs voting down.

The young woman's thumb made a slow feint upward to boos. Then, with a foxy smile, she thumbed decisively down. The cheer soared to the sky.

One of the guards strode over to the Ax and plunged a sword into his neck. A spurt of blood said that the Ax had not been quite dead yet. But he had been a gladiator so he got the sword, before Hades could poke him with a spear, and the slave with the hook came out to collect his carcass.

The *lanista* proceeded to the other gladiator. This time the crowd was demanding, "Live! Live! Live!" and the young woman obliged with a thumb up. The crowd cheered, though it really seemed too late. The bleeding from his severed femoral artery had stopped. That one was already dead.

Still, men rushed out with a litter and physically carried the fallen gladiator out of the arena at a run.

So that was what the bronze gladiator Xeno meant by *they like me.* If they like you or they need you, they don't let you stay dead. Roman medical technology for resuscitating the newly dead was unrivaled.

Steele's muscles were cooling, trembling a little from dehydration. The wound in his thigh *hurt* now. He was ready for a shower and one of those nice intradermic injections. *Come on, let's go, guys, take me in,* he thought.

He heard the *lanista* announcing something in Latin.

Crowd cheers spiked. Steele tried to see what was happening through the armed wall of his guards.

Got a glimpse of a gladiator in shining armor, bounding out the gate and collecting adoration, tens of thousand of voices chanting his name: XE-NO! XE-NO! XE-NO! The champion himself, back from the dead.

Steele's wall of guards started to separate around him. One commanded Steele to pick up his sword.

They were making him fight again.

33

STEELE PUSHED ASIDE MORTAL disappointment and picked up his sword from the sand.

Dissonance roiled within the crowd voices. Sympathy for the devil. This fight was fixed and their favorite villain deserved better. Their champion deserved better. They wanted to see Xeno go against the mighty *Adamas* in full strength, not a defanged tiger.

Instead they were getting the championship bout with the villain lamed. A champion was only as strong as his strongest enemy. Someone had seen fit to prechew Xeno's meal.

Steele's guards were leaving him, keeping their shields toward him.

The *lanista* was striding toward the gate. *I am tired of you and I hope you die.*

Xeno waited.

And Steele charged sideways, to hell with the pain in his thigh. He ran all out to catch up with the *lanista* headed for the gate. It was not wise to expend strength on someone without a weapon, but this man had already killed him. Steele could not survive this bout and everyone knew it. He was going to take his real killer with him.

The amphitheater filled with sounds of surprise, alarm, screams. The *lanista* became aware of his peril, looked back in time to see Steele's face just before Steele took off his ridiculous yellow hair and his head with it. It surprised even Steele that his blade went all the way through muscle and bone, but he didn't think he had ever been so angry. Through his blur of rage he heard the shrieks and laughter. And applause.

He turned to his opponent. Xeno was pounding his shield with his own sword. Took Steele a moment to realize that Xeno was applauding too.

Steele looked up to the crowd, gestured at the *lanista*'s body with his sword, soliciting a thumbs down.

And got it, with riotous laughter.

He turned to face Xeno across a length of sand. The noise died away, came back in a slow tide of chants and roars, rising and rebounding off the enclosing walls, to become a physical force.

Steele advanced at a walk to meet his fate, the Coliseum ringing. Xeno pointed his sword to Steele's helmet where he'd abandoned it. Steele shook his head, refusing it.

Xeno took a battle stance. Steele made the first charge. Could be his last. Pain and fatigue vanished in an adrenaline surge. He caught the downstroke of Xeno's sword with his shield, his own thrust deflected by Xeno's shield, and he charged past. Both spun round, exchanging places. Xeno was first on the counterattack, and Steele could only turn out and away from the thrust. He jumped back in for a return stroke that landed on Xeno's shield.

They traded hammering blows, till Steele got Xeno open—the sword stroke had gone *that* way, the shield *that* way—and Steele slashed.

Short! Scored Xeno's cuirass, nothing more. Xeno bowled him over with his shield. Sprang over him, but couldn't bring the kill home. Xeno's sword plunged into sand and wood as Steele rolled back to his feet.

Somewhere in the eternity of minutes the spring left Steele's legs. *This is it.* His strength was ebbing, limbs felt to be solidifying. Not even rage and noise were enough to keep his energy from slipping away.

He clashed against Xeno, shield to shield, sword hilt to sword hilt, pushed into his push. Xeno grunted behind his shield in American, "Put up a finger, Adamas. I bet they spare you." He pushed off to the side.

They leaped apart. Xeno shouted at Steele, pointed his sword, demanded to know if he would yield.

Steele shook his head. Spoke the only Latin he cared to know, *"Semper fi."*

Steele lifted his sword high, charging in for a mighty slash. His shield felt to be lifting itself as the blade sliding in underneath it ran him through.

He hit the ground twitching, spitting blood. He'd pitched over onto his back. Couldn't breathe. Diaphragm severed. Blood in his head sang for oxygen. The gladiator stood over him with his blade poised over his throat. Steele's trembling fingers felt round in the sand to find his sword. Found the hilt, closed his hand round it in a shaky grip but could not lift it. The muscles in his abdomen would not let him lift anything. Didn't even know if he still had muscles down there. Nauseous and his muscles wouldn't even contract to let him vomit.

He stared up at the blade over him. Kept trying to lift his own blade. Managed only to flip it over on its other side. The crowd noise peaked.

Sand was growing warm and wet around him. He knew what the wetness was. The victorious gladiator's face was turned toward Caesar's box, waiting on the verdict. Xeno was wide open. He left a perfect opening and Steele couldn't take it, his vision narrowing down to a tunnel.

The crowd was in tumult. At least half the voices chanting *Live. Live. Live.* As the light faded.

The evading Marines had moved their camp far away from where they hid the Roman bodies.

Kerry Blue dragged back from her foraging mission, late and empty-handed. She gave a sniffle as if suffering an allergy to something Roman.

"What kept you!" Carly whispered a cry as Kerry Blue flopped down to sit by the small fire.

"Oh. Um." Blue brushed the back of her hand under her nose. Shrugged. "I, uh, had sex with some guys I didn't wanna."

Kerry Blue was well known for not saying no. She stood by for the snotty remarks to come rolling in. The bull mastiffs were a tough crowd.

"Hell!" Twitch cried.

Cain said, "I'm so *sorry*, Blue!"

Kerry broke into tears. Carly looked over, scolded Cain, "What did you say to her!"

Kerry was smiling through her sobs. She grabbed Twitch and Cain in turn by the head, and kissed whatever part of the head met her lips, 'cause she couldn't see for tears. "I love you guys."

Twitch wore that helpless look that guys get when a woman is hurting and they're, well, helpless.

"You left 'em alive?" Cain asked Kerry.

"Not my choice."

The Marines passed round the food they'd gathered from the woods. A share came round to Kerry Blue. She pushed it away. Sniffled over her knees. "Hell of a way to treat a Russian student," she mumbled.

Cain crouched near her, afraid to touch her. "If you see 'em again, point 'em out, Kerry. I'll hit 'em where they don't ever wanna be hit."

"I don't care where you hit 'em as long as it's fatal," said Kerry Blue.

"You got it, gal."

Kerry shook back her hair. "Don't tell the Old Man, 'kay?"

Startled them. They exchanged glances. Did she not remember that Steele was dead?

Carly answered her carefully, as if she were breakable, "If that's what you want, *chica*."

Steele came to awareness coughing up liquid on the hard white floor. Must've got a thumbs up from the pretty thing standing in for Caesar. He had been counting on it when he'd let himself open for that thrust. Thought it an incredibly dumb idea as the blade was going through him. Looked now as if it could pay off. He knew where he was.

This time around he recognized the moment when it came. Only two medics with elephant pikes and a locked door contained him. When the warm water spray subsided, he grabbed both pikes and hauled both medics down to the slick floor with him. He cracked their heads hard on the floor and hacked off one's ear with a blade he found in a drawer.

The ear won him a green light on the door lock. The color made him pause a moment. Green still meant go in Rome. Only the U.S. fleet had flipped its colors for the siege.

The door opened for him without alarms, and Steele let himself out to the corridor.

He knew the way to the POWs' cage from here. He paused at the alcove by the stairs to pull out one of the beam cannons, then ran to his Marines. Immediately said, "Gimme a language module."

Icky Iverson, dumbfound, surrendered his through the bars, as the others rose in astonishment. Not just alive but Steele was naked, wet, and armed.

A Roman passed a tunic out through the bars of the gladiator cage. "Here. No one wants to look at that."

Ranza said, "I'm not having a problem with it."

Keeping his distance, Steele snatched the tunic out of the offering hand.

Icky said, "Sir, you have an extra ear."

Steele used the ear to unlock the cage. He passed his cannon to Ranza, then he let the criminals out.

As Steele pulled the tunic over his head, one of the criminals snatched the medic's ear away from him and ran with it.

The gladiators, still caged, were yelling for guards. Steele would have left them locked in there even if he still had the ear. He was leaving this circus behind him.

They heard the criminals running into guards. Heard shouts and gunfire.

Ranza passed the cannon back to Steele, and the Marines headed up a cross corridor. Dak took point.

Coming to a corner, Dak glanced round first, startled to see a face *right* there. Dak grabbed the owner of the face by the front of his tunic and hauled him back round the corner with him Dak wrapped him up in a tight headlock before he saw what he had.

A young black man in Roman garb. He had a cultured look about him, not like the evils of society they had just set free from the other cage. This one was not burly as a gladiator. His skin was soft as a baby's.

There followed from around the corner sounds of more beings coming up the corridor. Dak jumped out into the intersection, hiding behind his hostage and warned, "Don't come any closer!" He pretended he had a weapon at the Roman's back.

There were four armed human guards. They stopped, but one of them laughed.

The captive locked within the crook of Dak's elbow advised Dak in perfect, if strangled, Americanese, "You chose your hostage unwisely."

"Nuh uh!" said Dak. "You can't pretend you're one of us."

"I cannot because I am not," said his hostage, sounding altogether *stately*. "But an escaping political prisoner just won't give the effect you are looking for."

Ranza, hunched against the wall around the corner hissed: "Oh, no! You're not the guy who got burned with Captain Carmel!"

"I am that guy," said Gaius Americanus.

The guards were grinning, inching forward.

Steele reached round the corner with the beam cannon. "Dak, get down."

Dak hunkered down, hauling his hostage down with him. Steele pointed the cannon blindly over Dak's head.

"Aim a little lower, Colonel," said Dak. "There. Four of 'em. And I don't see any personal fields on 'em."

The four Romans kept grinning. "Are you playing Russian roulette, Yank?"

U.S. weapons only fired for their authorized owners. There were nineteen U.S. beam cannons in the alcove.

Steele growled at Dak, "Is there anything out there I shouldn't shoot?"

"Nothing but Romans. You're good, sir. Fire at everything."

"You think that weapon is yours?" said a Roman, closing in. "Your weapon was not in the stack, Colonel Steele."

Steele gunned down all the smiles.

"They're all mine," said Steele.

Marines checked the bodies to make sure they were

dead. They took the four Roman weapons. Ranza carved off one guard's earlobe with his own knife, and gave the capsule from inside it to Steele, then started on the other three. "Romans, lend me your ears."

Steele turned back to Dak's prisoner, Gaius Americanus. He remembered a distinguished older man. He told Gaius, "You look different."

"So does Captain Carmel," said Gaius Americanus.

That was true. Steele motioned for Dak to loosen his grip a little. "What are you doing here?"

"My door opened," said Gaius. "So I think: I have a friend or I have an enemy baiting me. Either way, I decided not to cower in my cage."

"You're not coming with us," said Steele.

"No," Gaius agreed. "I am not."

Automatons, a full dozen, came marching down the stairs. Steele turned, clutching the guard's capsule. He spoke in halting Latin. "I have these prisoners. Go catch the others. Move."

The automatons immediately turned and retreated double time.

Steele stared after them, astonished that they actually obeyed.

Ranza let out a cackle, showing her gapped teeth. "It can't be that easy!"

Steele snarled, hand to his midriff. "Marine? Be careful what you call easy."

From somewhere within the enormous building, weapons' fire and shouting sounded. "Mister Americanus, what's the best way out of here?"

"I've never been down here before," said the Senator. "I didn't know this was here. This is outrageous."

"If we get to the first floor, would you know the way?"

"Yes," Gaius said provisionally. "I think the loading dock would be my choice. If your ear pieces haven't been disallowed by the time we get there."

Steele hadn't considered that. The instant that someone with human intelligence found the guards dead with bloody ears, the capsules they carried would turn from authorizations into targets. They needed to move fast.

They rushed up the stairs where the automatons had just

gone. Gaius, after a momentary pause to get his bearings, led the way to the dock.

At their approach, automatons on the dock kept working, loading and unloading hover trucks. Except one, dressed as a guard. That one turned toward them with a gun. Said, "*Domni*, do you require assistance?"

"No," said Steele.

They descended some concrete steps from the dock to the ground, where Gaius murmured to Steele, "Kindly order me to go now."

Steele and Dak exchanged looks. What to do with the Roman Senator? Killing seemed the safest option.

As if reading their minds, Gaius said softly, "With Augustus dead, I am now Romulus' worst enemy. You want me alive. I opposed the war."

Himself, Steele would have voted for the war.

He motioned to Dak to release Gaius. "Go," Steele commanded.

Gaius walked quietly away into the city.

The Marines could not do that. They could not blend.

They draped a cargo tarp over themselves and left the dock on the flatbed of one of the hover trucks.

When the scenery was nothing but trees on either side, they baled out, leaving the guards' capsules in the truck.

In moments, backup lights appeared up the road.

"Oh, skat!"

The truck was coming back.

The truck came to a stop next to the Marines, and in a machine voice, the truck informed the disembodied capsules riding in it that the truck had lost part of its load right here.

Steele picked up a capsule, verbally authorized the offloading of things at this point, and ordered the vehicle to continue on its way.

As they watched the truck go, the Marines realized that the Romans would have an easy job of tracking them to this location. The first task was to get as much space between themselves and this place as fast as they could. Not sure which way to go.

From this point forward, the escape plan was a little on the nonexistent side.

34

SENATOR QUIRINIUS OPENED the back door of his villa to find a young black man who smelled rather strongly and would do well with a haircut and a shave. Recognition poked about the Senator's consciousness but did not set in until the young man spoke in an older voice, "Will you help me?"

"Gaius!" Open flew the door. "Gaius! I would be no kind of man if I did not! Come in! Come in."

"You are harboring a fugitive," Gaius warned, crossing the threshold.

"And honored and proud to do so!" Quirinius shut the door. "Where have you been?"

"Locked in a place that does not exist."

On hearing a sound from outside, Quirinius moved quickly to a rear window to peer out, and Gaius asked, "Is your house under watch?"

"No," said Quirinius, seeing nothing. "I could wish it were. I am troubled by vandals. They steal my lambs, and I don't know what has become of my dog."

Quirinius offered his guest a chance to clean up, but Gaius said, "If you can stand my stench a while longer, can we speak first?"

"Yes, yes." Quirinius beckoned him to the courtyard. He did not fear satellite surveillance. Could thank the Americans for that.

A colonnade enclosed a private garden. Vines twined up the columns. A mosaic of dolphins swam in the fountain at the center of the courtyard. A stone table and comfortable chairs sat on a circle of polished terra-cotta tiles.

A human slave brought refreshments. Quirinius had no automatons. He never cared for false people. He told the girl to prepare a bath, fresh clothes, and a bedchamber for his guest.

Then Gaius and Quirinius listened in horror to each other's tales, tales of deeds within the prison, and worse without.

Quirinius had not thought he could be more disgusted with Romulus. "I would say that Caesar is insane except that he appears to have complete command of all his faculties. I can only conclude that he is evil."

Quirinius had no idea there were any Americans in Roman captivity other than the famed *Adamas*, which was revolting enough. Quirinius had no idea that the American POWs had escaped—twice now—and there had been no public warning. The cover-up was abominable.

"Half the world is still dark. The Americans drop out of FTL at will and snipe at our repairs as soon as we are ready to go live again. We have citizens boiling water—*boiling water* in this century, because we cannot provide purification. We have lost surveillance on our colonies. And Caesar plays his games."

"Is that truly Caesar?" Gaius asked.

The question jolted Quirinius. "Why? Why ask?"

"I have heard the gladiators complain that they don't fight before Caesar. Why doesn't Caesar witness his own games? Has he been involved in affairs of state?"

"He has not come to the Curia," said Quirinius. "But he does introduce the games."

"*Does* he?" said Gaius.

Quirinius sat back, reviewing his recent memories of Caesar. Caesar appeared only briefly at the start of the games, reciting formal declarations before ceding his seat to a young woman. Now that Quirinius thought about it, an automaton could do that much convincingly.

Quirinius rose and went inside to his home office. He

opened up vid com to the Imperial Palace and demanded an audience with Caesar.

The *major domus* refused him, informing Quirinius that he was on a list of those forbidden from entering the palace.

Quirinius demanded a video audience instead. "Unless I am forbidden to look upon the visage."

He meant it as sarcasm, but that demand was denied without explanation.

Quirinius shut off his vid com. Looked up at Gaius, who had been listening from behind the camera. Gaius commented, "This begins to smell worse than I do."

Quirinius said, "Perhaps I am less than wise making these inquiries from my home. And I think now I should *not* use the com to inform my lady wife that we have a houseguest. I am going out. I shall leave you in the care of my slave. Anything you want, ask or help yourself. This is your house."

Gaius nodded his gratitude.

Quirinius put on his Senatorial toga. He instructed the slave to inform the lady Ludmillia face-to-face that they had company.

Quirinius tracked down the identity of one of the young ladies who filled in for Caesar at the games. He located the woman herself, and accosted her coming out of a dressmaker's shop.

Because Quirinius was a Senator of some rank the woman welcomed the attention and answered all his questions.

Of the man who appeared at the games and gave his seat to her, she confided in a conspiratorial whisper, "That is not really Caesar." She put her finger to her lips and winked.

Quirinius nodded that her secret was safe with him, while near bursting with outrage. Caesar was expected at the games if he were in Rome. How dare he stage this barbaric circus and not attend in person? The man forgot that he was not an autocrat; he was servant of the People.

"Where *is* Caesar?" Quirinius tried to sound casual asking that one.

The young woman shrugged, jingling her new earrings.

The question had been a long shot. Of course she would not know.

Upon returning home, Quirinius found Gaius shaved, washed, dressed in clean clothes, and having coffee in the courtyard with Ludmillia.

Ludmillia rose to kiss her husband, then sat back down to hear what Quirinius had learned in the city. Quirinius had few secrets from his wife and did not try to exclude her. She was safer knowing what he was about.

Quirinius reported that he could gather no verifiable sighting of Caesar within the last several days. And that the man who was introducing the games was not Caesar, and was not even a man.

Ludmillia speculated, "It is possible that Romulus has fallen to Claudia's malady?"

"What is Claudia's malady?" Gaius asked.

Quirinius sat forward, appalled. "Have they told you nothing, Gaius?"

"I have been in a cage beneath the Coliseum. I heard gladiators' gossip. The Americans are very careful to speak nothing of importance, not that anyone can hear."

Ludmillia explained that Claudia was in intense pain and calling for her father. Her sickness started after she had touched something of the patterner Augustus.

"I'm not sure if she is calling her father," said Quirinius. "I saw the woman, and that cry sounded like fear. Her pain and her delusions are being driven by nanites from the patterner. The data receptacle inside Augustus' head was infected with nanites."

Gaius had not even known Augustus was dead, killed by John Farragut in the first siege of Palatine.

Gaius at least knew that Palatine was under attack. He had gathered that from the prisoners under the Coliseum.

Gaius said, "If that is not Caesar opening the games, then who is sending out the replica of Caesar and who is running Rome?"

"It must be Romulus, from wherever he is," said Quirinius. "There is no one who could or would use Romulus as a front."

"I concur," said Gaius.

"Romulus is up to something," said Quirinius. "Something *more*, I should say."

"But where is he?" said Gaius.

"Maybe he is visiting the ravaged cities on the dark side of the world, giving solace and succor to the victims," said Ludmillia.

Quirinius touched her hand, appreciating the irony, but he could not laugh.

Quirinius went out again, this time to pay a call on Romulus' comrade in the Senate, Senator Ventor.

Ventor did not admit his visitor into his house. Did not even let him within the perimeter of the heavily monitored grounds. So right there at the ornamental front gate, Quirinius asked Ventor when last he had seen Caesar.

"Scheming, Quirinius?" Ventor asked back.

"Just tell me that the holder of your leash is in Rome," Qurinius challenged.

The question seemed to surprise Ventor, and he did not answer, which left Quirinius to wonder if the silence came from Ventor not knowing the answer, or was it because Caesar was not in Rome?

More direct still, Quirinius demanded, "Where is Caesar?"

A twitch moved the corner of Ventor's eyelid. Ventor did not answer. He turned his back on his caller and boarded an elevated carriage to carry him back up the long drive to his house.

Quirinius could read that answer clearly.

Ventor didn't know.

After much internal doubt and debate, Munda's successor as head of Imperial Intelligence sent a resonant signal on Caesar's private harmonic.

The new magister had been instructed not to make contact except in cases of dire importance. In his message, the magister stated only, "Gaius Americanus escaped."

Important enough. Caesar did not rebuke him for the contact, and responded, "Was he shot?"

"No, Caesar. Senator Americanus successfully escaped. With an American group of prisoners of war and several violent criminals."

"Well, now he is obviously a traitor," Caesar sent back. "Have Gaius Americanus shot on sight."

*   *   *

TR Steele took point. He moved through the forest at night. Three moons in various phases added light to the faint glow from the city below. His eyes had grown accustomed to the dark, so he spotted the figure ahead on the rise — a female silhouette in tunic and boots framed between trees against the sky of midnight blue.

Steele stopped. He blinked at the vision of exactly what he wanted to see. Was this Roman bait set out for him?

What Roman could know the one thing TR Steele wanted to see more than anything in the universe?

He wanted too badly to believe his eyes, so he didn't dare. Yet he knew that loose rangy build, those wide shoulders for a woman. He recognized the way she moved when she shook out her hair, the way she jerked her head back to bat away a bug in her face. That was not an automaton. That was nothing that could be duplicated by PanGalactic or anyone else.

The figure suddenly froze, like a deer hearing a twig snap, even though Steele hadn't made a sound.

He had seen that wary stance from her many times on Hive watch. Her right hand had frozen in the act of reaching for her sword, which wasn't at her side now.

Steele cupped his hands round his mouth and whispered, "Blue. Kerry Blue!"

She didn't move. Steele slowly emerged from the underbrush so she might see him.

The silhouette stayed mapped against the night sky like a still photograph, immobile. A tremor rippled the image.

And suddenly she dropped out of her stance, hurtling down the incline at a twig-snapping, leaf-crushing run.

Steele caught her jumping into his arms.

Her arms, her legs wrapped round him tight.

He held her hard, trying not to crush her. His hands found every part of her. He tangled his fingers in her wet hair. She had bathed in a stream; her skin was damp and a little chilled. He felt her heart pounding close to his. Her life in his arms. He kissed her neck, her hair, her ear, her face. Held her head, and kissed her mouth with a hunger deeper than the need for water or air.

At last he came up from the kiss, crushed his face against the side of her head, and whispered with difficulty, like requesting she remove something vital from his chest, "Let go of me, Marine."

She lowered her feet to the ground, pulled back to look at him in the dark, her eyes half-drowned with happy tears, smiling giddily. She touched him several times with her palms, just to make sure he was really really here and hadn't vanished.

"How many of you are there?" he whispered.

"Eight," she said. "We're eight. Everybody."

All eight of the Marines who escaped on the night he was shot still lived. He thanked God again.

"I have ten," Steele told her. "I'm bringing them. Tell yours not to shoot us."

"We don't have guns," she whispered. "The Roman crap we got don't work for us."

He seized her head, kissed her fiercely, and let her go.

Kerry dashed up the rise to tell the others.

Steele went back to get his team.

At the approach of Steele's group, Kerry Blue's group hid themselves behind trees. Carly grabbed Kerry and dragged her behind an uprooted tree with her. Scolded, "How could you bring them! They're Roman fakes! That can't be Steele! He's dead!"

"He's real," said Kerry. "Oh bitch, babe, you gotta trust me on this."

Carly shook her head wide, pitying. *"Chica, chica—"*

Cain Salvador stepped out of hiding, making himself a clear target for whatever approached. "I have to believe Kerry on this one." He strode down to meet Colonel Steele. Saluted, "Sir!"

"As you were, Marine."

"But you died!" Carly called from behind her tree. "Sir."

"Twice!" Ranza called back, flanking Steele. "He died twice."

Steele ordered the two groups of Marines to ask each other personal questions, the answers to which the Romans could not know. His men needed to trust each other.

A lot of questions were exchanged, with quite a lot of

laughter at things they dredged up to establish their identities.

Carly asked Kerry, "How'd you know Steele was alive?"

Kerry screwed up her face at her. "*Carly!* I been with you the whole time. Why you asking *me* a question?"

"I just want to know how you knew," said Carly.

Carly hadn't been at the knee wall when the colonel had been shot during their escape. But Twitch had told her about Kerry's anguished scream.

Thomas.

Carly hadn't known TR Steele's name was Thomas.

Hadn't seen him lock gazes with Cain Salvador at the end and order Cain to get Kerry out of there.

Okay, so Kerry fell in love stupid. And Steele even stupider back. Didn't explain how Kerry Blue, who saw him dying, knew he was alive. "So how'd you know?"

"I got no idea how." Kerry shook her head. "He just had to be."

Colonel Steele nodded to Flight Sergeant Cain Salvador. His voice dropped down a choked octave. "Good job, Salvador."

Cain had kept Kerry Blue alive. Steele's gratitude was profound, suffused with an intensity that could not be faked ever. The embarrassment, the depth of raw emotion, the trust.

Weird having charge of your CO's girlfriend, who was also your comrade-in-arms. Awkward. That's why there were rules against this kind of skat.

Yet the difference here was the difference between *Hey soldier, cover my ass while I shoot off some unauthorized ordnance*, and an order spoken with his dying breath to protect the woman he loved. No matter that he was not allowed to love her. There was no distinction in the military code of conduct, but the difference on the human level was huge and definite. Unwritten, understood, and recognized when it was thrust upon you as something you must do, a pact from man to man. And you accept it. Because you're human.

Cain shrugged as if it were no big deal. This had probably been a Neolithic ritual. The shrug to say it was nothing, which really meant, *Thank you for admitting that you put a hell of a load on me and I went off grid for you.*

Sudden harsh white lights fell on all of them from above.

Threw hard black tree shadows out on the ground. Illuminated more figures among the surrounding trees.

A loud voice from behind the light commanded in Latin: *"Do not move."*

Oh, hell, not again.

Civilian space traffic into Western Europe had been on an alarming increase for months. Italy got the bulk of it. Italy was not at war with Palatine, either as a nation for herself, or as a member of the League of Earth Nations. At first the Italian authorities did not object to civilians of the Empire of Rome visiting their country. But they did not mean to invite quite this *many* Romans.

And did not seem to be able to stop them.

Italy, France, Spain, Portugal, Morocco and Algeria had huge numbers of Roman visitors.

Captain Carmel on board *Wolfhound*, orbiting Earth with the home guard, signaled Jupiter Control regarding a new raft of Italians. "Are we sure these are all civilians?"

"We are sure there are enough Italian citizens on board those ships that we can't shoot at them."

And because the ships were not attempting to land in the United States, Calli could not buzz them away from entering Earth's atmosphere.

Italy would not authorize the U.S. military to come in on the ground to repel their excess visitors, much less allow them to drop any ordnance on Italian soil.

Most of the visitors did not have proper admittance documents. They were obviously Roman. They spoke flawless Italian or French or Portuguese or Spanish or Arabic depending on the country they visited. Immigration was not inclined to incarcerate masses of orderly people. The visitors gently bypassed immigration. Italy did not authorize the use of force against them, and the immigration officials did not attempt to make any arrests. The Romans were breaking immigration law, but they were well dressed, friendly, said hello, and brought nice gifts. Colonial wine was very fine, and a confection that rivaled chocolate for divinity was a nice gift.

The visitors submitted to searches. They carried no weapons, they had adequate currency, did not look as if they would be a burden, and there were just too many of them and not enough reason to get belligerent with them.

Wolfhound could only watch all those wolves coming in among the lambs.

"That's cheating," said Red Dorset at the com station.

"You tell 'em," said Tactical. "Bet you'll really hurt their little feelings with that one."

The Romans had staged a mass Exodus from Earth a century and a half ago. "Is this the Eisodos?" Red wondered out loud.

Tactical straightened up at his station, yelped, "You mean they're all coming *back*?"

Red Dorset passed a message from Jupiter Control to Captain Carmel. Per instructions from Captain John Farragut a week ago, Jupiter Control reported the approach of an Italian ship bearing Italian colors, Italian ID, and a passenger manifest of children.

Calli ordered Red Dorset to contact his buddy Guglielmo in Italy to recheck the ship's identity while she took *Wolfhound* closer for a look at the target.

Merrimack was in Palatine's atmosphere, making decoy drops on the planet's surface. Any time *Merrimack* dropped to sublight speed she had all the Roman ships' attention. The Romans knew by now that *Merrimack* was often used as a diversion, sent down only to draw fire. And the diversion always worked, because Roman defense could not afford to ignore her.

Captain Farragut gave his XO the deck so he could take Calli's hail. "Little busy here, Cal. You still at Earth?"

"Yes, I'm still here, and your Italian school group is here."

Farragut remembered the school group leaving Palatine. A busload of ten year olds going home. "Did I miss that call?" he asked. He had already vetted that bus, and lain off it as civilian. Still he had known something was wrong with it.

"It's a bone fide school group and it's Italian," said Calli. "But they've got a Roman passenger."

"Can't start shooting for one Roman," said Farragut. "Not children."

"I know," said Calli. "But you were right, and I sure wish I had your patterner friend with me."

"What's wrong?"

"The Roman passenger. I got a bead right through the view port. John, I'm looking at him. It's Romulus."

35

SHOCK SELDOM SLOWED DOWN John Farragut. He responded immediately "That's not real likely, Cal. Caesar is in Roma Nova. He's been holding games." Had to suppress anger at that. He had seen a recording of Steele's last contest in the arena and wanted nothing better than to run Romulus through with a sword.

Calli sent back, "Are you sure you've got the real Caesar there?"

"Are *you*?" Farragut returned.

"Actually, *yes*," said Calli. "I am. I know Rom. This is Rom. I just want you to argue with me."

"I—" had to consider carefully. The Caesar whom Farragut had seen on the recordings only made cameo appearances to introduce the games. "—can't," he finished. And added significantly, "Your guy is hiding behind children."

"I've got the real Romulus," said Calli.

"Numa's shooting at me," Farragut sent and had to break communication.

"Give him my worst," said Calli.

Wolfhound received orders to wear off from the Italian school ship at the stratosphere.

In her place, U.S. Rattlers swarmed up and took positions on either side of the descending spacecraft. The Rattler pilots could see the children through the viewports. The children did not appear frightened. Did not seem aware of the Rattlers. The ship must have one-ways activated on the viewports so the children could not look out and see gunships and start screaming.

Calli listened to the transmissions between the Rattlers and Ground Control.

Control: "Is Romulus on board?"

Rattler 6: "Looks like him, sir."

Control: "What is he doing?"

Rattler 6: "Singing, sir."

Control: "What?"

Rattler 6: "*Frère Jacques*, sir."

Romulus had a flock of the children around him, and one on his knee. The viewports were only occluded one-way instead of fully opaqued. Romulus wanted the world to see this.

He let the children teach him the song. Pretended not to know the words. The children were eager to show off their mastery of foreign words to the Roman Emperor.

Control: "What are they doing now?"

Rattler 6: "Rounds, sir."

Control: "What load?"

Rattler 6: "No. Rounds. They're singing *Frère Jacques* in rounds."

The lead Rattler hailed the school ship, demanded the pilot stop.

The Italian pilot hotly demanded the U.S. gunships cease menacing his craft.

Caesar added his own message to that, "No harm shall come to these children. They are under my protection."

Hearing that, Calli had to walk away from the com, incensed.

"Skata! They don't even know they're hostages! *He* is under *their* protection! With those children around him, we don't dare aerate his head!"

They were singing *Alouette* now. The children giggled as Romulus kept pointing to the wrong body parts of the plucked lark, his fingertip to his elbow when they were singing beak, to his knee when the children sang neck. The emperor was being very silly.

When the ship set down at the spaceport in old Rome, it was greeted not just by parents of the schoolchildren, but by such a mass of people that there was no controlling them. With his people around him, Romulus went anywhere he wanted. People reached out to touch him like a sports hero or the Pope. Or a conquering Caesar.

Snipers in space could not get a clean shot on his eminence. Romulus was wearing a two-stage personal field, which protected him from beams, projectiles, and even thrown rocks, none of which were headed his way. Joy and adoration surrounded him.

Anything the Americans could send down there capable of penetrating his personal field would take out a wide radius around him as well. The Pentagon was debating the pros and cons of doing so.

Unfortunately the people closest to Caesar were not Romans. They were Italian civilians caught up in mob fervor. Not that the Romans were not part of the masses.

There were hundreds of thousands of Roman tourists in Italy. They had come without weapons.

But weapons could always be bought. Civilians could become soldiers. Their commander in chief was here.

Caesar proceeded on foot to Vatican City where the Swiss Guards forbade him and his thousands entry. Tried to forbid. The titanic crowds made the gates part for him. Romulus walked past them.

Romulus walked into Saint Peter's Square with his legions of civilians around him. And the guards could not bring themselves to wreak violence on unarmed people.

Romulus advised the unhappy guards to ask God to smite him, if He objected to his being here.

The guards were more concerned with the flouting of international borders and possible lifting of Vatican treasure than they were with God's will.

The U.S. had been denied entry into Vatican City airspace, so there was nothing but blue sky and the glint of high distant spacecraft overhead. And a dark swarm of approaching aerial news craft.

Romulus stopped at the Vatican obelisk, which stood in the center of the square. In actuality it was Caligula's obelisk. A soaring red granite phallic symbol brought here a thousand years ago by Sixtus V. The Catholics had stuck a cross on top of it. Sixtus V had been Roman.

Romulus announced that he wanted to sit on the Throne of the Fisherman. He pretended not to know the way. By involving the people in his quest, he took ownership of their hearts. The throng directed him to the palace. The mob, swept up in the sense of this historic moment and the grandeur of the place, made sure Romulus got whatever he wished. Excitement crackled like lightning within a thunderhead, common sense swept aside by the rapture. This moment had been thousands of years in the coming. A Caesar had returned to Rome.

Romulus strode into the Papal palace and up to the chamber like returning royalty. The Vatican ran a lean organization, so there were few people to stand in his way.

The Pope did not come out to oppose him, but his personal secretary, the monsignor, did. The people cleared the path for Caesar. Romulus strode up the steps of the dais and sat on the red velvet cushion of the gilded throne.

Someone brought him a scepter like a shepherd's crook, which he accepted. He refused the miter. He wore his own crown of gilt oak leaves.

Media transmitters shoved their way into the chamber. Caesar requested the curtains be parted so the airships could get their views through the windows. Romulus used the public media to transmit a greeting to the President of Italy.

He also said into the cameras, "Someone can tell Sampson Reed that We are here if he has anything to say to Us." He was speaking in royal plurals now. Omitted Sampson Reed's title of President of the United States.

And he posed for people to record images of him.

He glanced toward the window. "Can we get some white smoke out there?"

The crowd outside roared, because his words were carried everywhere instantly on the news media. And soon white smoke issued from the chimney that normally announced a new Pope.

Cheers resounded from Saint Peter's Square.

*   *   *

Merrimack pulled back from her battle with *Gladiator*. Jumped to FTL, then slowed back down to sublight speed again in a new location and transmitted to *Gladiator*, "Time Out."

Time *Out?* The Romans on *Gladiator*'s command deck were mystified. They looked to each other as if their language modules were malfunctioning. "Did he say Time Out?"

Numa Pompeii took up the com: "Do you think this is an American game of football, Captain Farragut?"

Farragut returned, "Numa, just stop shooting for a minute and turn on any news broadcast from Earth."

This was possibly a trick, but this was also John Farragut. Numa was curious now. He nodded to his command crew to comply.

Everything in the universe was stopping to watch the news from Earth. The signals from Vatican City were broadcast by resonant pulse, so the feed was immediate and everywhere.

White smoke.

"What does that mean?" Numa asked the air, because he could not expect anyone around him to have the answer. "Is that Romulus? Did he just take possession of Vatican City?"

Difficult to be Pope when Romulus wasn't Catholic. Though historically there had been Popes with dim claims to the faith.

When Caesar had collected the attention of the better part of the known galaxy, he rose from the Throne of the Fisherman. He spoke to anyone who would know, "Show me the way to that balcony. I need to give my address *Urbi et Orbi et Cosmi.*"

"That balcony" was description enough to get him where the Pope traditionally spoke his message to the City, the World, and the Universe.

By the time his procession wended it way from the palace to Saint Peter's Basilica, up the stairs, and to the doors that led out to the central balcony, the sky over Saint Peter's Square was clogged with camera ships. The pilots angrily signaled to each other to get out of the picture.

Curtains over the doors to the Loggia of the Blessings moved. The human ocean down below roared.

Romulus stepped onto the balcony, sunlight on his oak leaves. He collected the voices, the immense sound of Biblical thunder.

Romulus stepped to the railing, made eye contact with individuals in the crowd, waved and smiled. The cheering only intensified, resolving into a chant that rocked the earth: CAE-SAR! CAE-SAR! CAE-SAR!

Romulus was in no hurry for silence. The streets before him had become rivers of humanity. People clustered on the rooftops. Faces filled all the windows. Small craft jockeyed for positions in the sky.

Romulus gripped the railing, bowed his head, collecting himself to address the multitude. At length the crowd allowed itself to go quiet, listening. The galaxy held its breath.

Romulus looked out.

His focus faltered, swam away. He held tight to the railing for balance.

A murmur rolled back in a wave.

His lips moved, no sound coming forth at first, confusion, disgust, and fear moving on his face.

Romulus reached forward, his hand out to empty air over the square, his eyes fixed in profound horror. Blood appeared on his palm, not like the wound of a nail, but blood all over both hands. He screamed at something no one else could see.

"Pater!"

PART FIVE

The Outer Darkness

36

STEELE AND HIS RECAPTURED MARINES sat on the floor in a boxcar. The compartment smelled like sheep. Every surface felt greasy with lanolin. There was no light.

After several hours, a voice in the dark sounded, moaning, "Just how long does it take to get to the Coliseum?"

It was probable they were not going back to the Coliseum after two escapes.

They didn't seem to be going anywhere.

Daybreak brought light and nothing else. Time wore on. There was no food. There was still a carton of water, which they were relunctant to drink because there was no crapper in here.

"Did you see the light, sir?" Dak Shepard asked.

Steele looked to either side of himself for some other "sir" who might answer the question. He squinted at Dak Shepard. "What?"

"When you died," said Dak.

"I saw it once," said Kerry Blue. "The light." She had been drowning.

Dak turned to her. "See anyone at the end?"

Kerry shook her head. "I didn't get very far before a medic was squishing water out of me."

"Sir?" Dak turned back to Colonel Steele. "Did you?"

Steele slowly nodded. "Saw my mom. She told me to go back."

Dak nodded, liking that answer. But it was only part of what Steele heard from the light.

What Ma Steele actually said was, *Boy, you go right back there and get her.*

The sun was past zenith when the boxcar set down, and the door lifted open. Automatons and human guards herded the Marines into a clean Spartan dormitory, some place where the season was autumn. The guards locked the Americans in by themselves.

There was a security system all around the building, but no locks on the doors to the individual rooms. Once locked inside, the prisoners had free run of everything. There were dry showers, cots with air mattresses, food, drinking water, heads, a first aid kit, and a dry laundry.

Cain blurted, "Wow! Was there a regime change?"

Steele supposed the League of Earth Nations must have stepped in to enforce conventions of treatment of POWs.

Dak looked around for a video. That was asking too much. But there were decks of cards.

So the Marines played cards, talked, making up stories of what could have changed about the war to land them here. Except for Steele, Ranza, and Cain who spent the daylight inspecting their confines, searching for a way out.

There were two cots in each sleeping room, but enough rooms for each Marine to have his own private space.

At nightfall Kerry Blue came to Flight Leader Ranza Espinoza's room, and stood in the doorway hugging a pillow. "Can I stay here?"

Kerry Blue hadn't had her own room *ever* and discovered she didn't like it. On *Merrimack* there would be eight women stacked into a space this size. And there would be Dak Shepard snoring right on the other side of the thin metal partition that walled Kerry's pod from the guys' rack.

The private room felt like exile.

Ranza was trying to make her thick cloud of freshly cleaned hair lie down. She shot Kerry a sneer through the mirror. "You mean you're not going to bunk with *Thomas*?"

Ranza had been in the arena when Kerry screamed the colonel's name over the wall.

Kerry asked, "You gonna bust me, Ranza?"

"Nah. Can't. Take that cot. I got this one."

"Thanks," Kerry came in. She sat on her cot. Thought to ask, "You *can't?*"

"Can't," said Ranza. " 'Cause if the Old Man wanted to frat with me, I'd be there in a half a heartbeat."

Wolfhound had not received new orders since Caesar's collapse, so she maintained orbit around Earth. When the wolfhunter ship finally received a message other than a general broadcast, it wasn't from Command.

Red Dorset at the com reported, "Captain Carmel, I have a resonant hail coming in on a disallowed harmonic. Claims to be Gaius Americanus."

"I'll take it," said Calli.

The transmission came with a video. Calli saw the face and let out an involuntary, "Oh."

Gaius Americanus touched his own young face. "Oh, yes." He had forgotten, as had she, that they hadn't seen each other since they had both been burned. "That's what my wife is going to say, I'm afraid."

"What's happening, Gaius?"

The Roman appeared to be debating how much to say, "You saw the transmission from the Vatican?"

"The whole universe saw that," said Calli.

"Our nations are talking."

"Who is speaking for the Empire?"

Last seen, Romulus was screaming incoherently.

"The Senate."

Calli noticed that Gaius was wearing a red-bordered Senatorial toga.

"No interim Caesar?"

"Not a chance."

That meant Rome was working in a power void—which would be more of a power glut if you counted all the Senators. No one could expect that many ambitious brains to agree on anything, except that they all distrusted anyone who might seize control as deftly as Romulus had upon Magnus' death.

"What is the purpose of this call, Senator?" Captain Carmel kept her words formal.

"A personal favor, if at all possible," said Gaius. "Check on my wife and children at Fort Eisenhower? I know you can't carry a message. If you could just see that they are well?"

"I think I can accommodate that," Calli said.

Seeing him, and speaking of Fort Ike, memories of their doomed flight in the shuttle came back to her. The attack. The fire. "I'm sorry the war might be ending without my getting a chance to kill Numa."

"He's right here," said Gaius.

"No, no, don't pass me over to— What do *you* want?"

The vastness of Numa Pompeii filled her com screen. "I wanted to let you know I had the warrant for your arrest lifted, Callista."

"What warrant?"

"For your arrest for the murder of Caesar Magnus."

That nonsense? She had assumed Claudia's accusations were long behind her. "That wasn't I."

"I know that," said Numa.

"Why isn't there a warrant out for *your* attempted murder of Gaius?" said Calli. "And why is he even talking to you? Gaius! Where's Gaius! Put Gaius back on!"

"You ridiculous American cowgirl," Numa's deep voice rolled like mumbling thunder. "Had I wanted Gaius dead, he would be dead. I would have let him board *Gladiator* and executed him with my own sword. I would not have hatched a sniveling plot in the dark using a disgraced moron from Daedalus Station and Romulus' other toadies."

What he said made sense, but Calli was never good at backing down or giving Numa Pompeii the benefit of any doubt. She said back, "What was Romulus hoping to achieve here?"

"I was not privy to Caesar's plans and would not tell you if I knew. I like your new face by the way."

"Don't be cruel."

"I mean it," said Numa. "It lets the strength behind it show through. Before you were just pretty."

* * *

Sound and lights outside the POWs' dormitory woke the Marines, who had become light sleepers anyway. Ranza rolled off her cot to look out the window. A lander descended, right next to the building. Leaves and dust fanned out beneath it. *"It's one of ours!"*

Kerry ran to the window, looked for the Roman guards. Found them at the periphery of the lights, standing there, looking surly.

"No one's shooting!" Kerry marveled. *"We're going home!"*

Home meant the *Merrimack*.

She was afraid that their evader status might exclude them from fighting the rest of the war. But they learned upon boarding *Merrimack* that there might not be much more war left. Other Marines from the 89th were being picked up from the field.

With the return of seven hundred plus Marines, *Merrimack* reverted to its noisy, crowded familiarity.

Colonel Steele spent extra time in quarantine, having died and been resurrected by Roman medics—like Augustus had been.

"I am not Augustus!" Steele bellowed. But TR Steele distrusted Romans more than anyone, so he submitted to the extra scrutiny to make certain he carried nothing of them aboard.

"So God struck Romulus down," said Marcander Vincent at his tactical station on the command deck of *Merrimack*.

"Didn't look like God's work," said Systems. "Looked more like Augustus' work."

The helm nodded, murmured, "Same thing that got Claudia."

"Augustus' nanites laid out Claudia on Palatine," said Marcander Vincent. "How could those nanites get to Vatican City?"

Captain Farragut, listening to the crew chatter, caught in a breath in sudden epiphany.

Vatican City. The seat of the old Catholic religion.

I know a Catholic.

He knew a Catholic who had personal nanites exempted from the sterilization of the *Merrimack* at the outbreak of the war. The nanites had been set outboard while the space battleship was scoured. The nanites had been picked up by their owner in space after he separated from *Merrimack*.

I know a Catholic who had an audience with the Pope.

"Young Captain!" Jose Maria de Cordillera greeted John Farragut's hail cheerily. He wore a fine white shirt and a waistcoat the color of pure gold. He appeared to be on the coast of Spain, on a terrace of a villa on the sea, tranquil as if nothing momentous were happening anywhere in the galaxy.

"Are you still on Earth?" Farragut asked looking at the scene behind him.

"No. I have been to Earth and I have been home to Terra Rica since last we met. I am in transit now to another destination. This is *Mercedes*." He motioned to his surroundings.

Mercedes was Jose Maria's little racing yacht, named for his late wife, lost on board the Roman ship *Sulla* years before, the first victim of the Hive.

The turquoise sea, the white birds, the yellow sun, the villa were all a holoimage.

Sun glanced off the water.

Farragut finally got round to asking innocently, "How did your audience with the Pope go?"

"Very well," answered Jose Maria with the same false innocence.

Farragut asked outright: "How did you get the nanites onto the Papal throne?"

"I did not." Jose Maria sipped red wine, his dark eyes impish. "I put them in the holy water."

Farragut shook his head. He had watched the recordings of Romulus' entrance to the Vatican. Romulus never dipped his hand in a stoup or in a baptismal font. He never picked up an aspergillum. "Romulus doesn't use holy water."

"But the Pope does," said Jose Maria. "The hand that touches the water is the hand that rests on the arm of the throne, the hand that grips the scepter, the hand that touches the rail of the balcony. God does intervene in the affairs of humankind. But heaven helps those."

"You are a holy bastard, Jose Maria."

"I did penance just in case it was not heaven doing the helping of those who helped themselves."

Farragut remembered Augustus' first shot at Romulus, the one that pierced the seat and the headrest of the throne in Caesar's bunker during the American siege of Palatine. That attempt never quite felt right. It wasn't enough for Augustus to shoot Romulus through the head. And it had never seemed like it had a high likelihood of success.

That shot had been the announcement to Romulus that Augustus was coming.

Death was not enough. Augustus needed to show blood on Romulus' hands and to make him face his father.

For that there were the nanites left in Augustus' data bank, which he knew would be excised from his head upon his death. That trap required Caesar to touch the data bank, and Caesar hadn't.

Had Augustus ever meant for Romulus to touch it? Or had he foreseen Romulus avoiding that trap as well?

"How could Augustus be certain Romulus would come to Vatican City?"

"Certain?" said Jose Maria. "I do not know that he was certain, young Captain. Romulus had expressed an interest in giving a speech *Urbi et Orbi et Cosmi* from the Loggia. But for all we know there are more nanites elsewhere. As the nanites are only triggered by a combination of DNA in common with Magnus and memory of patricide, then any other traps, if such exist, will never be activated, never be found. I must believe Augustus created other backups. Redundancy is good."

"Redundancy is good," said Farragut. That was why there were six engines on the *Merrimack*.

"Was *that* the purpose of your audience with the Pope?" said Farragut. "To set Augustus' trap for Romulus?"

"Oh, no. My delivery of the nanites was a last favor to Augustus. That was not the reason for my visit to the Vatican. The reason for my journey was personal."

"May I ask?"

"I must share, young Captain," said Jose Maria, becoming quietly animated, "The Vatican has always conducted scientific research, much of it in the field of astronomy and space exploration—the search for the fingerprints of God in His cosmos. The Riverites are not the only ones who see God in His Creation. To the Riverites Creation, not the gospels, is the firsthand testament of God. It is both, of course. Outer space doth make gnats of us all. I went to the Vatican because I funded a research project for them."

"Success?" Farragut asked.

Jose Maria nodded. "I am on my way to see the results of their exploration for myself even now. The Vatican ship is waiting for me at the site."

Jose Maria set aside his wine, looked meditative. Emotions shone in his face—wonder, sorrow, and something else.

He gave a sad smile. His voice came out surreal, as if he could scarcely believe what he was saying—speak it and it will cease to be. "They found the *Sulla*."

The Roman Empire was in the control of a Senate without a unified head to make decisions. The Senators proceeded cautiously this time, with much debate. No one was afraid to express disagreement with anyone else. Charisma was ill regarded now, so Senator Trogus got his floor time, and Numa Pompeii had to rein in his eloquence.

If anyone's voice carried more authority, it was Gaius Americanus. The others were willing to pause now and consider why Magnus chose this man to succeed him. Gaius Americanus became, if not their leader, then their moderator.

Negotiations with the United States were strained. The United States tried to take advantage of the situation and gouge out terms, which was why Caesar Magnus had surrendered his Empire to Captain Farragut, not to the United States, during the Hive crisis.

The nations were going to be a while pounding out an Armistice. First thing the Roman Senate wanted was to stop the shooting and the sabotage on the ground. Then they wanted to collect their power plants, which had been bounced out of orbit by U.S. warships, and to reestablish communications with their colonies.

The U.S. troop carriers had already withdrawn from the Palatine system. The armies had been confined in their spaceships for months. They would not be landing on Palatine any time soon if ever.

The U.S. permitted a Roman hospital ship to retrieve Caesar Romulus from Earth.

The immediate collapse of the Roman war effort upon Caesar's incapacitation left John Farragut to wonder how Romulus had ever planned to establish his claim to any part of Earth. Something was missing.

There gaped a giant hole in the available information where something strategic belonged.

Sulla. She waited in the Abyss. A cenotaph traveling faster than light.

Her speed had leveled out at cruising velocity, her direction toward nowhere. She was nearly impossible to find.

And there she was.

She was surprisingly close to Near Space. She would have passed by unseen had no one been intently looking for her. The Vatican ship found her bound on a northerly route that would carry her out of the galaxy.

It appeared that the last act of the crew of *Sulla* had been to take the ship off her homeward course and away from humanity.

Objects traveling faster than light do not fall out of FTL. Passing the light barrier required energy—the same energy to decelerate below the barrier as to accelerate above it.

The Vatican ship had found *Sulla* traveling FTL with a dead engine, no energy emanating from her, no residual heat left about her. Her antimatter in its magnetic container had been blown out the back, magnets and all, somewhere hundreds or thousands of parsecs back.

Without intervention, the dead hull would travel on at this speed forever.

Jagged rents in her hull, as if the metal had been peeled open, confirmed the stories and suspicions. *Sulla* had in fact been humankind's first Hive victim.

The racing yacht *Mercedes* made rendezvous with *Sulla* and the Vatican research vessel in the Abyss. The Vatican ship had been awaiting the arrival of their patron, Jose Maria de Cordillera, before boarding the wreck.

The *Mercedes* matched speed and attitude with *Sulla* and lined up an air lock opposite one of the large holes in her hull.

As he suited up, Jose Maria felt an irrational desire to carry a sword. But he had given his sword to Captain Farragut upon leaving *Merrimack*.

Feeling naked without a weapon while going into the Hive-scarred wreck, Jose Maria slid a short blade into his calf holster, like a diver's knife. Then, as if he were actually going to Mercedes' rescue, he strapped on a beam knife and slung a welding torch pack across his back. Part of him felt ridiculous. Another part called out in silence, *My love, I come!*

He stood in the air lock of his racer as the air was sucked out and the artificial gravity lifted away.

The Vatican researchers had anticipated the possible state of *Sulla*'s hull, and had come equipped with a polymer spray to blunt the sharp metal edges around the holes in the ship. An exo-suit's personal field would not protect it against a sharp edge approaching slowly.

The safety coating appeared blue against the ship's black hull.

Jose Maria opened *Mercedes*' air lock and turned on his suit lights.

He crossed the short void between ships with a slow push out of the air lock. He did not need his suit's directional jets, but gently floated straight across and caught the blunted opening.

Carefully, he ducked inside and looked for something on which to attach the line he had carried from his own ship. He fastened the tether to an overhead conduit, then surveyed the scene around him.

His lamps shed cheerless light that could not push back the black from this space. The cold illumination threw out fanged shadows of torn metal wherever he looked.

His thickly gloved hands propelled him at a floating crawl through the ravaged corridors. He kept his com link open. The researchers in the Vatican ship could hear him breathing. They allowed him his silence. They watched the video feed from his helmet as he progressed through the flying tomb.

He found her chamber. Knew it by her clothes. Her field garb, sand-colored, synthetic, was inedible by gorgons. Those small boots. How tiny her feet had been. He hugged the boots.

He did not find teeth in her sleeping compartment. His Mercedes would not have died hiding under a bed.

He found the control room, a scatter of teeth there. He collected all that he found and tucked them into a sealed pocket in his suit. He pulled data receptacles out of the communications station and fit those inside another pocket.

Then he found an incisor. He knew it immediately. How many times had he gazed at her smile across a table?

There was no gravity here, but still came the impulse to fall to his knees. He curled round one knee, his head bowed, floating. He held the tooth to his chest.

My love. My love. I am taking you home.

The colossus that was the Jupiter Monument was lit up to be visible from Earth. With the naked eye it appeared like a bright pinpoint moon to the planet.

Seen through a scope, dark specks appeared, moving across the face of the monument like black ash.

An observer on Luna Station spotted the specks first and asked, "What the hell is that?"

The United States and the rest of Earth went on immediate maximum alert.

Wolfhound turned her scanners toward Jupiter to mutters of "Those treacherous bastards."

The specks looked like incoming small craft. Thousands upon thousands of them, moving near light speed. Calli Carmel couldn't believe it. A Roman double cross.

Tactical refined the image. The specks weren't Roman ships.

A cricket in a tiny cage on the command deck, left over from the Sagittarius campaign, chirped madly.

"Hive!"

37

IMAGES FROM THE JUPITER MONUMENT reached the U.S. Fleet at Palatine, images of gorgons crawling on the monument in a black mass that all but obscured the bright lights. Images of more gorgons headed toward Earth. Not in spheres. The new generation Hive hadn't figured out spheres. These monsters were strewn about in gaggles, ribbons, clumps, and nets.

Captain Farragut on the *Merrimack* hailed Admiral Mishindi on Earth. "A Hive emerged on *Jupiter*?"

"No," Mishindi responded, harried. "Jupiter is where the monsters are entering the solar system."

The Jupiter Monument was a resonant source. Naturally it would attract the Hive.

But other than on the planet Thaleia, which was heavily monitored and contained, the Hive had no known presence anywhere near Earth. The Hive had no other history in Near Space at all.

"Their actual point of origin is the 82 Eridani system," Mishindi told Farragut. "The third planet, Xi."

"*Xi!*"

Xi was a dead planet. Long, long, long dead.

There was no arguing the improbability of it, since the fact was chewing on the Jupiter Monument even now.

The 82 Eridani system was damned close to Sol in astronomical terms. Which made it close to the Roman worlds of Thaleia and Palatine as well. But so far no gorgons had started in those directions. They were all headed toward the closest resonant target, Earth.

And they had arrived, falling from the sky in a spidered rain.

It would take any ship of the attack Fleet a week at best to return to Earth to fight the Hive. Captain Farragut wanted to be there yesterday. Then the side thought struck him.

"He knew," he said out loud.

Gypsy lifted dark brows toward her captain. "Sir?"

"*Romulus knew!* He knew the gorgons were coming. He knew when they would get to Earth. He timed his visit so he could be there when the Hive arrived and the United States Fleet wasn't!"

Gypsy's brow furled all the way up to her shaved scalp. "Why would Romulus want to be on Earth when the gorgons came?"

"To be our savior. Romulus meant to collect our surrender under a Hive siege. *God bless America!*"

And Farragut guessed how Romulus meant to get weapons to all those unarmed Roman tourists who had come to Earth. He was going to make the United States and the rest of the world arm them for him.

Romulus had not figured on Augustus striking him down from beyond the grave.

"But how did Romulus get the gorgons to Xi?" said Gypsy.

"He didn't." Farragut spoke it as he realized it himself. "They've been there! They've been there for three quarters of forever!"

"Since the galaxy's first civilization? That can't be. If gorgons were there, why didn't they eat the archaeological team who found the Xi tablet decades ago?"

"Because the gorgons of the ancient Hive moved on a long long time ago, and the new swarms didn't hatch until the original swarms died!"

"But most of the second generation swarms woke up months ago. What took these so long to hatch?"

"I'm getting the idea they don't hatch until there's something they can eat. Remember Telecore was clear when we went there. The gorgons only woke on Telecore when we brought edible things down to the surface. Something edible came to Xi. And I would stake anything that Romulus sent it."

Gypsy followed the argument. "Whatever Romulus sent to Xi got eaten, and Romulus didn't tell anyone. He's worse than Calli said he was, and she had nothing good to say about that man ever."

"It's looking like a new Hive can pop up *anywhere* the last Hive ever was. I need to ask Jose Maria—" He stopped. Cold. "Oh, for Jesus."

Sulla.

Inertia carried Jose Maria up—which was the same as down, which was the same as sideways in this weightless place—into the ship's overhead.

His lamplight fell on a very large, black lump like a charcoal mass crusted on the conduit.

Jose Maria uncurled in panic reflex. He bounced off the deck, clutched a grate to stop his motion. He spoke into his helmet com with restrained urgency, "Get clear of the *Sulla* immediately. I have Hive presence."

He tucked Mercedes' tooth into the pocket at his chest. He planted his feet to take a stand on a wall, anchoring himself against the hatchway, and drew his knife from its sheath at his calf. He faced the uncurling mass of tentacles emerging in the overhead.

Captain Farragut fought down the impulse to signal a warning to Jose Maria's little ship *Mercedes*. The Hive had the ability to home on any reception point of a res pulse. If the Hive did not already know where Jose Maria was, Farragut's signal would give his location away.

Farragut sent an urgent message to the Vatican Observatory, warning them, "Do *not* contact the research ship that found *Sulla*. When is the last time you heard from the crew?"

"You cannot know how much I welcome this communication, Captain Farragut," said the monsignor who took his call. "You are a Godsend. We have lost contact with our research vessel. I pray to God that He did not send you to us too late." The monsignor provided Captain Farragut with the Vatican ship's last known vector.

Farragut hailed Admiral Mishindi again. He did not need to beg to be cut out from the Fleet and assigned to the rescue mission. "*Sulla* has been classified as a plague ship," said Mishindi. "It must not be allowed to advance into Near Space. *Merrimack*, you are clear to separate from the Fleet to stop the Hive incursion and attempt a rescue of the Vatican vessel and Doctor Cordillera."

Merrimack blazed out to the Abyss at threshold speed.

"We should be able to see her," said Gypsy as *Merrimack* closed on the projected course of the Vatican ship.

Tactical sang out. "Occultation! Dead ahead! Got him!"

The plot turned out to be a solo ship. Not the *Mercedes*. Not the *Sulla*. It was the Vatican ship, alone, running Earthward.

Merrimack veered to make intercept. The Vatican ship appeared intact. *Merrimack* hailed her on a tight beam instead of resonating so not to alert the Hive of their location.

"Is Jose Maria with you?" Farragut demanded.

The Vatican personnel told him that the Hive had emerged on *Sulla*. Jose Maria had ordered the Vatican ship to run.

"Where is he!"

The Vatican pilot gave *Merrimack* Jose Maria's vector. It led galactic north, fastest route out of the galaxy.

As *Merrimack* blazed away, the pilot's benediction followed, "May God be with you."

After a chase that took far too long, with John Farragut stalking the corridors of his ship as if he were pushing her along, *Merrimack* caught up with another solo ship.

It wasn't Jose Maria's *Mercedes*.

It was *Sulla*.

She was an image out of a nightmare, a mass of torn metal, riddled with jagged holes, cold as space. Dead.

"Where is Jose Maria?"

"No other ships detected, Captain," Tactical reported.

"Did we cross a heat trail?"

"No, sir. There's no one else out here except *them*."

Alongside the ghost ship *Sulla*, a Hive sphere traveled on a parallel course at matched speed. The swarm was a small one, the sphere only about three quarters the size of *Merrimack*.

"The new Hive has learned spheres," Gypsy noted gravely.

The sphere was the most heat conservative shape possible, giving the highest survivability rate to the swarm's members.

"No! They haven't learned skat!" Tactical cried. "That's not a Hive sphere! That's *Mercedes*!"

A scan revealed a ship at the core of the sphere. The scan also alerted the gorgons that *Merrimack* was here.

The sphere was a writhing nest of black tentacles. Monster crawled over monster trying to get to the core where *Mercedes* was encased in their hunger. The outer tentacles now lifted toward *Merrimack* like hesitant squirrels, gauging whether they could make the jump.

Commander Dent called *Merrimack* to battle stations.

Mister Hicks at the Com could not establish contact with *Mercedes*.

"I'm sorry, sir," said Hicks. The young man sounded as if he might cry.

"That doesn't mean he's dead," said Farragut.

It mustn't mean he was dead. It only meant Jose Maria was not answering, or the Hive had overwhelmed *Mercedes'* com system.

"Those Star Racers have strong force fields," said Systems.

There was still hope. He might still be in time. This Hive might not have figured out insinuation yet. The ability to slowly penetrate an energy field was one of many exotic characteristics of the parent Hives.

"We do know Jose Maria will have put full power to his energy field," said Farragut.

Gypsy picked up that cue. "Fire Control, power up hydrogen jets."

Mercedes with her field at full could withstand a hydrogen jet.

"Fire Control, aye. Powering hydrogen jets, aye."

Mister Hicks sent another tight beam to *Mercedes*. "Doctor Cordillera, this is *Merrimack*. Can you respond?"

Receiving nothing but silence, Mister Hicks turned to the XO and shook his head.

"Command. This is Fire Control. Hydrogen jets powered and standing by."

"Fire!" said Gypsy.

Merrimack, like an enraged archangel, hurled pillars of purest hellfire on the sphere.

Gorgons burned, peeled away, layer on seared layer to reveal an intact energy screen underneath.

But there were gorgons within the shield itself, distorted, impossible, squashed figures, slowly insinuating their way through the energy barrier in toward the ship.

"They've learned insinuation!"

Worse. A jagged hole showed clearly in *Mercedes'* hull. The gorgons had already eaten through the hull.

The monsters were on board *Mercedes*.

One man could not stand long against a swarm. There was no telling how long ago the gorgons had gained entry to the ship, how many gorgons were already inside.

One more gorgon, preserved from the hydrogen blast by being inside the force field, oozed itself free on the inside of the field and scuttled into the ship through the hole in the hull.

"Get an energy lever through that field and spread an opening for soft dock at that hole," Farragut ordered. "All possible haste. Colonel Steele! I need a boarding party, suited for potential vacuum and armed for Hive. Yesterday!"

John Farragut had to believe they were in time.

Never say die.

Never say die until you're dead.

Time that could be clocked in seconds passed in abysmal slowness before soft dock was achieved and Marines charged through the flexible tunnel to board *Mercedes*.

Armed with swords, the Marines slashed off any tentacle

that pierced the flexible docking tube, and they boarded the yacht through the gorgon hole. The Marines found the ravenous enemy on board and engaged them at once.

Several Marines stationed themselves at the hole to hack down flankers that were still emerging from the force field. Other Marines on *Merrimack* stood by for boarders coming back their way.

Colonel Steele was in the fore of the boarding party, Captain Farragut bringing up the rear, sword in hand, a second sword in a hanger at his side.

Gravity was rock solid and uniform on the Star Racer.

Farragut ran down a side corridor. He kicked open a compartment. Found masses of monsters within what looked like a bedchamber, chewing on leather and wood and linen with all their mouths.

Oh, God. Too late.

So close. Oh, for Jesus. Late by how long? Minutes?

Farragut cut down gorgons in a fury.

Then the full import of the scene before him caught up with him. There was a lot in here left to eat.

A lot left to eat.

And Jose Maria would not be standing still.

Farragut shut the compartment, tore his helmet off and bellowed: *"Jose Maria!"*

No answer. Yet Jose Maria must be here. Alive. An experienced gorgon fighter, Jose Maria would be the very last thing on board to get eaten. Certainly there were a lot of gorgons inside the ship, but their numbers were not yet overwhelming. *Mercedes'* force field must have been only recently penetrated. Jose Maria must be alive.

"Jose Maria!"

Farragut opened another hatch. He could not possibly have arrived here just seconds too late. God would not allow it.

Then again God often called the best people home early.

"Jose Maria!"

No one answered.

Dammit. Dammit Dammit.

Farragut whirled and slashed down a gorgon that intruded on his damnations.

He raced forward to the cockpit.

He found a sight that made his flesh creep.

Mercedes' res chamber was active, sending a resonant pulse. The ship's resonance would be drawing the gorgons to her.

Horror gave way to puzzlement.

Jose Maria knew the effect resonance had on the Hive.

Jose Maria would know what he was doing.

Jose Maria, what are you doing?

Farragut tried to back figure what had happened here.

Jose Maria found gorgons on *Sulla.*

He had ordered the Vatican ship to run.

And where did Jose Maria go?

Farragut spun away from the console.

He never left Sulla!

Farragut opened his com link with *Merrimack.* "Gypsy! Hook *Sulla!* Get a Marine detail on *Sulla* yesterday!"

The instant that soft dock was achieved, John Farragut charged on board *Sulla.* He was in the fore this time. He hacked through the gorgons that met him at the ragged opening.

Were gorgons still here because they were still hatching? Or were they here because there was still one thing left on board to eat?

Farragut barreled through the tight, ravaged corridors. "Jose Maria!"

And from somewhere he heard the jet of a gas torch and a muffled voice, *"Aqui!"*

Farragut dashed to the head of a ladder, looked down the hatch.

Jose Maria, on the deck below, backed against the bottom rungs of the ladder, wielded a failing blowtorch against a mob of gorgons.

"Jose Maria!"

Jose Maria looked up through the hatch, saw what Farragut had, reached up. Caught the sword—his own El Cid colada—as it dropped into his hand.

38

JOSE MARIA SALVAGED a few bottles of aged wine from *Mercedes* and set those on the captain's table at dinner on board *Merrimack*. Jose Maria was in good spirits but moving gingerly from multiple burns, cuts, and gorgon bites.

Chef Zack was thrilled to be creating dishes for *Don* Cordillera's palate again. Not that John Farragut lacked refinement but Jose Maria's taste was extraordinarily subtle, not one of the top fifty words ever used to describe the captain.

They had left *Sulla* behind in a dead calm, the galactic coordinates of her location recorded, and a finder beacon activated on board. *Sulla* could be collected after the Hive emergency passed. *If* the emergency ever passed.

Merrimack now raced back toward Near Space at flank speed with *Mercedes* in tow. The sturdy little Star Racer was in good working shape. Her amenities however were a bit ragged.

Earth's state of emergency shocked Jose Maria. "How did gorgons get to Earth so fast? Was the outbreak on Thaleia that much worse than we ever thought possible?"

"No," Farragut told him. "The gorgons attacking Earth didn't hatch on Thaleia. They came from the planet Xi."

Which meant that a dormant gorgon egg, or whatever the next generation Hive sprang from, could remain coherent longer than most rocks.

Xi was the site of the galaxy's most ancient civilization. The Xi civilization had fallen to an unknown catastrophe an unimaginably long time ago.

It was clear now that the mysterious catastrophe had been the Hive.

Agent of entropy, Augustus called the Hive. Entropy was a constant throughout the universe. From the first instant of the Big Bang there had been entropy. Entropy governed all things from the turning of leaves, to coffee growing cold, to iron rusting, to objects breaking to pieces rather than piecing themselves together, to all human things turning to dust and ash.

"Xi was Origin," said Farragut.

Jose Maria tilted his head quizzically. "Origin?"

Farragut gave his head a wake-up shake. "I don't know why I keep forgetting you weren't with us at the Myriad."

In the globular cluster IC9870986, a/k/a the Myriad, *Merrimack* had encountered a race of beings from a distant planet known as Origin. Origin turned out to be distant in time rather than space. Origin was Xi a long time ago.

"The Myriadians tried to go back in time to their Origin and change their history."

"Of course they changed nothing," said Jose Maria.

"How do you know?" Farragut asked. "How do we know this isn't an alternate timeline?"

"Now you are being fanciful, young Captain. The Xi civilization is still extinct. Chaos changes the details, but in the grand design the end is inevitable."

"Except that it hasn't ended yet," said Farragut. "Extinction of everything may be inevitable, but it doesn't need to be now. Even someone as fatalistic as Augustus fought the Hive."

When John Farragut first met Augustus, they did not meet face-to-face. Augustus had come in his Striker to the Myriad, where he was presented with a clear shot at *Merrimack*'s stern. And Captain Farragut made no move to defend his ship, because it meant dropping hold of a lifeline to two of his Marines in a small craft. Had he dropped his Marines, the encounter could have been a battle. As it was, the Striker had a simple shot at a foe who refused to defend himself.

"Augustus never told me why he didn't shoot me at the Myriad."

It had been a defining moment, when Augustus had John Farragut's back and did not take the shot.

Jose Maria said, "He told me."

"He *did?*" Farragut stared at him, astonished. And asked at last, "So *why?*"

"Because he wanted you to exist. Augustus did not believe in John Farragut. And he wanted to."

"I don't understand."

"A parable, young Captain," Jose Maria proposed. "Once upon a time, a great hunter came upon a tigress with her cubs trapped in a ring of fire. Never mind the nonsense of how that situation came to pass, there it is. Put yourself there. The tigress can jump free. She has one cub in her mouth but she will not leave the other cubs. She is an easy mark. Does the hunter take the shot?"

"No," said Farragut.

"You say that without the hesitation of even a moment. Did you mark that, young Captain? Romulus would take the shot. A lot of men would take the shot. And a sensible tigress would have jumped out, saving one cub." A mild scold there.

"But the tigress was not sensible," Jose Maria went on. "She was stupidly courageous, and you are correct, the hunter could not shoot her. You put it all on the line not to abandon your own Marines. Because you knew the good hunter could not take the shot. And you only knew the hunter was good because you are good and the thoughts of the petty and cowardly did not occur to you in the ring of fire."

Augustus had not been able to shoot John Farragut in the back while he was trapped in the act of something non-sensically heroic.

"So I guess I really *didn't* outdraw him at Palatine," Farragut had to admit. Some not too deeply buried part of him had thought he was Superman.

"No one outdraws a patterner," said Jose Maria.

At Palatine, Farragut and Augustus had guns pointed at each other once again. No backs turned that time. No one else in the balance. The showdown at Palatine had been a gunfight in the street. A moment for choosing loyalty.

I chose country. Augustus chose me.

"Does he still need me to exist?" Farragut wondered out loud.

"I cannot say."

"He was, without a doubt, the most obnoxious, cynical, abrasive, bad-tempered man I have ever known. I miss him."

"Do we know what became of the mortal remains of Augustus?" Jose Maria asked, speculative.

"Except for the black box, which was man-made anyway, I think Romulus had Augustus atomized."

"Something of his first incarnation I would expect to be interred at the Corindahlor Monument with the other two hundred and ninety-nine of the Roman Tenth," said Jose Maria. "One only needs a finger to lay someone to rest."

"And they had more remains than that," said Farragut.

The brain and his spinal cord had been walking around in a second incarnation as Augustus. But there was more than that left of Flavius Cassius' body, which had fallen over the side of the bridge.

"I believe he rests with his cohort," Jose Maria concluded. "Though some souls spend time in purgatory before moving on."

Farragut hesitated. "Augustus always claimed Flavius Cassius was not he."

"And we both know he was—how do you say?—full of shit. Corindahlor is not far from here."

"No, it's not," Farragut agreed, sounding wistful. "Be all kinds of irresponsible to take a quick detour to Corindahlor with Earth under siege."

"I have a racing craft, young Captain."

The smaller mass of *Mercedes* gave her a much higher threshold velocity than the titanic space battleship.

"Is she that fast?"

He meant was she fast enough to make a side trip to Corindahlor and still catch up with *Merrimack* without losing time.

"We can make it a race," said Jose Maria.

Farragut lifted his wrist com. "Farragut to Command."

Gypsy's voice responded, "Command, aye."

"Commander Dent, you have the ship."

"Aye, sir," said Gypsy, accepting the order, only then questioning, "What are you doing, sir?"

A reminder there that the Hive was on Earth.

"Going to see Augustus."

"He's dead, sir."

"I'm not."

I'm not. Why am I not?

Why did he let me live the third time?

Corindahlor, a planetary system known less for itself than for one of its bridges, lay just to the galactic south of *Merrimack*'s homeward course.

Decades ago, a Roman cohort made a heroic stand at the bridge. They lost the battle. The valiant three hundred died to a man. But the heroic defeat set in motion events that won Rome the world.

The famous stand had been recorded—by the victors of that battle, to their eternal dismay. It was a picture of Roman heroism.

Augustus had been one of the three hundred in his past life.

The Roman Horizon Guard granted the unarmed neutral Terra Rican ship *Mercedes* permission to enter Corindahlor airspace and set down.

The Bridge.

Gray and massive. Two miles long. A choke point connecting land masses. The proud inhabitants had left the beam fire scars unrepaired and the bullets lodged in the original railings.

Augustus always had cynical things to say of the three hundred and the monument to youthful gullibility. He said it reinforced witless credulity so that future generations of prime stupid youth would not hesitate to answer the call to serve their country. *Isn't it grand to be dead?*

Farragut had told Augustus that he demeaned his empire's war dead by speaking so. Augustus said, "Do I? Because I know what it is."

The monument was stirring in its simplicity. Built on the defender's end of the bridge. Large, not colossal. The Roman Tenth had been the Few against overwhelming odds. The memorial was simple. Enduring. Steadfast. It bore three hundred names.

Farragut found him in the Flavian century list. He lifted his fingers toward the name. Cyprian Flavius Cassius.

Hesitated.

Touched the name.

Heard Jose Maria's gasp. Then a voice:

"John you flaming idiot Farragut."

Farragut was not sure why he didn't jump. That voice, those words seemed the most natural thing in the world for him to hear. And weirdly comforting.

He turned to the holoimage of Augustus that had given Jose Maria such a start.

The image's mouth moved. The voice sounded from somewhere nearby, "Here you are. Some things are just inevitable."

Augustus appeared as he had the day he left *Merrimack*. A battered sardonic warrior. In black. A ruby showed like a drop of blood on his chest where soldiers wore their medals.

"What is it about touching a name on a grave monument that makes you think you can contact a spirit? This is not a spirit. I am not here. This is a recording.

"This recording will appear only for you, John Farragut, and only after Romulus is effectively dead."

Captain Farragut supposed Romulus' current condition qualified as death.

"You are the only one I can trust—obscene and absurd as that notion is. I'm giving you this for the same reasons Caesar Magnus chose you to take Rome's surrender. Do not use this information for political or tactical advantage. If you do, you will end like Romulus. You see, I really don't trust anyone. And I didn't let you live because I like you."

A hiss sounded from the span of the bridge. Smoke rose off

its surface with an acidic smell. Red marks began to appear on the bridge. The marks took the shapes of numbers etching themselves into the concrete.

"Rome has these figures from my black box and the Striker, but I don't know if they have put the knowledge to use or not, because, as you have noticed, I am dead. Get these to Jose Maria if he's not standing next to you."

Farragut and Jose Maria glanced at each other. Exchanged the same thought: *Patterner*.

"I shall meet you in the Outer Darkness," said Augustus. And he was gone.

Farragut and Jose Maria stepped onto the bridge to read the smoldering figures burned into the stone. "Can you read that, Jose Maria?"

"It may be an algorithm," Jose Maria said provisionally, his eyes still roving up and down the numbers. He withdrew a computer from his pocket.

Farragut was receiving a signal from Gypsy on *Merrimack*. "Admiral Mishindi for you, Captain," she told him.

Farragut waited for Gypsy to pass through the signal, expecting to hear piss and brimstone for his separating from *Merrrimack*, though Farragut could not believe Gypsy would sing on him. And when Farragut answered the hail, Mishindi did not seem to be aware that Farragut was not on board the *Mack*.

Admiral Mishindi sounded more surprised and confounded than angry. "John! What did you do?"

Farragut foundered. The admiral hadn't demanded, "Why aren't you on your ship? Or where the hell are you?"

Puzzled, Farragut asked back, "What did I do?"

"I've got reports coming in from all over Earth and the Deep End of gorgons melting and gorgons freezing solid in space. Just like the last time you erased the Hive. You mean this is nothing you did?"

"I . . . may have done." He looked to Jose Maria, who was casting round the bridge supports for something. "I'll report when I have something definite, sir." Clicked off.

Jose Maria hiked up from under one end of the bridge. "I have found it."

"It?"

"The resonant chamber. You touched the name. Your action did not just trigger the holoimage of Augustus. You triggered two resonant pulses."

Farragut asked, "Can I assume those two pulses are on harmonics complementary to the two new Hive harmonics?"

"From what your admiral says, it would seem that they are."

A harmonic pulse and its complement cancelled each other out so that neither existed.

A Hive lived by its harmonic resonance. Without its resonance, a Hive ceased to exist.

"Augustus killed both Hives."

Just like that.

Augustus had waited until Romulus was dead — effectively dead — to do so. A little high-handed, that. To allow the Hive to flourish while Augustus waited for his revenge.

But then again, allowing the Hive to flourish was not all Augustus' doing.

Rome has these figures.

"Rome could have done this much sooner," said Farragut. "Other than Romulus, who in Rome would have access to Augustus' data?"

Jose Maria placed his hand over his breast pocket. Spoke, resentful, "Roman Imperial Intelligence counts among its members some of my least loved acquaintances under God's heaven."

Waiting for Farragut to touch the name had not been a delay in getting the cure to the disease. It was the backup plan to make sure the cure got to the disease somehow, in case someone in Rome decided to withhold it for his own purposes.

Redundance is good. Redundance is good.

There had been a period of time when no one knew where Augustus was. Between the time he left *Merrimack* in the Deep End and his reappearance over the Roman Curia.

Sometime in that range Augustus had come here to walk over his own grave.

And to plant this recording and these res signals.

"If I didn't come here and trigger those two resonant pulses, Rome has . . ." Farragut looked to the numbers on the bridge. "What exactly does Rome have there?" The figures looked like more than just two harmonics. There were equations.

"I think," Jose Maria answered slowly because he hadn't had time to verify what he thought, "this is an algorithm for calculating the shift in harmonic between the old Hives and their successor Hives. The difference between the old and new generations in both Hive entities share a progression. Should a third generation emerge—may God forbid—then this algorithm should calculate the new harmonics, and allow us to destroy them as well."

Augustus had been programmed to serve Rome, and so he had done to the end.

"He saved his Empire and our Earth," said John Farragut. "And no one but you and I will thank him for it."

"Augustus did not believe in heroes," said Jose Maria.

"Oh, he crabbed a lot, but there's a reason he came back here."

Back here to the place he first died. To the monument from a grateful nation.

Farragut touched the name again. The image did not come again. Only a voice: "Get the hell out of here. I am still dead, and you are still an idiot."

39

A T THE DINNER DANCE in honor of his promotion, Rear Admiral Farragut made his entrance with a young thing on his arm. He had been dreading the ground posting as district commander until his future tripped and fell on him on the steps at the inn where he was staying.

She was twenty-five years old, brown hair, moderately pretty face, the nose a little pointy, a bright genuine smile. Blue-gray eyes. You could see at once that someone was home behind the eyes. She was athletic, very thin, a bit angular. Pretty as only a laughing woman of that age wearing an evening dress and making an entrance on the arm of a hero admiral can be.

Farragut could have carried less weight, and he had fifteen years on her, but the two looked good together. That Farragut smile, those blue eyes never looked brighter. He looked amazingly buoyant, even for John Farragut.

He had intended to come to the party stag. Until this young woman tripped over him. He'd caught her.

"I didn't trip," Kathy confessed at the party in a circle of admirals. Her name was Kathy.

"I knew that," Farragut confessed back.

They danced a lot of the dances. Kathy got introduced to everyone. Looked you right in the eyes.

After the toasts to the rear admiral's success, John Farragut in turn toasted Captain Calli Carmel on her new post as captain of the space battleship U.S.S. *Merrimack*.

Not altogether sure about leaving his command to an officer known as "Crash," he added at the end of his toast, "Don't bend my boat, Cal."

Lieutenant Colonel TR Steele made a brief appearance. Stiff. Steele was always stiff at formal events, especially when the room was full of brass. It was worse when all those senior officers made way for him and the chant started, "A-da-mas! A-da-mas!" His head burned red and bright enough to serve as a port sidelight.

Steele extended congratulations to Rear Admiral Farragut and to Captain Calli Carmel, and quickly left.

Kathy watched him go. "That was fast. That was the gladiator, wasn't it? Does he have a *date*?"

"I try not to know," said Commander Gypsy Dent.

Calli asked, "Is that Marine girl still on board the *Mack*? What was her name?" She remembered the young woman, good-tempered, eager, and moral as a cheerful dog. Steele snarled at her all the time. "Kerry Blue. Is she—?"

Gypsy hummed and took an interest in the light fixtures.

Farragut asked Kathy to dance.

"Ah," Calli said, and nothing else.

Captain Calli Carmel, who had come to the dance stag—or doe—spent much of the evening discussing Roman strategy with a cluster of admirals. They had been following the many speculations over who would be Caesar's successor. Bookmakers had odds on the front-runners. Odds on Rome reverting to a republic were fairly steep.

Calli snorted at the mere suggestion of republic. Rome needed its Caesar. And to Calli, Gaius Americanus was the obvious choice.

But she also recognized that the Empire did not think as she did.

Though Romans had respect for a man who survived an assassination attempt and who came back to confront his attacker and endured imprisonment for it, Gaius had spent much of the war in hiding and in an American hospital—not good places for a leader to be. He had been the one to speak openly against Romulus. He had walked onto the Senate floor to certain doom and denounced the madman.

The Senate *had* chosen Gaius as moderator for the debates concerning the Empire's future course.

But while Gaius' integrity was beyond question, his ordeal did not make him quite the man of action Romans preferred. Gaius was also an extreme moderate, and the middle ground was always a good place to get shot in the Roman Empire.

The field of possible successors was wide open.

Senator Quirinius was a strong possibility. He was philosophically similar to Gaius. He had given shelter to Gaius upon his escape from prison. A protector was a more attractive image than an evader.

Numa Pompeii had always been quintessentially Roman. But he had been bested in battle by the *Merrimack* and by Calli Carmel. He had obeyed Romulus—as had everyone except for Gaius. But more was expected from the mighty Triumphalis.

Among the dark horses was the father of Herius Asinius, the heroic commander of Legion Draconis who had died fighting the Hive. Also among the long shots was Senator Trogus, who had resisted Romulus, but he was a very very long shot because no one could love him.

A Senator Siculus was making a bid for the supremacy, but Siculus was just not a popular name.

A serious contender was Flavia Irena. Irena was an ironic name for a Flavian, as it meant Peace. This Irena, like most Flavians, was a hardcore hawk. Irena was the feminized clone of one of the fallen at Corindahlor—but not of Augustus.

No one was considering any clones of *his*. A mind could not be cloned—thank all the gods.

A strange and alarming number of Romans were not recanting their support for Romulus' agenda. It went against human nature to back down from a public stand. And denial was often stronger than reason, so there was an odd litter of Julians vying for the top position.

The admirals asked Calli for her prediction.

Calli shook her head. All things being equal—and things were never equal—the Senate should elect Gaius.

She answered, "I guarantee Rome will surprise me."

*　　*　　*

Jose Maria de Cordillera came later in the evening to offer his congratulations to Rear Admiral Farragut and to kiss Kathy's hand.

Jose Maria and John Farragut toasted Augustus, because no one else would.

"Augustus finally found his way to the Outer Darkness," Farragut said sadly.

He and Jose Maria used to speak of such things. Rather a lot of alcohol was usually involved in those dialogues.

Jose Maria offered one more opinion, "I believe not."

John Farragut objected, "Augustus was obnoxious, but I can't think he belongs in *hell*."

"Neither can I," said Jose Maria. "I believe he is with God in heaven."

"Isn't that completely at odds with your creed?"

Jose Maria demurred, "It is a core belief of Catholicism that Man was given free will. Augustus did not have it."

Augustus had been altered and programmed. His choices were not entirely his own.

"What does that make Augustus?" Kathy asked.

"An agent of God's will," Jose Maria proposed. "Perhaps sent to stop the Hive from destroying all God's children. God shall take his angel back to Him."

"Augustus? An angel?" Farragut's eyebrows could lift no higher. "That's some real creative theology there, Jose Maria." But Farragut drank to the idea anyway.

When Kathy left John Farragut's side to fix her brown hair, which was kind of all over by now, his eyes followed her till she was out of sight.

Gypsy asked, "You going to marry that girl, Admiral?"

"Yes, I am."

"She know that yet, sir?"

"Not yet."

"How long have you known her?"

Farragut checked his chron. "Nine hours now."

"What's taking you so long?" said Gypsy.

Gypsy's husband, Marshal Dent, widened his eyes at that question, silently asking his wife, *Long?*

Gypsy, Calli, and Farragut explained to the civilian Marshal Dent in unison, "See the target, acquire the target, secure the target."

There was no time for fox-trotting around in between.

Farragut said, "I'm just not sure I've got a lock on the target."

Gypsy patted his broad shoulder. "Oh, you have tone, sir."

The band chose that moment to play one of those songs to which anyone who had someone special must take the floor. That left Calli on the sidelines while John Farragut danced with his young woman, Gypsy Dent with her man. TR Steele, not here, was out somewhere breaking all kinds of rules to be with his someone.

As the celebration wound down, Calli told John Farragut like an afterthought, in a bad attempt to sound casual, "While I was in the burn tank I kept having a recurring dream. Kind of funny." She made a motion to slide a long lock of hair that wasn't there anymore behind her ear. "I dreamed Rob Roy was reading to me. *Through the Looking Glass*, if you can believe it. Then it was *Vingt mille lieues sous les mers*, I think. Different books, but the dream was always that Rob Roy was reading to me. What do you think that means?"

"You weren't dreaming, Cal," Farragut told her.

Unfamiliar expressions moved across Calli's new face.

John Farragut saw Kathy home. Walked her to her door.

They had come to that moment which probably hadn't changed ever since the invention of doors. They lingered at the threshold.

Kathy uttered the words, "Do you want to come in?"

Farragut looked up at the stars. "There is a God."

In the morning, when Kathy looked stellar wearing just his admiral's jacket, John Farragut asked her to marry him.

She asked him what took him so long.

The new captain of the *Merrimack* marched into the Navy lawyer's office in the main station of Fort Eisenhower, dropped documents straight down on his desk so that they made a decided slap upon landing. "Orders," she said as the lawyer looked up from his writing. "You've been reassigned."

His face was very very young for a thirty-eight-year-old man. The beard stubble did not age him. His opaque brown eyes assumed a quizzical expression that made him look even younger. He recognized her immediately, though last time he had seen her, she had no skin.

Rob Roy Buchanan set aside his stylus and considered the top document. "I see there is a provision in the budget for a legal officer on board an RBS."

RBS. Really Big Ship. *Merrimack* was one.

No one had asked Rob Roy if he wanted to be reassigned from his post at Fort Eisenhower. *Merrimack* had gone a long time without finding need for a legal officer. "Why does *Merrimack* need a legal officer now?"

"Captain wants one."

Rob Roy looked up from the orders. "This could be construed as harassment, Captain."

"Yeah?" said Calli. She sat on the corner of his desk. "Read the next one."

She was wearing tailored trousers. One long leg crossed over the other. Her foot twitched like the tip of a cat's tail. Calli never twitched.

Rob Roy read. Read again. Brown eyes moving back and forth.

Calli's foot was really twitching now.

Rob Roy stared at the document.

"Speak now, Robbie. There can be no hesitation on a space battleship."

"It's not hesitation. It's—" looking for a word. And it better be a good one. "Wonder." He picked up a stylus and signed his name to the second document. He handed it up to Captain Carmel. "Don't call me Robbie."

She slid off the desk. She gave her head a habitual toss as if she still had long tresses to swing over her shoulder instead of those cowlicked tufts that lay in a sassy mess on her head. "Can you find us a judge? I need to buy a dress. I think I want to look like a girl for this."

There was no waiting period in the Deep End.

"You didn't come prepared?" Rob Roy said, rising. "Inefficient, Captain."

"I wasn't sure what you'd say."

"You were sure."

"I can get scared."

"I can find a judge before you can find a dress."

It was nearly a tie. Calli appeared outside the judge's chambers wearing a short champagne number. Legs same as ever, only with softer skin. She found Rob Roy waiting, clean shaved, in dress blues. Flowers and a ring box in hand. He tried to stand up straight, which made him as tall as she was in heels.

She took the flowers, took his arm.

"Is this your dream wedding, Calli?" Rob Roy asked.

A crease appeared in her smooth forehead, considering. She nodded. "Pretty close. My dream wedding was Dad's holding the ladder and Mom's holding the shotgun."

"Do we have vows?"

Calli shook her head. "Let's go traditional. Honestly, all I can think of is, 'See the target, acquire the target, secure the target.' "

Epilogue

MERRIMACK'S NEW LEGAL OFFICER reported to the space battleship. The quartermaster showed him to the captain's quarters, where he saluted the captain.

A courier had brought a small package wrapped like a wedding gift addressed to the captain of the *Merrimack*.

"We got a wedding gift from Rome," said Calli.

"Are we sure we want to open that?" said Rob Roy.

Because it originated on Palatine, it had been through all the scanners. Twice.

It was heavy for a small box. Calli pulled back the gilt wrapping to reveal a life-sized solid gold locust.

"Son of a bitch."

Calli picked it up. It had the heft of solid gold. She turned it over.

Greek characters, engraved in the golden locust's thorax, read: *To Callista*.

"Son of a bitch," she laughed.

Inscribed in Greek as it was, her name was not her name but the inscription on the golden apple—the infamous gift at the wedding of Peleus and the goddess Thetis that started the Trojan War.

Translated, it really read: *To the fairest*.

Calli was not sure if he was calling her beautiful or picking a fight.

"Son of a bitch."

Rob Roy took the card that came with it. It bore only the signature, engraved in gold. Made his eyes go wide.

"Oh, that can't be a surprise," said Calli, reaching for the card. No one in this universe would give her a locust but Numa Pompeii.

"Oh, it is a surprise," said Rob Roy. "A little anyway. It seems you're not the only one with a new title, Captain Callista Carmel Buchanan." He passed her the card.

The gold letters identified the sender:

CAESAR NUMA.